The Cartel

DON WINSLOW
The Cartel

125 YEARS

WILLIAM HEINEMANN: LONDON

1 3 5 7 9 10 8 6 4 2

William Heinemann
20 Vauxhall Bridge Road
London SW1V 2SA

William Heinem~~an is part of the Penguin Random House group~~ of companies
whose add~~ress can be found at global.penguinrandomho~~se.com.

Penguin
Random House
UK

Copyright © Samburu, Inc. 2015

First published by William Heinemann in 2015
(First published in the United States by Alfred A. Knopf,
a division of Penguin Random House LLC, New York in 2015)

www.randomhouse.co.uk

A CIP catalogue record for this book is available from the British Library.

ISBN 9780434023547 (Hardback)
ISBN 9780434023554 (Trade Paperback)

Printed and bound by Clays Ltd, St Ives plc

Map by Mapping Specialists

Penguin Random House is committed to a sustainable future for our
business, our readers and our planet. This book is made from
Forest Stewardship Council® certified paper.

MIX
Paper from
responsible sources
FSC
www.fsc.org FSC® C018179

This book is dedicated to—

Alberto Torres Villegas, Roberto Javier Mora García, Evaristo Ortega Zárate,
Francisco Javier Ortiz Franco, Francisco Arratia Saldierna,
Leodegario Aguilera Lucas, Gregorio Rodríguez Hernández,
Alfredo Jiménez Mota, Raúl Gibb Guerrero, Dolores Guadalupe García Escamilla,
José Reyes Brambila, Hugo Barragán Ortiz, Julio César Pérez Martínez,
José Valdés, Jaime Arturo Olvera Bravo, Ramiro Téllez Contreras,
Rosendo Pardo Ozuna, Rafael Ortiz Martínez, Enrique Perea Quintanilla,
Bradley Will, Misael Tamayo Hernández, José Manuel Nava Sánchez,
José Antonio García Apac, Roberto Marcos García, Alfonso Sánchez Guzmán,
Raúl Marcial Pérez, Gerardo Guevara Domínguez, Rodolfo Rincón Taracena,
Amado Ramírez Dillanes, Saúl Noé Martínez Ortega, Gabriel González Rivera,
Óscar Rivera Inzunza, Mateo Cortés Martínez, Agustín López Nolasco,
Flor Vásquez López, Gastón Alonso Acosta Toscano,
Gerardo Israel García Pimentel, Juan Pablo Solís, Claudia Rodríguez Llera,
Francisco Ortiz Monroy, Bonifacio Cruz Santiago, Alfonso Cruz Cruz,
Mauricio Estrada Zamora, José Luis Villanueva Berrones, Teresa Bautista Merino,
Felicitas Martínez Sánchez, Candelario Pérez Pérez,
Alejandro Zenón Fonseca Estrada, Francisco Javier Salas, David García Monroy,
Miguel Angel Villagómez Valle, Armando Rodríguez Carreón,
Raúl Martínez López, Jean Paul Ibarra Ramírez, Luis Daniel Méndez Hernández,
Juan Carlos Hernández Mundo, Carlos Ortega Samper,
Eliseo Barrón Hernández, Martín Javier Miranda Avilés,
Ernesto Montañez Valdivia, Juan Daniel Martínez Gil,
Jaime Omar Gándara San Martín, Norberto Miranda Madrid,
Gerardo Esparza Mata, Fabián Ramírez López,
José Bladimir Antuna García, María Esther Aguilar Cansimbe,
José Emilio Galindo Robles, José Alberto Velázquez López, José Luis Romero,
Valentín Valdés Espinosa, Jorge Ochoa Martínez,
Miguel Ángel Domínguez Zamora, Pedro Argüello, David Silva,
Jorge Rábago Valdez, Evaristo Pacheco Solís, Ramón Ángeles Zalpa,

Enrique Villicaña Palomares, María Isabella Cordero, Gamaliel López Cananosa,
Gerardo Paredes Pérez, Miguel Ángel Bueno Méndez,
Juan Francisco Rodríguez Ríos, María Elvira Hernández Galeana,
Hugo Alfredo Olivera Cartas, Marco Aurelio Martínez Tijerina,
Guillermo Alcaraz Trejo, Marcelo de Jesús Tenorio Ocampo,
Luis Carlos Santiago Orozco, Selene Hernández León,
Carlos Alberto Guajardo Romero, Rodolfo Ochoa Moreno,
Luis Emmanuel Ruiz Carrillo, José Luis Cerda Meléndez,
Juan Roberto Gómez Meléndez, Noel López Olguín,
Marco Antonio López Ortíz, Pablo Ruelas Barraza, Miguel Ángel López Velasco,
Misael López Solana, Ángel Castillo Corona, Yolanda Ordaz de la Cruz,
Ana María Marcela Yarce Viveros, Rocío González Trápaga,
Manuel Gabriel Fonseca Hernández, María Elizabeth Macías Castro,
Humberto Millán Salazar, Hugo César Muruato Flores, Raúl Régulo Quirino
Garza, Héctor Javier Salinas Aguirre, Javier Moya Muñoz, Regina Martínez Pérez,
Gabriel Huge Córdova, Guillermo Luna Varela, Esteban Rodríguez,
Ana Irasema Becerra Jiménez, René Orta Salgado, Marco Antonio Ávila García,
Zane Plemmons, Victor Manuel Báez Chino, Federico Manuel García Contreras,
Miguel Morales Estrada, Mario Alberto Segura, Ernesto Araujo Cano,
José Antonio Aguilar Mota, Arturo Barajas Lopez, Ramón Abel López Aguilar,
Adela Jazmín Alcaraz López, Adrián Silva Moreno, David Araujo Arévalo—

Journalists murdered or "disappeared" in Mexico during the period
covered in this novel. There were others.

And they worshiped the dragon, for he had given his authority to the beast, and they worshiped the beast, saying, "Who is like the beast, and who can fight against it?"

—Revelation 13:4

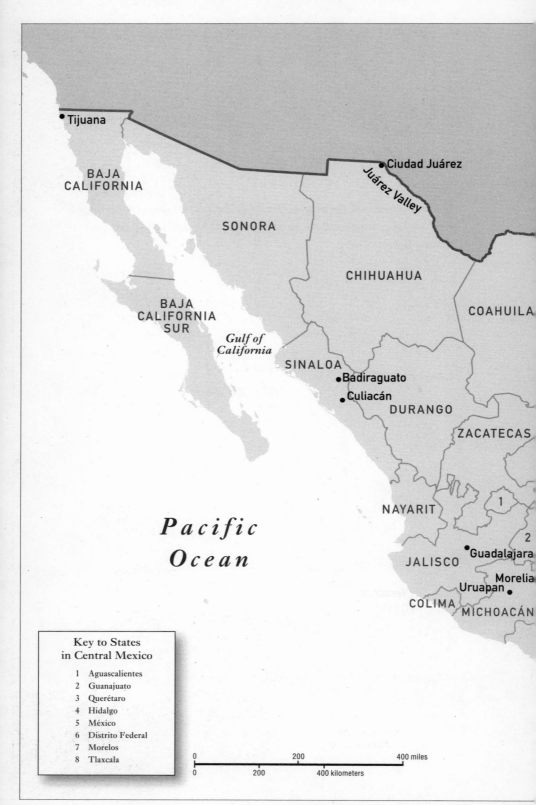

Tijuana

BAJA
CALIFORNIA

SONORA

BAJA
CALIFORNIA
SUR

*Gulf of
California*

SINALOA

Badiraguato

Culiacán

Ciudad Juárez

Juárez Valley

CHIHUAHUA

COAHUILA

DURANGO

ZACATECAS

NAYARIT

*Pacific
Ocean*

JALISCO

COLIMA

Guadalajara

Uruapan

Morelia

MICHOACÁN

Key to States
in Central Mexico

1   Aguascalientes
2   Guanajuato
3   Querétaro
4   Hidalgo
5   México
6   Distrito Federal
7   Morelos
8   Tlaxcala

0		200		400 miles

0	200	400 kilometers

The Cartel

Prologue

Keller thinks he hears a baby cry.

The sound is just audible over the muted rotors as the helicopter comes in low toward the jungle village.

The cry, if that is what he's hearing, is shrill and sharp, a call of hunger, fear, or pain.

Perhaps loneliness—it is that loneliest time of the night, the predawn darkness when the worst dreams come, the sunrise seems far off, and the creatures that inhabit both the real world and the darker edges of the unconscious prowl with the impunity of predators who know that their prey is helpless and alone.

The cry lasts only moments. Maybe the mother came in, picked up the child, and cradled it in her arms. Maybe it was Keller's imagination. But it's a reminder that there are civilians down there—women and children mostly, a few old men and women—who will soon be in harm's way.

The men in the chopper check the loads on their M-4 rifles to make sure the clips are solidly fixed and another one firmly duct-taped to the handle. Underneath the combat helmets and night-vision goggles and "bone-phones," their faces are blackened. Below the ceramic-plate protective vests they wear camouflaged cargo pants with big pockets that hold tubes of energy gel, laminated satellite photos of the village, compression pads if things go bad and they have to stanch the bleeding.

An assassination mission on foreign soil—things could go bad.

The men are in another world, that pre-mission tunnel vision that natural fighters go into like a trance. The twenty-man team—split up in two MH-60 Black Hawks—are mostly former SEALs, Delta Force, Green Berets—the elite. They've done this before—in Iraq, Afghanistan, Pakistan, Somalia.

Technically, they're all private contractors. But the shell company, a security firm out of Virginia, is a thin screen that the media will rip right through if this goes sick and wrong.

In a few moments the men will lower themselves down fast ropes into the village near their target. Even with the element of surprise, there'll be a fire-fight. The narco gunmen are protecting their boss and for him they'll give up their lives. And the *sicarios* are well armed with AK-47s, rocket launchers, and grenades, and know how to use them. These *sicarios* aren't just thugs, but special forces veterans themselves—trained at Fort Benning and elsewhere. It's possible that some of the men in the chopper trained some of the men on the ground.

People will be killed.

Appropriate, Keller thinks.

It's the Day of the Dead.

Now the men hear another sound—the pop of small-arms fire. Look-ing down, they see muzzle flashes cut through the darkness. A firefight has broken out in the village prematurely—they hear shouted orders and small explosions.

It's bad—this wasn't supposed to happen. The mission is compromised, the element of surprise gone, the chance of completing the job without tak-ing casualties probably gone with it.

Then a red streak comes up out of the night.

A loud bang, a flash of yellow light, and the helicopter jolts sideways like a toy that's been hit by a bat.

Shrapnel sprays, exposed wires spark, the ship is on fire.

Red flame and thick black smoke fill the cabin.

The stench of scorched metal and burned flesh.

One man's carotid artery spurts in rhythm with his racing heartbeat. Another keels over, shrapnel obscenely jutting from his crotch, just below his protective vest, and the team medic crawls across the deck to help.

Now the voices come from grown men—howls of pain, fear, and rage as tracers fly up and rounds smack the fuselage like a sudden rainstorm.

The chopper spins crazily as it falls toward the earth.

Southport Library
The Atkinson
Checkout summary

Name: Deryck Marsden
Date: 26/02/2024 13:04

Loaned today
The Atkinson
Title: Don't want to miss a thing
ID: 002823434X
Due back: 18/03/2024

Title: The cartel /
ID: 002916415X
Due back: 18/03/2024

Title: Kiss /
ID: 002961064X
Due back: 18/03/2024

Total item(s) loaned today: 3
Previous Amount Owed: £0.00
Overdue: 0
Reservation(s) pending: 0
Reservation(s) to collect: 0
Total item(s) on loan 4
Item(s) you already have on loan

Title: Silencer
Item: 00224 027X
Due back: 15/03/2024

For renewals and information
Tel 0151 934 8118
Email.
southportlibrary@sefton.gov.uk

PART ONE

To Arise from Sleep

It is high time for us to arise from sleep.

—Romans 13:11

1

The Beekeepers

We think we can make honey without sharing in the fate of bees.
—Muriel Barbery
The Elegance of the Hedgehog

Abiquiú, New Mexico
2004

The bell rings an hour before dawn.

The beekeeper, released from a nightmare, gets up.

His small cell has a bed, a chair, and a desk. A single small window in the thick adobe wall looks out onto the gravel path, silver in the moonlight, which leads up toward the chapel.

The desert morning is cold. The beekeeper pulls on a brown woolen shirt, khaki trousers, wool socks, and work shoes. Walking down the hall to the communal bathroom, he brushes his teeth, shaves with cold water, and then falls in with the line of monks walking to the chapel.

No one speaks.

Except for chanting, prayers, meetings, and necessary conversation at work, silence is the norm at the Monastery of Christ in the Desert.

They live by Psalm 46:10—"Be still and know that I am God."

The beekeeper likes it that way. He's heard enough words.

Most of them were lies.

Everyone in his former world, himself included, lied as a matter of course. If nothing else, you had to lie to yourself just to keep putting one foot in front of the other. You lied to other people to survive.

Now he seeks truth in silence.

He seeks God in the same, although he has come to believe that truth and God are the same.

Truth, stillness, and God.

When he first arrived, the monks didn't ask him who he was or where he came from. They saw a man with saddened eyes, his hair still black but streaked with silver, his boxer's shoulders a little stooped but still strong. He said that he was looking for quiet, and Brother Gregory, the abbot, responded that quietude was the one thing they had in abundance.

The man paid for his small room in cash, and at first spent his days wandering the desert grounds, through the ocotillo and the sage, walking down to the Chama River or up onto the mountain slope. Eventually he found his way into the chapel and knelt in the back as the monks chanted their prayers.

One day his route took him down to the apiary—close to the river because bees need water—and he watched Brother David work the hives. When Brother David needed help moving some frames, as a man approaching eighty did, the man pitched in. After that he went to work at the apiary every day, helping out and learning the craft, and when, months later, Brother David said it was finally time to retire, he suggested that Gregory give the job to the newcomer.

"A layman?" Gregory asked.

"He has a way with the bees," David answered.

The newcomer did his work quietly and well. He obeyed the rules, came to prayer, and was the best man with the bees they'd ever had. Under his care the hives produced excellent Grade A honey, which the monastery uses in its own brand of ale, or sells to tourists in eight-ounce jars, or peddles on the Internet.

The beekeeper wanted nothing to do with the business aspects. Nor did he want to serve at table for the paying guests who came on retreats, or work in the kitchen or the gift shop. He just wanted to tend his hives.

They left him alone to do that, and he's been here for over four years. They don't even know his name. He's just "the beekeeper." The Latino monks call him "El Colmenero." They were surprised that on the first occasion when he spoke to them, it was in fluent Spanish.

The monks talked about him, of course, in the brief times when they were allowed casual conversation. The beekeeper was a wanted man, a gangster, a bank robber. No, he'd fled an unhappy marriage, a scandal, a tragic affair. No, he was a spy.

The last theory gained particular credence after the incident with the rabbit.

The monastery had a large vegetable garden that the monks depended upon for their produce. Like most gardens, it was a lure for pests, but there was one particular rabbit that was wreaking absolute havoc. After a contentious meeting, Brother Gregory gave permission for—in fact, insisted upon—the rabbit's execution.

Brother Carlos was assigned the task and was standing outside the garden trying to handle both the CO_2 pistol and his conscience—neither very successfully—as the other monks looked on. Carlos's hand shook and his eyes filled with tears as he lifted the pistol and tried to pull the trigger.

Just then El Colmenero walked by on his way up from the apiary. Without breaking stride, he took the pistol from Brother Carlos's hand and, without seeming to aim or even look, fired. The pellet hit the rabbit in the brain, killing it instantly, and the beekeeper handed the pistol back and kept walking.

After that, the speculation was that he had been a special agent, an 007. Brother Gregory put a stop to the gossip, which is, after all, a sin.

"He's a man seeking God," the abbot said. "That's all."

Now the beekeeper walks to the chapel for Vigils, which begin at 4:00 a.m. sharp.

The chapel is simple adobe, its stone foundations hewn from the red rock cliffs that flank the southern edge of the monastery. The cross is wooden and sun-worn; inside, a single crucifix hangs over the altar.

The beekeeper goes in and kneels.

Catholicism was the religion of his youth. He was a daily communicant until he fell away. There seemed little point, he felt so far from God. Now he chants the Fifty-first Psalm along with the monks, in Latin: "O Lord, open up my lips, and my mouth shall proclaim your praise."

The chanting lulls him into a near trance, and he's surprised, as always, when the hour is over and it's time to go to the dining hall for breakfast, invariably oatmeal with dry wheat toast and tea. Then it's back to prayer, Lauds, just as the sun is coming up over the mountains.

He's come to love this place, especially in the early morning, when the delicate light hits the adobe buildings and the sun sets the Chama River shimmering gold. He revels in those first rays of warmth, on the cactus taking shape out of the darkness, on the crunch of his feet on the gravel.

There is simplicity here, and peace, and that's all he really wants.

Or needs.

The days are the same in their routine: Vigils from 4:00 to 5:15, followed by breakfast. Then Lauds from 6:00 to 9:00, work from 9:00 to 12:40, then a quick, simple lunch. The monks work until Vespers at 5:50, have a light supper at 6:20, then Compline at 7:30. Then they go to bed.

The beekeeper likes the discipline and the regimentation, the long hours of quiet work and the longer hours of prayer. Especially Vigils, because he loves the recitation of the Psalms.

After Lauds, he walks down into the valley to the apiary.

His bees—western honeybees, *Apis mellifera*—are coming out now in the early morning warmth. They're immigrants—the species originated in North Africa and was transported to America via Spanish colonists back in the 1600s. Their lives are short—a worker bee might survive from a few weeks to a few months; a queen might reign for three to four years, although some have been known to live for as long as eight. The beekeeper has grown used to the attrition—a full 1 percent of his bees die every day, meaning that an entirely new population inhabits a colony every four months.

It doesn't matter.

The colony is a superorganism, that is, an organism consisting of many organisms.

The individual doesn't matter.

All that matters is the survival of the colony and the production of honey.

The twenty Langstroth hives are built of red cedar with rectangular movable frames, as convenience dictates and the law demands. The beekeeper takes the outer cover from the honey-super of one of the hives and sees that it's thick with wax, then carefully replaces it so as not to disturb the bees.

He checks the water trough to make sure it's fresh.

Then he removes the lowest tray from one of the hives, takes out the Sig Sauer 9mm pistol, and checks the load.

Metropolitan Correctional Center
San Diego, California
2004

The prisoner's day starts early.

An automated horn wakes Adán Barrera at 6:00 a.m., and if he were in the general population instead of protective custody, he would go to the dining quad for breakfast at 6:15. Instead, the guards slip a tray with cold cereal and a plastic cup of weak orange juice through a slot in his door of his cell, a twelve-by-six-foot cage in the special housing unit on the top floor of the federal facility in downtown San Diego where for over a year Adán Barrera has spent twenty-three hours a day.

The cell doesn't have a window, but if it did he could see the brown hills of Tijuana, the city he once ruled like a prince. It's that close, just across the border, a few miles by land, even closer across the water, and yet a universe away.

Adán doesn't mind not eating with the other prisoners—their conversation is idiotic and the threat is real. There are many people who want him dead—in Tijuana, all across Mexico, even in the States.

Some for revenge, others from fear.

Adán Barrera doesn't look fearsome. Diminutive at five foot six, and slender, he still has a boyish face that matches his soft brown eyes. Far from a threat, he resembles more a victim who would be raped in ten seconds in the general population. Looking at him, it's hard to credit that he has ordered hundreds of killings over his life, that he was a multibillionaire, more powerful than the presidents of many countries.

Before his fall, Adán Barrera was "El Señor de los Cielos," "the Lord of the Skies," the most powerful drug *patrón* in the world, the man who had unified the Mexican cartels under his leadership, gave orders to thousands of men and women, influenced governments and economies.

He owned mansions, ranches, private airplanes.

Now he has the maximum-allowed $290 in a prison account from which he can draw to buy shaving cream, Coca-Cola, and ramen noodles. He has a blanket, two sheets, and a towel. Instead of his custom-tailored black suits, he wears an orange jumpsuit, a white T-shirt, and a ridiculous pair of black Crocs. He owns two pairs of white socks and two pairs of Jockey undershorts. He sits alone in a cage, eats garbage brought in on a tray, and waits for the show trial that will send him to another living hell for the rest of his life.

Actually *several* lives, to be accurate, as he faces multiple life sentences under the "kingpin statutes." The American prosecutors have tried to get him to "flip," to become an informer, but he's refused. An informer—a *dedo*, a *soplón*—is the lowest form of human life, a creature that does not deserve to live. Adán has his own code—he would rather die, or endure this living death, than become such an animal.

He's fifty—the best-case scenario, extremely doubtful, is that he gets thirty years. Even with "time served" he'll be in his seventies before he walks out the door.

More probably he'll be carried out in a box.

The slow trudge to trial drags on.

After breakfast he cleans his cell for inspection at 7:30. By nature an almost obsessively orderly person, he keeps his space neat and clean anyway—one of his few comforts.

At 8:00, the guards start the morning count of the prisoners, which takes about an hour. Then he's free until 10:30, when they slip lunch—a bologna sandwich and some apple juice—through the door. He has "leisure time activities," which for him means sitting and reading, or taking a nap, until 12:30, when they do another count. Then he has three and a half more hours of tedium until another count at 4:00.

Dinner—"mystery meat" with potatoes or rice and some overcooked vegetables—is at 4:30, then he's "free" until 9:15, when the guards count yet again.

The lights are turned off at 10:30.

For one hour a day—they vary the schedule for fear of snipers—guards lead him handcuffed out to a wired pen on the roof for fresh air and a "walk." Every third day he's taken for a ten-minute shower, sometimes tepid, more often cold. Occasionally he goes to a small meeting room to consult with his attorney.

He's sitting in his cell, filling out his order on the commissary form—a six-pack of bottled water, ramen noodles, oatmeal cookies—when the guard opens the door. "Attorney visit."

"I don't think so," Adán says. "I have nothing scheduled."

The guard shrugs—he does what he's told to do.

Adán leans and presses his hands against the wall as the guard shackles his ankles. An unnecessary humiliation, Adán thinks, but then again, that's probably the point. They get into an elevator and ride down to the fourth floor, where the guard unlocks the door and lets him into a consultation room. He unshackles Adán's ankles but chains him to the chair that's bolted to the floor. Adán's lawyer stands across the table. One look at Ben Tompkins and Adán knows something is wrong.

"It's Gloria," Tompkins says.

Adán knows what Tompkins is going to say before he says it.

His daughter is dead.

Gloria was born with cystic lymphangioma, a deformation of the head, face, and throat that is eventually fatal. And incurable—all Adán's millions, all of his power, could not buy his daughter a normal life.

A little over four years ago, Gloria's health took a turn for the worse. With Adán's blessing, his then wife, Lucía, an American citizen, took their twelve-year-old daughter to San Diego, to the Scripps clinics that housed the best specialists in the world. A month later Lucía phoned him at his safe house in Mexico. Come *now*, she said. They say she has days, maybe only hours . . .

Adán smuggled himself—like his own product—across the border, in the trunk of a specially outfitted car.

Art Keller was waiting for him in the hospital parking lot.

"My daughter," Adán said.

"She's fine," Keller said. Then the DEA agent jabbed a needle into Adán's neck and the world went black.

They were friends once, he and Art Keller.

Hard to believe, but the truth often is.

But that was another life, another world, really.

That was back when Adán was (is it possible to have been that young?) twenty, an accounting student and wannabe boxing promoter (*Dios mío*, the foolish ambitions of youth) and not even thinking of joining his uncle in the *pista secreta*—the drug trade that flourished then in the poppy fields of their Sinaloan mountains.

Then the Americans came, and with them Art Keller—idealistic, energetic, ambitious—a true believer in the war on drugs. He walked into the gym that Adán and his brother Raúl ran, sparred a few rounds, and they became friends. Adán introduced him to their uncle, then the top cop in Sinaloa and its second biggest *gomero*—opium grower.

Keller, so naïve then, knew Tío's first role and was blissfully ignorant (a notable trait of Americans, so dangerous to themselves and those within their flailing arms' reach) of the latter.

Tío used him. In all fairness, Adán has to admit that Tío made Keller his *monigote*, his puppet, manipulated him into taking out the top tier of the *gomeros*, clearing the way for Tío's rise.

Keller could never forgive that—the betrayal of his ideals. Take faith from the faithful, belief from the believer, and what do you have?

The bitterest of enemies.

For, *más o menos*, thirty years now.

Thirty years of war, betrayals, killings.

Thirty years of deaths—

His uncle.

His brother.

Now his daughter.

Gloria died in her sleep, her breath cut off by the weight of her heavy, misshapen head. Died without me there, Adán thinks.

For which he blames Keller.

The funeral will be in San Diego.

"I'm going," Adán says.

"Adán . . ."

"Make it happen."

Tompkins, aka "Minimum Ben," goes to see federal attorney Bob Gibson, an ambitious ballbuster who prefers to be known as a "hard charger."

The sobriquet "Minimum Ben" reflects Tompkins's success as a "drug lawyer"—his job isn't to get his clients acquitted, because that usually isn't going to happen. His job is to get them the shortest possible sentence, which is less about his skills as a lawyer than it is about his skills as a negotiator.

"I'm sort of a reverse agent," Tompkins once told a journalist. "I get my clients less than they deserve."

Now he relays Adán's request to Gibson.

"Out of the question," Gibson says. Gibson's nickname isn't "Maximum Bob," but he wishes it were and is a little envious of Tompkins. The defense attorney has a macho handle and makes a lot more money. Add to that the fact that Tompkins is a cool-looking dude with raffish silver hair, a surfer's tan, a house on Del Mar beach, and an office that overlooks the ocean up in Cardiff, and it's obvious why the civil servants in the prosecutor's office hate Minimum Ben.

"The man wants to bury his *daughter*, for Christ's sake," Tompkins says.

"The man," Gibson answers, "is the biggest drug kingpin in the world."

"Presumption of innocence," Tompkins counters. "He's been convicted of nothing."

"If I recall," Gibson says, switching tack, "Barrera wasn't too squeamish about killing *other* people's kids."

Two of his rival's small children, thrown off a bridge.

"Old wives' tales and unsubstantiated rumors," Tompkins says, "passed around by his enemies. You can't be serious."

"As a midnight phone call," Gibson says.

He refuses the request.

Tompkins goes back and tells Adán, "I'll take this in front of a judge and we'll win. We'll offer to pay for federal marshals, the cost of security . . ."

"There isn't time," Adán says. "The funeral is on Sunday."

It's already Friday afternoon.

"I can get to a judge tonight," Tompkins says. "Johnny Hoffman would issue an order—"

"I can't take the chance," Adán says. "Tell them I'll talk."

"What?"

"If they let me attend Gloria's funeral," Adán says, "I'll give them everything they want."

Tompkins blanches. He's had clients snitch before for lighter sentences— in fact, it's SOP—but the information they gave was always carefully prearranged with the cartels to minimize damage.

This is a death sentence, a suicide pact.

"Adán, don't do this," Tompkins begs. "We'll win."

"Make the deal."

Fifty thousand red roses fill St. Joseph's Cathedral in downtown San Diego just blocks from the Correctional Center.

Adán ordered them through Tompkins, who arranged the funds through clean bank accounts in La Jolla. Thousands more flowers, in bouquets and wreaths—sent by all the major narcos in Mexico—line the steps outside.

As do the DEA.

Agents walk up and down past the floral arrangements and take notes on who sent what. They're also tracking the hundreds of thousands of dollars in Gloria's name contributed to a foundation for research into cystic lymphangioma.

The church is filled with flowers, but not mourners.

If this were Mexico, Adán thinks, it would be overflowing, with hundreds of others waiting outside to show their respect. But most of Adán's family is dead, and the others couldn't cross the border without risking arrest. His sister, Elena, phoned to express her grief, her support, and her regret that a U.S. indictment prevented her from attending. Others—friends, business associates, and politicians on both sides of the border—didn't want to be photographed by the DEA.

Adán understands.

So the mourners are mostly women—narco-wives who are American citizens already known to the DEA, but who have no reason to fear arrest. These women send their children to school in San Diego, come here to do their Christmas shopping, have spa days, or vacation at the beach resorts in La Jolla and Del Mar.

Now they stride bravely up the steps of the cathedral and stare down the agents who take their photos. Dressed elegantly and expensively in black, most walk angrily past; a few stop, strike a pose, and make sure the agents spell their names correctly.

The other mourners are Lucía's family—her parents, her brothers and sisters, some cousins, and a few friends. Lucía looks drawn—grief-stricken, obviously—and frightened when she sees Adán.

She betrayed him to Keller to keep herself out of jail, to keep Gloria from being taken by the state, and she knew that Adán would never have done anything to harm his daughter's mother.

But with Gloria gone, there's nothing to stay his hand. Lucía could simply disappear one day and never be found. Now she glances anxiously at Adán and he turns his face away.

Lucía is dead to him.

Adán sits in the third row of pews, flanked by five U.S. marshals. He wears a black suit that Tompkins bought at Nordstrom's, where Adán's measurements are on file. His hands are cuffed in front of him, but at least they had the decency not to shackle him, so he kneels, stands, and sits as the service requires as the bishop's words echo in the mostly empty cathedral.

The Mass ends and Adán waits as the other mourners file out. He's not allowed to speak to anyone except the marshals and his lawyer. Lucía glances at him again as she passes by, then quickly lowers her head, and Adán makes a mental note to have Tompkins get in touch with her to tell her that she's in no danger.

Let her live out her life, Adán thinks. As for financial support, she's on her own. She can keep the La Jolla house, if the Treasury Department doesn't find a way to take it from her, but that's it. He's not going to support a woman who betrayed him; who is, in effect, stupid enough to cut off her own lifeline.

When the church clears, the marshals walk Adán out to a waiting limousine and put him in the backseat. The car follows Lucía's behind the hearse out to El Camino Memorial Park in Sorrento Valley.

Watching his daughter lowered into the earth, Adán lifts cuffed hands in prayer. The marshals are kind—they let him stoop down, scoop up a handful of dirt, and toss it on Gloria's casket.

It's all over now.

The only future is the past.

To the man who has lost his only child, all that will be is what already was.

Straightening up from his daughter's grave, Adán says quietly to Tompkins, "Two million dollars. Cash."

To the man who kills Art Keller.

Abiquiú, New Mexico
2004

The beekeeper watches the two men come down the gravel path toward the apiary.

One is a *güero* with silver hair and a slightly stiff gait that comes with age. But he moves well, a professional, experienced. The other is Latino, brown-skinned and younger—graceful, confident. They walk a few feet apart, and even from a hundred yards, the beekeeper can discern the bulges under their jackets. Stepping back to the hives, he takes the Sig Sauer from its hiding place, jacks a round into the chamber, and, using the arroyo as cover, starts moving down toward the river.

He doesn't want to kill anyone unless he has to, and if he has to, he wants to do it as far from the monastery as possible.

Kill them at the river's edge.

The Chama is swollen, and he can pull the bodies into the water and let the current take them away. Sliding down the muddy bank, he turns over on his stomach, peers over the edge, and watches the two men cautiously make their way toward the beehives.

He hopes that they stop there, and that they don't damage the hives out of carelessness or spite. But if they keep coming, he'll let them into pistol range. More out of habit than thought, his hand swings back and forth, rehearsing the first two-shot burst, and then the second.

He'll take the younger man first.

The older one won't have the reflexes to react in time.

But now the two men spread out, widening the angle as they approach the hives, making his four-shot pattern harder. So they're professionals, as he would have expected, and now they pull their weapons and approach the hives with their guns pointed out in front of them, in the two-handed grip that they're all taught.

The younger one juts his chin at the ground and the older one nods. They've seen his footprints that lead down to the river. But fifty yards of flat ground with only ankle-high brush for cover leading to a sheltered riverbank where a shooter could hit them at will?

They don't want it.

Then the silver-haired man yells, "Keller! Art Keller! It's Tim Taylor!"

Taylor was Keller's boss back in the day in Sinaloa. "Operation Condor" in 1975, when they burned and poisoned the Sinaloan poppy fields. After that he was in charge of Mexico when Keller was shredding it up in Guadalajara, becoming a superstar. He watched as Keller's trajectory shot right over him.

Keller thought he'd be retired from DEA by now.

He keeps the Sig trained on Taylor's chest and tells him to holster his weapon and put his hands up.

Taylor does it and the younger man follows suit.

Keller gets up and, pistol pointed, moves toward them.

The younger man has jet-black hair, fierce black eyes, the cocky look of a street kid. The kind of agent they recruit from the barrio for undercover work. Just like they recruited me, Keller thinks.

"You went off the radar," Taylor says to Keller. "Hard man to find."

"What do you want?" Keller asks.

"You think you could put the gun down?" Taylor asks.

"No."

Keller doesn't know why Taylor is here or who sent him. Could be DEA, could be CIA, could be anybody.

Could be Barrera.

"Okay, we'll just stand out here with our hands in the air like jerk-offs." Taylor looks around. "What are you, some kind of monk now?"

"No."

"These are what, beehives?"

"If your boy there moves to the side again I'll shoot you first."

The younger man stops moving. "It's an honor to meet you. I'm Agent Jiménez. Richard."

"Art Keller."

"I know," Jiménez says. "I mean, everyone knows who you are. You're the man who took down Adán Barrera."

"All the Barreras," Taylor corrects. "Isn't that right, Art?"

Accurate enough, Keller thinks. He killed Raúl Barrera in a shootout on a Baja beach. He shot Tío Barrera on a San Diego bridge. He put Adán—goddamned Adán—in a prison cell but sometimes regrets that he didn't kill him too, when he had the chance.

"What brings you here, Tim?" Keller asks.

"I was going to ask you the same thing."

"I don't answer to you anymore."

"Just making conversation."

"Maybe you didn't notice," Keller says, "but we're not big on conversation around here."

"Vow of silence sort of thing?"

"No vows." Keller's disappointed with himself in how quickly he fell into verbal fencing with Taylor. He doesn't like it, doesn't want it or need it.

"Can we go someplace and talk?" Taylor asks. "Out of the sun?"

"No."

Taylor turns to Jiménez and says, "Art's always been a hard case. A real asshole—the Lone Ranger. Does not play well with others."

That was always Taylor's beef with him, from the moment Keller—freshly transferred from CIA to the new DEA—arrived on Taylor's turf in Sinaloa thirty-two years ago. He thought Keller was a cowboy, and wouldn't work with him or let other agents work with him, thereby forcing Keller to be exactly what he accused him of—a loner.

Taylor, Keller thinks now, virtually drove me into Tío Barrera's waiting arms. There was nowhere else to go. He and Tío made a lot of busts together. They even "took down"—a euphemism for "killed"—Don Pedro Áviles, *gomero número uno.* Then DEA and the Mexican army sprayed the poppy fields with napalm and Agent Orange and destroyed the old Sinaloan opium trade.

Only, Keller thinks, to watch Tío create a new and vastly more powerful organization out of the ashes.

El Federación.

The Federation.

You start, Keller thinks, by trying to cut out a cancer, and instead you help it to metastasize, spread from Sinaloa throughout the whole country.

It was just the beginning of Keller's long war with the Barreras, a thirty-year conflict that would cost him everything he had—his family, his job, his beliefs, his honor, his soul.

"I told the committees everything I knew," Keller says now. "I have nothing left to say."

There'd been hearings—internal DEA hearings, CIA hearings, congressional hearings. Art had taken down the Barreras in direct defiance of orders from CIA, and it had been like rolling a grenade down an airplane aisle. It blew up on everybody, and the damage had been tough to contain, with *The*

New York Times and *The Washington Post* sniffing around like bloodhounds. Official Washington couldn't decide if Art Keller was a villain or a hero. Some people wanted to pin a medal on him, others wanted to put him in an orange jumpsuit.

Still others wanted him to just disappear.

Most people were relieved when, after all the testimony and the debriefings were concluded, the man once known as "the Border Lord" did it on his own. And maybe Taylor is here, Keller thinks, to make sure I stay disappeared.

"What do you want?" Keller asks. "I have work to do."

"Do you read the papers, Art? Watch the news?"

"Neither."

He has no interest in the world.

"Then you don't know what's going on in Mexico," Taylor says.

"Not my problem."

"It's not his problem," Taylor says to Jiménez. "Tons of coke pouring across the border. Heroin. Meth. People getting killed, but it's not Art Keller's problem. He has bees to take care of."

Keller doesn't answer.

The so-called war on drugs is a revolving door—you take one guy out, someone else grabs the empty chair at the head of the table. It will never change, as long as the insatiable appetite for drugs is there. And it's there, in the behemoth on this side of the border.

What the suits will never understand or even acknowledge—

The so-called Mexican drug problem *isn't* the Mexican drug problem. It's the *American* drug problem.

There's no seller without a buyer.

The solution isn't in Mexico and never will be.

So once it was Adán and now it's someone else. After that it will be somebody else.

Keller doesn't care.

Taylor says, "The Gulf cartel stopped two of our agents in Matamoros the other day, drew weapons, and threatened to kill them. Sound familiar?"

It does.

The Barreras had done the same thing with him back in Guadalajara. Threatened him and his family if he didn't back off. Keller responded by sending his family back to San Diego and pushing harder.

Then the Barreras killed Art's partner, Ernie Hidalgo. Tortured him for weeks for information he didn't have and then dumped his body in a ditch. Left a widow and two little kids.

And Keller's undying hatred.

Their feud became a blood feud.

And it wasn't the worst thing that Adán Barrera did.

Not by a long shot.

That was what, Keller thinks, twenty years ago?

Twenty years?

"But you don't give a damn, right?" Taylor asks. "You live in this ethereal world now. 'In it but not of it.'"

When I was in it I was *too* in it, Keller thinks. I got Ernie killed and then I got nineteen innocent people killed. He'd made up an informant to protect his real source and Adán Barrera slaughtered nineteen men, women, and children along with the phony *soplón* to teach a lesson. Lined them all up against a wall and shot them.

Keller will never forget walking into that compound and seeing children dead in their mothers' arms. Knowing that it was his fault, his responsibility. He doesn't want to forget, not that his conscience will let him. Some mornings the bell wakes him from the memory.

After the El Sauzal massacre he wasn't in it to stop drug trafficking, he was in it to get Adán Barrera. To this day he doesn't know why he didn't pull the trigger when he had the gun to Adán's head. Maybe he thought that death was too merciful, that thirty or forty years in the hell of a supermax prison before he goes to the *real* hell was a better fate for Adán.

"I have a different life now," he says.

A Cold Warrior, then a Drug Warrior, Keller thinks.

Now I'm at peace.

"So here in your splendid isolation," Taylor continues, "you haven't heard about your boy Adán."

"What about him?" Keller asks, despite himself. He wanted to have the strength not to ask.

"He's gone Céline Dion," Taylor says. "You can't stop the guy from singing."

"You came here to tell me that?" Keller asks.

"No," Taylor says. "There's a rumor that he's put a two-million-dollar bounty on your head, and I'm legally obligated to inform you of a direct threat on your life. I'm also obligated to offer you protection."

"I don't want it."

"See what I mean?" Taylor says to Jiménez. "Hardass. You know what they used to call him? 'Killer Keller.'"

Jiménez smiles.

Taylor turns back to Keller. "It's tempting—my share of two mil, I could buy a little place on Sanibel Island, get up every morning with nothing to do but fish. Take care of yourself, huh?"

Keller watches them walk back up the hill and then disappear over the crest. Barrera a *soplón*? There are a lot of things you can call Adán Barrera, all of them true, but a snitch isn't one of them. If Barrera is talking, it's for a reason.

And Keller can guess what it is.

I *should* have killed him, Keller thinks more out of fatigue than fear. Now the blood feud will just go on and on, like the war on drugs itself.

World without end, amen.

He knows it won't end until one or both of them is dead.

The beekeeper is not at dinner that night, he doesn't go to Compline afterward. When he doesn't show up at Vigils in the morning, Brother Gregory goes to his room to see if he's sick.

The room is empty.

The beekeeper is gone.

Metropolitan Correctional Center, San Diego
2004

The thing you have to admire about the North Americans, Adán thinks, is their consistency.

They *never* learn.

Adán has been as good as his word.

After the funeral, he sat down with Gibson and gave him gold. He sat across the table from DEA, with federal, state, and local prosecutors, answered every question they asked, and some they didn't know to ask. The information he provided led to a score of huge drug seizures and high-level arrests in the United States and Mexico.

This scared the shit out of Tompkins.

"I know what I'm doing," Adán assured him.

He saves the best for last. "Do you want Hugo Garza?"

"We're on Viagra for Garza," Gibson answers.

"Can you *give* them Garza?" Tompkins asks, rattled. His client is offering to give up the head of the Gulf cartel, the most powerful drug organization in Mexico now that Adán's old Federación has been taken apart.

This is why Tompkins doesn't like to let clients in on the haggling. It's like bringing your wife in with you to buy a car—sooner or later she's going to say something that costs you. Clients have a right to be present, but just because you can doesn't mean you should.

But what Adán says next—it goes way over the top.

"I want to be extradited," Adán says. "I'll plead guilty here, but I want to serve my sentence in Mexico."

Mexico and the United States have a reciprocal arrangement to allow prisoners to serve their time in their home countries for humanitarian purposes, to be near their families. But Tompkins is aghast and hauls his client out of the room. "You're a *snitch*, Adán. You won't last five minutes in a Mexican prison. They'll be lining up to kill you."

"They'll be lining up in American prisons, too," Adán observes. The prisons on this side of the border are filled with Mexican narcos and *cholo* gangbangers who would jump at the opportunity to move up in the hierarchy by killing the world's biggest informer.

Security arrangements for Adán have played a major role in the plea agreement that Tompkins has been negotiating, but Adán has already balked at going onto the "protected prisoner" units with child molesters and other informers.

"Adán," Tompkins pleads, "as your lawyer—as your *friend*—I'm asking you not to do this. I'm making progress. With judicial notice of your cooperation, I can possibly get your sentence down to fifteen years, then the witness protection program. Time served, you're out in twelve. You can still have a life."

"You *are* my lawyer," Adán says, "and as your client, I'm instructing you to make this deal—Garza for extradition. If you won't, I'll fire you and get someone who will."

Because this deal has to be made, and Adán can't tell Tompkins why. Can't tell him that delicate negotiations have been going on in Mexico for months, and that yes, it's a risk, but it's a risk he has to take.

If they kill him, they kill him, but he's not going to spend his life in a prison cell.

So he waits while Tompkins goes back in. Adán knows it won't be simple—Gibson will have to go to his bosses, who will go to theirs. Then the Justice Department will talk to the State Department, who will talk to the CIA, who will talk to the White House, and then the deal will get done.

Because a former occupant of that same White House authorized the arrangement back in the '80s by which Tío trafficked cocaine and gave money to the anticommunist Contras, and no one wants Adán Barrera pulling *that* skeleton from the closet to the witness stand.

There will be no trial.

They'll take the Garza bait instead.

Because the North Americans never learn.

Three weeks later, the Mexican *federales,* acting on information provided by the DEA, capture Hugo Garza, the boss of the Gulf cartel, at a remote ranch in Tamaulipas.

Two days later, U.S. marshals take Adán out of San Diego in the middle of the night and put him on a plane to Guadalajara, where *federales* in black uniforms and hoods whisk him off the plane and drive him to serve his sentence at the Puente Grande Correctional Facility—"the Big Bridge"—outside the city that his uncle had once ruled like a duchy.

A convoy of two armored cars and a personnel carrier rumble up the Zapotlanejo Freeway toward the guard towers of the prison, its searchlights glowing silver in an otherwise silk black night.

The lead armored car stops under one of the towers by a large sign that reads CEFERESO II. Coils of razor wire top the high fences and concrete walls. Machine gunners in the towers train their sights on the convoy.

A steel door slides open and the convoy pulls inside a large supply bay. The door slides shut behind it. They say that once you cross the Big Bridge, you never cross back.

Adán Barrera is looking at twenty-two years here.

It's cold, and Adán huddles inside the blue down jacket they gave him as the guards take him by the elbows and help him out of the personnel carrier. His hands are cuffed in front of him, his ankles shackled.

He stands against a concrete wall as guards snap his picture, fingerprint, and "process" him. They take off his cuffs and shackles, then the jacket, and he shivers as he changes into the brown prison uniform with the number 817 stitched on the front and back.

The warden gives a speech. "Adán Barrera, you are now an inmate of CEFERESO II. Do not think that your former status gives you any standing here. You are just another criminal. Abide by the rules, and you will do fine. Disobey them, and you will suffer the consequences. I wish you a successful rehabilitation."

Adán nods, and then they take him from the processing area into the COC, the Observation and Classification Center, to be evaluated for a permanent housing assignment.

Puente Grande is Mexico's harshest and most secure prison, and CEFERESO II (Federal Social Rehabilitation Center) is its maximum-security block, reserved for the most dangerous criminals, kidnappers, narco kingpins, and convicts who killed in other prisons.

The COC is the worst section of CEFERESO II.

This is where the *malditos*—the damned—go. Usually their indoctrination consists of being beaten with hoses, shocked with electric wires, or drenched with water and left to shiver, naked, on the bare concrete floor. Perhaps even worse is the isolation—no books, no magazines, nothing to write on. If the physical torture doesn't destroy them, the mental torment usually takes their minds. By the time the evaluation is completed, they are usually, and accurately, classified as insane.

The guard opens the door of a cell, Adán steps in, and the door closes behind him.

The man sitting on the metal bench is huge—six foot eight, heavily muscled, with a full black beard. He looks at Adán, grins, and says, "I'm your welcoming committee."

Adán braces for what he knows is coming.

The man gets up and wraps him in a crushing bear hug. "It's good to see you, *primo*."

"You, too, cousin."

Diego Tapia and Adán grew up together in the Sinaloan mountains, among the poppy fields, before the American war on drugs—a saner, quieter time. Diego was a young foot soldier—a *sicario*—when Adán's uncle formed the original Federación.

Adán's physical opposite, Diego Tapia is broad-shouldered, whereas Adán is slight and a little stooped, especially after a year in an American jail cell. Adán looks like what he is—a businessman—and Diego looks like what *he* is, a wild, bearded mountain man who wouldn't seem out of place in those old photos of Pancho Villa's riders. He might as well have bandoliers crossed over his chest.

"You didn't have to come personally," Adán says.

"I won't stay long," Diego answers. "Nacho sends his regards. He'd be here, but . . ."

"It's not worth the risk," Adán says. He understands, but it's a bit annoying, seeing as his becoming an informer vastly increased Ignacio "Nacho" Esparza's wealth and standing.

The intelligence Adán provided the DEA created fissures in the rock of the Mexican drug trade, cracks that Diego and Nacho have seeped into like water, filling every vacancy created by the arrest of a rival.

(North Americans never learn.)

Now Diego and Nacho each have their own organizations. Collectively, as the so-called Sinaloa cartel, they control a huge portion of the trafficking business, shipping cocaine, heroin, marijuana, and methamphetamine through Juárez and the Gulf. They also managed Adán's business for him in his absence, trafficking his product, maintaining his connections with police and politicians, collecting his debts.

It was Nacho who negotiated Adán's return to Mexico from the Mexican side, delivering large payments and larger assurances. Once that was arranged, Diego saw to it that most of the prison staff was already on Adán's payroll by the time he arrived. The majority of them were eager for the money. For the reluctant, Diego simply came into the prison and showed them their home addresses and photos of their wives and children.

Three guards still refused to take the money. Diego congratulated them for their integrity. Each was found the next morning sitting primly at his post with his throat cut.

The rest accepted Adán's largesse. A cook was paid $300 American a month, a senior guard as much as a thousand, the warden $50,000 above and beyond his annual salary.

As for the men lining up to kill Adán, there *were* several of them, all beaten to death by other inmates wielding baseball bats. "Los Bateadores"—"the Batters"—Sinaloan employees of Diego, would be Adán's private security squad inside Puente Grande.

"How long do I have to be here?" Adán asks.

Diego answers, "In here we can guarantee your safety. Out there . . ."

He doesn't need to finish—Adán understands. Out there are people who still want him dead. Certain people will have to go, certain politicians have yet to be bought, *cañonazos*—huge bribes—have to be paid.

Adán knows he'll be in Puente Grande for a while.

Adán's new cell, on Block 2, Level 1-A, of CEFERESO II, is 635 square feet, has a king-sized bed behind a private partition, a full kitchen, a bar, a flat-screen LED television, a computer, a stereo system, a desk, a dining room table, chairs, floor lamps, and a walk-in closet.

A refrigerator is stocked with frozen steaks and fish, fresh produce, beer, vodka, cocaine, and marijuana. The alcohol and drugs are not for him but for guards, inmates, and guests.

Adán doesn't use drugs.

He saw his uncle become addicted to crack and watched the once power-ful *patrón*—Miguel Ángel Barrera, "M-1," the genius, the progenitor of the cartels, a *great man*—become an addled-minded, paranoid fool, a conspirator in his own destruction.

So a single glass of wine with dinner is Adán's only indulgence.

A closet holds a rack of Italian-made, custom-tailored suits and shirts. Adán wears a clean white shirt every day—the dirty ones go to the prison laundry and come back pressed and folded—because he knows that in his business, as in any business, appearances are important.

Now he goes about the business of putting back together the pieces that Keller shattered. In his absence, the Federación has splintered into a few large groups and dozens of smaller ones.

The largest is the Juárez cartel, based in Ciudad Juárez, just across the border from El Paso, Texas. Vicente Fuentes seems to have won the battle for control there. Fine—he's a native Sinaloan, tight with Nacho Esparza, whom he allows to move his meth through the Juárez plaza.

The next in importance is the Gulf cartel—the Cartel del Golfo, the "CDG"—based in Matamoros, not far from the entry points in Laredo. Two men, Osiel Contreras and Salvador Herrera, reign there now that Hugo Garza is in jail. They're also cooperative, allowing Sinaloan product, via Diego's organization, to pass through their territory.

The third is the Tijuana cartel, which Adán and his brother Raúl ran before, using it as a power base to take the entire Federación. Their sister, Elena—the only surviving sibling—is trying to maintain control but losing her grip to a former associate, Teo Solorzano.

Then there's the Sinaloa cartel based in his own home state, the birth-place of the Mexican drug trade. It was from there that Tío built the Fede-ración, from there that he divided the country into plazas that he handed out like fiefdoms.

Now three organizations collectively comprise the Sinaloa cartel. Diego Tapia and his two brothers run one, trafficking cocaine, heroin, and mari-juana. Nacho Esparza has another, and has become the "King of Meth."

The third is Adán's own, made of old Federación loyalists and for which Diego and Nacho have been the dual placeholders, awaiting Adán's return. He in turn insists that he has no ambition to become the boss of the cartel, just the first among equals with his fellow Sinaloans.

Sinaloa is the heartland. It was the black loam of Sinaloa that grew the poppies and the marijuana that first gave birth to the trade, Sinaloa that provided the men who ran it.

But the problem with Sinaloa is not what it has, it's what it lacks.

A border.

The Sinaloan base is hundreds of miles from the border that separates— and joins—Mexico from the lucrative American market. While it's true that the countries share a two-thousand-mile land border, and that all of those miles can and have been used to smuggle drugs, it's also true that some of those miles are infinitely more valuable than others.

The vast majority of the border runs along isolated desert, but the truly valuable real estate are the "choke point" cities of Tijuana, Ciudad Juárez, Nuevo Laredo, and Matamoros. And the reason lies not in Mexico, but in the United States.

It has to do with highways.

Tijuana borders San Diego, where Interstate 5 is the major north–south arterial that runs to Los Angeles. From Los Angeles, product can be stored and moved up the West Coast or anywhere in the United States.

Ciudad Juárez borders El Paso and Interstate 25, which connects to Interstate 40, the main east–west arterial for the entire southern United States and therefore a river of cash for the Juárez cartel.

Nuevo Laredo and Matamoros are the twin jewels of the Gulf. Nuevo Laredo borders Laredo, Texas, but more importantly Interstate 35, the north–south route that runs to Dallas. From Dallas, product can be shipped quickly to the entire American Midwest. Matamoros offers quick road access from Route 77 to Interstate 37, then on to Interstate 10 to Houston, New Orleans, and Florida. Matamoros is also on the coast, providing water access to the same U.S. port cities.

But the real action is in trucks.

You can haul product through the desert—by foot, horse, car, and pickup. You can go by water, dumping loads of marijuana and vacuum-sealed cocaine into the ocean for American partners to pick up and bring in.

Those are all worthwhile methods.

Trucking dwarfs them.

Since the 1994 NAFTA treaty between the United States and Mexico, tens of thousands of trucks cross the border from Tijuana, Juárez, and Nuevo Laredo *every day*. Most of them carry legitimate cargo. Many of them carry drugs.

It's the largest commercial border in the world, carrying almost $5 billion in trade a year.

Given the sheer volume of traffic, U.S. Customs can't come close to searching every truck. Even a serious effort to do so would cripple U.S.-Mexican trade. Not for nothing was NAFTA often referred to as the "North American Free Drug Trade Agreement."

Once the truck with drugs in it crosses that border, it's literally on the freeway.

"The Fives"—Interstates 5, 25, and 35—are the arterial veins of the Mexican drug trade.

When Adán ruled the trade, it didn't matter—he controlled the border crossings into El Paso, Laredo, and San Diego. But with him out of power, the Sinaloans have to pay a *piso*—a tax—to bring their product across.

Five points don't sound like a lot, but Adán has an accountant's perspective. You pay what you need to on a flat-fee basis—salaries and bribes, for instance, are just the cost of doing business. But percentages are to be avoided like debt—they suck the life out of a business.

And not only are the Sinaloans paying 5 percent of their own business—which amounts to millions of dollars—but they aren't collecting the 5 percent of other people's businesses, the *piso* that was theirs when *he* controlled all the plazas.

Now you're talking serious money.

Cocaine alone is a $30 billion market in the United States annually. Of the cocaine that goes into the United States, 70 percent of it goes through Juárez and the Gulf.

That's $21 billion.

The *piso* on that alone is a billion dollars.

A year.

You can be a multimillionaire, even a billionaire, moving your own product and paying the *piso*. A lot of men do, it's not a bad life. You can get even richer controlling a plaza, charging other traffickers to use it and never touching or even going near the actual drugs. What most people don't understand is that the top narcos can go years or even their entire business lives without ever touching the drugs.

Their business is to control turf.

Adán used to control it all.

He was the Lord of the Skies.

Adán's days in Puente Grande are full.

A thousand details require supervision.

Supply routes into Mexico from Colombia have to be constantly refreshed, then there's transportation to the border, smuggling into the United States.

Then there's money management—tens of millions of dollars flooding back from the United States, in cash, that need to be laundered, accounted for, invested in overseas accounts and businesses. Salaries, bribes, and commissions that need to be paid. Equipment to be purchased. Adán's operation employs scores of accountants to count the money and keep an eye on each other, dozens of lawyers. Hundreds of operatives, traffickers, security lookouts, police, army, politicians.

Adán hired a convicted embezzler to digitize all his records so he can track accounts on computer, laptops that are swapped out once a month and freshly encoded. He uses scores of cell phones, changed every other day or so, the replacements smuggled in by guards or other of Diego's employees.

Los Bateadores are in charge of managing Block 2. The rest of Puente Grande is a bedlam of gangs, robberies, assaults, and rapes, but Block 2 is quiet and orderly. Everyone knows that the Sinaloa cartel runs that part of the prison on behalf of Adán Barrera, and it is a sanctuary of calm and quiet.

Adán rises early, has a quick breakfast, and then goes to his desk. He works until 1:00 p.m., when he has a leisurely lunch, then goes back to his desk until 5:00. Most evenings are quiet. His chef comes in every day to cook his dinner and select the appropriate wine. It seems to matter a great deal to the chef—it matters less to Adán.

He's not a wine snob.

Some evenings Los Bateadores convert the dining hall into a cinema, complete with a popcorn machine, and Adán invites friends in to watch a movie, munch popcorn or eat ice cream. The guests call these sessions "Family Nights" because Adán prefers PG films—lots of Disney—because he doesn't like the sex and violence that come with most Hollywood films these days.

Other nights are less wholesome.

A prison guard cruises the Guadalajara bars and comes back with women, and then the dining hall is converted into a brothel, replete with liquor, drugs, and Viagra. Adán pays all the "fees" but doesn't take part in these evenings, retreating to his cell instead.

He's not interested in women.

Until he sees Magda.

Sinaloans like to brag that their mountain state produces two beautiful things in abundance—poppies and women.

Magda Beltrán is certainly one of the latter.

Twenty-nine years old, with a tall frame, long legs, blue eyes—Magda is a mixture of the native Mexican people and the Swiss, German, and French who migrated to Sinaloa in the nineteenth century.

Seven Sinaloanas have been crowned Miss Mexico.

Magda wasn't one of them, but she was Miss Culiacán.

She competed in beauty pageants since she was six years old and won most of them. In doing so, she attracted the attention of agents, film producers, and, of course, narcos.

Magda was no stranger to that world.

Her uncle was a trafficker in the old Federación, and two cousins had been *sicarios* for Miguel Ángel Barrera. Growing up in Culiacán, she simply knew traffickers; most people did.

She was nineteen when she started dating them.

Narcos flock around local beauty queens like circling vultures. Some of them even sponsor their own pageants, *narcoconcursos de misses,* to bring out the talent. When some other pageant officials expressed concern about the girls associating with drug traffickers, one local wag asked, "Why would you not want these women representing the state's biggest product?"

It's a natural combination—the girls have looks, and the narcos have money to treat them to gourmet dinners, clothes, jewelry, expensive vacations, spas, beauty treatments . . .

Magda took them all.

Why not?

She was young and beautiful and wanted to have a good time, and if you wanted good times in Culiacán, if you wanted to hang with the *cachorros*—the jet-set kids of the drug barons—you had to go where the money was.

Besides, the narcos were fun.

They liked parties, music, dances, concerts, and clubs.

If you were on the arm of a narco, you didn't stand in line behind the rope; they opened the rope for you and showed you into the VIP room with the Cristal and the Dom, and the owners—if the narco himself didn't own the club—would come over to greet you personally.

Some of the girls found themselves enmeshed with the older narcos who became obsessed with them, but Magda avoided that trap. She watched what happened to girls a few years ahead of her. A fifty-year-old *chaca*, a boss, would become enamored, make the girl his mistress, and make sure no other man—especially a young, handsome one—came near her. Sometimes he would "marry" her in a faux ceremony, fake because he was already married (at least once). The poor girl would waste her youth imprisoned in a luxury condo somewhere until the narco went to prison, was killed, or simply grew tired of her.

Then she would have money, yes, but also regrets.

Magda had none.

She was nineteen when Emilio, an up-and-coming twenty-three-year-old cocaine trafficker, came to one of her pageants, swept her off her feet and into his bed. He was handsome, funny, generous, and a good lover. She could see herself with him, marrying him and having his babies when she was done with the pageant world.

Magda was heartbroken when Emilio went to prison, but by that time she was competing for Miss Culiacán and gained the attentions of Héctor Salazar, a younger associate of her uncle's. Héctor sent a dozen roses with a diamond in each one to her dressing room, stood politely in the shadows as she was crowned, and then took her to Cabo.

Emilio was a boy, but Héctor was a man. Emilio was playful, Héctor was serious, about business and about her. Emilio had been puppy love—her first and therefore beautiful in that way—but with Héctor it was different, two adults building a life together in an adult world.

Héctor was very traditional—after Cabo he went to Magda's father to ask permission to marry his daughter. They were planning the wedding when another narco who was also very serious about business put four bullets into Héctor's chest.

Technically Magda wasn't a widow, but in a way she was, and expected to play the part. She was heartbroken, she knew that, but she also knew that somewhere, in a secret part of her mind, she was at least a little relieved at not having to take the role of wife and presumably mother so early in her life.

She also learned that black became her.

Jorge Estrada, a Colombian who had been one of Héctor's cocaine suppliers, was at his funeral and noticed her. A respectful man, he waited what he considered a decent interval before approaching her.

Jorge took her off to Cartagena, to the Sofitel Santa Clara resort, and while, at thirty-seven, he was older than Emilio or Héctor, he was just as good-looking, and in a manly rather than a boyish way. And where Héctor had money, Jorge had *money*—generational wealth, as they say—and he took her to his *finca* in the countryside and his beach house in Costa Rica. He took her to Paris and Rome and Geneva, introduced her to directors, artists, important people.

Magda wasn't a gold-digger.

The fact that Jorge was rich was just a bonus. Her mother—as generations of mothers have—said, "It is just as easy to fall in love with a rich man as a poor one." Jorge did give her things—trips, clothes, jewelry (a lot of jewelry)—but what he didn't give her was a ring.

She didn't ask, didn't demand or nag or even hint, but after three years with the man she had to wonder why. What was she not doing? What was she doing wrong? Was she not pretty enough? Sophisticated enough? Not good enough in bed?

Finally she asked him *that* question. In bed one night in a suite on the beach in Panama, she asked him where this was headed. She wanted marriage, she wanted children, and if he didn't, she would have to get on with her life. No hard feelings, this has been wonderful, but she would have to move on.

Jorge smiled. "Move on where, *cariño*?"

"I'll go back to Culiacán, find myself a nice Mexican man."

"Are there such creatures?"

"I can have any man I want," she answered. "The trouble is, I want you."

He wanted her, too, he said. Wanted to give her a ring, a wedding, babies. It was just . . . business had been bad lately . . . a couple of shipments seized . . . debts unpaid . . . but after these small reversals were ironed out . . . he was hoping to pop the question.

There was just one small thing.

He needed a little help.

There was some money, cash, in Mexico City. He'd go himself, but things were . . . difficult . . . there at the moment. But if she would go, perhaps visit her family, see friends, and then pick up the money and fly it back . . .

Magda did it.

She knew what she was doing. Knew that she was crossing the line from "association" to "participation," from dating a drug trafficker to money laundering. She did it anyway. Part of her knew, deep down, that he was using her, but another part wanted to believe him, and there was yet another part that . . .

. . . wanted in.

Why not?

Magda grew up around *la pista secreta,* learned about the trade from Emilio, learned much more about it, and on a much higher level, just being with Jorge. She had the experience, the brains—why did she always have to just be eye candy on the arm of some male narco?

Why couldn't she be a narca?

A *chingona,* a powerful woman on her own?

Other women—admittedly few—had done it.

Why not her?

So when Magda packed two suitcases with $5 million in American cash and headed for Mexico City International Airport, she couldn't really say, then or later, if she was going to deliver the money to Jorge or steal it from him to start her own business. She had a ticket to Cartagena and a ticket to Culiacán, and she didn't know which she was going to use. Go to Colombia and see if Jorge was really going to marry her, or go back to Sinaloa and fade into the protective cradle of the mountains, where Jorge would never dare come to demand his money back. (Really, what was he going to do? She would simply say that the police seized the money, and what was he going to do?)

She never had the chance to decide.

The *federales* arrested her as she was walking into the terminal.

So she could truthfully tell Jorge that the police seized his money. They made a big show in front of the news cameras over the seizure of $1.5 million and the arrest of a "major money launderer for the Colombian cartels."

The media loved it.

They plastered Magda's mug shots all over the front pages and television with split-screen images of her under arrest and her standing on the stage in her tiara. News announcers shook their heads and *tcch'd* cautionary, let-this-be-a-lesson tales for other young women tempted by the narco-world of "glitz and glamour."

Even some American papers picked it up, with headlines reading BEAUTY AND THE BUST. Or, in the tabloid version, THE BUST AND THE BUST.

Magda was less amused, although her police interrogations were ridiculous. The focus of the *federales'* questions was not so much on what she was doing taking $5 million in cash through Benito Juárez Airport, but what she was doing taking $5 million in cash through Benito Juárez Airport without paying them first.

She admitted that it was a naïve mistake, that she should have known better, and if she had it to do over again—that is, if they gave her the chance to do it over again—she would certainly do so.

That led directly to the next round of questions—did she, in fact, have any more money?

She didn't.

Magda had a few thousand in the bank, some jewelry on her fingers and around her neck and a little more in a safe-deposit box in Culiacán, but that was about it. But hadn't they made enough from her already, stealing three and a half million dollars?

As it turned out—no.

They did let her try to call Jorge to see if something could be arranged, but he didn't answer his phone and appeared to have gone on an extended trip to Southeast Asia.

That was bad luck, the *federales* commiserated.

Bad luck for them, worse luck for her, and she ended up getting charged, and convicted, of multiple counts of money laundering, advising and abetting a drug kingpin, and narcotics trafficking.

The magistrate sentenced her to fifteen years in maximum security.

As an example to other young women.

Her processing into CEFERESO II was brutal.

Of the five hundred inmates of the prison block, three of them are women, so Magda was a novelty to begin with, never mind being a (former) beauty queen. She was stripped, "internally searched" numerous times for contraband, scrubbed with disinfectant, and then hosed down. She was poked, prodded, felt up, patted down, hit on, and told over and over again about the multiple gang rapes that awaited her inside, both from guards and from inmates. By the time they carted her to COC, clad in male sweat clothes, she was almost catatonic with shock and terror.

The other convicts hooted "compliments" and threats as the guards walked her to COC.

This is when Adán sees her.

"Who is she?" Adán asks Francisco, the head of Los Bateadores and his personal bodyguard.

"The *dedo* was Miss Culiacán," Francisco says. "A few years back."

She certainly doesn't look like a beauty queen at the moment. No makeup, her hair dirty and stringy, her body disguised in the oversized sweatsuit, shuffling along the corridor with her ankles bound.

But Adán sees her eyes.

Blue as a Sinaloan mountain lake.

And the classic bones of her face.

"What's her name?" Adán asks.

"Magda something," Francisco answers. "I don't remember her last name."

"Find out," Adán says. "Find out everything about her and get back to me tonight. In the meantime, make sure they give her a blanket. And have a doctor attend her. And not one of the prison butchers—a real doctor."

"*Sí, patrón.*"

"And no one touches her," Adán says.

The word—greatly disappointing as there have already been knives out over who gets to rape her first—goes out: Any part of you that touches her gets the chop. You touch her with your hand, you lose the hand. You violate her with your dick . . .

She's the *patrón*'s woman.

Everyone knows this but Magda.

When the blanket arrives, from a guard who seems uneasy even being in her presence, she thinks it's normal. Same when a respectful woman doctor comes into the cell and asks to examine her. The doctor gives her a mild sedative to help her sleep and says she'll call back to check up on her.

At first Magda is afraid to close her eyes for fear of the threatened rape, but the sedative takes hold and, anyway, a guard posts himself outside her cell with his back to her, his eyes never on her.

She starts to suspect that she's receiving special treatment when breakfast comes on a tray and it's actually edible, but she attributes it to her celebrity.

Two days later a guard comes in with a set of new and quite decent clothing—two dresses, some blouses and skirts, some pants, a nice sweater—with labels from chic Guadalajara shops. Magda asks the guard who sent these things and gets just a shrug in response. The clothes are in her sizes, and Magda wonders if her family got them in, or maybe Jorge did it.

She hasn't heard from him, nor from her family, but the prison shrink also told her that she'd be held incommunicado in COC, so perhaps there are phone calls or messages waiting for her.

The clothes make her feel a little better, but she can't shrug off the profound depression, imagining even a few months in this place, never mind fifteen years. She expresses this at her first evaluation with the prison psy-chiatrist, who insists that the door remain open and sits behind his desk as if it's a barrier.

He tells her that these feelings are perfectly normal, that she'll adjust, especially when she's out of COC and integrated into the general popula-tion. But Magda can't imagine how that could even happen in a place with thousands of men, and wonders if they'll put her in a cell with the two other women, and doesn't know if that would be a good or a bad thing.

Cosmetics arrive the next day. Expensive makeup, exactly the kind she normally uses, with a small hand mirror. At the bottom of the box she finds a note—"Courtesies of a fellow Sinaloan."

So much for Jorge.

But who is it?

Magda is not stupid.

She knows the narco-world and its players. There are dozens of Sinaloans in Puente Grande, but maybe a handful with the means to pull off the sort of privileges she's experiencing. Like most Sinaloans in the business, she knows that Adán Barrera, the former Señor de los Cielos, is a resident here.

Could it be?

Step away from yourself, she thinks, looking into the mirror as she applies the makeup, such a simple thing that is now a great pleasure. He's *Adán Barrera*—he could bring in the most beautiful women in the world if he pleased.

What would he want with me?

Magda makes a frank self-assessment—she's still beautiful, but closer to thirty than to twenty. Women her age back in Sinaloa are considered old maids.

But three afternoons later, a bottle of good Merlot arrives with a glass, a corkscrew, and another note: "A few friends and I are having a 'movie night' and I wonder if you'd like to come as my guest. Adán Barrera."

Magda has to laugh.

Inside the most brutal prison in the Western world, the man is *courting* her as if they're high school students.

He's asking for a *date*.

To "movie night."

She laughs even harder when she realizes what else she's thinking—oh, God, what should I wear?

The guard stands there, clearly waiting for an answer.

Magda hesitates—is this just a setup for a gang rape?

If it is, it is, she decides. She has to take the chance, because she knows that she can't survive fifteen years in this place as a "normal" inmate.

"Tell him I'd love to," Magda says.

What first strikes Magda about Adán Barrera is how shy he is.

Not a quality you usually see in a *buchone.*

His entire affect is subdued, from the tone of his voice to his clothes—tonight a black Hugo Boss suit with a white shirt.

Adán's a little shorter than she is; there are a few flecks of silver in the temples of his black hair. He smiles shyly and then looks down as he shakes her hand and says, "I'm so glad you came. I'm Adán Barrera."

"Of course," she says. "Everyone knows who you are. I'm Magda Beltrán."

"Everyone knows who *you* are."

Adán notices the wine bottle and glass in her left hand. "You didn't like the wine? I'm sorry."

"No," Magda says. "I just didn't want to drink it alone. I thought it would be more fun if we drank it together."

She'd decided on one of the blue dresses that he sent. At first she went with the sweater and slacks as appropriate for a "movie night," then decided that he'd sent dresses for a reason, and didn't want to disappoint him.

Adán walks her to the front of five rows of folding chairs that have been set in front of a large-screen television. She notices that their whole row is empty, but that the others are filled with inmates who try to look at her without staring. Other inmates stand by the door of the dining hall, clearly on guard.

Adán pulls out a chair for her, she sits down, and he sits beside her. "I hope you like *Miss Congeniality.* Sandra Bullock?"

"I like her," Magda says. "It's about a beauty pageant contestant, isn't it?"

"I thought . . ."

"That's very considerate of you."

"Would you like something? Popcorn?"

"Popcorn and red wine?" Magda asks. "Well, why not?"

Adán nods to an inmate, who hustles to a popcorn machine and comes back with two bowls. Another inmate hands Adán a corkscrew and another glass.

He opens the bottle and pours. "I know nothing about wine. It's supposed to be good."

She rolls the glass and sniffs. "It is."

"I'm glad."

"Do I have you to thank for the clothes?" she asks. "The cosmetics?"

Adán dips his head in a slight acknowledgment.

"And my safety?" she asks.

He nods again. "Nobody will touch you in here unless you want him to."

Does that include you? she wonders.

"Well, I'm very grateful for your protection," Magda says. "But may I ask why you're being so generous?"

"We Sinaloans have to look out for each other," Adán answers. He nods to an inmate and the movie starts.

She doesn't go to bed with him that night.

Or the next, or the next.

But Magda knows that it's an inevitability. She needs and wants his protection, she needs and wants the things he can give her. It's no different in here than out in the rest of the world, but it's entirely different in the sense that he is her only choice.

Magda wants and needs affection, companionship—admit it, she tells herself, sex—and he is the only choice. She knows that he will never accept anyone else having her. It would be not only a rejection and a disappointment, but a humiliation.

Magda has been around enough to know that a man in Adán Barrera's situation cannot allow himself to be humiliated. It could be literally fatal—if you're humiliated, it's because you're weak. If you're weak, you're a target.

So if she wants a man, it has to be Adán.

And why not?

True, Adán's older and not beautiful like Emilio or handsome like Jorge, but he's kind of cute and not at all repulsive like some of the older bosses she's seen. He's nice, he's polite, he's considerate. He dresses well, he's smart, interesting, and well-spoken.

And he's rich.

Adán can provide her with a life in this prison vastly better than she could otherwise have. With him, she's protected, privileged, and she has the "little" things that make life in this hellhole just tolerable.

Without him, those things go away, along with—much more important— his protection. If he withdraws that, she knows that sexual assaults will quickly follow, and she'll become a pass-around item among first the guards and then the prisoners.

She sees it happening with the other two women.

They have sex for liquor, food, and drugs. Especially drugs. One of the women looks catatonic most of the time, the other—clearly psychotic now—sits naked in her cell and displays her genitals to anyone who passes by.

So Magda knows that it's just a matter of time before she gives herself to Adán, and while she tells herself that it's not rape, she's also smart enough to know that it's definitely a power relationship with her on the bottom.

Adán has the power, so he can have her.

They both know this, neither speaks it, and he doesn't press things. But she knows that she can't let it go on until it becomes a joke, until laughs and whispers go around the prison that she is making a fool of the lovesick *patrón*.

If Adán ever heard one of those jokes, she knows her throat could be slit and her body tossed literally to the dogs.

He would have to do it, to restore his honor.

Magda has heard the stories about the woman who spurned Adán's uncle and ended up with her head cut off and her children tossed to their deaths off a bridge. This man Adán, she reminds herself—this polite, shy man—threw two small children off a bridge.

Or so the story goes.

So when, after four "dates," he asks her to dinner in his cell, they both know that the evening is going to end in his bed.

Adán looks across the table at Magda.

"Are you enjoying your dinner?" he asks.

"Yes, it's good."

It should be, Adán thinks. The swordfish was specially flown in from Acapulco packed in ice. The wine should meet her approval. He knows all about Magda by now, of course, about her background, her youthful affair with the young cocaine trafficker; more important, her longer relationship with Jorge Estrada.

The Colombian had made a foolish mistake in not paying Nacho to bring product in through the airport. It would have been a simple matter of setting up a meeting, paying a modest fee, and Nacho would have graciously offered the use of his turf.

But Estrada was too arrogant or greedy to do that, and his willful disrespect had gotten his woman thrown into prison. Worse, he knew there was a problem, that's why he sent her instead of doing it himself. Now it was too late—her case, like his own, was too high-profile for a quick, quiet fix.

Magda is staring at him.

"I'm sorry," he says. "A business distraction."

"Do I already bore you?" she asks, with the practiced, pretty pout of a pageant contestant.

"Not at all."

"If there's something you'd like to talk about . . ." She reaches across the table and touches his hand.

It's an intimate gesture. "Adán, I don't want to wait anymore."

She stands up and walks to the partitioned area that comprises his bedroom. Turning her back to him, she starts to unzip her dress, but then stops, looks over her shoulder in a way that makes her neck long and elegant, and says, "Help, please?" because she knows that he wants to unwrap her like a gift.

Adán steps behind her and pulls the zipper down, past her shoulder blades and the small of her back, then he leans in and kisses her neck.

"If you do that," Magda says, "I can't stop you."

He keeps kissing her neck and then pushes the dress down below her shoulders and cups her breasts. Then he slides the dress over her hips and down her legs until it pools like water at her feet.

She steps out of it and turns to him.

"Turnabout is fair play," she says, unzipping his fly. "What do you like?"

"Everything."

"That's good," Magda says, "because I *do* everything."

Her love with Emilio had been pure passion.

Simple and direct.

With Jorge had come more sophistication, and he taught her things in bed, things he liked, things that any man would like.

Now she uses them all on Adán, because this cannot be, *cannot be*, a one-night stand after which he figures he's had what he wanted and throws her back into the pool. He has to know that the whole sexual world is in her fingers, her mouth, her *chocha*, and that she could give him things no other woman can.

But it's also clear that he's had some experience himself, because Adán knows his way around a woman's body and isn't selfish. Magda is surprised when she feels a climax building inside her, more surprised when she feels herself toppling over that waterfall, even more surprised that he's still hard.

When she looks at him curiously, he says, "I was always taught, ladies first."

There's something in his eyes, this small superior glint, that makes her competitive with him, so she does something that she was going to save up for another time and she watches his eyes go wide, feels his breathing get hard, then hears him moan (you're not distracted *now*, are you?), and she keeps him there for a moment and cranes her neck up so her mouth is by his ear and demands, "Say my name."

He doesn't and she stops what she's doing and feels him tremble.

"Say my name."

"Magda."

She starts to move. "Say it again."

"Magda."

"Scream it."

"Magda!"

She feels him come inside her.

It feels like safety.

They start a life of odd domesticity, given their circumstances.

Officially transferred from COC into the unit with the two other women, Magda actually moves to the cell next to Adán's and spends most of her nights with him.

He gets up early to work and then joins her for breakfast. She goes back to her cell to read or work out, then they lunch together. He goes back to work and she reads more or watches television until they have dinner together.

Some afternoons he takes an hour or two off and they go out into the yard and join one of the volleyball games with other inmates, play basketball, or just get some sun. In the evenings it's television or movie nights, although more and more often he wants to go to bed early and make love.

He's enamored of her.

Lucía was pretty, petite, and thin. Magda's body is lush—full hips, heavy breasts—a fruit orchard on a warm, damp morning.

And she's smart.

A bit at a time, Magda reveals the extent of her knowledge about the business. She lets drop small bits of information about the cocaine trade, people she's met—friends, acquaintances, connections. She casually mentions the places she's been—South America, Europe, Asia, the United States—to show that, while she's a proud Sinaloan, she's no mere *chuntara*, hillbilly, either.

That she could be an asset to him, and not only in bed.

Adán doesn't doubt that, actually.

It isn't a matter of doubt, it's a matter of trust.

Magda sees the blade.

A glint in the sunshine.

"Adán!" she screams.

He turns as the small, thin man—perhaps in his thirties—steps toward him, knife leveled horizontally and held back at the waist like a professional. The man thrusts the blade, Adán pivots, and the knife slices the small of his back. The attacker pulls back the blade to try again, but two of Los Bateadores are already on him, pin his arms behind him, and start to drag him off the volleyball court.

"Alive!" Adán yells. "I want him alive!"

He reaches around and feels the hot, sticky blood seep through his fingers. Francisco grabs him, then Magda, and then he blacks out.

His would-be assassin doesn't know who hired him.

Adán believes him, and didn't think that he would, actually. Juan Jesús Cabray is a good man with a knife, serving a pair of sixty-year sentences for dispatching two rivals in a Nogales bar with a blade. He did a couple of jobs for the old Sonora cartel back in the day, but that means nothing now. Now he's tied to a pillar in a basement storage room as Diego lazily shoulders a baseball bat and prepares to swing.

"Who hired you, *cabrón*?"

Cabray's head lolls forward like a broken doll, but he manages to shake it feebly and mutter, "I don't know."

Adán sits uncomfortably on a three-legged stool. The seven stitches itch more than hurt, but his side is starting to ache. Whoever hired Cabray used multiple layers of cut-outs to approach him. And they chose a man who had nothing to lose. But what would he have to gain? That his impoverished family would receive a bundle of cash—money that he could no longer provide. So he would keep his silence, use the one resource that God gave to the Mexican campesino—the ability to suffer. Diego could beat this man to death and it wouldn't matter.

"Stop." Adán edges his stool closer, and says softly, "Juan Cabray, you know you're going to die. And you will die happy, thinking of the money that will go to your wife and family. That's a good thing, you're a brave man. But you know . . . Juan, look at me . . ."

Cabray lifts his head.

". . . you know that I can reach out to your family, wherever they are." Adán says, "Listen to me, Juan Jesús Cabray, I will buy your wife a house, I will get her a job where she doesn't work hard, I will send your son to school. Is your mother alive?"

"Yes."

"I will see that she is warm in the winter," Adán says, "and that you have a funeral that will make her proud. So, the only question is, do I take your family under my wing and make them *my* family, or do I kill them? You decide."

"I don't know who hired me, *patrón*."

"But someone approached you," Adán says.

"Yes."

"Who?"

"One of the guards," Cabray says. "Navarro."

Two of Los Bateadores hustle out.

"What did he offer you?" Adán asks Cabray.

"Thirty thousand."

Adán leans in and whispers into Cabray's ear, "Juan Jesús, do you trust me?"

"*Sí, patrón.*"

"Save us time," Adán says. "Tell me how to find your family."

Cabray whispers that they are in a village named Los Elijos, in Durango. His wife's name is María, his mother is Guadalupe.

"Father?" Adán asks.

"*Muerto.*"

"He is waiting for you in heaven," Adán says. Wincing a little as he stands up, he says to Diego, "Make it quick."

As Adán walks out of the room, he hears Cabray mutter a prayer. From the hallway, he hears the *tiro de gracia*, the mercy shot.

"Who?" Adán asks Diego.

They're sitting back in his cell. Adán sips on a glass of scotch, to ease the ache in his side.

Diego looks at Magda sitting on the bed.

"We can speak in front of her," Adán says. "After all, *she* saved my life, not your men."

Diego flushes but has to acknowledge this truth. The men responsible for guarding Adán have been transferred to Block 4, the worst unit in the prison, where the child molesters, the murderers, the lunatics go. There will be no movie nights, no women, no parties. They'll be fighting and killing over scraps of food.

New men will be coming in over the next few days.

They're volunteers, men who willingly get themselves convicted and sent to prison, knowing that when they get out in a few years they'll be offered opportunities to traffic drugs, to make fortunes that they could never otherwise dream of.

The guard Navarro ran as soon as word got out that the attempt failed. They're tracking him now. The warden was apoplectic with apologies, promising a full investigation and increased security. Adán simply stared at him. He would do his own investigation and provide his own increased security. Even now, five Bateadores stand outside the door.

"Suppose it was Fuentes," Diego says, naming the *chaca* of the Juárez cartel. The Juárez plaza was always connected to Sinaloa, and now Vicente Fuentes might be concerned that Adán wants it back. But he had asked Esparza, related by marriage to Fuentes, to reassure him that Adán Barrera only wants to make a living from his own territory.

Or the murder attempt could have come from Tijuana, Adán thinks. Teo Solorzano led a revolt against my sister in my absence and might well be afraid of the consequences now that I'm back. This could have been a preemptive strike.

"What about Contreras?" Magda asks.

"He has no reason to kill me," Adán says. "Contreras is better off with Garza in prison. He's the co-boss of the Gulf cartel now, he makes more money, and has me to thank for that."

And I sent Diego personally to speak with Contreras, to assure him that I have no designs on the Gulf or ambitions to take back my old throne.

But Contreras has ambitions of his own, Adán thinks.

It could have been any of the three, but we won't know, Adán thinks, until we find Navarro, and maybe not even then. If this attempt came from any of the men they're thinking about, the guard is probably already dead. Some man he trusted offered to get him out, then took him somewhere and killed him.

He looks at Diego and smiles. "We'll see who comes first."

Diego smiles back. Each of the three groups will send an emissary to deny responsibility. Whoever comes first is probably the most nervous, and for good reason. If they'd succeeded in killing Adán, they'd be in negotiations with Diego Tapia and Esparza already.

But having missed, they'd be at war with them.

Not a good place to be.

"This village of Cabray's," Diego says, "I'll have it bulldozed to the ground."

"No," Adán snaps. "I gave the man my word."

Find the family, Adán tells him, and set them up with exactly what I said. And put a school in the village, or a clinic, or a well—whatever it is they need—but make sure they know who it came from."

After Diego leaves, Magda, flipping through Mexican *Vogue,* says, "Perhaps you're looking too far away."

"What do you mean?"

"For the people who tried to kill you," Magda says. "Maybe you should be looking closer. Who was in charge of protecting you? Who failed to?"

The suggestion makes him angry. "Diego is blood. More like my brother than my cousin."

"Ask yourself, who has the most to gain by your death?" Magda asks. "Diego and Nacho have their own organizations now, they've become used to being their own bosses. Has Nacho even come to see you?"

"It's too risky."

"Diego came."

"That's Diego," Adán says. "He doesn't give a damn."

"Or he does."

Not Diego, Adán thinks. Maybe the others, although I doubt it. Nacho was a close friend and adviser to my uncle, and was as good an adviser to me. He's married to my sister's brother-in-law's sister. He's family.

But maybe.

But Diego?

Never.

"I'd bet my life on Diego," he says defensively.

Magda shrugs. "You are."

He sits down on the bed next to her.

"If they tried once," she says, "they'll try again."

"I know," he says. And one day, they'll succeed, he thinks. I'm a stationary target in this prison. And, whoever it is, if they really want me dead, I'm dead. But there is no use dwelling on it. "*You* saved my life today."

She flips a page and says, "It's a small thing."

Adán laughs. "What do you want in return?"

Magda finally looks up from the magazine. "You've saved my life many times over."

"Christmas is coming," Adán says.

"Such as it is"—she sighs—"in this place."

"We'll make the most of it," he promises.

If we live long enough.

Matamoros
Tamaulipas, Mexico
November 2004

Heriberto Ochoa watches from a pew in the third row of the church as Salvador Herrera holds the baby girl over the baptismal and the priest says the words. As is tradition, both infant and godfather wear white, and Herrera's squat form reminds Ochoa of an old refrigerator.

The church is packed, as befits the *bautizo* of a powerful narco's daughter. Osiel Contreras stands to the side of the font and beams in paternal pride.

Ochoa remembers the first time he met Osiel Contreras, over a year ago now. A soldier then, Ochoa was a lieutenant in Mexico's elite Airborne Special Forces Group, and Contreras had just risen to the leadership of the Gulf cartel after Garza's arrest and extradition.

They met at a barbecue on a ranch south of the city, and Contreras mentioned that he needed protection.

"What kind of men do you need?" Ochoa asked. He sipped his beer. It was cold and crisp.

"The best," Contreras answered. "Only the best."

"The best men," Ochoa said, "are only in the army."

It wasn't bragging, it was a simple matter of fact. If you want gangbangers, drug addicts, thugs, and *malandros*—useless layabouts—on your payroll, you can pick them up on any corner. If you want elite men, you have to go to an elite force. Ochoa was elite—he'd taken counterinsurgency training from the American special forces and the Israelis.

The best of the best.

"What do you make a year?" Contreras asked. When Ochoa told him, Contreras shook his head and said, "I feed my chickens better."

"And do they protect you?"

Contreras laughed.

Ochoa deserted the army and went to work for the Gulf cartel. His first task was to recruit others like him.

The Mexican army was rife with desertion anyway. Armed with *cañonazos de dólares*—cannonballs of money—Ochoa easily seduced thirty of his comrades away from their long hours, shabby barracks, and lousy pay. Within weeks he'd brought over four other lieutenants, five sergeants, five corporals, and twenty privates. They brought with them valuable merchandise—AR-15 rifles, grenade launchers, and state-of-the-art surveillance equipment.

Contreras's terms were generous.

In addition to a salary, he gave each recruit a bonus of $3,000 U.S. to put in the bank, invest *el norte,* or buy drugs.

Ochoa bought eighteen kilos of cocaine.

Now he was well on his way to becoming a rich man.

The work itself was relatively easy—guard Contreras and enforce the *piso.* Most paid willingly, the recalcitrant were taken to the Hotel Nieto in Matamoros and persuaded, often with a pistol barrel shoved down their throats.

Just a few months into the job, Contreras ordered him to eliminate a rival trafficker. Ochoa took twenty men and besieged the man's compound. The occupants of the fortified house, maybe a dozen of them, returned fire and held Ochoa's men off until he dashed to the back of the compound, found the propane tank, and blew it up, immolating everyone inside.

Mission accomplished.

The resultant bonus from a grateful Contreras bought more cocaine, and the story gained them useful notoriety.

And now they have become far more than just bodyguards. The original thirty are now over four hundred, and Ochoa has begun to worry a little bit about the dilution of quality. To counter that, he's set up three training bases on cartel-owned ranches out in the countryside, where the new recruits sharpen their skills on tactics, weapons, and intelligence gathering, and are indoctrinated into the group culture.

The culture is that of an elite force.

On missions, they blacken their faces and wear black clothing and hoods. Military protocol is strictly observed, with ranks, salutes, and chain of command. So is loyalty and camaraderie—the ethic of "no man left behind." A comrade is to be brought off the field of battle, dead or alive. If wounded, he gets the best treatment by the best doctors; if killed, his family is taken care of and his death avenged.

Without exception.

As their numbers grew, their role expanded. While mission one is and always will be the protection of Osiel Contreras and his narco-turf, Ochoa's force has gotten into lucrative side markets. With the boss's approval—and why not, he gets thick envelopes of cash—the men have moved into kidnapping and extortion.

Shopkeepers, bar owners, and club proprietors in Matamoros and other towns now pay Ochoa's men for "protection," otherwise their businesses might be robbed or burned to the ground, their customers beaten up. Gambling dens, brothels, *tienditas*—the little stores that sell small amounts of dope to junkies—pay off.

They're scared not to.

Ochoa's men have a well-earned reputation for brutality. People whisper about *la paleta*, said to be a favored technique of Ochoa, in which the victim in stripped naked and then beaten to death with a two-by-four.

But to be truly famous, a group needs a name.

In the army, Ochoa's radio call signal was "Zeta One," so they went with that and called themselves the Zetas.

As the original Zeta, Ochoa became known as "Z-1."

The original other thirty took their nicknames from the order in which they came over—Z-2, Z-3, and so on. It became a hierarchy of seniority.

Z-1 is tall, handsome, with a thick head of black hair, a hawklike face, and a muscular build. Today he wears a khaki suit with a deep blue shirt—his army-issued FN Five-seven pistol tucked into a shoulder holster under his left arm. He sits in the crowded church and tries to stay awake as the priest drones on.

But that's what priests do—they drone.

Finally, the service comes to an end and the participants start to file out of the church.

"Let's go for a ride," Contreras says.

A fiend for intelligence, Ochoa knows his boss's history. Born dirt poor and fatherless on a shitty ranch in rural Tamaulipas, Osiel Contreras was raised by an uncle who resented the additional mouth to feed. The young Osiel worked as a dishwasher before running off to Arizona to deal marijuana, only to end up in a *yanqui* prison. When NAFTA came along, Contreras, with scores of others, was transferred to a prison back in Mexico. The legend goes that he had an affair with the warden's wife, and when the warden found out and beat her, Contreras had him killed.

When he got out of jail, Herrera ostensibly got him a job in an auto body shop but really as a trafficker for Garza. The two men earned their way to the top. It was often said that they sat at the feet of God—Herrera on the right, Contreras on the left.

"Herrera is coming with us," Contreras says now.

Lately, Contreras has become more and more annoyed with his old friend. Ochoa can't blame him—Herrera had always been high-handed, all the more so since assuming the head chair, and he's started to treat Contreras more as a subordinate than a partner, interrupting him at meetings, dismissing his opinions.

Still, the two men are friends.

They washed dishes together, served time together, came up the hard way under Garza, a hard man.

The three of them get into Contreras's new *troca del año*, a Dodge Durango. "You can take the boy out of the country," Ochoa muses as he squeezes his long legs into the pickup's narrow rear compartment. Contreras gets behind the wheel—he loves to drive a truck.

In the rural shitholes they grew up in, you were lucky to have a pair of shoes. Even a *baica* was a dream. You'd stand there in the dust and watch the *grandes* speed by in their new pickups and think, one day that's going to be me.

So Contreras has fleets of trucks and SUVs, he has drivers, he even has a private plane with a pilot—but when he gets the chance to get behind the wheel of a pickup truck, he's going to do it.

As they head out of town toward Contreras's ranch, Herrera wants to talk. "Did you hear the news? Someone tried to kill Adán Barrera."

"It wasn't me," Contreras says. "His people pay the *piso*. If Adán increases volume, it's more money for us."

"What if he wants the throne back?" Herrera asks.

"He doesn't."

"How do you know?"

"He sent Diego Tapia personally," Contreras answers.

"He didn't come to see *me*," Herrera says. "You should have told me."

"I'm telling you now," Contreras says. "You think I just like chauffeuring you around?"

Herrera pouts for a few moments and then changes the subject. "A beautiful ceremony, I thought. Although I prefer weddings—you get to fuck the bridesmaids."

"Or try, anyway," Contreras answers.

" 'There is no try.' " Herrera chuckles. " 'Just *do.*' "

"I hate those fucking movies," Osiel says.

Ochoa quietly pulls his pistol from the holster and lays it by his side.

"It's my big dick they like," Herrera says. "You should—"

Ochoa sticks the pistol into the back of Herrera's head and pulls the trigger twice.

Brains, blood, and hair splatter onto the windshield and the console.

Contreras pulls over and puts the truck in park. Ochoa climbs out of the cab and pulls Herrera's body in the bushes. When he comes back, Contreras is fussing about the mess. "Now I'll have to have it detailed again."

"I'll just dump it someplace."

"It's a good truck," Contreras says. "Have it steam-cleaned, replace the windshield."

Ochoa is amused. The *chaca* spent about thirty-seven minutes working in a body shop and thinks he's an expert on auto repair.

He's also cheap.

Ochoa understands that—he grew up poor, too.

He was born on Christmas Day to campesinos in Apan, where life promised little opportunity except to make *pulque* or go into the rodeo. Ochoa didn't see a future in either, or as a tenant farmer, so the day he turned seventeen he ran away and enlisted in the army, where at least he'd have clean sheets, and if the meals were bad, at least there were three of them a day.

A natural soldier, he liked the army, the discipline, the order, the cleanliness so different from the constant dust and filth of the impoverished *casita* he grew up in. He liked the uniforms, the clean clothes, the camaraderie. And if he had to take orders, it was from men he respected, men who'd earned their positions, not just fat *grandes* who'd inherited their estates and thought that made them little gods.

And a man could rise in the army, rise above his birth and his accent and make something of himself—not like in Apan, where you were stuck in your class, generation after generation. He watched his father work his life away, come home red-eyed and staggering from the *pulque*, whip out his belt, and take it out on his wife and his kids.

Not for me, Ochoa thought.

"There was only one man born in a stable on Christmas who ever made anything of himself," Ochoa liked to say, "and look what they did to him."

So the army was a refuge, an opportunity.

He was good at it.

His father had made him insensitive to pain; he could take anything the training sergeants could dish out. He liked the brutal training, the hand-to-hand combat, the survival ordeals in the desert. His superiors noticed him and plucked him out for special forces. There they gave him skills— counterinsurgency, counterterrorism, weapons, intelligence, interrogation.

He made his reputation putting down the armed rebellion in Chiapas. It was a dirty war in a jungle, like any guerrilla conflict it was hard to tell the combatants from the civilians, and then he found it didn't really matter—the response to terror is terror.

Ochoa did things, in clearings, in streambeds, in villages, that you don't talk about, that you don't trumpet on the evening news. But when his superiors needed information, he got them information, when they needed a guerrilla leader dead, he made it thus, when a village needed intimidation, he snuck in at night, and when the village awoke at dawn, it found its headman's body strung from a tree.

For all this, they made him an officer, and, when the rebellion had been put down, transferred him to Tamaulipas.

To a special antinarcotics task force.

That's when he met Contreras.

Now a white Jeep Cherokee comes down the road. Miguel Morales, aka "Z-40," gets out, tosses Ochoa a quick salute, and gets behind the wheel of the Durango. Ochoa and Contreras get into the Cherokee.

"I'll have someone come out and bury him," Ochoa says, jutting his chin toward Herrera's corpse.

"Let the coyotes enjoy his big dick," Contreras answers. "What about the others?"

"It's taken care of."

There will be two more killings—of Herrera loyalists—before the sun goes down. When it comes back up, Osiel Contreras will be the sole, undisputed boss of the Gulf cartel.

And he'll have a nickname—El Mata Amigos.

The Friend Killer.

Ochoa will gain a new *aporto* as well.

El Verdugo.

The Executioner.

2

Christmas in Prison

It was Christmas in prison
And the food was real good

—John Prine
"Christmas in Prison"

Wheeling, West Virginia
December 2004

Keller presses himself against the wall by the door of his motel room and waits.

He listens to the footsteps coming up the stairs to the second floor and knows now that there are two of them and that they made him in the sports bar across the highway where he had a burger and fries. He could tell from the overlong sideways glance of one, and the studious indifference of the other, that they had tracked him down.

To Wheeling, West Virginia.

Keller has been on the move since he left the monastery. He didn't want to leave, but staying would have put the brothers in danger and brought his world of violence into their world of serenity, and he couldn't let that happen.

So he moves, like any wanted man, with his head on a swivel.

To a man with a price on his head, no other man is innocent. The Mexican guy at the Memphis gas station who checked out his license plate, the desk clerk in Nashville who looked twice at his (phony) ID, the woman in Lexington who smiled.

He'd hitchhiked from Abiquiú to Santa Fe, getting picked up by two Navajo men driving down from the rez, then caught a bus to Albuquerque where he bought an old car—a '96 Toyota Camry—from a tweaker who needed cash.

From Albuquerque he drove east on the 40, the irony not escaping him that this was "Cocaine Alley," one of the main arterials of the drug trade from Mexico through the southeastern United States from I-35, to I-30, to I-40.

Keller holed up in a motel in Santa Rosa for a couple of days, slept most of the time, and then continued east—Tucumcari, Amarillo, Oklahoma City, Fort Smith, Little Rock, Memphis. At Nashville he left the 40 for the 65 and headed north, turned east on the 64, north again on the 79.

Keller's travels have been random, and it's better that way—hard to figure out or anticipate.

But eventually terminal, a dead end, as it were.

Barrera has the best killers in the world at hand. Not just Mexican *sicarios* or *cholo* gangbangers, but mob assassins, special forces veterans, and just plain freelancers looking to bank a seven-figure windfall in a numbered account.

It could be anyone.

A drug dealer looking to do a favor for the Lord of the Skies, a junkie praying for a lifetime supply, a convict's wife wanting to get her husband a pass in prison.

Keller knows that he's a walking lottery ticket.

Winner, winner, chicken dinner.

At an SRO in Memphis, Keller thought they had him. The guy who checked in to the room next door followed him into the common shower. Could have been looking for company, could have been looking for two mil. Keller sat up all that night on his bed with his legs stretched out in front of him and his Sig Sauer on his lap. Took off before the sun came up.

Now they do have him.

Trapped in his room.

After a while, motel rooms become like jail cells—claustrophobic, with the same sense of isolation, hopelessness, and loneliness. The television, the bed, the shower, the creaky air conditioner or heating unit that bangs all night, the coffee maker with the plastic cups in plastic holders, the packets of sugar, powdered "cream," and artificial sweeteners, the clock radio that glows by the bed. The diner across the parking lot, the bar down the street, the hookers and the johns three doors down.

His aimlessness wasn't just a tactic but also a state of mind, a condition of the soul. He had to be on the move, running from someone he couldn't know, looking for something he couldn't identify or name.

Yeah, that's bullshit, Keller had to admit. You know what you're running from—and it's not Barrera—and you know what you're running *at*.

Same thing you've been charging for thirty years.

You're just not willing to accept it yet.

He became his own blues song, a Tom Waits loser, a Kerouac saint, a Springsteen hero under the lights of the American highway and the neon glow of the American strip. A fugitive, a sharecropper, a hobo, a cowboy who knows that he's running out of prairie but rides anyway because there's nothing left but to ride.

Lexington, Huntington, Charleston.

Morgantown, Wheeling.

The loneliness didn't bother him, he was used to it, he liked the quiet, the solitude, the long days in his own capsule speeding through space with just the sound of the wheels and the car radio. He didn't mind eating alone with just a book for company—paperbacks that he bought in secondhand shops and Goodwill stores.

So he sat alone and ate and read, with an eye always toward the door and the windows, careful to leave a tip neither small nor large enough to attract notice, always paying in cash, always getting it from an ATM in the middle of his day and never where he's spending the night.

With the exception of his marriage and the years spent raising his children, Art Keller was pretty much a loner, an outsider. The son of an Anglo father who didn't want a half-Mexican kid, he always had one foot in each world, but never both feet in either. Raised in San Diego's Barrio Logan, he had to fight for his half-gringo side; at UCLA, he had to prove that he wasn't there on an affirmative action pass.

So he boxed in the barrio, boxed in college, and also verbally sparred in class with California Anglo "legacy" kids for whom Westwood was a birthright and not a privilege, and when CIA started to court him in his junior year he let himself be seduced. When he went to 'Nam on Operation Phoenix he felt like he was finally an American. When he "swapped alphabets," as his wife, Althea, put it, and transferred to the new DEA, of course they sent him to Mexico, because he looked the part and spoke the language.

The Mexicans in Sinaloa had no doubt who he was—a *yanqui*, a *pocho*—but he didn't he really belong to the DEA community either, who saw him as a CIA plant and isolated him. When he finally made an ally, it was young Adán Barrera and then his *tío* Miguel Ángel. Once again Keller had a foot in both worlds, two floating islands that inevitably drifted far apart and left him once again alone.

For a while, he had Ernie Hidalgo—his partner, his friend, his ally against the Barreras. But the Barreras killed him—not before torturing him over the course of weeks—and after that, Keller didn't much want another partner.

He had Althea and his kids, but she (sensibly, understandably) left him and took his children with her.

And Keller became "the Border Lord," running the drug war along the entire length of Mexico, his power as aggrandized as his soul was attenuated, his ruthlessness out of control.

And he did something for which he's still ashamed—used the illness of a little girl, Barrera's daughter, to lure him across the border. Told a man that his child was dying to entrap him. And enlisted Barrera's wife to help him do it.

Such was the depth of their hatred.

Was? Keller asked himself.

You've tried to put it all in the past—how you bagged Barrera, killed his brother and Tío, your old mentor. How you had a gun to the side of Adán's head but didn't pull the trigger.

Barrera went to prison and Keller went into exile, finally finding the only serenity he'd ever known in the simple job of tending the beehives, in the quiet comfort of routine, the solace of prayer.

But the past is a dogged pursuer, a pack of wolves relentlessly running you down. Maybe it's better to turn and face it.

And now you are, he thinks with grim humor, whether you want to or not. His back literally against the wall, he waits.

They kick in the door.

The little chain snaps and flies off.

Keller slams the butt of the Sig into the first guy's temple and brings him down like a poleaxed bull. Pulling the second guy in, Keller snaps his wrist and then shatters his nose with the gun barrel. The guy drops to his knees, Keller kicks him in the head, and the man flattens out on the floor, maybe dead, maybe not.

Both were carrying cheap revolvers, not professional gear, Keller thinks, but that might be cover. Maybe they're just robbers, meth heads, maybe not. He should put a bullet in each of their heads, but he doesn't. If they're closing in, they're closing in, he thinks, and two more corpses on my karmic tab won't change that.

Killer Keller.

He walks out, gets into his car, and drives the short distance to Pittsburgh, where he dumps the car and walks to the bus station, that refuge of the American lost, and gets on a Greyhound to Erie, where they used to forge iron and steel.

As he walks to find a motel, the hard snow crunches under his shoes, the wind coming off the lake stings his face. Sad windowfront displays in dying department stores advertise sales, bars promise warmth and the companionship of lost souls, and Keller is glad to find a hotel where they accept cash. The adrenaline of fear and violence fading, he falls asleep.

He gets up and goes out again to midnight Mass at an old Catholic church of tired yellow brick, an old lady whose children have moved out to the suburbs and rarely visit.

It's Christmas Eve.

Puente Grande Prison
Guadalajara, Mexico
Christmas 2004

The walls of Block 2, Level 1-A have been painted a fresh bright yellow, red lanterns hang from the ceilings, and lights are strung along the corridors. Adán Barrera promised that Christmas would be festive, and the *patrón* is throwing a party.

Despite, or perhaps because of, the threat on his life.

As Adán had expected, the guard Navarro was found in a ditch fifty miles away with two bullets in the back of his head, so he had nothing to say about who ordered the attempted assassination.

Osiel Contreras did.

The boss of the Gulf cartel reached out to Diego, and then got the okay to phone Adán directly. Typical Osiel, he started with a joke: *"It's a sad day when a man isn't safe in his own prison."*

"I shouldn't play volleyball, I'm getting too old," Adán answered.

"You're a young man," Osiel said. *"Adán, I cannot believe it. Thank God they didn't succeed."*

"Thank you, Osiel."

"Anyway, I took care of it for you."

"What do you mean?"

Adán already knew what he meant—Contreras killed his own partner. That's how cold-blooded and ruthless Contreras is, and Adán made a mental note not to forget it, especially now that Contreras was assuring him of his friendship.

"I wanted to tell you this before you heard from someone else," Osiel said. *"I*

wanted to tell you personally. Adán, I'm ashamed and embarrassed, but it was Herrera who ordered the attempt on your life."

"Herrera? Why?"

"He was afraid of you, now that you're back."

"I've been back for almost a year," Adán answered. "Why now?"

"Your business has been growing," Osiel said. *"You've been doing very well."*

"Very well for you, too," Adán said. "And for Herrera. The *piso* that I pay you—"

"I tried to explain that to him," Osiel said. *"He wouldn't listen. So you can relax and enjoy the holidays. Herrera won't be bothering you anymore."*

Adán clicked off and went back into the "bedroom," where Magda sat doing her nails. "It was Contreras."

Magda looked up from her nails.

"He was the one who tried to have me killed," Adán continued, "and when it didn't work out, he shifted the blame on Herrera and bragged about killing him for my sake. It's a win-win for him—he gets the CDG all to himself and has an excuse for it."

If Magda was disturbed, she didn't show it. She just seemed to accept treachery as a fact of life. "Why now?"

"I asked him that," Adán said, sitting down beside her, "and he actually answered, vis-à-vis Herrera. Apparently my business is doing too well."

Magda finished applying polish to a finger, held it up for inspection, and apparently approved. "It's nonsense, of course. Contreras is ambitious. He wants to be El Patrón, and knows that he can never be while you're alive."

"I have assured him—I have assured *everyone*, time and again, that I have no—"

"But that's the problem, isn't it?" Magda asks. "No one believes you."

"Do you?"

"Of course not," Magda says, starting in on another fingernail. "How can I? Not even you believe you. You knew, whether you admit it or not, even to yourself, the moment you manipulated your return to Mexico that you would have to take back the throne. Some people welcome that; others—like Contreras—will fight you for it. Kings don't resign, Adán. They either remain king or they die. And not in bed."

Magda's right, Adán thinks.

About all of it.

Contreras *will* have to try again. *It's a sad day when a man isn't safe in his own prison.* And he has the power to do it, with his private army, the so-called Zetas.

But now Adán sets those concerns aside for the party. It's Christmas, time to celebrate. A mariachi band is setting up in the dining hall. Brightly wrapped presents are stacked up against the walls. Trucks have prime rib, lobster, and shrimp. Others are bringing wine, champagne, and whiskey.

Still another will be delivering his family.

Such as it is.

He hasn't seen his sister, Elena, in years. Nor his own nephew, Salvador, Raúl's son—a teenager now.

No, it's been too long.

Too long.

The Tapia brothers and their wives are coming (Adán has strictly banned mistresses and whores from the party; this is meant to be a family day), as are a few of the narcos and favored prisoners—friends of Adán's—in Puente Grande. The warden has been invited, and some of the higher-ranking guards and their families.

Security is tight outside.

Both additional prison guards and Diego's people patrol outside the main gate. They've pulled an armored car sideways across the road to block unwanted vehicles, its machine gun trained to shred any attacker that comes up the highway.

Nacho Esparza is not at the party. He's in Mexico City to deliver a Christmas present.

It's in a suitcase he carries as he gets out of his car on Paseo de la Reforma in the Lomas de Chapultepec neighborhood of Mexico City.

He's familiar with Lomas, a wealthy neighborhood of businesspeople, politicians, and drug traffickers northwest of downtown and literally above the ring of pollution that keeps the city itself in a soup bowl.

Nacho is as smooth as Diego Tapia is rough, his bald head as slick as his speech. Clean-shaven, immaculate, he favors linen suits and Italian loafers. Today, in honor of Christmas, he's added a tie.

He walks to the Marriott hotel on Hidalgo and goes into the lounge, which is quiet on a Christmas afternoon.

The government official is already there, sitting in an easy chair by a glass table with a drink set on it. Nacho sits across from him and sets the suitcase down. "You're aware that certain people want this to happen. Tonight."

"What certain people want is beyond the scope of my authority," the official says. "What I can promise is that there will be no interference."

"So if something should happen with our friend in Puente Grande . . ."

"Then it happens."

Nacho gets up.

He leaves the suitcase.

A semi truck rolls up to the gate of CEFERESO II.

Two of Diego's men, AR-15s in their hands, walk up to the driver. They talk for a few seconds, Diego's men bark some instructions, and the prison guards back off into the shadows of the walls. The blocking truck pulls aside, the metal door slides open, and the semi truck backs its rear door to the entrance.

Salvador Barrera hops out of the truck in his black leather jacket and jeans and looks around with all his father's bluff arrogance. It almost brings tears to Adán's eyes. Salvador *is* his father's son—thick, muscled, aggressive.

Aggression had been Raúl's role in the organization. In the terms of cheap journalism, Adán was the brains, his brother Raúl was the muscle. A generalization, of course, but fair enough.

Raúl had died in Adán's arms.

Well, that's not quite accurate, Adán thinks as he embraces his nephew. Raúl, gut-shot, died from a *tiro de gracia* that I fired into his head to end his agony.

Another memory he owes to Art Keller.

"You've grown," he says, holding Salvador by the shoulders.

"I'm eighteen," Salvador answers, just the slightest trace of resentment in his tone.

I understand it, Adán thinks. Your father is dead and I'm alive. I'm alive and the empire your father died for is shattered. If he were alive, the empire might still be intact.

And you might be right, my nephew.

You might be right.

I will have to find a way of dealing with you.

Salvador turns away to help his mother from the truck. Sondra Barrera has taken on the trappings of a stereotypical Mexican widow. Her severe dress is black and she clutches a rosary in her left hand.

It's a shame, Adán thinks.

Sondra's still a pretty woman, she could find another husband. But not looking like a nun waiting for death. A nice dress . . . a little makeup . . . maybe an occasional smile . . . The problem is that Raúl has become a saint in her memory. She has apparently forgotten his endless infidelities, violent bursts of temper, the drinking, the drugs. Among the many names Adán remembers Sondra calling her husband when he was alive, "saint" was not one of them.

He kisses Sondra on her cheeks. "Sondra . . ."

"We always knew," she says, "that we'd end up here, didn't we?"

No, we didn't, Adán thinks. And if *you* did, it never stopped you from enjoying the houses, the clothing, the jewelry, the vacations. You knew where the money came from—it never stopped you from spending it.

Lavishly.

And, to my knowledge, you never turn down the package of cash that arrives at your house the first of every month. Nor the tuition payments for Salvador's college, the medical bills, the credit card payments . . .

One of Diego's men reaches up and helps Elena Sánchez Barrera down from the trailer. Wearing a red holiday dress and heels, she looks wryly amused—a (deposed) queen arriving in a slum. "A trailer truck? I feel like a delivery of produce."

"But safe from prying eyes." Adán steps up to greet his sister with a kiss on each cheek.

She hugs him. "It's wonderful to see you."

"And you."

"Are we going to stand here proclaiming our mutual affection," Elena asks, "or are you going to give us something to drink?"

Adán takes her by the arm and leads her to the dining hall where Magda stands nervously beside the head of the table, waiting to greet them. She looks quite fetching in a silver lamé dress that is, strictly speaking, a little too short for Christmas with a little too deep a décolletage, but that shows her to great advantage. Her hair is upswept and lustrous, held in place with cloisonné Chinese pins that give her a touch of the exotic.

"Leave it to you to find a rose in a sewer," Elena whispers to Adán. "I've heard rumors, but . . . she's magnificent."

She offers her cheek to Magda for a kiss.

"You're so beautiful," Magda says.

"Oh, I'm going to like her," Elena says. "And I was just telling Adanito how lovely *you* are."

This is going well, Adán thinks. It could as easily have gone the other way—Elena's mouth is a jar of honey with a sharp knife in it, and she has already gotten through an entire sentence without alluding to Magda's youth or his lack thereof. Perhaps she's mellowed—the Elena he knew would have already asked Magda if he helps her with her homework.

And the "Adanito"—"Little Adán." Nice touch.

"I *love* your dress," Magda says.

Women, Adán thinks, will always be women. In the middle of one of the bleakest prisons on earth, they'll act like they bumped into each other at an exclusive mall. They'll be shopping for shoes together next.

"I'm leaving my children *nothing*," Elena says, displaying the dress. "I'm going to spend it *all*."

"Now the party can begin!" Diego yells, making an entrance.

Everyone smiles at Diego, Adán thinks.

He's irresistible.

Today he's dressed in his Christmas best—a leather sports coat over a leather vest. A bolo with his purple shirt takes the place of a tie. And he has new jeans—pressed—over silver-tipped cowboy boots.

Diego's wife, Chele, is a bit more subdued in a silver-sequined dress and heels, her black hair in an updo. She's thickened in the hips a little bit, Adán observes, but she's still *una berraca*—hot stuff.

And a match for her husband, equally blunt. Chele will say anything that's on her mind, such as her opinions about Diego's numerous *segunderas*—she's all for them. "Better than him wearing me out all the time. *Dios mío*, I'd have a *chocha* wider than one of his tunnels."

She walks up, hugs and kisses everyone, then steps back and looks at Magda from toe to head. "*Dios mío*, Adán, you've become a mountain climber! Darling girl, don't the *pitones* hurt?!"

From anyone else, it would have been a horribly awkward insult; but it's Chele, so everyone, even Magda, laughs.

They've brought their children, three boys and three girls ranging from six to fourteen. Adán has given up on keeping their names straight but has made sure that he has a nice gift for each of them.

Adán had questioned the wisdom of bringing children to the prison, but Chele was firm about it. "This is our *life*. They need to know what it is, not just the good parts. I won't have them being ashamed of their family."

So the children, impeccably dressed in brand-new holiday clothes, came, and now line up to kiss or shake hands with their *tío* Adán.

They're nice kids, Adán thinks. Chele's done well with them.

Diego's youngest brother is a (much) smaller version of him, the classic case of the sibling becoming the oldest brother, only more so. Alberto Tapia's one concession to Christmas is a red bolo in his otherwise totally narco-cowboy, *norteño* outfit—black silk shirt, black slacks, lizard cowboy boots, black cowboy hat.

Short as he is—and he's shorter than Adán by at least two inches—the get-up looks comical on him, like a child playing cowboy. No one is going to say that to Alberto, though, because his fuse is shorter than he is.

Adán worries about Alberto's violent temper, but Diego assures him that it's nothing to worry about, that he has his little brother under control.

I hope so, Adán thinks.

Alberto seems convivial today, all laughs and smiles, and Adán wonders if he snorted up on the way here. Certainly his wife did—Lupe's black eyes are pinned and her tight, short dress is wildly inappropriate. Another example of Alberto's recklessness, Adán thinks. You *sleep* with strippers if that's your taste, but you don't *marry* them.

"Just because he bought her tits," Chele once observed, "doesn't mean he had to buy the rest of her." Lupe's remarkable breasts—cantilevered precariously on her petite frame—notwithstanding, she looks almost childlike, vulnerable, and Adán makes a mental note to be kind to her.

Former stripper or not, she is Alberto's wife and therefore family.

Martín Tapia is the perfect middle child, as different from his brothers as the tyranny of genetics will allow, and the family joke is that a banker crept in one night and impregnated his mother while she was asleep.

The financial manager and diplomat of the Tapia organization, Martín is soft-spoken, quiet, conservatively dressed in an expensively tailored black suit and white shirt with French cuffs.

He and his wife, Yvette, have just moved to a big home in an exclusive Cuernavaca neighborhood, close to Mexico City to be nearer to the politicians, financiers, and society types whom they need to cultivate for business.

His job is to play tennis and golf, have drinks at the nineteenth hole, go to parties at the country club, be seen at expensive restaurants, and throw soirees at their home. Yvette's job is to look pretty and be the charming hostess.

They're both perfect for their jobs.

Yvette Tapia is another former beauty queen—impeccably dressed in an expensive, stylish black dress on her svelte body—the personification of class. Her hair is cut in a short bob, her makeup is subtle, a slash of red lipstick makes it all sexy.

She's perfect.

"Yvette," Chele has said, "has the beauty and warmth of an ice sculpture. The only difference is that an ice sculpture eventually melts."

In Adán's day, they would have been called "yuppies." He's not sure what the word would be now, but they're politely tolerant, if mildly embarrassed, at being at the prison party. Yvette smiles thinly at Chele's jokes, Martín finds topics of conversation that he can share, mostly about *fútbol*.

They can't complain about the meal.

While it isn't the nouvelle cuisine they search out in Cuernavaca (they are both self-admitted foodies), but heartier, simpler Sinaloan fare, fresh and beautifully prepared filet mignon, shrimp, lobsters, roast potatoes, and green beans served with expensive wines that even Martín and Yvette can't find fault with.

Dessert is the traditional flan, with *galetas de Navidad,* then *champurrado* and *arroz dulce,* after which the piñatas are hung and the children go at them with sticks, and the dining room floor is soon covered with candy and little toys.

As the evening settles into the post-feast languor, Adán nudges Elena and says, "We should talk."

They sit in one of the consultation rooms.

Adán says, "The situation in Tijuana—"

"I've done the best I could."

"I know."

Elena took charge only because she was the last Barrera sibling not in a grave or a jail. A number of their people would have rebelled just because she was a woman. Some of the others were Teo's people anyway. Once he broke away, they went with him. So did a number of the police and judges, who no longer had Raúl or Adán to fear.

The miracle of it is that Elena has held on as long as she did. She's a good businessperson but not a war leader. Now she says, "I want out, Adanito. I'm tired. Unless you can give me more help on the ground . . ."

"I'm in *prison,* Elena." They're in a staredown, as they so often were in childhood. "Do you trust me?"

"Yes."

"Then trust me on this," Adán says. "It will work out, I promise you. I'll deal with it. I just need a little time."

They stand up and she kisses his cheek.

Diego interrupts playing with his children to take a phone call.

He listens and nods.

The Christmas present is on its way.

———

"May I have a word?" Sondra asks Adán.

Adán suppresses a sigh. He wants to enjoy the party, not endure Sondra's gloom, but, as the head of the family, he has responsibilities.

It's Salvador, she tells him when they retreat to a quiet corner. He's disrespectful, angry. He stays away for nights at a time, he's cutting classes. He parties, he drinks, she's afraid he might be doing drugs.

"He won't listen to me," Sondra says, "and there's no man at home to set him straight. Will you talk to him, Adán? Will you, please?"

She sounds like an old lady, Adán thinks. He does his math—Sondra is forty-one.

Salvador is none too pleased when his uncle comes up and asks to talk with him, but he grudgingly follows Adán back to his cell, sits down, and looks at Adán with a combination of resentment and sullenness that is almost impressive. "My mother asked you to do this, right?"

"What if she did?" Adán asks.

"You know what she's like."

Yes, I do, Adán thinks. I truly do. But he's the head of the family so he asks, "What are you doing, Salvador?"

"What do you mean?"

"With your life," Adán says. "What are you doing with your *life*?"

Salvador shrugs and looks at the floor.

"Have you dropped out of college?" Adán asks.

"I've stopped going to class."

"Why?"

"Seriously?" Salvador asks. "I'm going to be an architect?"

It's so Raúl, Adán almost laughs. "Your father had a medical degree."

"And he did a lot with it."

Adán gestures to the cell. "Do you want to end up here?"

"It's better than where my father ended up, isn't it?"

It's true, Adán thinks, and they both know it. "What do you want, Salvador?"

"Let me work with Tío Diego," he says, looking Adán in the eyes for the first time in this conversation. "Or Tío Nacho. Or send me to Tijuana. I can help Tía Elena."

He's so eager, so sincere all of a sudden, it's almost sad. The boy wants so badly to redeem his father, Adán hurts for him.

"Your father didn't want this for you," Adán says. "He made me promise. His last words to me."

It's a lie. Raúl's last words were his begging to be put out of his gut-shot misery. He said nothing about Salvador, or Sondra. What he said was *Thank you, brother* when Adán pointed the pistol at his head.

"It was good enough for him," Salvador says.

"But he didn't think it was good enough for *you*," Adán insists. "You're smart, Salvador. You've been to the funerals, the prisons . . . you know what this is. You have money, an education if you want it, connections . . . You can have a *life*."

"I want *this* life," Salvador says.

As pigheaded as his father.

"You can't have it," Adán says. "Don't try. And don't think of freelancing—if I catch anyone selling to you, I'll have their heads. Don't make me do that."

"Thanks."

"And straighten up," Adán says, the stern uncle now, and, anyway, he's bored with this. "Start going to class, and keep a civil tongue in your head with your mother. Are you doing drugs? Don't even bother to lie to me. If you're not—good. If you are—stop."

"Are we done?" Salvador asks.

"Yes."

The young man gets up and starts to walk away.

"Salvador."

"Yeah?"

"Get your degree," Adán says. "Show me you have the discipline to finish your education, stop being a pain in the ass, and then come back to me and we'll see."

Salvador is going to get into the *pista secreta* one way or the other, Adán thinks. He might as well do it through me, where I can at least keep an eye on him.

But not yet.

This will kick the can down the street for a couple of years, anyway. By that time he might find a nice girl, an interest, a career, and not want what he thinks he wants now.

Adán goes back into the party room and looks at his guests—his extended family, or what's left of it.

His sister, Elena.

His sister-in-law, Sondra, and his nephew Salvador.

His cousins, the Tapia brothers—Diego, Martín, and Alberto—and their wives, Chele, Yvette, and Lupe, respectively. Diego's children . . . This is his family, his blood, all that he has left.

Without me, he thinks, they go where a deposed king's family go in this merciless realm—to the slaughterhouse. Your enemies will kill them just after they've killed you. And unless you take back your rightful place, all the death, all the killing, all the terrible acts for which you're going to hell, were all for nothing.

He's heard it said that life is a river, that the past flows downstream. It isn't true—if it flows, it flows through the blood in your veins. You can no more cut yourself away from the past than you can cut out your own heart.

I was the king once, I will have to be the king again.

Life, he muses, always gives you an excuse to take what you want anyway.

Adán's relieved when they're gone.

When the mandatory oohs and ahhs over presents have been exchanged, the equally obligatory confessions over having eaten too much, the hugs and busses on the cheeks, the insincere promises that we need to do this again sooner, Diego finally manages to herd them all back into the truck and they leave him to the peace of his prison.

He flops face first down on the bed beside Magda.

"Families are exhausting," he says. "It's easier to manage a hundred traffickers than one family."

"I thought they were nice."

"You don't have to meet their needs," Adán says.

"No, only yours."

"Are they a burden on you?"

"No, I like your needs," she says, reaching for him. "*Feliz Navidad*. Do you want your last present?"

"Not now," he says. "Pack a few things."

She looks at him oddly. "What do you mean?"

"Just a few," he says. "Not your whole wardrobe. We can buy more clothes later. Go on—we don't have a lot of time."

Diego walks into the cell. "You ready, *primo*?"

"For years."

Diego points to his ear—*listen*.

Adán hears a shout, then another, then a chorus of shouts. Then the banging of wooden bats on steel bars, feet pounding on the metal catwalks, alarms.

Then shots.

A *motín*.

A prison riot.

Los Bateadores are rampaging through Block 2, Level 1-A, attacking other inmates, attacking each other, creating chaos. The guards are running back and forth, trying to contain it, radioing for reinforcements, but it's already too late—inmates are busting out of cells, running down the cell block, spilling out into the yard.

"We have to go!" Diego says. "Now!"

"Did you hear that?!" Adán yells to Magda.

"I heard!" She comes out with a small shoulder bag while trying to put on a different pair of shoes, flats. "You might have given a lady some notice."

Adán takes her arm and follows Diego onto the block.

It's as if they're invisible. No one looks at them as they move through the swirling fights, the noise, the guards, and Diego leads them to a steel door that has been left unlocked. He ushers them into a stairwell and they climb to another door that opens onto the roof.

The guards aren't watching them, they have their guns and lights aimed down at the yard and don't even seem to notice when the helicopter comes in and lands on the roof.

The rotors blow Magda's hair into a mess, and Adán puts his hand on her back and pushes her down a little as they step into the open door.

Diego climbs in behind them and gives a thumbs-up to the pilot.

The helicopter lifts off.

Adán looks down at Puente Grande.

It's been five years of negotiations, diplomacy, payoffs, establishing relationships, waiting for the other bosses to accept his presence, for some of them to die, for others to be killed, for the North Americans to move on and become obsessed with another public enemy number one.

Five years of patience and persistence and now he's free.

To resume his rightful place.

Erie, Pennsylvania

Outside a diner the next morning, going in for the breakfast special of two eggs, toast, and coffee, Keller sees it.

A headline behind the cracked glass of a newspaper box.

DRUG KINGPIN ESCAPES.

Almost dizzy, Keller puts two quarters in the slot, takes out the paper, and scans the story for the name.

It can't be.

It *can't* be.

The letters spring out at him like shards of metal from a tripwire, booby-trap grenade.

"Adán Barrera."

Keller lays the paper on top of the box and reads the story. Barrera extradited to a Mexican prison . . . Puente Grande . . . a Christmas party . . .

He can't believe it.

Then again, he can.

Of course he can.

It's Barrera and it's Mexico.

The irony, Keller thinks, is as perfect as it is painful.

I'm a prisoner in the world's largest solitary confinement.

And Barrera is free.

Keller tosses the paper into a trash can. He walks the streets for hours, past piles of dirty snow, closed factories, shivering crack whores, the detritus of a Rust Belt town where the jobs have gone south.

At some point, late in the afternoon with the sky turning a harsh, threatening gray, Keller walks into the bus station to go where he knows he's always been headed.

The Drug Enforcement Administration headquarters are in Pentagon City. Which, Keller supposes, makes perfect sense. If you're going to fight a war on drugs, base yourself in the Pentagon.

He's in a suit and tie now, his only one of either, closely shaved and his hair freshly cut. He sits in the lobby and waits until they finally let him up to the fifth floor to see Tim Taylor, who successfully masks his enthusiasm at seeing Art Keller.

"What do you want, Art?" Taylor asks.

"You know what I want."

"Forget it," Taylor says. "The last thing we need right now is some old vendetta of yours."

"Nobody knows Barrera like I do," Art answers. "His family, his connections, the way his mind works. And nobody is as motivated as I am."

"Why, because he's hunting you?" Taylor asks. "I thought you had a different life now."

"That was before you guys let Barrera out."

"Go back to your bees, Art," Taylor says now.

"I'll go down the road."

"What do you mean?"

"If you let me walk out of here," Keller answers, "I'll go to Langley. I'll bet *they'd* send me."

The rivalry between DEA and CIA is bitter, the tension between the two agencies horrific, the trust virtually nonexistent. CIA had at least helped to cover up Hidalgo's murder, and DEA had never forgotten or forgiven it.

"You and Barrera," Taylor says, "you're the same guy."

"My point."

Taylor stares at him for a long time and then says, "This is going to be complicated. Not everyone is going to welcome you back. But I'll see what I can do. Leave me a number where you can be reached."

Keller finds a decent hotel up in Bethesda by the Naval Hospital and waits. He knows what's happening—Taylor has to meet with higher-ups at DEA, who then have to go to their bosses at Justice. Justice has to talk to the State Department, and then it would have to be coordinated with CIA. There will be quiet lunches on K Street and quieter drinks in Georgetown.

He knows what the arguments will be: Art Keller is a loose cannon, not a team player; Keller has his own agenda, he's too personally involved; the Mexicans resent him; it's too dangerous.

The last argument is the toughest.

With a $2 million reward on Keller's head, sending him down to Mexico is dangerous, to say the least, and DEA can't afford the media storm that would ensue if another agent were killed in Mexico. Still, no one can reasonably question Keller's potential value in the hunt for Adán Barrera.

"Give him a desk at EPIC," a White House official determines, referring to DEA's El Paso Intelligence Center. "He can advise the Mexicans from there."

Taylor relays the offer to Keller.

"I'm pretty sure," Keller says, "that Barrera isn't in El Paso."

"Asshole."

Keller hangs up.

The White House official who was listening in explodes. "Since when does some *agent* tell us where he will or will not go?!"

"This is not 'some agent,'" Taylor responds. "This is Art fucking Keller, the former 'Border Lord.' He knows where the bodies are buried, and not just in Mexico."

"What about the danger?"

Taylor shrugs. "It is what it is. If Keller gets Barrera, great. If Barrera gets him first . . . It puts other things to bed, doesn't it?"

Keller knows what happened in 1985. He was there. He busted the flights of cocaine, saw the training camps, knew that NSC and CIA had used the Mexican cartels to fund the Nicaraguan Contras, with full approval of the White House. He perjured himself in his testimony before Congress in exchange for a free hand to go after the Barreras, and he destroyed them and put Adán Barrera away.

And now Barrera's out, and Keller is back.

If he gets killed in Mexico, he takes some secrets with him.

Mexico is a cemetery for secrets.

After more phone calls, more classified memos, more lunches, and more drinks, the powers-that-be finally decide that Keller can go to Mexico City with DEA credentials, not as a special agent, but as an intelligence officer. And with a simple mission statement—"assist and advise in the capture of Adán Barrera or, alternatively, the verification of his death."

Keller accepts.

But they still have to sell it to the Mexicans, who are skeptical about Keller being sent to "assist and advise." It touches off a bureaucratic pissing match between the Mexican attorney general's office, the Ministry of Public Security, and an alphabet soup of other agencies, all variously cooperating and/or competing within overlapping jurisdictions.

On the one hand, they want his knowledge; on the other hand is the notorious, if understandable, Mexican sensitivity about the perception that they're "little brown brothers" in the relationship, as well as aggrievement over the constant—and one-sided—American insinuations of corruption.

Taylor lectures Keller about it. "Perhaps you missed it when you were off playing Friar Tuck, but it's a new day down there. The PRI is out and PAN is in. The federal law enforcement agencies have been reorganized and cleaned up, and the received wisdom—which you *will* receive, Art—is that Los Pinos is reborn with a bright shiny new soul."

Yeah, Keller thinks. Back in the '80s, the received wisdom was that there was no cocaine in Mexico, and he was ordered to keep his mouth shut about the all too tangible evidence to the contrary, the countless tons of blow the Colombians were moving through Barrera's Federación into the United States. And Los Pinos—the Mexican White House—was a wholly owned subsidiary of the Federación. Now the official word is that the Mexican government is squeaky clean?

"So Barrera's escape was a Houdini magic act," Keller says. "No one in the government was bought off."

"Maybe a prison guard or two."

"Yeah, okay."

"I'm not bullshitting you," Taylor says. "You are not going to go down there and make onions. You assist and you advise, and otherwise you keep your mouth shut."

A battle of e-mails, meetings, and confidential cables between Washington and Mexico City ensues, the result of which is a compromise: Keller would be on loan to, and under the supervision of, a "coordinating committee" and would serve in a strictly advisory capacity.

"You accept the mission," Taylor says, "you accept these conditions."

Keller accepts. It's all bullshit anyway—he's fully aware that one of his roles in Mexico is that of "bait." If anything would bring Adán Barrera out of the woodwork, it would be the chance to get Art Keller.

Keller knows this and doesn't care.

If Adán wants to come after him—good.

Let him come.

The words of a psalm they used to chant at Vigils comes back to him. Romans 13:11.

"And do this, knowing the hour,
That now it is high time for us to arise from sleep."

3

The Hunting of Man

There is no hunting like the hunting of man.

—Ernest Hemingway
"On the Blue Water"

Los Elijos, Durango
March 2005

The sun, soft and diffuse in the haze, comes up over the mountains on this Holy Thursday.

Keller sits in the front of an unmarked SUV tucked into a stand of Morales pines on the edge of a ridge, fingers the trigger of the Sig Sauer he isn't supposed to have, and looks down into the narrow valley where the little village of Los Elijos, wedged between mountain peaks, just starts to appear through the mist.

The thin mountain air is cold and Keller shivers from the chill but also from fatigue. The convoy has driven all night up the narrow twisting road, little more than a goat path, in the hope of arriving here unseen.

Looking through binoculars, Keller sees that the village is still asleep, so no one has raised an alarm.

Luis Aguilar shivers behind him.

The two men don't like each other.

The first meeting of the "Barrera Coordinating Committee," held the day after Keller arrived in Mexico City, was inauspicious.

"Let's have things clear between us," Aguilar said as soon as they sat down. "You are here to share your knowledge of the Barrera organization. You are not here to cultivate your own sources, take independent action, or do surveillance or any other intelligence gathering. I will not have another gringo wiping his boots on my turf. Do we understand each other?"

Everything about Luis Aguilar had an edge to it—from his aquiline nose, to the press of his trousers, to his words.

"We have resources of our own," Keller answered. Satellite surveillance, cell phone intercepts, computer hacks, information developed in the States. "I'll share them with you unless and until I see that intelligence leaked. Then it's cut off and you and I don't know each other."

Aguilar's sharp eyes got sharper. "What are you trying to say?"

"I'm just getting things clear between us."

As sharp as Aguilar was, Gerardo Vera was that smooth. He laughed and said, "Gentlemen, please, let's fight the narcos instead of each other."

Luis Aguilar and Gerardo Vera head up the two new agencies charged with the task of cutting through the Gordian knot of corruption and bureaucracy to finally, seriously take on the cartels.

Aguilar's SEIDO (Subprocuraduría Especializada en Investigación de Delincuencia Organizada)—the Assistant Attorney General's Office for the Investigation of Organized Crime—was created to replace its predecessor, FEADS, which the new administration had disbanded, labeling it "a dung heap of corruption."

Similarly, Vera disbanded the old PJF—the *federales*—and replaced it with the AFI, the Federal Investigative Agency.

The heads of the two new organizations were a study in contrast—Aguilar short, slim, dark, compact, and tidy; Vera tall, heavy, blond, broad-faced, and expansive. Aguilar was a lawyer with a reputation as a hard-charging prosecutor; Vera a career cop, trained by, among others, the FBI.

Vera was a regular guy you'd swap stories over a few beers with; Aguilar a quiet academic, devout Catholic, and family man who never told tales. Vera wore custom-made Italian suits; Aguilar was strictly Brooks Brothers off-the-rack.

What they had in common was a determination to clean things up.

They started with their own people, making each investigator pass a background check and a polygraph asserting that he never has been, nor is he now, in the employ of the narcos. Aguilar and Vera were the first ones to take the test, and they released the (clean) results to the media.

Not everyone passed. Aguilar and Vera fired hundreds of investigators who failed the test.

"Some of these bastards," Vera told Keller, "were working with the cartels *before* they came to us. The cartels *sent* them to enlist, do you believe that? Fuck their mothers."

Aguilar winced at the obscenity.

"Now we all take the test once a month," Vera said. "Expensive, but if you're going to keep the stable clean you have to keep shoveling out the shit."

The shit tried to shovel back.

Vera and Aguilar had each received scores of death threats. Each had half a dozen heavily armed bodyguards who escorted them everywhere; sentries patrolled their houses twenty-four/seven.

DEA was encouraged.

"We've finally found people we can work with," Taylor told Keller in his predeployment briefing. "These guys are honest, competent, and *driven*."

Keller had to agree with that.

Still, Keller and Aguilar knocked heads.

"Your organizational chart," Keller said one day after it took an exchange of thirty-seven memos to approve a simple wiretap, "is about as straightforward as a bowl of day-old spaghetti."

"I don't eat stale food," Aguilar answered, "but perhaps you can enlighten me as to the exact delineations between DEA, ICE, FBI, Homeland Security, and the plethora of state and local jurisdictions on your side of the border, because, frankly, I haven't noticed them."

They argued about the Puente Grande escape.

The prison system now came under Vera's bailiwick, but prosecutions of prison staff had to be done under Aguilar's authority. So Vera had appointed his own man to investigate the escape, while Aguilar had ordered the arrests of seventy-two guards and staff, including the warden. Interrogations were conducted by a top AFI official named Edgar Delgado, but Aguilar and Keller were allowed to sit in. Aguilar was humiliated by what he heard— that Barrera basically ran the prison.

Keller took it as a given.

"Because all Mexicans are corrupt," Aguilar huffed.

Keller shrugged.

Aguilar went home that night too late for dinner but in time to help his daughters with their homework. After the girls went to bed, Lucinda set a plate of lamb *birria*, one of his favorites, at the table.

"How is the North American?" she asked, sitting next to him.

"Like all North Americans," Aguilar answered. "He thinks he knows everything."

"I didn't know you were a bigot, Luis."

"I prefer to call myself parochial."

"You should invite him over for dinner."

"I spend enough time with him," Aguilar answered. "Besides, I wouldn't inflict him on you."

His new job had been hard on his wife. A school principal, she wasn't used to the bodyguard who now took her to work and back, or to the guards who patrolled the house. The girls were easier with it—their young minds less set in their ways, and, besides, they thought it was kind of "cool," and any numbers of their fellow students at their private schools had bodyguards.

Some were the children of government officials. Others, Aguilar knew with chagrin, were doubtless *buchones*—the sons and daughters of narcos. Never mind, he thought now, you can't blame the child for the sins of the father.

"How's the lamb?" Lucinda asked.

"Excellent, thank you."

"More wine?"

"Why are you buttering me up?"

"I'm sure," Lucinda said, "that he's not so horrible."

"I didn't say he was horrible," Aguilar answered. "I just said that he was North American."

He finished his dinner and his wine, played two moves in a chess match against himself, and then went upstairs to bed.

Lucinda was waiting up for him.

The next morning they started fresh.

"Let's work," Aguilar said, "on the assumption that the Tapias, acting in concert with Nacho Esparza, took Barrera out of Puente Grande."

"Fair enough," Keller agreed.

"What is the operational corollary of that assumption?" Aguilar asked.

"We hit them," Vera said. "Make it too expensive for them to hide him."

They went at it hard.

Using SEIDO intelligence and information that Keller provided from DEA intelligence packages, they raided properties that Tapia or Esparza owned in Sinaloa, Durango, and Nayarit. They tracked down and questioned dozens of the two men's associates. They busted growers, dealers, shippers, and money launderers.

They turned up the heat, busting a shipment of Diego Tapia's cocaine, then a freighter full of the precursor chemicals that Esparza needed to cook his meth.

They made their agenda clear. The AFI troopers would throw the arrested men to the ground and scream, "Where is Adán Barrera?!" Then they turned them over to the SEIDO agents, who asked, over and over again, "Where is Adán Barrera?"

No one told them anything.

The raids netted drugs, weapons, computers, cell phones, but no solid leads as to Barrera's whereabouts.

Aguilar threw it right back on Keller.

"You're the Barrera expert," he said with no effort to disguise his sarcasm. "Perhaps you'd gift us with your expertise to find him."

Keller picked up the glove.

When he first arrived in Mexico City he checked in to his official housing near the embassy, but then went out and found a furnished apartment on the second floor of an art deco building on Avenida Vicente Suárez in Colonia Condesa, within walking distance of the embassy but not close enough to be an American diplomatic ghetto. The bohemian neighborhood was all sidewalk cafés, bars, nightclubs, and bookstores.

A native Spanish speaker, Keller blended in easily. He moved his few things into the Condesa apartment and rarely went back to the official housing. The apartment was well stocked—his Sig Sauer, a 12-gauge Mossberg Tacstar 590 shotgun strapped under the bed, and a U.S. Navy Ka-Bar combat knife taped to the toilet water tank. I might be bait, he thought, but that doesn't mean I have to be a sitting duck.

After weeks of the futile search for Barrera, Keller burrowed himself into the Condesa apartment and went to work. Barrera had escaped from Puente Grande, so Keller started there, poring over the thousands of pages of transcript from the guards who had been arrested and interrogated.

If he didn't know better, the accounts were almost the stuff of fiction— Barrera's well-stocked luxury cell, the "movie nights," the imported prostitutes, Los Bateadores. Keller read about the former beauty queen Magda Beltrán, the family Christmas party, the riot the night of the escape. It was fascinating but shed no light as to where Barrera might be.

Keller started over, reading, rereading, and reading again the stories about Barrera's time in Puente Grande.

Then it hit him—a passing mention to a rumored attempt on Barrera's life that had happened, if it happened at all, on the volleyball court. The would-be assassin's body was later found with a neat bullet hole in the back of the head.

Keller phoned Aguilar. "Can you pull the file of a former prisoner, now deceased, Juan Cabray?"

"Yes, but why?"

"I need it to employ my expertise."

"Well then, by all means."

Keller went to the SEIDO offices to pick up the file.

Cabray was a career criminal who had worked for the old Sonora cartel and was apparently good with a knife. Not good enough, though, Keller thought. He set aside the question of who had ordered a hit on Barrera to consider Cabray.

Assume the story is true, Keller thought. Cabray took a stab, as it were, at Barrera and missed. Barrera's people executed him. Looking at the photo of Cabray's corpse, the bullet wound was clear, but Keller was more impressed by what he didn't see.

Signs of torture.

They would have worked on Cabray pretty good to find out who hired him, but the photo showed no bruises, no broken bones, no burn marks.

Cabray cooperated.

Keller dug deeper into his file and found out that Juan Cabray was from Los Elijos, in Durango state. He logged on to the computer and quickly got satellite images of the little village, tucked in a valley among remote mountains.

Durango was part of the so-called Golden Triangle, the mountainous intersection of Sinaloa, Durango, and Chihuahua that made up the prime opium and marijuana areas in Mexico.

It was in the heart of the Sinaloa cartel stronghold.

Keller convened a meeting of the Barrera Coordinating Committee and requested permission to ask for a U.S. satellite run over Los Elijos. It was a delicate suggestion, the Mexicans reluctant to accept foreign satellite surveillance over their country.

"It's absurd," Aguilar said. "Why would Barrera think of hiding in the village of a man who tried to kill him, moreover a man whom he ordered killed?"

"Just humor me," Keller said.

"Your expertise?" Aguilar asked.

"We're not making progress anywhere else," Vera said, shrugging. "Why not?"

"We can just send a plane over," Aguilar said.

"It has to be high-altitude," Keller said, "not a low flyover. I don't want to spook him. Let me ask for a satellite run."

Aguilar snorted but gave the necessary permission, Keller got on the horn to Taylor, and the satellite run was okayed.

Two days later, Keller was back at SEIDO with the photos laid out on the conference room table. He pointed to a small circle, a larger square, and a yet larger rectangle.

"This could be a new well," he says. "This . . . I don't know, maybe a school? The third shape, maybe a clinic. In any case, it's all new construction."

"What's your point?" Aguilar asked.

"This is a poor village. Suddenly there's all kinds of new construction on things that they need?"

"We have social development programs all over Mexico," Aguilar said.

"Can we find out—quietly—if there have been any in Los Elijos?" Keller asked. "Because if there haven't, I have an idea as to who's funded these projects."

"Let me guess—Adán Barrera," Aguilar said. "Oh, please."

"Where are you from?" Keller asked.

Aguilar looked surprised, but answered, "Mexico City."

Keller turned to Vera. "You?"

"Same."

"I spent years in the Triangle," Keller said. "I know the people, I know how they think, I know the culture. I've known Adán Barrera since he was twenty years old."

"So?"

"So the people of Los Elijos will think that Juan Cabray acted honorably," Keller said. "They'll further think that Adán Barrera responded nobly. Go from the supposition that, before he died, Cabray accepted Barrera as his *patrón*. Barrera has acted the role of *patrón* in the village—a well, a school, a clinic. They'd shelter him."

"I think you're reaching," Aguilar said.

"Do you have a better idea?" Keller asked.

Aguilar made some discreet calls and found that neither the federal nor state governments had development projects in Los Elijos. Likewise, there were no church or NGO activities there that he could discern.

Vera made the decision—AFI would launch a surprise dawn raid on Los Elijos.

Further satellite intel narrowed Barrera's most likely location down to the largest house in the village, at the end of a dirt road, a single-story limestone structure with a tiled roof and a low wall around the periphery.

"I hope that the beauty queen is with him," Vera said. "I would like to lay eyes on that specimen."

Keller looked at the satellite photos of the house in Los Elijos and said, "I'm going on the raid."

"We cannot run the risk of a North American agent being killed on Mexican soil," Aguilar said, although Keller suspected that what he really meant was that they couldn't run the risk of a North American agent killing a Mexican citizen on Mexican soil. Barrera's capture would be an exclusively Mexican operation, Aguilar asserted. No mention would be made of the DEA intelligence.

Advise and assist, Keller thought. "If anything happens to me, just bury me in the mountains."

"As tempting as that sounds," Aguilar said, "I'm afraid it's impossible."

"It was my intel that made this possible," Keller agued.

"How is that relevant?"

"Collegiality," Vera answered. "We owe him the courtesy as comrades-in-arms."

"If you're willing to take the responsibility," Aguilar huffed.

They were on a military flight to El Salto, Durango, that afternoon, and from there the AFI troopers got into trucks and SUVs and headed for the mountains. After driving all night, they arrived at the ridge above Los Elijos.

Now Keller sits shivering beside Aguilar.

Vera is in another vehicle with five of his troopers. The tactical plan is simple. At first light, Vera will give the word over the radio and the eight vehicles will race down the road into the village but drive straight through and then surround the large house at the end of the road and go in.

Hopefully, Barrera will be inside. If not, if he's somewhere else in the village, they'll have him isolated in the countryside and then can run him down.

That's the plan, anyway.

Aguilar's not buying it.

"This whole idea that Barrera has found sanctuary in Cabray's village is a romantic conceit," he said on the tortuous drive through the mountains, which aggravated his stomach as well as his psyche. Now he chews an antacid and looks down at the village.

With nothing else to do but wait, they actually start to talk, if only to break the tension and monotony. Keller learns things about the taciturn lawyer that he hadn't known, or maybe, he considers, never bothered to find out.

Aguilar has a wife and two teenage daughters, he attended Harvard as an undergraduate and thought it overrated, he's an ex-smoker, a devout Catholic, and almost as devout a fan of the Águilas de América *fútbol* team.

"You?" Aguilar asks.

"Soccer? No."

"Family, I meant."

"Divorced," Keller answers. "Two kids—boy and a girl—grown up now."

"This job," Aguilar says, "is hard on family life. The hours, the secrecy . . ."

Keller knows that this is Aguilar trying to be kind and to find common ground. It's almost friendly, so he responds, "They say that DEA issues you a gun and a badge, not a wife and kids."

"I couldn't live without my family," Aguilar says, and then quickly adds, "I'm sorry, that was unkind, and I didn't mean it to be."

"No, I get it."

They're quiet for a while and then Aguilar ventures, "I've heard the stories about you and Barrera."

"Well, there are a lot of them."

"I think," Aguilar says, "that it is important to distinguish between revenge and justice."

Just when I was beginning to like you, Keller thinks, you have to get sanctimonious on me. "Have you ever been in a firefight before?"

"No," Aguilar answers. "Nor am I likely to now."

"I just wondered if you were nervous," Keller says. "It's understandable."

"All my previous combats have been in court," Aguilar says. "But, no, I'm not nervous. I'm merely irritated at this monumental waste of time and resources, neither of which we have to spare."

"Okay."

Aguilar glances at the Sig Sauer. "You are not to discharge that weapon, except in the most extreme exigency of self-defense."

"Where did you learn your English?" Keller asks.

"Harvard."

"Makes sense."

"I have no idea what that means."

"I know."

Aguilar might not be nervous, Keller thinks, but I am. Barrera *is* in that village. I know it for a reason that Aguilar would contemptuously dismiss—I can just feel it. I've been hunting Adán Barrera in one form or another for over thirty years—we're connected by the psychic hip—and I can *feel* him there.

In twenty minutes, thirty minutes, this could be *over*. And then what? Keller wonders. What do you do with your life then?

You're getting ahead of yourself.

First get Barrera.

Keller nervously fingers the trigger.

Then there's crackle of the radio signal open and he hears Vera order, "Stand by."

"Are you ready?" Aguilar asks.

Fuckin' A, Keller thinks.

Vera gives the signal and the car lurches ahead and pitches down the steep grade. The AFI driver makes no concession to the sharp curves and sudden edges that could send the vehicle somersaulting hundreds of feet down.

But they make it into the village and race down the main and only street. A few early risers stare at them in shock and Keller hears one or two raise the alarm *"Juras! Juras!"*

Police! Police!

But it's too late, Keller thinks as the car speeds past the new well, the new school, the new clinic, and races toward the house at the end of the road. If you're here, Adán—and you are here—we've got you.

The car comes to a stop in front of the house while other vehicles circle it like Indians in a bad western and then form a circle. The AFI troopers in their dark blue uniforms and baseball caps spill from the cars with American-made AR-15s and .45 pistols, bulletproof vests and heavy back combat boots.

With Vera in the lead, they storm the house.

Keller jumps out of the car and trots toward the back door. Aguilar keeps up with him, looking awkward with a .38 in his hand. Keller goes through the door, his Sig Sauer out in front of him.

It's the kitchen, and a terrified cook raises his hands over his head.

"Where is Adán Barrera?!" Keller shouts. "Where is the *señor*?!"

"No sé."

"But he was here, wasn't he?" Keller presses. "When did he leave?"

"No sé."

"Was a woman with him?" Aguilar asks.

"No sé."

"What was her name, *'no sé'*?" Vera walks in, pulls his pistol, and jams it against the cook's cheek. "Do you know now?"

"He's terrified," Aguilar says. "Leave him alone."

"I'll put you and your whole family in jail," Vera growls at the cook as he pushes him away.

"There is no criminal statute that I'm aware of that prohibits making black bean soup," Aguilar says, looking at the stove. "What do you think—that Barrera told his cook where he was going?"

Keller goes through the house.

The bedrooms, the bathrooms, the sitting room, anywhere. He looks under beds, in closets. In one bedroom he thinks he smells the scent of expensive perfume. The AFI troopers rip up bathtubs and floor tiles, looking for tunnels.

There isn't one.

They sweep the house for cell phones and computers and find nothing. Walking back to the vehicles, Aguilar mutters to Keller, "I told you so."

As they drive back through the village, Keller sees that the troopers are going through each house, tossing the people out into the road, smashing windows and furniture.

He gets out of the car.

"I'll burn this shithole to the ground!" Vera yells, his face flushed with fury.

The same mistakes, Keller thinks. Vietnam in the '60s, Sinaloa in the '70s, we make the same dumbass mistakes. No wonder these people shelter the narcos—Barrera builds schools and we wreck houses.

The troopers are lining people up against the stone wall of the little cemetery, dishing out slaps and kicks as they interrogate the villagers and demand to know where El Señor is.

Keller walks up to Vera. "Don't do this."

"Mind your own business."

"This *is* my business."

"They know where he is!"

"They know where he *was*," Keller says softly. "This will do more harm than good."

"They need to be taught a lesson."

"Wrong lesson, Gerardo." Keller walks over to the line of people, who look terrified and resentful, and asks, "Where is the family of Juan Cabray!?"

He sees a woman put her arms around her children and turn her face away. It has to be Cabray's wife and kids. An elderly woman standing next to them looks down. He walks up to her, takes her by the elbow, and walks her away from the group. "Show me his grave, señora."

The woman walks him to a new headstone of handsome granite, much better than a campesino could afford.

Juan Cabray's name is carved into the stone.

"It's beautiful," Keller says. "It honors your son."

The old woman says nothing.

"If El Señor was here," Keller says, "shake your head."

She stares at him for a moment and then shakes her head violently, as if refusing to answer.

"Last night?" Keller asks.

She shakes her head again.

"Do you know where he went?"

"No sé."

"I'm going to handle you a little roughly," Keller says. "I apologize but I know you understand."

He takes her elbow, shoves her away from the grave and back to her family. The villagers lined up against the wall avoid his look. Keller walks back to Vera and Aguilar, who is arguing with his colleague to "stop this fruitless and illegal barbarity."

"He was here last night," Keller says. "You know that if you burn this village, every campesino in the Triangle will know about it within twenty-four hours and we'll never get their cooperation."

Vera stares at him for a long moment then snaps an order for his troopers to stand down.

Barrera slipped out of this one, Keller thinks. But at least they have a hot trail, and now Vera turns his energies to directing the hunt and ordering resources. Army patrols go out, local and state police, helicopters and fixed-wing aircraft go up, covering the roads.

But Keller knows that they aren't going to find him. Not in the mountains of Durango, with its heavy brush, impassable roads, and hundreds of little villages that owe more loyalty to the local narcos than to a government far removed in Mexico City.

And Barrera owns the local and state police. They aren't hunting him, they're *guarding* him.

As they drive away from the village, Aguilar says, "Don't say it."

"What?"

"What you're thinking—that Barrera was tipped off."

"I guess I don't have to."

"For all you know," Aguilar snaps, "it could have been someone from DEA."

"Could have been."

But it wasn't, Keller thinks.

———

Adán got out just before they came.

He was at the house in Los Elijos when Diego sent word that the AFI was on the way. Now he's tucked away in a new safe house across the state line in Sinaloa.

"Someone tipped them off," Adán asks Diego. "Was it Nacho?"

Maybe he decided to turn the tables, cut a deal of his own.

"I don't think so," Diego says. "I can't imagine it."

"Then who was it?" Adán asks.

"I'm not sure it was anyone," Diego says. "Listen, the government has brought someone in."

"Who?"

Adán can't believe the answer.

"Keller," he repeats.

"Yes," Diego says.

"In Mexico."

Diego shrugs an assent.

"In what capacity?!" Adán asks, incredulous.

"There's something called the 'Barrera Coordinating Committee,'" Diego says, "and Keller is the North American adviser."

It makes sense, Adán thinks. If you're going to trap a jaguar, get the man who's trapped a jaguar before. Still, the nerve of that man is outrageous, to come down to Mexico and stick his head in, as it were, the jaguar's mouth.

And just like him.

Keller had once risked his own life saving Adán's. It was back before Adán was even in the trade, but was caught up in an army sweep of the Sinaloa poppy fields. They beat the shit out of him, poured gasoline up his nose until he thought he was going to drown, then threatened to throw him out of a helicopter.

Keller stopped them.

That was a long time ago.

A lot of blood under the bridge since then.

"Kill him," Adán says.

Diego nods.

"You can't," Magda says.

Those aren't words Adán is used to hearing, and he turns around and asks, "Why not?"

"Isn't there enough pressure on you already?"

Truly, the pressure has been as heavy as it was unexpected. After taking off from the prison, the helicopter flew just a few miles and dropped them off in a small village. They rested for a few hours, then left in a convoy. They'd been gone for just an hour when the army and police pulled in and burned every house in the village as a punishment and an example.

It didn't do any good.

The government set up a "Barrera Hotline" that got a call every thirty seconds, none of them accurate, none of them from people who had actually seen him. Half the calls were "flak," made by Diego's people to create hundreds of false leads that the police had to waste time chasing down.

Diego even hired three Barrera lookalikes to wander the country and provoke more false leads.

For weeks Adán moved only by night, changing safe houses as often as he changed clothes. He dressed as a priest in Jalisco and as an AFI trooper in Nayarit. All the time, the pressure was brutal. Helicopters flew over their heads, they had to skirt army checkpoints, taking back roads that were little more than ruts.

Finally Adán had the brilliant idea to go to Los Elijos, where the campesinos, far from resenting him for killing Juan Cabray, welcomed him as a benefactor who had done Cabray honor and helped their village. Adán and Magda moved into the best house in town, small but comfortable.

No one in Los Elijos or the surrounding countryside breathed a word about El Señor and his woman being there. But the hunt continued, and the government brought in Art Keller, who came within a couple of hours of capturing them.

And now Magda is objecting to having Keller killed.

"You of all people should know," she says, "what happens when a North American agent is killed in Mexico. Be patient and all this will die down, but kill this Keller person and the North Americans will never quit—they'll force the government to keep after you. I'm not saying 'no,' I'm saying 'not now.'"

He has to admit that she's speaking wisdom. That smart son of a bitch Keller knows that he's safer here in Mexico than he was in the States. Knows that if you stick your head far enough into the jaguar's mouth, it can't clamp its jaws shut.

"I won't stay my hand forever," Adán says.

Magda is smart enough to suppress a smile of victory, but Adán knows that she's won, and in doing so, saved him from his rasher impulses.

Diego hadn't even wanted to include her in the escape.

"It's going to be hard enough to hide the most famous narco in the world," he said. "The most famous narco in the world and a former beauty queen? Impossible."

"I'm not leaving her in Puente," Adán said.

"Then at least split with her," Diego said. "Go separate ways."

"No."

"*Dios mío, primo,*" Diego said, "are you in love?"

I don't know, Adán thinks now, looking at Magda. I might be. I thought I was acquiring a beautiful, charming mistress, but I got a lot more—a confidante, an adviser, a truth-teller. So he asks her, "What should I do about Nacho?"

"Reach out," she says. "Set up a meeting. Offer him something that he wants more than he fears the government."

Nacho agrees to meet at a remote hilltop *finca* in the jungles of Nayarit.

They stay in the field.

Rather than return to Mexico City and start over, the "Committee" decides that Barrera couldn't have gone far, so they return to the base at El Salto and try to develop more information.

The army and air force maintain radar scans for any unlogged flights. Roadblocks are set up. SEIDO monitors cell phone and computer traffic with assistance from EPIC.

This is critical.

A bird makes noise when flushed from the bush.

Keller knows that if you force a major narco to move, especially in a hurry, you also make him communicate. Arrangements have to be made, security set up, travel routes planned, the right people notified.

They have to scramble, they have to talk to each other. They try their best to mask it—using cell phones only once, using SAT phones, text, e-mails, routing phone calls through international Internet services, but the less time they have, the harder these things are to do.

Even a sophisticated operation like EPIC can't keep track of every individual communication, can't intercept every e-mail or listen in on every phone, but what those guys can do is monitor traffic volume.

They already identified certain hot spots—geographical areas and cell phone towers combined with websites and servers that they know the narcos use—and if something is happening, those areas light up with increased traffic.

Now one of those hot zones goes absolutely Christmas tree.

The scans show a dramatic increase in traffic from a tower associated with one of Nacho Esparza's frequent hiding areas in Jalisco. Several of the calls, all made from different phones, go to a tower in Nayarit, in remote jungle mountains south of Sinaloa. Geographically, it makes sense. Nayarit is close, a short drive or flight from Durango.

The Esparza element makes sense, too. There have been rumors for months about possible tension between Barrera and Esparza—Nacho's absence at the company Christmas party was noted—and that Esparza was concerned Barrera was still an American snitch. Nayarit lies between their respective bases in Sinaloa and Jalisco—could they be planning a summit meeting to clear the air?

Keller looks at a map of the area served by the cell phone tower and then coordinates it with Google Earth. There's only one significant residence in the area, a *finca* of several buildings carved out of the rain forest on the top of a hill.

It's a perfect place.

Aguilar keeps his SEIDO people in Mexico City working twenty-four/seven tracing the ownership of the property. They track it back through several individuals until they find out that it's owned as a "hunting resort" by a investment firm in Guadalajara.

The firm is a holding company already under suspicion for laundering money for Nacho Esparza. Armed with that information, they get a tap on the phone coming from the *finca*.

> INCOMING CALLER: *You have guests arriving.*
> RECIPIENT: *When?*
> INCOMING CALLER: *Two tonight. One tomorrow morning.*
> *(Pause)*
> RECIPIENT: *Three men.*
> INCOMING CALLER: *You know who. And their people. No one else comes in or out. You understand?*
> *(Call terminates)*

Keller understands. "Three men—Barrera, Tapia, and Esparza?"

"It's possible," Aguilar says.

Vera is ecstatic. "We have him now. We *have* him. *Dios mío*, we might get all three of them."

That night, fifty heavily armed men, with Aguilar, Vera, and Keller, board a SEIDO plane, its flight plan logged for Jalisco. The men all passed polygraphs that afternoon, and Aguilar confiscates all their cell phones as they board.

When they're ten minutes in the air, Aguilar orders a change of course, telling the pilots that they're flying to Nayarit instead. He has personally located an airstrip in a defunct logging camp only eight kilometers from the *finca*.

The landing is rough but successful.

"Go radio silent," Aguilar orders the pilots.

"We should report—"

"I said go radio silent," Aguilar snaps. "Any transmissions you make will be monitored."

The men deplane and begin the hike up to the *finca* in the dim light of predawn. Keller is reminded again of Mexico's amazing diversity—from deserts to rain forests—as they head up the rough, wet terrain through thick green jungle.

Aguilar struggles in front of him. He's not really an operational guy, Keller thinks, his tennis shoes more suitable to a walk in the park than a slog in the mud. But Aguilar keeps going and doesn't complain.

The sun is fully up when they reach a plateau that has been cleared for grazing. A few curious cattle look at them as they deploy into a semicircle for the approach to the compound of houses that stand about three hundred yards away, through a low silver mist.

No lights glow from the windows. Is it possible, Keller wonders, that we've caught him sleeping?

"You will wait here," Aguilar says to him. "I want Barrera alive."

"I'll bet you do."

Men are getting ready, clicking clips into place, checking loads—one or two cross themselves and whisper prayers.

Adán steps out of the house and walks down to the broad, cleared grounds in front.

He and Diego arrived last night by car, having left Magda in the safe house in Sinaloa. He would have brought her with him, but he's not sure how safe this meeting is going to be. And he's annoyed that he had to arrive first—he knows that it's Nacho showing that he's not subservient.

Nacho arrives in a helicopter, and Adán has to wonder if it was a precaution or a deliberate act of noblesse oblige. Now Nacho emerges from the chopper flanked by bodyguards, like a president, looking cool and breezy in a linen suit. If Diego is the soldier of the Sinaloa cartel, Esparza is its diplomat. He strides over to Adán and his first words are, "We shouldn't stay long."

"I know you're busy," Adán answers.

The irony is apparently lost on Nacho, or he simply chooses to ignore it. "It's good to see you, Adán."

"Is it?" Adán asks.

Nacho smiles as if he doesn't understand what Adán could possibly mean. "Of course."

"Because I've been back for quite a while," Adán says. "You could have had the pleasure of seeing me earlier."

Unflustered, Nacho answers, "There's a two-million-dollar reward on my head. I was concerned that if I walked into Puente Grande, I might never have left."

"Funny, I had the same concern."

"I delivered a million and a half reasons why you shouldn't have had any concerns," Nacho says.

"Then why all this pressure?" Adán asks. If Nacho delivered the right money to the right people, there shouldn't *be* any.

"I could ask you the same question, Adanito," Nacho answers. "*Why* all this pressure?"

Adán ignores the diminutive version of his name. "You're worried that I'm a *soplón*? An informer?"

"I'm thinking that you did it before."

"And you were the beneficiary," Adán answers. "I didn't hear any complaints then. Nacho, you were my uncle's best friend and closest adviser, and then you were mine. There shouldn't be tension or suspicion between us. I've given up nothing about you. We have to use the authorities as we can—no one is better at this than you—and any connections I have are your connections as well."

"I hope you know that's mutual, Adán."

"I do," Adán answers, "and I understand other concerns that you might have, so let me tell you what I've already told Diego. I have no ambition to be *patrón*. I understand that you have your own organization now. I only want to be, at most, the first among equals."

Nacho opens his arms and they embrace.

"You know that I value you," Adán says. "Your wisdom, your experience. I rely on you. Tell me what you want."

"The Tijuana plaza," Nacho whispers.

"It's my sister's," Adán says.

"She can't hold it," Nacho answers. "And I want it for my son."

Then Adán hears a tremendous roar in the sky.

Keller looks up to see a Mexican air force fighter fly directly over the ranch.

Low.

"God *damn* it!" Keller yells.

Lights come on in the *finca*.

"Go!" Vera yells.

They rush forward.

Keller goes with him, Aguilar's prohibition forgotten in the rush to get there before Barrera can get away. It's still possible, Keller thinks as he runs across the pasture. There's only one road out and we have it covered.

Adán looks up and sees a fighter jet zooming in low.

Nacho's eyes widen. He pushes Adán away and runs back toward his heli-copter. Stumbling on a rock, he falls and stains the knee of his linen slacks. A bodyguard picks him up and leads him into the chopper.

The rotors start.

Diego unslings his AK and looks for something to shoot at.

Adán sees men moving across the pasture toward him. He runs for the helicopter, which hovers just a couple of feet above the ground. Nacho looks out at Adán and then signals the pilot to take off.

"Nacho, please!"

"Let him in," Esparza says.

One of his guards hauls Adán up, and Diego jumps in behind.

The helicopter takes off.

As it circles the *finca*, Adán sees the troopers moving in below. He isn't sure—it must be his imagination—but for a second, he thinks he sees Art Keller. He leans across and, over the throb of the rotors, shouts to Nacho, "Tijuana is yours, if you can take it from Teo!"

Keller sees a helicopter come up from the mist.

It circles the compound once and then takes off in the other direction.

Barrera has slipped the noose again.

"That was deliberate!" Keller yells at Aguilar when they get back to the plane.

"It was an unfortunate mistake," Aguilar answers. "It was supposed to be a high-level reconnaissance flight . . ."

An "unfortunate mistake," my ass, Keller thinks. It was deliberate, the only way of warning Barrera that someone could think of.

But who?

Four federal agents are waiting when the helicopter lands at a ranch farther down in Nayarit.

Adán looks at Nacho. "I guess you'll take Tijuana on your own. And the rest of it."

"Come on," Nacho says.

They get out of the helicopter and follow the agents into the house.

Four million dollars later, the helicopter takes off again, with Nacho Esparza, Diego Tapia, and Adán Barrera on board.

Keller has a cup of coffee in a Condesa café, and then does a little shopping at El Pendulo bookstore. He picks up an Elmer Mendoza novel, then walks along Avenida Amsterdam, which used to be part of the old racetrack, and stops in at Parilladas Bariloche for a reasonably inexpensive dinner of *papas con amor* and *arrachera*. Sitting there perusing the Mendoza, he knows that he's the image of the lonely, middle-aged divorced man—reading alone at a table for one.

Maybe, Keller thinks, I've become too used to solitude.

Maybe I like it too much.

He finishes dinner and then walks over to the Parque México.

Barrera has gone radio silent—no calls, no e-mails, no sightings, not even any rumors.

The trail is cold and dead.

The next meeting of the Barrera Coordinating Committee has the feel of a postmortem. Keller looks at his colleagues and wonders which, if either of them, has been tipping off Barrera.

He's also aware that he's been told to keep his big mouth shut about it—Mexican law enforcement has its shiny new soul—and Art Keller is not going to besmirch it. And the truth is that he doesn't have anything solid, just his suspicions.

And his gut feeling that both of these men are about to throw in the towel.

Aguilar is actually right when he points out to Keller that the search for Barrera is only one part of a multifaceted effort, and that neither SEIDO nor

AFI can commit all their time and resources for what seems to be an increasingly quixotic quest.

Keller hears the subtext—we're going to get you the hell out of here—and he's too smart to hasten the process of his own demise by making noise about corruption.

"Let me tilt at one more windmill," he says.

Keller and Vera watch from behind the one-way glass as Aguilar interviews Sondra Barrera.

She looks like hell, Keller thinks.

The Black Widow.

"You were present at the Christmas party in El Puente prison," Aguilar says.

"I don't know anything about that," Sondra answers.

"Well, you were there," Aguilar says. "We have witnesses."

Sondra doesn't respond.

"You were there with your son Salvador and other members of the family," Aguilar says.

"I don't know—"

"Where is Adán Barrera?"

Sondra laughs.

"Did I say something funny?" Aguilar asks.

"Do you think Adán would tell me where he is?" Sondra asks. "Do you think I would tell you if I knew?"

"*Do* you know?"

Sondra Barrera has no love for her brother-in-law, Keller knows, but she's not going to give him up, even if she could. He's her paycheck, her pension, her social security.

"My husband is dead," Sondra says.

"I'm aware of that," Aguilar answers. "What are you getting at?"

"That Adán has an instinct for survival," Sondra says. "Other people die for *him*. You'll never find him."

"Is he in touch with your son, Salvador?"

"Leave my son alone."

Keller sees the alarm in her eyes. Aguilar must have seen it, too, because he presses, "Tell me where Adán is and I won't have to speak to your son."

"He's good," Vera says to Keller. "Whatever else you can say about the persnickety bastard, you have to admit he's good."

"Please leave my son alone," Sondra says, on the verge of tears.

"I wish I could."

"You're bastards, all of you."

"You're hardly in a morally superior position, Señora Barrera," Aguilar says. "Do you know how many people your late husband killed?"

Sondra doesn't answer.

"Would you like to know? Does it matter to you? No, I thought not." He hands her his card. "This is my number. If Adán contacts you, I hope you will call me. And please have Salvador make an appointment. I don't want to pick him up on campus and embarrass him."

After Sondra and her lawyer leave, Aguilar comes into the room and sits with Keller and Vera. "Well, that was useful."

"It was," Keller says. "I know Sondra—she'll panic."

"Do we have a trace on her phones?" Vera asks.

"Of course," Aguilar answers. "And her son's."

"Luis is getting into the game," Vera says, getting up to leave.

"I've been in the game," Aguilar answers.

But Vera is already out the door.

Aguilar turns to Keller and says defensively, "I've *been* in the game."

Sondra calls a number in Culiacán. "*. . . they're talking about obstruction charges.*"

"*They're bluffing.*"

"It's not Adán's voice," Keller says.

"No," Aguilar agrees.

"*I will not go to prison. I will not have my son go to prison.*"

"*Relax. We'll fix it.*"

"What does that mean?" Keller asks.

"I don't know," Aguilar snaps.

"*Call him.*"

"*That's not necessary. We can take care of it.*"

"*He's not leaving us hanging out there.*"

"*You know he wouldn't do that.*"

"*I don't know that.*"

"*Sondra—*"

She hangs up.

"Who was she talking to?" Keller asks.

"Esparza?" Aguilar asks. "Tapia? I don't know."

But now they have the number she called, and it's a simple matter of technology to tap its calls.

They sit through a long night. Finally the man in Culiacán, now code-named "Fixer," makes a call to the 777 area code—Cuernavaca. *"Sondra's panicking."*

"Tell her to calm down."

"You don't think I did? She wants us to talk to him."

"To say what? Just fix it."

"Obviously. If she gives us the time."

"What can she tell them?"

"Who knows what she knows?"

"Silly bitch. What about the kid?"

"He's his father's son."

"The man loves him."

"Then we should tell him."

Keller feels a jolt shoot through his body. The men on the phone call are about to contact Adán.

The next minutes are agony.

Aguilar orders an underling, "Get Vera in here."

The AFI chief shows up twenty minutes later, disheveled, in a tracksuit and sweatshirt. "This had better be good. I've been seducing this woman for weeks."

Aguilar briefed him.

They sit in silence, watching the phone monitor.

Hoping, praying.

Then it lights up.

"Cuernavaca" is on the phone.

"Jesus," Vera says. "It's 555—a Mexico City number. Barrera's *here*."

Here, Keller thinks, in Mexico City. He's so goddamn smart, Barrera, he flies under the radar by getting under the radar's shell. You have to hand it to the son of a bitch, it's as clever as it is arrogant.

Classic Adán Barrera.

Keller listens as "Cuernevaca" says, *"It's me."*

"What is it?"

"Is that Barrera?" Aguilar asks.

"Can't tell," Keller answers.

They listen as "Cuernavaca" describes the problem with Sondra Barrera. Then the recipient of the call says, *"The* pendejos, *why do they have to interfere with families?"*

Keller nods. It's him.

"What do you want to do?" "Cuernavaca" asks.

"Just tell her you spoke with me and we're fixing it. Send them on vacation or something."

"Atizapán," the technician says, naming a town on the outskirts of Mexico City, "5871 Calle Revolución."

"Cuernavaca" says, *"Do you think . . . we should . . ."*

"She's my brother's wife."

The call goes off. Vera grins. "Did we just hear 'Cuernavaca' suggest killing Barrera's sister-in-law?"

Keller is already on the horn to DEA to request a satellite run.

By early morning they have a hit.

"Look at this," Keller said.

He shows them a grainy video image of Adán Barrera standing on the roof of the house, gazing out over the neighborhood, a cup of coffee in his hand. He only stayed a minute, and then went in.

"It's him," Keller says.

"Are you sure?" Aguilar asks.

Keller has come to learn that the head of SEIDO is a cautious man, constantly checking and rechecking the "facts" to make certain that they are indeed facts, and not rumors or deliberate misinformation. The image is grainy but Keller is reasonably sure it's Adán—the short stature, the shock of black hair across the forehead . . .

"Put a percentage on it," Aguilar presses.

"Eighty-five," Keller says.

"Eighty-five is good," Vera comments.

Keller wants to go in right away. He requests and receives another satellite flyover with mega-audio capability and sits listening to what he believes is Adán's voice inside the house.

Talking to a woman.

"Do you want red or white?"

"Red tonight, I think."

"Is that her?" Keller asks. "Magda Beltrán?"

The beauty queen.

Aguilar shrugs. "Narcos have a lot of women."

"Not Adán," Keller says. "He's more of a serial monogamist."

They run the audio against DEA recordings of Adán and come up with a close match.

"We know that he's inside the house *now*," Keller says. "Let's *do* it now."

"It's too risky," Aguilar says.

Vera—usually the more aggressive—agrees. "Too much chance of my men hitting each other in a crossfire."

"Or a civilian," Aguilar says.

It's frustrating—the AFI troopers are good, more and more of them have received training at Quantico, but Keller yearns for American special forces, with their high level of training and equipment. He knows it will never happen—D.C. would never send, nor would Los Pinos ever accept, American troops on Mexican soil—but Keller would give a lot right then for special operators who *preferred* to fight at night.

But this is the Mexicans' call to make, and they decide to wait until dawn. Aguilar puts his best surveillance team on the scene, and Vera sends an AFI plainclothes team in case Barrera tries to leave the house.

"We have him penned in," Vera reassures Keller. "He's not going anywhere. He'll be there in the morning."

Keller hopes so.

Adán hasn't stayed free this long by being careless, and he doubtless has men watching from the house, as well as *halcones*—"falcons," lookouts—on the street. Not to mention an average, misguided citizen who sees Barrera as some kind of Robin Hood and who could get very rich very quickly by warning the *patrón* about strangers in the neighborhood.

But now the "strangers" are in place—four armored vehicles filled with AFI troopers with black hoods and Kevlar vests—parked blocks away from the building. The troopers are armed with automatic rifles, flash-bang grenades, and tear-gas canisters. Two helicopters stand by to take off as soon as the raid starts, and they'll drop more AFI troopers onto the roof.

Keller urges the sun to hurry the hell up.

The house will be full of *sicarios*, and, sleepy or not, they'll fight to protect Barrera, and there will be gunfire. And when the shooting starts, Keller thinks, the distinction between justice and revenge tends to get blurred.

Then Vera's voice comes over the radio.

"Two minutes."

The plan is straightforward, perhaps too much so, Keller thinks. At the "go" command, the vehicles will charge up to the building and AFI troopers will get out, bludgeon open the door, and go in while others guard the back entrance and seal off the streets. The SEIDO agents will follow to make arrests and gather intelligence and evidence—cell phones, computers, cash, and weapons.

Aguilar checks the load on his service revolver, and tightens his Kevlar vest. Then he turns to Keller and says, "You will remain in the vehicle. We will bring Barrera out and you will identify him. Is that clear?"

"I heard you the fifteenth time."

They sit in silence for an interminable ninety seconds, until they hear Vera say, "Go."

Aguilar starts to follow his men out of the car.

Keller watches him go down the block, then pulls his gun and follows.

"Juras! Juras!"

Keller hears the *halcones* shout that the cops are coming, but the lookouts—most of them kids—run away as the AFI troopers pour out of the vehicles.

Gunfire blasts from the windows and the roof.

Vera seems oblivious to the bullets zipping around him. Pistol in hand, he urges the men with the battering ram to hit the door. More afraid of him than the bullets, the troopers pick up the ram and run it into the door.

The door comes off its hinges, pulling the trip wires on the grenades attached waist high to the sill.

Keller sees the red blast as two troopers fly back.

"Muévanse!" Vera yells at the stunned survivors.

Move!

They balk as bullets zip out through the doorway and they look at their two comrades lying in the street, limp as puppets.

"Rajados! Cowards!" Vera yells. *"I'll* go!"

He runs in.

His men follow him.

So does Keller, who trots toward the house, remembering Vietnam and his Quantico training—*don't run to your death*—and saves his oxygen for the firefight.

And, like 'Nam, he hears the choppers coming in.

The house is a bedlam.

The power out, faint light comes through the few windows—screams of pain and bursts of automatic weapons fire cut through the darkness. The carnage is horrific, although it's hard to make out the narcos from the AFI troopers. Keller hears Vera's voice in front of him, toward the back of the house, shouting orders.

Stepping over the bodies of dead and wounded, Keller looks for the stairs. Adán wouldn't be on the ground floor or on the top. He'd be on the second, in the back, with the possibility of getting out a window.

If he's even here, Keller thinks. This was an ambush—a booby-trapped ambush—and they were ready for us.

But the voice track said he was here. *Was* here, anyway, Keller thinks as he finds the stairs and starts up, pistol pointed in front of him.

Then he trips over Aguilar's legs.

The lawyer sits on the landing, his back against the wall, his legs stuck straight out, his left hand grasping his right arm, the glassy look of the wounded in his eyes.

He sees Keller.

"You're supposed to be in the car," Aguilar says softly.

Keller crouches beside him. The wound is jagged—shrapnel, not a bullet. Keller rips Aguilar's sleeve and uses it as a tourniquet. "The medics are on the way. You won't bleed out."

"Go back to the car."

Keller continues up the stairs.

A grenade clatters down the steps.

Before he can move, it goes off by his ankles. The smoke explodes up, choking him, blinding him. Staggering up the stairs, he hears gunfire above him, as the AFI troopers fight their way down from the roof. A *sicario* appears through the smoke in front of him. He looks confused when he sees Keller, then throws his AK up to his shoulder.

Keller fires twice into his chest and the man goes down.

Pushing past him, Keller makes it to the top of the stairs. He opens the first door he can find and sees—

Adán—

—standing by the bed—

—a pistol in his right hand.

"Don't," Keller says.

Hoping he does.

Barrera raises the gun.

Keller fires.

The first bullet takes off the bottom of Barrera's jaw.

The second goes through his left eye.

Blood sprays against the wall.

The woman screams.

Keller lowers his gun.

Vera walks up behind him.

Together, they look down at the corpse.

The black hair, the slightly pug nose, the brown eyes.

Well, *one* brown eye.

"Congratulations," Vera says.

"It's not him," Keller says.

"What?!"

"It's not fucking him."

Adán used lookalikes before, at least three of them during his war with Palma, and when Keller sees the body up close, remote from the chaos, adrenaline, darkness, and smoke, he realizes that it wasn't Adán and that the whole raid has been a setup.

Keller, Vera, and the AFI troopers tear through the house, and in one of the bedrooms they find it.

The bathtub has been torn up and there it is—the entrance to a tunnel.

Keller jumps down.

Pistol in front of him, he moves down the tunnel, which is wired for electricity and has lights. He hopes that Barrera is in here, cowering somewhere, but the greater likelihood is that if Barrera's down here, he has an army of *sicarios* protecting him.

Keller keeps pushing anyway.

Vera is right behind him, his gun also drawn.

They walk under the street and then come to the end of the tunnel and another metal ladder. Keller climbs up and pushes open the trapdoor into another house.

It's empty.

Barrera is gone.

They do the press conference that afternoon. Aguilar questioned the wisdom of making a public show of what had been a desperate shootout near the nation's capital, but Vera insisted.

"We must not only combat the cartels," Vera said, "we must be *seen* to be combating the cartels. That's the only way to restore the public's confidence in their law enforcement agencies."

Keller watches on television at the embassy as Vera describes the daring raid, the intense firefight, and memorializes the brave men who gave their lives. He goes on to praise the diligent work of SEIDO, and introduces Luis Aguilar, "who, as you can see, shed his blood in the pursuit of this criminal."

Aguilar mumbles through a typed statement. "We regret our failure in this instance. However, we assure the public that the battle will go on and we must . . ."

Vera throws his arm around his colleague's shoulder.

"We're Batman and Robin." He looks straight into the cameras. "And he's right—the battle is just beginning. We won't relent in our hunt for Barrera, but now I'm talking to the rest of you narcos out there. We're coming after you. We'll be in Tijuana next."

"What about the beauty queen?" a reporter asks. "What about Miss Culiacán?"

Vera steps back in. "She wasn't in the house. But don't worry—we'll find her and give her a new sash."

The reporters laugh.

The fight starts the next day.

"You're going home," Aguilar tells Keller.

"Absolutely," Keller answers. "The moment Barrera is back behind bars or on a slab."

"*Now*," Aguilar insists. "It's too dangerous—not only for you but for other people. The booby-trapped door could have been meant for you. Other men paid with their lives."

"That's what soldiers do," Vera says.

"They were policemen, not soldiers," Aguilar says. "And this is a law enforcement action, not a war."

"Don't kid yourself," Vera answers.

"I object to the militarization of—"

"Tell that to the narcos," Vera says. "If Keller is willing to stay until the job is done, I'm willing to have him. If he's willing to stay."

Keller's willing.

Adán Barrera is still out there, in his world.

La Tuna, Sinaloa

Adán walks out onto the little balcony off the master bedroom of his *finca*.

The ranch was his aunt's, abandoned back in the '70s when the American DEA came in and devastated the poppy fields with fire and poison. Thousands of campesinos and *gomeros*—now refugees—fled their mountain homes.

Tía Delores's *finca* stood empty for years, a home for only ravens.

Since his return to Mexico, Adán has poured millions into renovating the main house and the outbuildings, and more millions turning the ranch into a fortress with high walls, guard towers, sound and motion sensors, and casitas that serve as living spaces for the servants and barracks for the *sicarios*.

For Adán it is a return to innocence, of sorts, to the idyllic day of his teenage years when he would come up here to escape the heat of the Tijuana summer and dive into the cold waters of the granite quarries. Of family dinners at large tables under the oak trees, listening to the campesino men play tamboras and guitars, and the old women, the *abuelas,* tell stories from a time beyond his memory.

A good life, a rich life, a life that the North Americans destroyed.

It is good to be home, Adán thinks.

Despite Sondra's stupidity.

Stupid, vapid Sondra was a perfect pawn for both white and black. As it turned out, it wasn't a problem. He and Magda went to the safe house in Atizapán, he let himself be seen and heard, and then he slipped out of the net that had been thrown around the house.

The lookalike was already there, a happy idiot thrilled to have a nice house and a beautiful woman for a few days, an expensive whore who resembled Magda in all the most superficial ways.

Adán will take care of the lookalike's family.

The only downside is that Keller didn't die in the ambush. It would have been perfect—the North American killed in a botched raid that couldn't have been blamed on me. But Keller is still out there, alive, and Magda is still urging that he be left out there. Too much at stake now, Magda says, too much happening to take another chance.

Adán maintains the "stay of execution" but insists that it's just that. Unlike the United States, Mexico has no death penalty, but Adán likes to think of Keller just inhabiting a mobile cell on death row.

After the raid, Adán deemed it safe to move to the ranch in Sinaloa, outside La Tuna, high in the Sierra Madre. His convoy made its way up winding roads—dusty now but often impassable with mud in the rainy season—through tiny hamlets made of spare odds and ends of wood and corrugated tin.

Despite its wealth in drug production, the Triangle is still one of the poorest parts of Mexico. The vast majority of the people are still campesinos—peasant farmers—as they had always been. The fact that they grow poppies and *yerba* instead of corn is only a detail.

For most, life never changes.

It was good to be home.

"Is there where you grew up?" Magda asked, looking at the expanse of green field with the mountains in the background.

"Summers," Adán said. "Actually, I'm a city boy."

The car pulled through the gate then up the macadam road lined with junipers, tall and straight like soldiers on parade. It stopped in the crescent gravel driveway outside the main house.

"No moat?" Magda asked.

"Not yet."

Magda looked at the main house, a two-story stone building with a central structure flanked by two wings that came out at a forty-five-degree angle. A large portico with marble columns stood at the front of the central structure; balconies were cantilevered from the second floors of the wings.

"It's a mansion," Magda said.

"More than I need or want," Adán answered, "but there are expectations."

A king must have a castle, whether he wants one or not. It's *expected*, and if the king doesn't build one, he can be certain that his dukes will.

Designing the renovation became a hobby of sorts in prison—Adán met with architects and builders, approved plans, even drew a few sketches of his own. It gave him something to look forward to.

So many of the narco-mansions are monuments to bad taste. Adán did his best to avoid gaudy, ostentatious displays, retaining the classic lines of old Sinaloa while still making sure that the house revealed the proper level of wealth and power.

The Barreras, after all, came to the Sierras in the early seventeenth century as hidalgos—Spanish gentlemen of fortune—and conquered the local Indians over centuries of brutal, bloody warfare. They were aristocrats, not *indios* like so many of the new nouveau-riche narcos.

So Adán felt an obligation toward restraint.

It was in his nature anyway.

He showed Magda around the house and then they went up to the master bedroom. The thick walls kept it cool in the summer and warm in the winter, and the maids had sprinkled the sheets with ice water.

After she and Adán made love, she asked, "So what do I do now?"

"Live?"

"As the lady of the house?" Magda asked. "Supervise the staff, organize parties, go shopping in Culiacán with the wives, get my hair and nails done? I'll die of boredom. I need something else. Something to make money."

Adán looked at her long, slender form stretched out like a cat and saw that she was fully awake and not going to let him sleep. "Money is not your problem in life."

"It will be one day," Magda said. "I'll lose my looks, or you'll grow tired of me, or I'll grow tired of you, or you'll start looking for some young *pura señorita* to start a new family for you. What am I supposed to do then?"

"I'll always take care of you."

"I don't want to be 'taken care of,'" she answered, "like some worn-out *segundera* put out to pasture. I want into the trade."

"No."

"You can't stop me."

"Of course I can," Adán said. But he admired her for trying.

"I could be useful to you."

"Oh? How?"

"I could help you reestablish your Colombian cocaine connections," Magda said.

"Nacho and Diego's connections are my connections," he answered.

"Please listen to yourself," Magda said. "It only goes to show how much you need me."

She's making sense, Adán thought. Magda would be an effective ambassador. The Colombians would find a beautiful, intelligent woman hard to resist, and her advice to him had always been clearheaded.

"And what would you want for these services?" he asked.

Magda smiled, knowing that she'd won. "A piece of the cocaine I bring in. And the protection to make it worth something."

"What else?" He could tell from the look in her eye that she wasn't finished.

"A seat at the table," Magda said.

"Which you already have."

"Not the dining table," she said. "The *men's* table."

"They won't accept you."

"I'll make them accept me," Magda said.

Now, as Adán looks out over the hills, he realizes both that he believes her and that it might not matter. Osiel Contreras wants him dead and has the men and the means to do it.

I need more force.

I need an alliance.

———

The table is set in the back room of an exclusive restaurant in Cuernavaca.

Meeting in neutral territory was Nacho's idea, to put Vicente Fuentes at ease. Nacho has guaranteed everyone's safety—Fuentes, the Tapias, Adán, and the twenty other important associates from Sinaloa.

Even so, everyone comes armed.

Plainclothes Cuernavaca police guard the door from other police, the media, and from the important narcos who haven't been invited—Teo Solorzano and Osiel Contreras.

Adán makes a point by not even mentioning Magda's presence, as if it's a given and literally unremarkable. But she *is* remarkable—stunning in a gold lamé dress with a deep décolletage that if Vicente Fuentes doesn't remark upon, he's certainly thinking about as he leans over to kiss her hand.

Vicente looks up at Adán and says, "It must be Easter."

"Why is that?"

"You've risen from the dead." The line gets a laugh from the guests who've already come into the room. Encouraged by his audience, Vicente goes on. "You look good, Adán, for a corpse."

The Fuenteses are originally from Sinaloa, and the family has ruled the Juárez plaza for years. Vicente doesn't have the charisma or brains of his late uncle—he's dissolute, flamboyant, too busy with coke and women to run his business well.

And he's lazy, Adán thinks. Too lazy to work out solutions to difficult problems, so his only reaction is the easiest one—killing. He orders up murders like takeout Chinese food, and a lot of his people are tired of it. Afraid that a casual word or a misunderstanding could make them next, a lot of them came over to Adán after his return to Mexico.

Vicente resents it and sees Adán as a threat. Maintaining the relationship with Nacho, who moves vast weights of meth through Juárez, is the only reason he agreed to this meeting.

"When Nacho told me you were alive," Vicente says now, "I wept."

I'll bet you did, Adán thinks.

Vicente asks, "Is Elvis here, too?"

The joke doesn't sit well with Alberto Tapia. "You want to *meet* Elvis, Vicente? Because maybe we can work that out."

Vicente reaches for the gun at his hip.

So does Alberto.

Nacho steps in. "Don't make a liar of me, gentlemen."

Vicente eases his hand away.

He believes he's too handsome to die, Adán thinks, that it would be too great a loss to a world in need of beauty. Alberto waits for Vicente to back down first, and then, grinning, takes his hand away from his gun.

But it could have happened that fast, Adán thinks. Plans that I've spent years constructing could have fallen apart in a stupid exchange of insults. We run a billion-dollar business and act like nickel gangbangers. He makes a mental note to tell Diego to get his little brother under control.

Martín Tapia steps into the awkward gap. "Gentlemen—and lady—dinner is served."

They take their seats.

Adán hates making speeches.

It was his uncle's speech almost thirty years ago—at a dinner like this—that created the Federación, and Adán knows the men at the table are expecting an equal performance.

He's afraid that he's not up to it.

"We Sinaloans created the *pista secreta*," Adán says. "The trade is in our blood, in our bones, in the water we drink and the air we breathe. We made it flourish. When the *yanquis* destroyed our homes and our fields and scattered us like dry leaves in the wind, we refused to die. We re-formed, we created La Federación, we divided the country into plazas and ran it."

The men around the table nod in agreement.

"When Sinaloa ran the drug trade," Adán continues, "it ran efficiently and everyone made money. It was a *business*."

He's telling them what they already know, letting them remember his uncle and the reign of peace and plenty—brief but beautiful—he engendered.

"Now we are going to take back what is ours," Adán says. He lets it sink in for a moment, and then says, "All the plazas, all the so-called cartels—the big ones and the small ones—I intend to reunite under our leadership. They will be run by us—by Sinaloans and only Sinaloans. That is why you're here tonight. We are blood. Therefore I want to propose an alliance. An *alianza de sangre*. An alliance of blood."

Adán waits for a few seconds to let the precisely chosen words sink in. An alliance of equals, not an empire with himself at its head. An alliance based on the old family and cultural relationships that go back centuries. He lets them also hear what he didn't say. No mention of the Cartel del Golfo—they are not Sinaloans.

He's talking to all the men in the room, but his real target is Vicente.

The Tapias are already on board, of course, so is Nacho, but if Adán is going to achieve what he wants, he needs Vicente, he needs the Juárez plaza through which to move his product.

"How exactly would it work?" Vicente asks. "This 'alliance of blood'?"

Adán answers, "We will protect each other's interests, defend each other in the case of an attack from outsiders, agree to allow each other to move product through our plazas, with a *piso*, of course."

"But Adán doesn't have a plaza," Vicente says to the others, pointedly ignoring Adán. "Barrera is offering something he doesn't have. I hear he doesn't even have Tijuana anymore."

You "hear"? Adán wonders. Or you're behind Solorzano? But he doesn't say it. Instead, he turns toward Vicente and says, "What we have is product and protection. We have police and politicians. We are willing to share. But only with blood."

Vicente won't let it go. "Are you saying you'll only move your product through Juárez? Not Laredo, not the Gulf?"

Diego has had enough. "We'll move our product where we want."

"Not through Juárez," Vicente answers. "Not if I don't allow it. Not when Adán is already poaching on my territory, stealing my people."

This is starting to go badly, Adán thinks. Not what he wanted at all.

Then Magda says, "We are all friends here, we are all family. Families have little quarrels—they mean nothing. Let's be honest—at the end of the day, we all need family. Family is all we can trust."

She touches her hand on Vicente's.

He hears what she's saying. His territory is flanked on the east by the Gulf cartel, on the west by Tijuana, where Solorzano may have ambitions of his own. But it's the Gulf that worries him—Contreras's power is growing every day, and it's only a matter of time before he starts glancing at the rich plaza next door.

Vicente needs protection, and if Adán is offering that . . . well, what are a few defectors, especially if Adán is guaranteeing that they will all pay the *piso*. If they pay Adán as well, it's money out of their pockets, not his.

An alliance of blood is an alliance against Contreras. Not a declaration of war—that would be foolish—but a statement of strength that might prevent an invasion. It might discourage Tijuana. And Adán's woman, by framing it as a matter of family, has given him the chance to step down from this argument without losing face.

Adán can virtually watch the man think. Finally—*finally*—Vicente speaks up. "Blood is blood. If Adán will agree that anyone moving product through our plaza will pay the *piso*—"

"I will," Adán says.

"—and offer us the benefit of his connections, then we will join in this *alianza de sangre*." Vicente stands, raises his wineglass, and proposes a toast. "To the *alianza de sangre*."

Adán clinks his glass.

"To the *alianza de sangre*."

Adán stretches out on the bed next to Magda.

The meeting almost turned into a disaster, which Magda averted but at the end he got what he wanted—an alliance that will counterbalance Contreras and make him think twice about another assassination attempt.

The *susurro* is that Contreras is making a move on Nuevo Laredo, right on Fuentes's doorstep. Since the old Chinese opium days at the turn of the century, Nuevo Laredo has been controlled by two families, the Garcías and the Sotos, and the Barreras have happily done business with the Garcías for years, at a discounted *piso*. The CDG owning Laredo would be a catastrophe, costing us billions, Adán thinks. Worse, it would give Contreras yet more power.

It can't be allowed to happen.

Magda runs her index finger along his temple. "That mind of yours—doesn't it ever get tired?"

"It can't."

She leans over and unzips his fly.

"Even when I do this?" Then she stops for a second and asks, "Are you still thinking?"

"No."

"Liar."

"I need you to go to Colombia now," Adán says.

"Right now?"

"Not *right* now."

"Oh."

Later he asks, "Where did you learn that?"

Magda gets out of bed. "I'll pack tonight, leave in the morning. You'll miss me."

"I will."

"You'll find another woman," Magda says, "some silly virgin. But no one who could do *that* to you."

He will miss her.

But he'll be busy.

It's almost time to move against Contreras in the Gulf. I have justification, Adán thinks—Contreras started the war when he tried to kill me in Puente Grande.

First the Gulf.

Then Tijuana.

Then Juárez.

The new *alianza de sangre* will become the old Federación.

And I'll become El Patrón.

Keller lies on the bed in his apartment.

His loneliness is a faint ache, like the reminder of an old wound, a scar you no longer notice because it's just a part of you now.

Like your Barrera obsession? he asks himself. Is there a legitimate purpose, a reason, a *cause,* or is it just part of you now, a disease of the blood, an obstruction of the heart?

It felt good, didn't it, pulling the trigger on the man you thought was Barrera. Seeing the fear in his eyes. At the end of the day you have to account for the fact that it felt good.

Aguilar's right—the ambush at the house was probably meant for me. Kind of funny, when you think about it, that Barrera and I each thought we'd killed each other.

And were both wrong.

PART TWO

The Gulf War

They bought up half of southern Texas,
That's why they act the way they do.

—Charlie Robison
"New Year's Day"

1

The Devil Is Dead

Some say the devil is dead,
The devil is dead, the devil is dead
Some say the devil is dead
And buried in Killarney.
I say he rose again,
He rose again, he rose again . . .

—Irish folk song

Nuevo Laredo, Tamaulipas
2006

Keller watches the girl writhe on the pole in a pathetic parody of lust.
He's sitting by himself at a cantina in La Zona—the "Zone of Tolerance," more commonly known as Boy's Town—a walled-in section of bars, strip clubs, and brothels frequented mostly by teenagers and college kids coming over the bridges from Laredo, Texas, just across the Rio Grande.

Los dos Laredos, Keller thinks.

The Two Laredos.

One in Mexico, the other just across the river in Texas.

Collectively the two cities form the busiest inland port in the hemisphere. Something like 70 percent of all Mexican exports to the United States pass through Nuevo Laredo into its sister city across the border.

That includes dope.

Lots of dope.

Keller sits and watches the girl tiredly do a routine that is almost prophylactic in itself. She's young and thin, her eyes vacant even as they try to stare down men into slipping money under her ill-fitting yellow G-string, her motions more robotic than erotic.

The girl is on autopilot and Keller bets that she's high.

The joint is almost impossibly depressing. Drunk American college kids, sad middle-aged men, sadder bargirls and whores, and, of course, narcos. Not top guys, but low- and midlevel traffickers and wannabes, most of them dressed in full *norteño* narco-cowboy gear.

Keller takes another sip of beer. This bar, like most of them in La Zona, serves only beer and tequila, and he chose a bottle of Indio.

These are bad and brooding days for Art Keller.

Adán Barrera's trail is colder than a bill collector's heart.

After the Atizapán shootout, Barrera went off the radar. No cell phone or Internet traffic, no discernible movement, no "Adán sightings" that used to light up the phone boards like Times Square at sunset. Keller can't get a solid lead, just rumors, some of which say that Barrera has retired from the *pista secreta* and is content to live out his life in peace and seclusion.

Keller doesn't buy it.

If Barrera is quiet, he has a reason, and the reason is always bad. Adán's not playing bridge, going on Carnival cruises, or working on his golf swing. If he's lying low, it's because he's about to make a move.

The question is where.

Barrera needs a piece of the border.

A plaza.

Keller thinks it's going to be the Gulf.

The CDG, the Cartel del Golfo, aren't Sinaloans so don't qualify for the "we are family" love-fest. The cartel's boss, Osiel Contreras, is a Matamoros homeboy who lacks the Culiacán pedigree that is the usual prerequisite for narco-royalty. So he's fair game. Especially when Adán figures that *he* put Contreras on the Gulf throne anyway, by dropping a dime on his predecessor.

Barrera views Contreras as a placeholder.

Contreras doesn't.

He sees himself as the next *patrón*.

His power is growing—the CDG recently expanded from its Matamoros and Reynosa bases to threaten Nuevo Laredo, absorbing the Soto family that used to run the east side. And Contreras has his own private army—the Zetas—trained by us, Keller thinks with chagrin.

At Fort Benning.

To combat drug trafficking.

So now Contreras's CDG has the whole state of Tamaulipas, effectively making him the predominant narco in the country.

But it's the same old story, Keller thinks, as a new girl—this one older, even more tired, if that's possible—takes her rotation on the pole. Sources say that Contreras has started to use his own product, is snorting piles of cocaine, and that it's fueling his paranoia.

And his rage.

It recently caused him to seriously fuck up.

Two DEA agents in Matamoros had an informant in their car. Contreras had some of his men surround their Ford Bronco, then he got out of his own vehicle and, gold-plated AK-47 in hand and golden-gripped Colt pistol tucked into his waistband, swaggered up to the trapped DEA men and demanded that they turn the informant over to him.

When they refused, Contreras said he would kill them.

DEA agents in Mexico aren't allowed to carry weapons, so these guys were helpless.

They toughed it out, though, and said that they wouldn't surrender the man, seeing as how they were going to die anyway. The agent's exact words to Contreras have already become agency lore. "Tomorrow and the next day and the rest of your life, you'll regret anything stupid you do now. You're fixing to make three hundred million enemies."

Everyone still remembered the massive manhunt launched after Ernie Hidalgo's murder. They especially recalled that Keller's obsessive quest for revenge brought down the Barreras.

Contreras remembered that, too, and backed off.

Washington overreacted, putting Contreras near the top of the Most Wanted list, just below bin Laden, and placing a $2 million reward on his head. Then they bought armored Suburbans for each of the eight DEA offices in Mexico. The vehicles were a gesture, the reward symbolic—no one in his right mind would try to collect on it.

But Osiel Contreras has leapfrogged Adán Barrera as target *número uno*. Indictments on multiple counts of trafficking have been handed down on both sides of the border. All that remains is to arrest the man.

But they simply can't lay their hands on Contreras, even though he's reported to be operating openly in Tamaulipas. His arrogance is galling, the reason for it humiliating, especially to Vera and Aguilar:

Contreras owns the police.

Municipal police in Matamoros, Reynosa, and Nuevo Laredo, police chiefs in a hundred smaller towns and villages, and state police in Tamaulipas are on the CDG payroll.

The problem is intractable—you can't just fire three-quarters of the police force. Traffic would come to a halt, public order would be compromised, robberies, rapes, and murders would go uninvestigated.

Vera and Aguilar tried to effect the necessary change from above, Vera appointing new AFI commanders from Mexico City, Aguilar sending in teams of trusted SEIDO agents.

They met with a hostile reception from the local police, who considered them "outsiders," ignorant of local conditions, men sent to disrupt their normal operations, including the cozy relationship with the CDG.

And the Zetas' military discipline and reputation for torture have made seizures difficult, informers impossible, and the CDG impenetrable.

They've effectively stunted the campaign to bring down Osiel Contreras.

But Gerardo Vera and Luis Aguilar—"Batman and Robin"—are *shredding* the Tijuana cartel.

Every week brings a new seizure or a major arrest. A tunnel found under the border at Otay Mesa, three thousand pounds of marijuana seized, key players captured. Every seizure and prisoner is paraded in front of the media, and each arrest yields intelligence that so far have led to the arrests of over one thousand members of the Tijuana cartel.

Whom the AFI can't capture, they kill.

They gun down one of Solorzano's lieutenants in a firefight in Mazatlán. A firefight in Rosarito takes down his chief of security.

Vera's new AFI is a collective Dirty Harry—the narcos have to decide if they feel lucky—and Vera isn't shy about voicing his philosophy to the public. "They surrender or they die. That's their only choice. *Los malosos*—the bad guys—are not going to run Mexico."

The media love it. Every arrest and seizure makes headlines in the American newspapers, especially in California. One went as far as to chirp, BATMAN AND ROBIN CLEAN UP THE MEXICAN GOTHAM.

Add to that the fact that Nacho Esparza has launched his own campaign against Solorzano. Adán's former partner has reportedly sent his son, Ignacio Junior, to run the war to retake Adán's old plaza.

But Keller is convinced that Barrera is about to make a move on the Gulf; he said so at one of the increasingly infrequent meetings of the Barrera Coordinating Committee and saw both Aguilar and Vera roll their eyes.

"This Barrera obsession of yours," Aguilar said.

"It doesn't seem that long ago when it was a Barrera obsession of *ours*," Keller answered.

"And we'll get him," Vera said. "But the fact is that he's a spent force, a hunted fugitive content just to be free for another day. We have to concentrate on the *active* narcos."

Vera referred him to a map of Mexico. "We have a strategy. We get control of Tijuana, west of Juárez. Then we beat down the CDG, east of Juárez. We'll have Fuentes in a vise, and we crush *him*. When you really think about it, the capture of Barrera is more symbolic than strategic."

It isn't symbolic to me, Keller thought.

It's personal.

"If we're not going after Barrera," he asked, "what am I doing here?"

"*Excellent* question," Aguilar said.

"We're not giving up the hunt for Barrera," Vera said. "I'm only saying that, absent any development, it has to . . ."

"Go on the back burner?" Keller asked.

Vera shrugged, an eloquent gesture.

The weekly meetings of the Barrera Coordinating Committee had already been suspended, to be held only when "developments" warranted.

But there were no developments.

Barrera had gone to ground.

Some rumors had him holed up in Sinaloa, others in Durango, still others—among them the Mexican president—hinted that Barrera was actually hiding in the United States.

Keller did what he could to develop leads, but he couldn't do much. Even DEA got on board with the "Barrera as spent force" theory, which soon gained the status of received wisdom.

"Barrera's old news," Taylor said over the phone just this afternoon.

Literally true, Keller thought. Barrera vanished from the media just as he disappeared off the radar—and Washington, in the peculiar ADD fashion of the American news cycle, seems content to let him slip out of the public consciousness.

So does Mexico City.

It has mostly to do with the elections.

After over seventy years of PRI monopoly of Los Pinos, the Mexican White House, the PAN party finally won a national election and seized control of the federal government. Now PAN's first term is coming to an end—Mexican presidents can only serve a single six-year term—and PAN's new candidate, Felipe Calderón, is in a close election race to hold Los Pinos against PRI.

So PAN is more than happy to sweep the Puente Grande prison escape scandal under the rug, and PRI's history of narco-corruption prevents them from bringing it up as an issue.

Nobody wants to talk about Adán Barrera.

Batman and Robin are happier subjects, especially with Vera providing irresistible quotes like, "Contreras has his own army? So what? I have *my* own army—we'll see who wins."

"I didn't come here for Contreras," Keller told Taylor.

"We're thinking the same thing," Taylor said. "It might be time to pull you out. The bees probably miss you, right?"

I'm on the endangered species list, Keller thought when he hung up the phone. The ax is looming over my head and Luis Aguilar can't wait to swing.

On the other hand, Gerardo Vera has become something of a friend.

Well, not exactly a friend—Keller has no friends in Mexico, will allow himself no real friends among colleagues whom he doesn't trust—but they do share an end-of-the-day beer from time to time, and Vera is as gregarious as Aguilar is closed.

Almost everything Keller assumed about Vera turned out to be wrong. He'd thought that Vera was from your typical privileged Mexico City upper crust, when in fact he came up the hard way and had been a beat cop in one of the city's most notorious slums.

He'd fought his way up the ranks, gaining attention from his superiors for cleaning up tough neighborhoods, and when PAN took over and was looking for someone to clean up the scandal-ridden corrupt *federales*, they turned to Gerardo Vera.

"Oh, I gained some sophistication along the way," he joked to Keller one afternoon over beers at the Omni Hotel bar. "I learned which fork to pick up when, where to buy my suits . . . Mistresses mostly taught me things. I was sleeping with a higher class of women, and they cleaned me up so that I'd be more suitable material for scandalous gossip."

He never married or had children.

"Never had the time or interest," he said. "Besides, families make you vulnerable. I prefer married women and expensive whores. You have a nice meal, a few laughs, a good fuck, and then you each go back to your own lives. It's better that way."

So he took Keller out for a drink and asked him to go to Nuevo Laredo on an errand. "Alejandro Sosa. Osiel Contreras's personal pilot. We've had him under surveillance for months."

"I'm here for Barrera."

Vera was ahead of him. "We both know that the clock is running on you. If you help me get Contreras, you'd be untouchable. You could stay in Mexico."

True, Keller thought. But his brief was strictly the Barrera Coordinating Committee, the CDG was other agents' turf, and he'd be trespassing, a poacher. "Why do you want me?"

Vera was silent for a few seconds before he answered. "You and I, we're very much the same. You and I know that you can't punch the narcos with gloves on. It's a bare-knuckle fight. I want you in the alley with me. These people are scum. Garbage to be hosed off the streets. By any means necessary."

"What's your way into Sosa?" Keller asked, knowing that he was walking down an alley where he shouldn't go. It was in violation of his working agreement, in violation of DEA practice, and in violation of his own better sense.

But he wanted to stay in Mexico, and Vera was offering him the chance.

Vera chuckled. "It's a little complicated, almost baroque. One of those things that might just be crazy enough to work, but very embarrassing if it doesn't. Like your CIA sending poisoned cigars to Castro."

Now Keller looks at the casually but well-dressed man who looks to be in his thirties. Sandy hair, light-complexioned, he sits at the bar, sips on a beer, and watches the strippers. Sosa looks soft to him. Thin, unmuscled, a man who can fly a plane but hasn't seen a lot of life. Maybe it's the green pastel polo shirt or the pressed white jeans. Maybe it's the sandy hair, thinning already—Sosa is what, thirty-nine?—and it looks like he might be using Rogaine or something.

A few minutes later—thank God—Sosa flips a few bills on the bar and walks out onto Cleopatra Street, where he window-shops along the cribs of younger attractive prostitutes that line the street.

The older hookers are on the back streets.

Keller doesn't feel like waiting for the man to get laid, so he makes his approach. "Alejandro Sosa?"

Sosa turns around and looks puzzled, not recognizing this man. "Yes? How can I help you?"

"I don't need your help," Keller says. "You need mine."

"What do you mean?"

"Your boss," Keller says, "Osiel Contreras. You probably know that he goes to a gypsy, right? A fortune-teller?"

"Yes . . ."

Keller says, "She told him that someone very close to him—light-skinned, light-haired—was going to betray him. You know anyone close to him with light skin and light hair?"

Sosa's skin turns lighter. Like *white.* "Oh my God."

"You're on the hit list, my friend."

"What can I do?"

"Run," Keller says. "I guess in your case fly."

"Who are you? Why are you telling me this?"

"You don't want me to flash my DEA badge here, do you?" Keller asks. "Let's walk, talk, like two guys in La Zona looking to catch the clap."

It's the critical moment.

Keller has flipped scores of informants, and he knows that there's a moment in which you literally have to make the man come along with you, get him into the habit of doing what you say. He starts to walk away, and is relieved a moment later when Sosa falls in with him.

"Look around you," Keller says. "Do you see trees with ornaments on them? Bulbs? Candy canes?"

Not hardly. What he sees are sleazy bars, hookers, their customers, young punks, drunk students, and narco lookouts.

Keller continues on the classic bad-cop routine. "Do I look like a jolly fat man? Am I wearing a red suit? I guess what I'm getting at here, Alejandro—this isn't Christmas. There are no presents under the tree. Do you know what the definition of a present is? Something for nothing. You want me to get you out of Mexico, get you a snitch visa on the other side, you're going to have to give me something I want."

"I can give you a lot of information about Contreras."

Keller stops in front of a window and runs his eyes up and down the body of a young woman in a purple negligee. "I *have* a lot of information about Contreras. I have *warehouses* of information about Contreras. I bet I know more about him than you do. You're going to have to do better than that."

"Like what?" Sosa asks. He's scared.

"Look at the woman, not at me," Keller says. "His location."

"I never know," Sosa answers. "He only tells me a few minutes ahead of time. To get the plane ready."

"Well," Keller says, "when he does, you can tell me."

Sosa shakes his head. "I can't go back there. He's going to kill me."

"Then if I were you?" Keller says. "I'd call me at the first possible opportunity."

"I won't do it."

And then there's that moment with an informant where you pull the carrot away and just show him the stick. You have to let him know he's trapped, and the only way out is you.

I am the truth and the way.

"Yeah you will," Keller says, smiling at the woman behind the glass. "Or I'll put it out that you were talking to DEA. Then Contreras won't need any goddamn gypsy to tell him to kill you. He'll turn you over to Ochoa to find out what you told me."

"You evil motherfucker."

"Hey, you could have chosen to fly for the friendly skies," Keller says, walking down the street with Sosa at his side like a puppy. "Now, you have options: The *federales* arrest you right now and you go to a jail where Contreras's guys kill you; you run until Ochoa finds you and tortures you to death; or you go back, you do your job like nothing happened, you call me when you know where your boss is going to be, and I put you in the 'program.'"

Sosa chooses door number three.

Now they just have to wait for him to call.

Keller flies back to Mexico City.

Luis Aguilar finally broke down to his wife's imprecations and invited the North American to dinner, albeit not without some rearguard resistance. "It would be unkind."

"How so?" Lucinda asked.

"The man lost his own family," Luis assayed, "and it would be unkind to confront him with our happiness."

"Is that the best you can do?" Lucinda asked. "How do you win any cases?"

"I'll call him."

Keller got the call at his desk and was too surprised to think of an excuse. He showed up that night at Aguilar's with a bottle of wine and flowers, both of which Lucinda graciously accepted.

If Keller expected Luis Aguilar's wife to be, well . . . dull . . . he's disappointed. In a word, she's striking. A head taller than her husband, with long chestnut hair and an aquiline nose, subtly but elegantly dressed.

The daughters, luckily, favor their mother. Tall, thin, each resembling a ballerina (which, he learned over dinner, was accurate), Caterina and Isobel, sixteen and thirteen respectively, are lovely, perfect combinations of their father's reserve and their mother's graciousness.

They politely answer Keller's polite questions over a meal that starts with a delicious soup made of cactus tenders, followed by diced chicken in a creamy almond sauce over wild rice, and then a coconut flan.

"You went to a lot of trouble," Keller tells Lucinda.

"Not at all. I love to cook."

At a subtle nod from their mother, the girls excuse themselves after dinner and Lucinda says she's going to "finish up" in the kitchen.

Keller starts to say, "Let me—"

"We have help," Aguilar says as he takes Keller into his study. "Do you play chess?"

"Not very well."

"Oh."

"We can play."

"No," Aguilar says, "not if you don't play well. It wouldn't be a challenge."

A maid—Keller learns that her name is Dolores—brings in coffee, which Aguilar laces with cognac. They sit down, and with nothing else to talk about, the conversation turns to Vera.

"Gerardo runs roughshod on the law," Aguilar complains. "It looks good in the media, I suppose it gets results, but sooner or later it comes back and bites you in the ankle."

Keller is a little skeptical about Aguilar's by-the-book pretense. The lawyer hasn't been exactly reluctant to use the information that Vera's none-too-gentle interrogations produce. Half the time, the suspects actually confess, and Keller hasn't noticed Aguilar asking too many questions as to how those confessions were induced.

He doesn't tell Aguilar about his trip to Nuevo Laredo for Vera.

"And this 'Batman and Robin' business," Aguilar says, "it's silly and demeaning."

"But it gives the media a hook," Keller says.

"I'm not in the media business."

"Sure you are."

Lucinda comes in and rescues them from another debate, steering the conversation to film, sports, and Keller. He finds himself telling them about his background—the absentee Mexican businessman father, his days at UCLA, meeting Althea, Vietnam . . . Then he sees Aguilar glance at his watch. "And I should be going. Thank you for a wonderful evening."

After he leaves, Lucinda says, "See, he isn't so bad. I like him."

"Hmmmm," Aguilar says.

Gerardo Vera spends the evening with his latest mistress. Good wine, good food, better sex.

Drink, food, and women. What else is there in life?

"God?" Aguilar asked him when he'd spouted this philosophy over lunch.

"That's the next life," Vera said. "I'll worry about that when I get there."

"Then it will be too late."

"Yes, Father Luis."

Luis believes in heaven and hell, Vera knows that there is neither. You die and that's it, so you have to suck the marrow out of life. The American, Keller, he likes to pretend that he's lost his faith, but it's still there, tormenting him with guilt over his supposed sins.

Vera has no such torments.

He doesn't believe in sin.

Right and wrong, yes.

Courage and cowardice, yes.

Duty and dereliction, yes, but these are parts of being a *man*. A man does the right thing, does his duty and does it bravely.

Then he drinks, eats, and fucks.

The woman tonight is a charmer, her husband a government official too busy with his work to do *his* duty at home, and Vera is the grateful beneficiary of this neglect, cheerful to hang horns on a fool.

It's an epidemic in Mexico these days, what with these Ivy League technocrats bringing the absurd American "work ethic" back with them. They have volunteered to become cogs in a machine, and they forget why it is that they work.

Vera doesn't forget.

He's ordered a fine meal delivered to this Polanco love nest, has put fine champagne on ice, music on the stereo.

Discreet, trusted sentries stand guard outside.

Vera pours the woman a glass of champagne, just enough now to make her giddy but not sloppy, then savors the perfume of her elegant neck, then reaches down to feel her equally elegant ass.

She freezes but doesn't stop him, and he lifts the silk up and then reaches around to feel the essence of her, and she doesn't object but leans back and lays her head on his shoulder as he strokes her and whispers filth into her ear.

The rich ones, their husbands are too tame, they like to hear words that come from the slums.

Luis hopes for heaven.

Keller fears hell.

Vera fears only death, and that because he takes such pleasure in life.

Sosa calls that night.

"I'm taking Contreras from Nuevo Laredo to his niece's birthday party in Matamoros tomorrow," he tells Keller. "After that, he's going to have a party of his own at one of his safe houses."

"I need an address."

Sosa gives it to him—a three-story apartment building on Agustín Melgar in the Encantada district.

"Anyone flying with him?"

"Ochoa," Sosa says. "And Forty. And another Zeta named Segura. Crazy guy who wears a grenade on a chain around his neck. Other Zetas are coming to the party. Look, I don't want to stay on the phone too long."

"Okay," Keller says. "Here's what you do. You drop Contreras off. You go downtown. You walk across the Puente Nuevo into Brownsville. A DEA agent will be waiting for you on the other side."

"You promise?"

"You have my word."

Keller gets on the horn to Vera. Thirty minutes later, he's sitting in the SEIDO office with him and Aguilar.

"What do you have to do with this?" Aguilar asks Keller.

"He helped me with the informant," Vera says.

"That's not—"

"You want Contreras or not?" Vera snaps.

"I should have been informed of this operation," Aguilar says. "My God, gypsy fortune-tellers . . . what's next?"

"What's next is that we take Contreras," Vera says, "and three top Zetas."

Aguilar warns, "They won't give up Contreras without a fight."

"Good," Vera says.

"I want him alive," Aguilar says to Vera.

Keller gets on the phone to Tim Taylor. "I'm going to need an agent to pick up an informant on the New Bridge in Brownsville. And I'm going to need an S-visa for him."

"What the hell, Keller? What are you doing in Matamoros?"

"The op is out of Mexico City."

"What does it have to do with Barrera?"

"Nothing," Keller says. "It has to do with Contreras."

"*Keller—*"

"You want him or not?" Keller asks, echoing Vera.

"*Of course we want him.*"

"Then get an agent there tomorrow afternoon," Keller says. "He's picking up an Alejandro Sosa and putting him into protective custody. Then get the extradition papers going for Contreras."

"*Gee, is that all? Anything else?*"

"Not right now." He hangs up and turns back to Aguilar and Vera. "We'd better get going."

"You're not coming," Aguilar says.

"Do you know the address of the safe house?" Keller asks.

"No."

"Then I guess I'm coming."

Vera laughs.

Matamoros makes cars.

Perched on the south bank of the Río Bravo where it flows into the Gulf, the city is home to over a hundred maquiladoras, many of which build parts for GM, Chrysler, Ford, BMW, and Mercedes-Benz.

Once the odd combination of a cow town and fishing village, Matamoros came of age during the American Civil War, when it became an alternate port from which to ship Confederate cotton after the North closed New Orleans. Now it has the feel of an industrial city, with factories, warehouses, pollution, and endless rows of trucks carrying its products across four bridges into Brownsville, Texas, just across the river.

Matamoros is the home of the Gulf cartel, and Osiel Contreras is throwing a party.

Ten o'clock in the morning, Ochoa thinks, and the boss is sound asleep, naked, wedged between two similarly unconscious and unclad thousand-dollar whores in a bedroom on the second floor of the safe house.

It was a hell of a fiesta.

The women were exceptional.

But he's starting to worry more and more about Contreras. The boss is doing too much cocaine, his paranoia is becoming treacherous, and his ego has led to acts of terrible misjudgment.

The assault on the American DEA agents had come one second from what would have been a catastrophe. Even what did happen put the CDG on the radar in ways that just aren't good.

Ochoa doesn't like it—it's bad for business, bad for his money. And Ochoa has come to like his money.

"Patrón, patrón." Contreras had ordered his plane to be ready by eleven. They have business in Nuevo Laredo. *"Patrón."*

Contreras opens one jaundiced eye. *"Chíngate."*

Okay, fuck me, Ochoa thinks, but—

Miguel Morales, whom they call Forty, comes up the stairs. A thick, squat man with a thick mustache and curly black hair, he's pulled on his jeans but nothing else and he looks both hungover and fucked out.

And alarmed.

Which in turn alarms Ochoa, because Forty isn't one to panic. He's risen quickly in the Zeta ranks despite not being one of the original special-ops veterans. In fact, he's half American, a *pocho* from Laredo, with no military experience but a long history with the Los Tejos gang along the border. He took to the military training like he was born to it and didn't blink at the rougher stuff.

A story going around has it that Forty once tore the heart out of one of his living victims and ate it, saying that it gave him strength, and while Ochoa doesn't really believe the story, he doesn't really disbelieve it, either. So when Forty says, "There's a problem"—there's a problem.

He follows Forty to the window and looks out.

Police and soldiers are everywhere.

The Zetas fight.

For six hours, fifteen of them, surrounded, hold out against over three hundred AFI, SEIDO, and army troopers trying to storm the house.

Ochoa never goes into any building without working out fields of fire, and his disciplined men are laying it down. First they drive the *federales* from the door, then across the street, but that's the best they can do.

The soldiers have armored cars, and after an initial burst of overexcited, incontinent fire, they've settled down and are picking their targets. They've fired tear-gas grenades through the shattered windows, and the helicopters have swept Zeta snipers off the roof.

If we could hold out until dark, Ochoa thinks, there's a slim chance of getting Contreras out in the confusion, but we can't hold until dark.

He looks at his watch.

It's only 1:30 in the afternoon.

They already have one KIA and two wounded, and they're running out of ammunition.

A bullhorn once again demands Contreras's surrender.

Vera lowers the megaphone.

"It's time to storm the house," he says.

"Why?" Aguilar asks. "We have them surrounded. They're not going anywhere."

"It makes us look weak," Vera says. "The longer they hold out, the worse it makes us look. I can hear the *corridos* already."

"Let them sing," Aguilar says. "We'll have Contreras. Without him, these Zetas are nothing."

He's missing the point, Keller thinks. Vera *wants* bodies, the more the better. Contreras and his troops in handcuffs sends one message—Contreras and his troops in pools of their own blood sends another:

If you form an army, we don't arrest you.

We kill you.

You want a war, you get a war.

"Strap your vest on," Vera says. "Five more minutes and we go."

"You should reconsider that," Keller says.

Vera looks at him, surprised.

Same with Aguilar.

But for once, Keller thinks, the lawyer is right. Contreras is trapped, he can't possibly escape. Those aren't just narcos in that house, they're highly trained elite soldiers.

"Whatever message you want to send," Keller tells Vera, "it's not worth a bloodbath. Which there will be if we storm the house."

Vera stares at him.

"Make them surrender," Keller presses. "Make them come out with their hands in the air. That's the footage you want. Dead, they're martyrs; alive, they're bitches. That's the song you want sung. That's what makes some kid look at you and not them as the hero."

"Quite a speech, Arturo," Vera says. "But you still don't understand Mexico. Five minutes."

"They're moving!" Forty yells.

Ochoa crawls back to the window and peers out. Forty is right—there's movement behind the armored cars.

He recognizes the signs of an imminent assault.

"They're coming," Ochoa says.

Segura fingers the grenade around his neck. He's a giant of a man, six-seven and built like a tree. He's worn his "grenade necklace" ever since Ochoa can remember, since they served together in Chiapas. "If they get in, I let them get close and pull the pin. We go to the devil together."

"It will be a good time," Forty says. "All the best women are in hell."

"Don't be idiots," Contreras says. "I'm going to surrender."

"Not me," Segura grunts. That's why he wears the grenade.

"I didn't say you, I said me," Contreras snaps. Turning to Ochoa, he says, "Take your best men out the back. I'll go to the front with my hands up, make a big show. You might have a chance in the excitement."

"They'll gun you down," Ochoa says.

The AFI are murderers.

"Maybe not in front of the cameras," Contreras says. "Ochoa, listen to me, this is the right decision."

Ochoa knows that it is. Contreras can still run the organization from prison, but only if he still has an organization to run.

Which means the Zetas surviving.

Contreras says, "My brother will take over the day-to-day running of the organization."

Despite the grimness of the situation, Ochoa almost has to laugh. The "little" brother is little only in the sense of "younger." Héctor Contreras is known as "Gordo," who is only impressive in that he manages to be obese despite an addiction to cocaine. The man has no self-discipline whatsoever, and therefore Ochoa has no respect whatsoever for him.

Gordo "running the operation" in reality means that I'll be running the operation, Ochoa thinks. There are worse things.

"You know who's behind this," he says.

"Of course," Contreras answers. "It was the right move."

"Hell will wait," Ochoa says.

Keller tightens his Kevlar vest.

Aguilar stares at him. "I wonder who you are sometimes."

"You and me both, Luis." He checks the load on the Sig Sauer, hoping not to use it, and wishes that Aguilar would stay behind the vehicles. I don't care that much about you, Luis, he thinks, but I do like your wife and kids, and I don't want the next time I see them to be at your funeral.

Keller feels that moment of calm he always has before going into a fire-fight. The fear subsides, the pins-and-needles pricking of anxiety goes away, and he feels this cool rush in his brain.

His only regret is that it's not Barrera.

He gets his weight solidly under his feet and gets ready to push off.

Then the front door of the house opens.

Contreras steps out.

His hands high over his head.

At least two hundred weapons are trained on him.

So are a dozen news cameras.

"Me rindo!" Contreras yells. "I surrender!"

Vera stares across the street for a moment. Then he yells, "Hold your fire! Don't shoot!"

Keller hears a burst of fire, then an explosion from the back of the house. For a second it seems like everything is going to fall apart. Contreras drops to his knees, yelling, "Don't shoot! Don't shoot!"

The gunfire stops.

Vera strides across the street. He grabs Contreras by the wrists, turns him, kicks him to the ground, and handcuffs him. "Osiel Contreras, you are under arrest!"

"Go fuck yourself," Contreras says quietly. "You *and* your bosses."

Canelas, Sinaloa

Eva Esparza is seventeen and beautiful.

Long, wavy black hair, brown doe eyes, high cheekbones, and a figure that is just beginning to fulfill its promise. She's just a little taller than Adán, who holds her loosely in his arms as they dance to the music of Los Canelos de Durango, a band that Nacho had flown in for the occasion.

The occasion is a dance to raise support for his daughter's candidacy for Miss Canelas, which she'll probably win anyway by virtue of her beauty and charm, but Nacho isn't taking any chances. He's sponsored this dance and handed out gifts to the judges.

Adán wouldn't be interested in a runner-up.

A king can only marry a queen.

Or, better, a princess.

Adán finds Nacho's solicitude a little amusing. His ally has at least six families scattered across Sinaloa, Durango, Jalisco, and God knows where else, but Eva is clearly his favorite, Daddy's little girl.

Holding her, smelling her hair and her perfume, Adán can see why. The girl is intoxicating, and he's grateful that Nacho's favorite daughter inherited his charm and not his looks.

When the subject first came up, Adán wasn't exactly sanguine.

"We're not getting any younger," Nacho had said, at the end of a long discussion about the war in Tijuana.

Adán smelled a trap. "I don't know, Nacho, you look younger than I've ever seen you. Maybe it's the money."

"Don't let's kid ourselves," Nacho answered. "I take the Viagra, you know."

Adán let the chance to exchange confidences pass. Erectile dysfunction was not an issue with Magda in his bed, although she was now in Colombia, setting up a cocaine pipeline.

"Still," Nacho said, "I'm not making any more children."

"Jesus, Nacho, get to the point," Adán snapped.

"All right," Nacho said. "What's all this for, this empire building, if we don't have anyone to leave it to?"

"You have a son."

"You don't."

Adán got up from his desk chair and walked over to the window. "I had a child, Nacho."

"I know."

"The truth is," Adán said, "I don't know if I could live with that kind of heartbreak again."

"Children are life, Adanito. You still have time."

"I don't think Magda would be interested."

"It can't be Magda," Nacho said. "Don't get me wrong, no offense, but she's been around."

"This from *you*?" Adán asks.

"It's different with a woman and you know it," Nacho said. "No, your wife has to be a virgin, of course, and the mother of your children must be from an important family."

Then Adán got what Nacho was really driving at. "Are you suggesting—"

"Why not?" Nacho asked. "Think about it. An Esparza and a Barrera? Now *that* would be an *alianza de sangre*."

Yes, it would be, Adán thought. It would lock Nacho in. I would not only get his undying loyalty, but, in a sense, the Tijuana plaza back with it. But . . .

"What about Diego?" he asked.

"Have you seen his eldest daughter?" Nacho asked. "She'll have a heavier beard than he does!"

Adán laughed in spite of himself. *Diego, always sensitive of his position, might feel threatened if I move closer to Esparza.*

Nacho said, "I have a daughter, Eva. Seventeen years old—"

"That's young."

"We're about to hold a dance for her," Nacho said. "Just come and meet her. If you don't like her, if she doesn't like you, it's one day out of your life. This is all I'm asking."

"And what will Eva think about this?" Adán asked.

"She's seventeen," Nacho answered. "She doesn't know what she thinks."

Now, as the music stops, Adán wonders what she *is* thinking. *Here's this young girl, the center of attention at a party in her honor, and suddenly two hundred armed men in black hoods and masks roar in on ATVs and block off all the roads. Then six small planes land on a field nearby and I get out of one of them, with an AK slung over my shoulder, and now two helicopters circle overhead.*

She's either totally taken with it all, or totally disgusted.

And I'm more than thirty years her senior, what does she think about that? I'm guessing it's not the honeymoon night that she's dreamed of. She's probably not even thinking of marriage—she wants to date, go to clubs, hang out with her friends, go to college . . .

Adán feels like one of those old-time Sinaloan *grandes,* exercising his droit du signeur, and it makes him feel creepy. *Still, it would be an important marriage. Twenty years or so down the road I'll be ready to retire, and by then there might be a son, and he would have it all.*

Adán walks Eva over to a table for an *agua fresca.*

He's not as gross as Eva feared.

When her father came home with the news that Adán Barrera was going to be a "special guest" at her dance, Eva cried, sobbed, threw a temper tantrum, and then sobbed some more. After her father stormed out of the room, her mother held her, dried her tears, and said, "This is our life, *m'ija.*"

"Not mine, *Mami.*"

Her mother slapped her.

Hard, across the face.

She'd never done that before.

"Who do you think you are?" her mother asked. "Everything you have—the clothes, the jewels, the pretty things, the parties—come to you because of this life of ours. Do you think that God just *chose* you?"

Eva held her hand to her cheek.

"If this man wants you," her mother said, "do you think you can reject him? Do you think your father would allow his most important ally to be humiliated by his own daughter? He would take you out and beat you and I would hand him the belt. He would throw you into the road and I would pack your bag."

"*Mami*, please . . ."

Her mother held her tight, stroked her hair, and whispered, "Not everyone would cry for you. You would have money, houses, position, prestige. You would be a *queen*. Your children would have everything. I am going to go pray that this man likes you. You should do the same."

Eva didn't.

She only prayed that he wouldn't be hideous, and, in all fairness, he isn't. He's not bad-looking for an old man, he's polite, gentle, and charming in an old-fashioned way.

Eva can't imagine having sex with him, but she can't imagine having sex with any man. Unlike so many of her *buchona* friends, her parents haven't let her run wild, go to overnight parties, or on skiing weekends away.

They've kept her under tight wraps, and now she knows why.

Her virginity isn't going to be given away.

It's going to be negotiated.

"So?" Nacho asks Adán after he returns from dancing with Eva.

"She's charming."

"So you'd like to see her again," Nacho presses.

"If she wants to see me."

"She will."

"I don't know," Adán says.

"She's my daughter," Nacho insists, "and she will do what I say."

Sometimes, Adán thinks, I forget how old-school Nacho really is. "Let's go see Diego."

They find him having a beer at the refreshment table, and walk away to have a private conversation. The big man has a beer in each hand, foam on his mustache, and is feeling no pain. Seeing Adán, he raises one glass. "To fortune-tellers."

"For a hundred dollars," Nacho says to Adán, "you brought down an empire."

"Not yet," Adán answers.

Unfortunately, infuriatingly, Contreras is still alive, and will doubtless do his best to run the CDG from prison. The sooner the North Americans can extradite him, the better. Still, the situation is different with Contreras at least hobbled. El Gordo is a joke, and the Zetas? Without Contreras they're just toy soldiers—line them up and knock them down.

It's taken months and months of patience. Kissing Contreras's ass, pretending to believe that he didn't try to kill you, pretending to tolerate his taking Nuevo Laredo—all to put him at his ease until you could figure a way to topple him.

A bribe to a fortune-teller, Adán muses.

It's a funny world.

And now everything is ready.

Well, almost.

"On another topic," Adán says, "why is Keller still alive?"

Diego and Nacho look at each other uncomfortably. Finally, Nacho says, "Now is not the time, Adán."

"When *is* the time?" Adán snaps. It never seems to be "the time."

"Not now," Nacho answers. "Not when you want to make a move on the Gulf. Not while there's a presidential election—a *close* election in which we have a lot at stake. We simply cannot afford to antagonize—"

"I know, I know." Adán waves his hand as if to brush away the unwanted concession.

"We know where Keller is," Diego says. "We won't lose track of him again. You can have him anytime you want."

"*After* the election," Nacho adds.

They talk for a few more minutes, mostly about inconsequential things, and then Adán walks over and says goodbye to Eva.

He kisses her hand.

Then he gets back in his plane and flies off.

Eva wins the pageant.

The press conference is classic, Keller thinks, watching it on television from the American consulate in Matamoros. Vera presents Osiel Contreras to the public like Ed Sullivan introducing the Beatles.

Contreras plays his role.

His hands cuffed in front of him, he looks down at the ground sullenly as Vera makes a speech . . . *another victory for society . . . for order . . . a lesson to all those who would defy the laws of the land . . . this is the way it will always end . . . the jail cell or the morgue . . .*

The corpse of one of the Zetas is propped up on a gurney. Two others were wounded. Sadly, one AFI trooper and one soldier died heroically for their country. Their murders will be relentlessly, mercilessly prosecuted.

One cheeky reporter, Pablo, points out that there was a gun battle in the street following Contreras's surrender.

"Pablo"—Vera smiles at the reporter—"some of the Zetas did attempt a breakout."

"Well," Pablo follows up, "they *did* break out, isn't that correct?"

Ochoa, Forty, and Segura fought their way out, Keller knows from the statements of the two wounded Zetas.

Glaring at the reporter, Vera answers, "Some of these criminals escaped, but don't worry, we will bring them to justice."

Vera moves on to introduce Aguilar, who stumbles through a statement expressing his grief for the fallen, his thoughts and prayers for the families, and his satisfaction that Osiel Contreras will be put through the due process of the law.

It's all very good, Keller thinks, but he can't help getting the feeling that Vera is disappointed that Contreras is alive.

Keller's bosses at DEA aren't disappointed. Champagne corks pop, cake is brought in, congratulatory phone calls go from El Paso to D.C. And to Keller, in Brownsville, where he dutifully delivered Alejandro Sosa to Tim Taylor.

Taylor hands Keller the phone. "The big boss."

"Art," Keller hears. "Fantastic job. Needless to say we're all thrilled here. Teach these guys to threaten our agents. Extradition papers are already in the works . . ."

Keller mumbles a thank-you and zones him out. Taylor takes the phone back and Keller vaguely hears him taking a verbal bow. When the boss clicks off, Taylor says, "Not everyone here is so happy with you poaching other agents' hunting grounds, Art."

Keller says, "If we think this is the end of the CDG . . ."

"No one thinks that," Taylor answers, "but it's a huge step. Take out enough of the number one guys, pretty soon no one is going to want the job."

Yes they will, Keller thinks.

They'll fight for the top job, they'll kill for it.

"Contreras's brother is a cokehead dumbass," Taylor says. "Not exactly the A Team taking over."

"Okay."

"Jesus Christ," Taylor says, "take a minute to celebrate, would you? It's a good day and we don't get a lot of them. Let's at least crack a smile when we do."

"Sure."

Taylor shakes his head. "Don't be smug. You just saved your own ass, and you know it."

Yeah, they both know it. Taylor wouldn't dare call him back now, not the guy who just took down Osiel Contreras.

Keller doesn't say what else he's thinking.

That the Contreras operation wasn't a successful arrest.

It was a botched execution.

2

Los Negros

Leave by the Gulf Road
In the gray dawn.

—James McMurtry
"The Gulf Road"

Nuevo Laredo
2006

W
hen Eddie Ruiz thinks back, he likes to think about Friday nights.
Friday night lights, baby.
Under a satin Texas sky.

The crowd chanting his name, the cheerleaders creaming for him under those short skirts, the sweet sharp adrenaline rush of sticking a QB under his pads and driving the bitch into the Texas turf.

Laredo Uni High.

(Just across the river, but a million miles away. Just eight years ago but an eon since they were division champs.)

Eddie loved to hear the QB's grunt of pain, feel the air go out of him, and with it the heart and the will. Take away his breath, you take away his legs, his arm, his game.

And you hear your name.

Eddie, Eddie, Ed*die*.

He misses it.

Good times.

Good times.

Friday nights.

Now he sits in Freddy's, a place where they know Eddie well, unless a stranger comes asking for him, in which case they don't.

Nuevo Laredo, Eddie thinks, "Narco Laredo," "the NL," "the 867," call it what you want.

Just a bridge—well, three bridges, four if you count the rail bridge—from

Laredo, Texas. But definitely Mexico, in a thin finger of Tamaulipas state that sticks up like Tamaulipas giving Chihuahua the bird.

Some people call it the Parrot's Beak, but Eddie thinks that's stupid.

What are we, pirates?

Who has a parrot anymore?

Anyway, he's been coming to the 867 all his life. As a kid to visit cousins, as a teenager after games on Friday nights to drink beer and get loaded and party. Popped his cherry with a whore in Boy's Town (shit, who didn't?), and he brought Teresa to a hotel down here where she (finally) gave it up to him, where he (finally) got under that sweet short cheerleader skirt and pulled down those panties and got into her and it doesn't seem possible they've been married for coming on seven years now.

Seven years and two kids.

How did *that* happen?

And he was driving home from the 876 when that other thing happened.

He was eighteen, in what should have been his sweet senior year, and he swerved his pickup onto the wrong side of the road head-on into that middle-school teacher's Honda.

The teacher died.

They charged Eddie with negligent homicide, but the charges got dropped and he was back at practice when two-a-days started, and it was after that he started dealing weed.

A shrink could call that a "causal relationship," but the shrink would be wrong.

It was an accident, that's all.

An accident is an accident, nothing to feel guilty about.

Eddie, Eddie, Ed*die*.

No one stopped cheering when he drilled the QB or came up on the run and stuck his man.

Eddie likes to think about that.

He looks sharp now. Eddie never could stand that *norteño* look—the cowboy boots, the hats, the belt buckles big as a baby's ass. For one thing, you looked like a tool, for another thing, you might as well take an ad out that you were a narco.

Eddie likes to keep it tight, clean, under the radar.

He wears polo shirts and nice slacks, makes his crew dress nice, too. Some of the *norteño* types don't like it, give him shit about it, are always busting his balls that he looks like a fag, but fuck them.

And he's sober and straight.

No drinking, no doping on the job.

One of Eddie's rules.

You want to get high on your own time, that's your business—but do not make it mine.

And Eddie don't drive an SUV, either. Used to have that cliché black Cherokee with tinted windows, but then he grew up. Now he drives a Nissan Sentra. Less conspicuous and it gets great mileage. He tells his guys, you change the oil in a Nissan, you just can't kill it. *You'll* die before that car will.

Used to have a pickup, of course, back in Texas.

When Eddie's mom was drinking, which was like when she was *awake,* Eddie used to drive out to the ranches at night, rope a couple of steers, and then go sell them like old-time rustlers. Then take the money and cross the river to the 867 for some brews and some girls.

Good times.

Now he looks at his watch because he don't want to keep Chacho waiting.

Chacho García has been his supplier for years, even before a U.S. federal indictment sent Eddie across the International Bridge for good. Seven hundred pounds of weed shipped to Houston—business as usual, except Eddie had a snitch in his crew, so he had to put the Nuevo in the Laredo and cross the river to the other side, as the Boss might say.

The Rio Grande if you're a *yanqui,* the Río Bravo if you're looking at it from the Mexican side.

Eddie has been a full-time resident of the 867 for what, six years now, and it's worked out pretty good. He graduated from weed to coke and now he ships two tons a month, most of it to Memphis and Atlanta. That's a lot of blow and a lot of dough, so he don't mind that he has to buy through Chacho and pay him $60K a month in *piso.*

You ship two tons of coke a month, $60K isn't chicken feed, it's chicken *shit.* Chacho keeps it cheap because he has about twenty "Los Chachos" buying his coke and paying his *piso,* so he's raking it in without ever touching the drugs.

The García family had been in the smuggling business here since the product was whiskey, so Eddie figures it's Chacho's due, his inheritance. Besides, most of the *piso* goes to paying off customs agents so the trucks can roll across the World Trade International Bridge ("Commercial Trade Only"—well, there's no shit) and onto the old 35.

Anyway, over the years him and Chacho have become *cuates*—buddies. It was Chacho who gave him a warm welcome to the 867 when he really didn't have to, Chacho who took him around, introduced him, provided a *pocho* with a layer of protection from the locals.

Chacho is his best friend, maybe his *only* real friend in Mexico.

Eddie Ruiz is twenty-six and a freaking millionaire.

His dad wanted him to go to college, even offered to pay for it, which for Eddie's old man was a big deal, but Eddie had basically said, "I'm good, Pops."

He was shipping weed in 120-pound lots, so the thought of sitting in class taking Accounting 101 or Introduction to Shakespeare seemed counterproductive.

Pops was an engineer, had him a good-paying job, a house in the burbs, a nice car, so Eddie wasn't one of those *cholos* who grew up in the barrio. He was a middle-class kid who went to a good school and played football with other chicanos and with white kids, so he had none of the usual excuses to start dealing dope.

Eddie didn't need an excuse—he had a reason.

It made money.

("With my mind on my money and my money on my mind.")

Four years of college would have just put him behind.

You want to live the high life, man, be a high school football star in Texas. Be a good-looking blond chicano kid with blue eyes and a killer smile, have a blond, blue-eyed drop-dead gorgeous chicana on your arm, and you're going to know what the view is like from the top of the world.

That's why he started dealing dope, you want to know the truth.

At five foot ten, 210, he knew he wasn't going Division I, at least not at a Texas school, so what was the point in going at all? Be a second-stringer in some I-AA in Ditchweed, Iowa?

No thanks.

You get used to the penthouse, you don't want to move to the third floor. You want to keep your view after the Friday night lights go out, there are only two things that can keep you there—

Division I or—

Money.

Maybe money can't buy happiness, but it can rent it for a long time. Now Eddie has $60K of happiness in a briefcase, and he walks out of Freddy's to his Nissan to deliver it to Chacho.

Except he don't.

Because when he gets to the sidewalk three guys stick guns in his grill, hustle him to a black Suburban, and shove him into the backseat. Two of the guys get in on either side of him, the other gets in the front passenger seat, and the driver pulls out.

Eddie knows the guy sitting beside him.

Mario Soto.

The Soto family have had a piece of Laredo as long as the Garcías have. They worked it out a long time ago—Los Chachos had the East, Los Sotos the West. Plenty for everybody, everybody got along.

Eddie's partied with Mario on many occasions.

Good times.

Mario don't look like he's in a party mood right now.

He looks jacked up.

Eddie don't know the other guy in the backseat—big head, long hair, and, seriously, a *hand grenade* hung like a chain around his neck—which can't be *good* news.

The driver is squat and thick—looks like a linebacker.

The guy in the front passenger seat looks like a hawk—with a hawk's hooked beak and a hawk's sharp, observant eyes. Thick, jet-black hair, movie-star handsome. He turns around, looks at Mario, and says, "Tell him."

"Tell me what?" Eddie asks.

"You don't pay Chacho anymore," Mario says. "You pay the CDG."

"The fuck, Mario? Laredo ain't Gulf territory," Eddie says.

"It is now," Mario says.

Christ on a pogo stick, Eddie thinks. If Los Sotos have gone with the Gulf cartel . . .

"You're a *pocho*, right?" Movie Star says. "A North American?"

"So?"

"Your life doesn't change," Movie Star says. "You can do business as usual. The only difference is that you'll pay Mario instead of Chacho."

Oh, that's the *only* thing? Eddie thinks.

That's a big freakin' thing.

"That sixty thousand you have in the briefcase," Movie Star says, "belongs to us. Osiel Contreras wants you to know that he appreciates your loyalty in his time of current trouble and assures you of his protection."

"From who?"

"Anybody."

"You're making me choose—"

"No one is giving you a *choice*," Movie Star cuts him off. Mario takes the briefcase and the Suburban pulls back up beside Eddie's car. "Sixty thousand, the first of every month, don't be late."

Eddie's a little shaken when he gets out.

He's heard the stories, he knows who these guys are.

The Zetas.

Now Chacho, he *looks* like a narco.

With a bright patterned silk shirt that had to go a bill and a half, white chinos, loafers, gold chains, he's either an actor in a soap opera or a narco, and he ain't no actor in no soap opera.

Eddie went straight to Chacho's "office"—the second floor of an empty warehouse in Bruno Álvarez—and the narco immediately notices Eddie don't have nothing in his hands.

"You forget something?" Chacho asks him.

"I don't have it," Eddie says. He tells Chacho about what happened with the Zetas, and what they said.

"What," Chacho asks, "you just let them take my money from you?"

"They had guns."

"You don't got a gun?"

Yeah, Eddie got a gun, up in the attic of his house. He never needed a freakin' gun. "I don't carry one."

"Well maybe you fucking should," Chacho says. He looks around to the six or seven Los Chachos hanging around the room for agreement, then pulls his Glock. "See? I carry a gun."

All the Los Chachos show their guns. Of course they carry guns, Eddie thinks. Shit, four of them are Nuevo Laredo cops.

Chacho says, "You pay *me*."

"For protection," Eddie answers. "You call what just happened to me 'protection'? Because I don't, Chacho."

"I'll take care of it," Chacho says. "Maybe Soto's afraid of the CDG. I'm not."

"What about the Zetas?"

Chacho answers, "What are we, ten-year-olds running around with walkie-talkies? 'Come in, Z-1. Over-and-out, Z-2'? I gave up playing with GI Joes when I discovered my dick."

His boys laugh.

Eddie don't. "I hear some sick shit coming out of Matamoros."

Stories about what goes on in the Hotel Nieto and the safe houses the Zetas supposedly have. Special "interrogation techniques" they learned in the army. Torture shit.

"This isn't Matamoros," Chacho says. "This is the 867. You pay *me*."

"The people you're supposed to be protecting me from took it off me," Eddie says.

Chacho says, "We're friends and all that, Eddie, but business is business."

Eddie picks up Angela and bounces her on his shoulder while Teresa tries to shovel some nasty-looking carrot shit into Little Eddie's mouth. The boy turns his head away, clamps his mouth shut, but grins like it was a joke.

"Why don't you take the kids," Eddie says, "go visit your parents for a few days?"

Teresa turns to look at him, the spoon poised in her hand. She knows what this means, knew it when she married Eddie.

But what was she going to do?

She loved him.

Didn't mean it wasn't hard sometimes.

He sees all of that in her look, the way married people do. It hasn't been so great lately, even in bed, where it was always great. But couples go through phases, he knows, just as he knows it can't be easy with a three-year-old and a rambunctious rug rat. And he's out a lot at night, and sleeps in the day, and even though she knows that the clubs are part of his work, she still has her suspicions about where he is and what he's doing.

Comes with the territory, he thinks.

And I like a little strange pussy—freakin' shoot me.

Teresa knew the deal, took the good with the bad. She gets the money, the shopping trips to Laredo, the vacations to Cabo.

The house—a nice house, brand-new, but not one of those gaudy McMansions some of the other narcos puked up.

A quiet neighborhood—doctors, lawyers, businesspeople.

A good school down the street.

So that's the deal and she knows the deal. Her whole family does. When she first started dating Eddie, they didn't like him. When they found out he dealt dope, they flipped out and forbade her to see him. But when the money started rolling in, they changed their tune.

Now Teresa's mother helps launder the cash.

So Teresa gets it, just like she gets it that his suggestion to go to Laredo for a few days means there's a problem.

"It's okay," he says off her look, not wanting her to worry. "Just for a week or two."

"First it was a few days," she says, "now it's two weeks."

He shrugs.

The fuck does she want from him?

Angela screams into his ear. *"DaddyDaddyDaddy!!!"*

He nuzzles his nose into her neck, makes her giggle, and then sets her down. She toddles off to grab a Barbie they just bought. She's four, Eddie thinks. Isn't it a little early for that shit?

"When should I go?" Teresa asks.

"Now would be good," Eddie says.

After Teresa and the kids leave, Eddie goes into the attic and pulls out $60K in cash.

He also pulls out a gun.

Nine-millimeter Glock.

Finds a larger size polo shirt so the butt of the gun don't stick out. Doesn't look good, doesn't look tight, but there it is.

He goes back to Chacho's and hands him the bag.

Chacho grins. "I want to show you something."

Eddie follows him into the back room.

Mario Soto's body is laid out on the floor, his hands duct-taped behind him, his ankles taped together, blood pooling out of the wound in his head. Two other Los Sotos are leaned against the wall, their eyes wide in death.

Eddie has never seen a dead man before. Well, except on a highway that one time. "Chach—what did you do?"

"I told you I'd take care of it." Turns out four Nuevo Laredo cops—all Los Chachos—pulled over Mario's car at a traffic stop and drove him to the warehouse. "Nuevo Laredo, baby, we defend our turf. *We* have the police. We can put a hundred men on the streets."

Brave talk, Eddie thinks. Chacho can afford brave talk—he don't have a wife and two kids to think about.

"How is this going to help?" Eddie asks.

Because Chacho don't see what's happening.

The Big Guys are coming back.

The bosses. *Los buchones.*

Contreras in the Gulf, pulling the strings from a prison cell.

Solorzano in TJ.

Fuentes in Juárez.

And now Barrera is out and put together "the Alliance"—shit, it sounds like freakin' *Star Wars*—with Nacho Esparza, the Tapia brothers, and Fuentes.

Big guys have big appetites and they're going to eat up the world. The CDG wants the 867—they already swallowed Los Sotos. If we want to survive, we're going to have to go with one of the big guys.

But Chacho he don't get that.

"I gotta know whose side you're on," Chacho says. "You with me or you with them? You gotta choose."

Chacho hugs him tight. "The 867, *'mano*. Us against the world."

"The 867," Eddie echoes.

Outside, he knows he has to act cool, like nothing happened. Who knows, maybe Chacho's right. Maybe this will back the CDG down.

Yeah, not so much, because a week later, the Nuevo Laredo police find four burning gasoline drums on the outskirts of town. Nothing unusual there, you can find old gasoline drums all over the shabbier parts of the city. People start fires in them for heat, for cooking, for light, or just for the hell of it.

What's unusual is that there's a body in each of these drums. The four cops who bagged Mario Soto have been beaten, tied up, stuffed into the drums, and burned alive. The Nuevo Laredo police don't go out looking for the men who did this to their comrades. They already *know* who did this to their comrades, and they do the smart thing.

They change sides.

Eddie and Chacho leave town.

Monterrey sits in a valley dominated by the Cerra de la Silla, which Eddie knows as Saddle Mountain. Eddie's bilingual but he usually thinks in English. Now in either language he's in deep shit.

Stuck up to his neck.

Even in Monterrey, which a lot of people think is the most "American" of Mexico's cities. Whirlpool is there, and Dell and Boeing, and a lot of other corporations like Samsung, Sony, Toyota, and Nokia.

Monterrey is rich while Nuevo Laredo is poor, and Eddie knows why—the men who sit in those corporate offices decided that the products that used to be made by cheap labor in Nuevo Laredo could be made by even cheaper labor in China.

So Nuevo Laredo dried up and blew away while Monterrey built skyscrapers and opened new restaurants where Mexican yuppies could complain about the hollandaise sauce.

Eddie and Chacho ran to Monterrey because Chacho has a safe house in the suburb of Guadalupe and because, narco-speaking, it's an open city. No one has a strong presence there, even the CDG, and there's an unspoken agreement that Monterrey is neutral ground, safe turf. Narcos go there to sit on the sidelines when they need to, or park their families when things heat up in their own plazas.

And things have certainly heated up, so to speak, in Eddie's plaza.

Or what *used* to be our plaza, Eddie thinks as he goes down into the Metro. Los Sotos have gone over to the CDG—so have most of the city cops and state police. So has the army, although the army has always been pretty much its own gang anyway.

Eddie knows he can't live in Monterrey forever. And that he can't go back to the 867—other than as a human torch—unless he works something out. Fucking Zetas, man. Nobody *does* shit like that. Sure, every once in a while things get out of hand and someone catches a bullet, but *burning guys alive?*

That's some sick shit.

That's *way* out of bounds.

Serves a purpose, though, he has to admit. If the purpose was to scare people, it worked.

I'm scared.

Eddie rides the subway to Niños Héroes and then walks the rest of the way to the baseball stadium where the Monterrey Sultanes are playing his own Tecolotes. He isn't really a fan—he'll watch baseball if he can't get a Cowboys game on satellite.

He buys a ticket along the first-base line, finds his section, and makes his way down the row to where he sees a heavyset man with a big beard eating peanuts between gulps from a paper cup of beer.

Has to be Diego Tapia.

No one else looks like that.

Eddie and Chacho had reached out. The Tapias did business through Laredo. We gotta go with someone, Eddie knows, and now they're the only game in town. The *alianza de sangre* is their only chance.

The man next to Tapia gets up when he sees Eddie, who takes his seat.

"I like to watch the pitchers," Diego says. "A lot of people don't like low-scoring games. I do. You want a Modelo?"

Eddie don't really want a beer but he don't want to offend Diego Tapia, either, so he nods, and Diego gestures to the guy, who goes up to get Eddie a beer. Then he asks, "Where's Chacho?"

"I didn't think it would be smart for you to be seen with him," Eddie answers. "Nobody really knows *me*."

Diego looks at Eddie as if he's reevaluating him. Eddie knows that look from football coaches who thought he was too small until they saw him hit someone. Then they took that second look.

"You like baseball?" Diego asks.

"It's okay."

"You're a *yanqui*," Diego says. "I thought all *yanquis* liked baseball."

"I'm more of a football guy."

"Which kind?"

"The *good* kind," Eddie answered. "The kind where something happens occasionally."

He'd rather watch grass grow and die again than sit through a soccer game.

"How about them 'Boys?" Diego says in English.

"Something like that."

Diego's man puts a beer in Eddie's hand.

The Tecolotes pitcher hangs a curve and the batter connects. It's a solid hit, but Eddie can tell from the crack of the bat that it don't have the legs, and it dies in the center fielder's glove.

Then Diego asks, "Are you here for yourself, or Chacho?"

It's risky. Diego has to know that it was Chacho who killed Mario Soto and the others and caused all this hassle. So Chacho is about as popular as herpes right now. But Eddie's here to offer Diego his loyalty, so if he acts *dis*loyal to Chacho . . .

"Both of us," Eddie answers.

Diego takes this in. "And what do you think I can do for you?"

"We had some trouble in Laredo."

"You boys are in the shit," Diego says. "You should have come to me *before* blood got spilled. Harder to fix now."

But Eddie notices that he left the door open. "Harder" to fix, not "impossible." He says, "You and Chacho always had a good relationship. You've moved product through Laredo."

"Chacho doesn't control Laredo anymore," Diego says. "He can't fight the CDG."

"But you could."

"But I won't," Diego says. "Why should I go to war to pay the *piso* to Chacho instead of Contreras?"

"We'll lower the rate."

Diego just smiles.

Eddie drinks his beer because suddenly his throat is dry. If Tapia thinks he's a clown, the conversation is over and he'll end up in a fifty-gallon drum filled with gasoline.

Fuck baseball, it's time to blitz.

"You back the CDG off of us," Eddie says, "you use our turf, no *piso*."

"You have balls." Diego laughs. "You come to me for protection and then want to charge me rent on property you don't own."

The batter smacks a sharp hit to the shortstop, who digs it out of the dirt and throws a beautiful ball to the first baseman for the out.

"Slider," Diego says. "He *wanted* the ground ball. If I back the CDG off you, you go to work for *us*. You handle our product, you manage the plaza, if you move your own product, you pay *us* eight points."

The next batter swings on the first pitch. It's a curve that hung up there a millisecond too long, and now is headed over the left-field wall.

Eddie accepts the offer.

Diego sits over a plate of *cabrito*, a Monterrey specialty—kid goat slow-cooked over a bed of embers.

He and Heriberto Ochoa are sitting in the back room of a restaurant in the exclusive Garza García neighborhood in Monterrey's south end, below the Santa Catarina River. Two plainclothes policemen guard the door.

"Why are we here?" Ochoa asks.

It's rude, but he's impatient. They've talked about baseball, the weather, the food, the wine, baseball again, and now the food. It's time to get on with it.

Diego sets his fork down and looks across the table.

"We don't want trouble with you," Diego says. "We're willing to forget that Contreras tried to have Adán Barrera killed."

"Someone's been telling you lies."

"Someone is always telling me lies," Diego says. "If I don't get lied to by lunchtime, I feel deprived."

"It wasn't us," Ochoa lies. "But whoever did it was doing you a favor. You'd be better off, wouldn't you, with the Boy King in the dirt?"

Again, Diego lets the insult slide. "We're doing business with Chacho García."

"What business do you have in a cemetery?" Ochoa asks.

Diego picks up his fork again. Looks down at his food as he says, "At the end of nine innings, if you're ahead, the game is over. You don't keep playing after you've already won."

It's a remarkable admission, Ochoa thinks—Diego Tapia has just conceded that Nuevo Laredo now belongs to the CDG.

"What business do you have with Chacho?" Ochoa asks.

"We move product through his old plaza," Tapia says. "He has the men, the machinery, the customs agents. Why reinvent the wheel? All we're asking of you is the courtesy. Of course, I didn't come with empty hands. It goes without saying that we'd pay you the traditional *piso*."

"Of course."

"Then we have no problem?"

"Yes, we have a problem," Ochoa said. "This Chacho killed Soto and two of his men."

"And you killed four back."

"But Chacho's family isn't weeping," Ochoa answers.

"You made your point. Leave it now." A lesson Diego learned from Adán—strike fast, strike hard, and then be content with victory. Don't grind the survivors into the dust and make more enemies.

Ochoa took a different lesson away from Chiapas. Winning isn't enough—the losers have to fear you or they try again. He says, "If you want to keep the Laredo plaza open for your shipments—tell us where this *malandro* Chacho is."

"That's assuming I know," Diego answers.

"If you don't," Ochoa asks, "what do we have to talk about?"

Diego had argued with Adán about this.

"How long do we eat the CDG's shit?" he'd asked Adán.

"As long as necessary."

"That's not an answer."

"Do you have a better one?" Adán asked.

"I can have fifty good men in Matamoros tonight," Diego said. "We kill Z-1, then Z-2, then Z-3 . . ."

"No," Adán said. "We cooperate with them, let them think we're afraid of them. I want them complacent, arrogant, secure."

Diego has learned not to second-guess Adán. Every move he's made since coming out of Puente has been right. So if Adán wants him to play ball with the Zetas, that's what he'll do.

He hates to do it, but Diego tells Ochoa where he can find Chacho.

———

On Sunday they do *carne asada*.

Carne asada and beer, man, that's Sunday. *Carne asada* means "meat" and it also means "cookout," and there's really no difference because you ain't got one without the other.

It's a tradition, and anyway, they're celebrating the deal with the Alliance, which Eddie persuaded Chacho to accept.

Now Eddie is busting Chacho's balls, trying to make the best of it, put a smile on it, telling Chacho how he'll get a weekly paycheck now, benefits, health insurance—eye and dental, paid vacations, a 401(k).

"Maybe a gym membership," Eddie says.

"I do my workouts with *her*," Chacho said, pointing his thumb at Yolanda, who's sitting out on the deck in just a red bra and panties ("What's the difference between this and a bikini?"), and from what Eddie can see—which is a lot—he can't blame Chach for doing his push-ups with her.

Anyway, he likes Yo.

She's been with Chacho about two years and is a very cool chick, very laid-back. Low-maintenance, which is a plus in their line of work. Doesn't hassle him about where he's been, what he's been doing, who he's been doing. Teresa could take some lessons from her, and Eddie makes a mental note to introduce the two of them. And maybe Yo can teach her a few new tricks in the bedroom, too, freshen things up a little.

Chacho flips the meat on the grill and they get into one of those Tex-Mex border skirmishes about the marinade.

"You beaners use too much lime," Eddie says between swallows of *cerveza*. "Shit, if I wanted fruit juice, I'd get a V8."

Chacho says good-naturedly, "You *pochos* wouldn't know good meat if it hung between your legs, which it don't."

"You want to see?" Eddie asks.

"Didn't bring my magnifying glass," Chacho says.

It goes like that, ball-busting and horsing around, and then they sit down to eat. Eddie can't help but sneak a few peeks at Yo's tits as she bends over to get some salsa, and she sees it and just smiles.

Cool *chica*.

They're going to eat and pack it up and then get in the car and head back to Nuevo. Eddie's eager to call Teresa and tell her to get her ass back home. Anyway, they eat and clean up the kitchen and load the car and they're about to pull out when a black Ford Explorer pulls behind them, another one roars up in front and cuts them off. A third comes in from the side.

At least twenty men get out.

Dressed in black.

Black hoods.

The boogeymen.

Fast, so fast. It's over before it even starts. Eddie don't even have time to reach for his gun before they pull him out of the door and shove him into one of the SUVs.

Where he gets a black hood of his own.

The room smells like gasoline.

Eddie, naked, is duct-taped, wrists and ankles, to a wooden chair, Chacho beside him.

Yolanda is already dead.

They taped Chacho to the chair and then made him watch as they did what they wanted with her and then shot her in the head. Now she lies dead at his feet, her red bra and panties tossed into a corner of the room. Looks like a living room, but except for the wooden chairs, there's no furniture.

The white walls are bare and the blinds are pulled.

Three Zetas are in the room now. Grenade Guy is there—Eddie heard the others call him "Segura." The linebacker is there, too. They called him "Cuarenta"—"Forty"—which Eddie thinks is odd because he'd heard there were only thirty Zetas. He speaks English like he's spent some time in Texas.

Ochoa leans against the wall.

That's Movie Star's name—Ochoa.

"Z-1."

The fact that they hadn't bothered to disguise their faces or their names tells Eddie that they're going to kill him, too.

He only hopes it's quick.

Then he sees white T-shirts soaking in a dishpan full of gasoline, and Ochoa says, "You boys like *carne asada*, don't you? We had to sit out there for hours, smelling it. Made us hungry. So we're going to have *carne asada* of our own."

He nods to Forty, who takes one of the T-shirts from the pan, wrings it out, then walks behind Chacho and lays the T-shirt on his bare back. The legs of Chacho's chair rattle on the wooden floor, he's shaking so bad. He shakes worse when Forty takes a Bic lighter out of his pocket and waves it like he's at a concert.

Jesus, Jesus, Jesus, Eddie thinks. He feels like he's going to piss, and his right leg starts to quiver and he can't stop it.

Forty steps behind Chacho and talks into his ear. "You killed Soto. Now you burn in hell."

He lights the T-shirt.

Flames shoot up like a flare.

Chacho screams.

His chair bounces.

Segura laughs. "He sounds like a girl."

The fire goes out, the shirt seared into Chacho's raw skin.

Burning flesh scorches Eddie's nose, then his lungs, his soul.

Ochoa walks over from where he was leaning and lifts Chacho's chin. "You think you hurt? You don't hurt yet."

Stepping behind Chacho, he takes remnants of the T-shirt between his thumbs and his forefingers.

"You don't hurt yet," he repeats.

Then he tears the fabric out of Chacho's burned skin.

Chacho bellows.

A rhythmic, animalistic huffing.

The veins in his neck look like they're going to burst, his eyes like they could pop out of his face.

"*Now* you hurt," Ochoa says.

Forty laughs. He seems to think this is hysterical. Segura fingers the grenade around his neck like it's a rosary. When Chacho finally stops howling, exhausted, Forty takes another shirt from the pan and lays it on his back.

"Please," Chacho murmurs.

"Please what?" Ochoa asks.

"Please don't . . . do it again."

They do it three more times, set him on fire, rip off the shirt, and with it his burned flesh. By the time they finish, Chacho is meat, Eddie thinks. Nothing more than burned meat.

Carne asada.

Steam comes off his back.

Then Eddie hears Ochoa say the worst thing he's ever heard in his life.

"You're next."

Forty walks behind Eddie and lays a gas-soaked shirt on his back. Eddie, he tries to control himself but he can't. He feels his urine run down his leg and then sees it pool on the floor.

"He pissed himself." Forty laughs.

Segura fingers his grenade. "Like another girl."

Eddie blubbers, "No, please."

Like he's talking from far away, like through an old cardboard tube or something you used to shout through when you were a kid.

Forty flicks the lighter.

"No!" Eddie screams.

Forty closes the lid.

"We're going to let you go," Ochoa says, holding Eddie by the chin. "You go and you tell people what happens when you disrespect the Zetas. Now stop crying, faggot, and get dressed."

They cut the tape off and Eddie scrambles into his clothes and runs down the stairs.

He hears them laughing behind him.

"Segura," Eddie tells Diego, verbalizing what has become an internal chant, a prayer, a mantra, "Forty, Ochoa. They're mine. I'm going to kill each one of them personally."

Diego just smiles. He likes this young man, likes his spirit.

Eddie ran to Badiraguato after the Zetas finished with him. They dumped Chacho's body out in the street, clad only in Lupe's underthings, to embarrass him, shame his family, call him a *joto* who died like a girl.

A big joke.

Funny assholes.

So Eddie came to Badiraguato, to the heart of the Sinaloa cartel, to tell the Big Man that he was in, that he'd come in with the cartel, he was their guy for the war against the Zetas and Contrerases.

The big bearded man just looks at him and says, "No war."

Eddie can't believe what he's hearing. "I told you what they did. In Monterrey, which is supposed to be neutral ground."

"I said no war."

"I'll do it on my own, then," Eddie says, getting up. "Without you."

"You think you and a few Los Chachos can go up against the Zetas?" Diego asks. "This time they *will* kill you."

It was him who asked Ochoa not to kill this young *pocho*, to let him live to run the business.

"At least I can die like a man," Eddie says.

"*Think* like a man," Diego says. "A man has responsibilities. You have a wife, you have kids to take care of."

"I got no way of taking care of them anymore."

"You'll run Laredo for us, pay our *piso* to Ochoa," Diego says.

"You want me to suck his cock, too?"

"That's up to you, *m'ijo*," Diego says. "What I'm trying to tell you is, don't be stupid. Don't let your emotions get in the way of doing the smart thing. Sit down."

Eddie sits down. But he says, "They killed my friend. In front of me. Burned him to death."

Diego already knows what happened in that room. It was awful, disgusting, unnecessary. But done. Now he says, "You know how many friends *I've* lost? You grieve, you put food on their graves on the Day of the Dead, you move on. I'm offering you a plaza. You're a *pocho* and I'm offering you a plaza. In exchange, I'm asking you for one thing—"

"To eat shit."

"To bide your time," Diego says.

You eat shit, you smile. You deliver the *piso* to Ochoa and smile some more. You're happy and grateful to still be alive and still be in business.

In the meantime—quietly, smartly—you recruit men. Not in Laredo, not even in the Gulf, but in Sinaloa, Guerrero, Baja. And not coke-snorting *malandros*, either, but police, soldiers, serious people.

Slowly, quietly, you move them into Laredo.

You build up a force, an army.

"The CDG has the Zetas," Diego says. "We'll have—"

"Los Negros," Eddie says.

The Blacks.

Black.

The color of burned flesh.

It takes months.

Months of recruiting, secretly renting safe houses, moving men and weapons into Nuevo Laredo, months of kissing CDG ass, delivering payments to the men who had tortured his friend to death, grinning like a stray dog who's been tossed a scrap from the table.

But finally, it was ready.

Adán Barrera gives them the green light.

El Señor says the word, Diego gives it to Eddie like a gift, and Eddie gets on the phone to Ochoa. "You have one week to get your asses out of Nuevo Laredo and Reynosa. You can keep Matamoros so you can eat, but that's it."

Eddie relishes the long, stunned silence. Then Ochoa asks, "What if we don't?"

Eddie's answer is simple.

If you don't—

—we'll burn you.

One week later Eddie stands on a Nuevo Laredo roof with five men dressed in police uniforms, lets off bursts of rifle fire into the air, and shouts, "We are Los Negros, Adán Barrera's people, and he is here . . . in Nuevo Laredo!"

Keller reads the headlines and can't help smiling.

The devil was dead.

But he wasn't dead for long.

3

Los Dos Laredos

The blues is my business
And business is good.

Todd Cerney
"The Blues Is My Business"

Nuevo Laredo
2006

It's civil war in Nuevo Laredo.

Keller goes there because Adán Barrera has announced himself there, literally from the rooftops.

Everyone keeps waiting for Barrera to show up in Nuevo Laredo. A rumor, repeated to the point that it's become "fact," is that his men came into a Nuevo Laredo restaurant, confiscated all cell phones, locked the doors, and politely said that no one could leave. The story goes on that Barrera came in, had dinner in the back room, paid everyone's check, and then left. The cell phones were restored to their owners, who were then allowed to leave.

Keller knows it's bullshit, but finds it revealing that such a story could be considered true. He knows that Adán Barrera will come nowhere near the war zone until the shooting is all but over.

Surrogates fight his battles, surrogates like Los Negros and the Tapias, and they might, just might, be a route into the man himself.

Back in the day, Keller muses . . . back in *my* day, he admits . . . the narcos used to shoot it out themselves when they had a beef. Adán's brother Raúl was at the front of every fight. Now they have "armies"—the CDG has the Zetas, Tapia has Los Negros, Fuentes in Juárez has something called La Línea. The narcos become little states and the bosses politicians sending other men to war.

Civil war in this case.

Cop-on-cop violence.

The Nuevo Laredo municipal police are in the pocket of the CDG and their Zeta allies fighting against Barrera's *alianza de sangre* and the *federales*. Not that the latter two entities are allies, it's just that when Gerardo Vera sent an AFI commander to restore order in Nuevo Laredo, the CDG's paid police ambushed him as he came back from a shopping trip across the bridge, killed him, and wounded his pregnant wife.

Keller had been gracious enough not to gloat about Barrera's resurrection, and both Vera and Aguilar had been decent enough to admit that they were wrong, that what they'd dismissed as rumors about Barrera's creation of an *alianza de sangre* were in fact true.

As was Keller's prediction that Barrera was about to move on Laredo.

Into the space that we created for him, Keller can't help but think, when we busted Contreras.

The CDG boss was barely checked into his cell before Barrera made his move, so it had to have been years in the planning, maybe even before the escape from Puente Grande. Was Adán just waiting for Contreras to fall, or did he have something to do with it, using the AFI as his witting or unwitting agents?

And now the CDG kill an AFI commander.

In retaliation for Contreras's arrest, or because they view the AFI as Barrera's allies? Keller wonders. The television reports said something about the Nuevo Laredo police "turning over every stone" to find the killers.

"That shouldn't be hard," Vera said. "All they have to do is look in their own precinct house."

He was white with fury—his own handpicked man dead, the wife wounded. He gave a press conference of his own at which he declared, "This was no less than an attack against the government and people of Mexico. And I swear to you that it will not go unanswered."

Later in the day, AFI agents and the Nuevo Laredo police opened fire on each other in the streets.

Civil war.

Eddie stands across from the Otay Restaurant.

The street is quiet at 1:15 on a Wednesday morning.

Through the plate-glass window, Eddie sees the three cops, the only customers, sitting at the same table eating a night-shift policeman's dinner. He turns to the four guys standing with him. "You guys ever see *The Godfather*?"

They look at him blankly.

"What I thought," Eddie said.

They're Salvadorans, members of Mara Salvatrucha—MS-13—a gang known more for its pure viciousness than its knowledge of film. These boys probably don't know toilet paper. What they do know is tattoos and killing—Eddie made sure of the latter when he recruited them for Los Negros.

"So we're basically going to Al Pacino them," Eddie says, more to himself than to them. "Got it?"

Of course not.

"I'm the *palabrero*, got *that*?" Eddie asks.

Palabrero—Salvadoran for "the boss."

They nod.

They're nervous. Probably, Eddie thinks, more about going into a restaurant than killing three guys. Truth is, he's nervous, too. He's never killed anyone before—well, not intentionally, anyway.

And it's not like the cops inside are exactly innocent. These are the guys who gunned down an AFI commander—shit, shoot a pregnant woman? There went the million and a half bucks he and Diego had paid for the commander to protect them.

Shit, he couldn't even protect himself.

But now there has to be payback.

"Okay, let's do it," Eddie says.

They cross the street.

Eddie goes into the restaurant first.

The cops—a commander, a lieutenant, and one flunky officer—look up but then go back to the serious business of eating.

Never, Eddie thinks, get between a cop and free grub.

The owner says, "We stopped serving."

"Can we just use the bathroom?" Eddie asks.

The owner juts his chin toward the back. It would be more trouble to throw these punks out than to let them take a piss.

"Thanks," Eddie says.

He walks past the cops' table, then turns, pulls his pistol, and blasts the commander in the back of the head. The MS-13s do the same on the lieutenant and the cop, then all five of them walk out, leaving forty-three cartridge cases on the restaurant floor.

A white SUV pulls up and they hop in and take off.

"In the movie," Eddie says, "Pacino did it coming *out* of the bathroom, but I figured, what the fuck?"

They look at him blankly.

"Shit," Eddie says.

There's blood on his new polo shirt.

Ochoa and Forty sit outside under a ramada at a ranch three miles off the highway south of Matamoros.

Across the table sit the governor of Tamaulipas and two of his staff. Ten suitcases are set beside the table, two and a half million dollars in cash inside each one.

The war, Ochoa knows, has gone beyond Nuevo Laredo now—it's going to be the whole state of Tamaulipas now. Ostensibly, that fat fuck Gordo Contreras is in command of the CDG, but unless the Sinaloans and the *federales* have *carnitas* in their hands, Gordo isn't going to go after them very hard.

The governor and his staff leave with the suitcases.

"Get up to Nuevo Laredo," Ochoa tells Forty. "You're in charge up there. Hold the city."

"We should have killed that Eddie when we had him," Forty says.

We should have, Ochoa thinks. We burned the wrong guy.

"Kill him now," he says.

Two days later, the Tamaulipas state legislature appeals to the federal government for help against an "invasion" from El Salvador of Mara Salvatrucha gangsters. A week after that, the bodies of five MS-13 members are found dumped in a vacant lot with a note on one of the corpses: "Adán Barrera and Diego Tapia: Send more *pendejos* like this for us to kill—Los Zetas."

Eddie takes them up on it.

He drives down to Matamoros with four surviving Salvadorans, a Sinaloan ex-*federal,* and two of Diego's *sicarios* from Durango.

"Let's play on their side of the field for a while," Eddie says.

They roll up on a club called the Wild West where Segura's silver Jeep Wrangler is parked right out front, right where they were told it would be.

Careless, Eddie thinks. Grenade Guy is careless and complacent on his home field.

Good.

The two Mexican guys go into the club for a while and come back out to report that Segura is in there drinking and dancing with three teenage girls. Nice, Eddie thinks. It's 4:30 in the morning and this perv Segura is clubbing with young girls?

But the important thing is that he's in there. Eddie can still smell Chacho's scorched flesh, see his terror and the anguish in his eyes.

Eddie's mantra: Segura, Forty, Ochoa.

Three names.

Time to make it two.

Eddie tells the Salvadorans to go in through the back. They're eager—they have their own to pay back now. And it's not pistols this time—it's AKs and AR-15s—they're not taking a chance on being outgunned.

The Salvadorans move down the alley toward the back. Two minutes later Eddie hears shots and screams. Segura comes out the front door blasting, the girls behind him, wobbling on their high heels, terrified.

They get into the Jeep.

Eddie shoots the tires out.

Segura starts the engine and throws the Jeep into gear but Eddie and Los Negros go Bonnie and Clyde on it.

The Jeep rattles like a jonesing junkie.

Segura screams as the bullets strike him.

"You sound like a girl!" Eddie yells. He inserts a fresh clip into his AR and walks toward the Jeep.

Segura lies halfway out the open door.

"You remember Chacho, you sick fuck?" Eddie asks him. "This is for him."

Segura reaches for the grenade around his neck and tries to pull the pin but Eddie's blast severs his hand.

Its lifeless fingers clutch the pin.

The Salvadorans walk up to the Jeep from the other side and look into the backseat.

Two of the girls are wounded, moaning.

The third, blood-spattered, wails.

The Salvadorans open up on the girls. One of the Salvadorans laughs as he shoots. "Look, they're dancing!"

Eddie makes himself look.

Then he walks away.

Segura, Forty, Ochoa.

One down.

New mantra—Forty, Ochoa.

Two nights later, the Zetas find Eddie's house in Nuevo Laredo and burn it to the ground.

Eddie's not there.

Neither is his family. Teresa has stayed in the other Laredo. She ain't coming back, Eddie knows, and it's the right call, things being what they are.

This is no way for a family to live.

A wanted man—the Zetas have a million-dollar reward on him—he moves from safe house to safe house, from one cheap hotel to another, which he basically turns into barracks with fifteen or twenty Los Negros in each.

Well, in most of them.

The Zetas hit one of the houses in a full military raid, snatch fifteen Los Negros, throw them into trucks, and drive them away.

Eddie knows they ain't coming back, either.

They're not.

They're taken to an isolated ranch near the border where Forty tortures them for information—the location of Eddie Ruiz being a prime topic. When they're drained of everything they know, Forty's guys drench the bodies with gasoline and burn them.

What Eddie does next sets records for sheer balls, even in the storied annals of narcotics traffickers.

What he does is he takes out a full-page ad in *El Norte,* Monterrey's biggest daily newspaper.

In the form of an open letter to the president of Mexico, Eddie implores him to "intervene to resolve the insecurity, extortion, and terror that exists in the state of Tamaulipas, especially in the city of Nuevo Laredo, carried out by a group of army deserters who call themselves the Zetas."

The ad goes on, "Seriously, dude, the Mexican army, the *federales,* and the attorney general lack the means and tools to handle these guys? I'm no angel but I take responsibility for what I've done."

And he *signs* it.

"Sincerely, Edward Ruiz."

The ad gets some attention.

It wins him the nickname "Crazy Eddie."

Which Eddie don't really like.

It also earns him even more unwanted attention, so Diego decides that Eddie maybe better cool it for a while and move his command post all the way south and west to Acapulco.

———

Eddie chills out on the beach in a seventh-floor condo overlooking the Pacific. Two bedrooms, Jacuzzi tub, flat-screen television, and PlayStation.

Runs Los Negros from there because it's too risky for him in the 867, and, dig this, the public relations value of his being killed would be too much a victory for the Zetas. So Eddie shifts from condo to condo, plays tennis and video games, and, like *Call of Duty,* runs his part of the war by remote control.

Acapulco is cool because it's now Tapia territory. Diego has clubs, brothels, restaurants, and police, and Eddie and Diego are tight now. He has a dozen Los Negros watching his ass, and Diego has the local *federales* on the lookout, too.

So life is weird but life is also good, if you don't count that he never gets to see his wife and kids because him and Teresa are now officially separated. Separated or no, her and her family are still hooked on the money, so Mom still flies the cash down, which is also weird.

Eddie misses his kids like crazy, but Teresa?

Uhhh . . .

Fact is, Eddie is getting more pussy than he can shake his dick at, so to speak.

He's a good-looking guy and there's tourist pussy in all the bars and the clubs, or just on the beach. The cruise ships offload pussy like it's cargo, so Eddie has no problem hooking up. Mexican girls, American girls, French, Swedish, Spanish, Brits—they're all coming for the sun, the sand, the margaritas, and vacation sex.

So when they find a blond, blue-eyed, tight-looking guy who speaks the language, gets them into the VIP rooms, and doesn't mind spending a few bucks on them, they're all over it. But if he doesn't feel like making the effort, he goes to one of Diego's clubs or whorehouses and just lays down the cash. The pros down here are amazing. These girls can go around the world in twenty minutes.

And cash is no problem.

War or no war, the money just keeps flowing.

Cocaine north, cash south.

So Eddie's living large in Acapulco.

Misses Chacho, though. Chacho should be here to enjoy this shit. Because what Eddie don't have is friends. He has flunkies, he has gofers, he has hangers-on, but he don't have friends. Don't really want any, because friends just get killed. He sends his flunkies out on errands—get more champagne, bring home some girls. One day he hands to gofers thousands in cash and tells them to buy up every video game they can find and he spends a week alone in his condo slamming those buttons.

Eddie's chilling out one Sunday in his crib, watching a little football, tossing back a couple of beers, when one of the Acapulco *federales* stops by.

"You wanna beer?" Eddie asks.

The *federal* takes a beer and Eddie asks him what's up. The guy didn't just drop by to watch the 'Boys blow a fourth-quarter lead.

"Some men came into Zihuatanejo," the *federal* says. "Zetas."

Zihuatanejo is a small beach resort up the coast.

"What do they want?" Eddie asks.

Like he don't know what they want.

The plaza.

And me, Eddie thinks.

"Where are they?' Eddie asks.

"They have a safe house down by the beach."

Yeah, except the house ain't so safe. The *federales* and city cops hit it just before dawn and scoop up four Zetas. One of these guys apparently thought he was going to mix whacking Eddie with a little vacation, because he brought his wife and two-year-old stepdaughter. The fuck, Eddie thinks, I'm living in Disney World? What am I supposed to do now with the wife and a kid?

He has them all taken to a four-story house he owns not that far from the beach back in Acapulco. Keeps the wife and kid down on the first floor and stores her husband and the other three Zetas on the top floor. Eddie has his guys cut up black plastic garbage bags and tape them to the floor and walls because, well, it's going to get messy up there and bloodstains on the floor and walls don't do great things for the resale value.

Then he gets one of his ideas.

If a full-page ad was cool . . .

He goes upstairs with a Glock and a Sony.

The Zetas are sitting on the black plastic with their backs against the wall (literally) and their hands plastic-tied behind them. They don't look like elite stud supermen to Eddie—they looked like scared jackoffs. He'd heard that the Zetas were now recruiting civilians and then training them at camps in the desert, and he has to wonder if these guys even made it through basic.

Two of the Zetas look to be in their thirties, the other two look like kids, barely out of their teens. Scraggly mustaches, T-shirts, they look like shit. Of course, they've been smacked around pretty good, too.

"Bad idea, guys," Eddie says to them as he sets the camera on its tripod and sets up his shot, "coming down here."

He frames the shot so that all four are on camera and then turns it on. "This is like *The Real World*, right? You guys get MTV? No?"

If people think the Zetas are heroes, Eddie thinks, I'm going to show them different. Framing the guy farthest to the left, he asks, "When do you start with the Zetas, and what do you do?"

The guy wears a faded green T-shirt that shows his pot belly (where'd he do his training, Eddie wonders, Popeye's?), khaki shorts, and tennis shoes with no socks. He looks up at Eddie like, are you kidding? but then he starts talking.

"I have contacts in the army," he says, "and I warn the Zetas about patrols and operations."

Eddie moves down to the second guy. Red T-shirt and jeans, bad 'stache, curly black hair. This guy smiles at Eddie, like he's figured out this is some kind of joke, that they're all friends here.

"I'm a recruiter," he says.

"Who do you recruit?"

"You know," the guy says, "men who need work."

"Soldiers?"

"Sometimes. Sometimes police. Sometimes just guys."

Just like us, Eddie thinks. He slides down to the next one. This guy isn't wearing a shirt, just a pair of old shorts and flip-flops.

"I'm a *halcón*," he says.

"What's that?" Eddie asks.

"You know."

"*I* know," Eddie says, playing the television host, "but our audience might not."

"A falcon is sort of a scout," the guy says. "I keep an eye out on the street. I tell where to find people."

"Then what?"

"We pick them up."

"And . . ." Eddie cues.

"Then the boss tells me whether or not to do *el guiso*," the guy says.

"What's *el guiso*?" Eddie asks.

"It's when they kidnap someone," the guy says, "and they torture him for information, about moving drugs or money, and then they take him to a ranch or somewhere and execute him. They shoot him in the head and then they throw him in a barrel and burn him with gas or diesel or something."

"Tell me about the Zetas," Eddie says. "Tell me about the nasty shit you guys do."

The guys start talking. It turns into a regular *Jerry Springer Show* as they start talking about murders, kidnappings, rapes. The bare-chested guy talks about killing that woman reporter.

"That radio woman?" Eddie asks.

"Yes."

"Why?"

"She took our money," the guy says, "but then said bad things about us."

"What about the reporter whose hands you broke?"

"That was Ochoa."

"What did that reporter do?" Eddie asks.

"He just made Z-1 mad."

Eddie steps over beside the fourth guy. Making sure that only the pistol is on camera, but not himself, Eddie asks, "What about you, buddy?"

The Zeta looks up at the gun barrel.

Fuck it, Eddie thinks, and pulls the trigger.

Good thing he put the plastic up.

"Get rid of the rest of these assholes," Eddie orders. He takes the video camera and goes back downstairs.

The little girl is in the pool, wearing inflatable water wings.

Having a great time.

Eddie goes out, sits next to the wife. "What's her name?"

"Ina."

"Cute. What's *your* name?"

"Norma," the woman says.

She's pretty, maybe an eight. Not an Acapulco Eight, where the ratings are inflated, but sort of a national eight.

Eddie's phone rings.

"Eddie Ruiz?"

"How'd you get this number?" Eddie asks, getting up and walking into the kitchen.

"You think if I can get your number, I can't get you?" Forty asks.

"Yeah, how's that working out for you?"

"I'm warning you," Forty says. *"Don't hurt the family."*

Eddie looks out the window to the girl swimming in the pool and her mother dangling her feet in the water.

"I'm not you," Eddie says. "I don't hurt women and children."

"I'll tell that to those girls in Matamoros."

"That wasn't me."

"No, it was those jungle bunnies, right?" Forty asks.

"You running out of Rambos?" Eddie asks. "Because you sent F Troop down here."

Forty laughs. *"You gotta lay off Nickelodeon, Crazy Eddie."*

"No, I like it."

"Let the family go."

Eddie clicks off as Norma and her daughter come in.

"Is she hungry?" Eddie asks. He turns to one of his flunkies. "What we got? For a kid?"

"I don't know. Cheerios, maybe. A banana?"

"Then give her Cheerios and a banana," Eddie says. "What are you standing there for?"

The girl sits down at the table and eats hungrily. Eddie watches her. When she's done, he reaches into his pocket and gives Norma a thousand pesos. "Bus fare. My guys will run you to the station."

She takes the money.

"What about my husband?" Norma asks.

"He said to tell you that he loves you," Eddie says.

Actually, he didn't. Eddie doesn't even know which one he was, but what the fuck, right? Make the woman feel a little better, something to tell her friends. After they leave, he slips the videocassette into an envelope, addresses it to the *Dallas Morning News*, and has one of his guys drop it off at FedEx.

Then he goes back to Acapulco and thinks about maybe starting a new career.

Filmmaking.

His phone rings and it's Diego. *"You have someone's wife and kid?"*

"I did."

"Oh shit, Eddie."

"No, not that," Eddie says. "I put them on a bus home."

Diego sighs with relief and then asks, *"What about the men?"*

Eddie says, "Let's go to the videotape."

Santa Marta, Colombia

This time Magda went to Benito Juárez Airport to catch a flight bound for Colombia and actually made it on board.

Which was a definite improvement and the difference between being connected, via Adán, to Nacho Esparza and not being connected. Technically still a fugitive on the Most Wanted list, she used a different passport, but no one even took a second look, even though her photo was once plastered over every front page in the country.

True, she dyed her hair blond and had sort of a Christina Aguilera, Shakira thing going on, but that wouldn't fool anyone who didn't want to be fooled, and she did it more as a style statement than an effort at disguise.

It was refreshing, different, and she wanted to see if men reacted to her differently as a blonde.

The reaction was actually pretty much the same, the men's eyes went from her hair to her boobs to her legs and then made the trip back up again, but it is fun to be a blonde for a change.

In any case, she breezed through check-in and passport control and took her seat on the plane.

First class, of course.

She accepted a mimosa and settled back into the cushioned seat and started in on her stack of magazines—Spanish editions of *Vogue*, *WWD*, and *Cosmo*—which featured photos of clothes that she could actually afford now.

With Adán's money.

But Magda doesn't want Adán's money.

She wants her own money. Like that Destiny's Child song, right? She sings the lyrics to herself—

The shoes on my feet, I bought 'em
The clothes I'm wearing
I bought 'em.

That's what Magda wants, because at the end of the day men are like stockings—no matter how well you take care of them, they eventually run on you.

It was a short flight into Simón Bolívar International Airport in Santa Marta, and as Magda "deplaned," as they say, she vaguely recalled from high school history classes that Bolívar was born here or died here, one of the two.

Jorge used to take her here a lot, to this, the oldest city in Colombia, with its beautiful beaches on the Caribbean and its fine hotels. They would come for a week or just a weekend and lie on the sand, and then get a little drunk at some bar on the beach, and then go back to the cabana and make love.

Then they'd have dinner and go out to one of the clubs on the Parque de Los Novios and dance until the sun came up.

It was nice.

Jorge is surprised to see her, to say the least, when she appears at the terrace of the hotel bar overlooking the sea.

He always liked to have lunch here, so Magda had no trouble finding him. And he's still handsome—the hair a trifle thinner—and still stylish in a sky-blue shirt tucked into white jeans. Hasn't gained a pound, has Jorge, his stomach is tight, his tan rich, his eyes match the color of his shirt as he takes off designer shades to make sure he's seeing what he thinks he's seeing.

"Magda?"

She just smiles, knowing that she looks, well, fetching in her white sun-dress cut to maximum advantage and her white sunhat.

"I'm glad," he stammers, "that you're out."

"From the prison you abandoned me to? Thank you so much."

Magda enjoys his discomfiture. She likes that oh-so-cool Jorge looks afraid, almost as if he expects Adán Barrera and his gunmen to appear any second. He knows, of course; he has to have heard that she's made a powerful connection. "It's all right. I haven't come to kill you."

"You'd be within your rights." He smiles.

Same old Jorge, still charming.

But now his charm eludes her.

Magda would still fuck him, if that's what it takes, but it would just be part of the job. Hopefully mildly diverting, perhaps even providing some sexual release, but there was no longer any question of loving this man. She can't imagine now that she ever found him anything but pathetic.

"Adán did send me to see you, though," she says, watching him turn pale. "Are you going to offer me a drink?"

"Of course," Jorge says. "What would you like?"

"You don't remember?"

"Gin and tonic."

"No lime."

He orders two and his drink settles him down a little, at least enough to ask, "What can I do for Barrera?"

"It's what he can do for you," Magda says.

"What's that?"

"He can make you wealthy, or he can make you dead." She smiles at him and adds, "*You* choose, *cariño*."

Jorge chooses the money.

"Of course," he says, "as much product as Barrera wants. Depending on the quality, I can give it to him at around, say, $7,000 a kilo."

Magda knows her math, knows that the same kilo can be turned around in Mexico for about $16,000, around $20,000–$24,000 in the northern towns along the border.

"You're not 'giving' anything," Magda says, "you're selling. And you're going to sell it to me at six."

"And you'll tell Barrera it was seven?" Jorge smirks.

"No, Adán will pay retail for whatever of your product he wants," Magda says. "If I want to buy additional kilos on my own, the price will be discounted to six."

Jorge smirks. She used to think of it as a charmingly sardonic smile, but now she sees it's a smirk as he says, "And why should I do that?"

"Because you owe me," Magda says.

"Would you like another drink?" Jorge asks. "I would. Listen, *cariño*, certainly I owe you something, for old time's sake, but not that much. To be perfectly honest, at the risk of hurting your feelings, you weren't *that* good in bed."

"I'm not talking about the sex," Magda says. "I'm talking about the months I spent in prison."

"You knew you were taking a chance," Jorge says. "All right, I'll tell you what I'll do because I'm still so fond of you—let's say six-five to you for the first ten kilos, but after that, I'm afraid it has to be seven."

"And I'll tell you what I'll do because I'm still so fond of you," Magda says. "Six for the first ten kilos, but I'm afraid it has to be five-five after that."

"Or your boy Barrera will send gunmen to kill me?" Jorge asks.

"No," Magda says. "I will."

She gets up from the table.

"I'll be at the Carolina," Magda says. "Send me your answer there. And send it, don't come yourself, because that's just not going to work anymore."

"Prison changed you."

"Oh, no kidding, Jorge," Magda says. "And don't look so forlorn, *cariño*, you're going to make a lot of money with me."

She walks away, knowing that he's looking at her ass.

She thinks about going out that night to one of the clubs, to dance and maybe find someone to bring back, but decides to settle for a good room-service dinner, a bath, and an evening of solitude instead.

The message is in her mailbox in the morning.

Jorge is honored to accept her offer.

Magda's pleased, because it will make her rich and she didn't really want to have him killed. She would have done it, though, to teach the next prospective seller a lesson. She would have taken the bonus money Adán is paying her to set up the connection and used it to buy *sicarios* to come to Colombia and kill Jorge.

Either way, the story will get around and the men will respect her. She leaves the hotel humming—

Ladies, it ain't easy being independent.

It may not be easy, Magda thinks.

But it's good.

Mexico City

Even from the faint hallway light, Keller can see that his door has been jimmied.

The bedroom lamp is on in his apartment and the light shines under the door. He pulls his Sig Sauer and kicks the door open.

A man sits in his one chair and looks calmly at him. "Señor Keller?"

Keller trains the sight on his chest. "Who are you and what do you want?"

The man slowly holds up an eight-by-ten photograph of a young woman who looks into the camera, terrified. "Her name is María Moldano, she was kidnapped off the streets today, and she will be killed in a brutal way if you don't come with me."

"And if I do?"

"I give you my word that she will be released," the man answers, and then adds, "Intact. We know who you are. "So we know you will make this trade."

Keller lowers his gun.

They put him in the back of a Navigator, then pull a black hood over his head and make him lie down on the floor. Keller got a glimpse of the license plate and knows it will make no difference. Even if he does survive, the plates will turn out to have been stolen.

The men are well trained and don't talk.

Keller tries to time the drive but he knows that fear and adrenaline will speed up his mental clock.

He doesn't try to initiate conversation or ask questions. *Who are you? Where are you taking me? What do you want?* It would do no good and only show weakness. If they want two million dollars of Adán Barrera's money they're going to get it.

They drive for a long time—Keller estimates two hours—out of the city and into the country. Traffic noises gradually fade and then Keller can feel them leave tarmac and go onto a bumpy gravel road. He can hear goats and chickens. He feels the car go uphill, the driver shift into first, and then a sharp curve to the right.

The car stops.

Doors open, hands reach down and lift him out.

If they're going to kill me, he thinks, they're going to do it now. Shove me to my knees and put a bullet in the back of my head. It isn't the worst result. The other possibility is torture, the kind that the Zetas described on Crazy Eddie's video clip.

It's hard to be brave in the face of that. Any man who says he's not afraid of torture is lying, and Keller feels his legs quiver as they walk him away from the car and then into a building.

Hands push him down onto a stool.

Keller gets a faint whiff of something familiar.

Gasoline.

The place smells of gasoline and it smells of something else, too.

Death.

It's palpable, and Keller feels it the way that perhaps cattle feel a slaughterhouse, a sympathetic sense that members of your species have suffered and died in this place.

He shivers.

Then he hears a man sit down across from him. His tone is strong, calm, authoritative. "Señor Keller, I'm Heriberto Ochoa. I'm sorry to have brought you here this way. But we have no one else to go to, and we didn't know if you'd come otherwise."

"Release that girl," Keller says.

"She's already in a taxi on her way home," Ochoa says. "I'm a man of my word."

"What do you want?" Keller asks, steeling himself to be interrogated. The names of informants? The status of investigations? A way to get to Aguilar or Vera? He flashes back to Ernie Hidalgo's body, showing the marks of torture, his face frozen in a grimace of agony. How long can I hold out, he wonders, before I give it to them?

"We have something in common," Ochoa says.

"I doubt that."

"We both want to take down Adán Barrera," Ochoa says. "You know the old saying, 'The friend of my enemy is my friend.'"

"I'm not your friend."

"You could be."

"No."

"Barrera will kill you."

"Or I'll kill him."

"You're exactly who they said you are," Ochoa says. "That rarest of creatures—an honest cop."

"Well, you should know about cops," Keller says. "You own enough of them."

"I don't own the *federales*," Ochoa says. "Barrera does."

"If you have evidence of that, give it to me," Keller says. "I'll see that it gets into the right hands."

Ochoa laughs. "Those hands are too full grabbing Barrera's money."

So I guess we do have something in common, Keller thinks. We don't trust anyone.

"All we want is a level field," Ochoa says, "for the government to treat both sides the same. If we lose, we can respect that, but we can't tolerate the government applying the law only against us."

"*Do* you have incriminating evidence?"

Ochoa stands up. "You're the super-cop. Find it. If I were you I'd start with the Tapias. I'm sorry you rejected my friendship. It might have been mutually beneficial."

Back in the vehicle for the long drive back to the city. They stop a block from his apartment, remove the hood, and let him out. He goes up to his apartment, sits on the bed, and shakes. It lasts only for a few seconds, then he checks under the bed. The shotgun is there—they didn't take it. So is the knife.

Everything Ochoa said rang true.

The near misses on Barrera, the apparent fact that he's living in perfect safety in Sinaloa, Batman and Robin's war on Barrera's enemies in Tijuana, the arrest of Osiel Contreras, the AFI and SEIDO fighting against the CDG-owned cops in Tamaulipas . . . all those facts would support a theory that the administration is backing Barrera at the cost of the other cartels.

But which parts of the administration?

Aguilar?

Vera?

Neither? Both?

And how do you find out? And how do you prove it?

Start with the Tapias, Ochoa said.

Face it, Keller thinks, the hunt for Barrera is going nowhere and now Batman and Robin, disingenuously or not, are bogged down in the Gulf War and they've taken you with them.

Start with the Tapias.

Again, how?

Although the night isn't cold, Keller can't seem to get warm.

He gets into the shower and turns it up hot, to warm up but also to scour away the place where he met Ochoa. Some places hold horror in them, it seeps into the walls, it permeates the air, its smell stays with you after you leave, as if it wants to seep through your pores into your blood, into your heart.

Pure evil.

Evil beyond the possibility of redemption.

Jesus the Kid

You got a one-way ticket to the Promised Land

—Bruce Springsteen
"The Ghost of Tom Joad"

Laredo, Texas
2006

J esús "Chuy" Barajos didn't grow up in the nice part of Laredo.

He was raised in the projects, in a wooden shack set on cinder blocks, with nine brothers and sisters. His father did construction jobs to feed his family, his mother cut hair. Hardworking people, loving parents who knew they were too busy supporting their kids to spend enough time with them.

Chuy played *fútbol* in a park across the street and wanted to be a professional player or a Navy SEAL. He and his best friend Gabe would talk about that a lot, especially after 9/11. Chuy wanted to fight for his country, Gabe wanted to learn how to beat the hell out of his abusive alcoholic father.

Neither one ever joined the navy, never mind the SEALs.

Gabe started hanging out on Lincoln Street with the *mota* dealers. Chuy, he ran away from home, got picked up for marijuana possession, which was no big deal.

The gun was.

Chuy was kicking the ball around in a vacant lot when he saw the brown paper bag in a bush along the chain-link fence. He opened the bag and hefted the heavy pistol, silver and pretty, in his hand. If you find a pistol like that, what else are you going to do except shoot it?

You *have* to.

Chuy fired the gun into the air.

A neighbor lady called the cops.

In the "interview room" at the precinct house, Chuy admitted to what he'd done. When he repeated his admission in court, the judge put him in juvie for a year, eight months with good time.

The "Gladiator Academy" was a learning experience.

The older boys taught him things he never wanted to know. He was small and skinny and weak, and they took him in the showers, took him in the bathroom, took him in his cell at night. He tried to fight back, he begged, he pleaded . . . and learned that fighting back was futile and that begging and pleading just made you more of a punk, made you a bitch.

More a bitch.

What they did to him made him a bitch, and they never stopped telling him so, calling him a bitch, a girl, a *joto*.

Every time he sees his face in the mirror, that's what he sees. You don't forget what they did to you, what they made you do to them. That fire doesn't go out, it just smolders, and you remember every face.

When Chuy got released, he started slipping across the border to Nuevo Laredo—not much of a slip, right across the bridge. A lot of the *pochos* did it, Chuy and Gabe and a dozen others.

Mostly hung out in a disco called Eclipse.

Doing his best to dance to the reggaeton music, working up the nerve to talk to one of the girls in their tight, slinky dresses, looking in admiration at the narcos in their *crema*, with their chains and their watches and their money and their cars parked out front.

None of those narcos live in a wooden house on cinder blocks. None of them share a bathroom with eleven other people, with a toilet that doesn't flush half the time, a trickle of a cold shower, with a father who shows up late at night and leaves before the sun comes up, a mother who looks as tired as she is.

The narcos have houses, condos, apartments. They have new cars and hot girls and *money*.

A lot of money, which they throw around like it's nothing.

Like it's *nothing*.

Like it doesn't come from lugging concrete, digging ditches, laying pipe. Like it doesn't come from holding a scissors until your hands are bent and cramped like a Halloween witch, your shoulders stooped, your neck aching.

Chuy knows where this money comes from.

A simple trip back across the bridge.

He makes it all the time, and he knows that you can make it empty and that's what you get, or you can make it heavy, and that's another reason— along with the music and the lights and the girls—he hangs out at Eclipse, hoping to catch on.

Hoping one of the narcos will notice him and give him a chance.

That's what Gabe said.

"We hang out long enough," Gabe advised, "someone will take notice and give us a shot."

Finally, one of them does.

One of the older narcos, guy named Esteban, maybe in his twenties, gives them each a little packet of coke and tells them to carry it back across the bridge, go to this house, and give it to this guy.

Chuy does it.

Of course he does it.

It's easy.

Strolls right across the bridge, goes to the address he was given, and gives the packet of *perico* to the guy who comes to the door. Guy takes the packet and hands Chuy a hundred-dollar bill.

Tip money.

Chuy goes back to Eclipse and starts making more trips.

Him and Gabe both, heavier and heavier amounts, and they start walking around with money in their pockets.

It isn't enough.

"We're making chump change," Gabe complains. "We'll never break into the big time this way."

"So how?" Chuy asks.

The Zetas, Gabe tells him. "The Zetas are looking for people. We catch on with them, we're made."

"So how do we catch on with them?" Chuy asks.

Gabe says he'll put the word out.

He does but nothing happens.

For months, they keep going down to the 867, making dope runs back, collecting chump change.

"We're getting nowhere," Chuy says.

"We gotta be patient, *'mano*," Gabe says. "They're watching us."

Finally, Chuy's hanging out at Eclipse when Esteban, the guy who gave him his first dope run, comes up and says, "You still looking to get hooked up with some people?"

Chuy feels his throat tighten. He can barely breathe.

He just nods.

"Come on then," Esteban says.

He takes Chuy out to a black Lincoln Navigator and blindfolds him. They drive maybe an hour before he takes Chuy out of the car and walks him into a house, then takes the blindfold off.

Chuy sees a squat, muscled man in a black shirt and black jeans. He has thick, curly black hair and a thick black mustache. He also has a .38 pistol in a holster on his belt, and he looks at Chuy with an expression of wry amusement.

"This is Señor Morales," Esteban tells Chuy. "Z-40."

Chuy just nods.

Esteban nudges Chuy. "Tell him *your* name."

Chuy hears his own voice—high and squeaky. "Chuy—Jesús—Barajos."

Forty laughs. "Where you from, Chuy Jesús Barajos?"

"Laredo."

"A *pocho*," Forty says. "So, Chuy, do you think you have what it takes to work for the Zetas?"

"Yes."

"Well, you'll have to prove it," Forty says.

Chuy looks around the room. Five other Zetas are standing around, looking at him. Then there's another man, sitting on a wooden chair, his hands tied behind his back, dried blood at the corners of his mouth.

"You see that man?" Forty says. "He owed us money that he didn't want to pay. He wanted to pay it to someone else. Do you understand?"

"Yes."

"Now he has to pay," Forty says. Forty takes the pistol from his holster and puts it in Chuy's hand. "You ever shoot a gun before?"

"Yes."

"You ever kill anyone before?" Forty asks.

Chuy shakes his head.

"You will now," Forty says. "If you want to work for us. If you don't, well, *m'ijo*, you've seen what you've seen, do you understand?"

Chuy understands. He either proves he can kill someone or someone else comes in and proves it on him.

"I don't think the scrawny little shit can do it," Forty says to the others.

Chuy isn't sure either. Like, it's one thing to fire a gun into the air, another thing to . . .

Esteban whispers into his ear, "Gabe did it."

Chuy lifts the gun. It's heavy, solid, real, and he points it at the kneeling man's head, looks into the man's eyes and sees the terror as the man begs and pleads for his life. The trigger is heavy, harder to pull than with the gun he found in the brown paper bag.

"If you don't do it," Forty says, "you're a punk. A bitch."

Chuy fires.

Puts the man's lights out.

It feels good.

Chuy Barajos just turned eleven years old.

He's not a Zeta yet.

Him and Gabe find themselves in the back of a truck, rumbling down a dirt road in the boonies out near the little Tamaulipas town of San Fernando. Six other recruits bounce with them in the back of the truck, a couple of them are in their twenties, a couple are teenagers.

The truck pulls down into a broad valley where Chuy sees a ranch enclosed by a fence topped with barbed wire and a strand of electrified tape. Stopping at a gate, the driver speaks with a guard armed with an AK-47, and then goes through.

Esteban's there to greet them.

"Out!" he yells.

Uniformed men scream at them, hustle them out of the truck, yell at them to pick up their packs, and then shove them into a long one-story building with bunk beds along the walls.

Chuy's seen this shit in movies.

These are barracks and this is basic training.

He's there for six months.

And loves it.

First of all, the food is good and there's plenty of it. You have to take a quick shower—thirty seconds—but the water is piping hot. And the barracks are clean—spotless—the instructors see to that. Everything is squared away, and Chuy finds that he likes that.

He even likes the training.

They run, at first with shorts and tennis shoes, later with heavy packs and boots. They do calisthenics, they belly-crawl under barbed wire, then graduate to martial arts and hand-to-hand combat.

Then they get guns—AKs, AR-15s, Glocks, Uzis—and learn how to shoot, really shoot, not like a bunch of gangbangers, but like soldiers. Chuy becomes a hell of a marksman, one of the best with his *"erre,"* his AR-15. What he aims at, he hits, and it's a source of pride.

They handle explosives, learn how to build a car bomb, an IED, a C-4 charge to blow off a door. They throw grenades, shoot grenade launchers, learn how to attach a grenade to a door so that it will take an intruder's head off.

They learn discipline—mostly through the *tablazo,* a whack on the ass with a wooden paddle. You don't answer a radio call, you get two whacks. You don't go to headquarters when you're called, you get ten.

Most of all, they're indoctrinated into the group culture.

That of an elite force.

Military protocol is strictly observed, with ranks, salutes, and chain of command. There are the top-tier commanders, like Ochoa and Forty and the commanders of regions and then plazas. Then there's the next level—*los licenciados*—the lieutenants. Under them are sergeants, each in charge of an *estaca*—a cell—of five to seven men, because that's how many you can fit, with weapons, into a single vehicle.

Loyalty is demanded and camaraderie prized—the ethic of "no man left behind" is an absolute. A comrade is to be brought off the field of battle, dead or alive. If wounded, he gets the best treatment by the best doctors; if killed or jailed, his family is taken care of, receiving $1,000 every two weeks.

And his death avenged.

Without exception.

Their instructors are Zetas and Israelis, former U.S. Marines, and ex–special forces from Guatemala known as Kaibiles, truly scary dudes who specialize in teaching how to kill with a knife.

The instructors teach them surveillance, countersurveillance, how to follow a car, how to lose a tail, how to bug a building or a room, wiretap a phone, hack into e-mail. They preach that cell phones are like women—you use them once or twice and then throw them away.

"We're like James Bond," Chuy enthuses to Gabe one night. "We're 007!"

Some of the recruits wash out.

They can't handle the physical demands or they just can't learn. Chuy feels a little bad for them because their futures are bleak—they become lookouts, at best, or maybe do some lightweight dope runs.

They aren't going to move up in the world.

Him and Gabe, they do well.

Very well.

They catch the attention of Esteban and Forty, who runs a section of the camp that a lot of rumors come out of.

Ugly rumors about what goes on there.

Deliveries come in the back of covered trucks and some of the recruits whisper that those trucks are full of people.

"Bullshit," Gabe says. "Anyway, it's none of our business."

Chuy knows that if you want to stick here, one thing you do is mind your own business. You don't talk about shit you shouldn't even know about, and you don't ask about it, either.

You just do what they tell you.

They're headed for graduation night and Chuy isn't going to fuck that up by shooting his mouth off about stuff he isn't supposed to know.

The dining hall is decorated with lighted paper lanterns and real white table-cloths. Real plates and wineglasses.

The dinner is the best Chuy's had in his life. A big steak all to himself, roast potatoes, vegetables, flan and *tres leches* cake for dessert.

And wine.

By the time dinner is over, Chuy's a little lightheaded.

And proud.

He's lean and mean, in terrific shape, and has a feeling that he's earned membership in a brotherhood of elite warriors.

It feels wonderful.

After dinner, the instructors lead them up a little knoll to a building none of them were allowed to enter during their training. One by one, they're led into a room in the back of the building. Chuy sits and waits. One by one, the recruits come out and walk right past him. None of them speak, but look straight ahead and walk out of the building.

Finally, it's Chuy's turn. Esteban comes and gets him, opens the door, and ushers him into the room.

Forty and Heriberto Ochoa, Z-1, El Verdugo himself, are there to greet him and tell him what he has to do to graduate. A man, his hands tied behind his back, kneels on the floor. One of the Kaibiles stands behind him, and he hands Chuy a serrated knife. For the rest of his life, whenever he *can* sleep, Chuy will have nightmares about what happened in that room.

What he sees is the man's face.

Chuy ain't living in no shack anymore.

No cinder blocks, no cold shower.

He's living in a rented five-bedroom house on a leafy cul-de-sac in an expensive suburban Laredo subdivision. Chuy and Gabe each have their own bedroom, the living room has a flat-screen TV with an Xbox, the kitchen has a fridge full of food. Three Mexican dudes live there with them, but they're pretty quiet and don't go out much.

Esteban comes over every Friday and hands each of them $500 in cash, their weekly salary.

For doing nothing.

So far all they've done since they got back from the training camp is sit on their asses, play *Call of Duty* and *Madden,* go to the Mall del Norte, hit Mrs. Fields, and try unsuccessfully to pick up girls. (This is frustrating to Chuy. He can't tell them that he's a man, a killer, an elite trained warrior. To them he's just a middle schooler.) Otherwise, they sit around, drink beer, smoke weed, jerk off, and sleep until noon.

It's teenage boy heaven.

Except for the nightmares, it's a good life.

One Friday Esteban comes around and says he has a job for them. There's a guy living in Laredo who's been messing around with a woman of Forty's.

"Guy's gotta go," Esteban says.

Tell the truth, Chuy's a little disappointed. He thought he was a soldier, fighting in a war against the Alliance ("It's like *Star Wars,* bro"), but the first mission they send him on is over some *chica.*

But orders are orders and five hundy a week is five hundy a week and if you're going to live in a nice house you pay the rent, so he and Gabe go out in a car the Mexicans stole for them to the address that Esteban gave them.

"You drive and I'll pull the trigger," Gabe tells him.

"Why don't you drive and *I* pull the trigger?"

"Because I'm older."

"By a year."

"Year and a half," Gabe says.

"Big deal."

But Chuy drives. He don't have no license, but they're going to kill a guy, so he's not exactly sweating the underage driving thing. He pulls up on the curb, Gabe checks the load on the 9mm and gets out. "I'll be back in a sec."

"Cool."

"You better be here."

"I'll be here, bro. Just go do your thing."

Chuy watches Gabe put the pistol behind his back, walk up to the door, and ring the bell. Door opens, Gabe pulls out the 9 and shoots twice, then walks back to the car.

"Mrs. Fields?" Gabe asks.

"Sure."

They dump the car at the mall.

Mission accomplished.

Except it's not.

Esteban comes over in the morning, wakes them up, and he's *pissed*. Shows them the morning newspaper. "You *malandros* fucked up! You didn't shoot the guy, you shot his son!"

Chuy looks at the picture in the paper.

Kid was eleven.

"*Told* you I shoulda done it," he says to Gabe.

"This is *serious*," Esteban says. "Forty wanted me to whack both of you, but I talked him out of it. But you idiots are on a short fucking leash. Your next chance is your last chance, *comprende*?"

They *comprende*.

Chuy's disconsolate.

"We had our chance to prove ourselves and we fucked it up," he says to Gabe. "Couldn't you see it was a kid?"

"The door opened and I shot."

"You were too jacked up, bro," Chuy says. "You gotta chill out."

They wait months for their next chance. Then Esteban tells them, "The three of us are going on a mission together. Can I trust you not to fuck up?"

"You can trust us, man," Chuy says. "One hundred percent."

It's important, Esteban tells them. This former Nuevo Laredo city cop flipped and went over to the Alliance. Now he's in Laredo, providing protection for the opposition. Before we can get to them, we gotta take this guy out.

Tonight.

Chuy gets into the work car and sees it's serious because Esteban hands him an *erre*.

"You remember how to use this?" Esteban asks.

"Sure."

"I hope so."

Gabe drives. They wait outside a strip club out by the airport until the guy comes out and then follow his Dodge Charger along an access road along a bunch of factories and warehouses. Esteban takes out a police flasher, puts it on the car roof, and sets it off.

"Bad boys, bad boys," Gabe sings, "whatcha gonna do . . ."

"Shut up," Esteban says.

The Charger pulls over.

Chuy sees the dome light come on but can't make out whether the guy is reaching for his registration or a gun. He don't wait to find out. As they pull up alongside, he rolls the window down, sticks out the AR, and *melts* the guy.

It's the small hours of the morning, though, so Mrs. Fields is closed.

That's okay—Esteban gives them each ten grand in cash instead.

Chuy and Gabe don't play *Call of Duty* so much anymore. After you've done the real thing, a video version is . . . boring.

Their next job is big.

A big step up.

"'Bruno,'" Gabe says when they get the assignment. "Isn't that, like, a cartoon character?"

"I thinks that's 'Bluto,'" Chuy says. He watches a lot of Cartoon Network.

Bruno Resendez ain't no cartoon. He's a major marijuana dealer based in Rio Bravo, Texas, right on the border, and he's with the Alliance. He's so much with the Alliance that what he does is finger Zetas on the Mexican side for assassination. Esteban figures Bruno's responsible for about a dozen dead Zetas.

Forty wants him dead.

"You guys take Bruno out," Esteban tells them, "you're *gold*."

They spend a week scoping out the town and blend right in because of the five thousand or so citizens of Rio Bravo, about four thousand nine hundred and ninety-eight of them are Hispanic.

Bruno tools around Rio Bravo like he owns it.

Maybe he does, Chuy thinks.

Bruno rolls up and down Route 83 in his black Ford pickup, in a straw cowboy hat, with his nephew in the passenger seat. No bodyguard, no follow car, so he must think he's safe on this side of the border.

The man has a routine as he makes his rounds. Bruno waits in the truck, the nephew goes in and picks up the money. Nephew looks to Chuy like he's fifteen, sixteen. Nice work, riding around with your *tío* picking up the cash.

"How you wanna do this?" Gabe asks Chuy.

"I dunno, the highway?"

"What about the nephew?" Gabe asks. "Nobody said nothing about him."

"Fuck the nephew," Chuy says.

They take Bruno on the 83.

Bruno don't want to be caught. Must have seen trouble in the rearview mirror because he takes that Ford up to eighty, then ninety. Gabe's gotta be doing a buck ten in the Escalade when they pull into the lane beside Bruno's truck.

Chuy laughing like a motherfucker as he rips off a clip from the AR. Hears the nephew scream like a little girl. Sees Bruno slumped over the wheel, the cowboy hat slammed over his face.

Truck swerves and then flips.

Does a double roll and then goes into the ditch.

Gabe eases off on the gas. "Think they're dead?"

"We gotta make sure."

Gabe flips a U-ey and they go back. Get out of their Escalade and walk over to the ditch, where the truck is upside down.

Bruno is dead, no question.

Half his head is crushed, the rest of it shot away.

The nephew is whimpering. Trapped in the passenger seat, jaws-of-life candidate, he don't look so good. He stares up at Chuy and moans, "Please."

"Doing you a favor," Chuy says. Even if the nephew makes it, gonna be a helper-monkey situation.

He fires into the kid's head.

When they get back to Laredo, Esteban gives them $150,000.

And Chuy gets an *aporto*.

They call him Jesus the Kid.

La Tuna, Sinaloa

Adán's reaction to Magda's meeting with Jorge is typically male.

"Did you sleep with him?" he asks when she comes back.

"Do you need the coke connection?" Magda asks.

"Yes."

"Then I slept with him," Magda answers. "Or I didn't, whichever turns you on more."

She still likes to turn him on, maybe all the more so because she no longer has to. It's now a matter of choice, not survival, and the distinction is important. Whether or not she slept with Jorge—or anyone else for that matter—is none of Adán's damn business, so she leaves the question unanswered.

Let him twist.

Besides, she's heard all about his courtship of Nacho's daughter, Eva, the little virgin. It's not surprising, but a little disappointing, Adán playing the stereotypical Sinaloan *señor*, plucking a rose from the beauty pageant garden. Still, he hasn't really plucked her yet, has he, if the rest of the rumors are true. Our Adán, every inch the gentleman.

Magda chose a basic black dress for this reunion, with a diamond necklace that she bought for herself. It does more than draw his eye to her décolletage, it makes a point—I bought this, Adán darling, with my own money. I don't need you to drape jewelry around me anymore.

Or a blanket.

Magda got a bonus of twenty kilos of cocaine for setting up the Colombian connection. Of course Adán knows that she's already sold all twenty kilos and used the profit to buy more discounted coke from Jorge, which she'll parlay into a larger fortune. Nothing happens in Sinaloa that Adán Barrera doesn't know about. Still, numbers are numbers to an accountant—it helps to have a little visual aid. "Do you like what you see?"

"I always have," Adán says.

"I meant the necklace."

"I know." He understands—Magda is asserting her independence. It's not such a bad thing, given that he's probably going to have to cut her loose anyway. She's doubtless heard all about Eva, and her pride will make her pull away before she's pushed. "It's lovely."

"Would you like me to take it off?"

"No," Adán says, his throat tightening. She doesn't need him, and it makes her wildly attractive. Like Nora. "Just the dress. Please."

"Oh. 'Please.' In that case . . ." The dress slides off her like water. The diamonds dig into his chest as he makes love to her.

Chuy has about $120,000 in the bank (well, not in the bank, he can't open his own account), but what does an eleven-year-old buy with $120K?

Can't buy a house.

Can't buy a car.

Can't buy a ticket to an R-rated movie.

He can buy clothes, he can buy Air Jordans, he can buy video games. He can buy a woman, or rent one, anyway. Him and Gabe go across the bridge and through the guard shack into Boy's Town down Calle Cleopatra where Esteban hooks them up with a brothel. And not a house where their next stop is a pharmacy, but to a really good house where the women are beautiful and really know what to do.

Which is a good thing, because Chuy really don't.

Next morning he revisits the car issue.

"You want a car?" Esteban asks. "No problem."

They get back to the other Laredo, Esteban takes Chuy to a dealership and lays down the kid's cash for a new Mustang convertible, black. It's in Esteban's name, but it's Chuy's car, and Esteban hands him the keys.

Chuy's *rolling*.

He has money, clothes, a brand-new ride. He has dreams that would sear the inside of your eyelids. Speaking of eyelids, Gabe does something really weird. Comes home one night, and his eyelids are tattooed with images of eyeballs.

"So when I *close* my eyes," Gabe says, demonstrating, "it looks they're still open."

What it looks like is creepy, Chuy thinks. Especially because Gabe's real eyes are brown but his tattoo eyes are blue.

It gets creepier.

Gabe gets called across the river to do some "work." Calls one night and he sounds messed up, really high, and he's talking some weird shit about kidnapping this kid they knew, Poncho, who was dealing for the Alliance, and his girlfriend.

Gabe, he's just riffing. *"You should have seen Poncho, dude. He was crying like a fag. 'No! I'm your friend! I'm your friend!' I was all like, 'What friend, you son of a bitch, shut your fucking mouth!' and then—POOM—I just slashed him, dude. Just took this motherfucking beer bottle and slit his whole fucking belly open! You should have been there, dude, you should have seen it. He was bleeding? And I took this plastic cup and held it under his belly and filled it with blood and then I drank it, dude! Right in front of him I drank it and held it up and dedicated it to Santísima Muerte, and then I went over to the girl and did the same thing."*

"So they're both dead?" Chuy asks.

"Yeah, they both bled out. They died and shit, dude."

"You really cooked them?"

"Of course, dude. Right there at the house." Fifty-gallon drum and gasoline. *"They're soup, dude."*

Chuy clicks off and goes back to *Grand Theft Auto*. He didn't know Gabe was into that weird Santísima Muerte shit. Chuy's a Catholic, man, he believes in the Father, the Son, and the Holy Ghost.

Eddie's having a relaxing evening cocktail at the Punta Bar down by the beach in Acapulco, scoping out this *tourista* chick who looks like she's either Danish or Swedish or Norwegian, but definitely a Scandinavian Ten.

Blond hair.

Rack.

Yoga ass.

Eddie knows he's looking tight—new plum-colored polo, white jeans, huarache sandals. It's annoying that the shirts have to be a size too large these days to accommodate the Glock, but war is hell.

The chick is drinking a mojito—of course she is—and Eddie has the bartender set up another for her. She looks over at Eddie, lifts her glass in thanks, and Eddie smiles back.

He's going to get up in that tonight.

Then an explosion goes off.

Chuy goes in heavy.

Okay, a little too heavy.

Okay, a *lot* too heavy.

He knows Ruiz's rep. He's seen the video and doesn't want to star in Ruiz's next movie, and he knows that the Punta Bar is a Tapia hangout and that Ruiz will have people there.

Chuy got orders to go to Acapulco to take out this guy, this Eddie Ruiz.

Because what the fuck, right?

Why not?

Ruiz is looking for men, Zeta *sicarios*. He's not going to have his eyes open for some eleven-year-old kid. Plus, this is a *chance*. If Bruno Resendez was worth $150K, Eddie Ruiz—public enemy *número uno*—has to have a price tag of what, half a million? A mil? More? And if Esteban could buy him a car, he could also buy him a house. Two houses—one for him and one for *Mami* and *Papi*.

It's Chuy's fantasy, rolling up on the house in his sled, walking in and saying, *No more digging ditches, Papi, no more cutting hair, Mami*—and handing them the keys to their new house on the other side of Laredo. A nine-bedroom house—a room for everyone and a Guatemalan maid to keep it clean.

If he takes Eddie Ruiz off the count, Forty and Ochoa will throw him a party, give him coke, make him an officer, give him his own plaza to run. He'll boss Gabe around, shit, he'll boss Esteban around. People will treat him with respect, whisper, *That's the guy who did Eddie Ruiz. That's Chuy Barajos, Jesus the Kid, the* macho *who walked into the Punta Bar on his own and . . .*

Chuy opens the door and tosses in a grenade.

Then he unslings the *erre* and opens up.

———

Eddie jumps on Ilsa, throws her to the floor, and lies on top of her.

Pulls the Glock and looks up.

It's ugly. People hold their bleeding faces, shards of glass sticking out. One of his flunkies looks down, staring, at his severed left arm. Bottles behind the bar shatter and then the mirror goes. Bullets zing, people go down, women scream, *men* scream . . .

Fucking Zetas, Eddie thinks—the place is *packed* with civilians. This is not the way you do things. He looks for the shooters but only sees one, a spindly-looking little dude standing in the doorway spraying fire like this is some sort of video game.

Ain't no replay, asshole, Eddie thinks.

He sights the bead on the shooter's chest.

The shooter sees him, swings his rifle, and fires.

Chuy drops the AR and *runs.*

Runs the way that only a scared boy can run, fast and fluid, through the streets. Doesn't dare turn his head to see if they're coming after him.

Tells himself you gotta be alive to spend the money. Gotta be alive to buy your mom and dad the house. Except the Zetas will take care of them—that was the promise, that was the oath. A soldier falls in combat, his family will be taken care of. Ochoa told him that himself, on graduation night before . . .

Chuy runs until he's out of breath.

Stops and looks around.

Hears the sirens, sees the ambulances speed past him, going the other way, toward the Punta Bar.

An hour later he's on a bus, heading up the coast to the port of Lázaro Cárdenas, Zeta country, to collect his beautiful reward for killing Eddie Ruiz.

Four dead, twenty-five wounded.

A real mess.

It takes Eddie three hours to get Forty on the phone, but when he does he says, "What the fuck? You're so desperate for men now you're using midgets?"

"What are you talking about?"

"That pygmy you sent," Eddie says, "was even smaller than your dick. Good job, by the way—he hit a dozen civilians and one of them's dead. Lobbing a grenade into a public place? Is this the way we play now?"

Forty hangs up.

Eddie turns to Ilsa, who's sitting on his bed.

The sex had been incredible—something about that near-death experience thing, he guesses.

"Crazy night, huh?" he says.

Chuy goes to the address of the safe house they gave him.

Gabe and Esteban are there waiting for him, and Chuy smiles at them.

"Forty wants to see you," Esteban says.

Chuy smiles. Of course Forty wants to see him. When he gets into the room, Forty stands up and slaps him so hard across the face Chuy thinks he might black out. His head spinning, he says, "But I killed Ruiz."

"No you didn't," Forty says. "You missed."

"I saw—"

Forty slaps him again. "A *grenade*?! You throw a grenade into a bar full of tourists, and then start shooting?! Are you stupid?! Are you crazy?!"

"I'm sorry."

"Make it hurt," Forty snaps.

Gabe and Esteban grab Chuy and drag him up the stairs. They strip him, tie his wrists to a rope, run the rope through a pulley, haul him up until he's barely on his toes, then tie the other end of the rope off on a bolt in the floor.

Esteban hands Gabe a thick leather strap. Walking behind Chuy, Gabe says softly, "Sorry, dude."

He takes a swallow of Coke, the good Mexican Coke in a bottle with all the sugar, then starts in with a leather strap on Chuy's back, on his ass, on his legs. Takes another hit of Coke, sets the bottle down on the floor, and starts whipping him again.

Chuy tries not to scream, but his determination doesn't last past the third stroke.

It hurts bad.

He screams and twists and cries.

Begs.

Like the little bitch he knows he is.

Finally, Esteban says, "Enough."

He picks up a length of two-by-four and shows it to Chuy. "You know what I'm going to do?"

Chuy knows.

La paleta is a Zeta specialty they taught at the training camp.

You take a piece of board and hit someone in the lower back. Slowly, rhythmically, again and again. The victim wants to die a long time before he does. Sometimes they stop before they kill him, and then the man is a cripple, barely able to walk, groaning every time he takes a piss.

Chuy had seen those guys and laughed at them.

Now Esteban steps behind him.

Chuy breaks down sobbing.

"Bitch," Esteban says. "You're nothing but a little bitch after all."

"Bitch," Gabe chimes in. "Fag."

"You think about it," Esteban says. "You think about what's going to happen to you, *perrita*."

He unties the rope and Chuy falls to the floor.

"Forty wants to do it himself," Esteban says.

Chuy lies fetal on the floor.

His blood sticks to the wooden planks.

Gabe sits with his back propped against the wall. "I'm sorry, dude."

Chuy don't answer.

"You don't know," Gabe says. "You don't know what they make you do. At the ranch. One after the other. One after the other. Like a machine, dude. Then we burn them. Put them in drums and burn them."

Chuy don't want to listen, don't want to feel sorry for Gabe. Fuck him, they aren't about to beat *him* to death. He closes his eyes and doesn't open them again until Gabe finally shuts up.

He looks over at Gabe's eyes.

His *blue* eyes.

Staring back at him, unseeing.

Chuy wriggles across the floor like a snake. Grabs the Coke bottle and smashes it against the wall. It wakes Gabe up but Chuy is already on top of him and slashes the jagged glass across his throat.

Gabe tries to keep his blood in, but it spurts out his carotid artery.

Tries to yell, but his throat is cut.

Naked, his wrists still bound together in front of him, Chuy jumps out the window.

Morelia, Michoacán

A whore finds Chuy two weeks later, sleeping in a Dumpster in the alley off the street she works.

Flor is young and Guatemalan. She came up from the Petén when the Kaibiles came in and forced her family off their land. They rode a train into Mexico, hoping to make it to the U.S., but somewhere in Quintana Roo, police stopped the train and forced them off.

The men took her father and brothers away—she doesn't know where.

They took her, too, to the city of Morelia, and told her that she'd have good work as a waitress, that she would make money that she could send to her family. She did work in the restaurant, washing dishes and the floor, but they told her that she owed the money she made as rent for the room above the restaurant she shared with twelve other girls.

She learned the truth from these girls.

Learned that the men—the "Zetas"—would put her on the street to have sex with men who paid them.

At first she didn't believe them, but then she learned to believe.

One at a time, men taught her to believe.

In the front seats of cars, they taught her to believe. In cheap dirty rooms, they taught her to believe. Bent over trash cans in an alley, they taught her to believe.

Now Flor stands under the pools of streetlamp lights in clothes that shame her, and she calls to the men in cars in words that shame her, bidding them to do things that shame her, for money that shames her.

She doesn't send money to her family. The men told her that they would help her find them, but never did.

The money her shame makes goes for rent, goes for food, for clothes, for makeup, it goes to the doctors for medicine, it goes to pay for the train that she rode. The money goes to the "interest" on her debt that grows every day, no matter how much shame she makes at night.

The money used to go for drugs.

She started shooting heroin that washed away her shame like a moist and soothing cloud full of rain, that brought dreams of her beautiful home in the Petén, her parents, her brothers. Her heroin dreams were green and soft and beautiful like her home.

But heroin cost money.

The men would always give it to her, but they would add it to her "tab," and as she got deeper and deeper into addiction she fell deeper and deeper in debt, until the men had her working all the time and she shamed herself ten, twelve, fourteen times a night.

Not that she felt shame any longer.

Not that she felt anything.

Then Flor found the Lord.

Not the Catholic god of her childhood, but a loving Lord.

Jehovah God.

A man bought her on the street one night, took her to a dim and dirty room, but instead of taking her, asked, "Child, my sister, do you know the Lord?"

He read to her from the Bible, and then *gave* her a book, the one written by the leader, a man named Nazario. He came to see her every night, when the men weren't watching, when the other girls weren't watching, and he told her that Jesus loved her, that the Lord loved her, Nazario loved her, and that if she accepted that love she would see her family again in heaven. She read the book and he took her to meet other people, other brothers and sisters, in a house where they live and call themselves a family.

One night there Nazario walked over to her, rolled up her sleeves, and saw the needle tracks, and he gently said, *"You don't need this, my sister,"* and that was the truth and she believed. He taught her to believe.

That while her body might be a slave, her soul is free.

She gave up the heroin.

This night Flor is standing at the edge of the alley and she hears something in the Dumpster and thinks it's a rat, but then she sees this boy climb out, this child. He looks startled to see her and starts to run, but she asks, "Are you hungry?"

The boy nods.

"Wait here," she says.

She goes into the restaurant's kitchen and asks the cook for some scraps— some meat, a little chicken, a corn tortilla—and brings it out into the alley.

The boy is still there and she hands him the food.

He eats like a ravenous dog.

Flor asks, "What's your name?"

"Pedro," he lies.

"Do you have a place to stay?" Flor asks him.

Chuy shakes his head.

"I can take you to a place where you can sleep," she says. "Jesus loves you."

This is how Chuy joins La Familia Michoacana.

Now Chuy lives in an old house with twenty or so other people, most of them young, most of them otherwise homeless. Some are girls, or even boys, who work the street. Others sell candy, flowers, or newspapers from traffic islands.

Chuy gets a different job, delivering food to orphanages, homeless shelters, and drug clinics. He hops in a van or a pickup truck in the morning and spends the day unloading boxes of rice, pasta, powdered milk and cereal, big vats of soup, cookies and candies, all labeled "With love from La Familia."

At the drug rehab clinics they deliver something else in addition to the food—copies of the Book: *The Sayings of Nazario.* Sometimes an adult stays behind at the clinic to talk to the addicts, tell them about Jehovah God and Jesus Christ and Nazario. As the weeks go by, Chuy notices that some of the patients he saw at the clinic come to live at the house or work on the delivery trucks.

At night, Chuy has supper at the house, and then goes to the meeting where they discuss the Bible and the Book, and then sometimes he hangs around the restaurant near the block where Flor works or he sits at home and slogs painfully through the Book, because he was never very good at reading, in Spanish or English. But with Flor's help, he makes it through, and memorizes key sayings. His favorite is, "A true man needs a cause, an adventure, and a good woman to rescue."

On Sunday mornings everyone goes to church, and on special occasions Nazario himself comes to preach—the good word about Jehovah God and Jesus Christ and how to live right and do the right things, and Chuy sees Flor's eyes light up when she gazes at Nazario, and after the service they line up to get his blessing and Chuy is excited in a way he hasn't been since he first met Ochoa, which now seems like a lifetime ago, because now he has a new life—he loves Jehovah God and Jesus Christ. He loves Nazario.

He loves Flor.

But the Zetas are still very much a part of his new life.

They're part of everybody's.

As Chuy moves around the city, he sees their gunmen on the street, sees them go into the bars and the clubs, into the brothels and the *tienditas*—the little stores—and he sees that they collect protection money from everyone.

The Zetas run Michoacán.

"Didn't you know that?" Flor asks him one night.

"I thought they were just narcos," Chuy says.

"They run everything now," she says. "It was them who took me off the train, brought me here, put me to work. The money I make goes to them. All the girls pay them or they beat you, maybe kill you."

She knows girls who have just disappeared.

The Zetas rule Michoacán like a colony.

So as Chuy works, he literally keeps his head down. As he goes in the truck all around the city, even out to the little villages in the countryside where La Familia delivers food and clean water, digs wells, and builds day-care centers, he keeps an eye out for Zetas.

If they recognize him, he knows they'll kill him.

And not quick.

But other than that, life is good. He likes living at the house with his new friends, likes spending his spare time with Flor, even finds he likes going to church, singing the hymns, hearing Nazario preach.

One of Nazario's sayings is, "You are only as sick as your secrets," and Flor urges Chuy to go speak to one of the counselors, the man who brought her into La Familia, to do a "cleansing," because it's wonderful and he will feel better.

"I feel okay," he says.

"You have nightmares," Flor says. "You wake up weeping. If you do the cleansing, the nightmares will stop. Mine did."

A few nights later, Chuy does his cleansing. He goes into a small room with the "counselor," a man in his forties named Hugo Salazar.

"Tell me your sins," Hugo says. "Get them off your soul."

Chuy balks, says nothing.

Hugo says, " 'You cannot climb a mountain with a sack of garbage on your back.' "

"I've done bad things."

"God already knows everything you've done and everything you will do," Hugo says, "and He loves you, anyway. This is not a confession, it's a liberation. Nightmares can't live in the light."

"I've killed people."

"You look like just a boy."

Chuy shrugs.

"How many people?" Hugo asks.

"Six?"

"You don't know?"

"I'm pretty sure six."

"Were they innocent people?" Hugo asks. "Women? Children?"

"No."

"How did you come to kill?" the man asks.

"I worked for narcos."

"I see," Hugo says. "Anything else?"

Chuy wants to tell him about his nightmare, what he did with Ochoa that night, but he's too ashamed, and afraid. The Zetas might be looking for him, and if he tells, he might be identified, because only Zetas do that kind of thing.

"Yes," Chuy says. He stares at the floor. "I killed my best friend."

"Why, my young brother?"

"He was going to kill me."

Hugo lays a hand on his shoulder. "Nazario says that this world is full of evil, which is why we must not be fully part of this world, but always have an eye on the next one. In an evil world, sometimes we have to do evil to survive, and God understands this. The point is that we try to do the right thing, with a pure heart. Go back now, my brother, and do what's right."

Chuy leaves and finds Flor on the street.

"Was it wonderful?" she asks, beaming at him. "I'm so happy you did it."

It was good, Chuy thinks.

He does feel lighter.

The nightmares still come, but less often, and he knows the reason that he still has them is because he didn't cleanse what he did with Ochoa that night. Maybe someday, he thinks, I'll have the courage to say.

Three days after his cleansing, Hugo approaches him.

"We have a new job for you, little brother."

The Family needs warriors.

Because La Familia Michoacana traffics drugs.

Nazario is the *chaca*, the boss.

But under the Zetas. Just as the Zetas run Michoacán, La Familia is also under their thumb. But the Family has its own trafficking business, mostly in meth, and it's bringing in vast amounts of money.

La Familia pays a tax to the Zetas, so are allowed to exist. Nazario was good friends with Osiel Contreras, who sent his Zetas to train Nazario's gunmen. Then the Zetas took over.

Chuy don't like the idea of working for Forty again, even indirectly, and he tells Hugo that the Zetas are evil.

"In an evil world," Hugo tells him, "you have to do evil to do good. The drugs we send to America pay for the food for orphans, the water for the villagers. Do you understand?"

"Yes."

"God needs warriors in this world," Hugo says. "You've read the Bible."

Chuy hasn't but doesn't say so.

Hugo says, "David was a great warrior. He killed Goliath. The Family needs Davids. Like you."

Chuy looks at him, puzzled.

"Don't you see, my brother?" Hugo asks. "All those bad things in your past, those things you were ashamed of, God takes and turns into good. When you fight for Nazario, you fight for the Lord. Your soul shines like the armor of a knight."

"But I'd be fighting for the Zetas," Chuy argues.

"The will of God is a mystery," Hugo answers, "that we humans can't always solve. Nor should we. We should only listen to His voice, and if you listen, Pedro, you will hear Him calling you."

Chuy hears the call.

He becomes a warrior of God.

Every night they meet for Bible study or to discuss the Book. They don't work on Sundays—instead they attend a massive outdoor service at which Nazario preaches.

"Every man needs a cause!" the leader bellows. "A cause, an adventure, and a good woman to rescue!"

His disciples cheer, then sing a hymn.

After the service there's a large dinner and then silent time—they spend four hours in quiet, contemplating their souls, their mission, the meaning of their lives, the sayings of Nazario. Sunday evenings they meet in the hall and chant the sayings over and over.

They watch videos, listen to tapes, and learn the strict rules—no smoking, no drinking, no drugs. A first offense will earn a beating, a second brings a severe whipping, a third means execution.

Three strikes and you're *out.*

One day the leaders bring Chuy a man they snatched off the streets—a child molester, the worst of the worst—and order Chuy to kill him.

No problem.

A warrior of the Lord, he strangles the man with his hands.

Now Chuy has a different job.

Now he doesn't deliver groceries.

His five-man cell patrols three city blocks. They watch who comes and goes, report anyone suspicious to their superiors, keep things tight, clean, and orderly. They deliver protection money to the local Zeta boss, who hangs out with his underlings in the office of a local auto body shop.

Instead of boxes, Chuy carries a Glock. He gets a salary. It's not much, but enough to rent a small room where he moves in Flor. They buy a bed at a junkyard, find a little table at the dump, get a lamp from a secondhand store. And Chuy has a different status—as a warrior, he has respect that earns him a right to make a request.

"I want to take Flor off the streets," he tells Hugo. "Let her work as a waitress."

"She isn't your wife," Hugo answers.

"She's going to be the mother of my child," Chuy answers. Flor told him, shyly and not without fear, that she had missed two periods.

Part of him was scared, part of him was thrilled. He took her in his arms and held her gently. "It will be all right. I'll take care of you."

"You don't have to."

"I will," Chuy promised. "I'll take good care of you both."

Now Hugo argues, "That child could be anyone's, little brother."

"Flor is my woman, so it's my child," Chuy answers.

That simple.

"I'll have to ask," Hugo says.

"The Zeta boss?"

"Yes."

"Don't ask," Chuy says. "*Tell* him that the mother of a warrior's child can't be a whore."

The Zeta boss's answer comes three nights later.

With four other Zetas, he walks into the restaurant after closing, when Flor is wiping down the tables and setting up for the morning.

"Everyone out," he orders, then looks at Flor. "You stay."

The others quickly walk out, their eyes on the floor. One of them, a former whore herself, runs to find Pedro.

"Are you Flor?" the boss asks.

Terrified, Flor nods.

"Take off that dress."

"I don't do that anymore."

"You're a whore," he says, "and you'll do what I tell you. You still owe us money."

"I'll pay you."

"Yes, you will. Right now."

He nods and the four men grab her, strip the dress from her, and pin her onto one of the tables.

"Pedro! Pedro!"

Chuy sees the girl running toward him.

"What is it?"

"It's Flor! Come quick!"

He runs.

Chuy lifts Flor's body off the table and cradles her corpse on his lap. She's still warm, her skin is still warm.

People say that you could hear Chuy's howl through the whole *colonia*.

They say they can never forget the sound.

Chuy stands outside the *yonke*, the auto shop where the Zeta *peces gordos*— the big bosses—hang out.

He hears them laughing inside.

The clink of bottles and glasses.

Well trained, Chuy checks the clip on his *erre*. Then he kicks the door in and sprays the five of them before they can as much as move.

Crouching beside the wounded Zeta *chaca*, Chuy takes the man's hair in one hand, like Ochoa did with the man that night. He takes out his knife, like the one the Kaibile handed him that night, pulls the boss's head back so that his neck is taut, and presses the serrated blade against his throat.

He's lived this over and over again.

More than the times that the boys hurt him, raped him, made him their girl. More than those things, his nightmares are of that night, when they handed him the knife and told him what to do—

—so now he knows and as if in a dream he saws the blade back and forth as the Zeta boss who raped and murdered Flor screams just as the man screamed that night and the blood spurts out in hot jets as Chuy saws through the arteries, and then the boss is quiet, just gurgling as Chuy saws through cartilage and bone like he did that night, and the bone and cartilage and skin pop as he severs the head.

He sets it down and starts in on the other four. Two are already dead. One tries to crawl away, but Chuy grabs his hair and pulls him back. The last man cries and slobbers and begs but Chuy tells him, "Shut up, bitch."

Chuy is sitting on the floor with the five decapitated bodies when Hugo bursts in. "*Dios mío*, Pedro, what did you do?!"

"My name is Jesús," Chuy says numbly. Over Hugo's shoulder he sees Nazario, with several men behind him. "Kill me."

Hugo pulls his gun, ready to oblige. The fallout from one of theirs killing five of the Zeta overlords will be horrific. If they can at least turn over a corpse . . . He points the gun at Chuy's head.

"Stop!" Nazario yells, knocking Hugo's hand down.

"The calf and the yearling will be safe with the lion," Nazario quotes from scripture, "and a little child shall lead them all."

He lifts Chuy up.

"It's time," Nazario says.

Chuy leads five La Familia warriors into the Sol y Sombre disco where a lot of the Zetas party.

The music throbs, the lights strobe.

Chuy fires a burst from his AR into the ceiling.

As the revelers dive to the floor, two of Chuy's men open a black plastic bag and dump out its contents.

Five human heads roll across the black-and-white-tiled floor.

Chuy reads from a cardboard sheet, "The Family doesn't kill for money! It doesn't kill women, it doesn't kill innocent people! Only those who deserve to die, die! This was divine justice!"

He tosses the sheet down and walks out.

The revolution—the rebellion of La Familia Michoacana to throw the Zetas out of their homeland—starts that night. Nazario writes press releases and takes out advertisements in the major newspapers to the effect that La Familia is not a public menace but just the opposite, a patriotic organization doing what the government cannot or will not do—"cleanse" Michoacán of kidnappers, extortionists, rapists, meth dealers, and foreign oppressors such as the Zetas.

Chuy doesn't care about any of that.

All he knows now is killing, and it's all he wants to know.

Eddie sees the story about the Sol y Sombre nightclub on the news.

"Nice," he says to the flunkie playing *Madden* with him. "Beheadings? Like . . . *beheadings*? I thought that was Muslim shit. Al Qaeda."

A few days later Eddie hears that the beheadings might have been carried out by the same guy who attacked his nightclub.

"Jesus the Kid."

The boy changed jerseys, I guess, Eddie thinks.

A midseason trade.

And some of the narcos are saying that the kid is really a *kid*, eleven, twelve years old.

Junior varsity.

Suddenly, Eddie feels old.

Then he gets the word—

—okay, the order—

—to go make nice.

—The word comes down from AB, El Señor, through Diego.

Eddie gets it—the Zetas have fought them to a bloody stalemate in Tamaulipas—tit-for-tat trench warfare that promises nothing but more of the same. So if these La Familia whackadoodles can draw some troops away from Tamaulipas, okay, good.

It doesn't stop Eddie from arguing. "They're religious nuts. You know this Nazario's *aporto*? 'El Más Loco'—the Craziest."

"As long as he's killing Zetas," Diego says.

"He's doing that," Eddie says. "He's also our biggest competitor in the North American meth market."

"Plenty of *helio*-heads to go around," Diego answers.

Well, that's a big chunk of truth, Eddie thinks. The Mexicans have finally found a drug that white trash likes and can afford. And one thing you ain't never gonna run out of is white trash.

That stuff makes itself.

They get made in the backseats of junk cars, and then they live in them.

So a week later Eddie Ruiz looks across a table at Chuy up in Morelia, Michoacán.

And he really is a kid.

An actual *kid*.

"I should be really pissed at you," Eddie says. "That stunt in Acapulco— very bad shit."

Feels like he should put him in "time out."

Chuy doesn't respond. Eddie looks into his eyes and sees nothing there— it's like staring at a snake. This kid, he has to remember, this freaking junior varsity water boy, cut the heads off five men and rolled them across a disco floor like he was duckpin bowling.

Guilty feet ain't got no rhythm, Eddie thinks.

But Diego said to work with these born-again Bible-thumpers, so—

"Hey, 'Texas forever,' right?" Eddie says. "We *pochos* have to stick together. Now let's you and me go bag ourselves some Zeta assholes."

"I kill for the Lord."

"Okay, then," Eddie says.

In the next ninety days, over four hundred narcos will be killed in Uruapan, Apatzingán, Morelia, and Lázaro Cárdenas.

The new tag team of Crazy Eddie and Jesus the Kid account for more than a few of them.

5

Narco Polo

Must be the money.

—Nelly
"Ride wit Me"

Mexico City
2006

Keller sips his white wine and looks over the glass at the exquisite woman smiling at him across the lobby of the movie theater.

Yvette Tapia is stunning in a short silver dress, her black hair cut in a severe pageboy, her lipstick a dark, daring red. If she meant to invoke the age of the flapper, a Zelda Fitzgerald combination of sophistication and sexiness in a Mexican milieu, she's succeeded. As one of the film's financial backers, she moves fluidly through the crowd, smiling and chatting and charming.

Desperate men, Keller reflects, make desperate moves.

And he's desperate.

His hunt for Adán Barrera is at a standstill, frozen on an investigational tundra of no leads, mired in bureaucratic entropy. His colleagues on the Barrera Coordinating Committee are bogged down elsewhere, simply too busy trying to cope with simultaneous wars in Baja, Tamaulipas, and now Michoacán.

Keller has to admit that the violence is unprecedented. Even at the height (the depth?) of Barrera's war against Güero Méndez, back in the '90s, the fighting was sporadic—brief sudden peaks of violence—not a daily event. And not spread across three broad areas of the country, with multiple and interconnected antagonists.

The Alliance fighting Teo Solorzano in Baja.

The Alliance fighting the CDG/Zetas in Tamaulipas.

La Familia (with, apparently, Alliance help) fighting the Zetas in Michoacán.

The war back in the '90s encompassed a few dozen fighters at a time. Now the cartels are mustering literally hundreds of men, maybe thousands—most of them military veterans, former or current police officers, in any case, trained fighters.

AFI and SEIDO are trying to take them all on.

Unless you believe Ochoa, Keller thinks, in which case the lineup looks a little different:

The Alliance and the federal government fighting Teo Solorzano in Baja.

The Alliance and the federal government fighting the Zetas in Tamaulipas.

La Familia (with, apparently, Alliance help) and the federal government fighting the Zetas in Michoacán.

Keller doesn't want to believe it. Was there official collusion in Barrera's escape from Puente Grande? Doubtless. Complicity in his close escapes? Likely. Entrenched corruption that keeps him protected wherever the hell it is he's "hiding"? Inarguable.

But a coordinated federal effort to assist Barrera in taking over the entire Mexican drug trade? That's a grassy knoll that Keller can't climb.

He and Ochoa do agree on one thing.

Start with the Tapias.

I have nowhere else to start, Keller thinks as he watches Yvette come toward him in the lobby.

It's in direct violation of his working agreement with both DEA and the Mexicans. *You are not here to cultivate your own sources, take independent action, or do surveillance or any other intelligence gathering.*

Yeah, well, Keller thinks, I'm not here to sit on my ass and do nothing while you guys work on everything but Barrera, either. Nothing changes if nothing changes, so it's time to start a little change.

He'd used an embassy connection to get into the film, and it came with an invitation to the post-premiere reception where everyone stands around thinking of nice things to say. Keller sought Yvette out, complimented her on the movie, and they got to talking.

"Yvette Tapia," she said. "My husband, Martín, and I helped to finance the film."

"Art Keller."

If she recognized the name, she didn't show it. "And what do you do in Mexico City, Art?"

"I'm with the DEA."

Give her credit, she didn't flinch. Her in-laws are some of the biggest drug traffickers in the world and she didn't as much as blink. Instead, she smiled charmingly and said, "Well, that must keep you very busy."

They made small talk for a little bit, and then she moved on to work the crowd. Now she makes her way back to him and says, "Art, we're having a post-party party at the house. Very casual. Won't you come?"

"I'm by myself," Keller answers. "I don't want to be a fifth wheel."

"You'd be a *twenty*-fifth wheel," she says. Her husband comes up and stands at her shoulder, and she turns to him and says, "Martín, we have a poor lonely diplomat here who's resisting my invitation. Make him come."

Martín Tapia looks like anything but a narco. He wears a carefully tailored dark blue suit with a white shirt and tie, and the word that comes to Keller's mind is "polished."

Martín extends his hand. "My wife has invited all the usual suspects, so a little fresh blood would be very welcome."

"Always happy to be a transfusion," Keller says. "Where . . ."

"Cuernavaca," Martín says.

Hello, "Cuernavaca," Keller thinks, remembering the series of phone calls that led to the ambush at Atizapán. "I don't have my car with me."

"I'm sure we can arrange a ride with someone," Martín says.

So Keller hops in a car with a film agent, and rides out to the modern house in a gated community in the hills of Cuernavaca.

The small crowd can only be described as "glittering." Literally, in the case of the actresses in sequined dresses—one of whom he thinks he recognizes from American films—metaphorically in the case of the writers, producers, and financiers. He's been standing around for about ten minutes when Yvette comes over to him.

"Let me see," she says, scanning the room. "Who here is right for you? Not Sofía, she's a wonderful actress but quite insane . . ."

"Maybe not an actress."

"A writer, then," Yvette says. "There's Victoria—stunning, isn't she? She's some sort of financial journalist, but I think she's married, and, anyway, she lives in Juárez . . ."

"You really don't have to play matchmaker for me."

"But I enjoy it so much," Yvette says, "and you wouldn't deprive a staid married lady of her small pleasures, would you?"

"Of course not."

"Come on, then," she says, taking him by the arm, "let me introduce you to Frieda. She writes film criticism and we're all *terrified* of her, but . . ."

Yvette skillfully dumps him off on Frieda, and Keller chats with the film critic as he watches Yvette move from guest to guest, charming everyone.

But she's here to do just that, Keller thinks.

So is her husband.

Martín Tapia is a successful young entrepreneur on the rise, and making high-level connections is his business. Or his brother's, Keller thinks. The Tapias could be Diego's link to Mexico's upper crust. And if they're Diego's, they could very well be Adán's.

It's not much, but it's the only thread Keller has. It's pretty ballsy, though, he has to admit, injecting himself into the Tapia household. I wonder what Adán would think, if he knew I was here.

Maybe he already does.

Keller makes polite conversation with the film critic for a moment and then wanders off and grabs another glass of wine.

"You look as lost as I feel."

The woman beside him is stunning—a heart-shaped face, high cheekbones, dazzling brown eyes, auburn hair that falls to her shoulders, and a figure that Keller can't help but notice under her classic little black dress.

"I don't know how you feel, but, yes, I do feel lost," Keller says. He offers his hand. "I'm Art Keller."

"Marisol Cisneros," she says, shaking his hand. "North American?"

"With the embassy."

"Their Spanish instruction is better than it used to be," Marisol says. "Rosetta Stone—Latin American version?"

"My mother was Mexican," Keller says. "I spoke Spanish before I spoke English."

"Are you a friend of the Tapias?"

"I just met them at the film opening," Keller says.

"I don't know them at all. I came with a friend."

Keller's surprised that he feels a slight pang of disappointment until he hears her say, "I think you met her. Frieda?"

"The terrifying film critic."

"*All* critics are terrifying," Marisol says. "That's why I became a mortician."

"You don't look like—"

"I'm a doctor," she says. "One step removed from a mortician."

Keller sees her blush.

"I'm sorry," she says, laughing at herself. "That was a stupid joke. I think I'm nervous. This is sort of my coming-out party."

"Coming out from . . ."

"My divorce," Marisol says. "It's been six months and I've done that bury-yourself-in-your-work thing. Frieda dragged me to this. I'm not very comfortable with the beautiful people."

But you're beautiful, Keller thinks. "Me neither."

"I can tell." She blushes. "There I go again, being socially awkward. What I meant was . . . I don't know . . . you don't seem . . ."

"The beautiful people type?"

"I meant it as a compliment, believe it or not."

"I'll take it as one." They stand there—awkwardly—and then Keller thinks of, "Do you live in Cuernavaca?"

"No, the city. Condesa. You know it?"

"I live there."

"I moved from Polanco after the divorce," she says. "I like it there. Bookstores. Cafés. You don't feel so . . . pathetic . . . going into those places by yourself."

Keller can't imagine that she's by herself that much. If she is, it's by choice. He says, "I was reading a book the other night while eating—alone—in a Chinese restaurant, and the book talked about a man so lonely that he eats alone in Chinese restaurants."

"So sad!"

"But you're laughing."

"Well, it's funny, too."

"I got up and left," Keller says. "Totally demoralized."

"This past Valentine's Day?" Marisol says. "I sent out for a pizza. Sat in my condo and watched *Sabrina* and cried."

"That's pretty bad."

"Not as bad as your Chinese restaurant."

They look at each other for a second and then Keller says, "I think this is where I ask you for your phone number. So I can . . . call . . ."

"Right." Marisol reaches into her purse.

"I'll remember it," Keller says.

"You will?"

"Yes."

Marisol tells him her number and he repeats it back. Then she says that she'd better collect Frieda and head back to the city—she has clinic hours in the morning. "It was nice to meet you."

"You, too."

As she starts to walk away, Keller asks, "Anne Hathaway or Audrey Hepburn?"

"Oh, Audrey Hepburn. Of course."

Of course, Keller thinks.

Of course.

———

"What do you think of the North American?" Martín Tapia asks as he steps out of the shower later that night.

Yvette sits in front of the mirror, carefully taking off her makeup and checking for wrinkles around the eyes that are as inevitable as they are undesirable. It might be time, she thinks, to check in with her cosmetic surgeon about Botox or a procedure.

"Keller?" she answers. "He's nice enough."

"Don't get fond. Adán wants him dead."

"That's a shame," Yvette says. "He could be useful."

"How?"

"Let me ask you something," Yvette says as she gets into bed. "Do you trust Adán?"

Keller starts with Martín Tapia the next morning.

To all appearances, the middle Tapia brother is a successful young entrepreneur who does what successful young entrepreneurs do.

Most days Martín leaves the house midmorning and drives downtown. He has meetings, he has lunches, he has more meetings. He plays golf at the Lomas Country Club. He goes to banks and corporate offices. Some evenings, usually with his lovely wife on his arm, he's seen in trendy restaurants, at the theater, at the ballet or the opera. On other evenings they just stay home and enjoy a quiet dinner—the pool, the Jacuzzi, the tennis court—and retire early.

On Sundays, he and Yvette go to brunch at the Hotel Aristo with the other smart couples. Their list of friendships, acquaintances, and associates is a Who's Who of the capital. But after a month of surveillance, Keller never sees Martín meet with a policeman or a politician.

Maybe I'm wrong, he thinks. Maybe Martín is clean, not involved in his brothers' business. Or maybe he's taken some of the money and used it to launch himself in legitimate business.

Maybe.

Keller switches his attention to Yvette.

And again, to all appearances, she does what the wife of a successful young entrepreneur would do. She gets up and does yoga or swims laps, she takes tennis lessons from a private coach. She goes out to lunch with other wives, serves on charitable committees.

She plays golf.

Yvette Tapia is a serious golfer, going two or three times a week to the La Vista Country Club.

Keller can't follow her into the club without being stopped at the gate, but he parks across the road. Switching rental cars every day or so, he gets an idea of her schedule—every Monday, Wednesday, and Friday she drives her white Mercedes to the club, plays nine holes, and usually drives home, unless she goes somewhere to have a drink with friends.

Maybe I'm wrong, Keller thinks again.

The next afternoon, Keller doesn't track Yvette from the house but waits on the road outside the club for her to finish. This time she doesn't drive home or to a restaurant, but to a residential street that flanks the golf club.

Keller watches the white Mercedes pull into a driveway.

He notes the address—123 Vista Linda.

Probably a friend, Keller thinks.

He drives past and watches through the rearview mirror as Yvette gets out of the Mercedes, takes a small case from the passenger seat, and walks up to the front door. Then he pulls over on the other side of the street as she lets herself in with a key.

Jesus, he thinks, is Yvette Tapia having an affair?

But there's no other car in the driveway. Maybe, Keller thinks, the guy is cautious enough to park down the street and walk to the assignation. Feeling like a sleazy private detective, Keller shuts off the motor and waits.

If Yvette is having an affair, it lacks passion, because she comes right back out.

Sans suitcase.

Having to choose whether to follow Yvette or stay on the house, he decides on the house.

An hour later, a blue Audi pulls into the driveway and a well-dressed man who looks to be in his midthirties gets out and lets himself into the house. He's only there for a few minutes, then comes out with the small suitcase and drives away.

Keller gives him a few hundred feet, and then follows.

Yvette Tapia isn't having an affair.

She's a bagman.

Keller could use help.

Surveillance isn't a one-man job.

It's hard to follow a car and not lose it or get "made," harder still to follow it through the labyrinth of heavy traffic that is the Mexico City metropolitan area, especially when you're relatively new to the area and don't know its intricacies. At least the Audi isn't trying to lose him—the driver seems confident, complacent, unaware that he might be followed.

That helps, but Keller knows that a successful surveillance operation needs a team—two or three cars to trade off the tail, a helicopter, communications and tech support. He could get any of this—all of this—through SEIDO or AFI, but . . .

. . . he can't.

For one thing, he's not supposed to be doing his own investigation, much less active surveillance. For another thing, he doesn't know whom he can trust.

Vera? Aguilar?

Every time—every time—they came close to Barrera, he slipped away. Then there was the Atizapán ambush. Did one or the other know? Did they both?

Keller could get some support from DEA, but he can't even go there because (a) he isn't supposed to be doing this, (b) they'd want to know why he isn't working with the Mexicans, and (c) he doesn't know whom he can trust.

For all he knows, *this* could be a setup and the blue Audi is leading him into a trap.

I'm bait, Keller thinks.

Now maybe the bait's been set for me.

He thinks of breaking off the tail. He has the license plate and could probably run it through EPIC without drawing too much attention. Find out who the driver is and proceed from there.

It's not a bad plan. Maybe smarter than losing the track now or, worse, getting made.

Or driving into an ambush.

The Audi takes a left.

It's the chance to let it go.

Keller follows.

The whole long way to Lomas de Chapultepec.

The man tosses the car keys to the valet outside the Marriott and goes inside, the suitcase in his hand.

This is where Keller could really use a teammate, someone to go inside. If anyone in that lobby knows him, it's over. But he doesn't have an option, so he hands the valet his keys and some peso notes. "Keep it close."

He walks into the lobby and goes straight to the bar.

His man is sitting in the lounge with the case at his feet.

"A Cucapá, please," Keller says.

He can see his man in the bar mirror. Watches him order a drink, watches as the waiter brings him what looks like a gin and tonic, watches as the man finishes his drink, leaves some bills on the table, and leaves.

The suitcase stays.

Seconds later, another man—in his forties, in a charcoal-colored suit— sits down, looks around briefly, and then picks up the suitcase and walks out.

Keller would give a lot for photographic surveillance.

He quickly pays for his beer, heads for the door, and watches the man get behind the wheel of a white Lexus. It's too late to get his own car and follow, but he does get the license plate.

The next morning, Keller runs both plates through EPIC. The first plate, the blue Audi that picked up the suitcase at 123 Vista Linda, is registered to a Xavier Cordunna, a junior partner in a Mexico City investment banking firm.

The second plate, the white Lexus that picked up the suitcase at the hotel, belongs to a Manuel Arroyo.

A commander in AFI.

Keller punches in Marisol Cisneros's number.

"I was beginning to think that you'd forgotten it," she says when she answers.

There's a little starch in her voice and he hears it—this is not a woman used to being ignored, and she's going to let you know it.

"No," Keller says. "I just didn't want to be pushy. I'm sorry, I'm sort of out of shape in the dating thing. I don't know what the rules are anymore."

"I'll send you the book."

"Seriously?"

"Another nervous joke. Bad habit."

"So," Keller says. "I was thinking if we're going to have dinner alone, we could have it alone together."

"That was very good." Marisol laughs. "Did you practice that?"

"A little."

"I'm flattered."

"So . . . yes?"

"I would love to." Her voice is deep and sincere now—warm—and it sends a little jolt through him.

"Where would you like to go?" Keller asks.

"We could go back to your Chinese place," she says, "and redeem you in front of the waiters."

"It's kind of a dive. Maybe someplace nicer."

They settle on a little Italian place they both know in Condesa, and agree to meet there rather than for him to pick her up. "That way if we don't like each other," Marisol says, "it will be easier for one or both of us to escape."

There's no need to escape. Again, a little to his surprise, the conversation flows easily and he finds that he likes Dr. Marisol Cisneros very much.

Over linguine with clams, served family style, a mozzarella salad, and a bottle of white wine, he learns that she's originally from Valverde, a little town in the Juárez Valley just along the Río Bravo. Her family has been there "forever," at least since the 1830s, anyway, when they were given land to settle in exchange for fighting the Apaches who were always raiding from the north.

The Cisneros clan has still been prominent in the Valverde area—not one of the "Five Families" that still dominate the valley, but more upper middle class than most of the people who live there—planting cotton and wheat down along the river, and running cattle and horses on the drier plateaus.

Marisol always knew she didn't want to be a *ranchero*'s wife, so she studied hard and won a scholarship to the Universidad Nacional Autónoma de México in Mexico City. Then she went to Boston University Medical School and did her residencies at Massachusetts General and Hospital México Americano in Guadalajara, specializing in internal medicine.

She married a contract lawyer from Mexico City, moved back here, and went into practice with three partners in lucrative Polanco, although she volunteers time at a clinic in Iztapalapa.

"Rough neighborhood," Keller says.

"The people look out for me," Marisol says, "and it's only on Saturday mornings. The rest of the week, I take care of rich people's small complaints. But I've been talking and talking. What about you?"

He tells her a little more than he did at the Tapias' party, "confessing" that his job at the embassy is with DEA.

"We know a little bit about drugs in the valley," Marisol says. "The Juárez people have been operating there for years through the Escajeda family."

"Is it a problem for you?"

"Not really," she says. "Over the years, you work out a modus vivendi. You know how it is—you leave them alone, they leave you alone."

"I work mostly on bilateral policy issues," Keller says.

"I like the U.S.," Marisol says. "Let me see, I've been to El Paso, of course, San Antonio, New Orleans, and New York. Lived in Boston. Of these, I liked New Orleans the best."

Why? "I've never been."

"The food. The gardens."

The divorce, she tells Keller, was more her fault than her husband's. He thought he knew what he was marrying, and so did she. In all fairness, he gave her the life she thought she wanted—a two-professional household in a trendy neighborhood, successful friends, dinners out at the best places . . . status.

"He was exactly what I wanted him to be," Marisol says, "and I punished him for it. Anyway, that's what my therapist said. I was a real bitch toward the end—I think he was quite relieved when I moved out.

"I always thought that Valverde wasn't enough for me," Marisol continues. "Then it turned out that it was Mexico City that wasn't enough for me. I was bored and boring—I was just a consumer. I need to . . . I don't know . . . contribute something. So what's your story?"

"The usual cop story," Keller says. "I was married more to my work than to my wife. You've seen it in a dozen movies. It was my fault entirely."

"Well, we're both just guilty bastards, aren't we?"

They finish the linguine.

"Do you want to escape?" Keller asks. "Or would you like dessert?"

"I'd very much like dessert," Marisol says, "but I'd also like to walk this meal off. Perhaps we could go for a stroll and find a place?"

"Sounds great."

Keller pays the check, likes that she doesn't offer to split it, and they walk down to the Pendulo bookstore. He enjoys watching her prowl the aisles, seriously perusing the volumes on the shelves.

She looks good in glasses.

"I love doing this of an evening," she says. "Looking at books, having a coffee. This is a very nice date, Arturo."

"I'm glad."

Marisol picks out a volume of Sor Juana's poems and they sit at a table in the little café and have coffee and *pan dulce*.

"There's a bakery in Valverde," she says. "Best *pan dulce* in the world. Maybe I'll take you there sometime."

"I'd like that."

Afterward, they stroll down Avenida Nuevo León.

"This is what they did in the old days," she explains. "A courting couple would walk on the paseo in the evening. Of course, the watchful *tías* would walk behind—out of earshot but within sight—to make sure that the boy didn't try to steal a kiss."

"Are there any *tías* behind us now?" Keller asks.

She turns around. "No."

Keller bends down and kisses her. He's just about as surprised as she is, and he doesn't know where he found the nerve to do that.

Marisol's lips are soft and full and warm.

Two days later, Keller answers his phone to hear Yvette Tapia say, *"Please tell me that you're free on Sunday."*

"I'm free on Sunday."

"Good," she says. *"And do you like polo?"*

Keller laughs. *Polo?* Seriously? "I've never been asked that before."

"Martín plays," Yvette says, *"and we're getting up a group to go watch and then a little party at our place afterwards. Shall we say Campo Marte at one?"*

We shall, Keller thinks.

But he doesn't know why.

Campo Marte sits on a plateau in Chapultepec. A rectangle of green field with the high-rises of the city looming in the background.

Keller sits with Yvette Tapia in the shell of an amphitheater that makes up the spectators' section. She's resplendent in a white summer dress that shows off her legs and a white bonnet that sets off her jet-black hair.

The rest of the hundred or so spectators are equally well-heeled—the rich, beautiful people of Mexico City—sipping champagne or mimosas, nibbling on hors d'oeuvres served by white-liveried waiters.

"Explain polo to me," Keller says to Yvette.

"To the extent that I understand it myself," she answers. "Martín just took it up about two years ago, but already I think he is quite good, a 'one' handicap, whatever that means."

"Do you own the ponies," Keller asks, "or rent them like bowling shoes?"

"You're making fun of us," Yvette says. "That's all right. It is a bit much, isn't it? But Martín's passionate about it, and a wise wife never denies her husband his passions if she wants to stay his wife for long."

"And a wise husband?" Keller asks.

"*Lo mismo.*"

The same.

"Some husbands buy sports cars," Yvette says, "or planes, or whores for that matter. Martín buys horses, so I'm lucky. The horses are very pretty and we meet some very nice people."

Which is the point, isn't it? Keller thinks. Golf and tennis place you in one social circle, polo takes you into another stratum altogether.

Keller sits back and watches the flow of play, a swirl of color with the riders' bright green or red jerseys, and the horses themselves—varied shades of white and brown and black. He barely understands what's going on—four riders on each side try to knock the ball into the opponents' goal—but it's fast and dramatic.

And dangerous.

The horses bump each other or flat-out collide, and several times—to the gasps of the crowd—it looked like one or both were going down.

Martín does look like a good player, a graceful rider, and aggressive in going after the ball. Keller learns that he's a "number two" on his team, responsible for feeding passes to the leading scorer and also for defense. It's the most "tactical" role on the team, Yvette tells Keller, who's not surprised.

The score is tied 4–4 at the end of two chukkers—halftime.

Yvette stands up. "Come on."

"Where are we going?"

"It's a tradition."

With the rest of the crowd they walk onto the playing field for the "divot-stamping," replacing the sod that the horses' hooves kicked up. Everyone does it to make the field clean and safe for the second half, but also to socialize.

Yvette introduces him.

Keller meets bankers and their wives, diplomats and their wives, he meets Laura Amaro.

Laura and Yvette are good friends.

"Where is your husband today?" Yvette asks.

"Working."

"Poor man."

"The president keeps him busy." She turns to Keller. "My husband, Benjamín, works in the administration."

"Ah."

"I barely see him anymore," Laura says with a pout. "I live at Yvette's house more than I do at mine."

"Can you come to the house after?" Yvette asks.

"There's nothing stopping me," Laura says. "Maybe Benjamín can join us."

"Call him and say that I insist," Yvette says.

"Well, that should scare him."

They walk around, replacing divots and talking. Then Yvette points out a striking woman chatting with a tall, broad-smiling man in an impeccably cut Italian suit.

"Do you recognize the woman?" Yvette asks.

"No."

"The president's wife," Yvette says. "The first lady."

"Do you want to go over?"

Yvette shakes her head. "I'm not there yet. Anyway, there'll be a new first lady soon, won't there? God send her husband is PAN."

Halftime ends and they go back to their seats.

The second half is more intense than the first. The sporting atmosphere becomes more competitive, the play more physical. Once, when it looks like Martín's horse is about to topple, Yvette reaches over and grabs Keller's hand.

She keeps it there for several seconds, squeezes, and then lets go.

The match is a 6–6 tie when Martín bursts his gray horse forward, "hooks" the mallet of the opposing player, and blocks it. Shouldering the other player aside, he takes the ball and drives down the field.

Keller sees the intensity in Yvette's eyes as her husband gallops ahead.

One opponent stands between him and the goal.

Martín raises his mallet over his head, swings it down, and, at the last second, passes to his teammate, who scores the winner.

Laura Amaro's overworked husband doesn't show up at dinner, so Yvette sits Keller next to her at dinner as her "date."

"Benjamín books the president's travel," Laura explains, "so it's a seven-day-a-week job."

"Important, though," Keller says.

"Oh, yes, we're all very important," Laura answers. "Just ask us. Of course he might be out of a job soon."

"Do you really think PRD can win?" Keller asks. PRD is a left-wing coalition that basically replaced PRI as the main opposition party. Its presidential candidate, Manuel López Obrador, was the mayor of Mexico City and had seen a commanding lead in the polls fade against the PAN candidate, Felipe Calderón.

"I think it's going to be close," Laura says. "So does Benjamín. It would be a disaster for the country, though, if we lose. I think your people in Washington share this opinion, don't they?"

"I think so, yes."

Keller also thinks this—the center of the Mexican drug trade isn't in the frontline border cities of Tijuana, Juárez, or Laredo.

Or even in the heartland of Sinaloa.

It's here, in Mexico City.

"You're kissing a cobra," Martín Tapia says as he climbs into bed next to his wife.

"But it's so much fun."

"If Adán knew that Keller was a guest here . . ."

" 'Adán, Adán, Adán,' " Yvette says, " 'Upon what meat does this our Caesar feed that he is grown so great?' "

"Diego is devoted to him."

"I know," Yvette says, turning to her husband, "they were boys together. Diego's problem is that he doesn't see his own worth."

"He's loyal."

"Loyalty should extend both ways."

"Meaning?"

"Adán's getting closer and closer to Nacho Esparza," Yvette says. "First he gives him Tijuana, now he's sniffing around the daughter."

"She's seventeen."

"There's no harm in keeping Keller close," Yvette says. "He might come in handy for us, and if not, he's always worth two million on the hoof, isn't he? Not to mention the Emperor's undying gratitude."

Yvette slides down in the bed.

"Let me show you," she says, "how much fun it is kissing the cobra."

Keller waits outside the Marriott in a rented car.

Arroyo comes out with the case and gets into his Lexus. Up Paseo de la Reforma into Colonia Polanco, then onto Avenida Rubén Dario, flanking Chapultepec Park.

The Lexus pulls over by the park.

A woman walks out, the passenger door opens, and she takes the suitcase. Keller doesn't have to risk following the woman to learn her identity, because he's already had dinner with her.

He watches Laura Amaro walk away.

Jesus Christ, he thinks. Laura hands the money to her husband, Benjamín, who takes it to Los Pinos.

Three weeks later, on election night, Keller and Marisol join thousands of people gathered in the Zócalo to await the results.

The Zócalo is Mexico City's main square, one of the largest in the world. The Palacio Nacional, built on the grounds of Moctezuma's palace, flanks the square to the east, and on the west is the Portal de Mercaderes. The mundane Federal District office buildings are on the southern edge, while the north of the square is dominated by the Metropolitan Cathedral of the Assumption of Mary, the largest church in the Americas, the construction of which began in 1573. It's said that Cortés himself laid the cornerstone. Its twin bell towers made of red *tezontle* stone loom over the Zócalo like sentries.

The square itself is huge and empty, save for the actual *zócalo*, the base for a column that was never built which now supports a flagpole with a giant Mexican flag. It has been a gathering place for centuries, and Keller has learned that the Aztec center of the universe was said to have been just northeast of here, at the old Templo Nacher.

Standing in the Zócalo makes you feel very small; as an American, it makes you feel that your country is very young.

Marisol is a political animal, Keller has discovered, a passionate leftist. She wept during *Pan's Labyrinth*, first from anger at the Spanish Fascists and afterward with pride that such a beautiful film had been made by a Mexican director, Guillermo del Toro.

As the election neared, her conversation became more and more obsessed with politics, to the point where she would apologize, change the subject, and then get back to politics a few minutes later.

Keller didn't mind—he liked her passion, and the truth was that he couldn't help but compare her to Althea, a dyed-in-the-wool liberal for whom Richard Nixon and Ronald Reagan were demonic figures.

"You don't know what poverty is in the U.S.," Marisol said to him one night over dinner at an Argentine place.

"Have you seen the South Bronx?"

"Have you seen the *colonias* of Juárez?" Marisol countered. "Or the rural poverty out in the valley, where I come from? I'm telling you, Arturo, the conflict between right and left is different in Mexico."

So she detests PAN, is wholeheartedly and hopefully PRD, and the night before the election, she asked Keller out for a date.

To watch the results in the Zócalo.

Keller isn't a very political person, more wearily cynical after his experiences with Washington. Marisol knew this, and was very pleased when he agreed to go to the Zócalo, because she knew he was doing it for her.

Now they stand in the enormous public square with a crowd that Keller guesses to be about fifty thousand. The mood is tense, and all day they have heard rumors of voter fraud—ballot boxes stuffed, ballots tossed away, small rural communities threatened with the loss of government benefits if they vote PRD.

Everyone knows it's going to be close, so the air is electric as they wait for the results of a peculiar Mexican procedure known as the *Cuenta Rápida*—the "Quick Count." The election commission takes a sampling of votes from some seven thousand districts when the polls close at 10:00 p.m. If the margin for one candidate is greater than .06 percent, a winner would be predicted; if less, the election would be determined "too close to call" until a complete counting of the votes.

At 11:00 that night, the election commissioner goes on television to announce that the Quick Count showed that the results are "too close to call," but he refuses to give the actual numbers.

"We're being robbed," Marisol says as they make the slow walk through the crowd from the Zócalo. "Everyone knows that the people want the PRD. They're going to cook the books."

"You don't know that," Keller answers, although he's worried. Worried for her, that she'll be hurt and disappointed; worried for himself, that PAN will take the election—fairly or unfairly—and that it will be business as usual for the Tapia money network.

He's in a quandary about what to do with the information he has about the money pipeline going to Los Pinos.

If he tells Aguilar or Vera, he could be instantly expelled from the country.

Worse, he doesn't know if one or both are implicated.

He should take the information to Taylor, let DEA and the rest of the alphabet soup take over the investigation, then deal with its consequences on the highest level.

But who in DEA is going to take on Los Pinos? The issue would be kicked up to Justice, then over to State, and probably die a slow death in the hallways. Because Laura Amaro is right—the current conservative administration in the White House wants PAN to win this election. They'd do nothing to rock that boat and risk the Mexican election going to the left wing.

So the smartest thing to do for the time being is nothing.

Continue the investigation and keep it from his colleagues and superiors until after the election.

Everything depends on the election.

The official count starts three days later.

The election commission collects all the sealed ballot packages from the districts and examines them for signs of alterations. Representatives from the various parties are present and can make objections.

Marisol sits up all night by the television in her condo.

Keller waits with her. They drink coffee and make nervous conversation as the numbers start to come in and López Obrador jumps out to an early lead.

"I told you," Marisol says. "The country wants PRD."

Then the erosion begins. It's like watching a riverbank collapse under a slow flood of water. The lead dwindles and then collapses as results from the northern districts are slow arriving.

"That's me," Marisol says. "That's my home."

When the northern votes finally come in, they're strongly for Calderón.

"I don't believe it," Marisol says. "I know the people there, they're poor and they're not PAN."

Early the next morning, the official result is announced.

Calderón has won by a mere 243,934 votes.

0.58 percent.

A hanging chad, Keller thinks.

Marisol cries.

Then she gets angry.

They take to the streets.

Two days after the official tally, almost three hundred thousand people demonstrate in the Zócalo and listen to PRD speakers talk about voter fraud. A week later, the crowd swells to half a million people who demand that the courts order a recount.

Marisol is one of them.

Keller another.

He goes to protect her, but he also goes because it's just such a spectacle. When was the last time, if ever, that half a million Americans gathered to fight for democracy? He doesn't know if the accusations of voter fraud are right or wrong, but he's impressed—no, *moved*—that they care in those numbers, that it means something to them. He'd watched an American election stolen with barely a whimper.

The ambassador would shit bricks if he knew that Keller was there, Tim Taylor would probably hemorrhage through the nose, but Keller doesn't care. It's an historic moment and he's not going to miss it, and of course he's aware that there's something else.

He might be falling in love.

It seems unlikely at his age and place in life. Marisol is twenty years younger (although she would be the first to say that she has an "old soul") and a loyal citizen of a country he might get tossed out of any day.

They haven't slept together yet—their physical contact has been confined to kisses—but the physical attraction is there. He certainly feels it, and thinks she does as well, from the nature of those kisses and her sighs when they say good night.

But she's a Mexican woman of a certain class, and a Mexican woman of a certain class doesn't go to bed on the first date or the third. He knows that if it happens it won't be casual for her—she's been through the demise of a marriage and now she's going to take her time.

Art Keller is no lovestruck fool, no victim of a midlife crisis. He knows that there are problems, problems he hasn't talked to her about. How do you tell a woman you're reluctant to get involved because it puts her in danger? How do you deliver the melodramatic, surreal news that there's a multimillion-dollar price on your head that someone might try to collect any moment, and that you don't want her to be in range of an errant bullet?

It's surreal, like so much of the narco-world—and yet, like so much of the narco-world, all *too* real.

So Keller knows he shouldn't be seeing her at all.

Her, or anyone else.

But being with her feels too good, too natural, too "right," to employ a cliché from pop music. He likes Marisol, he respects her, he admires her (okay, yes, he lusts after her), he might be falling in love.

And the odds of anyone trying to collect Barrera's bounty are slim right now. In a strange way, the disputed election affords him a level of protection, because Adán is too cautious to rock the boat in the middle of a storm.

Still, Keller knows that his getting involved with anyone is a bad idea.

Two weeks later he joins her at the biggest demonstration yet—a march down Paseo de la Reforma to demand a recount. It's impossible to judge the number of marchers from inside the march—some observers put it at two hundred thousand—but the Mexico City police estimate that almost two and a half million people march that day to demand a fair election.

Two and a half million people, Keller thinks as he walks beside Marisol, who chants along with the crowd. Martin Luther King's March on Washington was about a quarter of a million strong; a protest against the Vietnam War in '69 might have had six hundred thousand.

Despite himself, Keller finds it compelling. *Anyone who says that Mexicans don't care about democracy should be here today*, he thinks, as the marchers file pass the statue to Los Niños Héroes and El Ángel de la Independencia, past the American embassy and the stock exchange.

It's stirring.

"They'll have to give us a recount now!" Marisol shouts happily to him over the chanting. "They'll *have* to!"

The march ends in the Zócalo, but this time people don't leave as thousands of them start a *plantón*, an encampment, refusing to vacate until a recount is announced. Keller is against Marisol staying. "It's dangerous. What if the police try to clear you out? You could get hurt."

"Go home if you don't want to stay," she says.

"It's not that—"

"After all, it's not your country."

It isn't but it is.

Keller has spent more of the past twenty years in Mexico than he has in the United States, and even his time at "home" was consumed with Mexico. He's shed blood here, had friends die here.

He stays.

The first night he spends with Marisol Cisneros is on a sleeping bag in the Zócalo with a thousand other people around them.

Things start to turn ugly the next day as the protestors snarl traffic on Paseo de la Reforma and other major thoroughfares. Fights break out with commuters, police make arrests. Keller urges Marisol not to get involved—she has a practice to protect, patients to see, he urges caution—but she won't quit. She reschedules her regular patients and only leaves the protest to make her clinic hours in Iztapalapa. That afternoon, the judges decide that there is enough doubt as to the legitimacy of the voting to justify a recount in 155 disputed districts. The recount will start in four days and take weeks, at least.

A celebration breaks out in the Zócalo. Guitars play, people hug and kiss, some cry in joy.

"Will you go home now?" Keller asks Marisol.

"Only if you come with me," she says.

———

"I want to take a shower," she says when they get to her condo. "I'm a filthy mess."

Keller waits on a sofa in the small living room. The condo is nice but not elaborate and has the barely lived-in look of the divorced person who spends little time at home. Through the thin walls, he can hear the water running. It finally stops and he thinks that she'll come out, but it takes forever.

It's worth the wait.

Marisol's amber hair hangs over her bare shoulders, above a black negligee that shows tantalizing glimpses of the body underneath. "Shall we go to bed?"

Keller thought that she'd be tentative, he thought they both would be. But their bodies take over and she quickly lets him know that she wants him inside her, and when he is she's surprisingly unladylike.

Later, her head on his shoulder, her hair splayed on his chest, Marisol says, "Well, you worry that the fantasy is going to be better than the actual event, but in this case . . . no."

"You fantasized?" Keller asks.

"You *didn't?*"

"I did."

"I should *hope* so."

A few minutes later Marisol sighs. "It's been a long time."

"Me, too."

"No," she says, "I meant since I've loved someone."

And that's it—*una locura de amor*, that's what they have.

A crazy love.

"I'm looking at some interesting intel photos," Taylor says over the phone, *"of you at a demonstration. Some people aren't happy, Art. They're wondering whose side you're on."*

"I don't give a fuck who's happy," Keller says. "As for sides, I'm on *my* side."

"Same old Keller."

"Don't call me anymore with this bullshit."

He clicks off.

August in Mexico City is wet.

The rains usually come in the afternoon, and many of those afternoons find them in bed together, when her practice and his work allow. They meet at Marisol's and make love as the rain spatters against the bedroom window, then they get up, make coffee, and wait for the shower to pass before venturing out.

The protests against the election continue during the recount. There are marches out to the airport, marches downtown—demonstrations break out in other parts of the country, including Marisol's beloved Juárez.

Keller keeps up his surveillance of the Tapia money machine—it rarely varies as money finds its way to Los Pinos, or at least to its senior staff. And he keeps playing his dangerous game, socializing with the Tapias, provoking a response.

The Zetas don't contact him again, but he figures that they're doing what everyone else is doing—waiting for the election results, which might render their government problem moot.

Mexico is holding its collective breath, and then on August 28, the election commission releases the final count. By the slimmest of margins, virtually identical to the original results, Calderón is declared the winner and PAN retains Los Pinos.

New president, same party.

Marisol is devastated.

"They stole the election," she tells Keller, citing the various allegations of fraud, voter intimidation, miscounts, and no-counts. "They stole it."

The confirmation of the election results is also the confirmation of everything she's feared about her country, that it's hopelessly corrupt, that power will always protect power.

The rain keeps coming down.

Marisol becomes depressed, morose. Keller sees a person he didn't know was in there—quiet, uncommunicative, remote. Her disappointment turns to bitterness, her bitterness to anger, and with no legitimate outlet to turn it on, she turns it on him.

She's sure "his" government is pleased with the results, maybe even complicit. "His" politics are a little further to the right than hers, aren't they? He's a man (Keller pleads guilty), and no man can really be a feminist, can he? Does he have to hang his shirt on the bathroom hook, does he have to read her the headlines from the paper (she can read herself, can't she?), can a North American man really understand a Mexican woman?

"My mother was Mexican," Keller reminds her.

"Do I remind you of your mother?" she asks, deliberately taking the argument sideways.

"Not remotely."

"Because I don't care to be a mommy figure to—"

"Marisol?"

"You interrupted me."

"Fuck off." He takes a breath and then says, "I didn't steal the election, if, in fact, it was stolen—"

"It was."

"—so don't take it out on me."

Marisol knows she's doing it. Knows it but can't seem to stop doing it, and she's not proud of herself for it. She did the same thing to her ex, blamed him for things that he couldn't do anything about—for her own dissatisfaction, her own anger, her rage that life isn't what it should be, when she doesn't even know what it should be.

And Arturo—this beautiful, wonderful, loving man—is just so . . . *North American.* He's not only a North American, he's a North American law enforcement official, a drug cop who does God knows what and now somehow he's come to embody her . . .

. . . anger.

She tries to be reasonable. "What I'm saying is that there are a thousand years of history here that you North Americans don't comprehend and you come here stumbling around in ignorance and—"

"I came down here to—"

"Down here?" she asks. "Do you even hear the paternalism and condescension implied—"

"I meant 'down' as in 'south.'"

"South of the border, down Mexico way."

"Jesus Christ, Mari, stop being such a—"

"Bitch?" she asks. "That's what a woman who stand up for her own opinions is, right?"

Keller walks out of the apartment. He's angry about the election, too, and for reasons he can't tell her.

The continuation of a PAN administration is going to force his hand vis-à-vis the Tapia money tube. He'll have to do something—trust Aguilar or Vera—or finally take it to Taylor, who is going to reasonably ask why he wasn't told sooner.

And pull you out of Mexico, Keller thinks.

And then what?

Do you ask Marisol to come with you? She loves her country, it wouldn't be fair to ask her. So far, she's put up with the secret part of his life. She's smart, she senses that his job is more than "policy liaison," and she doesn't ask where he goes or what he does when he's not with her.

But that can't last; it's no kind of life.

In a different life, he'd ask her to marry him, and he thinks she'd say yes. In a different life, he'd leave the agency and settle in Mexico, find something to do—a job in SEIDO, or a private security firm. Maybe he'd open a bookstore or a café.

But that would be a different life.

You've been at this for coming on two years now and you're no closer to getting Barrera than you were when you started. Adán is more entrenched in power than he ever was.

And it's more than that—the validated election result will free Barrera to come after you.

He'll hunt you down in the States, or Mexico, or wherever you go, and it isn't fair to ask Marisol to endure that.

You don't do that to someone you love.

Keller knows what he should do, and knows that he should do it soon. The holidays will be here soon, and it's cruel to break off a relationship then. It's going to be cruel anyway—on both of them—but he doesn't have a choice.

That night at her place in Condesa, he says, "Marisol, I want to tell you something."

"I want to tell you something, too." She walks him over to the sofa and helps him sit down. Then she gently sits down next to him. "I guess this isn't the best time, but I want to tell you that I've moving."

"Where?"

"Valverde," Marisol says. "I've decided to go home."

She feels useless here, she says, treating rich patients, when there is so much poverty and need back home. She could do something there, mean something to people there, be part of the struggle instead of just making symbolic gestures at protest marches. She can't live like this anymore.

"We can still see each other," she says. "I can come down here, you can come to Juárez . . ."

"Sure."

It's the sort of thing people tell each other when they both know it isn't really going to happen.

"Arturo, please understand," she says. "I feel like I'm living a lie here. That we're living a lie."

Keller gets that.

He knows about living lies.

Adán decides to make peace in the Gulf.

The CDG and their Zeta troops have proved to be a surprisingly tough and resilient enemy, even with Osiel Contreras in jail. There have already been seven hundred killings in Tamaulipas, another five hundred in Michoacán, and the Mexican public is growing tired of the violence.

"Do you think they'd come to the table?" Magda asks. She knows her role—play devil's advocate to let him test his ideas. So she asks, "Why make peace now?"

"Because we can get what we want now," Adán says.

"What about La Familia?" Magda asks. "They've been good allies, and they'll never make peace with the Zetas."

She's heard the story about the murdered young whore and the boy who loved her.

It's almost romantic.

"The Zetas can have Michoacán," Adán answers. "I don't want it."

Magda knows what he does want.

Eddie sits with Diego and Martín Tapia in the back of a Cessna 182 on its way to the meeting with the CDG and Zetas. After long negotiations, the Sinaloans had agreed to meet at a ranch Ochoa owns between Matamoros and Valle Hermosa.

"Let me teach you what my mother taught me," Diego says to him. "If you keep your mouth shut, no one can stick his dick into it."

"Your mom didn't teach you that, Diego," Eddie says.

Diego says, "What I'm telling you is, at this meeting, you keep your fucking mouth shut."

Eddie looks out the window at the sere landscape below. "If you think I'm just going to sit there with the people who tortured my best friend to death—"

"*Sí, m'ijo,* I think you are," Diego says. "Or you take your money, go back *el norte,* and open a Sizzler's or whatever."

"Maybe a Soup Plantation," Eddie mutters.

"Cheer up," Diego says. "Things might go bad and then we can kill everybody."

God knows they have enough firepower to do it. They didn't come light—

four airplanes full of automatic rifles, handguns, grenade launchers, and the people to use them. If this is a trap, they aren't going to be defenseless.

"Remember, I get Forty and Ochoa," Eddie says.

Gordo Contreras—aka Jabba the Boss—he could give a shit about either way, although it was Eddie who started the joke: "What happened when Gordo took over the Gulf?" "The water level rose three feet."

Martín has warned Eddie that if he wants to do jokes, he should find an open mike night at a comedy club, but definitely, definitely not try out his material at the peace table.

The plane lands on a strip on the west side of Ochoa's ranch. Eddie looks out the window to see a dozen jeeps, three of them with machine guns trained on the aircraft, and Forty on full alert.

"Yeah, I can feel the love here," he says.

"If that's you keeping your mouth shut, it's not working," Martín says.

The hacienda has a tiled roof and a broad, covered porch where a long table has been set with carafes of ice water, iced tea, and bottles of beer. Ochoa, looking like a matinee idol from one of those old movies, steps down from the porch and walks toward Adán as he gets out of the jeep.

It's a key moment, Adán knows. Everyone here knows that the whole thing could go south and the guns will come out. He looks Ochoa up and down and then says, "You're as good-looking as they said. If my gate was hinged on the other side, I'd marry you."

A moment of silence, then Ochoa cracks up.

Everyone laughs and then they go up onto the porch.

Gordo Contreras—the little brother who is now the putative head of the CDG—is sitting at the table, not having bothered, Adán notes, to haul his fat ass out of the chair. He's sweating heavily—it's disgusting. All the more so when he leers at Magda.

"I didn't know *segunderas* were invited," Gordo says. "I would have brought mine."

Adán is about to step in when Magda says, "*Partners* were invited, Gordo. Your *segundera* can stay home where he belongs."

The look on Gordo's fat face is priceless—slack-jawed and furious at the same time. He glares at Magda but she looks coolly back at him until he drops his eyes.

Advantage Magda, Adán thinks.

They sit down, Adán and Ochoa at respective ends of the table. Drinks are poured and then Nacho says, "I think we should limit our discussions as to how we move forward. I see no gain in bringing up the past."

"We didn't start this war," Gordo says.

"Your brother tried to have me killed in Puente Grande," Adán says calmly. "I considered that a declaration of war."

"There was a gap of several years before you acted on it," Gordo says, already huffing with effort. He leans over and gulps from a glass of ice water.

Adán shrugs. "I have a long fuse."

"Can we just focus on how to end the war?" Nacho asks.

"Sure," Gordo says. "You withdraw all of your people from Tamaulipas, and if you want to use the Laredo plaza, you pay us tax. And we want what-do-you-call thems . . . reparations."

"You're out of your mind," Magda says.

Adán notices that Ochoa has said nothing. The former soldier is sitting back, letting Gordo go through the preliminary nonsense. As Tío taught me, Adán thinks—*Él que menos habla es el más chingón.*

He who speaks least has the most power.

Speaking of nonsense, Vicente Fuentes weighs in with cocaine-inspired gibberish. "Profit is the blossom of the plant of peace. While we are watering the fields with blood, we should be . . ."

As Vicente goes on, Ochoa looks down the table at Adán, who wonders if he's really seeing what he thinks he's seeing. Ochoa's smile is subtle, almost undetectable, but it's there, and then Ochoa ever so slightly juts his chin at Vicente.

It's a question.

And Adán ever so subtly nods.

Yes.

The real deal of this meeting has been made—Juárez is a legitimate target and the CDG won't interfere. Adán stands up. "We're not going to withdraw from Tamaulipas nor are we going to pay reparations. But here's what we *will* do . . ."

A cease-fire will start immediately, with each side keeping the territories it has taken.

The CDG will keep all of Tamaulipas with the exception of Nuevo Laredo, which will be an open city. In addition, it will retain Coahuila, Veracruz, Tabasco, Campeche, and Quintana Roo.

The Alliance will move product through Laredo without paying a tax. It will retain control of all of its old territories—Sonora, Sinaloa, Durango,

Chihuahua, Nayarit, Jalisco, Ochoa, Guanajuato, Querétaro, and Oaxaca, as well as Acapulco, and it will acquire—as Diego had insisted to Adán—the Monterrey suburb of San Pedro Garza García, the richest municipality in Mexico.

The territories of Nuevo Léon, Federal District, State of Mexico, Aguascalientes, San Luis Potosí, Zacatecas, and Puebla will be neutral.

Gordo struggles to his feet. "Barrera graciously offers to give us what we already have. This is a waste of time."

"Sit down," Ochoa says quietly.

Gordo glares at him.

But he sits down.

An amazingly blunt show of power, Adán thinks. Which Ochoa didn't bother to disguise and so wanted me to see. Gordo Contreras will hold on to power for as long as Ochoa wants him to and not a moment longer. Then Ochoa says, "I'm sure Barrera wasn't finished with his offer and was about to say something about Michoacán."

Ochoa has grown at the game, Adán thinks, but he's still no Osiel Contreras. Osiel would never have brought up Michoacán proactively, tipping off his main concern like that.

"I don't control La Familia," Adán says. "They're loose cannons. But we would become neutral in that conflict."

"Your friends in the government aren't neutral," Ochoa answers.

"If we make peace, our friends will become your friends," Adán says. "At the very least, they won't be your enemies. The government might decide to focus its efforts onto La Familia."

"And what would these 'friendships' cost us?" Gordo asks.

Rudely.

"I don't ask guests to dinner," Adán answers, "and then hand them a bill."

Ochoa takes a moment to look over at Gordo as if to ask, *Do you understand the importance of this? What he's offering is more valuable than territory.* He looks back to Adán and says, "Still, you'll be polite enough to let us pick up the check every now and then?"

Adán nods.

He has to give in on this issue—it's not only a matter of Ochoa's pride, to pay his way, but he knows that the Zeta boss also wants to establish his own relationships with Mexico City.

That's a problem, but he'll work it out.

"At the same time," he says, "if we don't assist a rebellion against you in Michoacán, we wouldn't expect you to help rebels fighting against us in Tijuana."

"Agreed," Ochoa says.

"Are we done?" Adán asks.

"Not quite," Ochoa answers. He looks pointedly at Eddie. "This man has to leave Nuevo Laredo. His presence there is an insult."

Eddie keeps his mouth shut. It's hard because he's thinking, shit, I *took* Laredo for us. Now that we have it, I have to leave? It's hard, because as he looks at Ochoa, he sees Chacho's face, hears him howl in agony, smells his burning skin. What he wants to do is stand up and put a bullet between Movie Star's eyes, but he keeps his mouth shut.

"Agreed," Adán says.

They all get up from the table.

The Gulf War is over.

Adán has created peace among the narcos and divided the country into plazas.

He's become his uncle.

What follows is a bitchin' good party.

Adán and Magda left right away, which made the party even better, because El Patrón is notoriously stuffy about these things. But with Barrera gone, the wraps came off—champagne, weed, coke, hookers—it goes on all night into the next day.

Eddie is particularly taken with Las Panteras—the female contingent of the Zetas. These are some hot *chicas,* who went through the same training that the men did, and came out on the other side *smokin'.* They even have hot names. Eddie gets with the Panteras' leader, Ashley (no, seriously, a Mexican chick named Ashley), who calls herself La Comandante Bombón. "Commander Candy" carries a pink Uzi, which Eddie really digs. She likes to hold on to it while she rides him, threatening, "Let's see which goes off first, you or the Uzi."

Eddie's been with a lot of women, but there's a unique sexual thrill to banging a gash you *know* has canceled some guy's reservation. Like, literally killer pussy. Doing the midnight rodeo with a babe you know would waste you if she got the order adds a little Tabasco to the taco.

Commander Candy . . . shit.

Eddie still plans on killing both Forty and Ochoa, but he has to admit they know how to throw a party.

"Ruiz behaved himself," Nacho says to Adán on the flight back to Sinaloa.

"He did," Adán agrees. "Diego is going to bump him up, give him San Pedro Garza García."

"He'll do well."

"Nacho," Adán says, "I have something I want to ask you."

But he's looking at Magda instead of Nacho.

She arches a curious eyebrow at him, and then he turns back to Nacho. "Now that we have peace with the Gulf, I want to ask you for your daughter's hand in marriage."

Magda forces herself to smile.

Despite his amazing cruelty, to ask for another woman *in front of her*. She knows this is payback for her sleeping with Jorge—or not, as the case may be—and she accepts it as such.

But even Nacho—smooth, unflappable Nacho—is a little taken aback and stammers, "Adán, I'm honored."

"If she'll have me," Adán adds.

"I'm sure she will."

It's time, Adán thinks, to create another family.

"There's one other thing," he says.

"Anything."

"I don't want to hear that now is not the time, it's too politically sensitive, it's risky, *anything*," Adán says to both of them. "As soon as the new president takes office, I want Keller dead."

It's time for that, too.

Past time.

Yvette Tapia invites Keller to their house on inauguration eve for a celebratory dinner party.

"You're happy about the results?" Keller asks when she phones.

"*Of course,*" Yvette says. "*Six more years of PAN means six more years of prosperity, growing the economy, lifting people out of poverty. Genuine democracy.*"

"Even though it was decided by a federal tribunal?"

"*Sort of like your Supreme Court?*" Yvette asks. "*Come to dinner. We can talk about Florida, hanging chads, and voter fraud.*"

He might as well go, continue his dangerous courtship with the Tapias, all the more dangerous now that PAN will retain the presidency. It remains to be seen if Barrera money will continue to flow through the Tapias to the new president, whether either Vera or Aguilar will be retained in their positions or how the change of administrations, if not parties, will affect the drug situation.

The fighting in Tamaulipas, anyway, stopped as abruptly as it started, and there are rumors of a peace meeting between the Alliance and the CDG. It could be true, because Barrera has apparently withdrawn his men from Michoacán and the Zetas have stopped their public complaints about the government being prejudiced against them.

The intel coming out of Nuevo Laredo is that Barrera has use of the city without paying a *piso*. The common wisdom is that he "lost" the war against the CDG and had to "settle" for Laredo, but Keller knows that the common wisdom is bullshit.

Barrera, as usual, got exactly what he wanted.

Laredo.

A plaza.

At the same time, the war in Tijuana seems to be going Barrera's way, and the word is that he'll soon wrest control of the city back from Teo Solorzano, if he hasn't already.

Two down, Keller thinks, one to go.

And me.

Adán will be looking to settle the tab with me now.

At least Marisol is safely away from it.

She's in Valverde now, bought a house, opened her clinic. He helped her pack and move out of the Condesa place. They were both very civilized about it, and made mutual pro forma promises to visit when she got settled.

Which they haven't done yet.

Keller misses her.

They talk on the phone, but the calls are short and awkward, and he can tell she's very busy with her work.

It's good, he thinks, as he drives out to Cuernavaca.

It's the right thing.

The dinner at the Tapias' is large, loud, and celebratory, a gathering of the new rich Mexican entrepreneurial class—stockbrokers, hedge fund managers, film producers, with a few actors, singers, and artists tossed in to give the evening tone.

Laura Amaro is there, and this time, even her husband has found the time to attend.

"He's out of a job," Laura declares happily. "Unemployed."

Benjamín shrugs.

"But not to worry," Laura says. "He's been promised something even more likely to keep him away from home."

"Laura . . ."

"It's a victory for business," Martín says quickly, lifting a glass of champagne to the new president, "a victory for stability, growth, and prosperity."

"Even for the poor?" Keller asks, because he can't help himself.

"*Especially* for the poor," Martín says. "Seventy-five years of socialism did what for them? Nothing. In the past six years, we've started to create a middle class. In the next six, that middle class will solidify and expand. We'll be looking for cheap labor on *your* side of the border."

"We could use the jobs," Keller says.

After dessert and coffee, Yvette says, "Let's walk down to the pool."

"Where's Martín?"

"Did you notice that handsome young actor?" Yvette asks.

"Yes."

"So did Martín."

"Oh."

"We have an arrangement," Yvette says. "We're not as provincial about these things as you are up in the barbarian north. Martín does what—or whom—he wishes, and I do the same."

"Yvette—"

"Relax," she says. "This is not that kind of seduction."

They reach the pool, she sits down at the edge, takes off her shoes, and dangles her feet in the water. The pool shines blue and beautiful under the filtered lights. Sitting beside her, Keller asks, "What kind of seduction *is* it?"

"First of all," Yvette says, "could we drop the pretense? We know who you are, you know who we are. The dance has been amusing, but at some point the masquerade ends and we reveal our faces."

"All right."

Good, Keller thinks. Let's get on with it.

"We could be your friends," Yvette says. "Influential friends who could provide you with important information. That *is* your currency, isn't it? You'll note, please, that I haven't insulted you with an offer of money."

"How do you know I'd be insulted?"

"You're much too Catholic," she answers. "You couldn't live with the guilt. No, you'd have to be convinced it was for the greater good."

"Would it be?"

"You know what's out there," Yvette says. "Perhaps we're not the greater good, but we are the lesser of evils."

If I were as much a Catholic as you say I am, Keller thinks, you'd know I believe that evil is an absolute, without gradations. But he asks, "What would you want in return?"

"Friendship," she says. "We would never ask you to betray a colleague, reveal a source, anything like that. We would come to you only when our interests align. Perhaps just to be an 'ear,' someone to represent a point of view in Washington . . ."

"Whose point of view?" Keller asks. "Yours? Martín's? Diego's? Adán Barrera's?"

It's inconceivable to him that this is Barrera reaching out, probing for peace. There's too much blood between them. But the Tapias are Adán's creatures, his functionaries, his ambassadors to the outside world.

Or are they?

"Martín and I are truly partners," Yvette says. "We share everything. Diego? Diego is a dear sweet man and I love him like a brother, but he's a dinosaur. Diego still thinks that this is a culture, a way of life, he still thinks it's about the drugs."

"What is it about?"

"Money," Yvette answers. "Finance. Power. Connections. I'm speaking for myself and Martín."

"And Adán?"

"If we were representing Adán's point of view," Yvette says, "your head would be in a box of dry ice by now, on its way to Sinaloa, and we'd be two million dollars richer. But two million dollars is small change, no offense."

Is this a rift between the Tapias and Barrera? Keller wonders. Big enough for me to walk through? To get the evidence I need about Vera or Aguilar? Or Los Pinos? Big enough to bring Barrera down?

Yeah, Keller thinks, this is a different kind of seduction.

"You understand," he says, "that if we become 'friends,' that friendship cannot ever include Adán."

"Actually, I'm counting on it." She puts her hand out. "It's a complicated world. In a complicated world, everyone needs friends."

Keller takes her hand. "Friends."

Yvette gets up. "We should wander back. My husband's sodomies are passionate but short-lived."

———

The next morning, Felipe Calderón takes office.

On the same day, he appoints Gerardo Vera as commander of all federal police forces in Mexico.

Benjamín Amaro is appointed as Vera's liaison to Los Pinos.

Luis Aguilar is retained as head of SEIDO.

Twelve days later, the new president launches Operation Michoacán and sends four thousand army troops and a hundred AFI agents into the violence-torn state, his wife's native country, to suppress La Familia.

Three weeks later Operation Baja California sends thirty-three hundred troops into Tijuana.

Three weeks after *that*, Osiel Contreras is extradited to the United States.

It's the beginning of Mexico's war on drugs.

PART THREE

Good Night, Juárez

This isn't a city, it's a cemetery.
— Peggy Cummins as Laurie Starr
in *Gun Crazy*

1

Gente Nueva—The New People

And he that sat upon the throne said, "Behold, I make all things new."

—Revelation 21:5

Mexico City
May 2007

The *trajinera*, named *María*, is brightly decorated, its high arch painted in blue, red, and yellow, its gondola-like bow strewn with fresh spring flowers.

Keller and Yvette sit in the prow, out of hearing from the oarsman who steers the boat through the canal flanked by *ahuejote* trees. The narrow canals are all that remain of the once large lake of Xochimilco, where the Aztecs grew crops in the *chinampas,* floating gardens.

For the past five months, Keller and Yvette Tapia have had secret assignations. They'd meet in the Zócalo, in the museum at Chapultepec Castle, in the Palacio de Bellas Artes by the Orozco murals. Each time he went, Keller wondered if this was the time that she was setting him up, and each time he came back safely he was a little surprised.

Twice she warned him of an impending attack—*That Italian restaurant you like, don't go there. Take a different route home tonight.* It was risky. Adán was getting impatient, she told Keller, frustrated at the failed attempts, beginning to get suspicious.

Risky for Keller, too. Every meeting with Yvette increased the chance that Aguilar or Vera would find out what he was doing. At the very least, they'd expatriate him; at worst, if either or both were dirty, it would kill any chance of getting Barrera.

Then there was the sheer physical danger and the stress of being a hunted man again. He found his life becoming more and more constrained, limited, his world getting smaller as he went from his apartment to his office to the occasional rendezvous with Yvette or meetings in the SEIDO building or at AFI.

Before Marisol he was never lonely, in fact he reveled in his solitude. After she first left, they spoke over the phone every few days. She had set up her clinic—the only full-time doctor for twenty thousand people in the valley—and was happily busy. They talked about getting together—she coming to Mexico City for a weekend, he going to Valverde—but something always came up for her, and he didn't feel right about exposing her to the risk of being with him.

The phone calls started to fade to once a week, then once every ten days, and then once a month or so.

And he was getting nowhere on Barrera.

Just hanging in, hovering, hoping for a break.

Yvette was giving him bits of information that he knew had been approved and sanitized by Martín. Mostly "soft" intel—Diego was getting more involved in the Monterrey area, Eddie Ruiz's star was rising, Nacho had acquired yet another new mistress. The "hard" intel she gave him was mostly about Solorzano—safe houses, drug shipments, which cops he owned, which border—in the hope that he would pass it on to DEA.

She also bitched about Diego. Even Martín Tapia was getting fed up with his brother's antics. Diego comes to stay at the Cuernavaca house for weeks at a time, and the well-heeled neighbors have started to complain about the loud music, the strange men coming in and out at all hours of the night and day, the clouds of *yerba* smoke rising above the walls, the apparent squadron of hookers who arrive in the evening and depart in the morning.

Alberto was even worse, with his bejeweled pistols and *norteño* clothes, flashing his money around jewelry stores, nightclubs, restaurants, and discos. There have been *incidents*—fights in bars, shootings, alleged rapes—all of which cost money and favors to straighten out. And there are rumors of Alberto's involvement in kidnapping—the sons of wealthy businessmen—which, if it continues, *can't* be straightened out. The big money establishment won't tolerate that for long.

So Yvette gave up tidbits of family gossip, useful in its own way, but no hard information.

He knew that she was playing a cute double game—giving him enough to keep him interested but nothing that could hurt the Tapias or even Barrera. Just keep him on the hook in case things went sick and wrong with Adán and they needed an ally with a voice in Washington.

Keller played the same game with her. He fed her tidbits from DEA intelligence—similar information about Solorzano, gossip about their Zeta allies, general analysis of trends in U.S. drug policy.

"What about the Mérida Initiative?" she asked one time. "Is it going to pass?"

The Mérida Initiative was a proposed $1.4 billion U.S. aid package to Mexico to fight drug trafficking—cash, equipment, and training.

"I don't know," Keller answered. "It's controversial."

"Because of corruption?"

"That's part of it."

Even the questions they asked each other were risky, because each tried to discern the reason for the question, which in itself could provide information. Why were the Tapias interested in Mérida? Why did Keller want to know where Adán bought his clothes? Where was Magda Beltrán? Why did Keller want to know?

Now Keller is getting tired of the game. The string has to run out. Aguilar or Vera will find out about it, or Adán will, and then it will be over, and he has to make it pay off before that happens. So today, as the boat floats slowly along the green water of the canal, he presses. "Give me something I can actually use."

Yvette wears a long white dress today, and the effect is fetching and a little anachronistic, as if they were in a Monet painting of people on a Sunday along the Seine.

"All right," she says. "Adán is getting married."

"Really."

"To Nacho Esparza's daughter," she says, an edge in her voice.

The marriage will bring Adán closer to Esparza, Keller thinks. Are the Tapias concerned about it? Wondering if they're losing influence, that Adán is pulling away from them?

"The girl is just eighteen," Yvette sniffs. "A beauty queen, of course."

"Adán has a type."

"Apparently."

He keeps his tone casual as he asks, "When's the wedding?"

Yvette says, "We've been told to save three days—July first, second, or third."

"Where?"

"No one knows."

"You're lying." She has to know—Diego is doubtless in charge of security, and Keller tells her so.

"He hasn't told us," Yvette insists. "He just says that we'll be informed of the location the day before."

It's classic Adán, Keller thinks, a heady mixture of paranoia and arrogance.

He'll take every precaution, but his ego tells him—probably accurately—that's he's untouchable.

Even if an agency wanted to stage a raid on the wedding, it couldn't organize an assault on that scale inside twenty-four hours. Diego will have the site protected by rings of security, including local and state cops. Anyone who wants to get near that wedding without an invitation is going to have to shoot his way in, and even that's doubtful.

But God, the guest list.

It's a royal wedding—the Barreras joining with the Esparzas in a dynastic marriage. Adán knows that he has to go full bore, invite every major narco that he's not actively at war with, make a show of wealth and confidence.

And the invited know that they have to go, lest they offend the royal couple. A raid on the wedding could net almost the entire Most Wanted list, in Mexico and the United States.

It's a pipe dream, Keller thinks.

But even pipe dreams have their uses.

Keller does an analysis of orders from the scores of floral shops in Sinaloa and Durango. Every florist shows a vast increase in orders for July first, second, and third. Barrera has ordered flowers from all over the Golden Triangle.

The same situation exists for caterers. Every major caterer in the general area has been engaged.

So Barrera is going to throw himself a huge party, Keller thinks, with every major narco in the country, and there is nothing we can do about it.

Keller calls for a meeting of the committee.

"If I could get you a location with twenty-four hours' notice," Keller asks, "will you go in?"

"Yes," Vera answers.

"No," Aguilar says. "There would be no time for proper planning, we would be walking into a hornet's nest, never mind the possibility—no, the *probability*—of civilian casualties."

Vera says, "With a select force of my men—"

"You'd be risking a bloodbath," Aguilar says. "I mean, my God, do you really want images of a massacre *at a wedding* all over the television news? The public wouldn't stand for it, and I wouldn't blame them. Think about it. An errant bullet strikes a *bride*? It's not worth the risk."

"To get Barrera?" Keller asks.

"To get *anyone*," Aguilar says. "We do not defeat the narcos by becoming them, and by the way, not even the narcos have attacked a wedding."

"Who knew you were so sentimental?" Vera asks.

"I am not sentimental, I am correct," Aguilar sniffs. "A wedding is a holy sacrament."

"A demonic one in this case," Vera says.

"What crime has Eva Esparza been convicted or even accused of?" Aguilar asks.

"Oh, here we go again," says Vera.

"Yes, here we go again," Aguilar says. "There are right ways of doing things and wrong ways of doing things, and I am going to persist in insisting that we do things the right way."

"Then we're going to lose," Vera says. He turns to Keller. "*How* could you get us the location on twenty-four hours' notice?"

"Cell phone traffic," Keller says. "They'll have to let people know, and if we pick up a surge from a certain area, it might be indicative."

"So you don't have a source," Aguilar says.

"How would I have a source?"

"A good question," Aguilar says, "because I would hate to think that you're violating our working agreement."

"He could violate my sister if it would get us Barrera," Vera says.

"That's very nice," Aguilar says. "Thank you."

"So what should I tell Washington?" Keller asks. "That you *don't* want to take this shot at Barrera?"

"Well, there's a shot across the bow," Vera says. "Did someone say, 'Mérida Initiative'?"

Aguilar asks, "What does Washington know about this?"

"Nothing from me," Keller says, "but I'm sure EPIC has picked up soundings. And if you want satellite runs, I have to tell them something."

"Tell them," Aguilar says, "that it's an internal Mexican matter."

"It's not an internal matter if they're sending us a billion-plus dollars in weaponry, aircraft, and surveillance technology," Vera says. "If we're allies, we're allies."

"*If* we were to move against Barrera in this situation," Aguilar says— "and again, I remain opposed—we would have to get clearance from the very highest levels."

Which is as good as killing it, Keller thinks.

But instructive.

"Top secret" consultations take place involving the Mexican attorney general's office, the interior secretary, and a representative from Los Pinos, as well as the DEA chief and the American Justice Department.

The decision comes back down—SEIDO and DEA should make every effort to locate the time and place of Barrera's wedding, but it should be considered strictly an "intelligence opportunity" and not an "operational mandate."

Barrera's right, Keller thinks.

He's untouchable.

Keller has long believed that you have to be lucky to be good, but not good to be lucky.

But sometimes luck just rolls your way.

It's nothing you did, nothing you didn't do, and it can come from the most unexpected places.

Now luck rolls the other way.

From the unlikeliest of sources.

Sal Barrera is clubbing at Bali.

Not as cool as clubbing *in* Bali, but it is the coolest disco in Zapopan, and he and his buddies were ushered into the VIP section because they're *buchones*—Sal is Adán Barrera's nephew, of course, César is the son of Nacho Esparza's latest mistress, and Edgar's father is a big shot in Esparza's organization.

So they sit in the raised center of the club, which is decorated in Indonesian style, and scope out the talent around them.

"A little sparse tonight," César says. He's a good-looking dude—slim, with wavy black hair, and well dressed in a black Perry Ellis shirt over custom jeans.

"It only takes one," Sal answers, scanning the lower level where the plebes are. Sal is dressed to score, too—silk batik shirt, white jeans, Bruno Magli loafers. He's there to get his knob polished, at the very least. Figures he needs the release, because Nacho's been working him like a burro.

Adán was as good as his word—Sal finished his degree, and then went to his uncle.

"You've done everything that I've asked," Adán said.

"I gave you my word," Sal said.

"Don't think I haven't noticed," Adán said. "So I want you to serve as an apprentice to Nacho Esparza for one year. As such, you'll be present at important meetings and privy to the family's business. If that goes well, as I expect it will, I'll bring you in as my second in command here in Sinaloa. Be a sponge, soak up everything that Nacho has to teach you."

Sal blushed with the unexpected news. *"Sí, patrón."*

" 'Tío,' " Adán corrected. "I'm your uncle."

"Sí, Tío."

"To get you started," Adán said, "I'm giving you five kilos of cocaine. Market it through Nacho. He'll help you make a good profit and set yourself up in business. "

"Thank you, *Tío.*"

"Sobrino," Adán said, "the days ahead are going to be interesting . . . and dangerous . . . I'm going to rely increasingly on family. Do you understand? On *family.*"

"I'm honored, Tío Adán."

"Well, don't be *too* honored," Adán said, "until you see what it entails."

It's been a revelation to Sal how boring the drug business is. Yeah, there's the women, the money, the parties, the clubs, but at the heart of it are numbers.

Endless columns of numbers.

And not just the money coming in, but the money going out, which Nacho keeps a sharp eye on. The price of precursor chemicals, shipping costs, dock handling charges, equipment, transportation, labor, security . . . it goes on and on.

Sal spends most of his time double-checking figures that some worker bee has already checked, but when he objects to the redundancy of this "busy work," Nacho tells him that he's learning the business, and the business is numbers.

Then there are the meetings.

Holy fuck, the *meetings.*

Everyone has to sit down, everyone has to be given coffee or a beer, everyone has to be fed. Then everyone has to talk about their families, their kids, their kids' kids, their prostate problems . . . then they finally get to the tedious details. They want a lower *piso,* they want someone to pay them a higher *piso,* so-and-so is overpaying the truck drivers and fucking up the market for everyone else, some chemist in Apatzingán is fucking with the meth recipe . . .

It goes on and on until Sal wants to swallow his gun.

At least he has that.

At least Nacho lets him carry and feel like a narco instead of an accountant, and Sal has a Beretta 8000 Cougar tucked into the waistband of his jeans.

All the *buchones* carry—a piece on the hip is as mandatory an accessory as the gold chains around your neck. You just aren't a *buchón* without the *pistola*. You might as well not have a dick.

He scans the crowd and then sees this babe sitting at a table, sipping on some fruity drink.

She's with two guys.

No *problem*—the guys look like jerks, cheaply dressed, no style at all. And neither of them is Salvador Barrera.

"I'm going in," he says to César.

"She's with somebody."

"She's with nobodies," Sal answers. He pours a glass of champagne from the complimentary bar, descends to the floor, and walks up to the girl's table.

"I thought you might like a *good* drink," he says. "Cristal."

"I'm good," she says.

"I'm Sal."

"Brooke."

"What a nice name," Sal says, ignoring the two guys sitting there like crash test dummies. They look annoyed, a little bewildered, a little scared. They're both Mexicans, they know what's what. "Where are you from, Brooke?"

"L.A.," she says. "Well, Pasadena. *South* Pasadena."

She's pretty. Blue eyes, honey hair, turned-up nose, nice rack under a white blouse.

"What brings you to Mexico?" Sal asks. "Spring break?"

She shakes her head. "I'm a student at UAG."

Universidad Autónoma de Guadalajara, right here in Zapopan.

"A student. What do you study?"

"Pre-med."

Now *she's* looking a little nervous, like this guy is hitting on her, right in front of her friends, so Sal moves to close the deal. "How would you like to come up to the VIP section? It's better."

"I'm with friends," she says. "We're celebrating David's birthday."

"*Feliz Navidad*, David," Sal says to the jerk she points out. "Listen, you all three can come. It's cool."

They look at each other, like, what do you think? But Sal sees that David isn't having it. Jesus, is this plebe tapping that? Unbelievable. But she's looking at David, and he just slightly shakes his head, so Brooke looks up at Sal and says, "Thanks, but . . . you know . . . we're just having a little birthday party here. But thanks."

It pisses Sal off. "Well, how about a little later? I mean, *after* you shake these losers."

David makes a mistake.

He gets up. "The lady said no."

"Is that what the lady said?" Sal asks. "What are you, a tough guy?"

"No." His voice shakes a little, but he stands there in Sal's face. "Why don't you leave us alone and go back to the VIP section?"

"You going to tell me what to do now?" Sal asks.

"Please," Brooke says.

Sal smiles at her. "You know, you must be a *dumb* cunt, you can't get into pre-med in the States. It's okay, I'll still fuck you until you scream my name and come on my dick."

David shoves him.

Sal takes a swing and then bouncers are there, squeezing between them, and César and Edgar pull him back.

"*Big* mistake, birthday boy," Sal says to David.

Edgar's big and he gets his arms under Sal's and hauls him away, toward the door. "Come on, 'mano. This *chiflada* isn't worth it."

They wrangle him out the door. On the sidewalk, Sal says, "This isn't over."

"Yes it is," Edgar says. "Nacho—"

"Fuck Nacho." They get into Sal's red BMW, but Sal won't leave. "We *wait*."

"Come on, man," César says.

"You want to go, go."

"You're my ride."

So they sit and wait, and instead of Sal cooling off, he gets hotter and hotter. By closing time, 4:00 a.m., he is seething.

"Here they come," Edgar says.

Brooke, David, and her other friend come out of the club, walk into the parking lot, and get into an old Ford pickup truck.

"He's a *farmer*," Sal sneers.

"You'd better get over there, you're going to mess him up," Edgar says.

"Fuck that." Sal starts the car and follows the truck. It pulls onto the highway and Sal hits the gas, coming right up on the truck's bumper. The truck speeds up but the truck isn't going to outrun a BMW.

Sal laughs. "Now this is fun!"

He pulls up alongside the truck.

They're doing about eighty now.

"Let's fuck them up," Sal says.

"Come on, *'mano*," César answers. "It's enough. Let it go now."

"Can't let it go," Sal answers. "You think we can let people disrespect us in public like that?! Let it get around that we did nothing, and we're *pajearses*, jerkoffs."

He pulls his Beretta out and rolls the windows down. "You with me? Or are you pussies?"

They take out their guns.

"Duck," Sal says to César.

Then he opens up.

So do César and Edgar.

They put twenty shots into the truck before it rolls over into the ditch.

David and Brooke are both dead.

The other friend, Pascal, is badly hurt, but still alive.

He IDs the three shooters to a Jalisco state cop smart enough to know what he has and honest enough to know what he should do. The detective phones SEIDO and holds until Luis Aguilar himself comes on the line.

"We have Salvador Barrera in custody," he tells Aguilar.

"On what?" Aguilar asks, assuming it's a drug charge.

It's not.

"A double homicide," the Jalisco cop says.

Sal Barrera has that *me vale madre* attitude, but Keller can see that he's scared.

For good reason.

The Jalisco police have witnesses to the fight, and the third victim can identify the shooters. Sal dropped the gun out of the car but it has his prints and matches eight of the shots. And the paraffin test came up positive.

Sal's fucked.

Aguilar and Keller got on a SEIDO plane right away and flew to Guadalajara. Now Keller watches through the glass as Aguilar interviews Sal.

"I want my lawyer," Sal says.

"A lawyer is the last thing you want," Aguilar answers. He reviews all the evidence against him. "You killed a rich blond girl from California, Salvador. You're not going to walk away from that, I don't care who your uncle is. Let me help you."

"How can you help me?"

"We can make a deal for lesser charges," Aguilar says. "Maybe you do ten years instead of twenty. You're still a young man when you get out."

"What do I have to do?"

"Give us your uncle," Aguilar says.

Sal shakes his head.

"He's getting married, isn't he?" Aguilar asks. "To Eva Esparza. We can pick him up when he leaves the wedding. No one ever needs to know it was you."

"He'll know. He'll kill me."

Aguilar leans across the table. "He'll kill you anyway. You've put him in a very difficult position. If he even *suspects* that you might roll over, he might be tempted to . . . eliminate that possibility. We can't protect you forever. I can, however, get you extradited to the United States."

Sal asks, "You think my uncle couldn't have me killed in the States?"

"Then help me get him," Aguilar presses. "Save your life."

Sal shakes his head again and stares at the floor.

"Think about it. But don't take too long." Aguilar gets up and comes into the observation room. "So?"

"I think he's Raúl's son," Keller says. "He stonewalls."

"Do you really believe that Barrera would have him killed?" Aguilar asks. "Just on the chance that he *might* talk?"

"Don't you?" Keller asks.

Nacho stands in Adán's study, looking chagrined.

"You were supposed to be looking out for him!" Adán yells. "Teaching him!"

"I was. He was doing well."

"You call this 'well'?!" Adán yells. He takes a moment to collect himself, and then asks, "What can he give them?"

"A lot," Nacho answers. "You said to bring him into the business, educate him. I did."

"Shit."

"And he knows *this* place, Adán," Nacho says. "He could bring them right here. You'll have to go on the run again."

"May I remind you that I'm marrying your daughter in a week?" Adán asks. The phone rings and Adán checks the caller ID. "God damn it."

He hesitates, but picks it up.

Sondra is sobbing. *"Don't kill him, Adán! He's my son! I'm begging you, don't kill him!"*

"No one's talking about anything like that, Sondra."

"Is it true? Did he do it?"

"It looks like it."

She starts sobbing again. *"How could he? He's a good boy. I don't understand!"*

I do, Adán thinks. He's arrogant and young and thinks the world belongs to him, including any woman he wants. His father was the same way. And some of this is my fault. I should have known better. I should never have brought him into the business. "Sondra? That's his lawyer on the other line. I'd better go."

"Please, Adán. Please. Don't hurt him. Help him. Anything, I'll do anything. You can have all the money back, the house . . ."

"I'll call you," Adán says, "when I know something."

He clicks off and looks at Nacho. "I'm open to ideas."

Nacho has one.

Aguilar's phone rings. He listens for a moment, clicks off, and asks Keller, "Do you know an American lawyer named Tompkins?"

" 'Minimum Ben'?"

Keller hasn't been to San Diego in years.

He grew up here, in Barrio Logan, until he worked up the nerve one day to march into his estranged father's office downtown and demand money to go to college. He went off to UCLA, where he met Althea, and then it was Vietnam and CIA, and then DEA—Sinaloa and then Guadalajara—before he came back to San Diego as the "Border Lord," running the Southwest Task Force from his office downtown.

It's strange to be back.

He, Aguilar, and Vera flew to Tijuana, crossed on the pedestrian bridge at San Ysidro, where Minimum Ben is waiting for them.

Keller knows Ben Tompkins well, from the old Border Lord days, when they played sheepdog and the coyote together on dozens of drug cases. Now he sits in Tompkins's Mercedes—the two Mexicans in the back, Keller in the front passenger seat—because they don't want to be seen and no one is going to admit that this meeting ever happened.

Tompkins starts in full Minimum Ben mode. "First thing is, Salvador Barrera gets a pass."

"Call us when you sober up," Keller says, opening the car door.

Tompkins leans across him and closes it. "Dome light?"

"If Salvador can give us Adán Barrera," Aguilar says, "I would agree to a plea agreement under which Salvador would serve no more than ten years."

"You're asking Adán to exchange his life for Salvador's?" Tompkins asks.

"I'm not *asking* for anything," Aguilar answers. "I'm perfectly happy to prosecute Salvador for a double homicide and put him away for life. *You* called *me*. If you don't have anything serious to offer, I'd like to get dinner."

"What I'm about to say never leaves this car," Tompkins says. "And if you start a CI file, *I'm* the informant."

"Go on," Keller says.

"I can't give you Adán—"

"See you, Ben."

"But I can give you the Tapia brothers."

Shit, Keller thinks. It's a genius move, a classic Adán manipulation. He gave up Garza to get himself out of an American prison, now he'll give up the Tapias to get his nephew out of a Mexican one.

Tompkins starts selling. "If you look at the actual numbers, the Tapias—not Adán Barrera—are the biggest drug dealers in Mexico. That being the case, you'd be negligent in not accepting this arrangement. You're not trading down, you're trading *up*."

"We are talking about the senseless, brutal murders," Aguilar insists, "of two innocent young people."

"I understand that," Tompkins says calmly. "On the other hand, how many have the Tapias murdered? More than two."

Keller notices that Vera has uncharacteristically said nothing.

"We need to confer," Aguilar says.

"Absolutely," Tompkins answers. "Take your time, I'll just be getting some coffee."

He gets out of the car and crosses the street to the Don Félix Café and takes a booth by the window.

Keller feels a thrill shoot through his body.

Because he sees it now, sees it as clearly as he's ever seen anything—the breach in Barrera's stone wall.

Adán's move to throw the Tapias under the bus is brilliant and ruthless. There *is* a rift between him and the Tapias, as Yvette feared, and he wants to take them down. Then his nephew kills two innocent people, gets caught, and Adán sees the opportunity to solve two problems in one stroke.

Classic Adán.

Usually he sees the whole chessboard, several moves in advance, but this time he doesn't realize that he's put himself in checkmate.

Neither does Aguilar or Vera—that if they are working for either Barrera or the Tapias, or both, they're about to put themselves into exposed, vulnerable positions, knights moved forward too quickly.

And Adán's carefully built protective structure—his castle—will come tumbling down.

After the castle comes the king.

But Keller pretends to put up a fight, plays the role they expect of him. "You're going to allow Adán Barrera to manipulate your entire legal system and let his nephew walk for killing two people?"

"But you *would* let him walk in exchange for Adán," Aguilar says. "We have to face facts. Salvador is not going to give up his uncle, but Tompkins didn't come with empty hands. It's a very serious offer—capturing the Tapias would be a major blow that would disrupt trafficking to the States for months at least and take tons of drugs off your streets."

"Why would Adán turn on his oldest friend?" Keller asks, although he knows the answer.

"Because Salvador is family," Vera says. "His dead brother's son. He has three choices—swap places with him, kill him, or free him. What would you do?"

"But why the Tapias?"

"What else does he have to offer?" Vera asks. "Nacho Esparza is going to be his father-in-law. He can't go there. The Tapias are his only choice."

"We have two young people here," Keller says, "slaughtered for nothing. We have two grieving families. What are we supposed to tell them? That we have a better deal, and they just need to understand?"

Aguilar says, "Diego and Alberto Tapia are murderers many times over."

"You sound like Tompkins now."

"Even a North American defense lawyer is right sometimes," Aguilar says. "Like a broken clock, twice a day. I say that we should accept his offer."

So if you are *sucio*—dirty—Keller thinks, it's on Barrera's side.

"If I get a vote," Keller says, "it's no. Check that, it's *hell* no."

They look at Vera.

"Gentlemen," he says, "we deal in the art of the possible. Removing the Tapias takes out a full third of the Sinaloa cartel, and, most importantly, Barrera's armed wing. I would think that DEA would be delighted. I'm sorry, Arturo, but I agree that we should seize this opportunity with both hands."

If you were on the Tapia payroll, Keller thinks, now you've flipped.

And now you're fucked.

"This is wrong," he says.

"But you'll support it?" Aguilar asks.

Keller knows what he's concerned about. One of the victims is an American citizen. If Keller leaked this deal, there'd be an uproar in the States, one that could potentially kill the fragile Mérida Initiative.

They need him to sign off.

Keller is silent for a few seconds and then says, "I won't sabotage it."

Feeding them a line and feeding them line—the hook is set so let them run with it. I'll jerk the hook when it's good and set.

Three hours later Salvador Barrera and his buddies walk out of jail.

Free.

The parents of David Ortega and Brooke Lauren are told that law enforcement is doing everything in its power to find their children's killers.

Sinaloa
July 2, 2007

Eva wears white.

A spring bride, virginal.

Lovely and traditional, she wears a mantilla veil with the white dress and a bolero jacket entwined with white baby rosebuds. Chele Tapia, as the *madrina*, sewed the three ribbons onto the bride's lingerie—yellow for food, blue for money, and red for passion.

Adán hopes that there will be passion despite the difference in their ages.

Chele had tried to talk him into the bolero garb, but he'd picked up a few pounds lately and his vanity made him reject the tight pants. Instead, he wears a guayabera shirt of the *presidencial* style, with embroidered designs on the front and back, over loose drawstring trousers and sandals—traditional garb for a rural groom.

Now he stands and waits for his bride.

Eddie thinks Eva looks hotter than shit and wouldn't mind getting himself a little of that. He half thinks about asking Esparza if he has any other daughters, but the wedding day of Adán Barrera is no time to fuck around, and Esparza takes the virginity of his daughters very seriously.

Adán is going to pop a cherry tonight.

Anyway, the wedding is a target-rich environment, more Sinaloa Tens than you can shake a dick at, at least half of them beauty queens, former or current Miss Whatevers—Miss Guava, Miss Papaya, Miss Methamphetamine . . .

If you can't get laid at this wedding, Eddie thinks, you are a dickless gnome. That or you got no money—these babes are wearing more gold around their wrists and necks than old Cortés ever found in Mexico, that's for sure.

There's a lot of cash at this bash.

Anybody who's anybody in the narco-world is here, and Eddie knows that his presence signals a big leap in status.

Nacho is here, of course, with the wife who produced the lovely Eva. Diego is here with his wife, Chele (showing a lot of tit, a definite MILF), his brother Alberto and his hot wife, and his brother Martín and *his* hot wife, an iceberg that Eddie wouldn't mind crashing into.

Adán's family is here, or what's left of them.

Eddie thinks he recognizes Adán's sister, Elena—Elena la Reina—the former *patrona* of Tijuana. Then there's the nephew, Sal, a real hard-on, and his mom, who looks like she's been sucking on lemons. Then you got some second-tier narcos, Eddie thinks, like me, and then there are the politicians.

The head of PAN in the state.

A PAN senator.

The mayor of the local town.

At the wedding of the most wanted man in Mexico, a man the U.S. and Mexican governments swear that they just can't find. It's funny, Eddie thinks—these guys are afraid to be seen at Adán Barrera's wedding, but more afraid *not* to be seen.

And of course, the whole village is ringed with Diego's guys, and Eddie's. State cops patrol the roads in and out, and helicopters hover overhead, only moving away so the rotors don't wash out the actual exchange of vows.

There would be even more security, Eddie knows, except that we're relatively at peace, only at war now against the Tijuana boys, who aren't about to come down here to take a shot at Adán under these circumstances.

Peace is good, Eddie thinks, even if it meant playing kissy-face with those Zeta cocksuckers. But for the time being, it's nice not to have your head on a swivel, although it takes a little getting used to. Nice not to have to worry about a bullet or a grenade, or ending up *guiso'd*.

And nice to be making money again.

Nice to be sitting next to a hot woman, a genuine Sinaloa Ten, even if he's here as Adán's beard.

Magda Beltrán thinks that Eva Esparza looks pretty, too.

The tight-twatted little bitch.

That's not fair, Magda thinks. I'm sure she's a perfectly nice, sweet little girl, and, in all honesty, exactly what Adán needs at this moment. But still, a woman can't help but feel a *little* jealous.

Clever move, she has to admit, Adán bringing Nacho into the family. Peace breaks out and the king settles down to the business of getting a queen and cranking out some princes.

Your basic fairy-tale ending.

Real Walt Disney.

All we need are cartoon birds singing.

Then again, Adán always gets what he wants. He wanted Nuevo Laredo and he got Nuevo Laredo. Now he has a secure port through which to ship the cocaine she arranged for him—independent of Diego or his new father-in-law—and free of the burdensome *piso*, which he can now charge others.

And slowly, quietly, with Magda's help, Adán has been recruiting his own force, independent of both Nacho's and Diego's. The Gente Nueva—the "New People"—mostly former and current federal police—owe their allegiance only to Adán.

So he has his own cocaine supply and his own armed force.

He has Laredo, and Nacho is gaining ground in Tijuana, now connected to Adán again by family.

"How's your little virgin?" Magda asked Adán the last time she saw him, to go over some cost and pricing issues.

"She's my fiancée now."

"But still a virgin?" Magda asked. "Yes? No? Never mind—a gentleman doesn't tell. But you know Nacho will be watching for bloodstained sheets to be draped out the window."

Adán ignored the jibe. "My marriage doesn't need to change anything between you and me."

"Does your little virgin know this?" Magda asked.

"Her name is Eva."

"I know her name." After a while, she asked, "Do you love her?"

"She'll be the mother of my children."

"Mexican women." Magda sighed. "We're either virgins, madonnas, or whores. There are no other choices."

"Mistress?" Adán suggested. "Business partner? Friend? Adviser? Choose any. My preference is you choose all."

"Maybe," Magda said. His business partner she certainly is. As for the rest, she's not sure. She is sure that she wants to extract more of a price. "I want to be invited to the wedding."

It was fun to see Adán taken aback, if only for a moment.

"You don't think that would be awkward?" he asked.

"Not if you find me an acceptable escort."

So now Magda sits with this handsome young North American, who is very sweet and attentive but has a wandering eye for every attractive woman at the wedding, of whom there are many. She's not offended—he assumes that, as Adán's woman, she's out of bounds. It would serve Adán right if she slept with him. Maybe she will, but probably not. Magda can't help teasing him a little. "I've heard you have a nickname."

Crazy Eddie.

"I don't like it." She finds it funny that he pouts.

"Based on your wardrobe," Magda says, "I hear they call you 'Narco Polo.'"

Eddie laughs. "Well, I like *that*."

Diego Tapia has been a busy man.

Security for the wedding has been brutal.

First there was the problem of the multiple dates and locations. Just yesterday, Diego's people reached out from a network of cell phones all over the country, to call the guests and tell them the real location.

Then and only then did Diego distribute his *sicarios,* in concentric circles around the village, with special attention given to the roads in and out. He stationed more men at the local airstrips to meet the many guests who were coming in on private planes and take them to the wedding site.

All cell phones and cameras had to be politely but firmly collected, and each guest just as politely and firmly informed that they must not, under any circumstances, talk about the wedding afterward, not even to the extent of mentioning that they were present.

Adán is firm about this—he wants no pictures, no videos, no recordings, and no gossip afterward. The guest list alone would be a treasure trove for DEA and other enemies.

Arriving cars are searched far outside the village. Snipers are hidden in the hills above the village, with more heavily armed men standing by in vehicles that block roads at all compass points.

Nobody is going to go in—or out—of the village without Diego's knowledge and permission.

Not that they're expecting trouble now that there's peace with the Gulf. The only possible threat is from La Familia, which is deeply angered at Adán's abandonment of them. But they're too busy fighting off the army and the *federales*, and besides, not even Nazario is crazy enough to attack Adán Barrera's wedding ceremony in the heart of Sinaloa.

La Familia's *jefe* may be insane—he's not suicidal.

Now, watching Nacho walk Eva down the aisle, Diego is unsettled. Nacho got Tijuana. Now he's going to be Adán's father-in-law? It's like a screen door shutting in Diego's face. He can still see through it, but from the outside.

I shouldn't worry, he tells himself. I'm Adán's cousin, more like his brother. We've been friends since before our balls dropped. And Nacho is also my friend and my ally. We have interests together. Nothing has really changed.

Then why do you feel that it has?

"I'd like you to be in charge of our relationship with Ochoa," Adán said to Diego after the peace meeting with the CDG. "Make him your friend."

"Now you're pushing it."

"And meet with our friends in Mexico City," Adán said. "Make sure they know that the CDG is under our protection now, in Michoacán as well as Tamaulipas."

"I'll do it," Martín said.

"I want Diego there," Adán said, "so they'll know that there would be *consequences* for any betrayals."

Martín was the glove, Diego the fist inside.

"We'll both go," Diego said.

The meeting with the government assholes in Mexico City was funny. The suits just sat there while Martín Tapia carefully explained to them what the new world was going to look like.

"By all means," Martín said, "continue your campaign in Michoacán. La Familia is a dangerous threat to public safety—lunatics really—not to mention the largest purveyors of methamphetamine in the country."

"What about the Zetas?"

"They're under our protection now."

Amazing, Diego thought. The *federales* had been giving La Familia a pass and beating the Zetas like rented mules, but now they didn't even blink when they were told that they were going to switch sides.

But that's the way it is in this business.

Enemies one moment, friends the next.

Unfortunately, it also works the other way around.

Now Chele reads her husband's mind. "Don't worry. They chose *us* as their *padrinos*."

The *padrinos* are a married couple who mentor the newlyweds from the engagement throughout their entire marriage. It's an honor, Diego knows, in his case more symbolic than practical, because Adán has certainly not asked for marital advice.

Eva, on the other hand, has come to Chele to ask certain questions that Chele won't reveal and Diego can only guess at. He would have thought that modern girls didn't have these questions anymore, but from Chele's sly smiles, he guesses that Eva did.

"I just told her how to keep her man happy," Chele told him.

"And how is that?"

"Later, *marido*."

Chele didn't share it with the girl, but the sad truth is that Eva doesn't need to keep Adán happy in the bedroom—his spectacular mistress will see to that—she only needs to keep him happy in the delivery room.

Eva has to produce a son who will join the Barrera and Esparza organizations—rendering, however unintentionally, the Tapias outsiders. If Chele had a daughter of marriageable age, she would have shamelessly walked her to Adán's bed and tucked her in. But her daughter is too young, and anyway, inheriting more of her father's genes, unlikely to be as beautiful as the splendid young Eva.

Now Chele looks at Eva coming down the aisle between the rows of white chairs.

Nacho looks every bit the proud papa in his own black bolero jacket and tight-fitting pants as he walks her down the aisle, conscious of and gratified by the stares of envy both for his daughter's beauty and his good fortune.

Fortune my ass, Chele thinks—Nacho has been grooming the girl for this since she slid out between her mother's thighs.

It breaks Adán's heart.

Turning on his old friend.

On the other hand, he has reason to believe that Diego Tapia has turned on him. Not with law enforcement, true, but with the Zetas.

It's your own fault, Adán tells himself as he waits for his bride. You practically shoved Diego and Ochoa into bed together, made them meet, asked Diego to become the Zetas' "friend."

Well, he did that, all right. Adán's informants have it that Diego has been steadily shifting his operation into Monterrey, basing himself in the tony neighborhood of Garza García, and that he's welcoming the Zetas into the city.

Where they're selling drugs, setting up an extortion racket and a kidnapping operation.

Stupid, Adán thinks, to go for chump change that could interfere with the real money pipeline from the U.S. by alienating police, politicians, and the powerful industrialists in Monterrey who, at the end of the day, control them.

Stupid and shortsighted.

Almost as bad is their ostentatious behavior, displaying their wealth and power like *chúntaros*—hillbillies—instead of the billionaire businessmen that they are.

Adán was saddened to hear that his old friend is dipping into his own product, that, like Tío back in the bad old days, he has started snorting coke. If it's true, it's bad news, and certainly Diego's recent behavior supports the suspicion. Diego's been throwing huge, loud parties, and in the wrong places—Cuernavaca, Mexico City, where they can't escape the notice of the powers-that-be.

When will we ever learn? Adán wonders.

The cops, the politicians might be on our payroll; the financiers, bankers, and businessmen may be our partners in legitimate businesses; they might look the other way on our other activities—but you *can't rub their noses in it.*

Stupid and self-indulgent, Adán thinks. You can't be doing those things in a neighborhood like that. We have everything. Everything that money can buy. We can do whatever we want—only be subtle about it.

There are worse rumors about Diego, rumors that Adán doesn't want to believe. That he's started to follow Santa Muerte, the so-called Saint of Death, a cult that's sweeping the mostly younger narco ranks with blood sacrifices and God only knows what else.

Foolishness.

When he was young, Adán made a blood oath with Santo Jesús Malverde, the local Sinaloan drug trafficking martyr who became something of a religious figure with his own shrine in Culiacán.

Adán blushes at the memory of his youthful foolishness.

But Diego is no kid. He's a grown man with a wife and kids and adult responsibilities. He's the boss of the largest drug trafficking organization in Mexico and he's messing around with this foolishness?

Ridiculous.

And dangerous.

But not as dangerous as him flirting with an alliance with the Zetas.

Adán gets it—Diego feels threatened by Nacho's rise. You gave him Tijuana to take, you're marrying his daughter.

Adán thought of reaching out to make things right with Diego. Sit down and talk like the old friends they are, and work it out. Apologize for any seeming slights or neglect. But now it's too late.

Diego is the price for stupid, idiotic, undisciplined Salvador's life. And it's for the best, Adán decides. The Tapias have to go. Face it, you were going to have to do it anyway, and Sal's issues are a convenient pretext.

It's all set up and ready to go.

Simultaneous raids against Alberto and Diego in Badiraguato, take them both out in one swoop.

Martín they'll leave alone, for now.

He has too many connections—another stupid mistake of yours, Adán thinks, to let the Tapias gain so much political influence—and you can deal with him. He'll be reasonable.

As long as there are no deaths.

Adán has insisted that both Alberto and Diego must, at all costs, be taken alive. They are his friends, his brothers, blood of his Sinaloan blood.

The altar has been built under a bower of ficus trees. The chairs are set up on an emerald-green lawn clipped again that morning and lined with stacks of fresh flowers.

Adán stands by the priest. He smiles at Eva as Nacho releases her, kisses her on the cheek, and ushers her to the altar.

Opening a small wooden box, Adán pours thirteen gold coins—one each for Christ and the twelve apostles—into Eva's outstretched, cupped hands. Then he places the box on top of her hands. The coins signify his pledge to take care of her and her promise to run his household conscientiously.

They turn to the priest, who drapes the *lazo*—a long, decorated cord—around each of their shoulders, symbolizing that they are now attached to each other. They wear the *lazo* throughout the long ceremony, which includes a Mass, then the wedding vows, and finally the priest declares them man and wife.

Eva kneels at the little shrine that had been built to the Virgin of Guadalupe and makes the *ofrenda,* leaving a bouquet of flowers.

Then the bride and groom walk back up the aisle and the wedding party and guests follow them back to where the reception party will be held and the mariachi band—decked out in their finest costumes of black and silver—falls in behind, playing the *estudiantina* music.

Salvador Barrera has kept a low profile throughout the wedding.

After the unfortunate incident in Zapopan, Adán called him back to Sinaloa and put him on double secret probation.

"If you were not my blood," Adán said when he sat Sal down in his office, "you would be dead."

"I know."

"No," Adán said, his face tightening. "You will never know—and I mean you will *never* know—what your freedom has cost me."

"Thank you, *Tío.* I'm so sorry." Then he had to sit and let Adán lecture him for twenty minutes about respecting women and innocent people. This from the same man who's invited his whore to his own wedding? Who had a woman's head cut off and sent to her husband like a muffin basket? The guy that once threw two little kids off a bridge? I mean, come on. This guy's going to lecture me on family values?

But now Sal knows that he's being watched.

Eventually, he hopes, his uncle will forgive him and bring him back into the business.

Eva swoops in, takes Adán's hand, and pulls him toward the center of the reception area, a clearing in the middle of the dining and banquet tables.

It's time to *lanzar el ramo,* toss the bouquet.

As is traditional, the wedding guests form not a circle but a heart shape around the bride and groom. All the eligible women gather, and Eva tosses her bouquet back over her shoulder. It hits Magda right in the hands, but she squeals and bats it back up in the air, where it's caught by one of Eva's bridesmaids.

Then a chair is brought out, Eva sits down, and Adán—backed up by Diego, Nacho, and Salvador—kneels in front of her and, to ribald remarks from the guests, slides her dress up her thigh and pulls her garter back down her leg.

It feels odd, running his hand up her smooth skin, because heretofore they have done little more than kiss, and this feels oddly intimate. Then Adán stands up, throws the garter over his shoulder, and turns to see Salvador catch it.

Then the men swoop in, pick Adán up, and begin to throw him around and dance with him to the funeral music ("Your life is over!") that the band strikes up. When this stops, Salvador and the bridesmaid dance together, then Adán and Eva, then the entire party joins in the dancing. As they dance, married couples come up to the bride and groom, chat a little, and pin envelopes onto Eva's dress, money that will later be given to charity, as Adán Barrera and the daughter of Nacho Esparza hardly need money to start their married life. Eventually the dance turns into *la víbora de la mar*—"the sea snake"—the guests joining hands and "snaking" under Adán and Eva's outstretched arms as they stand on chairs.

Magda finds Adán alone in a bedroom, changing clothes to leave for his honeymoon.

"How convenient," she says.

"How so?"

"Well," Magda says, kneeling in front of him, "we wouldn't want you to disappoint your new bride, letting that tight virgin *chocha* make you come too quickly. The poor thing expecting a night of breathless passion and youthful endurance."

"Magda . . ."

"Don't be so selfish," Magda says as she unzips him. "I'm only thinking of her."

"You're very considerate."

"Besides," Magda says, "when she's all fat, splotchy, and bitchy, you'll remember that you have *this* to come to. Just don't get anything on my dress, do you hear, there are appearances to keep up."

Magda brings him to the point of climax and then stops.

"On second thought," she says, getting up, "disappoint her."

"Magda!"

"Oh, come here. Do you think I'd really leave you like this?"

She finishes him, then feels melancholy.

It could have been me, Magda thinks. It might have been nice, maybe, settling into a life of domesticity with him, allowing myself a few extra pounds around the hips and watching my babies scuttle around at my feet.

Be happy with what you have, she tells herself.

It wasn't that long ago you were thrilled with a blanket.

And now you're rich, and soon you'll be richer, independent of any man, including Adán. You can have other men, and fuck him when he comes around, and have your own house and make your own money.

You're a *narca*, a *chingona*.

Your own woman.

Magda knows that they're already calling Adán's bride "Queen Eva I." The more culturally aware have dubbed her "Evita" (Don't cry for me, Sinaloa). She also knows what they're calling *her*.

La Reina Amante.

The Queen Mistress.

There are worse things.

The meal was fantastic—chicken and pork dishes, potatoes and rice, *tres leches* and almond cakes, champagne, wine, and beer—and now the wedding party gathers to see the bride and groom off on their honeymoon.

Diego comes up to Eddie. "We'll be leaving soon."

"You headed back to Monterrey?"

"No," Diego says, "we're going to spend the night in the Badiraguato house. Come over if you want."

"I'm going to stay for *la tona borda*," Eddie says. "Too much pussy here to bail out now when they're all drunk."

He's had his eye on one of the bridesmaids, and then there's La Reina Amante. Christ, sitting next to her . . .

"Be careful what and who you do," Diego says. "You're in the country now. These old hillbillies will shoot your ass. And *not* El Patrón's woman, either."

"He just got married, for Chrissakes."

"Don't be stupid," Diego warns him.

Adán and Eva come out and walk to the helicopter waiting to take them to their honeymoon at an undisclosed location. They walk through the line of guests, shaking hands and kissing cheeks.

Adán comes up to Diego.

"Thank you, *primo*," Adán says, kissing him on the cheek. "Thank you for everything."

"You're welcome, *primo*."

It makes Diego feel better.

That Adán appreciates him.

They honeymoon at a house Adán owns in Cabo.

Adán had thought about Europe, but there are Interpol warrants in almost every country.

Mexico is his prison.

That's all right; everything he wants is here.

When they arrive at the house overlooking the Pacific, Eva excuses herself and goes into the bathroom. She comes out half an hour later in a blue negligee that sets off her eyes.

It's far more revealing than he thought it would be. Her hair hangs long and loose over her bare shoulders. Lovely, she presents herself to him but looks down at the polished parquet floor.

Adán walks over and lifts her chin.

"I want to make you happy," Eva says.

"You will," Adán says. "You do."

They're both shy in bed; she from youth, he from age. He spends a long time touching her, stroking her, kissing her cheeks, her neck, her breasts, her stomach. Her eighteen-year-old body responds easily despite her nerves, and when he feels she's ready he takes her, silently thanking Magda for her earlier ministrations as Eva bucks upward beneath him. Her energy can't trump Magda's experience, but he's grateful for it.

She's springtime to his autumn.

This is some weird shit, Eddie thinks as he watches Diego kneel in front of the statue of a skeleton in a purple robe, with human hair braided into her skull. She holds a globe in one hand and a scythe in the other.

Santa Muerte.

The Saint of Death.

The lady has a lot of names: La Flaquita—"the Skinny One"; La Niña Blanca—"the White Girl"; La Dama Poderosa—"the Powerful Lady." She sure as shit looks powerful now, Eddie thinks as Diego rubs goat blood (Jesus, Eddie *hopes* it's goat's blood) onto the statue's face.

They're in a back room of Diego's safe house in Badiraguato, and Eddie has just come back from the after-wedding party. He's fucked out, sleepy, but hungry as he watches Diego take a deep drag on a blunt and then blow the smoke into the Skinny Lady's face. He's already placed gifts at the little altar he had built in the house, like he has in all his houses now—candy, cigarettes, flowers, fresh fruit, incense, a fifth of single-malt scotch, cocaine, and cash.

This skinny bitch, Eddie thinks, makes out better than Diego's actual *segunderas*.

Now Diego lights a gold candle.

"For wealth," Diego explains.

Yeah, well, *that's* working, anyway, Eddie thinks. Diego has more money than God. The rumor is that he has more money than Adán Barrera, which can't make AB happy. And Diego's picked up a new *aporto* in certain circles—El Jefe de Jefes—the Boss of Bosses, which won't sit well in La Tuna either.

Diego lights another candle.

Black.

Like you buy at Party City for Halloween, Eddie thinks.

If you're a dweeb.

But he listens as Diego places the black candle on the altar and prays to Santa Muerte for revenge against his enemies and to protect his drug shipments. Maybe he should get more than one candle, Eddie thinks. He's hoping they're done, but Diego picks up a white candle.

"Protection," he says.

"Yeah, great."

Diego could use some protection, because he looks like pounded shit. El Jefe's doing blow, no question about it. Diego mumbles another prayer, then gets up and they walk into the living room.

"Adán called earlier," Diego says.

"What for?"

"Let me know he got into Cabo all right."

This gets Eddie's radar going. Barrera's usually all business, not your "shoot the shit" kind of guy. He's one of those geeks, when he calls you, you think he's reading from a four-by-six file card with an agenda on it.

He don't like that AB supposedly gets on the horn to chat like some housewife with a half hour to kill before her yoga class. And he don't like that Diego Tapia, who used to be so freaking sharp, seems indifferent and bored.

Diego used to have all the answers. Now he don't even know the questions. La Dama Poderosa, my ass.

"Hey, Diego?" Eddie says. "Let's get out of here."

"What for?"

"I dunno, man," Eddie says. "Get some air, some grub. I could use me some breakfast burrito action."

"It's two in the morning."

"So?"

"I'm not hungry."

"I am," Eddie says. "Come on."

Alberto Tapia is coming home from his *segundara*'s condo. Thought he'd use the occasion of the wedding to hook up.

His Navigator is full.

A driver and two other security guys. You want security when you're driving around at two in the morning carrying two suitcases with $950,000 in U.S. cash, and another case with a hundred grand worth of luxury watches.

Alberto likes his Rolexes and Pateks.

Maybe that's why he has an AK-47 across his lap. Wouldn't think you'd need it in Badiraguato, which is Sinaloa cartel country, but paranoia is not such a bad thing in his business. He also has his diamond-encrusted .45 holstered on his hip, the jewels spelling out the legend "Live Free" in Spanish. He's a little sleepy, though, after a long hard night of fucking. So he has his eyes closed and his head leaned back when the shit happens.

Four SUVs roar in from all directions and block the road. Alberto wakes up and flips his AK to full automatic, then hears, *"Federal police! Come out of the vehicle with your hands on your head!"*

Federales rousting him in *Sinaloa*? This has to be some sort of joke, or this *bola de idiotas pendejos* didn't get the word, and Alberto starts to get out of the car to tell them so when one of the security guys says, "What if they're Solorzano's people?"

Because it's possible, it's been done before—shooters dressed in AFI uniforms. Alberto sees a lot of rifle barrels sticking out at him from those cars, and then he hears, *"Come out now!"*

Rolling down the window, Alberto resorts to a line usually associated with Hollywood starlets who can't get a lunch table: "Do you know who I am?!"

"Step out of the vehicle!"

"I'm Alberto Tapia!" Like, you know how much food I put on your tables?

"We're not going to warn you again!"

Yeah, and I'm not going to warn *you* again. "You'd better talk to your boss and ask him—"

The bullet takes him squarely in the forehead.

A barrage quickly follows, after which all that remain intact in the Navigator are two suitcases full of cash and a case of expensive watches.

Still ticking.

Eddie watches the cars race up to the safe house.

AFI troopers jump out and move toward the house in military formation, rifles to their shoulders. He's seen this on TV, when they took Contreras down in Matamoros.

Diego is staring, wide-eyed for a nice change.

"Madre mía," he says.

No shit, your mama, Eddie thinks. He tosses his burrito wrapper in the trash can and says, "We'd better get out of here."

He walks Diego away from the sidewalk café. Luckily, the *federales* are focused on this house. Eddie hears them shout, *"Diego Tapia! You're surrounded! Come out with your hands on your head!"*

Eddie's a block away when Diego says, "You see? La Niña Blanca protected me."

Yeah, Eddie thinks.

It was that white candle.

No question.

Adán waits by the phone.

When it finally rings, he wishes it hadn't.

Alberto and three of his men are dead. Adán's furious—he had specifically ordered there was to be no killing, and now Alberto's dead? Diego's *brother* is dead?

He waits for the next call.

It comes quickly.

If the first call was a disaster, the second is catastrophic.

The *federales* missed Diego. They raided four safe houses and didn't find him. How could those *fugeda* idiots miss him? And now Diego Tapia is out there—grieving, outraged, and most likely insane for revenge.

Which he *will* get.

Adán goes into damage control.

"We have to find him," he tells Nacho over the phone.

Even Nacho sounds shaken up. "He's in the wind, Adán."

"Find him."

As it turns out, they don't have to find Diego. He phones Adán. *Alberto's dead. Those bastards turned on us. They killed Alberto.*

He's weeping.

"Diego, where are you?"

"They killed Alberto."

"We have to get you somewhere safe," Adán says. "Tell me where you are. I'll send people."

It's a terrible risk, Adán thinks. Diego has people, more than enough people to move him, hide him, protect him, and if he were thinking clearly, he'd know that I know that and be suspicious of the offer.

"I want them dead," Diego says. *"All of them. Dead."*

"Where are you?"

"I'm safe, primo. But I want to die."

"Don't do anything crazy, Diego."

"I want them dead."

Diego clicks off.

Keller gets a phone call at his desk from Aguilar. *"It's a mess. Totally botched. Gerardo is beside himself."*

It's a debacle, Aguilar goes on. Alberto Tapia is dead, Diego and Martín in the wind . . . The botched arrests are a shame . . . justice for two families tossed away . . . it's sickening . . .

It's working, Keller thinks as he clicks off.

This "debacle" is a keg of dynamite with a short fuse, sitting under Adán, the Tapias, the Mexican law enforcement establishment, even Los Pinos. All it requires is a match to set it off, and it will blow up the whole system that Adán has carefully built.

Keller walks outside the building and uses his own phone to contact Yvette Tapia. "I'm calling as a friend. There's something you need to know."

He lights the match.

"Adán Barrera flipped on your family," he says.

"Adán doesn't have a brother," Diego whines.

Dude is in bad shape, Eddie thinks—coked up, hasn't slept since he put his baby brother in the dirt. They're back in Monterrey, which is relatively safe, and the topic is revenge. Diego wants payback for Alberto's death, but the problem is . . . well, as stated.

Alberto's funeral was *ridiculous,* a display of hypocrisy that would have made a Louisiana televangelist blush. Adán and Queen Eva I showed up, hugged Diego, and gave the widow a fat envelope, and Diego hugged him back, pretending that he didn't know.

That sleazy cocksucker Nacho was there, too, looking all sad and grim and sympathetic, as if he hadn't put Barrera up to it.

All the top narcos came to pay respect, even though, truth be told, no one really liked Alberto all that much. He was a pint-sized pain in the ass—a mouthy, showy, yapping little shit like one of those mini-dogs that women like to bring to restaurants these days to aggravate everybody.

The only good thing about Alberto is his wife—his widow now—she of the hydraulically engineered rack.

She doesn't know, Eddie thought as he watched her accept Adán's condolences and cash. No stripper is that good an actress. The family hadn't told her that the man handing her the envelope sold her husband out.

At least Barrera didn't stick the envelope into her panties.

The Tapias will take care of her, Eddie knows that. They're not going to let her go back to the pole. Kind of a shame, though, because that is something that Eddie would truly like to see.

Not as much as he'd like to see Yvette Tapia out of that black dress she wore to the funeral. He bets she has a black bra and panties under that, and it's *hot.* And he knows just looking at her that the husband standing there beside her isn't delivering the goods on a regular basis.

Come to a cowboy, darlin'. Let me take you out of the gate. I'll stay on a lot longer than eight seconds, I'll tell you what.

Even the Zetas—who hated Alberto—showed up, and they're here now, helping Diego figure out how to go up against the Evil Empire. It's tricky, because Barrera has federal cops in his pocket, and politicians. They used to be in everyone's pockets—one big, happy family—but that's over now.

Martín says, "Before we can move directly on Adán, the ground has to be prepared. We have to get rid of certain powerful enemies in the police."

"Won't that alert Adán to the threat?" Ochoa asks.

They're allies now, Eddie thinks. The old quid for the quo is in—the Tapias have allowed the Zetas to take refuge in Monterrey; in return, the Zetas have agreed to join in a war against Barrera.

It's just the start, Eddie thinks. All the cartels will realign, and the relationships with the cops and the pols will shift. The deck is going to be reshuffled, and who knows where the aces and kings—the cops and the politicians—are going to end up? Right now they sure seem to be in Barrera's hand.

Eddie notices how Martín has taken over the meeting. Diego is still the chief in name, but it's Martín who's laying out the strategy.

Martín and Ochoa.

"We'll frame it as revenge for Alberto's killing," Martín says. "Let Adán think we believe that it was the police who betrayed us. By the time he figures it out, we'll have eliminated some of his key allies and be ready to move directly on him."

Yeah, Eddie thinks. Easy to say, harder to do. These aren't some local city cops, these are high-powered federal police with their own security details, men who didn't get where they are by being stupid or careless.

But we don't have a choice, Eddie knows. The feds took a swing at Diego and missed, so they'll have to try again. We have to get to them before they can, but it's going to take real planning—surveillance of their schedules, habits, security.

A war is a lot of work.

And Eddie has a feeling that from now on there's going to be nothing but war.

Roberto Bravo, the director of intelligence for AFI, parks his SUV outside his Mexico City home. Tomorrow is a day off, he's going to Puerto Vallarta, so he's let his bodyguard go. As he gets out of his car, a man steps up and shoots him twice in the head.

Less than twenty-four hours later the administrative director of the Federal Preventative Police, José Aristeo, chats with a woman neighbor on the sidewalk in front of his home in the exclusive Coyoacán neighborhood. Two men approach and try to drag Aristeo away from the woman into his car. When he fights back, they shoot him in the neck and chest.

At 2:30 the next morning, Reynaldo Galvén is coming home to his house in the rough Ochoa section of Mexico City. He chose this neighborhood because it's close to police headquarters, and Galvén is dedicated to his job. When you're an AFI commander with your own protection detail, you're not too worried about muggers.

Commander Galvén, the number two federal police officer under Gerardo Vera, is a little drunk after a wet evening at his club, but it's all right because he's flanked by two bodyguards. They walk him to the door, wait until he has his key in the lock, and then walk back to the car.

They shouldn't.

When Galvén opens the door a man points a .380 Sig Sauer pistol at him.

Galvén didn't become a top cop because he's weak. The first shot goes through his right hand, but he still manages to grab the gunman by the wrist and rip the gun out of his hand.

The assailant pulls a second pistol, puts eight shots into Galvén's chest and stomach, and runs. The bodyguards sprint back, subdue the shooter, and call for an ambulance, but it's too late.

Galvén dies in the hospital minutes after arriving.

The shooter, a thirty-two-year-old former Mexico City policeman, says under interrogation that the motive was robbery.

Nobody believes it.

Galvén commanded the operation that killed Alberto Tapia.

Sal Barrera wishes the mechanics would hurry the fuck up.

It's already coming on eight and, as stupid as it sounds, he has a curfew. Adán has him on a tight leash, but what's he going to do? Adán's not only his paycheck, he's also the *patrón* of the family, and if Sal has even a hope of getting back into the business he has to eat Adán's shit and smile.

So Adán basically put him on house arrest, but now unc is off breaking in his young bride and Sal was able to get out on the pretext of running errands in the city.

One of them is to pick up Adán's new truck, so he can ride around his *finca* like an old *gomero,* and now Sal hopes there'll be enough time to run by a club and have a little fun before he has to haul back to La Tuna. Might as well have a fucking ankle bracelet on. Finally, *finally,* the wrench monkeys lower the hydraulics and roll the truck off the skids.

Sal gets behind the wheel, Edgar slides in the middle, and César gets in and shuts the door. "Where are we going? Mandalay? Bilbao? Shooters?"

"Let's do Bilbao," Sal says. César's mother owns Bilbao, so they won't get a bill. It's early, probably too early for there to be any real talent yet, but he still has a couple of hours before the Lobo turns into a pumpkin, and some of these Culiacán girls still like the *norteño* pickup truck look.

He pulls out.

When Eddie left Diego at his safe house outside Cuernavaca, it got truly strange.

"Come see Santa Muerte with me," Diego said.

"That's okay."

"It will bring you luck," Diego pressed. "Her blessing for the success of your mission."

Diego insisted, so they had to troop into the little shrine to kiss the Skinny Lady's bony ass. Diego made Eddie toss her a twenty, and then they had to kneel while Diego lit enough colored candles to fill out a Crayola box. Then Diego dipped his arms into a bowl and came up with his hands dripping blood.

"*Human* blood," Diego said.

"Uhhh, where'd you get that?" Eddie had to ask, even though he really didn't want to know.

"From an enemy."

Well, I'm glad you didn't get it from a friend, Eddie thought as Diego smeared first La Flaquita's face and then his own with the blood and started mumbling some kind of voodoo shit or something. Then he reached toward Eddie's face, but Eddie backed away. "Yeah, no. I'm good."

"Your mission will succeed," Diego said.

Yeah, I know it will, Eddie thinks now, and not because I tipped La Flaquita but because I brought fifteen of my best guys to make goddamn sure that the mission succeeds.

Now he looks at Sal Barrera get into the truck. Kid kills two innocent people—including a girl—and gets a new sled.

Must be nice being a Barrera.

Eddie pulls the trigger on the bazooka.

The warhead hits the front of the truck and goes off.

The Lobo hops.

At first Sal doesn't know what happened.

His head bounces off the top of the cab, and then he looks over and sees Edgar's face stuck halfway through the windshield. The engine is on fire, shooting flame and smoke. César is rattling like he's amped on some kind of super crank, and then Sal sees bullets punching through the window and the door.

He bails. Gets out and runs toward the garage, and then he sees all the guns pointed at him.

"*Nooooo!*" he screams. Then, "*Mamaaaaa!*"

"Mama"? Eddie thinks.

Bitch.

Picking up his AR, he aims at what's left of Sal Barrera. He does this only because he promised Diego he'd do it himself, because there really isn't a lot left of Sal, who tumbles to the concrete and gets up to run because his body hasn't got the message that his brain already knows.

He tumbles again and then lies still, one arm stretched out in front of him, blood pooling beneath him.

People are screaming, shoppers drop their bags and run, the mechanics crouch beside other cars and watch wide-eyed. Eddie notices with approval that his guys are still firing—into the air—to frighten any potential witnesses.

If that doesn't do it, the truck exploding does.

Adán picks up the phone and hears Sondra's screams.

Over and over and over again.

It's been a day.

Adán had people on the phone to tame journalists all day, to reiterate that it was the Tapias who committed the cop murders. All the early stories had blamed the "Sinaloa cartel," and as the day went on and the national mood shifted, he had to make sure that the new stories referred to Diego Tapia specifically.

Drug traffickers, no less than guerrillas, "swim in the sea of the people," rely on the people for protection and information, and he can't afford public scorn.

So call after call went out, from "unnamed sources," on "deep background," giving the real inside story on the murders, that it was the Tapias taking revenge for Alberto's killing, that Adán Barrera had nothing to do with them, that he was, in fact, furious with Diego—to the extent that it might cause a permanent rift in the organization.

And calls had to go out to the politicians, too, reminding them of their obligations, of the liabilities that were now on them, as well. They would have to choose sides, and they should choose the side that is obviously going to win.

Some, no doubt, think that will be the Tapias.

After all, they're the larger organization, have more money, more *sicarios*. Diego and Martín are still at large, and Ochoa isn't taking Adán's calls, which is not a good sign—the probability is that the Zetas will align with the Tapias.

That leaves me with what?

"I need you to go to Michoacán," Adán says.

"I can't leave Carla right now."

"She's your mistress, not your wife."

"I know who she is, Adán, thank you."

"Just for a day," Adán says. "Meet with Nazario, renew the alliance with La Familia. We need more men, he can provide them."

"Nazario considers you a traitor," Nacho says. "The devil, actually."

"He'd make a deal with the devil if it meant beating the Zetas," Adán says. If Nazario could separate his emotions from his best interest, Adán thinks, he'd join with the rest of them until they've sucked all the marrow out of my bones, and then pursue his vendetta against the Zetas. But he can't—he believes he's waging some kind of holy war against the Zetas, so he'll side with me again.

El Más Loco, indeed.

Adán convinces Nacho to go to Morelia and then goes upstairs to talk to Eva. His young wife is understandably confused over how to feel about the murder of her father's mistress's son, but unabashedly grieving over Salvador.

She's known what her father's business is, but this is the first time any of it has really touched her directly, and now he has to tell her that they need to leave the *finca*, only the second home she's ever known, to go to another house in another part of the state.

Diego obviously knows where this house is, he knows the security system, he hired half the guards, although Adán has already replaced them with Gente Nueva. But it's not safe here, and now he walks into the bedroom to tell her so. She's been crying. Her eyes are red and puffy.

"For how long?" she asks when he tells her that they have to leave.

"I don't know."

"Days? Weeks?"

"I said I don't know," Adán snaps, and then regrets his tone when he sees the hurt look on her face. He's never spoken sharply to her before, and he has to remember that she's eighteen and this is all new to her. "I just want to make sure that you're safe."

He's tired. What he wants is a hot shower and a weak scotch and then to go to bed, because they have to be up and out very early. A caravan of state police is going to escort them to the next *finca*, one that Diego has no knowledge of. What he doesn't want to do is explain to his wife the realities of the life that she was born into.

Adán pours himself the drink, shucks off his clothes, gets into the shower, and sits on the tiled bench. He sips his scotch and enjoys the buildup of steam loosening his tight muscles.

Finishing his drink, he stands under the spray.

When he gets out and goes into the bedroom, he sees that Eva has completely misunderstood his mood, his need, and is lying in bed in a blue negligee, ready to give him sexual comfort.

He can't help thinking that Magda would have read him better.

She would have had the scotch poured and pretended to be asleep when I got out of the shower. But Magda isn't here—she's based herself in Mexico City now. Wealthy, independent, stubbornly insisting on paying him the *piso* to move tons of cocaine through Laredo, a long way from the traumatized girl he met in Puente Grande. She's come to Culiacán twice, and they met in a house for afternoon trysts, but he misses her.

Now Eva will feel hurt and inadequate if we don't make love, and the fact is that it's been more of a chore lately. She's so desperate to get pregnant, and the effort feels like just one more thing he has to do in his day.

"Eva, darling, we have to be up before the sun."

"I just thought you were stressed . . ."

I am, he thinks. God, I am.

". . . and that this would help," Eva says.

"I'm sad," he says, "and in mourning."

Which was stupid and cruel, he thinks, because now she's not only embarrassed but also ashamed.

Eva quickly turns her back.

Adán turns off the lights and gets in bed beside her. "It's all right," he says, holding her. "I love you and everything will be all right."

He's not sure he believes any of it.

God damn Salvador, he thinks.

Betraying the Tapias for Sal's freedom was a huge—and ultimately futile—mistake. Now Salvador is dead anyway, my oldest friend has become my worst enemy, I'm at war with the entire world and very likely to lose. It all hangs on a thread—if Mexico City goes against me . . .

Was I duped, he wonders? Did Nacho use me to get rid of what he perceived as a rival? And who told the Tapias about the deal? Who tipped them off?

Aguilar?

Vera?

Then it hits him like a punch to the stomach.

Of course.

Adán curses himself for his stupidity, his lack of foresight.

I handed it to him, he thinks.

I handed it to Keller on a silver platter.

Keller watches the honor guard flank the three flag-draped caskets of the slain police officers.

The AFI troopers wear their blue uniforms, flak jackets stenciled in white with POLICÍA FEDERAL, dark blue baseball caps, and black combat boots as if they were on duty, ready for battle.

Behind them stand the president, the secretary of the interior, the secretaries of the navy and defense, the attorney general, and Gerardo Vera, in his full dress uniform.

The three officers were his friends, men he appointed to their jobs, and he's personally leading the investigations into their murders, with support from SEIDO and liaison with Keller.

Aguilar is heading up the Salvador Barrera investigation. Now he stands beside Keller. Without taking his eyes off the coffins, Aguilar says, quietly from the side of his mouth, "Whoever leaked the information to the Tapias has blood on his hands."

"What are you getting at?" Keller asks, even though he knows what Aguilar's getting at, and that he's right. I leaked it, Keller thinks, and it's something I have to live with.

Three dead cops.

He doesn't give a shit about Sal Barrera.

The media haven't tripped to the deal that started it, their take is that Adán Barrera and Diego Tapia have fallen out over the latter's murder of four policemen in retaliation for his brother's death.

It would be funny, Keller thinks, if it weren't—this view of Adán Barrera as the morally outraged supporter of law and order, whose poor nephew has paid the price for his uncle's principled stand.

The Sinaloa cartel has broken into civil war, with Nacho Esparza siding with his son-in-law Adán. The Tapias will seek out alliances, but with whom? The Zetas and the Gulf? The Fuentes in Juárez? La Familia? Teo Solorzano?

Barrera will be looking for allies, too. Solorzano is out, but the Zetas, CDG, and Juárez could be on the table, as could La Familia.

Some of the shabbier papers are running odds as if it's a horse race, with the smart money saying that if all the other organizations side with the Tapias, or even stay neutral, we could finally be looking at the end of Adán Barrera.

That would be fine, Keller thinks, but that's not his bet, not even the game he's playing.

He's playing a *much* deeper game.

"This is what you wanted, isn't it?" Aguilar asks. "You couldn't get to Barrera yourself, so you set the Tapias to do it for you."

Keller doesn't answer. Let him come, let him press, let him make a mistake.

"*Was* it you," Aguilar asks directly, "who leaked our arrangement to the Tapias?"

"Is that a question or an accusation?" Keller asks. And now he knows that Aguilar wasn't on the Tapia payroll.

Maybe Barrera's, though.

"Both," Aguilar says.

On shouted orders, the honor guards snap their rifles to their shoulders. The sound is crisp and sharp.

"I guess we suspect each other, then," Keller says.

Aguilar's face goes red with anger. "Were you thinking that, when you were sitting at the table, with my family?"

Good, Keller thinks. It's out there. "As a matter of fact, I was."

The rifles crack.

Calderón makes a speech.

"Today I reiterate my promise not to retreat in the quest for a Mexico where order prevails," he says. "We must say, all Mexican men and women together, that enough is enough. We have come together to confront this evil. We can't accept this situation. Our fight is head-on. The capacities of the Mexican state are aligned to break the structures of each cartel. We are determined to recover the streets that should never have ceased being ours."

Gerardo Vera stands up and says simply, "We will not be intimidated."

"You're corrupt," Aguilar says to Keller as they walk away. "You're a corrupt man and a corrupt cop, and I'm going to bring you down."

Mutual, Keller thinks.

Christmas 2007
Sinaloa, Mexico

The Barreras come home for Christmas.

Adán has his new security system in place with the Gente Nueva, the government has come down hard on the Tapias, and while the war with them drags on, it's more the Tapias on the run than him.

The killings of three top police officials have shocked the nation. The public relations campaign has worked—people from vastly different demographics agree that the Tapias should be hunted down like rabid dogs.

The Tapias did the government a huge favor, Adán thinks. It's a game change—heretofore the public has been lukewarm on Calderón's war on drugs, some even protesting in the streets against it. But the disgust at the murders has aroused a feeling of patriotism and support for the government not seen in a very long time.

The Tapias have handed Calderón a mandate.

And me as well, Adán thinks.

Eva is glad to be home.

She decorates the *finca* in La Tuna with traditional poinsettias—unaware that they symbolize new life for fallen warriors. Sinaloa has a heavy German influence, so she and Adán put up a gigantic Christmas tree outside for the village children to come see because Eva wants to start a new tradition.

So they sponsor a *posada*, a children's parade from the village to the *finca*, where Eva has spent thousands on the tree with special carved wooden ornaments imported from Germany and a nativity scene with ceramic figures from Tlaquepaque.

The children, with two playing Mary and Joseph on a burro, march to the nativity scene, where Eva has hung up a gigantic star-shaped piñata from a ficus branch, filled with candy and toys.

After that, Adán and Eva host a feast for the village, with *buñuelos, atole,* tamales, and hot *ponche* spiced with cinnamon and vanilla.

Then they sing the *villancicos,* the Christmas carols.

Adán is a little surprised, but pleased, at how traditional Eva is. Christmas Eve, she insists that they go to the village church for the late-night Mass of the Rooster, and she delights in the fireworks set off after the service.

Then there's a midnight dinner, this time the traditional *bacalao,* dried cod in tomato sauce with onions—which Adán can't stand but tolerates because it reminds Eva of her childhood—and *revoltijo de romerita,* shrimp in *pepito* sauce, which he does like.

They spend Christmas Day itself quietly, sleeping late and getting up to eat leftovers.

Three days later comes Los Santos Innocentes to commemorate the boys that Herod slaughtered in his futile hunt for the baby Jesus. Tradition has it that anything borrowed on this day doesn't have to be returned, and Nacho phones up asking to "borrow" the Laredo plaza. Adán declines and they chat for a few minutes about inconsequential things before hanging up with best wishes for the New Year.

Los Santos Innocentes is also Mexico's "April Fool's Day," with the mandatory pranks, including phony newspaper stories, one of which announces that Adán Barrera, despite being rumored dead or employed as a sous-chef at Los Pinos, will nevertheless take over as host of *Atínale al Precio—The Price Is Right*. Eva hides the paper from him, but he laughs when he sees it and, to her delight, does a passable impression of Héctor Sandarti, replete with Guatemalan accent.

Adán doesn't really want to go out for New Year's Eve, but Eva very much does and he doesn't want her to think that she married a grouchy old man, so they fly to Puerto Vallarta, where his men go into the club first, collect all cell phones, apologize, and tell the other celebrants that they'll be locked in until El Patrón leaves, and then Adán and Eva come in and join the festivities. She looks more than wonderful in a short red dress and a silly New Year's Eve tiara, and she even talked Adán into a tuxedo on the promise that she would talk him out of it later.

Eva dances her head off and Adán does his best to keep up, although he has to admit—albeit only to himself—that he's quite ready for midnight to come when they do the traditional thing of feeding each other twelve grapes along with the strikes of midnight for good luck in the coming year.

They leave shortly afterward, and cell phones are restored to their owners, who have a new story to tell.

Epiphany—El Día de los Tres Reyes Magos, "Three Kings Day"—is the next festival in the liturgical calendar. That night, January 5, Eva, as she did when she was a girl, leaves a shoe outside the door where the Wise Men will enter to greet Jesus. That afternoon, the village children put messages inside helium balloons provided by Adán and Eva that explain why they have been good or bad that year and what they would like as a gift, and then loft them to the heavens with great hope.

And that night, five Nueva Gente armed with high-powered rifles and night scopes shoot to death five of Vicente Fuentes's key people in Juárez.

Holidays are hard on the solitary man.

The single, the widowed, perhaps most especially the divorced, to whose loneliness is added the bitter spice of regret.

Marisol invited Keller up to Valverde for Christmas, but he declined.

Although the threat against him has diminished—neither side is likely to kill a DEA agent and tip the scales—he prefers to be alone with his angst. Starting things with Marisol again won't solve any of the underlying issues, and there's no point in prolonging it for either of them.

It's been a miserable six months.

Luis Aguilar has been waging his own bureaucratic war on Keller, doing everything he can to get him recalled to the United States.

"You been fucking around with the working agreement?" Taylor asked Keller on the phone a few weeks ago. *"Going behind Aguilar's back, developing your own sources? Is the past prologue here, Art? Tell me you don't have some sort of relationship with the Tapias."*

"I've been a Boy Scout."

"Aguilar says you're taking money, Art," Taylor said. *"He says you're in the Tapias' pocket."*

"Jesus Christ, Tim."

"Could you pass a polygraph?"

"Could *he*?"

"What, you have evidence?" Taylor asked.

"No." Not yet. I don't have it yet, Keller thought, but I know it's coming. "You test me and I walk."

"That's not much of a threat at this point."

"Go to the videotape," Keller answered. He cited his record—Osiel Contreras sitting in a Houston supermax, Alberto Tapia on a slab, and the Sinaloa cartel split into pieces. "I shouldn't have to plead for my life here. The fuck, Tim? You think I'm dirty?"

He heard Taylor sigh. *"No, of course not. You're a lot of things—most of them bad—but you're not dirty. You do play the edges of the plate, though, and it's not helpful in trying to keep you there. If it weren't for Mérida, I'd have no fucking leverage. Play nice, Art, huh? If your usual dick-meter is at, say, 10, try to be, I don't know, a 5, okay?"*

Not easy, with Aguilar cutting him out of everything and Vera so obsessed with the Tapias that he's not paying attention. Add to that the fact that Aguilar has him under surveillance now, with SEIDO agents tracking him constantly. Keller has to assume that his phone is tapped, too.

Aware that he's wallowing in self-pity, Keller microwaves a Swanson "Hungry Man" turkey dinner with its little tub of cranberry sauce in a parody of Christmas dinner. Balancing the meal on his lap and washing it down with scotch, he watches Mexican television and remembers other Christmases in better times, when the kids were young, the family together and never thinking that they'd ever be apart.

He almost calls them but then thinks better of it, not wanting to tinge their day with his melancholy. Maybe they're with their mom, maybe they're with friends. Maybe Althea took them somewhere special—Utah to ski, Hawaii to lie in the sun. Maybe they're with Althie's family in California.

And I'm here, Keller thinks—Don Quixote tilting at windmills, Ahab chasing the great white whale—alone with my obsession. As hooked as any junkie in a shooting gallery, any crack whore on the stroll.

My personal war on drugs, my own addiction.

Two scotches later, he phones Marisol. *"Feliz Navidad."*

"Feliz Navidad to you," Marisol says. *"Are you having a good day?"*

"Not really."

"Are you drunk?"

"No," Keller says. "Maybe a little."

She's quiet for a second and then says, *"I asked you to come here."*

"I know."

"I miss you."

"I miss you, too," Keller says. Then, against his better judgment, "Do you want to come down here for New Year's?"

"I wish I could," Marisol says. *"But it's so busy here. Sadly, it's the domestic violence season as well. Could you come here?"*

He knows he's being a dick, but he says, "For the 'domestic violence season'? I think I'll pass."

If his intent was to piss her off, it worked. *"All right."*

"All right, well . . . I guess I'll talk to you."

"All right. Goodbye, Arturo."

Goodbye, Marisol, he thinks.

Keller gets good and drunk that night, for the first time in many years. The next morning, he showers and shaves and makes himself go into the office. The embassy is all but empty over the holidays, eerily quiet.

Settling himself behind his desk, he pores over intelligence reports, data spreadsheets, and analyses.

The Sinaloa civil war (the war you set in motion, Keller reminds himself) has spread corpses out all over Sinaloa and Durango, while the fighting in Michoacán goes on with no end in sight, and the trap Keller set has yet to be sprung.

But the intense pressure on the Tapias is going to accelerate that, Keller thinks. It has to, because the clock is winding down on you.

Going through the data, Keller tries to get a line on Barrera's next move.

He already has Laredo, Keller thinks.

He'll soon have Tijuana back.

There's only one other target left, the biggest jewel in the Mexican smuggling crown.

Juárez.

2

Journalists

Those were truly golden years my Uncle Tommy says,
But everything's gone straight to hell since Sinatra played Juarez.
—Tom Russell
"When Sinatra Played Juarez"

Ciudad Juárez, Chihuahua
2008

Pablo Mora has one of those hangovers where you see yourself in the mirror and think you look familiar.

The mirror's not his friend this morning. His unshaven face is puffy, his hair a rat's nest and badly in need of a cut, his eyes are bloodshot. He brushes his teeth—even that's painful—finds a bottle of aspirin in the medicine cabinet and swallows two of them, then shuffles back to the bedroom, finds his cleanest shirt on the bed, and then struggles into jeans and sits down to put on socks and shoes. He sniffs the socks—they're just on this side of acceptable—and notes that the shoes need a shine that they're not going to get.

The bed calls him to come back, but he has stories to get in and Óscar will not be happy if he misses another deadline.

And Ana, who'd had every bit as much to drink, would mock him as a pussy.

Making coffee seems like too much work—and he's not sure he has any left anyway—and the thought of breakfast is literally nauseating, so he decides to head downtown and go to the café across the street from the paper's offices.

The owner, Ricardo, is simpatico with hungover journalists.

He'd better be, Pablo thinks. It's half his business.

Pablo heads out the door of his second-floor apartment and gingerly navigates the stairs. The place has an elevator but Pablo doesn't fully trust it anyway and he's not sure he can handle the doors slamming shut.

God *damn* Jaime's, Pablo thinks as he walks out into the brisk January morning. He'd let Ana talk him into going there after work for one beer, although they both knew how that would turn out. He'd started at Jaime's with a Modelo, then graduated to dark Indio, at some point Giorgio joined up with them and shouted for tequilas, and, by the time they apparently thought it would be amusing to go to Fred's, they had graduated to some scotch older than Pablo's grandmother.

Which, he thinks now, they could afford neither physically nor financially.

Newspaper reporters in Mexico make basically shit, and city-beat reporters in Juárez make less than shit—about a hundred dollars a week, paid every Friday—and although his rent is cheap he has child support payments, and now he tries to remember if this is his weekend with Mateo.

Doesn't so much matter—he sees his son almost every day anyway. Mateo is almost four now, and getting to that point where his jokes are actually funny. Victoria is good about letting him see their child, and Pablo usually picks him up from preschool these days.

So his ex-wife is easy about that.

On other things? Not so much.

Then again, she's a *financial* journalist.

Whole different world.

He gets into his '96 Toyota Camry, which is decked out with all the reporter's essential equipment—two mostly empty cardboard coffee cups, several El Puerco Loco burrito wrappers (the smiling pig logo grinning up at him with derision), a mapbook of the city streets, which he doesn't really need, a two-way Nextel phone (provided by the paper), which he does, and a police radio scanner that provides the background track of his working life.

The Camry isn't in much better shape than Pablo. It isn't hungover, of course, but it is in need of a paint job to disguise the dings on all four fenders that Pablo has inflicted on it by getting in and out of literal as well as metaphorical tight scrapes. The back passenger window is cracked from a rock thrown by a disgruntled wino in Anapra, the rubber in the windshield wiper has long since melted in the summer sun, and a fine layer of khaki dust mutes the car's original blue.

"Why don't you get a nicer car?" Victoria asked him just last week.

"I don't want a nicer car," Pablo answered, even though a large part of the answer was that he can't afford a nice car.

Besides, a nice car is just a liability in his work. The residents of the poorer neighborhoods that he goes into get jealous and suspicious when they see an expensive car, and people are less likely to steal his old *fronterizo*, even though car theft is epidemic in Juárez.

The strange thing about Juárez car theft is that the cars turn up on their own—usually on the same day—which was a mystery to police until reporters like Pablo figured out that minor-league narcos were stealing cars, driving them across the border with drugs, coming back, and dumping them off.

Anyway, the Camry starts up and Pablo drives to the paper.

Pablo loves Juárez.

A true Juarense, he was born here, educated here, and would never live anywhere else. Admittedly, Juárez is surprisingly cold in the winter, miserably hot in the summer, and you just hope that either spring or autumn falls on a weekend so you get to enjoy it. The city is known more for its dust storms than its scenic beauty, more for its bars than its architecture, and its most famous invention is the margarita, but Pablo loves his town like a long-married husband loves his wife, as much for her flaws as for her virtues.

He's also a little defensive about her.

Maybe it's because Juárez has always been looked down on as a place you go through to get somewhere else. Even its original name, Paseo del Norte, proclaimed that it was just a place to cross the Río Bravo to the north, but Pablo likes to remind people—especially North Americans—that the city's mission of Our Lady of Guadalupe was founded in 1659, when Washington, D.C., was still a malarial swamp.

The name was eventually changed to Ciudad Juárez to honor the old democrat who threw the French out of Mexico, and it boomed in the late 1880s under the leadership of the Five Families—the Ochoas, Cuaróns, Provencios, Samaniegos, and Daguerres—whose descendants still dominate the city. They created the central business district—the old Calle del Comercio (now Vicente Ochoa) and 16 September Avenue, named to celebrate independence.

Then again—and Pablo is proud of this—Juárez has always been a hub of revolution. Old Pancho Villa hung out here, arriving in the city with eight men, two pounds of coffee, and five hundred bullets, but eventually becoming governor of Chihuahua, beating Díaz, and even invading the United States. The fighting destroyed Juárez, though—it was a burned-out shell by 1913 and the Five Families had to rebuild the whole thing, which accounts for the city's early-twentieth-century look.

Even the neoclassical cathedral was only built in the 1950s.

Then again, the '50s were Juárez's heyday, the old Tourist Zone, now called by the brutally ugly name PRONAF (Programa Nacional de Frontera), was the place celebrities went to have a good time.

People get sentimental—and, Pablo thinks, silly—about *el Juárez de ayer*, "Old Juárez," the freewheeling city of bullfights, brothels, and nightclubs where Sinatra and Ava Gardner would paint the town. At thirty-four, he's not sure he even knew the real "Old Juárez," but the city he grew up in was enough for him.

Not that it hasn't changed.

Enormously, and in two great waves, first in the 1970s when the maquiladoras—the factories from American companies—came to take advantage of cheap Mexican labor, and again in the 1990s when the maquiladoras left for even cheaper Chinese labor.

The first wave created gigantic slums as workers poured in from all over Mexico, but especially the poor, rural south. The city couldn't hope to keep up with the population boom, and the *colonias* had little, if any, infrastructure—decent housing, electricity, running water, or plumbing. And because the maquiladoras' management preferred women workers, it left thousands of men, shamed and bitter, to sit idly in the slums, drinking cheap beer and, increasingly, doing drugs.

The *colonias* were bad—when the maquiladoras left for even higher profit margins, they got worse.

Now most people—men and women—are unemployed.

And the desperately poor *colonias*—Anapra, Chihuahuita, and the others—edge the city like a necklace of worn beads, hard along the border with El Paso, just across the river.

Juárez has about a million and a half people, El Paso about a third of that, but El Paso has most of the wealth, unless you count the Mexican "partners" who got rich off the maquiladoras (and even most of them live in El Paso nowadays), or, of course, the narcos out in Campestre with their new McMansions, almost a parody of the American upwardly mobile suburban dream.

And that, whether Pablo likes it or not—and he doesn't—is the central fact of the city's existence: Juárez and El Paso are inextricably linked, in many ways one community divided by an arbitrary line.

A strong arm can throw a stone from Juárez's downtown—El Centro—to El Paso's, and you stand on one or the other side of the river and look across at the other city, the other country, and the other culture. But many residents of both towns have dual citizenship, almost everyone has family, or certainly friends, on the other side—El Paso is, after all, 80 percent Hispanic—and people go back and forth as a matter of course.

So the city's most important structures aren't its bars and clubs, its stores or office buildings, or even the old bullring or the *fútbol* stadium (Pablo's beloved *fútbol* stadium, home of his beloved Los Indios)—the central structures are the bridges.

Four of them.

More than two thousand trucks and thirty-four thousand cars cross those bridges every day, carrying $40 billion worth of legal trade in a given year. And somewhere between $1.5 million and $10 million worth of illegal drugs (Pablo finds the wide range of the estimate itself instructive) go over those bridges *every day*.

Cash comes back.

Well, cash and guns, Pablo thinks, but that's another story. Literally billions of dollars in cash—called "new money" in Juárez—comes back over those bridges, and a lot of it gets invested in the city's businesses and real estate.

Pablo didn't come from poverty or wealth. His parents—both university professors—raised him in genteel, comfortable middle-class shabbiness and have always been quietly disappointed that he didn't pursue a career in academia.

He's vaguely a "leftie," like most journalists (not Victoria, though—as a financial journalist she's a free-market true believer who thinks that PAN will be the salvation of the country; their political differences were symbolic of the other issues in their marriage).

So is Ana a leftist, but nothing like Giorgio, who with his long hair and wild beard is an out-and-out communist and presents himself as a latter-day Che except, as Pablo has pointed out to him, the photographer lacks Guevara's seriousness of purpose. Giorgio cannot leave a bottle undrunk or an attractive woman unfucked, and those activities tend to get in the way of revolution.

Pablo hopes that Giorgio has left Ana unfucked, although he suspects that he hasn't, because she's strangely quiet on the subject even though she's generally quite open about her love life.

Ana likes pretty men.

And I, Pablo thinks as he drives past the Plaza del Periodista—Journalists' Square—am decidedly *not* a pretty man.

Not ever, and especially not this morning.

The topic of him and Ana going to bed has come up on several sodden occasions, and they even teetered on the brink of that cliff a couple of times, although they backed away from the edge with the conclusion that they were too close, too good friends to risk it, but the attraction (he can understand his for her, but not hers for him) is mutual and always there.

And apparently noticeable, because Victoria used it as the cutting edge for several arguments, observing that Ana, not herself, was Pablo's true love.

That and booze (depending on her agenda), and chasing down sordid stories (ditto) of a degenerate street life that could only appeal to a degenerate readership, and why couldn't he cover stories that mattered (by which she meant international economic policy or politics, both of which bore the shit out of him). Pablo loves to write about the old man selling flowers at the traffic circle, the kids spray-painting murals, the mothers who strive to raise families in the *colonias.*

He writes mostly about crime, although if he can talk Óscar into it he'll do "color" features, human interest, travel stories, film critiques, and the occasional restaurant review—because it's a free and usually good meal—and all these extra stories pay him a few more pesos. If he's really in Óscar's good graces, the editor will send him to cover his beloved Indios *fútbol* matches out at Benito Stadium.

Pablo does American stories for his own paper—making the tedious slog across the border into El Paso for material—then freelances stories that are basically recirculated rumors about the narco-world back to American papers, which have a seemingly insatiable appetite for scary tales about the looming threat that is Mexico. Adán Barrera is usually good for an overdue utility bill. (We all, in our own way, he thinks now, profit off the *pista secreta.*)

Pablo drives by the statue of newsboys hawking papers (he admits to sentimentality over that), parks in the paper's lot, and crosses the square to the café, where Ana is hunched over the zinc-top counter by the window, nursing her hangover with shots of espresso.

He plops onto the stool next to her and she grunts a hello. Her face seems pained but otherwise she looks good. Then again, she always does. Ana is meticulous about her clothes, which are neat, stylish, and always pressed.

She's a trim, small woman who sometimes compares herself to a bird. No one would call her pretty—she has a bird's beak of a nose, her mouth is wide but thin-lipped, and she has no "figure" to speak of ("If you're looking for 'boobage,' you'll have to look elsewhere," she'll tell prospective lovers), but her short-cut black hair is thick, glossy, and, to Pablo, beautiful, and her brown eyes are warm (well, not this morning—they look like they ache) and intense.

Ana is interesting-looking, and Pablo never gets tired of seeing her, although he can get tired of listening to her because she can be something of a nag and she can get *overly* intense, especially about politics, which she covers with an energy and devotion that Pablo finds both incomprehensible and somewhat demonic.

This is where their professional worlds merge, because covering crime and politics in Mexico is, sadly, often the same thing, so they rely on each other's expertise and often share sources. With Giorgio giving images to their words, they make up what Óscar calls—inevitably—"Los Tres Amigos."

Ricardo gently sets a café con leche by Pablo's hand and just as quietly withdraws.

"You're a saint," Pablo says. He pours a stream of sugar from the glass container set on the counter.

"That's not going to help your waistline," Ana says.

Pablo knows he could stand to lose twenty pounds—okay, thirty—and that his muscle tone is the consistency of flan, but he's not going to start today. What he should do is go back to his former thrice-weekly evening *fútbol* sessions in the park.

That's what he *should* do.

"I blame you for this, by the way," he says.

"You're a big boy," Ana observes, staring blankly into her cup. "You could have said no."

"I stand with Oscar Wilde on the subject of temptation."

You seem quite able to resist *me*, Ana thinks sourly, then quickly attributes her sudden bitterness to the foul hangover. She'd invited him out last night with the full intention of finally seducing him into the sack, and then the alcohol took over.

Probably intentional, she thinks.

I mean, seriously, she asks herself, *would* you have? Even if he was, shall we say, persuadable? Would you have gone through with it or chickened out as you have in the past?

Probably the latter, she decides now. Still, it would have been nice of him to give you the choice. But probably better it didn't happen. Lovers are a dime a dozen, good friendships rare. No sense in literally screwing this one up.

Besides, Pablo goes for beautiful women, witness his ex-wife—a tall, thin, blond Sinaloan with a body honed in the gym. Hurrah for her discipline, anyway. Pablo was *smitten,* and pursued her with the relentlessness he would only normally devote to a good story, and all his friends could have told him (they certainly told each other) that it wouldn't work out, that Victoria was emotionally slumming, trying to find in him the warmer parts of herself, and that, for his part, he simply lacked the ambition that she would eventually need in a mate.

Ana likes Victoria. She's a damn fine journalist and actually very nice, even funny, once you cut beneath the frost layer. She's a wonderful mother to Mateo and has been very generous to Pablo on the visitation thing.

It just wasn't a match, that's all.

Victoria's career is rising with a bullet, and Pablo's . . .

Well, Pablo writes about itinerant poets who leave snatches of their verse under people's windshield wipers. He writes about the *ambulantes*—the street vendors. It's what makes him so lovable, like a big, ugly dog that you just can't keep from jumping up on the sofa.

"Do you want to come over tonight?" she asks. "I'm making a paella and having a few people in."

"I might have Mateo."

"Bring him," Ana says. "Jimena would love to see him. She's coming, and Tomás. Giorgio, probably. First we're going round to Cafebrería for Tomás's reading."

Cafebrería is one of Pablo's regular haunts—a bookstore-cum-coffeehouse where the city's artists and intellectuals gather. Pablo was going to hit Tomas's reading anyway, Ana's paellas are justly famous, and maybe Jimena will bring some *polvorones* from her bakery out in Valverde.

"I'll bring a bottle of wine," Pablo says.

"Just bring Mateo," Ana answers. She takes a last sip of her espresso and looks at her watch. "We don't want to keep El Búho waiting."

Pablo gulps down his coffee, wishing he'd left time for a bite to eat. He leaves money on the counter and, with Ana, crosses the street into the offices of *El Periódico.*

Óscar Herrera is the dean of Mexican journalism.

The last of the old-school editors, "El Búho"—the Owl—scans the city room looking for the red meat of a factual error, the scent of a stylistic sin, or the very whiff of literary pretentiousness.

His *aporto* is perfect, Pablo has always thought. El Búho's thick, heavy-framed glasses make his eyes large, he blinks at slow intervals, and the hair on the top of his ears makes him look—well, owlish.

Pablo has progressed from, as a new reporter, sheer terror of El Búho to now, ten years later, just vague anxiety in his presence. And vast admiration and respect. Óscar Herrera—*Dr.* Óscar Herrera, to be accurate—is a figure of courage and probity who has stood up to presidents, generals, and drug lords who tried to influence his coverage of their respective and unfortunately intertwined activities.

Nine years ago they tried to kill him.

Narcos (although Pablo has always suspected it was the army acting on behalf of the PRI, and Óscar's editorial colleagues joked that it was his own reporters) ambushed his car at a stoplight, killed his driver, and put three bullets into Óscar's left leg and hip.

Now he walks with a cane, which he famously brandished at the television cameras as he left the hospital, growling about the incompetence of bad marksmen. Then he went back to the office and brutally edited the stories about the attack, correcting trivial factual errors and improper syntax.

Not that Óscar is merely a hard man.

He's written three published volumes of poetry, as well as a critical appreciation of the novels of Élmer Mendoza, and Pablo knows that the man's Saturday morning ritual is to go out to breakfast and then sit in his living room listening to Mahler symphonies on vinyl.

Now he sits with his stiff leg propped up on the table beside his cane and blinks at Pablo. "And *why* do you think that story about itinerant musicians who play at bus stops might be of interest to our readers?"

"It interests *me*," Pablo responds truthfully.

Óscar blinks. There is some sense to that—when a reporter is interested in his subject, his research is more thorough and his writing more passionate. "But you would be writing about music, which our readers wouldn't be able to hear."

"They could on the e-edition," Giorgio says. "We could record a track and run an MP3."

Now Óscar frowns—he understands the technology, it's part of his job—but that doesn't mean he likes it. He's only reluctantly yielded to the mixture of video clips on the daily e-edition of his paper, his belief being that if people wanted to watch television, they should. But the business managers at the paper insisted, so now they have video and audio tracks.

Óscar prefers written words on paper.

And beautiful photographs that help tell the story.

Memorable, as opposed to fleeting, images.

He asks Giorgio, "Could you shoot this?"

To Pablo's gratitude, Giorgio answers, "I could shoot the hell out of it. Give you killer stills and video, if you want."

Giorgio is an amazing specimen, Pablo thinks, looking at the man. His cheeks are ruddy, his voice firm, he is none the worse for wear despite having outdrunk them all—and he looks like he just got off the slopes from a morning skiing. And he's positively glowing with energy this morning—Pablo suspects there was a woman involved in this—and it's disgusting.

Óscar blinks again and says, "Eight hours, not a minute more. On more substantive matters, the drug situation."

Pablo groans.

He's not behind in his rent, doesn't need a child support payment, so a narco story is simply an exercise in tedium. The truth is that the narcos are generally stupid, brutal thugs—once you've written about one of them, you've written about them all.

And anyway, who cares?

Apparently Óscar. "You object, Pablo?"

"Why give ink to these bastards?"

"Five Juárez police officers murdered?" Óscar asks. "I'd say that amounts to sufficient reason. I want to know what the 'street' says."

Pablo had covered the murders.

A little over two weeks ago, snipers with high-powered rifles killed five men in various parts of the city. Two of them, Miguel Roma and David Baca, were Juárez cops.

Two days ago, Juárez police captain Julián Chairez was shot twenty-two times while he was on patrol at the corner of Avenida Hermanos Escobar and Calle Plutarco Elías.

Then, yesterday morning, Commander Francisco Ledesma, the third-highest-ranking cop in the city, was pulling out of his driveway to go to work when a white Chevy van pulled up, a man got out, calmly walked up to Ledesma's car, and put four 9mm pistol rounds through the door lock.

Ledesma died before the EMTs got there.

His killing rocked the city. He was only thirty-four, charismatic and popular, and headed up a unit called Los Pumas, the city's antigang task force.

There are about eight hundred gangs in Juárez—most of them in the poor *colonias* that surround maquiladoras—with about fourteen thousand members. These gangs are recruiting grounds for the "big" gangs that operate the drug trade under the Juárez cartel—Los Aztecas, Los Mexicles, Los Aristos Asesinos, and La Línea.

Ledesma was going after those gangs, and Pablo guesses it got him killed. But the details bother him.

Gangbangers spray bullets around, but this was clearly a professional hit—experienced *sicarios* shoot through the lock because the bullets go through the door in a tight pattern, which professional gunmen take pride in.

Five city cops—Chairez, Baca, Romo, Gómez, and Ledesma.

Pablo can't blame Óscar for wanting the story.

Now El Búho turns to Ana. "Find out what our officials think. The governor is in town today, meeting with the mayor. Get quotes."

"Images?" Giorgio asks.

Óscar answers, "If Ana gets an interview with the governor—"

"*When* Ana gets an interview with the governor," Ana corrects.

Pablo drives out to the working-class Galeana neighborhood to find Victor Abrego, a Juárez cop he knew from the bad old days.

Something that Pablo has found almost impossible to explain to his American editors (because it's inexplicable, he thinks) is the byzantine structure of Mexican law enforcement.

As in the U.S., there are basically three levels of police—municipal, state, and federal—but the resemblance ends there. What's so different in Mexico is that the municipal police, the city cops, don't investigate crimes. Their role is basically preventative—patrol, traffic control, community relations. They're the first responders to a crime—assist the victims, secure the scene—but then their role ends.

The investigation of a crime is left to state police and prosecutors. A Juárez cop who responds to a murder call in Juárez turns the investigation over to a civilian state prosecutor or a state cop.

Unless it's a federal crime.

If it's a federal crime—there are allegations of organized crime or drug trafficking over a certain weight—the investigation is handed to the federal police and prosecutors.

So a narco killing in Juárez is handled at various times, often overlapping, by a combination of city police, state prosecutors and police, federal prosecutors and police, and a grab bag of intelligence agencies from the city, state, and national governments.

It's no wonder, Pablo thinks as he looks for a parking spot in Galeana, that so few crimes are ever solved.

Mexico is a very good place to be a criminal.

There's another factor at play in Juárez, and everyone knows it.

Most Juarenses are scared shitless of the city cops.

And for good reason. Not only can they be arbitrary and unpredictably violent, but the plain truth is that a lot of them work for two bosses—the chief of police and La Línea.

La Línea—"the Line"—was, until recently anyway, the chief enforcement arm of the Juárez cartel. Made up exclusively of current or retired city or state police, La Línea keeps the drug trade, well, in line. Someone tries to run a load through without paying the *piso*? La Línea collects. Someone loses a shipment and claims the customs agents seized it? La Línea learns the truth and deals out justice. Someone is a chronic problem or an unlicensed competitor? La Línea "lifts" him and makes him disappear.

And who are you going to go to for help?

The cops?

Pablo wouldn't say that all, or even the majority, of the fifteen hundred Juárez police are La Línea, but he's certain that a critical mass are, that those who are intimidate those who aren't, and those who aren't "go along to get along" if they want to keep their jobs or even survive.

Say that even two of the district commanders—there are six in Juárez—are La Línea. They control postings, they can shift La Línea cops to where they're needed at the moment, transfer out or fire clean cops. Say a state homicide investigator is La Línea. How hard is he really going to investigate the murder of some narco who fell afoul of the Juárez cartel, a murder that La Línea probably committed? Is he really going to pass critical evidence along to the *federales,* or is he going to lose it somewhere in the process?

It's an open secret in Juárez that the cops pass "066" calls—the anonymous tip line—right through to the cartel. So if a citizen tries to aid an investigation, that citizen is likely to become the subject of the next one.

But now the latest victims are cops.

Parking the car, Pablo gives the *parquero* at the corner a five-peso coin not to steal the tires, and walks down the street until he finds Abrego. He's in his powder-blue uniform with a dark blue flak jacket with white lettering: POLICÍA MUNICIPAL.

Pablo doesn't begrudge him the protective vest; he almost wishes he had one himself.

"I'm busy, Pablo," Abrego says when he spots Pablo walking up the street.

"I'm sorry about your people," Pablo says.

"No comment."

"Come on," Pablo says. "Usual deal—deep source, no attribution. What's going on?"

It's tricky, asking a cop questions after a brother officer has been murdered. They're angry, sensitive, easily offended, and Abrego is no different. "What's going on? Some narco garbage killed a police commander."

"Motive?" Pablo asks. "Leads?"

"I guess Ledesma was pushing too hard and got someone angry," Abrego says.

"Vicente Fuentes?"

Abrego shakes his head. "These weren't locals."

"How do you know?"

This pisses Abrego off. "Because I'd have *heard* something."

Pablo doesn't know if Abrego is La Línea or not. He guesses not, but he's not going to ask, either. "If they weren't locals, who were they?"

"Go to Sinaloa and ask."

"Adán Barrera?"

Abrego hesitates and then says, "Cops have been getting calls. On their personal cell phones. Or other cops have been approaching them . . ."

"And saying what?"

"That 'New People' are moving in," Abrego says. "The Sinaloa people, and you'd better get on the bus now."

If he's right, Pablo thinks, at least five guys missed the bus.

"Go away, Pablo," Abrego says. "I have work to do, then I have a funeral to attend."

Pablo takes a Chihuahua state homicide investigator to lunch.

Comandante Sánchez isn't fooled by the social gesture—in Mexico no less than the rest of the world, there is no such thing as a free lunch. So after polishing off a plate of excellent *camarones*, he looks across the table at Pablo and asks, *"Pues?"*

"What's going on in Juárez?"

"Why ask me?"

"Did you get a phone call, too?" Pablo asks.

"From whom?"

"The 'New People.'"

"Who told you about that?"

Pablo doesn't answer.

Then Sánchez says, "As a matter of fact, I did. On my private phone, and how did they get that number? What we're hearing is they approached division commanders with money. I guess Ledesma didn't take it."

"Would you like another beer? I think I would." Pablo signals the waiter and then turns back to Sánchez. "Are we looking at an invasion here?"

"You're so well informed, you tell me."

"Okay," Pablo says, starting to get annoyed with the game. "Is this Adán Barrera putting the empire back together?"

Sánchez says, "You were a kid then."

"I heard the stories."

The waiter sets two cold *cervezas* on the table and then, at a glance from Sánchez, steps away.

"Do yourself a favor," Sánchez says. "Don't hear stories now."

"What does that mean?"

"You know what it means."

"Oh, come on." The food has helped Pablo's general condition, as has the beer, but he still has a headache and all this silly subterfuge makes it worse. The whole world knows about Adán Barrera—there have been books, novels, movies, television shows. The narcos are a media franchise, for God's sake, this generation's version of the Mafia.

"That was the old days, wasn't it?" Pablo asks. "The cartels, the *patrones*— they're all dead or locked up. Even Osiel Contreras is in prison."

"But Adán Barrera is out."

Pablo is annoyed and eager to finish up the interview. "So what are you saying? There's going to be a 'war'? Barrera is moving in on Juárez?"

"I'm saying you'd be better off not hearing any more stories," Sánchez says. He reaches across the table for the bill.

A new one on Pablo.

He's never seen a cop pick up the check before.

It takes Pablo three hours to track down Ramón, but he finally finds his old schoolmate at the Kentucky, near the Santa Fe Bridge that crosses into El Paso.

Pablo plops down on the stool beside Ramón. *"Qué pasa?"*

"Nada."

Nothing my ass, Pablo thinks. If Ramón is hanging out by the border there's a reason—he has a shipment going over. And it speaks to another truth about Juárez—everybody knows someone in the drug business.

The Kentucky is classic Old Juárez. It came into being just a few weeks after Prohibition hit the United States as an easy place for gringos to come and get a drink. Sinatra used to hang out here, and Marilyn Monroe, and the legend—although Pablo doesn't believe it—is that Al Capone visited once after making a deal for bootleg whiskey.

But the bar is mostly famous for the birthplace of the margarita.

That's us, Pablo thinks, we're known for other contraband, other countries' movie stars, and fruity drinks.

He orders an Indio.

"Long time no see, *'mano*," Ramón says with a trace of resentment in his voice.

It's true, Pablo thinks—in high school they were buddies, hung out all the time, but then their lives took different turns. I got busy with work and other friends and Ramón went to prison.

Got caught jacking cars and did three years in Juárez's deservedly notorious CERESO.

If you wanted to survive there, you joined Los Aztecas.

Ramón wanted to survive.

The gang actually started in American prisons, where it's called Barrio Azteca, but when the U.S. started to deport convicts who were also illegal aliens, the gang quickly spread to Mexican prisons.

Then into the community.

There are roughly six hundred Aztecas in Juárez, but they use kids from a lot of the little gangs, and the word is that they're taking over more and more of the enforcement duties of the Juárez cartel. With La Línea, they control the drug trade in the northeast part of the city, while Los Mexicles and Los Aristos Asesinos control the southwest.

Pablo's heard the stories about how they exercise control—how they throw big parties and everyone cheers while they beat up a prisoner. Then they dig a hole, fill it with mesquite branches, throw the victim in, and light a match. Pablo doesn't quite believe those stories and doesn't believe that Ramón would do anything like that, but it's a fact that the Juárez cartel gives Los Aztecas a discount on the cocaine that they traffic across the border.

The gang makes a lot of money.

Los Aztecas have a military structure—generals, captain, and lieutenants—and the last time Pablo heard, Ramón was a lieutenant on the way up. He looks like an Azteca—crew cut with a blue bandana, white sleeveless T-shirt, tattoos up his neck.

Ramón looks Pablo up and down. "You look like shit, *'mano*."

"Rough night."

"Looks more like a rough *month*," Ramón says. "You need money?"

"No, thanks."

"How's Mateo?"

"He's good, thanks. Your guys?"

"Isobel's a little bitch on wheels," Ramón answers, "but you already know that. Dolores is almost walking, and Javier, he's playing *fútbol* now."

"No shit."

"You should come by sometime," Ramón says.

"I will."

"Watch a match on TV or something, burn some steaks . . ."

"Sounds great."

Ramón signals the bartender for a refill on his whiskey and then asks, "So what brings you here now?"

Pablo says, "A police lieutenant clipped."

" 'Clipped,' " Ramón says. "Listen to you, tough guy."

Pablo chuckles at his own pretensions, and then asks, "Who did it?"

Ramón knocks his fresh drink down with one gulp and then asks, "You want to do some blow?"

"I have to pick Mateo up," Pablo says, shaking his head. That's true, but the other truth is that he hasn't done drugs in years. Okay, maybe a hit of *yerba* from time to time, but even that's getting rare.

"Anyway, walk out back with me," Ramón says. Then he says to the bartender, *"Narizazo."*

Time to snort up.

Pablo follows him out the back door into the alley. Ramón takes a vial of coke out of his jeans pocket, scoops a little onto his fingernail, and takes a hit. "They say it's bad when you start using your own product. It's just I'm so fucking tired these days, I need a little pick-me-up in the afternoon. So what were you asking me?"

Pablo gets it. Yes, they came out here so Ramón could snort, but also to get away from the ears of the bartender. "These cop killings. Ledesma."

"Wasn't us, 'mano."

Pablo pushes the envelope. "Was Ledesma La Línea? The others?"

"Doesn't matter," Ramón answers. "Sinaloa wants this plaza, so they have to neutralize the cops. Clean cops, dirty cops, if they don't get on board with Sinaloa, Sinaloa is going to take them *off* the board."

So there's my story, Pablo thinks. The Sinaloa cartel has launched a systematic invasion and started with a strategic campaign against the Juárez cartel's central strength—La Línea.

It must have been in the planning for months—the intelligence and infiltration needed to get the officers' phone numbers, their addresses, their daily habits and routes. There had to have been surveillance, phone taps, informants . . .

Ramón shakes some more coke out on his finger and asks, "You sure?"

"Yeah," Pablo says. "So there's going to be a war."

"*Going* to be?" Ramón asks. "What do you call those bodies out there? There *is* a war. It's on."

"Los Aztecas in it?"

"The price we pay, man," Ramón says. "They don't give us the cheap coke because we're pretty. Up until now, it's been taking care of a few *malandros*, now it's going against Barrera's pros. The big-league batters. But we gotta do what we gotta do, and all that bullshit."

They're quiet for a few seconds, then Ramón adds, "I'm always proud of you, 'mano, every time I see your name in the paper. You did good for yourself."

Pablo doesn't know what to say.

Then Ramón grabs him by the elbow. "Don't get too close to this world, it's not anything you want. You need information, you come to me. Don't go around asking a lot of questions. People don't like it."

They say their goodbyes and talk about getting together maybe next Sunday, but they both know it isn't going to happen. Pablo goes back to the office, writes up the story, and then goes to pick up Mateo.

Pablo waits out in front of the preschool.

He really thought that Mateo was too young to start school, "pre" or otherwise, but Victoria argued successfully (of course she did; all of Victoria's arguments are successful) that it was never too early to start, especially if they wanted to get him into a decent elementary school.

Pablo suspects that the deeper motive was to free up more of her time for work. As she makes more money than he does, he was close to volunteering to give up the job at the paper, just freelance and be a stay-at-home dad for the next year or so, but some last vestigial trace of his machismo prevented him.

He didn't think that she would have agreed anyway, on the basis that Mateo's days under his father would not have been sufficiently organized. Which would have been true, Pablo thinks as he watches the children burst out of the door. They would have been wonderfully disorganized.

Mateo is the perfect combination of their union.

His jet-black hair, her piercing (ouch) blue eyes. Her keen intelligence, his warmth. The relentless curiosity comes from both of them.

Pablo is prejudiced, of course, but it is simply evident that Mateo is the handsomest child in the school. And the smartest, and the most charming, and doubtless, of course, the best *fútbol* player. Of course his entire future will be destroyed if he doesn't get into the right elementary school, so Victoria believes.

Mateo runs up and Pablo hugs him. It's amazing, he thinks, that he never gets tired of that sensation.

"How are you, *Papi*?"

"Very well, *m'ijo*. And you?"

"We colored zebras."

"Really?" Pablo asks. "Did they hold still for that?"

Mateo squeals with laughter. *"Papi!"*

"What?"

"They were *paper* zebras!"

"Paper zebras? I never heard of such a thing."

"Pictures of zebras!"

"I see now."

"Silly *Papi*!"

Pablo takes his hand and they start to walk toward the bus stop. This simple, normal activity is an intense relief from the insanity of "narco-world," as he terms it.

"Am I staying with you tonight?" Mateo asks now.

"Yes."

"How many sleeps?"

"What? Oh yes, for two sleeps."

"Yay." He tightens his grip. Then he asks, "What are we doing?"

"If you'd like," Pablo says, "I thought we'd go to the park and kick the ball. Then Tío Tomás is reading from his book. Would you like to go to that?"

"Can I bring coloring?"

"Of course," Pablo says. "Then Tía Ana is having a party. Tía Jimena will be there. Would you like to go to that?"

"Will Tío Giorgio be there?"

"Probably," Pablo answers.

Everyone loves Giorgio, he thinks.

Me too.

"Maybe he'll let me take a picture," Mateo says.

"I'm sure he would," Pablo says. "And if you get tired, you can fall asleep on Tía Ana's big bed."

"Can we go to the zoo?" Mateo asks.

"Saturday?"

"Well, not *today*."

"Yes."

"Good."

"What did you color your zebras?" Pablo asks.

"Orange and blue."

Good, Pablo thinks.

All this narco stuff is foolishness. All that matters is that his son is willing to color zebras in orange and blue.

The two rectangular boxes—one yellow, the other terra-cotta—of Cafebrería, sit on José Reyes Estrada Circle, just off the Plaza de las Américas and close to the university, and are the epicenter of the intellectual life of the city.

It represents everything Pablo loves about Juárez.

A coffeehouse, a bookstore, a gallery, a performance spot, a gathering place for everyone who cares about ideas and art and community, Cafebrería is almost literally the heart of the city for him.

He goes there to see friends, meet new people, find interesting ideas, get into discussions and debates (which occasionally turn into arguments but never fights), listen to music, hear readings, buy books that he can neither afford nor resist, not to mention just get an honest strong cup of coffee that doesn't come from a giant corporate chain, and sit in a quiet spot and read.

Now he sits in a metal folding chair with Mateo at his feet happily coloring (a magenta and turquoise tiger this time) and listens to Tomás read from his latest novel. It's a beautiful book and a beautiful reading, as one would only expect from Tomás Silva, whom Pablo regards as a national treasure.

One thing that Pablo loves about Tomás's readings is that there is no sense of irony in them. The author is serious about his work and reads it seriously, his sad eyes glowing from behind his glasses, his strong jaw set as if he's reconsidering his words as he speaks them.

Ana sits down the row with her eyes closed, shutting off visual stimuli to focus on the sounds of the words. Giorgio stands off to the side, quietly snapping photos of Tomás without the distraction of a flash.

Óscar has his bad leg propped up on the chair beside him, his cane hooked over the chair in front. He and Tomás go back to their university days—close friends still—and Pablo knew that El Búho wouldn't miss this reading.

Really, most of the Juárez intelligentsia are present for the event—writers, poets, columnists, and a scattering of serious readers who always show up for this kind of thing. Pablo recognizes a few local politicians, there to display that they have a brain and, supposedly, a soul, although he doubts both.

Victoria is not there, even though she loves Tomás, both professionally and personally.

Probably working, Pablo thinks.

Victoria is always working.

The reading ends and Tomás takes questions. There are many—some of them legitimately curious and wanting an answer; others more statements than interrogatives, meant to show off the questioner's knowledge or express a dogma. Tomás is patient and painstaking with all of them, but is clearly relieved when the Q&A is over.

Then there's coffee and wine and the usual standing around and schmoozing, but Pablo figures that he's probably used up his four-year-old's full store of patience and takes him across the boulevard into the park to run around and play before they go over to Ana's.

Four hours later, Pablo sits on the kitchen steps that lead into the small fenced-in backyard of Ana's little bungalow in Mariano Escobedo. Pablo has spent many a good evening out there, sitting on the kitchen steps or in one of the wooden chairs, or helping Ana to cook on the little charcoal grill.

Tonight, the house is packed.

Ana of course ended up inviting everyone who attended the reading, and most of them showed up. It didn't matter, she'd made enough paella to feed a small army, and a lot of her guests went out to dinner first before showing up at the party.

And most of them brought wine or beer, as did Pablo, so as not to put a financial strain on the hostess. That was just expected at Juárez gatherings, especially among a group that is mostly communist, or at least socialist, anyway.

Now Pablo sips on a beer and listens to Tomás and El Búho, just slightly in his cups, passionately discuss the romantic lyricism of Efraín Huerta as Giorgio debates the World Bank with an attractive woman whom Pablo doesn't know.

"Fiscal policy as foreplay," Jimena observes as she eases herself down beside Pablo, who slides over to make room.

Jimena is tall and thin, all awkward angles and sharp edges. One of nine brothers and sisters—her family have been bakers out in the Juárez Valley for generations—Jimena is also an activist. In her early fifties now, with two sons who are now young men, she spends more and more time on social causes, which often bring her to Juárez.

They met when Pablo was covering the *feminicidio,* as it came to be called— the disappearances and murders of hundreds of young women.

Three hundred and ninety, to be exact, Pablo thinks.

He covered at least a hundred of them. Saw the bodies—if they were indeed found— interviewed the families, went to the funerals and memorial services. It seems to have ended now, with no more answers than there were when it started. But Jimena, who lost a niece, helped to create an organization—Our Daughters Coming Home—to pressure police and politicians to close the cases.

Now she wryly observes Giorgio make his moves.

"He does have a certain charm," Jimena says. "What about you? Any romance in your life?"

"Not lately," Pablo says. "Between work and having a kid . . ."

"Mateo's getting big."

"He is."

"Such a nice boy."

And he loves his Tía Jimena, Pablo thinks. Mateo went to her the second they got into the house, climbed into her lap, and they had a serious conversation about zebras, tigers, and other animals.

Then she got Mateo a bowl of rice from the paella and, after securing Pablo's permission, some *polvorones de canela,* then eventually took him into Ana's big bed and read him a story until he fell asleep.

"How's Victoria?" Jimena asks.

"She's Victoria," Pablo answers. "Conquering the world."

"Poor world." She ruffles his hair. "Poor Pablo. Our big, shaggy puppy of a Pablo. Who is Giorgio seducing now?"

"Some lawyer, I think."

"Is he succeeding?"

"Just a matter of time," Pablo says.

But Giorgio breaks it off and comes to sit down with them, and the lawyer goes into the house.

"Neofascist dyke," Giorgio says.

"Now, now," Jimena warns.

"Left-wing lesbians are perfectly natural," Giorgio says, "but there's something about a right-wing lesbian that's, I don't know . . . almost North American. Sort of Fox News–ish."

They get El Paso television broadcasts in Juárez, and Giorgio is masochistically addicted to Fox News, which makes him simultaneously livid and horny.

"Tell me you don't want to do those women on Fox News," Jimena says.

"Tell me *you* don't," Giorgio counters. "Anyway, of course I do. I want to convert them through the subversive power of the orgasm."

"So it *would* be a political act," Jimena says.

"I am willing to sacrifice myself for the cause," Giorgio answers.

"How did she find her way to this party?" Pablo asks.

"She's a disciple of Tomás's," Giorgio answers. "She thinks he's 'important.'"

"He is," Jimena says. "And her supporting the World Bank doesn't necessarily make her a fascist any more than her resisting your doubtless charms makes her a dyke."

"I just couldn't imagine waking up with her," Giorgio says. "What would we talk about?"

"How wonderful you were in bed?" Jimena suggests.

"Certainly, but that gets boring after a few times," Giorgio says.

"*Pobrecito*. Such problems."

"*You* should go after her, Pablo," Giorgio says. "She's your type."

"But I'm not hers," Pablo answers.

"Pablo is giving up on love," Jimena says.

"Who said anything about love?"

"*What* about love?" Ana asks as she comes out the door. She sits down on Jimena's lap.

"Why do women love to talk about love?" Giorgio asks.

"Why don't men, is more the question," Ana says.

"You can either love," Pablo says, "or you can talk about it. You can't do both."

Ana whoops, then hollers, "Óscar, did you know that you have a young Hemingway working on your staff?"

Óscar blinks vacantly—he's much too involved in the discussion of poetry for this—but smiles politely before he turns back to make a point to Tomás.

"I'm a little drunk," Pablo admits.

"But you make a point," Giorgio says.

"Oh?" Ana asks. "So, Giorgio, can you either make love or photograph it, but not both?"

The edge in her voice makes Pablo certain now that they had sex.

"You should have seen Ana with our esteemed governor today," Giorgio says, changing the subject. "She had him sputtering."

Ana laughs, then does a rather good imitation of the Chihuahua state governor: "'On the subject of a so-called cartel in Juárez, it does not now nor never has existed, and moreover, my administration has made excellent progress in combating it if it does or has, which, of course, it doesn't and hasn't, unless you have evidence that you're about to show me, in which case I'm late for a very important meeting.' He's a great idiot, our governor, but very well bred. He kissed my hand."

"He didn't," Jimena says.

"He did," Ana answers. "I blushed."

"You didn't."

"No, I didn't," Ana answers. "But I didn't dislike it as much as I thought I would. It's been a long time since a man has kissed my hand."

Pablo leans across and touches his lips to her fingers.

"Oh, so sweet, Pablo," Jimena says.

Ana looks at him curiously, then recovers and says, "Anyway, certainly there are more important stories to cover, with PAN taking us into the brave new world of free-market economics just as all the jobs are going to China, and Bush killing every Muslim that moves."

"Bush speaks Spanish, you know," Giorgio says.

"That's the brother," Ana corrects him. "The one in Florida."

The conversation swings from the brothers Bush to the war in Iraq to the emerging rights of Muslim women to postfeminism to current cinema—Mexican, American, European (Giorgio goes spasmodically mad over Buñuel), and back to Mexican again—to the relative superiority of shrimp over any other kind of taco to the excellence of Ana's paella, to Ana's childhood, then to Jimena's, to the changing role of motherhood in a postindustrial world, to sculpture, then painting, then poetry, then baseball, then Jimena's inexplicable (to Pablo) fondness for American football (she's a Dallas Cowboys fan) over real (to Pablo) *fútbol,* to his admittedly adolescent passion for the game, to the trials of adolescence itself and revelations over the loss of virginity and why we refer to it *as* a loss and now Óscar and Tomás, arms over each other's shoulders, are chanting poetry and then Giorgio picks up a guitar and starts to play and this is the Juárez that Pablo loves, this is the city of his soul—the poetry, the passionate discussions (Ana makes her counterpoints jabbing her cigarette like a foil; Jimena's words flow like a gentle wave across beach sand, washing away the words before; Giorgio trills a jazz saxophone while Pablo plays bass—they are a jazz combo of argument), the ideas flowing with the wine and beer, the lilting music in a black night, this is the gentle heartbeat of the Mexico that he adores, the laughter, the subtle perfume of desert flowers that grow in alleys alongside garbage, and now everyone is singing—

México, está muy contento,
Dando gracias a millares . . .

—and this is his life—this is his city, these are his friends, his beloved friends, *these people,* and if this is all that there is or will be, it is enough for him, his world, his life, his city, his people, his sad beautiful Juárez . . .

—*empezaré de Durango, Torreón y Ciudad de Juárez . . .*

Pablo sings into the soft night.

Sundays are the worst.

They always are, but especially when he has to bring Mateo back to his mother. And Mateo is sad, too. Are they his own feelings? Pablo wonders, or is he picking up my melancholy?

Pablo makes them a simple breakfast of croissants, jam, and butter—Mateo has milk while he has café blanca—and then they walk over to the park to kick the ball around. They try to joke and laugh, but they're each aware that they're just killing time, postponing the sadness, and after a while Pablo asks Mateo if he's ready to go "home" and he says yes.

So Pablo calls Victoria and tells her that they're on their way, and they take a bus to her neighborhood and then walk down to her condo. It's a gated community but Pablo has the code, and anyway the guard recognizes them and passes them through.

Victoria is waiting out front.

She hugs and kisses Mateo, then says, "Honey, run inside and get ready for your bath, please. *Mami* wants to talk to *Papi*."

Mateo hugs his father and trudges inside.

"He's tired," Victoria says. "Did you let him stay up?"

"He went to bed at Ana's," Pablo says a little defensively. "At the usual time."

"Well, Ana has some sense," Victoria says. She looks tired herself and she's dressed professionally and Pablo is sure she took advantage of the free Sunday to get some time in at her desk. Tired or no, she looks beautiful, and Pablo is chagrined to feel the same old stir that he always feels.

Then she says, "Pablo, I've been offered a new job. A promotion."

"That's great. Congratulations."

"It's *El Nacional.* In Mexico City."

Pablo feels his heart stop. "Well, you're not taking it."

"Well, I am," she says. "A national newspaper? Editor of the financial desk? Come on."

"What about Mateo?"

She has the decency to look a little abashed. "He's coming with me. Of course."

"He's my son."

"I'm aware of that, yes."

Pablo feels anger welling up inside him. "Then you're also 'aware,'" he says, "that I have certain paternal rights."

"I was hoping you'd be reasonable."

"That *I'd* be reasonable?! You're talking about taking my son to live a thousand miles away!"

"Please keep your voice down."

"I'll yell if I want!"

"So mature."

"You're not taking Mateo away from me."

"I'm not staying in this . . . border town," she spits. "Not when I have the opportunity to go someplace else. And think of Mateo. Better schools, better friends . . ."

"His school and his friends are just fine."

"The problem with you—"

"Oh, just *one* problem today?"

"*One* of the problems with you," she says, "is that you can't see beyond this backwater. Nothing happens here, Pablo. No one who lives here makes any decisions about what happens here, because the people with the power all live somewhere else. This is a colony and you're a hopeless colonial. I don't want that for Mateo and I don't want it for me."

It's quite a speech and he's sure that she carefully rehearsed it. "But you're all right with him growing up without a father."

"You're a wonderful father. But—"

"Not a phrase generally followed by a 'but.' "

"—you have no ambition. And Mateo sees that." She looks down, and then makes herself look back up at him. "You can come on weekends—"

"I can't afford that."

"—or I'll bring him here," Victoria says. "When he's a little older, he can fly himself—"

"He's four!"

"The flight attendants take very good care of children," Victoria says. "I see it all the time."

"This is not going to happen," Pablo says.

"I've already accepted the position."

"Without talking with me first."

"You see what happens when we try to talk," Victoria says. "You won't listen to reason, you get emotional—"

"You're goddamn right I get emotional about losing my child!"

"You're not losing him!"

"Then let him stay here with me," Pablo says. "This is the only home he knows."

"That's part of the problem," Victoria says. "He can't live with you, Pablo. You're out half the night. Covering stories, drinking, doing God knows what . . ."

"I'm always there, sober, when he's with me!"

"Yes, I know."

"You're the one who's leaving, not me," Pablo says. "It isn't fair."

"You sound like a child."

"See if I sound like a child in court."

"You will," she says, because she can't help herself. "I was hoping it wouldn't come to that. But I have spoken to an attorney—"

"Of course you have."

"—and she tells me that I will have no trouble retaining custody of Mateo when I explain how this will improve the quality of his life—"

"You bitch."

"You could always move to Mexico City," Victoria says. "Get a job there and then you'd be close. I could talk to some people . . ."

"There are thousands of journalists in Mexico City," he says. "Natives. I know Juárez. I cover Juárez."

"And that's all you want."

"It's all I've ever wanted."

"And there we are."

She turns and walks away, leaving him standing there.

Victoria goes inside and lets herself cry for a minute before she calls Mateo for his bath.

Poor Pablo, she thinks.

Poor lost Pablo, adrift in a sea of his own sorrow.

He was never the same after the *feminicidio*, never the same and never even knew it. Day after day—more often night after night, or dawn after dawn—he would come home depressed, angry, tired, and sad.

As, one after another, young women disappeared and his beloved city became an abattoir. He could never understand it, never account for it, never explain it—to himself or to his readers—and when the killings faded away it seemed that he had faded away with them.

His drive, his ambition, his fierce love of life.

All muted or gone.

She tried to talk to him about it but he wouldn't talk, became angry if she even brought it up. He went out all the time, seeking answers, and if she complained then she was the heartless bitch.

The *feminicidio* killed their marriage.

Killed, to some extent, the woman inside her.

Because she could never understand, can still not understand, how he could love a city where that could happen.

If Sundays are the worst, Sunday nights somehow manage to achieve a less-than-zero, a negative "quality of life" number, especially when your ex-wife tells you that she's taking your son, and you decide to get a lawyer of your own and fight it, but when you know that you can't afford a really good lawyer and that she's going to win anyway.

And that a court fight will tear your kid apart.

And that there's no good answer.

He thinks of seeking Giorgio out to commiserate, or Ana, or even Ramón. Ramón would be good to drink with tonight, because he wouldn't intellectualize it, he'd just say, "Fuck that *segundera*" and "No one can take a man's son away from him" and things that Pablo wants to hear.

But he doesn't call Giorgio or Ana (would they fall into bed together on this sad night, him needing, her needing to offer, consolation) or Ramón. He just goes alone from bar to bar in old downtown, in Old Juárez, and has a whiskey in each, even though he knows it won't help his financial situation at all. He gets miserably, soddenly drunk, but at least manages to refrain from phoning Victoria and begging.

He makes it home, flops down on the bed, and sobs.

"You look horrible," Ana says the next morning at the café.

"That good?" Pablo asks.

"May I ask what . . ."

He tells her about Victoria and Mateo.

"That's terrible, Pablo. I'm so sorry."

He nods.

"Listen," she says, "Óscar has very good connections in the national media. I'm sure he'd put in a few calls. He wouldn't want to lose you, but—"

"Let's not kid ourselves, okay?" Pablo asks. "At least let's not start doing that."

A week later, Pablo stands in front of the monument to fallen police officers at the corner of Juan Gabriel and Avenida Sanders.

The bronze policeman has his eyes closed in prayer; at his feet is the cap of a brother officer. By the cap, held down by a rock, is a cardboard placard with big letters written in black magic marker: FOR THOSE WHO DID NOT BELIEVE—CHAIREZ, ROMO, BACA, GÓMEZ, AND LEDESMA.

The five Juárez cops shot to death earlier in the month.

Another banner reads FOR THOSE WHO CONTINUE NOT BELIEVING, and lists seventeen more Juárez police officers by name.

"You getting this?" Pablo asks.

Giorgio's too busy snapping away to give the obvious answer but, without taking his eye from the viewfinder, asks back, "Who do you think put this up?"

"The 'New People,'" Pablo answers. "Telling the Juárez cops—specifically, seventeen of them—that either they get on the Sinaloa cartel bus or get run over by it."

"It confirms your story," Giorgio says.

It does that, Pablo thinks. His story about the cop killings and the Sinaloa cartel has caused a stir. Some people believed it, others thought it was pure paranoid fantasy, something that Pablo Mora made up.

Apparently not, Pablo thinks as he copies the names down in his notebook.

The sixth on the list is his old source from the bad old days, Victor Abrego, who just a few days before told Pablo to get lost.

Shit, Pablo thinks.

The banners, which appeared overnight, have drawn a crowd of curious onlookers as well as media—television news trucks and stand-up radio announcers. Oscar will want the story filed quickly.

It will present El Búho with an ethical conundrum, Pablo thinks—whether to publish the names of police officers threatened with the choice between collusion and death, the old *plata o plomo*, "silver or lead," dilemma.

In a way, though, Pablo thinks, the New People have already published the names, haven't they? It's the new face of narco gang war, isn't it? They're becoming media savvy. They used to hide their crimes, now they publicize them. I wonder if they haven't taken a page from Al Qaeda. What good is an atrocity if no one knows you did it?

And maybe that's the lede on my story. "The crimes that used to lurk in shadows now seek the sunlight," or is that a little too "pulp"?

Óscar will decide.

Pablo goes out to Galeana to talk to Abrego. But what the hell am I going to ask him? Pablo wonders. *Are you worried about the threat on your life? Is the Sinaloa cartel threatening you because you're an honest cop causing them problems, or because you're La Línea?* Stupid questions that Abrego won't answer anyway. But maybe he'll give me something on deep background.

Yeah, except Pablo can't find him.

Not on the corner, not on the street, not in any of the restaurants, cafés, or bars that the cop usually hangs out in.

Abrego is in the wind.

Out of habit, Pablo checks his watch to see if it's time to pick up Mateo, then remembers that Mateo isn't here anymore, but in Mexico City with his mother.

A month has gone by, and the day that Victoria took his son away is as raw as a razor cut.

"Will you pick me up at school, *Papi*?" Mateo asked.

"No, *m'ijo*," Pablo said, kneeling in front of him. "Not every day."

"Who'll pick me up?"

"You'll have a very nice nanny," Victoria said.

"I don't want a nanny," Pablo cried. "I want my *papi*."

Pablo picked him up and hugged him tight. When he finally set him down, Pablo whispered into Victoria's ear, "I hate you for this. Do you understand? I hate you and I hope you die."

"Stay classy, Pablo." Then she put Mateo in the car seat of her Jetta and drove away.

Mateo waved at him.

It broke his heart.

It broke his goddamn heart.

Mateo has flown back to Juárez once, a frightened little boy getting off the plane with a flight attendant taking his hand. The weekend with Mateo was wonderful, but Pablo has to wonder if it's worth it, or if he's just being selfish, because the Sunday parting was so hard on Mateo, who started feeling anxious in the morning—he was sick to his stomach and didn't want to eat his breakfast—and was crying by afternoon.

And Pablo has come to *hate* the words *"Papi* will see you soon."

Pablo has given up his apartment—that money goes to the custody lawyer and to the visits to Mexico City. He crashes on Giorgio's couch, or, if the photographer is "entertaining" at home, on the sofa in Ana's living room, fifty feet and a thousand miles from her bedroom.

The police scanner squawks, *"Motivo 59."*

"Shit," Pablo says.

Fifty-nine is the code for a killing. He listens for another second and hears the dispatcher add, *"Two 92s."*

Two males.

He heads for the address.

The two corpses are out in Colonia Córdoba Américas in the middle of Vía Río Champotón, their hands bound behind their backs with adhesive tape.

"I'm getting nostalgic," Giorgio says, snapping away, "for the days I used to shoot *live* people."

"Do we have names?" Pablo asks. Óscar always wants names. ("We aren't going to yield to the cheap grotesquerie of the 'nameless dead,'" he says.)

"I'm just the photographer."

Pablo tracks them down through the cops who took their wallets and IDs. Their names are Jesús Duràn and Fernando González, twenty-four and thirty-two years old respectively.

"They're Sinaloans," Pablo tells Giorgio. "*New People.*"

"Not anymore they're not," Giorgio answers. It's hard, he complains, coming up with fresh angles.

Tell me about it, Pablo thinks as he hears the dispatcher: "*Motivo 59. One 92.*"

The last body is in the back of a pickup truck in Galeana.

It's Abrego.

His hands are plastic-tied, a filthy rag is stuffed in his mouth, and he's been shot in the back of the head.

What a lesser writer than Pablo would call "execution style."

Two days later, Pablo covers an army raid on a house in the Pradera Dorada neighborhood where the soldiers seize twenty-five assault rifles, five pistols, seven fragmentation grenades, 3,494 rounds of ammunition, bulletproof vests, eight radios, and five vehicles with Sinaloa plates.

The very next day the army raids another house, arrests twenty-one men, and seizes ten AK-47s, 13,000 hits of cocaine, 2.1 kilos of cocaine paste, 760 grams of marijuana, 401 rounds of ammunition, uniforms of the Mexican army and AFI, and three vehicles.

And a helicopter.

Pablo is in the city room the next morning when Óscar announces that they've received a press release from the Juárez Municipal Police Department.

"The police are no longer going to answer calls," Óscar says, "but stay in the station houses."

"So the people we pay to protect us," Ana says, "can't protect themselves."

But the retreat to the station houses doesn't do much good. The day after the press release, two Juárez police officers are kidnapped in separate incidents. Two days later, a Juárez police *comandante* is shot in the head in Chihuahua City.

The next day, Óscar sends Pablo and Giorgio out to Cocoyoc Street.

The house in the Cuernavaca neighborhood had been seized three weeks ago when the army found almost two tons of marijuana inside. Then an anonymous phone tip told them to dig under the patio.

When Pablo gets out there he gags and struggles not to throw up.

Three trunks of bodies, their arms and legs hacked off, are lined up on the lawn.

Beside them are two decapitated heads.

Throughout the course of a long day, the soldiers find a total of nine dismembered bodies under the concrete.

"I'm beginning to feel like a pornographer," Giorgio says as he takes the photographs.

Violence porn, Pablo thinks. He wonders if Óscar will really put these images on the pages of his newspaper.

A lot of papers do. It's become a new industry, *la nota roja*, tabloids with pictures of the dead—the bloodier the better—hawked by newsboys from street corners and traffic islands. You can make a lot of money taking photos for *la nota roja*, and Pablo wonders if Giorgio is tempted.

Now Pablo tries to get identifications of the dead, but the soldiers look at him like he's crazy. They haven't even matched the heads to the bodies; something, Pablo learns, that the coroner will try to do by matching the cut marks on the trunks and the necks.

"Decapitations?" Pablo asks Ana over a drink (okay, drinks) at San Martín that night. "When did we start doing *that*, cutting off heads?"

"It's not new," Ana said. "Remember that thing in Michoacán last year? Five heads rolled into a nightclub?"

"But that's Michoacán," Pablo answered. "Religious whack jobs."

"So to speak."

"Not funny."

"Sorry." It's *not* funny, Ana thinks. It's horrific, disgusting, and traumatic, and she worries about Pablo. Since Victoria took Mateo away, Pablo's treating himself like a refugee—staying out half the night, drinking too much, crashing on couches.

Including yours, Ana reminds herself. She's thought of going out there and inviting him into her bed, but it's a bad idea. Pablo is a train wreck waiting to happen—it would be simply self-destructive to get on board the Mora Express now. But she feels for him and worries about him, just as she worries about her city and, well, herself.

Admit it, Ana thinks.

You're scared.

Journalists have already been killed in Nuevo Laredo, and now the war has come here, and she feels this sense of threat that she can't seem to shake off. It's annoying—she's a tough "hard-bitten" reporter of the old school, and she's seen and reported *plenty*.

But this seems different.

Cops hiding in the station houses . . .

Decapitated, dismembered bodies under patios . . .

It's surreal, like one of those dreams you have after too much booze chased with spicy food.

The difference here is that the alarm clock doesn't seem to ring.

But the next morning, Pablo actually whoops with laughter.

The same press release in which the Juárez mayor's office announces that ninety-five people have been killed in the first two months of 2008 also announces a major crackdown on jaywalking.

Then the army comes in. The Juárez mayor didn't want them in the city but felt that he had no choice. With the police department dysfunctional he was simply out of men, and not only were the murders stacking up, but "ordinary" street crime was out of control.

So he made a deal with the federal government—Los Pinos would send in troops in exchange for a complete remaking of the city police department. The government launches "Operation Chihuahua" and sends 4,000 troops with 180 armored vehicles and an air wing that includes a helicopter gunship.

At first it does little good.

A city policewoman is struck with thirty-two bullets as she opens the door to her house. A police chief in the small town of El Carrizo on the Texas border is killed in his car as he pulls into his driveway. The army has to take over the town because every police officer quit or just ran off after that.

When police bring four narcos into a Juárez hospital, other narcos come in and execute them on their gurneys. Hospital staffers call police for three hours, but nobody comes.

It gets worse and worse.

A twenty-four-year-old woman is killed in a crossfire at the car wash where she works. Two Juárez cops are gunned down as they drop their kids off at school. A twelve-year-old girl is killed when narcos in a gun battle use her as a human shield.

The mayor of Juárez tells Ana in an interview that he knew "the killing season" was coming, had been informed that it would start in January, and that it was just a conflict between two rival gangs.

The governor announces that of the five hundred—*five hundred*—people killed in Chihuahua so far in the year, the mayor said, "only five" were "innocents."

Only five, Pablo thinks.

Does that count the baby in the young woman's womb?

It infuriates him, this killing, this death.

Infuriating that this is what we're known for now, drug cartels and slaughter. This my city of Avenida 16 Septembre, the Victoria Theater, cobblestone streets, the bullring, La Central, La Fogata, more bookstores than El Paso, the university, the ballet, *garapiñados, pan dulce,* the mission, the plaza, the Kentucky Bar, Fred's—now it's known for these idiotic thugs.

And my country, Mexico—the land of writers and poets—of Octavio Paz, Juan Rulfo, Carlos Fuentes, Elena Garro, Jorge Volpi, Rosario Castellanos, Luis Urrea, Elmer Mendoza, Alfonso Reyes—the land of painters and sculptors—Diego Rivera, Frida Kahlo, Gabriel Orozco, Pablo O'Higgins, Juan Soriano, Francisco Goitia—of dancers like Guillermina Bravo, Gloria and Nellie Campobello, Josefina Lavalle, Ana Mérida, and composers—Carlos Chávez, Silvestre Revueltas, Agustín Lara, Blas Galindo—architects—Luis Barragán, Juan O'Gorman, Tatiana Bilbao, Michel Rojkind, Pedro Vásquez—wonderful filmmakers—Fernando de Fuentes, Alejandro Iñárritu, Luis Buñuel, Alfonso Cuarón, Guillermo del Toro—actors like Dolores del Río, "La Doña" María Félix, Pedro Infante, Jorge Negrete, Salma Hayek—now the names are "famous" narcos—no more than sociopathic murderers whose sole contribution to the culture has been the *narcocorridas* sung by no-talent sycophants.

Mexico, the land of pyramids and palaces, deserts and jungles, mountains and beaches, markets and gardens, boulevards and cobblestoned streets, broad plazas and hidden courtyards, is now known as a slaughter ground.

And for what?

So North Americans can get high.

Just across the bridge is the gigantic marketplace, the insatiable consumer machine that drives the violence here. North Americans smoke the dope, snort the coke, shoot the heroin, do the meth, and then have the nerve to point south (*down,* of course, on the map), and wag their fingers at the "Mexican drug problem" and Mexican corruption.

It's not the "Mexican drug problem," Pablo thinks now, it's the North American drug problem.

As for corruption, who's more corrupt—the seller or the buyer? And how corrupt does a society have to be when its citizens need to get high to escape their reality, at the cost of bloodshed and suffering of their neighbors?

Corrupt to the soul.

That's the big story, he thinks.

That's the story someone should write.

Well, maybe I will.

And no one will read it.

Pablo is holding up pretty well under all this until the Casas murder.

Police captain Alejandro Casas was also named on the placard. He's leaving his house to drop his eight-year-old son at school on his way to work when five men with AKs attack his Nissan pickup truck in the driveway.

Casas is killed immediately.

A dozen 7.62 rounds shatter the boy's left arm.

The EMTs manage to get to him quickly, but he bleeds to death in the ambulance.

Pablo comes back from the emergency room, dutifully types up the story, and then leaves the office with the intention of getting very drunk. Out on the sidewalk, a man he doesn't know comes up to him and slips an envelope into the inside pocket of his rumpled khaki blazer.

"What are you doing?" Pablo asks, completely taken aback. "Who are you and what are you doing?"

"Take it," the man says. He has the face of a cop and the body to match. Barrel chest, wide shoulders that strain his gray sports coat. Pablo has met dozens of cops but he doesn't know this one.

"What is this?" he repeats.

"*El sobre,*" the man says.

The bribe.

"I don't want it."

The man's smile turns threatening. "I'm not asking you if you *want* it, *m'ijo*. I'm saying take it."

Pablo tries to give him the envelope back, but the man traps his wrist against his chest before he can get to it. "Take it. There'll be another like it every Monday."

"From who?"

"Does it matter?" the man asks.

Then he walks away.

Pablo rips the envelope open.

It's three times his weekly salary.

In cash.

Enough to hire a decent lawyer, if that's what he wants to do. Enough, if you add it up week by week, to take a flight to Mexico City twice a month and rent a modest room. Enough . . .

He recalls an old *dicho*—

When the devil comes, he comes on angel's wings.

3

Jolly Coppers on Parade

Oh, they look so nice
Looks like the angels have come down from Paradise

—Randy Newman
"Jolly Coppers on Parade"

Mexico City
2008

Keller walks down the center aisle to the Altar of Forgiveness.

As if, he thinks.

The altar allegedly got its name because victims of the Inquisition were brought there to ask for absolution before they were taken out and executed.

Yvette Tapia kneels there now, her head covered in a veil.

Keller kneels beside her.

She'd called an hour ago.

Not with the confident voice he's used to, but something different. Stressed, under pressure. Not surprising, given that she's on the run from both Barrera and the police. "Can we meet?"

The Metropolitan Cathedral in Cuernavaca is hundreds of years old, started in 1562—almost sixty years, Keller thinks, before the Pilgrims set foot on Plymouth Rock. The stones were taken from the destroyed temple of the Aztec god Huitzilopochtli, so, in a sense it's even older. The cathedral wasn't finished until 1813 and has survived floods, fires, and earthquakes.

They don't talk. He simply feels her hand reach out and put something in his. Keller slips it into his pocket.

Yvette crosses herself, gets up, and walks out.

Keller forces himself to wait long enough to mumble a decent prayer and then goes through the mockery of a confession with a Mexican priest.

Forgive me, Father, for I have sinned, he thinks. I have lied, been otherwise deceitful, and have touched off a war that has taken lives and will take more. In short, I have inspired men to murder, and I hold hatred in my heart.

He doesn't say that, but confesses instead to impure thoughts about women and receives the penance of a half dozen Hail Marys, which he says at the altar before he leaves the cathedral.

Back out on Madero Street, he refrains from the temptation of reaching into his jacket pocket to touch the item that Yvette gave him. He's seen it a hundred times from street dealers or buyers—that guilty "tell" where the contraband is. Instead, he stops at a street stand and buys a paper bag of *papas* with hot sauce and eats them while he checks the street for any surveillance that might have dropped Yvette in favor of him. The greasy potato chips taste good. He crumples up the bag, throws it into a trash can, and drives back to Mexico City.

It's a tape cassette.

Keller puts on headphones and listens.

"By all means continue your campaign in Michoacán. La Familia is a dangerous threat to public safety—lunatics really—not to mention the largest purveyors of methamphetamine in the country."

Keller recognizes the voice—Martín Tapia.

"What about the Zetas?"

Keller thinks he recognizes that voice, too.

Gerardo Vera.

The guards stop Keller in front of Aguilar's house.

It's late, after ten at night, and the guards are wary. They are asking what he's doing there when Lucinda comes to the door.

"Arturo?"

"I'm sorry to bother you," Keller says. "Is Luis home?"

"Come in, please."

As she ushers Keller inside, Aguilar walks in from the den and looks at Keller quizzically.

"Do you have a moment?" Keller asks.

"Do you know what time it is?"

"I wanted to wait until the kids were in bed," Keller says.

Aguilar stares at him for a long moment, and then says, "Ten minutes. Come into the study."

"Do you want coffee?" Lucinda asks. "A glass of wine?"

"No," Aguilar snaps.

Keller follows him into the study. Aguilar sits down and looks at Keller as if to ask, *So?*

"I came to apologize," Keller says. "My suspicions about you were wrong."

Aguilar looks surprised but unconvinced. "Thank you. But this doesn't change my mind about you. Is that all?"

Keller takes the audiocassette out of his pocket and sets it on the desk.

"What is this?" Aguilar asks.

"Play it."

Aguilar gets up and slips the cassette into a player. He sits back down and listens. *"By all means continue your campaign in Michoacán. La Familia is a dangerous threat to public safety—lunatics really—not to mention the largest purveyors of methamphetamine in the country."*

"Martín Tapia," Keller says.

"Well, *you* would know," Aguilar says. "And you didn't tell me about this because you suspected I was complicit."

He says this as a fact, not a question, and Keller doesn't answer.

"Did you tell Vera?" Aguilar asks.

"No."

Aguilar restarts the tape.

"What about the Zetas?"

Keller watches Aguilar's face turn pale and his jaw tighten as he rewinds the tape and listens again.

"It can't be," Aguilar says, stopping the tape.

Keller says nothing.

"Where did you get this?"

Keller shakes his head, then leans over and hits PLAY.

"What about the Zetas?"

"They're under our protection now."

"By 'our protection' you mean . . ."

"Us and Adán."

"He said this specifically."

"Adán sent us to inform you of this specifically, yes."

"Is there a problem?"

Keller stops the tape. "I don't know, but I'm thinking that's Diego."

Aguilar nods and starts the tape again.

"Turning government policy around like that . . . it's going to cost more money."

"We pay you half a million a month."

Keller thinks Aguilar's jaw might break.

"It's not for us."

There's a silence, then Martín Tapia says, *"We're willing to pay a reasonable bonus in addition to the normal payment, if that will help smooth over any rough patches."*

"I'm sure it would help."

"I'd think they'd be pleased to go after La Familia. You can't do business with religious fanatics."

Aguilar stops the tape. "Who are they talking about? How high does this go?"

It's time, Keller thinks.

To decide if he trusts this man or he doesn't. If Aguilar is clean, he'll work with me. If he's dirty, this tape disappears and I'm a dead man. He takes a deep breath and then tells Aguilar all about his surveillance of Yvette Tapia, and how it led to the Amaros, and, by inference, to Los Pinos.

Aguilar takes it in, realizing that his closest colleague is dirty, then sits quietly. Keller watches him work it through, a man considering a chessboard.

It's vastly complicated, Keller knows. Aguilar can't know how high up the corruption goes, or how thorough it is. His boss, the attorney general, was appointed by the president. And is his own organization, SEIDO, clean? He doesn't know if he can trust the people he works for, or the people who work for him. It isn't just bureaucratic backstabbing—the chance of losing a job or even a career.

It's life and death.

They could kill him.

"Luis," Keller says, "you have a wife and kids. If you want to walk away from this, no one would blame you."

"I would," Aguilar says.

He gets up, and Keller hears him tell Lucinda that he's going out and doesn't know when he'll be back.

They sit in a closed, locked room deep inside the SEIDO building and replay the tape again and again.

There are seven distinct voices at the meeting.

Martín Tapia is easy, but they still run it on voice recognition software against the tape of his phone calls from Cuernavaca, and it matches.

Aguilar locates old surveillance tape of Diego and matches that.

Then they run the voice that neither of them wants to run.

"Turning government policy around like that . . . it's going to cost more money."

"It's not for us." "I'm sure it would help."

Aguilar places this on one track, then on another runs, *"They surrender or they die. That's their only choice.* Los malosos—*the bad guys—are not going to run Mexico."*

Keller watches the parallel lines spike on the voice recognition screen.

It's a match.

Gerardo Vera.

Aguilar doesn't even pause, but goes to work on the other voices. It takes hours, but he finds tapes of Bravo conducting an interrogation, Aristeo doing a press conference when he was first appointed, and Galvén giving a speech to a community group.

Bravo, Aristeo, and Galvén match with voices making small talk in the meeting.

"So," Aguilar says calmly, as if discussing a theoretical law school problem, "we have a thesis: The Tapias were the paymasters for the Sinaloa cartel. Vera and the others were on that payroll, as were high-ranking members of the administration. Then Barrera made his arrangement with us to betray the Tapias in exchange for his nephew. Somehow"—he looks pointedly at Keller—"the Tapias found out, creating a break in the cartel. The Tapias murdered three police officers, as well as Salvador Barrera, in revenge for Alfredo and to improve their position in a war with Barrera. They either wouldn't or couldn't get to Vera, nor did they anticipate that public backlash would strengthen the government, which they view as Barrera's ally, so they leaked a tape incriminating the dead officers and Vera."

Sounds about right, Keller thinks.

The question is what to do about it.

Aguilar's first instinct is to arrest Vera, but it's a rash move and rashness is not on his operational menu. Gerardo has surrounded himself with security in the wake of the assassinations, and there could actually be a gunfight between his AFI men and Aguilar's.

Besides, Gerardo has the ear of the president, at the very least.

The prosecutor in Aguilar takes over. The tape isn't enough to nail him—he could challenge that the voice is his, he could claim that yes, he was at the meeting to "set up" the Tapias—the proof being that he ordered the raids on Alfredo and Diego, and why would he do that if he were on their payroll?

"He's not," Keller argues, "he's on *Barrera's* payroll."

"Prove it," Aguilar counters.

They need witnesses, someone to wear a wire, they need a complete investigation into Gerardo's finances. "And that just takes us as far as Vera," Aguilar says. "What about the president's office?"

They have information that could bring down a government. And that government isn't going to investigate itself.

Which begs another question.

"Do you intend to turn this over to DEA?" Aguilar asks.

"It's what I'm supposed to do."

"This is not what I asked you."

It's tricky, Keller thinks. He works for DEA, not SEIDO; for the United States, not Mexico. He's holding crucial information that directly impacts DEA operations and investigations, maybe even the safety of undercover agents, if DEA is giving Vera information that he might pass on to Barrera.

Certainly, Keller thinks, Vera has passed on information about you.

And DEA could do what SEIDO really can't: conduct an independent investigation of the Mexican government. It has the surveillance technology, the ability to hack computers and break codes, intercept communications. SEIDO can do that—to a certain extent—but without getting caught? Who knows what worms have been implanted in the SEIDO machine?

So DEA can do it—and what they can't, the CIA or NSA can—but will they?

They're in love with Vera. If he were a woman they'd marry him, and his supporters in Washington—and they are legion—will argue that he's getting results. It might not even matter to them that he's getting those results for Adán Barrera, as long as he's taking down the Tijuana cartel, the Juárez cartel—and now the Gulf, the Zetas, and La Familia. Keller can hear Taylor say it now—*So Vera's pulling in a half a million a month for taking down narcos? Good—we couldn't pay him that much.*

You're being too cynical, Keller tells himself.

One of the two men in charge of antidrug operations is dirty? Of course DEA wants to know. The president's office implicated? That goes to the White House. Billions of dollars are being considered in a major aid program. To fight drug trafficking.

But he knows what Aguilar is asking and why. The SEIDO chief is a patriot, fiercely protective of his country, and now he's ashamed. And he'd be even more shamed if the U.S. Big Brother steps in to fix it, condemning Mexican corruption. It's the worst of Aguilar's nightmares.

"It's going to come out, Luis," Keller says. "You know that. If we don't act, the Tapias will find someone who will."

Brave new world, Keller thinks. In giving me the tape, the Tapia cartel is, in effect, applying for American aid.

"A few weeks," Aguilar says. "Let me do what I can to complete the investigation. If I can develop the evidence I need, *I'll* meet with your superiors. We'll go together."

Keller makes the deal.

Three of the men in that meeting are dead.

But there was another voice on the tape.

A voice we haven't identified.

Who doesn't say much. A few times after Martín Tapia makes a point, you hear the voice agreeing, *Chido. Chido.*

Cool, cool.

They pull personnel records on every hire Vera made to AFI, and, since his promotion, to any federal police position, and find they have something else in common—all of them served together as beat cops in the tough *colonia* of Iztapalapa back in the '90s.

Galvén was there.

So were Bravo and Aristeo.

They find three other high-ranking officers: Igor Barragán, Luis Labastida, Javier Palacios. All served with Vera in Iztapalapa, all were hired when he started AFI.

Now Barragán is the AFI coordinator for regional security.

Labastida is the director of intelligence.

Palacios is director of AFI special operations.

All under Vera's umbrella. All passed lie detector tests validating that they were clean.

Vera brought everyone up with him, Keller thinks, but who did he bring to the meeting with the Tapias? In all probability it was one of these three men, who has to be feeling the heat now that three others have been killed.

Or did he flip and join the Tapias?

In either case, he could be the witness we need.

They look for voice records on any of the three men but find nothing.

Something Keller's learned over the years—if the answer isn't in the present, it's usually in the past.

You smell a slum before you see it.

Keller had a professor in college who said that civilization was a matter of plumbing. That basically, the infrastructure for moving clean water in and filthy water out is what allowed people to congregate in large populations in permanent dwellings and create cities and cultures. Otherwise, people had to be nomads to literally escape their own shit.

No such infrastructure exists in La Polvorilla, the worst slum in Iztapalapa. The smell of stagnant water is the least of it, the stench of urine and shit—dog, donkey, goat, chicken, and human—is an assault on the senses. The dirt streets are basically running sewers of shit and *agua de tamarindo*—"tamarind water," so called because of its brown color.

The lack of piped-in clean water demands a daily chore that only ensures that the women, at least, live in poverty. They wait for hours a day for the trucks to arrive, and on some days trucks don't make it at all because they've been hijacked in other Iztapalapa neighborhoods before they can get there.

Most of the "houses" are hovels—shacks and shanties with plywood walls and cardboard "roofs." Packs of feral dogs come out of the park at night looking for food. Most of the time it's garbage or a careless chicken, but the dogs have been known to carry away children.

The barrio is mostly famous for its dope, pickpockets, and prostitutes, and for an annual passion play that draws tens of thousands. I guess, Keller thinks, people will always show up to see someone put on a cross.

The streets are busy now.

Small-time drug dealers, hookers, gangs of kids. They watch Keller warily—he's not from here, doesn't belong here, only ventured into La Polvorilla to find a woman, buy heroin or coke.

Or maybe he's a cop.

Keller walks down a street, ignores the imprecations of the working girls and the kids selling *mota*, along the endless rows of shanties with tin roofs or old billboards serving the function of roofs.

He stops at a shack that has an old Coca-Cola sign for a door and pushes his way in.

The one room has a bare mattress and a single cane chair rescued from a garbage dump. A hot plate is wired to an old power strip—that and the single bare lightbulb hanging from the ceiling are connected to an illegal source in the street.

She's that rare creature, an old *jaladora*.

A crack whore.

Most of them don't live this long, Keller thinks, although it's hard to determine a crack addict's age. In their twenties they look like they're forty, in their thirties they look sixty, in their forties—if they live that long—they take on the indeterminate look of the very old. The wizened chin, the missing teeth, the vacant stare, which now looks at him blankly.

"Ester?" Keller asks. He's heard stories about her. Now it's taken him days to track her down.

Ester pats the mattress—an invitation. She offers him a half-and-half, an around-the-world, a hand job when she senses he isn't responding to the more expensive choices.

"Ester," Keller says, "you've been telling a story. About the policemen. About when you were young, and you were so pretty?"

"I was pretty."

"I bet you were," Keller says. "You're pretty *now*. Would you tell me the story?"

"*Un diabolito,*" she says, demanding a cigarette laced with crack.

"After you tell the story," Keller says.

Ester sighs.

She was pretty then and not a whore.

Long black hair, dark eyes, long lashes.

(There is a rose, Keller thinks listening to her, in La Polvorilla.)

Fifteen and a virgin when the policeman found her. Walking down the street with her cousin toward the butcher to buy goat meat for her mother because it was her little brother's first communion and they were going to have a special dinner. She was in her white dress, her legs brown, her ankles dirty from the dust of the street.

"*Ven aquí, chola,*" he called from the car.

"I'm not a *chola,*" Ester called back and kept walking. So many of the girls in La Polvorilla were in the gangs, but it wasn't for her to give her love and her body to some boy that would be dead soon.

"They will give you a disease or a baby," her mother warned. "Hook you on drugs, turn you out in the street."

Her mother would know, Ester thought, not unkindly.

This had been her mother's life.

It wouldn't be hers.

She was pretty and she knew it. She saw how boys looked at her, how men looked at her, she looked at herself in the dirty broken mirror in the shack that was her home when everyone else was asleep. She looked at her breasts and her stomach and her face and knew that men wanted her. One night when she was looking, she saw her older brother pretending to be asleep looking at her, and knew he wanted her, too.

Living in La Polvorilla, she had heard of such things.

Ester was a virgin but not a silly girl—she knew all about sex, had lain on her mattress and heard her mother with the men she brought home. Heard her mother's moans and the men's grunts and the whispered words. She had touched herself and known that pleasure, she had talked with girls who had done it, traded jokes and jibes with boys, but she knew she didn't want a boy but a man.

"Where are you going, little *mamacita*?" the policeman asked, driving the car slowly beside her.

She knew he was a policeman because only policemen drove cars like that in La Polvorilla.

"To get some goat," she said, and she and her cousin laughed, because "goat" in Spanish is the same as "cuckold."

The policeman laughed, too, and that's when she began to like him.

"From that thief, the butcher over there?" he asked.

"He's no thief."

"All butchers are thieves," he said. "You'd better let me come with you so he doesn't cheat you."

"You do what you want," Ester said, because a pretty girl can say things like that to men and get away with them.

"You want a ride?" he asked.

"In a cop car?" Ester answered. "What would the neighbors think?"

"'Lucky girl'!"

"I don't think so," Ester said. "They'd think I was in trouble or I was telling tales."

"What tales could you tell?"

"You'd be surprised."

By this time they were across the street from the butcher's. The policeman got out of the car and his partner took the wheel and parked it. He came in and stood there while Ester asked for two pounds of *cabra*. When the butcher put the meat on the scale the policeman said, "And keep your thumb off it, *'mano*."

The butcher, Señor Padilla, whom Ester had known all her life, frowned but said nothing until he told Ester the price.

"Wrap it up and give her *my* price," the policeman said.

Señor Padilla frowned but again said nothing, wrapped the meat in brown paper, and handed it to Ester. Confused, she started to hand him the money her mother gave her, but Señor Padilla shook his head and wouldn't take it.

The policeman stepped up to the counter. "Once a week, every Friday, you give her my price. Understand?"

"I understand."

"Chido."

Outside on the street, the policeman asked, "Aren't you going to say thank you?"

"Thank you."

"Is that all?"

"What do you want?"

"Un besito."

A little kiss.

She pecked him on the cheek.

The partner in the car laughed and then honked the horn. "We have work to do, lover boy!"

"What's your name?" the policeman asked.

"Ester."

"Aren't you going to ask mine?"

"If you want me to," she said. "What is it?"

"They call me Chido," he said, "because I say 'cool' a lot. Enjoy your dinner. I hope I see you again, Ester."

Walking away, her cousin said, "Ester, he has to be thirty!"

Ester knew.

She went home and they had their party. When Ester gave her mother the money back and she asked why Padillo didn't charge her, Ester said it was a present for Ernesto's communion. Her mother looked at her funny but didn't ask any more. When Ester touched herself that night, she thought of Chido.

He took her to dinner, he took her to clubs, he took her dancing. He introduced her to his police friends and they'd all go out together, her and Chido and the other cops and *their* girlfriends.

Chido bought her clothes so that she would look nice ("Your clothes should be as pretty as you"), and one of the other girlfriends took her out to buy makeup and taught her how to use it and how to fix her hair.

Every Friday she would go to Padillo's and he would have the package wrapped in brown paper and hand it to her and she would bring home the goat, or the chicken, even pork, and one time steak. And three times a week a man would come to their place with big blue bottles of clean water.

No charge.

"Have you fucked him yet?" her mother asked.

"Mama, no."

"When you do, make sure he uses something or he comes on your belly," her mother said. "He won't want you if you're fat with a baby."

A month after they met, he took her to what he called his "crash pad," an apartment that he shared with his partners.

"We come here in the day to get out of the heat," Chido explained. "You can't work all the time, and we need to relax."

He walked her into the bedroom.

It was clean, with nice sheets on the bed.

He laid her down and unbuttoned her blouse and she let him kiss her and his hand slid down and touched her where she had only touched herself and his lips touched lightly on her breasts and then her stomach and soon she spoke his name, *Chido Chido,* and he slid up and came into her.

He felt good, he felt so good, she wrapped her legs around him to keep him there forever but when he was close he pulled free and later he went into the bathroom and came out with a damp washcloth and wiped her stomach off and it felt cool and nice.

"We'll get you on the pill," he said. "I hate condoms."

"I got blood on your sheets."

Chido shrugged. "We'll get new sheets."

They had a woman who came in once a week to clean.

He got up again and came back with two bottles of beer and they lay on the bed looking out the widow at the sunbaked street and drank the beers and fell asleep and woke up and made love again.

When she got home that night her mother looked at her and said nothing, but her mother knew, because women know.

Ester was at a party at the crash pad when she found out Chido was married. This was about a year after she started going with him, and she was in the bathroom with Gerardo's girlfriend, sharing the mirror to put on makeup, when Silvia casually mentioned Chido's wife and kids, then saw Ester's expression in the mirror and said, "You didn't know, did you?"

Ester shook her head.

"Sobrina," Silvia said, "they're *all* married."

Ester went back out into the party and pretended nothing had happened, but when she confronted Chido about it later, in his car as he was taking her home, he said, "So? You have a good life, don't you? Don't I take care of you? Your family? Don't I give you nice things? Take you nice places?"

She had to agree these things were true, but she also said, "I thought *we* were going to get married someday."

"Well, that's not going to happen," Chido said. "You want to go back to waiting in line for water, eating posole, go ahead and marry some street cleaner. I'll send a nice gift to the wedding."

Ester went inside and lay down on her mattress, knowing that she wasn't a girlfriend but a *segundera*, a mistress.

"You treat me like a whore," she said to Chido one day.

Chido slapped her, grabbed her black hair in his fist, hauled her off the couch, lifted her face up, and said, "You want me to treat you like a whore, I will. I'll put you out on the street and then you'll *know* what it's like to feel like a whore. Now get dressed and try to look decent for a change. We're going out and I don't want you to embarrass me."

Ester fell asleep—passed out—at the crash pad that night and he left her there because he had night duty. He told her to go home and she said she would but then lay down for just a minute and fell asleep. She woke up to the sound of someone crying and cracked the bedroom door open to see Chido, Gerardo, and Luis and a fourth man she knew as a local car thief.

It was the fourth man who was crying—his clothes were torn, his face was bruised and bloody—and as Luis shoved him down into a chair, she heard Gerardo ask, "What did you bring him here for?"

"It's cool," Chido said. "No one saw us."

"Now we'll need a new pad," Luis said.

"Good," Chido answered. "I'm sick of this one anyway."

The man in the chair cried and Ester saw piss run down his leg onto the floor.

"Now we'll *really* need a new pad," Chido said.

"How many times did we tell you," Gerardo said to the crying man, "that you have to pay us?"

Ester wanted to shut the door but she was afraid to make a sound.

"I'm sorry," the man said. "I will, I will."

"Too late," Gerardo said.

Ester watched as Chido held the man's wrist so his hand was flat on the table, and then Gerardo took a hammer and brought it down on the man's hand. The man screamed and Ester thought she was going to be sick as she saw his bones stick up through his skin.

"Try stealing cars now," Gerardo said.

The man screamed again.

"Jesus, shut up," Chido said.

But the man wouldn't. He bellowed. Chido looked at Gerardo, who nodded. Chido grabbed the hammer and brought it down on the man's head.

Again and again.

They picked the man up and started to carry him out, and then Chido glanced back and saw Ester.

"I'll be right down," he said. He pushed Ester back into the bedroom, closed the door, and said, "What did you see?"

"Nothing."

"That's right," Chido said. "You saw nothing."

After that she didn't see him for three weeks.

That first Friday, she went to Padillo's for her package, and when he told her how much it cost she said, "I don't have that much," and he shrugged and took the package back. And when no water in the big blue bottles appeared, her mother said, "No wonder he dumped you. You look like shit. Go wait for the trucks—we need water to live."

She handed Ester a plastic bucket.

Three weeks later, Ester went looking for Chido. She knew the restaurant where he'd be on Friday nights and she got high on *viesca* and wine and walked into the restaurant and saw him at a table with Gerardo and Silvia.

And some other woman.

Ester went up to the table and asked Chido, "Can I speak with you?"

Chido looked surprised, angry. "Get out of here. Now."

"I just want to speak with you." Then she broke down crying. "I'm sorry. I love you, I love you. I'm sorry."

"You're drunk," Chido said. "High."

Silvia got up, took her by the elbow, and tried to walk her away. "Don't embarrass yourself, *sobrina*."

But Ester got mad and jerked her arm away, looked at the pretty girl sitting next to Chido, and asked, "Who's *this* cunt?"

"Enough," Chido said.

"They kill people, you know," Ester said to the girl, who sat there with her red-lipsticked mouth in a shocked *O*. "I saw them—"

Then Chido and Gerardo had her by the arms and she couldn't shake away and they walked her out of the restaurant into the alley and she saw Chido's face and it was red and angry and she saw his eyes and knew he was high on coke and she was suddenly sober and very afraid as they pushed her against the wall.

"What did you see?" Gerardo asked.

"Nothing."

"What did you see?"

When Ester didn't answer, Gerardo said to Chido, "You know what we have to do."

Ester started to run, but Chido grabbed her and pushed her back against the wall. Then he saw the bottle at their feet. A green bottle that had once been full of cheap wine. He smashed it against the wall and held the jagged neck to her face.

"I told you," he said, "that you saw nothing."

"I didn't."

"Lying bitch," Chido said. "Now you won't see anything."

He dragged the glass across her dark eyes and held his other hand over her mouth as she screamed and screamed.

When he let her go she slid down the wall and collapsed, pressed her hands against her eyes and felt nothing but blood. Then she heard Chido say, "She can't identify what she can't see. It's cool."

She heard them walk away.

They must have called a squad car, because a few minutes later two cops arrived, picked her up, put her in the backseat, and drove her to the hospital. The doctors did the best they could, but she would never see again, and she became the blind whore of La Polvarilla. As her mother said, you don't need to see a man's hard dick to put it inside you, and men came for the cheap thrill of getting done by a girl who couldn't see them, and when she went to the trucks to get water, some people, boys mostly, were mean and tripped her so the water spilled, but most people were kind and helped her.

She never heard from Chido Palacios again.

But that, she tells Keller, was when she was young and not a whore.

Javier "Chido" Palacios takes coffee at the same café just a few blocks away from AFI headquarters every day at four o'clock.

In nice weather, such as this May afternoon, he sits at a table outside, sips his espresso, and watches the world go by on the boulevard in front. His three bodyguards stand at various places by the iron fence or the door to the café.

Keller watches this for three days.

After a long debate with Aguilar, it was decided that it was Keller who would make the first approach.

"You can't," Keller told the prosecutor. "If he turns you down, he blows our cover. Besides, you don't have anything to offer him at this point. You can't protect him in Mexico."

Aguilar reluctantly agreed and Keller started his surveillance on Palacios, trying to find a time and place where he would be sufficiently alone. On this third afternoon, Keller walks in and takes a table next to Palacios. The bodyguards notice and watch, then apparently decide that he's not a threat.

If Palacios is nervous about his situation, he doesn't show it. His custom-made suit is pressed and clean, his black hair—with just flecks of silver at the temple—is carefully combed back. He looks cool, sophisticated, a man in charge of his world.

Keller sits and looks at him.

Palacios breaks first. "Do I know you?"

"You should, Chido."

Palacios flinches slightly at the old *aporto*. "Why is that?"

"Because I can save your life," Keller says. "May I join you?"

Palacios hesitates for a second, then nods. Keller gets up, the bodyguards start to close in, but Palacios waves them off.

"I'll bet you thought you left 'Chido' behind in La Polvorilla," Keller says when he sits down.

"I haven't heard it in years," Palacios says calmly. "Who are you?"

"I'm with DEA."

Palacios shakes his head. "I know all the DEA guys."

"Apparently not."

"You said something about saving my life?" Palacios says. "I wasn't aware it needed saving."

"Seriously?" Keller asks. "You just buried three of your buddies. The Tapias want to kill you. If they don't, Adán Barrera will. You have to know you're on the endangered species list."

"Your DEA colleagues would say that you're talking out of your ass," Palacios says.

I can't lose him now, Keller thinks. I can't make this cast and let him off the hook, because if I do he goes straight to Vera. So he says, "You were at a meeting last spring with Diego and Martín Tapia. During that meeting you agreed to provide protection to the Zetas and target La Familia instead. Also present at that meeting were Gerardo Vera, Roberto Bravo, and José Aristeo."

Palacios reverts a little to his La Polvorilla days. "You're full of shit."

"I have you on tape, motherfucker."

Palacios literally starts to sweat. Keller sees the beads of perspiration pop on his forehead, just below his carefully cut hair. He presses: "Think about it—you've got one foot on the Tapia dock and the other in the Barrera boat, and they're drifting apart. You're going to have to choose, and your guards can't protect you in Puente Grande, which is where you're going. The only question is, do they fuck you in the ass *before* they slit your throat?"

"I was at that meeting," Palacios says, "to gather evidence against—"

"Save it," Keller says. "You think Vera is going to protect you? I know you're boys and all that from the old barrio, but if you think Vera's going to put the life he has now on the line for old times' sake, you don't know your old friend."

"Maybe he's on that tape, too."

"Maybe he is," Keller says. "So that puts you in a little race with him, doesn't it, because the first one of you to cut a deal gets a snitch visa to the States and the other gets ass-raped. Which do you want to be?"

Palacios glares at him.

Keller gets up. "I came to you first because you can trade up, for Vera. I'm going to go to him in exactly twenty-four hours, unless I hear from you first."

He lays a slip of paper with a phone number on the table.

"Beautiful day for scoping the women, isn't it?" Keller asks. "By the way, Ester Almanza sends her regards, you piece of shit."

Keller holds his thumb and little finger to his face—*Call me*—smiles, and walks away.

There's little to do now but wait.

And prepare for the worst-case scenario, that Palacios runs to Vera and they launch a counteroffensive that could take several forms, the most likely of which is a raid on SEIDO to acquire the incriminating tapes, Aguilar's firing by pressure from Los Pinos, and even criminal charges against him.

Keller doesn't discount another possibility—an outright assassination attempt on Aguilar.

"Don't be ridiculous," Aguilar says when Keller suggests it over a brandy in his study.

Lucinda had prepared her usual excellent dinner, a fiery shrimp dish over rice, and the children were their charming selves, conversing easily about their ballet and horseback lessons, and shyly about boys they had met at an interschool dance. Keller had forgotten how simply lovely family life could be.

Then Aguilar and Keller went into his study to discuss business, and now Keller sits there with the cell phone in his pocket, urging it to ring. He'd bought it only for Palacios's call, and now it sits in his pocket like a time bomb you *want* to go off. Every second it doesn't increases the possibility that Palacios has gone to Vera, or, maybe worse, to the Tapias. "It's not ridiculous, Luis. In fact, I think you should consider moving your family out for a little while."

"How would I explain that to them, Art?" Aguilar asks. "Without terrifying them?"

"A vacation," Keller said. "We set you up in the States, DEA provides security."

"I don't think Gerardo would go so far as to hurt families."

"But Barrera would," Keller says, "and has."

"They'd make a threat first, no? To intimidate me into cooperating?"

"Probably," Keller admits. "But it doesn't hurt to be safe. Look, wouldn't the girls love a couple of weeks at some dude ranch in Arizona? They could ride—"

"Western saddles? And ruin their seats—"

"Luis," Keller says. "Galvén, Aristeo, and Bravo were killed outside their homes. Do you want to expose your family to that possibility?"

"Of course not."

"Well . . ."

"I'll think about it."

They go over other possibilities. If Aguilar's boss, the attorney general, calls him in and either fires him, shuts down the investigation, or both, it means he's in on it, in which case Keller gets out of the country as fast as possible with a copy of the tape.

The phone vibrates.

Aguilar watches as Keller digs it out of his pocket, listens for two seconds. "Parque México," he says. "Foro Lindbergh. One hour." He clicks off.

They meet under the pergola near the large columns in the Lindbergh Forum.

A smart choice, because it's out of sight. But dangerous, because the trees behind the columns offer ample cover for gunmen, especially at night.

Keller knows that he might be walking into a trap. But then again, he's pretty much in a trap already, so what's the difference? Nevertheless, he keeps his hand on the pistol under his jacket.

Palacios stands at the end of the pergola.

He appears to be alone.

"I want out tonight," he says.

"That's not going to happen." The moment Palacios crosses the border, he loses half his motivation to talk. Keller has seen it happen—the source sits on a chair in some office on the other side and spins useless bullshit stories until everyone gets tired of it and moves on. No, what they have to do is pick Palacios as clean as they can before they move him. Everything they get after that is gravy.

But they have to move fast.

"Here's how it's going to work," Keller says. "You're going to give us information. We check it out to see if you're telling the truth. When we have enough to nail Vera, you get your ticket."

Palacios stares at him. Then he says, "I want visas for myself, my wife, and my two adult children. And I get immunity, I get to keep my bank accounts."

The prick doesn't want to go into the program and become a greeter at a suburban Tucson Home Depot. He wants to come across and live the high life on the dirty millions he's taken from the Sinaloa cartel.

"That's up to your AG," Keller says.

It's a risk Keller has to take, and it might as well be sooner than later. Palacios might balk at the Mexican involvement, because he thinks he's been dealing exclusively with DEA.

Palacios says, "We're done here."

"You walk away now," Keller says, "you don't get far. You get busted before you leave the park. You think your old buddies are going to wait around to see if you flip?"

Keller knows his business, knows that there's a time to push and a time to pull, so now he softens his tone and says, "Look, you haven't committed a crime in the States. Neither has Vera. So the Justice Department can only offer you sanctuary as a courtesy to the Mexican AG's office. We do it through SEIDO, keep it under wraps."

"Luis Aguilar?" Palacios asks. "That sanctimonious prick?"

"He's your lifeline, Chido."

Palacios laughs. "Where is he?"

"In a car on Calle Chiapas."

"Let's go."

———

At first they meet in cars, in parks at night, but then Aguilar invents a new *segundera* for Palacios, actually an undercover SEIDO agent named Gabriela—drop-dead gorgeous, a *guapa* with long legs and a longer résumé—law degree, a master's in sociology, and a ruthless ambition. Aguilar provides Palacios with photos to show off to his buddies ("Look what I'm tapping") and arranges for them to be seen together at bars around AFI headquarters. He provides her with an apartment and makes sure she's seen leaving in the morning for her job at a local bank, and seen returning in the evening.

In the afternoons they meet with Palacios.

He plays games of his own, what Keller would call hide-the-ball, giving them a little information to shield more damaging information, having to be pressed, cross-examined, coddled, cajoled, threatened. He lets intelligence out like a fisherman lets out line to a fish, and they do the same with him, reminding him not too gently that *he's* the one who's hooked.

"You know we'll run you through a polygraph," Aguilar says.

"Yeah, I've taken them," Palacios says with a smirk. "Best test money can buy."

"This one will be legitimate," Aguilar says. "And if you lie about anything, our deal is null and void. Let's go over it again, Barrera's escape from prison."

"Who was in charge of prisons?" Palacios asks.

"Quit playing games."

"Galvén," Palacios says. "Nacho Esparza delivered $500,000 to Galvén and we cut it up."

"Did Vera get a share?"

"What do you think?"

"*I'm* asking the questions."

"It's a stupid question."

Aguilar sighs. "Humor me."

"Vera got the biggest share, as usual," Palacios answers. "Me, my motto is 'Eat like a horse, not like a pig.' That's not Gerardo's motto."

He's cute, Keller thinks. He knows the apartment is miked, and that he's playing to a crowd that will eventually include the Mexican AG and a host of *yanquis* in DEA and Justice.

When they get through the failed raids on Barrera after his escape, Palacios actually laughs. They have to go over it a dozen times before they get what they think is the whole truth, but then Palacios *laughs* and says, "Are you fucking kidding me? We *had* him."

"When? Where?"

"Nayarit," Palacios says. "When he got out by helicopter. He and Nacho paid us four million for the next leg of his flight."

"Did Vera—"

"Get his share? Of course."

You almost had Barrera in Apatzingán, Palacios tells them. But we got him out that night and put in the lookalike. After that, Barrera moved back to Sinaloa.

"Where?" Keller asks.

"My deal is on Vera," Palacios says, "not Barrera."

Anyway, he doesn't know, he claims. El Patrón moves from *finca* to *finca* in the mountains of Sinaloa and Durango. The police protect him, the locals protect him; he has his own private army now—Gente Nueva.

"Are they doing the fighting in Juárez?" Aguilar asks.

"You already know that."

The meetings go on. Sometimes Palacios meets Gabriela at her apartment, other times he treats her to a suite at a five-star hotel—the Habita, the St. Regis, Las Alcobas, the Four Seasons—but never the Marriott. They take a suite so Gabriela can wait in the sitting room, out of earshot, and leave just before or after Palacios.

"Try to look well-fucked," he says to her one day at the Habita. "I have a reputation to maintain."

Gabriela is too disciplined to respond.

At every session, Palacios plays peekaboo, but Aguilar and Keller doggedly work him, like a boxer walks his opponent into a corner. Keller was not a bad amateur middleweight in his youth. He was patient then and he's patient now, letting Palacios dance and shuffle, but always cutting off the ring and forcing him against the ropes where the truth gets told.

Palacios tells them how it worked.

A group of beat cops led by Gerardo Vera formed a drug, extortion, kidnapping, and car theft ring in Iztapalapa that they parlayed into a small empire, dealing dope internally for Nacho Esparza and the Tapias.

They had a monopoly in the eastern part of Mexico City that they enforced through threats, selective arrests, and—if that didn't work—assaults, kidnappings, and murders.

The Izta cartel.

The Tapias used their political influence to move Vera into the old, PRI-era federal police. He played it clean for years—the very model of the incorruptible cop. Eliot freaking Ness. He quietly brought his old boys up with him—they were the same choirboys—until they moved high enough up the ladder to really do the Sinaloa cartel some serious good.

When the new administration decided to reorganize the old, "corrupt" federal police, the Sinaloans hit the jackpot. Vera turned the organization inside out, firing anyone he couldn't control and hiring people loyal to him. And he put into high positions men from his old Izta cartel.

It was goddamn genius, Keller has to admit. Vera used the polygraphs to get rid of the undesirables, and then whitewashed the others to get the results he wanted. You could lie, just don't lie to Gerardo Vera. You could take money from narcos, just make sure they're the right narcos. Vera turned the entire AFI into an efficient, incorruptible institution serving the interests of the Sinaloa cartel.

Breaking Adán Barrera out of prison.

Making sure that no raid ever captured him.

Taking down Barrera's rival narcos like Osiel Contreras.

Going to war against the CDG cops in Nuevo Laredo.

Vera didn't have to worry about being investigated from below—his own people—or from above, thanks to Yvette Tapia's suitcase deliveries to the Amaros.

It was a beautiful system, smooth as a German railroad, even through the elections and the new administration, which only promoted Vera to an even higher position. It should have gone on forever.

The money flowed through the Tapias and was, as far as Palacios knew, made up of a collective fund from them, Esparza, and Barrera. It cost a flat mil to appoint a tame AFI boss to a region and another $50,000–$100,000 monthly salary to that guy, 20 percent of which he kicked up to the Izta cartel.

Five hundred thousand a month went to Vera, with step-down payments to the other high-ranking guys—Galvén, Aristeo, Bravo, and Palacios—depending on their rank.

"How much did you make?" Aguilar asks one afternoon at the Four Seasons, unable to keep the disgust from his voice.

"Two million a year," Palacios answers casually.

Special favors—the escape from Puente Grande, the close call after Nayarit, the takedown of Contreras, the raids on the Tapias—required extra money, Palacios tells them.

In those special cases, Esparza usually handled the payments.

"Where did the money come from?" Keller asks.

"El Patrón, I guess," Palacios says. "I didn't ask."

"How high does it go?" Aguilar asks.

Palacios shrugs. "All I know is Vera. What he does with the money afterward—above my pay grade."

"Los Pinos?" Aguilar asks. "We know that money went to Benjamín Amaro."

"Then you know more than I do," Palacios snaps.

Aguilar asks, his voice tight, "The attorney general?"

"I don't know."

At the next meeting at the St. Regis, Aguilar says, "Tell us about the meeting with Martín Tapia."

"Tell *me* when I go *el norte*."

"When we say you do," Keller says. But he understands Palacios's anxiety. Every day it gets more dangerous for him, every day he's at risk of getting gunned down by the Tapias, if not by Gerardo Vera. Keller doesn't really care if Palacios gets killed—good riddance to bad garbage—but not until they've stripped him of everything he knows, and he testifies.

"I want Arizona," Palacios says. "Not Texas. I like Scottsdale."

"It could be Akron for all I know," Keller says.

"And a car," Palacios adds. "Land Rover or Range Rover."

"The fuck you think this is?" Keller asks, "*The Price Is Right*?"

"Tell us about the Tapia meeting," Aguilar repeats.

"Can we get some lunch sent up?" Palacios asks. "I haven't eaten."

Gabriela calls down for some sandwiches. Palacios, munching on a *torta*, says, "The fuck you want to know? We met—"

"Was Vera there?"

"You know he was."

"Do *you* know he was?"

"He was sitting beside me."

"And—"

"And Martín told us that they'd made peace with the CDG and the Zetas," Palacios says, "and that we were to go after La Familia instead. The fuck did we care? A narco is a narco."

"Vera said that certain people would need more money," Aguilar says. "Which people?"

"I don't know."

"You don't?"

"Ask Gerardo."

At the next meeting, Aguilar opens with, "Tell me about the Tapia raids."

"You tell *me* about the Tapia raids."

"What do you mean?"

"All I know is that Gerardo wanted to meet," Palacios says. "Out of the office. Fine, we go out for a walk. He's shook, like I've never seen him. You know Gerardo—ice."

"And?"

"He tells me we have to go after the Tapias," Palacios says. "I about shit my pants. 'The Tapias, are you fucking kidding me? You know how much food they've put on our tables?' He says it comes from on high."

"And you ask him how high," Keller prompts.

"And he holds his hand way above his head," Palacios says. "So I say, 'Adán Barrera is not going to like this,' and Gerardo just stares at me, and then I get it—it *comes* from Barrera. And I say, 'I don't care, I'm not doing it, it's suicide, going after the Tapias,' and he says, 'That's why we better not fuck it up.'"

"Did he tell you why Barrera wanted the Tapias taken down?"

Palacios launches into a song-and-dance about how Gerardo didn't share it with him specifically, but it had something to do with Diego getting too much power, and Alberto being too flashy, and all of them being into this Santa Muerte shit, and Adán thought they were becoming a liability, a risk.

All of which is true, Keller thinks, but he can see that he's lying, that Vera told him about Salvador Barrera's double-murder beef, and that Palacios doesn't want Aguilar to know that he knows about the Tapia-for-Sal deal.

It's very dangerous knowledge, Keller agrees.

"But you did fuck it up," he prompts.

Palacios holds his hands up. "Not me—Galvén got stupid and blew Alberto away, and we just couldn't lay our hands on Diego."

"Couldn't or wouldn't?" Aguilar asks. "Are you still on his payroll? You're alive, after all."

"Shit," Palacios says. "You think the Tapias are going to take us back after we killed his little brother? You think we're going to double-cross Barrera? We're running for our lives here."

"You're having coffee at the same place every day," Keller says.

"When I'm not sitting here blowing you," Palacios says. "Do you think I'd be doing this if I'd made a separate peace with Diego? Jesus Christ, could that cunt remember the mustard for a change? How hard is that?"

———

The game goes on.

Aguilar wants names, numbers, he wants to see Palacios's bank accounts, his cell phone records, his e-mails. All the while, Keller plays a game of his own. He makes himself go out to lunch with Gerardo Vera, go out for drinks, listen to the man's problems.

A straight-up shooting war has broken out in Sinaloa and Durango between Barrera loyalists and the Tapias.

Eight killed in a gun battle on Tuesday.

Another four on Wednesday . . .

Two hundred and sixty killed by the end of June.

Then, just yesterday, seven AFI agents were killed storming a safe house in Culiacán filled with Diego's shooters.

And then, this morning, a banner appeared hanging from a Culiacán bridge that read THIS IS FOR YOU, GOVERNOR VILLA, EITHER YOU MAKE AN ARRANGEMENT WITH US OR WE'LL MAKE AN ARRANGEMENT FOR YOU. THIS WHOLE GOVERNMENT WORKING FOR BARRERA AND ESPARZA IS GOING TO DIE.

And other banners start to appear all over town with the message LIT-TLE TOY SOLDIERS AND STRAW POLICEMEN, THIS TERRITORY BELONGS TO DIEGO TAPIA.

"We have to move," Keller tells Aguilar after another dance session with Palacios. "This whole thing is going to blow up."

"You're friends with the Tapias," Aguilar says drily. "Tell them to give us a little time."

Then Palacios balks—digs his feet in and says that he won't give any more information until he's assured of asylum in the United States.

"You've been stringing me along for weeks," he says. "Enough."

And walks out of the room.

It feels strange, being back in the United States. After what, Keller thinks, three years?

Strange hearing the language, seeing the ugly green money.

Washington is hot and humid in June, and Keller is sweating before he can get into the cab to DEA. At least he managed to get a flight into National, so the cab trip isn't too long compared with the odyssey down from Dulles.

The announcement by Tim Taylor's receptionist that there's an Art Keller here to see him is greeted with the enthusiasm normally reserved for a colonoscopy. Taylor sticks his head out the door, sees that it's sadly true, and gestures for Keller to come into his office.

"Hold my calls," he says to the receptionist.

Keller sits down across from Taylor's desk.

"So," Taylor says, "how's the hunt for Barrera going? Not so good, huh?"

Keller takes out his copy of the Tapia tape, sticks it into Taylor's Dictaphone, and hits play. "One of the voices is Martín Tapia, the other is Gerardo Vera."

Taylor turns white. "Bull fucking shit. Where did you get this?"

Keller doesn't answer.

"Same old Keller," Taylor says. "How the fuck do you know that's Vera?"

"Voice recognition software."

"Inadmissible."

"And a witness."

"Who?" Taylor asks. He is not a happy man. He's a less happy man when Keller tells him that the witness is Palacios. "That's the third-highest-ranking cop in Mexico."

Keller tells him about the Izta Mafia, the killings of the three cops, and the highlights of Palacios's potential testimony.

"And you have this all on tape," Taylor says.

"Aguilar does."

Taylor gets up and looks out the window. "I'm pulling the pin in eighteen months. Bought one of those mobile homes with everything but a Jacuzzi in it, the wife and I are going to cruise around the country. I don't need this right now."

"I'll need a snitch visa for Palacios," Keller says. "Papers, a whole new package."

"No shit."

"Maybe one for Aguilar, too, if this goes south."

"Oh, it's already gone south," Taylor says. "Do you know how much intelligence, how much information we've shared with Vera?"

"I have an idea."

"No, you fucking don't," Taylor says, "because we specifically told him to keep most of it from you. If what you're saying is true, every op we have down there . . . and a bunch of them up here . . . have been compromised. We'll have to pull agents in, undercovers . . ."

"If what I'm saying is true," Keller answers, "and it is, the entire federal justice system of Mexico has been turned inside out."

"Palacios could be making up a story to get his ticket punched," Taylor says.

"He could be," Keller agrees. "But then, why would he need a ticket? If all this is bullshit, his life is in no danger."

Taylor thinks about this for a second, then goes off. "Your mission was very clear, very specific—assist in the pursuit of Adán Barrera. You were not authorized to launch an investigation of corruption within the federal police force of a foreign nation—"

"You *don't* want to know?" Keller asks. "You wanted me to hold it back until Vera gives Barrera one of your UCs to torture?!"

"Of course not," Taylor says. He sighs, tired. "Look, I'll need to go upstairs with this. You'll have to come in, do the dog-and-pony. Fuck. *Fuck.* I'd thought we'd finally . . . Okay, let me get on the horn with the director, make his week. You stay where I can reach you in a hurry. Anything else you want, or is ruining my life sufficient for today?"

"Reservations at a dude ranch in Arizona."

Taylor stares at him.

"For Aguilar's family," Keller says.

"See Brittany outside."

"Can you expense it through—"

"Yes. Get out."

Bureaucratic battles are bloody.

All the more so because it's usually other people's blood being shed, so what the fuck.

This is what Keller's thinking as he sits at a table with Taylor, the DEA director, and representatives from Justice, State, Immigration and Naturalization, and the White House. There's probably a Company guy in the room as well, sitting in the corner.

The DEA director chairs the meeting. "If Agent Keller's information is accurate, we have a crisis on our hands."

"Agent Keller," the Justice hack, a middle-aged lawyer named McDonough, weighs in, "has a dubious tape recording and an even more dubious witness. I, for one, would not jeopardize our relations with Mexico based on the tales of a dirty cop."

Keller knows McDonough—a former prosecutor in New York's Eastern District. He's gained more weight—his face is even redder, his jowls fatter, he's one jelly doughnut away from a triple bypass.

"Concur," the State Department rep says. Susan Carling has curly red hair, skin the color of chalk, and a PhD from Yale.

"What is the provenance of this tape?" McDonough asks.

Keller says, "The tape was handed to me by a source inside the Tapia organization, and that's as far as I'm prepared to go."

"You do not have the option, Agent Keller," McDonough says, "of withholding the source of your information."

"Fire me," Keller says.

"Now, *that's* an option," McDonough says.

"*Do* you have a source inside the Tapia organization?" the DEA director asks Keller. "Because it doesn't appear that you opened a file."

"I don't have a CI in the Tapia organization," Keller answers. "Someone handed me the tape and—"

"Do you have a relationship with them?" McDonough asks. "Because if you haven't opened a file, that's completely inappropriate and opens you to suspicions of—"

Taylor says, "Can we talk about the real problem here, Ed? If a source came to you with information that the number three guy in the FBI was on the Gambino family payroll, you wouldn't be sitting there picking him apart on procedural issues. I have *people* out there, who are now under horrendous risk."

"Potentially," McDonough says.

"Okay, you go to Tamaulipas under 'potential' risk, and tell me that you have time for this nitpicking shit," Taylor says. "Keller is protecting his source. He's an asshole, but that's what he's doing. Move on."

The White House rep says, "The Mexican government is extremely sensitive to accusations of corruption, especially from us. If we push an agenda on this, it might sabotage years of diplomacy that are now finally having some positive effect. It could scuttle the very antitrafficking efforts that DEA has worked so hard to establish. Not to mention embarrassing us on the Hill."

"I wouldn't want anyone to be embarrassed," Keller says.

"Be as ironic as you want," the rep says, "but the Mérida Initiative wasn't easy to push through Congress. It's what you guys wanted, isn't it??"

The Mérida Initiative is a three-year, $1.4 billion aid package, most of it to Mexico, to combat drug trafficking. Keller knows the details—thirteen Bell 412EP helicopters, eleven Black Hawks, four CN-235 transport planes, plus high-tech scanners, X-ray machines, and communications equipment. Not to mention training for police and Mexican military.

The same training, Keller thinks, we gave to the Zetas.

"Now you want us to do what?" the White House rep asks. "Go back to the Hill and tell them, 'Whoops, forget it'? Turns out we were going to give a billion and a half dollars in sophisticated military equipment to a cabal of corrupt cops? That, in effect, we were going to hand over Black Hawk helicopters to the Sinaloa cartel? No, this is not going to happen."

"We cannot disrupt the Mérida Initiative at this point," Carling says. "It's three days away from becoming law. The damage to our relationship with Mexico would be incalculable."

"So the option is what?" the director asks. "Letting our allies continue to live in the belief that their top police officer is honest when we know in fact—"

"Not in fact," McDonough says. "Allegedly."

"—that he's *allegedly* in the employ of the drug cartels?"

"If they don't already know," Keller says.

"We're not asking for an international incident," the director says, "just a 'Q' visa for Palacios."

McDonough leans forward. "This is an internal Mexican issue. Justice will only authorize action if and when the Mexican attorney general contacts us with a request. As for Mr. Palacios, we can't just accept his story at face value."

"You have Vera on tape," Keller says.

"There is no chain of custody on that tape," McDonough says. "We don't know its origin, it could have been doctored by the Tapia organization to sabotage its most effective adversary. They failed to take Vera out, so they're trying to have us do it."

"Palacios could have been planted on you," Carling says to Keller, "for the exact purpose of scuttling the Mérida Initiative."

"Which the cartels have to be extremely concerned about," the White house rep says.

"Yeah, they're quaking," Taylor says.

The director turns to McDonough. "What do you need to bring Palacios over?"

"Have him wear a wire," McDonough says. "Get me Vera on tape, incriminating himself on a record that we control, and then maybe we have something to talk about."

"*Can* you get Palacios to wear a wire?" Taylor asks.

"I don't know," Keller says. "Vera is smart, he's already freaked out . . ."

"We're talking a one-time event here," the director says, "not an ongoing operation."

"Give it a shot," McDonough says. "You get us a tape of Vera, we'll get you the visa."

He looks to Carling, who nods.

"What about Aguilar?" Keller asks. "Protection for him and his family."

"The head of SEIDO," McDonough says, "has ample reasons to confer with his counterparts here. If for some reason he were to decide not to return to Mexico, I'm sure something could be worked out."

"We can't have a Mexican intelligence officer shouting accusations across the border," Carling says, "and give him citizenship."

"But something could be worked out, couldn't it, Susan?" McDonough asks tiredly.

"The alternative being," Keller says, "that I *personally* drive Luis Aguilar across the border from Juárez and deposit him at the front door of *The Washington Post*, which would be happy to run an over-the-fold story about how this administration wouldn't lift a finger to protect an honest prosecutor and his family. And I'll be sure to spell your names correctly."

McDonough looks at Taylor. "You're right—he's an asshole."

Taylor shrugs.

Carling says, "I'm sure none of us wants to conduct foreign policy in the media. I didn't mean to suggest that we wouldn't welcome Mr. Aguilar into the country, only that we would want him to be discreet."

"Good," the director says. "Only question remaining—do we inform our Mexican counterparts of this operation now?"

"If we launch an operation on Mexican soil," Carling says, "against a high-ranking Mexican official without informing them—indeed, getting their permission—there's going to be diplomatic hell to pay."

"What?" McDonough asks. "They're going to turn the money down?"

"Possibly," Carling answers. "It would insult their pride and they'd think that we don't trust them."

"We don't," Taylor says.

"That is *exactly* the kind of attitude—"

Keller cuts her off. "If we inform them now, the operation could be compromised."

"A risk we have to take."

"It's not you taking the risk," Keller says. "It's Palacios and Aguilar. They and their families could be killed."

"Aren't you being a little dramatic?" the White House rep asks.

"No," Keller says. "I will not—repeat, *not*—send Palacios in with a wire if you give prior notice to the Mexicans, much less ask their permission."

McDonough looks at the director. "Do you run your organization or does Keller?"

"As the agent in the field," the director says, "Keller has the best knowledge of the situation and the people involved, and I trust his judgment and discretion."

"Send in a different agent," Carling says.

"Palacios would never cooperate with him," Taylor says. "Anyway, we're arguing over nothing—the Mexicans *do* know. The head of SEIDO is conducting the investigation, and we are merely cooperating as good neighbors. The burden of communicating with his superiors is on him, not us. There's your out. If the Mexicans scream, point at Aguilar and look innocent."

The quiet in the room indicates that a compromise has been reached. McDonough looks at his watch, then to Keller, and says, "You have your marching orders—get Palacios in a room with a wire."

"But not for three days," the White House rep says.

Keller gets it—in three days the Mérida Initiative becomes law.

State will be happy.

The White House will be happy.

DEA will be happy.

The Mexicans will be happy.

The arms manufacturers will be happy.

Adán Barrera will be happy, because he'll have new weapons in his war against . . . well . . . just about everybody now.

Keller stands up. "Thank you for your time."

He leaves the room.

"When this is over," McDonough says, "fire that guy."

"Go fuck yourself, Ed," the director answers.

Keller takes a red-eye back to Mexico City.

He's as grateful as he is surprised by the support that Taylor and the director gave him. But I shouldn't be surprised, he thinks—both men are true believers in what they do, both care about the safety of their people. And both are going to stick up for their organization in a bureaucratic border skirmish.

It didn't stop them from giving him holy hell after the meeting, but now they're fully invested in the operation, making logistical plans to bring Palacios across the border, working with Immigration on the paperwork, setting up a satellite run to photograph Vera's presence at the meeting with Palacios.

"We'll start a forensic analysis on Vera's finances," the director said.

"Justice will shit," Keller said. It will involve hacking computers, bank accounts, money transfers, real estate records.

"Let them shit," the director said. "I'll run it through NSA."

They plan to take preventative measures as well—call undercovers back in, sanitize any intelligence packages ready to go to AFI, suspend or at least slow down any operations against the Sinaloa cartel.

"Do you need more agents on the ground there?" Taylor asked Keller. "Surveillance, backup, communications?"

"Communications, maybe," Keller answered. "Otherwise, no. I don't want any extraordinary activity that might tip Vera off."

"Be careful," Taylor reminded him, dropping him off at Departures at National. "Remember, there's that five-million bounty on your head."

"I thought it was two million," Keller said.

"Barrera upped it," Taylor answered. "However much we put on him, he matches it for you. Stay in touch."

Keller had a rare late-night scotch to help him sleep, but it didn't do much good. He dozed a little, but was wide awake well before the plane started its descent, as they say, into Mexico City.

It feels more like home now than D.C., even though he knows that the airport cops have probably noted his coming and going for the Tapias or Nacho Esparza, depending which side they've taken.

Aguilar is at the airport, seeing his family off.

"I'll be there in a week," he tells his daughters, who look sad and a little dubious about the trip. "Maybe less."

"Why can't you come now?"

"I have just a little work to wrap up," Aguilar says. "Then I'll be there. What do you think I'll look like in a cowboy hat?"

"Why do we have to go to a *ranch*?"

"It's more of a spa," Lucinda says. "They have hot tubs, massages, yoga— you're going to enjoy it."

Her tone being more of a command than a prediction, the girls stop their objections and hug their father goodbye.

"A few days," he tells Lucinda quietly. "A week at the most."

"Be careful."

"Of course." He kisses her lightly on the lips and then watches his family go through security.

Keller stands off to the side and waits. On the drive back into the city, he says, "My bosses want Palacios to wire up."

"On Gerardo?"

"Yeah."

"That's risky."

Yes, it is, Keller thinks.

Palacios goes ballistic.

Yells, throws things at the wall, sits down, gets up, threatens to leave.

Aguilar remains perfectly calm. "You tell Gerardo you want to meet him. You express concern for your safety and ask him what he's doing about it."

"He's not an idiot," Palacios says. "He'll suspect."

"The second you get him on tape incriminating himself," Aguilar says, "we'll arrange transport for you and your family to the United States."

"I'm not doing it."

"Cut him loose," Keller says to Aguilar. "Who needs him?"

"You can't leave me hanging now!"

"Then wear the wire," Keller says.

"Fuck you."

"No, fuck *you*!" Keller yells. "You've been sitting in these rooms for three goddamn weeks, giving us as little as possible! The fucking minimum. Well, the minimum isn't good enough! I'll go have a beer with Vera *right now* and tell him we have a new CI!"

"You wouldn't do that."

"Try me!" Keller says. "If you don't wear this wire you are fucking worthless to me! And you know what worthless means? It means you're not worth a 'Q' visa, you're not worth a new identity, you're not worth the house, the car, you're not worth another one of my fucking sandwiches!"

He rips the food out of Palacios's hand and throws it against the wall.

"I guess we can't expect to come back to the Four Seasons," Aguilar says, surveying the damage.

"Two days," Keller says, calming down. "You set up your meeting with Vera, I'll set up your entry into the States. You wear the wire, you get us what you need, you disappear until you testify."

"You never said anything about testifying."

"The wire is no good without your testimony," Keller says. What did you think—you and Vera were going to be buddies anyway after this? You were going to bang girls together like the old days? Grow up."

Palacios agrees to wear the wire.

"Business as usual," Keller tells him. "Do everything you normally would, nothing out of the ordinary. Call me when you've set the meeting up."

The rest of the day goes by like a muddy, slow-moving river. It's well into night when Keller gets the call.

"Tomorrow at 6:30," Palacios says.

"Where?"

"Gerardo has a little love nest he keeps in Polanco," Palacios says. He gives Keller the address.

"We'll meet at five," Keller says. "Las Alcobas. We'll wire you up there."

"Do you think Gabriela would go for a farewell fuck?" Palacios asks.

"I doubt it."

There's a lot to get done. Aguilar arranges for SEIDO surveillance outside Vera's condo to get pictures of the AFI chief coming and going. Then he goes to work on the exit plan—a SEIDO Learjet 25 will be standing by at the 1st Military Air Station at Mexico City International Airport. The flight plan will be filed to the 18th Military Airbase in Hermosillo, Sonora, for Aguilar to confer with SEIDO personnel there. In Hermosillo, they'll change to an American DEA plane and fly to Biggs Army Airfield in El Paso. The DEA at EPIC will have arranged for the plane to clear American airspace and to pull into a classified hangar.

Palacios will be taken to EPIC, interviewed, and housed under heavy security at Fort Bliss.

Aguilar will join his family on vacation in Arizona and await developments. If Vera is arrested, Aguilar will return to Mexico to pursue the prosecution. If not, he'll consider staying in the United States, where a position in a D.C. consulting firm has already been quietly arranged.

During the operation, Keller will remain in a surveillance position in a car two blocks removed from Vera's condo, with remote audio sensor equipment allowing him to monitor the meeting.

He'll call Taylor at EPIC as soon as Palacios exits.

Palacios will walk the two blocks from the condo, and, if he's all clear, will get into an unmarked SEIDO vehicle and go out to the airport. If he's not clear, he'll walk to his own car, a late-model Cadillac, and his driver and bodyguard will take him.

That's all if Palacios gets what they need on tape.

If he doesn't, he'll simply go home and set up another meet with Vera to try again.

———

The day, which promises to be endless, begins with Keller having a late breakfast.

With Gerardo Vera.

It's part of the plan, to make Vera think that everything is as normal, keep him at ease. So Keller, feeling sleazy, sits with him at a sidewalk café out in Coyoacán. Keller is too edgy to be hungry, but he makes himself eat a large plate of *pollo machaca*. Vera goes for eggs Benedict and a Bloody Mary. He leans back in his chair, smiles at Keller, and says, "Big night tonight."

Keller feels his stomach tighten. Does Gerardo know something? Is he probing? "Yeah?"

"This woman," Vera says. "A famous beauty I've been seeing. Tonight I think I'm going to, as you say *in the States,* 'close the deal.'"

"How famous?" Keller asks.

"A gentleman doesn't name names," Vera says. He grins and adds, "Quite famous, really. For her beauty and her . . . sexuality."

He's boyishly pleased. Keller feels almost guilty, aware of the old adage that every successful operation ends in a betrayal. And he does feel guilty, irrationally, looking across the table at the broad, smiling face of a man who's thwarted every effort to get Barrera, who has taken tens of millions in *cañonazos,* a *matón*—a bully who held a young girl while his partner gouged out her eyes.

What the fuck do you feel guilty for? he asks himself.

"What about you?" Vera asks.

"What about me?"

"You have a woman?"

Keller shakes his head.

"You did, though, didn't you?" Vera asks. "She was a doctor or something, right?"

Is that a threat? Keller wonders.

"How do you know about that?" he asks, keeping his voice level.

"It's my business," Vera answers, "to know about everything. No offense, Arturo, nothing personal."

"Anyway, it's over."

"She left the city, as I recall."

He knows where Marisol is, Keller thinks. And it is a threat. Keller has an impulse—deep, atavistic—to just stand up and shoot him in that broad forehead right now.

"It was you, right?" Vera's asking now.

"Me who what?"

"You who told the Tapias about the Salvador Barrera deal," Vera says casually. "I know it wasn't me, and Luis is incapable of that sort of manipulation. So that leaves you."

Keller doesn't answer.

"No, congratulations," Vera says. "If you're going after Barrera, it was the perfect move. Split his organization in half, make people pick sides . . . Well done, *mi amigo*."

What's he doing? Keller wonders. Where's he trying to go with this? Is he threatening, testing, checking out the water? Shit, maybe he wants to come in, make a deal.

"I don't know what you're talking about," Keller says.

"Of course you don't," Vera says, still smiling. His lifts a finger to get the waiter's attention and then points at his empty glass. "Where are they?"

"You've lost me."

"The Tapias," Vera says. "If you're in touch with them, if you know where they are, now is the time to tell me."

He's working me the way you work an informant, Keller thinks. Shit, he's working me the way *I* work an informant. "I'm not in touch with them and I don't know where they are."

The waiter sets down a fresh Bloody Mary. Vera ignores it and says, "I think it's time for you to go home, Arturo. I think it's time for you to leave Mexico and go home."

Keller shakes his head. "Not until I get Barrera."

The smile comes off Vera's face and he says very seriously, "That is never going to happen. Listen to me, Arturo—that is never going to happen."

Jesus Christ, Keller thinks, he's doing everything but telling me that he's on Barrera's payroll.

Why?

Vera reaches out and lays his hand on top of Keller's. In another culture it would be interpreted as a homosexual gesture. Here it's a mark of strong friendship between two men.

"I respect you," Vera says. "I admire you. But you are never going to bring down Barrera, and your life is in danger now. Things are on the move and I am asking you—no, I'm *begging* you—leave the country as soon as possible. Tonight. I'm trying to save your life, Arturo."

And I'm trying to destroy yours, Keller thinks, the guilt coming back.

"Have a real drink with me," Vera says. "We'll toast to fighting the good fight. Then, if you're still here tomorrow, I'll have you arrested and deported. It's for your own good."

He orders two whiskeys and they drink to the good fight.

Keller goes back to the embassy and waits.

Eats a lunch that he can barely taste at his desk, leaves early, takes a walk through Parque México, and finally wanders over to the bar at Las Alcobas, where he nurses a beer before going up to Room 417.

Aguilar is already there with a Model G1416 body wire and a roll of medical tape.

Palacios is due in twenty minutes.

Chido Palacios sits at his usual table, sipping his usual espresso and watching women in their short summer dresses walk by.

They're beautiful—sleek and stylish with long, tan legs fit from the gym, and he's sorry that this is the last time he'll have this particular pleasure, but he knows that there are sidewalk cafés in Scottsdale, and, if not there, in Paris, and that there are beautiful women everywhere.

He's admiring a particularly stunning brunette when a man walks up to the fence, and, before the bodyguards can react, empties a .380 Cobra into his face and runs away.

The espresso spills on his lap as Palacios slumps in his chair, his dead eyes looking up at the blue sky, sightless.

Aguilar clicks the phone off.

"That was Vera," he says. "Palacios is dead. They killed him."

Things are on the move, Keller thinks.

They had started to worry when Palacios didn't show at the hotel, didn't answer his phone. Keller supposed that he was having second thoughts or had just decided to run on his own, but—

Gabriela didn't show up either.

They were trying to track her down when Vera called.

"They're already blaming the Tapias," Aguilar says. "Same MO, same weapon."

He gets up from the couch and carefully puts the recording equipment back in its case. "That's it. It's over."

"Gabriela—"

"Was the leak," Aguilar says.

"She's either dead or on her way to a country with which we have no extradition arrangements. Face it, Arturo, they beat us. It's over."

He's right, Keller thinks.

It is over.

For now.

"What are you going to do?" Keller asks.

"Go ride horses with my daughters," Aguilar says. "Talk to my wife and decide what career I want next. I know it's not this one."

He picks up the case and walks out of the room.

Keller is walking down Presidente Masaryk when his phone rings.

"It wasn't us."

Yvette sounds urgent, almost frantic.

"Please, Arturo, meet me."

Gerardo Vera opens the door of his condo to see Luis Aguilar standing there.

"How did you find me here?" Vera asks.

"Aren't you going to ask me in?"

They meet outside the Palacio de Cortés in Cuernavaca, one of the oldest structures in the Western world.

Cortés built it on the ruins of an Aztec temple.

"I thought you were out of the country," Keller says.

"I was. Martín is. We didn't kill Palacios."

"I know," Keller says. "Vera did."

"I gave you the tape weeks ago," Yvette says. "You haven't done a thing with it."

"Without Palacios, it's worthless."

"How can that be?" She's agitated, scared. "They'll never stop now. They'll track us down and kill us."

"If Martín wants to come in," Keller says, "and testify, I can guarantee his safety. And yours."

"And how many years in jail?" Yvette asks.

"A short time. Maybe none at all."

"He'd have to testify against his brother," Yvette says, "and he would never do that."

"This only ends one other way, and you know *that*," Keller says. "I can have you on a flight to the States tonight, Yvette. There are no charges against you there. Just tell us what we need to know and—"

"You'll extradite me back to Mexico," Yvette says. "I'm not going to Puente Grande, Arturo. I hoped you would help us."

"I'm trying."

She smiles bitterly. "They always win, don't they?"

"Who?"

"The polo crowd."

"They usually do."

"Laura Amaro doesn't know me anymore," Yvette says. "None of them do. We thought we were them. We're not, and they'll never let us be."

"Bring Martín in."

Yvette stares at him. "You got what you wanted, didn't you? You split Adán's organization in half so you can destroy it one piece at a time. And you don't care how many people get hurt, how many people get killed, as long as you get Adán. God save us from men of integrity."

She walks away.

His phone rings.

"I have it."

It's Aguilar.

"What do you mean? What are you talking about?"

Aguilar's voice is tight and excited. *"I have tape of Gerardo incriminating himself."*

"Luis, what did you do? What did you do?"

"Where are you?"

"Cuernavaca, headed back."

"Come to the airport. Hurry."

"Luis, what did you do?!"

"Just come. We can't wait long."

"Luis, go. Don't wait for me. Just go."

Keller drives 95 North back toward Mexico City.

The route takes him through El Tepozteco National Park, a winding road across the mountain, past lakes and meadows, now metallic in the moonlight.

What did you do, Luis? Keller asks himself. Then it hits him—Aguilar left the hotel room, miked himself up, and made the meeting with Vera himself. He must have solicited him, Vera agreed, and Aguilar got it on tape.

And he can testify to its authenticity.

But Vera is too smart to fall for that. He would have placated Aguilar to buy himself time to act.

But he'll act.

Headlights flash in his rearview mirror and Keller sees a car coming up behind him.

Fast.

The car starts tailgating him, dangerous on this winding road. Then it flashes its lights—it wants to pass.

"Hold on a second," Keller mumbles.

He finds a place to pull over and the car roars around him.

"Asshole," Keller says.

But then the car gets directly in front of him and slows down. At first Keller thinks the driver is just trying to teach him a lesson, get back at him, but then another pair of headlights appears behind him.

It comes up fast and then gets right on his bumper.

They have him boxed in.

Keller tries to pass the front car, but it slides out into the oncoming lane and blocks him and then the little parade races through a chicane, with steep slopes on either side, which opens onto a straightaway.

The car in front slows down.

The car in back—a Jeep Wrangler—pulls into the passing lane and comes even with Keller. He throws himself down on the seat as the muzzle flashes crackle red and bullets shatter his window.

Keller cranks the wheel to the left and hits the Wrangler, which flies off the road and crashes into the opposite slope.

The car in front slides sideways, stops, and blocks the road.

The natural instinct is to hit the brakes, but the natural instinct is only going to get him killed. He can already see the gun barrels pointed at him.

Keller hits the gas.

He aims straight for the driver's door.

The crash is horrific.

Keller's face slams into the airbag and his neck snaps back.

Dizzy, he reaches into the console and grabs his Sig Sauer. His right arm is weak, tingling, and he can barely grip the handle. With his left hand, he unhooks his seat belt and then pushes the door handle down.

To his relief, the door opens and he gets out.

Blood gushes out of his broken nose.

He can see that the driver of the other car is dead, his neck snapped. The passenger is getting out on his side. Seeing Keller, he rests the barrel of his shotgun on the roof of the smoking car and aims.

Shouldn't have taken the time.

Keller pops him twice in the head.

Then he staggers back to his car. His legs feel like water beneath him and he realizes that he's bleeding.

He collapses on the hood.

Aguilar clicks off the phone.

Keller didn't answer.

Where are you, Keller?

The pilot's voice comes over the intercom. *"Sir? We're cleared for takeoff. We only have a short window."*

Aguilar wants to tell him to wait. Hopefully, Keller will be there any moment. But the material he has in his case is too valuable to risk, and Vera could be on his way already.

"Go ahead," Aguilar says, settling back into a thickly upholstered seat.

It feels odd, being alone in the cabin, which can hold ten passengers. He watches out the window as the plane taxis, then picks up speed and takes off. Looking down at the lights of the massive Mexico City metropolis, Aguilar can't help but wonder if he'll ever come home again.

Adán looks at his watch.

He hasn't received the phone call he was expecting, the call to tell him that he would shortly have a body to view. There was a small risk entailed in coming to Mexico City, more from Tapias's *sicarios* than from the police—but it's worth it if he can look down at Keller's corpse.

Art Keller.

Holier-than-thou.

Mr. Clean.

Incorruptible.

You have to hand it to him, Adán thinks as he looks across the coffee table at Magda. He almost had me, he almost drove straight through the gap in my defenses, a gap that it's taken great effort to close up.

But it's almost closed.

Chido Palacios, the last of the Izta Mafia, is dead, the news all over the television, which is already blaming Diego Tapia.

The rest will be taken care of soon.

And Keller, by this time, should be in hell.

He glances at his watch again and Magda notices. Then again, she notices everything, something he admires about her. She's been a wonderful partner, maintaining relationships with the Colombians, assuring a smooth flow of cocaine, becoming wealthy and secure on her own.

"What?" Magda asks, seeing him look at her.

"Nothing."

Other than her, Adán really has no friends.

Nacho is an adviser, but also a father-in-law and a partner as well as a potential rival. Adán isn't afraid that Nacho would try to kill his own son-in-law, but Nacho definitely has his own agenda.

Adán can't relax with him, ever really let his guard down.

Only with Magda can he do that, and the truth is now that he'd rather talk to her than fuck her, not that he can't do both. He used to scoff at the old cliché about "the loneliness of command." He doesn't scoff now—he feels its truth. No one who doesn't have to make the decisions that he has to make can understand.

To order the deaths of scores of people.

The fight for Juárez has been far bloodier than he expected.

Vicente Fuentes is just a figurehead—hiding in his lairs, maybe even in Texas—but La Línea has fought hard and so has La Azteca. The Juarenses are ferociously protective of their turf.

Then there's the war with Diego.

A war that's your own fault, a situation that you brutally mishandled, almost fumbling the entire protective machinery into Keller's hands. But how could you have known that Martín Tapia taped his meetings with the Izta Mafia? How could you have known that Keller was working with the Tapias, maybe literally in bed with Yvette?

Stop giving yourself excuses—you should have known. It's your business to know.

You woke up—hopefully—just in time.

He looks at his watch again.

So much killing on both sides, so unnecessary. And exactly what he didn't need just as he was about to launch his campaign in Juárez. A needless distraction that saps resources away from the real battle. He has the resources to fight simultaneous wars against the Fuenteses, the Tapias, and the CDG with their Zeta mercenaries, but it stretches him thinner than he wants.

And he has bigger plans for Juárez, plans that go far beyond the city itself.

The Zetas are a problem.

The Zetas are going to be *the* problem. Of all his enemies, Heriberto Ochoa is the best of the lot—the smartest, the most ruthless, the most disciplined. He did the smart thing, siding with the Tapias. It was the right move. And he's doing the right thing staying out of the fighting in Juárez. Adán sees his strategy—let Fuentes and me bleed each other, then make his play.

At the end of the day, Adán thinks, it's going to come down to Ochoa and me.

Magda pours herself a glass of Moët, which he knows to have on ice for all their meetings. "You're thinking about Keller."

He shrugs. He's thinking about a lot of things.

"They'll call," Magda reassures him. She distracts him by going over business—prices per kilo, transportation issues, personnel decisions. Their relationship, while still sexual, has been more that of friends and colleagues recently. He's come more and more to rely on her advice, and she has new ideas to grow the business.

As for other men, Magda's had a few lovers, but fewer than anyone, herself included, might have expected. While a few men find her wealth and power an aphrodisiac, a surprising number find it quite the opposite, and she doesn't relish another night of coddling, as it were, another limp dick and assuring its owner that "it's all right, it's nice just to be close."

It isn't.

And she's not ready to go in the other direction, to the pretty younger men—boys, really—who see her as a source of cash and gifts, holidays and expensive meals. They're more than eager and able, and she has indulged once or twice, but she knows that her ego is far too healthy to accept the role of "cougar."

Nor, she thinks, am I a "MILF," lacking the "M" for "mother," and she's surprised that this is a source of increasing sadness. She wouldn't have expected that and supposes it's just some sort of biological thing, but she finds herself thinking about it, knowing that she's approaching the now-or-never moment, and she's increasingly pessimistic about meeting the right man to father her child.

For one thing, there's so little time in her busy days.

"Shouldn't he be here by now?" Adán asks Magda.

"He'll come." Magda smiles serenely. "I told him it was business, but he probably thinks it's more."

Doubtless he does, Adán thinks, knowing his man.

It's good to know a man's strengths.

Better to know his weaknesses.

The volume on the television picks up, the shrill tone of breaking news, and both Adán and Magda turn to the screen.

A Learjet 25, on fire as it plummeted from the sky, crashed into the busy financial district of Las Lomas at the corner of Paseo de la Reforma and Anillo Periférico, barely a kilometer from Los Pinos. It smashed into an office building, killing six people as well as the pilot, copilot, and the sole passenger on board.

Adán takes no joy in it.

From all accounts, Luis Aguilar was a decent man.

With a wife and children.

He hears voices downstairs as the guards stop someone, then start to walk him up to the second-floor apartment.

"I told you," Magda says.

The guard lets Gerardo Vera in.

He smiles at Magda, then his look turns to fear as he sees Adán sitting in the wingback chair.

"I didn't expect—"

"No," Adán says pleasantly. "You expected to have an assignation with my woman without my presence."

"It was a business meeting."

"It doesn't matter," Adán says, shaking his head. "It's not why I wanted to see you. Palacios is dead, Aguilar is dead, Keller should be dead by now."

"Then we're in the clear," Vera says.

"Not quite."

Vera looks puzzled at first, and then Adán sees the comprehension come across his face. "You let things get out of hand, Gerardo. You're compromised now."

"I see." Vera looks at the bottle of champagne. "May I?"

He pours himself a glass and then takes a long swallow. "It's good. Very good. I won't beg for my life."

"I didn't think you would."

"You know I have men just outside."

"Actually, they just left."

"We've come a long way, you and me," Vera says. "You were a little shit selling blue jeans off the back of a truck in Tijuana, I was a cop walking a beat in a slum. We've done all right for ourselves."

"We have."

"So why stop now?"

"You just had your oldest friend killed," Adán says, "and colluded in the death of your closest colleague. To be perfectly honest with you, Gerardo, I just can't trust you."

Magda stands up.

"Indulge me in one thing?" Vera asks. He leans over and puts his face close to her neck. "That's a lovely scent. Men debate about the prettiest part of a woman. I say it's the neck. Where it curves into the shoulder. Right here. Thank you."

She nods and walks out the door.

Vera reaches for the pistol in his shoulder holster.

The guard blows the back of his head off.

Adán gets up to leave.

It's all cleaned up now—there will be no "smoking gun," as it were, to tarnish PAN in the last administration or this one.

Only one thing troubles him.

He still hasn't received the phone call telling him that Keller is dead.

Keller comes to in the back of a black Suburban with tinted windows.

A medic in civilian clothes, but clearly military from his haircut and bearing, works efficiently and silently to clean and bandage his wounds.

"Who are you?" Keller asks.

The medic doesn't answer his question, just makes small talk as he tries to keep Keller awake. Desperate for sleep, Keller realizes that he must have a concussion, so they're keeping him conscious. This goes on all the way into Mexico City, where the car turns onto Paseo de la Reforma. Keller thinks that they're headed for the embassy but the car pulls off earlier, in a neighborhood of banks and corporate buildings, and at number 265 goes down a driveway to a steel door. The driver shows some identification to a guard, the door slides open, and the car goes into the parking structure.

They load Keller onto a stretcher, take him to a room that looks like a small infirmary, where an American medic, just as military-looking, takes over, does a preliminary examination, and then takes X-rays.

"Where am I?" Keller asks.

"A concussion, broken nose, dislocated shoulder, two cracked ribs, and a few scattered shotgun pellets," the medic says. "You're a hard man to kill, sir."

"Where *am* I?"

"Internal pain? Anything you haven't told me about, sir?"

"Where the hell am I?"

"Someone will be in to see you soon."

It's Tim Taylor.

"Aguilar called us," Taylor said, "when he couldn't get hold of you. We sent people out looking for you. What the hell were you doing in Cuernavaca?"

"Luis is okay, then," Keller says. "In El Paso."

"He's dead," Taylor says. He tells Keller about the plane crash and then says, "You didn't answer my question."

"I'm not going to," Keller says. "Vera had that plane brought down."

"Vera was found murdered," Taylor says. "Same MO as the other cops. He was having an assignation. Like Aguilar, his demise is being attributed to the Tapias."

"They didn't do either," Keller says. "Barrera did."

"We know that."

So it's over, Keller thinks.

Aguilar is dead, the tapes destroyed in the crash.

Palacios is dead.

So is Vera.

Barrera cleaned up his mess.

"So you're here to take me home?" Keller asks.

"Can you walk?"

"I think so."

Keller eases himself off the gurney, the effort setting his ribs on fire. His legs are wobbly from the shock and the meds, but he manages to follow Taylor down the hall and into an elevator that they take to the sixth floor. When they get out, Keller sees more military types, although in civilian clothes, and people who look like computer geeks and accountants.

None of the offices are marked.

All of the doors are closed.

"What you see here doesn't exist," Taylor says, "except officially as an accounting office to make sure that the taxpayers' Mérida money is being used properly. In reality, the hat racks in this building are pretty full—FBI, CIA, us, Alcohol, Tobacco and Firearms, Treasury, Homeland Security, the National Reconnaissance Office, NSA, Defense Intelligence Agency . . . you get the idea."

He opens the door to a room where a dozen technicians sit at desks in front of computers.

"Everything here is state-of-the-art," Taylor says. "Encryption equipment, counterencryption equipment, satellite surveillance, wiretapping, secure communications. Come on."

They go to a locked door at the end of the hall. Taylor looks into a retina scanner and the door slides open to what seems to be some kind of lounge, with comfortable furniture, a coffee machine, and a bar.

A man who looks a little younger than Keller sits on one of the sofas and sips a beer. His hair is black and cut short. A little under six feet tall, broad-chested, ramrod posture. He gets up when they walk in and extends his hand to Keller. "Arturo Keller—Roberto Orduña."

"Admiral Orduña," Taylor says, "is the commander of the Mexican marines' FES—special forces—roughly analogous to our SEALs."

"Let me first say how sorry I am about Luis Aguilar," Orduña says. "He was a good man. Would you like a drink? A coffee? This is your building but my country, so I feel that I should be a good host."

You made your point, Keller thinks. What do you want?

They all sit down.

"We're losing the war," Orduña says without preamble. "Drugs are more plentiful, more potent, and cheaper than ever. The cartels have more influence than at any time, have co-opted the major instruments of power, and threaten to become a shadow government. The war between them increases the violence to horrific levels. What we *have* been doing isn't working."

Keller knows this.

The strategy of drug interdiction is a broom sweeping back the ocean. The strategy of arresting traffickers at any level only creates a job opportunity that any number of candidates are eager to fill.

"We have to do something different," Orduña says. "The law enforcement model isn't working. We have to switch to a military model."

"With all respect," Keller says, "your president has already militarized antitrafficking. It's only made things worse."

"Because he's pursuing the wrong model," Orduña answers. "Are you conversant with the debate between counterinsurgency and antiterrorism doctrines?"

"Only vaguely."

Orduña nods. "Counterinsurgency—the model for fighting terrorism for the past thirty years—focused on defense, preventing attacks while politically building relationships with the local people so that they would not support the terrorists. That is roughly analogous to what we—and you—have been doing in regards to drug trafficking, if you can say that drug traffickers are analogous to terrorists."

"More and more they *are* terrorists," Keller says.

"Al Qaeda killed three thousand Americans," Taylor says. "This is going to sound callous, but that's a fraction of the harm that drugs cause every year. And we spend tens of billions on interdiction and incarceration."

"Exactly," Orduña says. "Counterinsurgency is expensive, time-consuming, and ultimately unsuccessful, which is why your military has recently evolved toward antiterrorist doctrine, which emphasizes the offensive—narrow, specific attacks on prime targets.

"As it exists now, we arrest a cartel leader—Contreras, for instance—another takes his place. There is great motivation to take the job, but little disincentive."

Taylor adds, "What we're finding is that fewer jihadists are stepping up for the top positions, because we've made it a death sentence instead of a promotion. You take the big chair, we drop a drone missile on your head, or special forces take you out."

"I wonder," Orduña says, "who would want to be the head of, say, the Sinaloa cartel, if his two predecessors were both killed. The message is, 'Go ahead and make your billions, but you won't live to spend them.' That's what we want to do, abandon counterinsurgency and adopt antiterrorism."

"You're talking about a program of targeted assassinations," Keller says.

"Arrest them if we have to," Orduña says, "kill them when we can."

Keller smirks.

"I know what you're thinking," Orduña says. "You've heard it before, and every piece of intelligence you gave Vera went straight to the Sinaloa cartel. The AFI was bought and paid for, but not my unit."

"That's what Vera said."

"Not in my unit," Orduña repeats. His men can't apply for the unit, he explains, they have to be selected, talent-spotted, picked from the chorus.

Then they're *trained*.

First at a secret camp in the mountains of Huasteca Veracruzana for *a year and a half* learning weapons, tactics—ambush and counterambush—evasive driving, surveillance, rappelling, explosives, survival.

If they make it through that session, they're sent to another secret camp in Colombia for specific anti–drug trafficking training. How to infiltrate the cartels' private armies, identify a drug lab, find stash houses, jump from helicopters, fight in jungles and mountains.

The men who pass that course then go on to a third school, on antiterrorism, in Arizona, on the "neutralization and destruction" of terrorist threats, where they're taught intelligence, counterintelligence, surviving capture and interrogation. They're put under intense physical and psychological pressure, and if they survive that, they're taught how to inflict it—"soft" and "hard" interrogation techniques.

Then they come back to Mexico where their salary is 30,000 pesos a month, plus a 20,000 bonus for every risky operation, which makes them far less likely to take bribes from the narcos.

Another incentive is, to be blunt, looting.

The FES marines get to keep a portion of what they capture—watches, jewelry, cash. Cops have done it forever, of course; Orduña's genius is to make it legal and actually encourage it.

His men aren't going to take bribes, they're just going to take.

"Any man of mine who takes a bribe," Orduña says, "knows that he won't be arrested, tried, and sent to jail. He'll just disappear out in the desert."

Orduña has created a dirty unit designed to fight a dirty war, Keller thinks. Whether he realizes it or not, he's formed his own version of the Zetas.

"We have a list of thirty-seven targets," Orduña says.

"Is Barrera on it?"

"Number two."

"Who's number one?"

"Diego Tapia. I'm sure you understand that the public, knowing nothing about the 'Izta cartel' scandal, expects it. Our honor demands it. But I swear to you, if you work with me, I will help you kill Adán Barrera." Orduña smiles and adds, "Hopefully before he succeeds in killing you."

"The operation is a cut-out," Taylor said. "No connection to normal DEA activities. Those will go on as usual, in cooperation, such as it is, with the Mexican government. This new unit will work out of here and only with the Mexican marines. The money has been siphoned off from Mérida, so there's no budget line item, no oversight committee. No State, no Justice—only the White House, which will deny its existence."

"Where would I fit in?" Keller asks.

"You'd run the American end of things," Taylor says. "You'll base yourself here and at EPIC. Only military flights back and forth. FES plainclothes security. Top-level clearance, top-level access."

"I get a free hand," Keller says. "I work alone. No handlers, no office spies."

"You get only the logistical support you request," Taylor says.

"And if this program comes to light, I get crucified."

"I have the nails in my mouth."

Jesus, Keller thinks, he's offering me a job as the head of an assassination program.

Just like the old days in Vietnam.

Operation Phoenix.

Except this time I'm in charge.

"Why me?" Keller asks. "You're not exactly the president of my fan club."

"You're a lonely, bitter man, Art," Taylor says. "The only guy I have driven, angry, and good enough to do this."

It's honest, Keller thinks.

And Taylor's right.

He takes the job.

Remembering what he once heard a priest say:

Satan can only tempt you with what you already have.

4

The Valley

Therefore, behold, the days come, saith the Lord, that it shall no more be called Tophet, nor the valley of the son of Hinnom, but the valley of slaughter.

—Jeremiah 7:32

The Juárez Valley
Spring 2009

They drive east out of Juárez on Carretera Federal 2.

The two-lane highway parallels I-10, just a few miles away across the American border.

Ana insisted on driving her Toyota, not trusting Pablo behind the wheel (certainly of his old heap), and to allow Giorgio to snap all the pictures he wants. Oscar has sent them out into the Juárez Valley to get the story of the increasing violence.

Two months ago, Calderón sent the army out there, a column of troops with armored vehicles and helicopters, to try to quell the fighting between the Sinaloa and Juárez cartels that has made the rural valley a battleground.

Pablo looks out the window at the green belt that flanks the Río Bravo. This used to be mostly cotton fields—cotton with some wheat—but the maquiladoras lured most of the labor away and the cotton plants have long since withered.

This is bandit country and always has been, Pablo thinks, looking past the green strip to the brown sierra to the south. Long controlled by the Escajeda family who migrated down when Texas gained its independence, most of the old families in the valley were refugees, fleeing the encroaching United States.

The Escajedas did what so many border families did—they raised and rustled cattle, participating in the time-honored tradition of two-way cross-border raiding, they fought off first the Comanches and later the Apaches, then turned to cotton when the end of slavery up north created opportunity.

They smuggled marijuana and opium at the turn of the century, then whiskey and rum during Prohibition. The Escajedas grew rich from the bootleg trade, but far richer when Nixon's War on Drugs made *la pista secreta* so profitable. You can drive or even walk to Texas from the little towns in the valley, and while the majority of drug trafficking still goes through Juárez, the value of this smuggling territory isn't to be sneezed at.

Until recently, two Escajeda brothers, José "El Rikin" and Oscar "La Gata," controlled the drug trade out here and maintained a fragile peace between Sinaloa and Juárez, allowing both cartels use of the plaza for a price.

So there was "peace in the valley," as it were, even while Juárez tore itself apart, until two months ago, when the army arrested La Gata, and the Sinaloa cartel took it as a signal to move in. The Sinaloan invasion forced El Rikin to choose sides, and he picked his local team, the Juárez cartel.

Now it's a war zone.

"I didn't sign up to be a war correspondent," Pablo says. "We should get extra pay."

Giorgio, of course, is thrilled with it. He would love to have been a war photographer, and looks like one, in a green shirt, khaki cargo pants, and a khaki vest. He quickly snaps an army convoy of three armored cars as it comes in the opposite direction.

Pablo sees Ana's hand gripped on the steering wheel. She's tense, sharing the road with farm trucks and military convoys, and you never knew when a vehicle could be filled with *sicarios* from one side or the other and when you might drive into a full-fledged firefight, maybe a three-sided one.

He's relieved when they reach the army checkpoint—a thrown-together post of sandbags, barbed wire, and plywood, outside of Valverde. It's hot out here now, sweltering really, outside the protective shade of the greenbelt, and Pablo is sweating heavily as Ana stops the car and the soldier walks over.

Pablo knows that it's more than the oppressive heat making the sweat come through the thin fabric of his white shirt—he's afraid. Military of any stripe have always made him nervous, all the more so when they're edgy. This one wears cammies, a combat helmet, and a heavy protective vest, and can't be happy in this heat.

Ana rolls down the window.

"What are you doing here?" the soldier asks.

"Press," Ana says.

"Tell him not to take my picture," the soldier snaps.

"Giorgio, for Chrissakes," Pablo mutters.

Giorgio lowers his camera to his lap.

"Identification?" the soldier asks.

They hand him their press IDs, and he scans them carefully, although Pablo doubts that the soldier can read. Most of them are rural boys who joined the army to escape hunger and drudgery, and most are illiterate.

"Get out of the car," the soldier commands.

Noooo, Pablo thinks, aware of the cardinal rule when confronted by cops or soldiers—*never get out of the car.* Once you're out of the car, only bad things can happen. Once you're out of the car, you're theirs—they can take you off into a ditch and beat you up, rob you. They can take you inside the post, they can put you into the back of a truck for a ride to the main base, and Pablo's heard stories about what happens to people who get taken to the base.

Now he sees two other soldiers, their interest aroused, get up and walk toward the car. One of them unslings his assault rifle and comes around to the passenger side.

"Get out of the car!" the first soldier yells. He brings his rifle to his shoulder and points it at Ana.

"No, no, no!" Pablo yells, throwing his hands up. "It's all right! We're reporters! Reporters!"

Giorgio slips Ana an American ten-dollar bill. "Give it to him."

Ana's hand shakes as she passes the soldier the bill. He lowers the rifle, stuffs the bill into his pants pocket, peruses the IDs for a few more seconds, and then hands them back. He waves his hand and a soldier lifts the barrier.

"Go ahead."

"Jesus Christ," Pablo says.

The little town of Valverde has around five thousand inhabitants and consists of about twenty blocks arranged in a rectangular gridiron in the desert flat. Its houses are small, mostly cinder-block with a few adobes, many brightly painted in vivid blues, reds, and yellows.

The Abarca family bakery is in the center of town on Avenida Valverde— a continuation of Highway 2, and the main street.

The bakery is in the center of town in more than just the purely physical sense—for three generations the rose-painted building has been a meeting place, a social center, where people go when they have an issue or a problem.

"Ir a ver a los panaderos," has long been a saying in town.

Go see the bakers.

If the landlord is pressing you for money you don't have, an Abarca will go talk to him. If you need a document completed and can't write, an Abarca will fill it out for you. If your child is having trouble at school, an Abarca will visit with the teacher. If the soldiers have taken your son away, an Abarca will go to the post to inquire.

There's been too much of that lately.

Jimena is waiting out in front for them.

"Did you have any trouble getting here?" she asks as they get out of the car. She wears a yellow smock over faded jeans, both smeared with flour.

"No," Ana lies.

Pablo hopes that they will go inside. Hot as he is, his nerves still jangled, the aroma coming from the bakery still tantalizes. He can smell the *pan dulce,* the distinct ginger of the *marranitos,* the anise of *semitas,* and he thinks he detects some empanadas.

It's almost lunchtime, but what he really wants is an ice-cold *cerveza.*

Jimena quickly dashes both hopes.

"Marisol is waiting for us," she says.

They follow Jimena to the largest building in town, the two-story town offices, and meet the councilwoman upstairs.

Marisol Salazar Cisneros, actually *Dr.* Marisol Salazar Cisneros, is a Valverde town councilwoman. When Jimena said they'd be meeting her, Pablo did his homework on the Internet—Cisneros was born to a middle-class family of planters outside of Valverde, went away to have a career in the capital, and then returned to open a clinic in the town.

Impressive, Pablo thought, fully prepared to hate the overachieving do-gooder.

What he isn't prepared for is her beauty. Marisol Cisneros is simply beautiful, to the point that Pablo feels almost intimidated as he shakes her hand. She invites them to sit down at the table, Giorgio instantly starts taking her picture, and Pablo feels a twinge of irrational but nevertheless powerful jealousy.

"You're friends of Jimena's," Marisol says.

"We've known each other since the *feminicidio,*" Ana says. "Pablo worked very closely with her in those days."

"I think I might have read your stories," Marisol tells him.

"Thank you," Pablo says, feeling stupid, and wishing that he'd gotten a haircut or at least shaved.

"And thank you for speaking to us," Ana says. "The mayor declined."

"He's a good man," Marisol says, "but he's . . ."

"Afraid?" Ana prompts.

"Let's say 'reticent,'" Marisol answers.

"Has he been threatened?" Pablo asks, finding his voice.

"I don't know."

"But you have," Pablo says.

A month ago, she tells them, she was driving back from Práxedis G. Guerrero, farther east in the valley, where she was doing checkups on pregnant women, and an SUV forced her car off the road. She was terrified—all the more so when three men in ski masks got out and fired AR-15 rounds over her head.

"You're sure they were ARs?" Pablo asks.

"Quite sure," Marisol says. "Unfortunately, we've all become experts at armaments around here."

The men told her that she wouldn't be so lucky the next time, so she'd better learn to keep her "stupid bitch legs open and her mouth" shut.

"What had you been saying?" Ana asks.

"It's not so much what I'd been *saying*," Marisol answers, "as what I've been *asking*. When person after person comes into your clinic with bruises, skull fractures from gun butts, signs of electric shock torture, you ask questions. I demanded answers from the commanding officers."

"What did they tell you?" Pablo asks.

"To mind my own business," Marisol says. "I told them that injured people are exactly my business."

"To which they responded—"

"That enforcing the law is theirs," Marisol answers, "and that they would greatly appreciate my not interfering with their work."

She told them that as long as their work consisted of hurting innocent people, it was her sworn duty—both as a physician and as a town official—to interfere.

"The army's working theory," Jimena says, "is that there is no such thing as an innocent person out here. They accuse us all of working with the Escajedas and the Juárez cartel."

They break into houses looking for narcos, drugs, weapons, money, Jimena tells them. They steal whatever they can lay their hands on, and if you object . . . you wind up at Marisol's clinic.

"If you're lucky," Jimena adds. "If not, they blindfold you, throw you in a truck, and take you to the base in Práxedis. There are eight young men from Valverde there now, and we can't even find out about their status."

"You've gone before a judge?" Ana asks.

"Of course," Marisol answers, "but normal law doesn't apply in a state of emergency. The valley is under martial law, so the army can do pretty much what it wants."

Talk about getting caught in a three-way firefight, Pablo thinks. The people in the Juárez Valley are trapped in a murderous triangle—the Juárez cartel demands their loyalty, the Sinaloa cartel demands that they change sides, and the army is a force of its own. So if the locals aren't *literally* caught in a crossfire—mowed down between narcos trying to kill each other—they're being squeezed from three sides.

Jimena takes issue with this analysis.

"There aren't three sides," she says, "there are two. The army and the Sinaloans are the same."

"That's a serious allegation," Ana says, scribbling notes.

"Here's how it works," Jimena answers. "The army raids a house on the pretext that it has drugs or weapons. They smash things up, maybe arrest people, but usually not. But that night, or the next, the New People come and kill everyone in the house."

"So you're saying that the soldiers are the Sinaloa cartel's bird dogs," Pablo says. "They sniff out the Juárez people, then the narcos come in and shoot."

"Sometimes the killers are wearing black masks, like the *federales* and the army do," Marisol says.

"The army is hunting down the Juárez people," Jimena says, "Los Escajedos, the Aztecas, what's left of La Línea. They're exterminating them. I don't see them hunting down Los Sinaloanos."

"It appears to be one-sided," Marisol adds.

They take a walk around the town.

The streets, even at midday, are mostly empty. A few old people and kids sit in the shade of a gazebo, a handful of soldiers peer out from a sandbag barrier. Pablo has the eerie feeling that people are peeping at him behind closed window shades. Some of the buildings are pockmarked with bullet holes, or chipped from grenade blasts.

Pablo sees a surprising number of empty houses. Some are empty shells, others still have all the furniture inside, as if the people are away on vacation.

"They're not coming back," Jimena says. "They've been threatened by one or the other cartel, or more likely by the army."

"Why would the army threaten them?" Ana asks.

"So they can steal their houses," Jimena says, "steal their land."

She sees Pablo's dubious look.

"Come on," she says.

They drive east to Práxedis.

Jimena joins them—Marisol stayed in Valverde for her clinic's office hours. It's a beautiful day, the sky an almost impossible blue, set off by pure white cumulus clouds.

Nevertheless, the drive is tense as they go farther into the desert, farther into bandit country. They pass through another army checkpoint (another ten-dollar bill, but at least no guns raised this time) before getting into the little town, even smaller than Valverde.

The look is similar, though—soldiers on the street, shot-up buildings, some of them abandoned.

"The narcos gunned someone down in there," Jimena says. "The owner got frightened and closed the store."

"Where do people go for groceries?" Ana asks.

"Valverde."

The army base is set up in what used to be a gymnasium. Now the building is surrounded by coils of barbed wire, sandbags, and a metal gate with a security shack in front.

"Don't pull up too close," Jimena warns.

They park a block away and walk to the guard shack.

"I'm here to see Colonel Alvarado," Jimena says.

The guard knows her. She comes most days making the same demands. "He's busy."

"We'll wait," Jimena says. "Tell him I'm with three reporters from a Juárez newspaper. No, *m'ijo*, seriously—he'll be mad at you if you don't tell him."

The guard gets on the phone.

A few minutes later a sergeant comes out and leads them into a makeshift office with a desk and a few folding chairs. Alvarado sets his cigarette in an ashtray, looks up from his paperwork, and gestures for them to sit. "Señora Abarca, what can I do for you today?"

He's a slick piece of work, Pablo thinks. Immaculately groomed and tailored, sandy hair brushed straight back, pale blue eyes that look right through you, the sort of person that Pablo has loathed—and, okay, yes, *feared*—his entire life.

"You still have eight young men from my town in custody here," Jimena says. She starts to run off the names—Velázquez, Ahumada, Blanco . . .

"I have told you and told you and told you that this is army business and you have no standing whatsoever to—"

Ana identifies herself and asks, "Have these men been charged with anything, and, if so, what?"

Alvarado looks at Giorgio's cameras. "Tell him not to take my picture."

"Don't take his picture," Ana says. "Have these men been charged with anything, and if so, what?"

"These men are still being interviewed," Alvarado says.

"Interviewed or interrogated?" Pablo asks.

"And who are you?"

"Pablo Mora. Same paper."

"It takes three of you?"

"Safety in numbers," Pablo says. "We have reports that people are being tortured in this facility."

"There is no truth to that," Alvarado says. "That is merely propaganda that the traffickers put out and some journalists are foolish enough to repeat."

"Then you won't mind," Ana says, "if we talk to these men?"

"Did I say 'foolish'?" Alvarado asks. "Perhaps I should have added 'corrupt.'"

"What does that mean?"

"That some journalists are on the cartels' payrolls," Alvarado says.

Pablo feels a deep flush come over his face and hopes that the others don't see it or chalk it up to the heat.

Jimena says, "The doctor in Valverde —"

"Dr. Cisneros?"

"Yes—has asked fifteen times to be allowed to examine these men," Jimena says, "and has received no response."

"We have perfectly qualified medical personnel here."

"She is their physician."

"Dr. Cisneros is a woman?" Alvarado asks.

"You've met her at least ten times," Jimena says.

"Can we see the prisoners from Valverde, yes or no?" Pablo asks.

"No."

"Why not?"

Alvarado says, "Something that they say and that you report might compromise an ongoing investigation."

"Don't *police* usually do criminal investigations?" Ana asks.

"These are different times."

"Are you concerned," Pablo asks, "that the local police are on the cartels' payroll, as well? And if so, which cartel?"

Alvarado doesn't answer.

"Suppose," Ana says, "we just see the prisoners but don't interview them?"

"Then what would you have to report?" Alvarado asks.

"That they haven't been tortured," Ana says.

Alvarado answers, "But you have my word. Isn't that good enough?"

"No," Ana says.

Alvarado glares at her with the hatred that a macho man feels toward an uppity woman.

So Pablo gathers up his courage and chimes in with rapid-fire questions—Do you intend to charge these men? If so, with what? When? If not, when do you intend to release them? Why won't you produce them? What, if any, evidence do you have against them? Why haven't they been allowed access to lawyers? Who are you? What's your background? Where did you serve prior to the 11th Military Zone?

Alvarado holds his hand up. "I don't intend to be interrogated."

"Is it torture for you?" Pablo asks.

"I have no comment for your paper."

"So we can print that you refused to answer," Ana says.

"Print what you like." Alvarado stands up. "Now, if you don't mind, I have real work to do."

"I've contacted the Red Cross and Amnesty International," Jimena says.

"It's a free country."

"Is it?" Jimena asks.

"Yes, unless you're a criminal," Alvarado says. "You're not a criminal, are you, Señora Abarca?"

The threat is clear.

He scribbles out a pass and hands it to Ana. "This will get you back to Juárez with no difficulties. May I suggest that you stay there? These roads can be very dangerous these days."

"Really?" Ana asks. "But we passed so many army patrols on the way."

"Those are two brave women," Ana says in the car on the way back to Juárez.

"Indeed," Pablo says.

"And you have a hard-on for the lady doctor," she adds.

"Who wouldn't?" Giorgio asks from the backseat.

"Me," Ana says.

"You would if your gate was hinged that way," Giorgio says. "It's not, right? You're not double-hinged, are you?"

"I wouldn't want to ruin your adolescent fantasies with a denial," Ana replies.

"They take my mind off things," Giorgio says.

"What things?"

"All of it," Giorgio answers. "The killing, the corruption, the oppression—the enervating *sameness* of it all. The fact that we've fought how many revolutions and end up with the same old shit. But here, check this out."

He leans forward and shows them the screen of his camera.

A beautiful close-up of Colonel Alvarado.

"How did you do that?" Pablo asks.

"While you were firing at him, so was I."

"Will Óscar print it?"

"With what?" Ana asks. "What story do we have? 'Colonel Denies Torturing Prisoners'? That's not news, that's the *opposite* of news. *News* would be 'Colonel *Admits* Torturing Prisoners.'"

"Yes, but there's a bigger story here," Pablo says. "If you accept Abarca's and Cisneros's version of events, the army is allied with the Sinaloa cartel to wipe out the Juárez cartel, and not only that, to move normal citizens out of the Juárez Valley."

If true, the Sinaloa cartel and the army are the same beast.

That night, Ana comes out on her back step, sits down next to Pablo, and lights a cigarette.

"When did you start again?" Pablo asks.

"I think it was when I started going to the morgues again," Ana says.

Pablo knows what she means—the cigarettes help get the smell out of your nose. Not entirely, nothing can do that, but it helps.

"What do you think about today?" Pablo asks.

"It's a hell of a story."

"Will Óscar print it?"

"Not the speculations," Ana says. "He'll run the fact that the army is holding prisoners in Práxedis without regard to legal rights."

They sit in silence for a while, enjoying the soft night and the faint sound of *norteño* music coming from someone's radio down the street. Then Ana asks, "Pablo, can I talk to you about something?"

"Of course."

"It's very awkward," Ana says, "and you can't say anything to Giorgio or Óscar about it."

"*Dios mío,* are you pregnant?"

"No," she snorts. "*No* . . . It's just that . . . while you were gone . . . a man came up to me outside the office and handed me an envelope."

Pablo feels his stomach flip. "An envelope?"

"He called it *la sobre.*"

"A bribe?" Pablo asks, choking on his own duplicity. "What did you do?"

"Well, I didn't know who he was," Ana says. "A cop, some politico's stooge, a narco . . ."

"So what did you do?"

"What else?" Ana says. "I shoved it back at him and told him that I wasn't interested."

Pablo tries to tell her, but shame stops him. Ana was always, he thinks, better than me. Every Monday, as promised ("threatened" is more like it), the man appears outside the office and gives ("forces on"?) Pablo the *sobre.* Pablo doesn't know what to do with the money, so he keeps it in an ever-growing manila envelope in his backpack.

You could just give it to charity, he told himself. Give it to the poor, give it to the homeless. (Shit, he thinks, you *are* the homeless.) Give it to the church if you can't think of anything better.

Then why don't you?

Because you could really use the money, is the answer. For trips, legal fees, court costs.

He hasn't so far, but still it sits there, a growing fund.

And the odd thing is that they haven't asked him for anything yet. They haven't demanded that he write a story, or kill another one, or give them a source, or anything. They just come every Monday, as inevitable as the post-Mateo hangover, and hand him the envelope.

He still doesn't know who they are. Juárez cartel? Sinaloa cartel? Somebody else?

Pablo was even tempted to talk to Óscar, but he feared what the reaction would be—contempt and disdain, maybe an immediate sacking—and he can't afford to lose this job.

So he kept his mouth shut.

And the money stacked up.

Betrayals start that way, with lies hidden in the shadows of silence.

"Are you on my sofa tonight?" Ana asks.

"If that's okay."

"Giorgio's probably driving back out to Valverde to bag that doctor."

"He's not her type."

"Oh," Ana says, both amused and annoyed at the easy assertion, thinking, I hate to tell you, bud, but Giorgio is about every woman's type. She gets up, tosses down the last of her beer, and crushes her cigarette out on the step. "See you in the morning."

Pablo sits for a while, enjoying the silence. Then he crashes on the sofa and indulges in a brief, consciously futile fantasy about Marisol . . . excuse me, *Dr.* Marisol Cisneros. Christ, he thinks, even my imagination knows that she's out of my league.

He and Ana go into the office in the morning and pitch the story to Óscar. He listens carefully, then tells them to cowrite a descriptive piece about the valley—what it looks like, how it sounds, the army patrols, the checkpoints, the bullet-riddled buildings.

Óscar says, "Ana, do the piece about the men being held in Práxedis. Quote the colonel's no-comment, call officials in these other towns and see if they have any people being held."

"What about what Jimena and Marisol told us?"

"On deep background," Óscar says. "Don't use their names, just write that some citizens in the valley believe that the army is favoring the Sinaloa cartel in the struggle, something like that."

All three articles run that week.

Juárez is a horror show.

The Juárez cartel and their Zeta allies put up banners promising to kill a police officer every forty-eight hours until the new police chief—a former army officer—resigned.

After the first two officers were murdered, the chief did resign. The Zetas then sent the Juárez mayor a message that if "you put in another asshole working for Barrera, we'll kill you, too." Signs went up around the city promising to decapitate the mayor and his family. He moved his wife and children to El Paso but, contrary to rumor, stayed in Juárez himself, albeit under heavy round-the-clock security.

The administration sent five thousand more troops into Juárez.

The new police chief was another former army general, and the mayor disbanded the entire municipal police force and announced that the army would take over all city police duties.

In effect, Juárez is under martial law.

Summer burns off spring.

Sweltering becomes scorching.

And the violence in and around Juárez goes on.

On the first official day of summer, eighteen people are killed in Juárez. Pablo, Ana, and Giorgio hop around the city like drops of grease on a hot pan. One of the bodies, found out in the desperately poor *colonia* of Anapra, just along the border, is decapitated and dismembered, just a trunk in a bloody T-shirt.

Pablo's glad that he, and not Ana, caught this call.

By week's end, three more are killed, although the headline story is that the $1.6 billion Mérida Initiative has gone into effect.

In July, the police commander in charge of antikidnapping is himself kidnapped, and the chief of Juárez's prison system is gunned down in his car along with his bodyguard and three other people.

By August, Pablo thinks he has seen it all when he gets a call to go out to the *colonia* known as First of September in the southwest part of the city to something called CIAD #8.

Center for Alcohol and Drug Integration.

A rehab clinic.

It's about 7:30 on a Wednesday night, still light out, enough to see the blood on the sidewalk outside the newly whitewashed little building. The metal gate that leads onto a front patio is open. Cops are everywhere.

Pablo counts seven bodies on the patio, and by now he's experienced enough to know that these men—recovering addicts and alcoholics—were dragged out here, shoved against the wall, and executed with shots to the back of the head.

He looks up.

A lifeless body, bullet holes punched in the back, still grips the rungs of a fire escape ladder.

The outraged neighbors are eager to tell the story. An army truck pulled up at the end of the block and stopped. Then another vehicle—some say it was a Humvee, others a Suburban, roared up and started blasting.

The neighbors screamed for help, phoned emergency services, ran down to the army truck and pleaded. The truck never moved, the soldiers didn't help, emergency services never came. The survivors and neighbors loaded the twenty-three wounded into the center's old van in shifts, until finally a Red Cross ambulance came to take several of the rest.

Pablo examines shell casings before the cops take them away. He's not concerned about contaminating evidence, knowing by now that there will be no arrests, never mind trials.

Like most Juarense reporters now, Pablo has become a semi-expert in forensics. The casings are from 9mms and 7.62s, and 5.56s. The 7.62s could be from AKs—the narco weapon of choice—or military weapons. The 5.56s are consistent with several of the NATO weapons used by the Mexican army. The 9s are Glock or Smith and Wesson sidearms.

Pablo sees a cop he knows from . . . who knows what recent killing. "You have any suspects?"

"What do you think?"

"There were soldiers fifty yards away," Pablo says. "They didn't do anything."

"Didn't they?"

True, Pablo thinks. They blocked the street, maybe they were lookouts, maybe they scared the police and the EMTs from coming.

"Why would anyone want to kill rehab patients?" Pablo asks.

"Because the cartels use them to hide gunmen," the cop says. "Or because they're afraid of what a clean and sober ex-gunman might confess to. I don't know. Unless you have some answers for me, Pablo, get the fuck out of my way. I have to collect evidence that will never be used."

"The weapons might have been military."

"Go have a beer, Pablo, huh?"

Pablo goes him eight better. He's working on nine when he gets a phone call from Ana.

The army has taken away Jimena Abarca's older son.

The sergeant at the gate won't admit them to see Colonel Alvarado.

But when they insist that they won't leave until they do, and that television trucks will be there soon, the colonel finally comes out to the gate.

At first, he denies any knowledge of Miguel Abarca.

"At least ten people saw soldiers throw him into an army truck," Jimena says.

"Unfortunately," Alvarado says, "the narcos sometimes use stolen army uniforms and vehicles."

"Are you really saying," Ana presses, "that you're so careless with your equipment that you allow it to be stolen by the very people you're supposed to be controlling? Do you have an inventory of these missing vehicles?"

Alvarado will neither confirm nor deny that his unit is holding Miguel.

"But you can check," Pablo says. "Presumably you keep better track of people than you do of equipment."

Glaring at Pablo, Alvarado sends a lieutenant to check the day's paperwork. The subordinate comes back with a report that they do indeed have an "Abarca, Miguel," age twenty-three, in custody.

"On what charges?" Jimena asks.

"Suspicion," Alvarado answers.

"Of being my son?" Jimena asks.

"Of colluding with narcotics traffickers."

"That's ridiculous," Marisol says. "Miguel is a baker."

"Osiel Contreras was a car salesman," Alvarado says. "Adán Barrera was an accountant."

"I want to see him," says Jimena.

"That's not possible."

"As an official of the Valverde town government," Marisol says, "I demand access to Miguel Abarca."

"You have no authority here."

"As his physician, then."

"Perhaps," Alvarado says, "if his mother weren't so busy attending demonstrations and spent more time supervising her children, her son wouldn't be in this difficulty."

"Is that what this is about?" Jimena asks.

"Isn't it?" Alvarado asks. "Aren't you just a publicity seeker? I noticed you brought the media with you."

"They're my friends."

"Exactly."

Pablo looks around and sees that the commotion in front of the gate has attracted a few onlookers. Within minutes word gets around, people start to walk down the dirt street toward the post, and a crowd forms around the gate. The people in Práxedis know the Abarcas, and Marisol Cisneros is their doctor.

Someone shouts an insult at the soldiers.

Someone else throws a rock.

Then a bottle smashes against the wire.

"Don't do that!" Jimena shouts.

"You see?" Alvarado says. "You're causing an incident."

Pablo sees that the soldiers are getting nervous. Rifles are unslung, bayonets fastened.

"Please, don't throw anything!" Marisol yells.

The missiles stop, but one of the townspeople starts to holler, "Miguel! Miguel! Miguel!" and the rest pick up the chant, *Miguel! Miguel! Miguel! Miguel!*

"These people are not doing your son any favors," Alvarado says.

But the chant keeps up—*Miguel! Miguel! Miguel!*—and more people come down the street. Cell phones come out—calls are made, pictures and video taken. The whole valley will be alerted soon.

"I will clear this street," Alvarado says to Jimena, "and hold you personally responsible for any civic unrest."

"We hold *you* responsible for civic unrest," Marisol says.

When Giorgio starts taking pictures of the crowd, Alvarado yells at Ana, "Tell him to stop that!"

"I've never been able to control him."

"Release my son," Jimena says.

"I do not respond to threats."

"Neither do I."

Arms outstretched, Jimena and Marisol move the crowd back about twenty yards from the gate, but more people keep coming until about two hundred are gathered in the long light of the summer evening.

Two television news trucks pull up.

"You'll be on the Juárez news tonight," Marisol tells Alvarado. "The El Paso news by morning. Why don't you just let him go? I know Miguel—he isn't even politically active."

"If Señora Abarca would agree to mind her own business from now on," Alvarado says, "perhaps something could be worked out."

"So Miguel is a hostage."

"Your word, not mine."

"I will call the governor," Marisol says, "I will call the president, if I have to. I am not without influence."

"Indeed, you are out of your social setting, Dr. Cisneros."

"Meaning that I'm not an *indio*?"

"Again, your words," Alvarado says. "I am only stating that I see you more in a Mexico City salon than on a dusty street in rural Chihuahua."

"My family have been here for generations."

"As landlords," Alvarado says. "As *patrones*. Perhaps you should consider acting as such."

"Oh, I am, Colonel."

Off to the side, away from the crowd, Jimena breaks down in Ana's arms. "They're going to hurt him. They're going to kill him, I know it."

"No they're not," Ana says. "Not now. There are too many eyes watching them now."

Pablo gets a call from Óscar. *"Are you all right? Are you safe?"*

"We're fine."

"How's Jimena holding up?"

"As might be expected."

"Tell Giorgio I need his photos."

"I will."

"Do you think they'll release him?"

"No," Pablo says frankly. "This Alvarado guy would lose too much face now."

It settles into a siege.

When darkness finally comes, the candles come out and the vigil begins.

Marisol calls the governor and is told that he will "certainly look into it." Then she takes the humiliating step of calling her ex-husband for help. He phones a friend, who phones a friend, who talks to someone at Los Pinos, who promises to "look into it."

They don't release Miguel that night, or the next morning.

The crowd fades away, but somehow it's arranged that a few people always wait by the gate, with signs demanding Miguel's release.

And Jimena Abarca goes on a hunger strike.

The hunger strike of Jimena Abarca doesn't make international news.

Or even national news.

Óscar, though . . . Óscar makes it a daily, above-the-fold headline, telling his staff, "If we're not here to cover something like this, we're not here for anything at all."

For three days straight he makes it front-page news, running stories under Ana's and Pablo's bylines about injustice in the valley, about the suspension of human rights, about the army running roughshod.

Pablo is there when the first phone calls start to come in. At first they're official—the general in command calls to ask Óscar why he's taking sides.

"We're not taking sides," Óscar says, perhaps a bit disingenuously. "We're reporting news."

"You're not reporting our side."

"We'd love to," Óscar says. "What is your side? You can give it to me over the phone or I'll send Ana right over. You know Ana, yes?"

"We're not giving interviews at this point."

"And if that's your side of the story," Óscar responds, "I'll print that."

A flack from the governor's office phones to ask basically the same question and to observe that the other papers aren't making this front-page news.

"I'm not the editor of other papers," Óscar answers. "I'm the editor of this one, have been for quite some time, and in my experience this is front-page news."

He hangs up, taps his cane on the side of his desk a few times, and then says, "The publisher will call next. Not until after lunch, though, when he thinks I'm mellowed by a glass of wine and a full stomach."

The call comes at 2:05, ten minutes after Óscar has returned to the office. El Búho listens to his complaints, sympathizes with the angry calls he's had to endure from the Defense Department, the governor's office, and even Los Pinos, and then kindly says he will do nothing different than what he's doing except to add an angry editorial for tomorrow's edition.

He puts the phone on speaker so Pablo and Ana can listen.

"News articles are one thing," the publisher says. *"Editorials are quite another."*

"I have built my professional life on that principle," Óscar says, smiling at Pablo. "I'm glad we agree."

"So you intend to commit this paper to the position that the army is committing an outrage in Práxedis."

"In the whole Juárez Valley," Óscar says.

"I don't know if the board can accept that."

"Then the board had better fire me," Óscar says.

"Now, Oscar, no one said anything about—"

"As long as I'm the editor of this paper," Óscar says, "I will *be* the editor, and, by definition, the editor writes the editor*ials*."

It's classic Óscar—firm, decisive, authoritative—but Pablo notices that he's aged. The mischievous glint in the eye has dimmed a little, his blinks are more frequent, his hip seems to hurt him a little more, and Pablo knows that the events in Juárez have played on their boss. On all of us, I guess, Pablo thinks.

Two more days into the hunger strike and Óscar's scathing editorial, the other calls come in.

The anonymous ones.

The threats.

"Stop what you're doing if you know what's good for you."

"Don't think bad things can't happen to you."

"I'm perfectly aware that bad things can happen to me," Óscar says. *"Dios mío,* they put three bullets into me."

"Then you should have learned."

"Ah, but sadly, I'm a slow learner," Óscar says. "My teachers in school despaired of me."

"Who are they from?" Pablo asks, guiltily conscious of the *sobres,* the envelopes.

"Narcos?" Óscar asks. "The government?"

"Is there a difference?" Ana asks.

"Until you can prove otherwise, yes," Óscar answers. He tells them to be careful, to watch their backs, and he increases security around the office. But he keeps running stories about Jimena Abarca.

For the first three days, Marisol explains, the body uses energy from stored glucose. It's painful of course, as anyone who has experienced hunger knows, but not lethal.

But after three days the liver starts to consume body fat, a process known as ketosis, which is dangerous and can cause permanent damage. If the hunger strike goes into a third week, the body starts to "eat" its own muscles and vital organs. There is loss of bone marrow.

This is called starvation mode.

Marisol then gives them the old "4-4-40" rough standard for human survival: four minutes without air, four days without water, forty days without food.

They are in day seven now.

Fortunately Jimena has agreed to drink water, but won't take vitamins or other supplements. She lies on a cot in a friend's house in Práxedis, not far from the army post, and grows weaker every day. A thin woman to begin with, she now looks emaciated.

The army shows no sign of releasing Miguel, demanding instead that Jimena be arrested and force-fed, if necessary.

"Are we just going to let her commit slow suicide?" Ana asks. She has taken turns with other women from the "movement" sitting with Jimena. More people sit outside to make certain that if the army tries to arrest Jimena, they won't do it easily and the seizure will be recorded.

"You're a doctor," Ana says to Marisol. "Don't you have an obligation to intervene? Certainly you can't assist in a suicide."

"I won't force-feed her," Marisol answers. "It's torture."

"As opposed to starvation?" Pablo asks.

Going back and forth between Jimena and Alvarado, Marisol feverishly tries to find a compromise. Will Jimena stop her hunger strike if Alvarado will let her see Miguel? They both refuse. What if the army turns Miguel over to the Chihuahua state police? Jimena agrees, Alvarado refuses. What if the AFI takes custody of him? Alvarado agrees, Jimena refuses.

Then they both dig their heels in.

Jimena won't quit until Miguel is unconditionally released, and Alvarado won't release him.

It turns into a grim siege of wills.

And tactics—on the eighth day, a note arrives from Miguel, asking his mother to stop her strike.

"I don't believe it," Jimena says.

"It's his handwriting," Ana says.

"He was coerced."

"He doesn't want his mother to die!"

"Neither does his mother," Jimena says, smiling as she lays her head back on the small pillow. "Neither does his mother."

Later that day, they put Miguel on the phone.

"Mama, I'm all right."

"Have they hurt you?"

"Mama, please eat."

"Are they forcing you to make this call?"

"No, Mama."

They take the phone away from him. Jimena's younger son, Julio, asks her, "Mama, are you satisfied now? Please stop."

"Not until they release him."

"Miguel said that they weren't hurting him."

"What else was he going to say?" Jimena asks. "If I give in now, they win."

"It's not a game," Ana says.

"No, it's a war," Jimena answers. "The same war it's always been."

Pablo gets that. It's the war between the haves and the have-nots, the powerful and the powerless. The one has the power to inflict suffering—the other only to endure it.

Their only weapon is shame, if the powerful can even feel it.

The people in the "movement" do their best—there are daily protests now outside the army post, the governor's office; a few allies in Mexico City even picket Los Pinos. The people in the small towns shun the soldiers, who can't buy so much as a candy bar, a beer, a postage stamp in the Juárez Valley.

Pablo hears whispers that some are talking about darker measures. If the army is taking the side of the Sinaloa cartel, why shouldn't we join with the Juárez people? La Familia Michoacana have attacked army posts, the Zetas have attacked prisons and freed convicts. If the army sees us as devils anyway, let's give them true hell. The talk turns from passive resistance to revolution, an old Chihuahua tradition.

Jimena gets wind of the talk and shuts it down.

"We do not beat them by becoming them," she says.

Others aren't so sure.

Marisol uses the weapons *she* has—her looks and charm—and literally attracts the media. The camera loves her, as they say, and she consciously takes advantage of that to get in front of television cameras in her white coat and with her physician's demeanor describe in graphic yet media-friendly terms what is happening to Jimena Abarca's body.

She knows exactly what she's doing, turning the Abarca ordeal into a soap opera—hoping that it will become a *telenovela* with a short run and a happy ending.

Marisol becomes "La Médica Hermosa"—the Beautiful Doctor. People turn on the news to see her, and Jimena's case starts to get national attention. It's hateful, Marisol tells Pablo and Ana privately—gross and demeaning— but it might be the way to save Jimena's life.

Then there are Giorgio's photographs.

It was a genius idea, Pablo thinks, Giorgio's concept to run a photo of Jimena's face every day, an increasing strip of them, so that readers could see the progression of her condition.

Day after day, people pick up their paper and *see* this woman starving to death. And the photos, they are *beautiful,* carefully, artfully composed in the half-light of the little house, each one a pietà of a mother grieving for her son.

The paper's circulation goes up.

It becomes water-cooler conversation—*Have you seen Jimena today?* Newsboys shout it from traffic islands—*Have you seen Jimena today?* House-wives talk about it at lunch—*Have you seen Jimena today?*

An anonymous donor pays for a billboard at the base of the Lincoln International Bridge, so that people coming in from El Paso are asked the question *Have you seen Jimena today?*

It speaks to the photos' effectiveness that no one has to ask what that means.

The army fights back with a public relations campaign of its own. The commander of the 11th Military Zone holds a press conference and says,

"This woman is not Mother Teresa. She's nothing more than a tool of the cartels."

Ana is there to ask the questions. "Do you have information linking Jimena Abarca to drug trafficking? And if so, why haven't you released it?"

"It might compromise ongoing investigations."

"If you have such information," Ana presses, "why haven't you turned it over to prosecuting authorities so that they can file charges?"

"We will in due time."

"What's 'due time'?"

"When we're ready."

"Will you be ready," Ana asks, "before or after Jimena Abarca starves to death?"

"We are not starving Señora Abarca," the general says. "She is starving herself. We will not be bullied or intimidated by these tactics."

The next morning, a photo of the well-fed general in his dress uniform appears next to a picture of the emaciated Jimena with the caption BULLIED AND INTIMIDATED?

The following day, an editorial appears in a major Texas newspaper under the title IS THIS WHAT THE MÉRIDA BILLIONS ARE PAYING FOR? A Democratic congressman from California stands up on the House floor and asks the same question. This prompts a call from the West Wing to DEA basically asking what the fuck is going on down there and demanding that whatever it is, DEA get a handle on it.

There's an election coming up, it's going to be close, and the incumbent party's candidate is from a border state with a lot of Hispanics. McCain was in Mexico City just last month, for Chrissakes, praising the Mérida Initiative as an important step, and the last thing he needs is the perception that the aid package he touted is being used to torture Mexican mothers.

The DEA director calls a colleague in the Mexican Defense Department, who listens and then says, "We can't let ourselves be beaten by one woman. What kind of message would that send?"

"That you're smart?" the director asks. "I suggest that if you want the helicopters and the aircraft to keep coming, you find a way to back down on this thing."

It's axiomatic that at certain points in any conflict, both sides think they're losing. It's true of wars and battles, lawsuits and strikes. It's true now. Jimena's supporters know nothing about the calls from Washington and don't realize the immense pressure being brought to bear on the army.

What they see is no movement from the military.

And Jimena failing.

Ana breaks down one night.

"I can't stand it," she cries to Pablo, who holds her in his arms and rocks her. "I can't stand the thought of her dying."

"She won't," Pablo says, even though he isn't so confident. "They'll break first."

"What if they don't?"

Pablo doesn't have an answer.

Adán watches La Médica Hermosa on television.

"She's so pretty," Magda says.

"I suppose." Adán is familiar enough with women to steer around the obvious pothole. But the woman on television is stunning. And effective—no wonder she's become a media sensation.

"And effective," Magda adds. They're lying in bed in her flat in Badiraguato, the one she comes to when she feels a need to be with him, less and less frequent now, he's observed.

"Do you think so?" he asks.

"Face it, *cariño*," Magda says. "It's a new world now. Every war you fight, you fight on three fronts: a shooting war; a political war; a media war. And that you can't win one without the others."

She's right, Adán thinks.

She's absolutely right.

He gets out of bed and phones Nacho. "Who is this Miguel Abarca, anyway? I've never even heard of him. Is he with Fuentes? Los Aztecas? La Línea?"

"He's a nobody," Nacho says. "A baker's kid."

"He's not a nobody anymore," Adán says. "Neither is the mother. The army has turned them into celebrities."

He's so tired of endless, needless *stupidity*. How the army could take a simple incident and let it grow out of proportion.

Adán has plans for the Juárez Valley, and they don't include creating a cause célèbre. He's winning the war against the Juárez cartel and now a bunch of morons in uniform find a way to screw it up.

"I don't want to read any more articles," Adán says. "I don't want to see this doctor on television. This needs to come to a quick and happy conclusion."

"Agreed."

"And we need better media control," Adán says. "For the money we're paying, you would think—"

"It's being worked on."

Isn't everything? Adán thinks after he hangs up and as he actually gets a chance to take a shower. The media are being "worked on," hunting down Diego is being "worked on," going after the Zetas is being "worked on." Killing Keller is being "worked on." I don't want something "worked on," I want something completed.

Marisol's phone wakes her in the small hours of the morning.

It frightens her, because at first she thinks that it's about Jimena, that her body has gone into crisis.

It is about Jimena, but it's Colonel Alvarado.

"I have a proposal," he says.

Óscar walks out into the city room.

"I just got a call that they released Miguel Abarca."

When Pablo, Ana, and Giorgio get out to the valley, Miguel and Jimena are already home in Valverde, with Marisol carefully easing Jimena back onto some solid food.

"I'm sorry I didn't inform you," Marisol says, "but that was the deal—no press coverage of Miguel's actual release. They didn't want film of him walking out to a triumphant crowd."

"We understand," Ana says.

"I hope you'll also understand this," Marisol says. "We can't let you interview Miguel or take photos."

"Why not?" Giorgio asks.

"He's on a gurney in my clinic," Marisol says. "Broken nose, two fractured ribs, and the soles of his feet have wounds consistent with *la chicharra*—burning with electrical wires. But he's alive, guys, and so is Jimena."

They drive back to Juárez and file a simple story stating that Miguel Abarca was released without charges, and that Jimena Abarca has ended her hunger strike. The story doesn't mention Miguel's injuries. The next day's edition features a photo of Jimena sipping a protein shake, and La Médica Hermosa makes what she assures reporters is a final appearance on the evening news and describes her patient's condition as stable.

The Abarca story disappears from the headlines because the Zetas throw grenades into an Independence Day celebration in Morelia, Michoacán, and kill eight people.

And in Juárez, the tired war of attrition goes on.

Pablo covers the killing of a police commander shot in a hotel parking lot, eleven gunned down in a bar, six killed at a family party, six more lined up outside a *tienda* and executed against the wall.

He writes the story about 334 Juárez city cops fired for failing polygraphs and drug tests.

All that is fine with the man who comes and slips him the *sobre*.

"I told you," Pablo says, "I don't want this."

"And I told *you*," the man says, "no one's *asking* you. Give the money to charity if you don't want it, but you're taking it."

Pablo's next call is to a headless body hanging from its feet off the Bridge of Dreams with the *narcomensaje* reading I, LORENZO FLORES, SERVED MY BOSS, THE DOG–FUCKER BARRERA.

"'Dog-fucker'?" Giorgio asks, trying to figure out his shot. "That's a new one."

"Zetas," Pablo says.

"How do you know?"

"Decapitation. That's their thing."

The head turns up later at the Plaza del Periodista.

Mexico City
December 2009

Only Keller knows the identity of the informant code-named "María Fernanda."

Through the miserable year of 2009, as violence and bloodshed spread through Mexico like an unstoppable virus, Keller stayed in the Mexico City bunker and, good as his word, focused on bringing down Diego Tapia.

Except you can't kill what you can't find.

It wasn't from lack of trying.

No "search and avoid" missions with the FES. Orduña even has his own satellite surveillance system, purchased from the French and operated by the European Space Agency.

It couldn't draw a bead on Tapia.

Neither could any of the American intelligence packages.

In regard to intelligence, Keller gets what he wants.

Taylor has seen to it.

"Let the word go forth from this time and place," Taylor pronounced. "There is no secret unit operating in Mexico City, and it gets everything it needs from you. If Keller asks you for something, you don't ask 'why,' you ask 'when.' If Keller wants a large pizza smothered with chocolate ice cream, French fries, and a cherry on top, you deliver it faster than Domino's, no questions asked. You have any questions, come to me, but don't have any questions. Are there any questions?"

There weren't.

Keller knew that a lot of this came from the fact that the new administration in Washington has a distinctly "antiterrorist" bent. The rumor was that the White House has a "kill list" on top jihadists, and this strategy had carried over into the war on drugs.

It's not so much that we've now defined the narcos as terrorists, Keller thought, but that there's more of a psychological leak from the war on terror into the war on drugs. The battle against Al Qaeda has redefined what's thinkable, permissible, and doable. Just as the war on terror has turned the functions of intelligence agencies into military action, the war on drugs has similarly militarized the police. CIA is running a drone and assassination program in South Asia; DEA is assisting the Mexican military in targeting top narcos for "arrests" that are often executions.

Mexico has formalized the militarization of the drug war; the U.S. is drifting in that direction.

Certainly, Keller thought, *my* war on drugs has changed over the years. It used to be all about busts and seizures, the perpetual cat-and-mouse game of getting the shit off the street, but now I barely think about the drugs themselves.

The actual trafficking is almost irrelevant.

I'm not a drug agent anymore, he reflected, I'm a hunter.

He came out of retirement to hunt Barrera—if he has to take down other narcos on the way to that, so be it. Mostly to stay on—however indirectly—Barrera's trail. The other reason is that he likes and actually trusts Roberto Orduña. Still mourning Luis Aguilar's death and enraged over Gerardo Vera's betrayal, Keller didn't want a close working relationship—never mind a friendship.

But that's what he got—a friendship, of sorts, based on a common understanding.

Revenge.

It came over a late-night drinking session after a long day of unsuccessfully tracking Diego Tapia. Single-malt scotch, very expensive, lowered inhibitions and provoked revelations.

Keller learned that Orduña came from an immensely wealthy family ("The reason I'm impervious to bribery"), and that they have something in common.

A grudge.

Felipa Muñoz.

Nineteen, a model, and a cheerleader for the local Tijuana *fútbol* team, Felipa was apparently friendly with a young man who was somehow associated with the Tapias.

Her decapitated body was found dumped on the soccer field—the trunk in two black plastic bags, the head in another. Her feet had been smashed in and her fingers cut off—the usual torture for a *dedo,* a snitch—although the clumsy nature of the wounds indicated that it was done by amateurs, not professionals. The two men who did it—Felipa's twenty-two-year-old "friend" and a forty-nine-year old associate—were arrested for speeding and the police found a video of the torture on their cell phone. They'd apparently heard that she was passing information along to a policeman and thought they'd kill her to garner favor with the bosses.

Felipa Muñoz was Orduña's goddaughter.

He'd held her in his arms as an infant, committed her soul to God.

"I hate the narcos," Orduña told Keller that night. "Tapia, Contreras, Ochoa, Barrera, all of them."

They touched glasses.

It was personal, Keller got that.

Keller knew "personal," so he started to trust Orduña.

Worked hard with him to bring down Diego Tapia.

At the end of the day, it came down to what it almost always comes down to.

A snitch.

The relationship, Keller thinks as he goes to meet María Fernanda at a movie theater in Mexico City, between an informant and "handler" is one of mutual seduction—if only in the basest of terms, because each is trying to fuck the other.

But it goes deeper than that.

You have to bring the informant in, convince him or her that your bed is warmer and safer than the one the informant is currently sleeping in. You have to be a friend, but not too friendly, you have to make promises, but none that you can't deliver. You have to keep your informants safe, but not hesitate to put them in mortal danger. You have to show them that there's a future beyond this, when you know that there probably isn't.

At the same time, the informant is seducing you—showing you a little leg, a glimpse beneath an unbuttoned blouse, promising that there's more. An informant is a great cock tease, knowing that her value is depleted as soon as she delivers all the goods. So she holds back, plays it coy, hard-to-get.

Keller makes his point very clear to María Fernanda as he sits behind the informant in the uncrowded matinee screening.

"Christmas is coming," Keller says. "I want Diego on the table with my turkey."

"Easier said than done."

"Didn't ask whether it was easy," Keller says, "and I don't care. You've been giving me appetizers—little snacks—and now I want to sit down and *eat*."

"I've given you over fifty arrests."

True enough, Keller thinks. Based on María Fernanda's information, the FES have captured a slew of Tapia soldiers, along with weapons, cash, and drugs. It's good, but makes it all the more urgent to get Diego, because every arrest shortens the informant's shelf life, and now Keller makes exactly that point. "I wouldn't want to be you when Diego figures out who you are. You need to put him away."

"I don't know where he is."

"I want Diego," Keller says. He walks away and heads back to the office thinking that the best time to nab Diego Tapia is coming up.

Narcos take the holidays very seriously. The *peces gordos* have to throw elaborate parties or they lose face. And none of them can afford to lose face, not this year, with loyalties and alliances on the fence, waiting to be tipped to one side or the other. Diego will throw a party and "María Fernanda" goddamn well better invite me.

María calls two weeks later.

"Ahuatepec. 1158 Avenida Artista. Tonight."

Keller puts up a photo of the address, a big house in a gated community outside Cuernavaca.

"He's an arrogant son of a bitch," Orduña says when Keller relays the phone conversation to him. Diego has invited dozens of guests, and hired twenty of Mexico City's highest-priced call girls and one of Mexico's most renowned *norteño* musicians to play at the party.

"We don't want a bloodbath," Orduña says. They both know the political reality—it's a far different thing to shoot up a wealthy suburb than some impoverished *colonia*. Maybe that's why Diego feels safe.

"We know where he is now," Keller said. "We can't lose him again."

Keller puts a call back in to María Fernanda.

Then sits back and watches the party from a distance.

Eddie hopes like hell it was goat.

Diego demanded that Eddie show up for his holiday party, and Eddie was all like "I'm busy" but Diego was like "Fuck that, *m'ijo*, you're showing up." So Eddie went and the usual crew was there—the bodyguards and some Zetas and the squadron of whores and they were all doing blow and then dinner was served.

Sitting around the table eating chili verde and Diego started talking about Manuel Esposito, this old Sinaloa cartel *sicario*—genuine tough guy stone-cold killer—who sided with the Barreras, and alone among the guests asked *Whatever happened to old Manuel* and Diego, he got this weird smile on his face and said, "Maybe you're eating him."

Everybody laughed, like, yeah, that's real funny, but then Diego looked all serious and said, "No. Maybe you're eating him."

Eddie set his spoon down.

Diego said, "I mean, they say you should eat what you kill, don't they? Besides, the flesh of a strong enemy makes you strong."

Eddie thought he might blow chunks right there at the table. He didn't eat any more chili, and probably Diego was kidding. But with Diego these days, who knows? And Eddie was pissed, because, well shit, did Diego just make him into a fucking *cannibal*?

That's just not right.

That could mess with a guy's head.

Turn him into a vegetarian.

Anyway, Eddie don't have time for this crazy shit.

He's got a business to run and he's married again.

Yeah, okay, well, *sort* of married, seeing as how he never got divorced. But he found himself another Tex-Mex honey, the daughter of one of his big-time coke runners, so they got "married" in Acapulco by a priest who wasn't anal about the paperwork and maybe wasn't really a priest anyway.

Honeymooned right there in Acapulco and she got knocked up, like microwave pregnancy. So now there's a kid on the way, so who has time for Diego's crazy death-worshipping maybe-I'm-a-cannibal-maybe-not bullshit?

And then there are these command performances he has to make when Diego requests his presence at one of the many safe houses he has in the greater Mexico City metro area, which he refuses to leave.

The visits to Diego are risky, because the *federales* have a hard-on for him like a fence post, and they're also a pain in the ass because El Jefe's always busting Eddie's balls about why he's not killing more of Barrera's people, "carrying more of his weight" in the war.

Well, in the first fucking place, it's not my weight to carry, Eddie thinks. I didn't start the war with El Señor, I only did what I was asked-slash-told and offed the nephew, and now *my* ass is on the line? *My* business?

Eddie don't want no part in the war, either in Sinaloa or in Juárez, because what's Juárez to him? He ain't gonna get a piece of the plaza, even if they win, so fuck that. So he's held back a little in the fighting—let his guys do a little here and there if they were eager to win their spurs, but that's about it.

So every time he goes to see Diego, it comes up.

And Diego is motherfucking *crazy* when he does coke, which he does more of every day, it seems. Coke and booze and hookers and the Skinny Lady, and it's getting stranger than strange.

The whole thing is jacked up, though. Killing cops. This is not what we used to do, this is not how we ran business. And this new stuff—the extortion, kidnappings, for Chrissakes—all this Zeta-type shit that Diego's into now.

It's not right.

It's not right and it's going to get us fucked up. And fucked up is something Eddie can't afford right now. Yeah, he's clearing over a hundred mil a year in coke sales north of the border, another twenty in Monterrey—it's not a money issue, it's a quality-of-life issue.

The DEA has put two million on his head, the Mexican government has matched it, and who knows which cop is on whose payroll anymore? It's chaos out there, not to mention that the Barrera faction has him high on their to-do list for canceling young Sal's reservation.

So he's on the move, splitting time between condos and apartments in Acapulco and Monterrey. Not only does he have to manage business in both places, he has to keep his ass moving lest it get shot off.

It's a hell of a party, though, Eddie has to admit now, looking down at the thousand-dollar blond head bobbing for apples on his lap. He's never been a fan of *norteño*—Eddie's taste runs more to Pearl Jam—but it is pretty cool to listen to a freaking Grammy winner sing "Chaparra de mi amor." Kind of like when Johnny Fontane sang at Connie's wedding in *One,* only better, because it comes with a blow job.

Even Diego's in a good mood, walking among the guests playing Santa Claus, handing out expensive watches, jewelry, and envelopes of cash—the *aguinaldos*—the yearly bonuses. He's also passing out raffle tickets with drawings later for cars and houses—this is how you keep the employees happy. And the women he brought in are fantastic, right out of Mexican *Playboy.* A little different from Barrera's parties where wives but not mistresses were invited. Wives were *banned* from this shindig.

What happens in Ahuatepec, Eddie thinks, stays in Ahuatepec.

A good thing, too, because guys are fucking women right out there in the open, booze flowing like water, coke everywhere, tables loaded down with food (Eddie only hopes that the chicken in the fajitas is really chicken).

It's like Six Flags for narcos.

The Mexico Ten finishes him off, he zips up and rejoins the party. Diego comes up to him and hands him a gift-wrapped box.

It's a diamond-studded Audemars Piguet.

Eddie figures the watch goes for about a half mil.

"I feel bad, Diego," Eddie says. What he got Diego for Christmas was a pair of Lucchese alligator boots, custom made. True, they cost him eight grand, and Diego's proudly wearing them now, but still.

"You got me Salvador Barrera," Diego says, and then wraps Eddie in a bear hug and says in his ear, "I love you, *m'ijo.*"

Now Eddie really feels bad about the boots.

They stay on Diego for five long days.

While Mexico City bustles with all the usual holiday activity, Keller and Orduña bunker down, track Diego Tapia's moves, and wait for him to go somewhere that they can take him. They have to be careful—the government won't tolerate another civilian casualty, nor do they have much stomach for one themselves.

The tracking device homes in on Diego, but he also makes several cell phone calls to María Fernanda, which they have monitored.

In the meantime, Diego doesn't go far, from one safe house to another in the Cuernavaca area. One is near a school—no good. Another near a busy shopping street—same. Finally he settles for two days in an apartment in one of five fifteen-story towers in the Lomas de Selva neighborhood of Cuernavaca.

"Elbus Complex, the Altitude Building," Orduña says. "But we don't know which floor."

Thirty minutes later, María calls.

"Where have you been?" Keller asks. "If you're playing some kind of double game here—"

"Nobody's playing."

"He's in the Altitude Building," Keller says. "Lomas de Selva. Which floor?"

"Second. 201."

Diego's planning a dinner with a general and three officers from the 24th Military Zone tonight. *"Maybe you won't chicken out this time."*

They have no intention of chickening out.

The FES are the elite troops that Keller wanted back in the early days of hunting Barrera. This is no clumsy AFI full frontal assault, but a highly professional, well-planned operation.

Plainclothes FES operatives move onto the street outside the complex, and report back that the forty Tapia *sicarios* are in three concentric circles— two of them around the building, the innermost in the lobby. Six additional men have gone inside the apartment, and listening posts outside Altitude confirm the presence of seven distinct voices in addition to Diego Tapia's.

The best FES marksmen take position on the rooftops of the surrounding buildings, ranged in on all exits, with permission to shoot if Diego comes out.

Orduña is taking no chances with civilian casualties. Over the course of five hours, starting at noon, the plainclothes ops start to quietly remove residents from the other buildings into the basements.

Others start removing Diego's security on the street, approaching with knives and pistols and quietly taking them away, putting on their clothes, taking their phones, replacing them. Diego's outer security ring is now Orduña's outer security ring.

And three officers from the 24th Military Zone, on their way to dinner, are stopped in their car and arrested.

Two hundred FES wait a kilometer away in armored cars. Others are loaded into Mi-17 helicopters. A pair of M1A2 Abrams tanks, part of the Mérida package, stand by.

Orduña is not fucking around.

Diego is pissed off that his guests haven't arrived.

Maybe, Eddie thinks, they heard about some of El Jefe's previous menu items. He's sitting at the table with Diego, waiting to eat. Five *sicarios* are on guard around the apartment, more in the lobby.

"I don't think they're going to show," Eddie says.

"Why not?" Diego asks.

He's stressed out, and Eddie gets it. The army is his protection—if they've flipped to Barrera, he's in deep shit. And now the army guys haven't shown up and aren't answering their phones.

"Fuck this," Eddie says. "I'm out of here."

"You're leaving?"

"I don't know, man," Eddie says. "I just don't feel good about this."

"Relax," Diego says. "I got forty men out there. What are you worried about?"

"I got shit to do, Diego," Eddie says. "The *waifa's* on my ass about getting a bassinette, baby clothes . . . I got two dealers in Monterrey need straightening out . . ."

"Go ahead," Diego snaps. "Get the fuck out."

"Diego . . ."

"How about that watch I gave you?" Diego asks. "You like that, right?"

"Yeah, it's beautiful. You're still wearing the boots, huh?" He kisses Diego on the cheek and gets up. "See you later, *Tío*."

"Later."

Eddie takes the elevator down, walks out onto the plaza.

Keller hears the radio call from the helicopter.

"Target acquired."

"Hold," Orduña says. *"Repeat, hold. Let him go."*

A long five minutes later, Keller hears him say, *"Go."*

The helicopter takes off, flies over the Lomas de Selva neighborhood, and lands on the roof of the Altitude Building. The roof secured, some of the FES evacuate tenants in the higher floors of the building while Keller and the others move down the stairwell toward the second floor.

Then the armored vehicles race up to the front of the building and start pouring 7.62mm rounds from the machine guns and M-16 fire into the lobby, mowing down Tapia's *sicarios* before they can react. Marines rush into the lobby, secure the wounded, and then head up to the second floor.

As the commandos burst into the second-floor hallway, one of the men inside apartment 201 throws a grenade out the door. Other *sicarios* fire out the second-floor windows at the troops outside the building, while the others make a fight of it in the stairway.

Keller is coming down the stairs behind a marine lieutenant when a grenade clatters into the stairway. The lieutenant takes the brunt of the blast and shards of the fragmentation grenade hit him in the neck above his Kevlar vest. Keller squats to feels his pulse, but there is none—the severed artery quickly bleeds him out.

Drawing his pistol, Keller fires down the stairway as other FES come in behind him. They're well trained, alternating cover and motion, and drive the *sicarios* back into the apartment.

Diego and his five men make a siege of it, holing up in the apartment. Through his headset, monitoring phone traffic, Keller can hear Diego calling Crazy Eddie Ruiz.

"Where are you, m'ijo*? We're getting fucked to hell here. We're about to get taken."*

"Give it up, Diego. There's nothing I can do."

"Fuck that. I'm fighting. Get over here with some men."

"It's no good, Tío. They've got hundreds of guys out there. Helicopters. Tanks. Give up."

Keller listens to a few moments of silence and then hears Diego say, *"Okay,* m'ijo, *you take care of my kids, okay? I'm going to take some of these* pendejos *with me. Last bullet for myself."*

They hold out for three more hours.

Tipping the tables and sofas on their side for cover, they use up most of the ammo for the AKs and AR-15s. Then all they have left are grenades. The FES, already furious at the death of the much-loved lieutenant, are in no hurry to take more casualties. They just keep up the pressure, keep tightening the noose, and force the narcos to expend ammunition.

At nine that night, when it's relatively quiet, Orduña gives the order to finish it.

A small C-4 charge blows the apartment door off.

Three FES go through the door, M-16s at their shoulders. Each kills a *sicario* with a two-shot burst to the chest. Keller sees another one of Diego's men put his pistol in his mouth and pull the trigger. The last jumps out the window, a burst of fire from a rooftop sniper catches him in midair, and he's dead before he somersaults onto the concrete courtyard.

Keller sees Diego go through a back door into the hallway toward a freight elevator.

I guess he decided not to fight it out after all, Keller thinks as he goes after him.

The elevator door slides open.

The two FES inside fire bursts of 5.56 hollow-points into Diego's chest. He staggers backward into the apartment and falls to the floor.

But still breathing, still alive.

Orduña comes in from the hallway. He stands over Diego and then looks at Keller.

Keller turns his back, then hears two shots. When he turns back again there are two neat bullet holes in Diego's forehead. El Jefe de los Jefes, La Barba, is dead.

He already looks like an anachronism—the long hair and beard, the tall frame, once heavily muscled, now as thin as some crippled beast starved over the course of a long hard winter.

Diego Tapia was from another time, and that time is gone.

Orduña walks out.

Keller squats down and pulls off Diego's boots.

He removes the monitoring device from the left boot and slips it into his pocket.

What happens next shouldn't have.

Inside the apartment, the FES discipline breaks down. Whether out of revenge, or adrenaline, or the sheer heady relief of surviving, some of the commandos yank Diego's black jeans down around his ankles and pull his shirt up to his neck, displaying his wounds. Then they take some money they find in the apartment—peso and dollar bills—and toss it on the body, then take photos and videos and start texting and tweeting.

By the time Orduña, furious, gets up there to stop it, the damage is done.

The images are out on the Net.

Keller walks away from Lomas de Selva to find "María Fernanda."

Crazy Eddie waits in the Zócalo in the shadow of the *fresno* trees. He looks cool and fresh in a plum polo shirt, white jeans, and loafers.

Narco Polo, Keller thinks. He walks up to Eddie and says, "He's dead."

Eddie nods. "Diego wasn't a bad guy, you know? The drugs fucked him up. And the Skinny Lady. I just couldn't go down with the ship."

"You have a chip with me," Keller says. "Why don't you cash it in now? I can bring you in safe."

" 'Let that pickup man haul in'?"

"I don't know what that means."

"Old song about rodeo," Eddie says. "No, I ain't done with my ride yet."

"You're on the list, Eddie."

Actually, he just moved up one slot.

"Right," Eddie says. "Because that's what you guys do now, isn't it? You just kill people."

"Doesn't have to end that way," Keller says.

"The Zetas," Eddie says, "that's who you *should* be going after. They're pure evil, man."

"Thanks for the advice."

"Fuck you." Eddie looks around the Zócalo for a second and then says, "You know? Someone's always going to be selling this shit. It might as well be someone who doesn't kill women and kids. If someone's going to do it, you guys might as well let someone like *me* do it."

Keller lets him walk away. Could have taken him right there, but that wasn't part of their deal.

Adán looks at the photos of his old *primo*'s bullet-shredded corpse and tells Nacho, "You'd think I'd be happier."

"We were all friends once."

"I think about Chele and the kids."

Nacho has no answer for that. He's fond of Chele, they all are.

"Drive home the message," Adán says.

They talk business for a few more minutes—Martín Tapia might keep up the fight, but will be at most an annoyance. Eddie Ruiz won't pick up Diego's fallen banner. He'll start his own organization, and as long as he stays out of the war, Adán is willing to let him be. Payback for Sal can wait until the war is over.

When Nacho leaves, Adán goes into his bedroom. Eva is already asleep, or pretending to be.

It's odd, Adán thinks, how life gets lonelier.

The next morning, two bound and beaten bodies of Tapia *sicarios* are found hanging by the necks from a bridge in Culiacán with a banner that reads THIS TERRITORY ALREADY HAS AN OWNER—ADÁN BARRERA.

Looking at the photos of Diego's body, Heriberto Ochoa, the head of the Zetas, is furious.

And concerned.

The government has finally figured out that to fight special forces you need special forces. No one saw it coming, and no one—not Diego or Martín, not even Barrera, managed to find out about this new unit, much less infiltrate or suborn it.

And this FES is very, very good.

A direct challenge to the Zetas.

As a special-ops vet, Ochoa recognizes the Lomas de Selva raid for what it was—not a law enforcement operation, but an execution.

Well done.

But *this,* he thinks, looking at the photos that are all over the Internet, this was unnecessary. To strip Diego and mock him, boast about murdering him, and then post pictures of it on the Net?

The FES needs to be taught a lesson.

Taught not to behave this way.

Taught that we're not going to be intimidated.

Taught that *we're* the ones who intimidate.

He gives the orders.

Keller stands to the side as six FES, in their cammie fatigues, with blue vests marked MARINA in white, carry the flag-draped casket of Lieutenant Angulo Córdova from the funeral home in his small hometown of Ojinaga, on the south bank of the Río Bravo in Chihuahua.

Trumpets and drums from a military band play as the casket is carried through the crowd of family, friends, and townspeople, who quietly applaud as the casket passes by. Middle-class or poor, Keller notices, they're dressed in their best clothes—the women in plain dresses, the men in jeans and white shirts. They're subdued and respectful, some weeping quietly, and Keller is struck again by the difference between Americans and Mexicans. Americans take their strength in victories, Mexicans' strength is in their ability to suffer loss.

One of the people is Marisol.

She and Keller look across the coffin at each other.

He can see her eyes beneath her black veil.

Keller falls in beside Orduña as the crowd follows the hearse to the little cemetery at the edge of town.

An honor guard of sailors in dress white marches behind the hearse, the band plays a dirge.

At least there's no wife and kids, Keller thinks. But there is a grieving mother, supported, literally, by Córdova's sister, brother, and aunt.

Marisol walks behind them.

The Christmas decorations on the street give the funeral parade an added poignancy.

Orduña gives a speech at the gravesite. Talks about Córdova's character, his courage, his service, his sacrifice. When he's done, an old man in a tattered vest and a knit cap raises his hand and asks to speak.

"I've known this man since he was a boy," the *viejo* says. "He was a good boy and a good man. He sent money home to his family. He died for our Republic. Our *Republic*. We can't give away our Republic to drug dealers and criminals. I'm sorry this man is dead, but he died fighting these animals. That is all I have to say."

Orduña thanks him and then signals the honor guard. The soldiers raise their M-16s to their shoulders and fire three salutes into the air. Then, at Orduña's orders, they attach bayonets and stand at guard. Two marines take the Mexican flag from the casket, fold it, and hand it to Córdova's mother.

A trumpet plays as the casket is lowered into the ground.

After the ceremony, Keller is unsure whether or not he should approach Marisol. It's awkward—they haven't spoken in a long time.

She solves his dilemma by coming up to him. "It's good to see you."

"You, too," he says. "I take it you know the family."

"Since I was a little girl," she says. "I'm their doctor now. What's your connection?"

Keller hesitates before he answers and then says, "I worked with him."

"Oh." The obvious question is right there in her eyes, but Keller doesn't answer it. Luckily for him, Córdova's younger sister walks up. "My mother would like you to come back to the house. Both of you."

"I don't want to intrude," Keller says.

There was a wake at the house the night before the funeral, when friends came to view the body and pay their respects. The time after the burial is usually reserved for the family.

"Please come," the sister says.

The house is modest, clean, and well kept. The aunts have laid food out on a table and Córdova's mother sits in an upholstered chair in the corner. Irma Córdova is a handsome woman, quietly elegant in a black tunic over black pants. Her iron-gray hair is pulled back into a bun. Keller can see where Angulo got his strength. She gestures Keller to come over.

"You were with my son when he died," Irma says.

"Yes," Keller says. "It was quick. He didn't suffer at all."

Irma takes his hand and closes her eyes.

"Your son was a brave man," Keller says. "You should be very proud of him."

"I am," she says. She opens her eyes. "But tell me, was it worth it?"

Keller squeezes her hand.

He stays for a couple of hours, talking with Córdova's family. A few of the cousins are there, and Orduña, and eventually they start talking about Angulo as a boy, and a teenager, and then the funny stories start, and the quiet laughter, and more tears. It's twilight when Orduña gets up to leave for the long drive to the airport and the flight back to Mexico City.

Marisol looks at Keller and says, "I'm driving back."

"To Valverde?" It's a long drive. Hours on a dangerous road through dangerous country.

"Yes."

"Alone?" Keller asks.

She thinks about it for a few seconds before saying, "I could use some company."

Keller goes to Orduña to tell him that he won't be driving back with him. Orduña smiles. "La Médica Hermosa? I can't say I blame you."

"We've known each other for a while."

"I know all about it, Arturo."

"You have a problem with it?"

"Only envy," Orduña says. "Go with God."

When Keller and Marisol go to leave, Irma insists on getting up and seeing them to the door.

"Thank you for coming," she says.

"It was my honor," Keller answers.

She takes Keller's hand again. "Arturo, you do not avenge a murder by killing—you avenge it by living."

It's ninety miles on Carretera 2 back to Valverde—every car and truck potentially full of narcos, potentially deadly, and army checkpoints that are just as dangerous. The soldiers at the checkpoints know Marisol and are prepared to give her a bad time but are confused by the gringo behind the wheel, especially when he shows them the DEA badge.

"They're afraid of you," Marisol says as they pull away from the checkpoint outside of Práxedis.

Keller shrugs.

"We don't think much of the army here in the valley," Marisol says.

She tells him the whole story—the land seizures, the arrests, the torture. If it weren't Marisol telling him, he'd think it was an exaggeration, liberal paranoia. But Marisol he believes, even when she concludes, "The army isn't fighting the cartels, the army *is* a cartel."

Keller tries to take it all in.

Then Marisol aks, "What were you doing with the FES? I thought you were some kind of policy wonk."

"No you didn't," Keller answers.

"No, I didn't," she says. "I only hoped."

"I can't do this with you, Marisol."

"Do what?"

"Play the cop–who–can't–talk–to–his–woman–about–what–he–does scene," Keller answers. "Played it once already. It didn't work."

"Then talk to me," she says. "Tell me."

He knows it's one of those moments. He either doesn't answer, or comes up with some half-clever evasion that won't fool her, and their relationship is over for good. Or he tells her, and their relationship is . . . what?

"I go after narcos," Keller says. "I kill them."

"I see."

Cold.

"And I'm not going to stop until I get Barrera."

"Why him so particularly?"

Keller starts to talk and then he can't stop. He tells her everything—about his friendship with the young Adán Barrera, how Barrera tortured and killed his partner Ernie Hidalgo. He tells her about Barrera throwing two children off a bridge to their deaths. He tells her about Barrera ordering the slaughter of nineteen innocent men, women, and children to punish a nonexistent informer that Keller invented to protect the real one.

"So you blame yourself," Marisol says.

"No, I blame him," Keller answers. "I blame both of us."

"And this is why you do what you do."

"He killed people I loved," Keller says. "He's evil. I know that's an old-fashioned concept, but I'm an old-fashioned guy. The truth of the matter is that he wants to kill me, too, and that's why I can't be with you."

They sit silently until they get to Valverde. Keller is shocked by the look of the little town—houses and shops boarded up, bullet-riddled stucco, army patrols rolling down the street in green trucks with searchlights sweeping to the front and sides.

She directs him to her house, an old adobe at the edge of town, and he pulls into the gravel driveway. Gets out of the car, opens the door for her, and asks, "Where's the hotel?"

"Do you prefer the Hilton or the Four Seasons?" she asks. "Another awkward joke. There's no hotel . . . I thought that you'd stay with me."

"I don't want you to think I was expecting that," Keller says.

"For God's sake, Arturo, come in," she says, "and if you mumble one word about sleeping on the couch I'll strangle you."

Keller follows her into the house and then into the bedroom, where Marisol starts to unbutton the black dress. "I've had enough of death today, I'm tired of death. Señora Córdova was right—you take revenge by living."

She steps out of the black dress and hangs it up in the closet.

"I want you inside me," Marisol says. "Let tomorrow worry about tomorrow."

Later that night, Zeta gunmen smash into Córdova's house.

His aunt, brother, and sister are asleep on the living room sofas and the Zetas shoot them first. Then they burst into the bedroom and blast Irma Córdova to death in her bed.

Before they leave, the Zetas take photos of the bodies and post them on the Internet with the message THIS WAS FOR DISRESPECTING OUR FRIEND DIEGO, YOU FES MOTHERFUCKERS. SINCERELY—THE Z COMPANY.

As they absorb the tragic news in the morning, Keller and Marisol come to a silent understanding, an acknowledgment that there is such a thing as evil, that the world holds horrors beyond their previous imagining.

There is an unspoken resolution between them now.

That they will face these horrors together.

And that they will live.

PART FOUR

The Jack of Spades and the Z Company

Gather up your tears,
Keep 'em in your pocket

—The Band Perry
"If I Die Young"

1

Women's Business

If that's all that troubles you, here, take my veil, wrap it round your head and hold your tongue. Then take this basket; put on a girdle, card wool, munch beans. The War shall be women's business.

—Aristophanes
Lysistrata

Ciudad Juárez
January 2010

Keller draws the cocaine up through the cotton into the hypodermic needle. He has three hundred of the small cocaine ampules, known as *colmillos*, ready to go.

He shows the needle to "Mikey-Mike" Wagner, a Zeta-affiliated meth dealer out of Horizon City, Texas, southeast of El Paso.

Mikey-Mike is terrified and he should be.

The day after the slaughter of the Córdova family, Orduña formed a new unit inside the FES, secret even from the navy, made up of the best of the best. Called "Matazetas," the men would be clad in black.

Their sole mission reflects their name.

Matazetas—Kill Zetas.

Keller signed on right away.

Mission one was to track down the Zetas who carried out the Córdova murders.

So Keller drove to Juárez and crossed the bridge in the Express Line using his SENTRI—Secure Electronic Network for Travelers Rapid Inspection—pass, then went to meet with a DEA undercover agent that Taylor turned him toward. Guy looked like a tweaker—long dirty hair, beard, rail thin—but Keller recognized him under the filthy red baseball cap as the guy who was with Taylor years ago when they came to warn him about Barrera.

"Jiménez, isn't it?" Keller asked.

"Yeah."

"You know what I'm planning to do?"

"Yes."

"And you're good with it?"

"I'm great with it."

"You know this could blow your undercover," Keller said.

"Know it?" Jiménez answered. "I'm *counting* on it. I can't wait to get away from these dirtbags."

They drove into the brush country to buy two pounds of meth from "Mikey-Mike" Wagner. Jiménez had a duffel bag with $50,000 in it, and they met Wagner among some old cracked concrete slabs that used to be home to a drive-in movie and now were home to jackrabbits.

Some old posts stuck up crookedly out of the ground like obstacles on a beachhead. The snack shack, denuded of color by the wind and sun, was still there. The roof was caved in but an old sign still depicted a cardboard container overflowing with popcorn.

Wagner pulled up in a Dodge van.

Of course it's a van, Keller thought.

Tweakers.

Meth used to be a local business, cooked in bathtubs and mostly sold by biker gangs. Then the cartels saw the profits that could be made and started to set up super-labs in Mexico, shipping the product north, and taking over the retail business. There were still some freelancers, but for the most part the meth trade was dominated by the cartels, and Wagner had a nice little deal going with the Zetas, selling them guns for a discount on the meth.

Looking at the chubby guy getting out of the van, Keller wondered if he'd sold the Zetas the guns they used to kill the Córdovas.

Wagner wasn't happy to see a second guy there.

"Who's this?" he asked.

"My partner," Jiménez said.

"You didn't say nothin' about a partner."

"I couldn't front the whole fifty myself," Jiménez said.

"You want to do this or not?" Keller asked.

"I don't want to sell dope to no narc," Wagner said, checking him out. Wagner was wearing an old black shirt and blue jeans and there was a definite ass-crack.

"Then go fuck yourself," Keller said. "We'll buy from someone else."

"Come on, Mikey," Jiménez said. "I got fifty K in cash right here. You think it was easy putting that together? Then we gotta drive all the way out here for nothing?"

"And how do we know this shit's any good?" Keller asked.

"You wanna see?"

"Fuck yes," Jiménez said.

Wagner went back to the van, came back out with a pound package wrapped in plastic. He took a knife out of his pocket, unfolded it, and slashed the plastic.

Keller looked. The meth was a nice blue color—transparent, not cloudy—good ragged shards.

"You wanna bleach it, go ahead," Wagner said.

"No, I want a hit," Keller said.

"Get out your pookie," Wagner said, digging into the package to take out a rock.

"Yeah." Keller reached into his jacket pocket for the glass pipe, pulled out a syringe instead, and jabbed Wagner in the carotid artery. Wagner sagged right away and Keller and Jiménez caught him, carried him to their car, and tossed him into the trunk. Wagner tried to get out but all he could do was mumble, "I have my rights."

Keller slammed the trunk closed.

He dropped Jiménez off in El Paso.

"There's thirty to life in the trunk," Keller said as Jiménez got out of the car. "If this goes south on us."

"No worries," Jiménez said. "There's not a prison in America where I'd last more than a week."

Keller crossed the border—"nothing to declare"—and went to a warehouse outside of Juárez where the FES had set up operations. They strapped Wagner into a wooden chair and waited until he came to.

Now Keller explains to Mikey-Mike that he doesn't, in fact, have any rights, that he's in Mexico now, and that the black-masked men around him are FES commandos who are very angry about the Zetas' murder of the Córdova family.

"If I turned you over to them," Keller says, "they'd skin you alive, and we're not speaking figuratively. Let me translate that for you, Mikey-Mike—they'd actually skin you."

"You're bluffing," Wagner says. "You're a cop. You can't just kill people."

"I can do any fucking thing I want down here," Keller says. The truth is he doesn't know what he's going to do if Wagner calls his bluff. Part of him isn't bluffing, part of him knows that he'll take it all the way. He hasn't felt this much anger, this much hatred, since they killed Ernie Hidalgo. Enough anger, enough hatred to kidnap an American citizen and haul him across the border. "Killing a grieving family, on the night of the funeral. That's about as low as it gets, isn't it?"

"I didn't have anything to do with that," Wagner says, shaking his head, still a little groggy from whatever they shot him up with.

"But you sold them the guns, didn't you?" Keller says evenly. "Or you know someone who knows someone who knows who did, and you're going to tell me."

"The fuck I am," Wagner says, eyeing the needle.

Keller says, "Here's how it's going to work. We're going to party like it's 1999. I'm going to start hitting you with *colmillos*. First couple of shots, you're going to feel great, better than you've ever felt in your life. After the next few, you're going to start getting sick. Really sick. You're going to get delirious, you're going to start seeing things that aren't there. And that was the good part, because then you're going to start to sweat, and then you're going to start to feel intense anxiety, and then you're going to panic.

"Which you should, because with the next few pops your blood vessels are going to constrict, your heart is going to start pounding, and then racing, and you're going to feel like it's going to explode right out of your chest, which is half right, because it is going to explode, but *inside* your chest. Then you're going to die.

"Then I'm going to drive your body back over the border and dump it, and the police will think that you stiffed the Zetas and they did this angry cocaine beehive thing on you, but they won't give a shit, because it's just one less meth dealer."

Keller jabs him with the first needle. "All you have to decide is where on this runaway train you want to jump off."

He jabs Wagner with two more needles. "Pure coke—'Rolex.' I took it off Diego Tapia myself. Feels good, doesn't it?"

Wagner throws his head back in pure pleasure as the drug bypasses his frontal lobes and hits right into his reptilian brain.

"You want to tell me now," Keller asks, "while we're all still happy?"

Wagner laughs. "The Zetas will kill me."

"Motherfucker," Keller says. "*I'm* going to kill you."

"You're going to kill me anyway," Wagner says as Keller pops him with two more hits.

"But you can go out happy," Keller says, laughing.

Wagner laughs. "True."

"Tell you what we'll do," Keller says. "You give me what I want, we dump you back high but alive."

"You're going to kill me so I don't tell," Wagner says.

"What are you going to tell?" Keller asks. "Some guys drugged you and took you down to Mexico and got you high? No one's going to believe you, and if they do, no one's going to care."

Two more pops.

"Oh, shit, that's good."

"Good *now*."

Wagner holds on, Keller has to give him credit for that, riding it straight toward the edge of the cliff in a game of chicken to see who blinks first. He holds on through the euphoria, the laughter, holds on as he starts to get the shakes and then he starts seeing all kinds of shit that isn't there.

"Make it stop!" Wagner yells.

God knows what the hell he's seeing, Keller thinks.

"You make it stop," Keller says. "Give me a name."

Mikey holds on. Literally, his bound hands grip the arm of the chair, his knuckles go white, he shakes his head back and forth.

Keller hits him with three more pops. Doesn't want to, but then he makes himself picture the photos of Irma Córdova, chopped to pieces with machine-gun fire, and that makes it easier to jab this fucking mutt with the needle.

You think *you're* seeing things, Mikey?

You want to see what *I* see?

And my shit's *real*.

Wagner starts sweating. First it pops out of his forehead in little dots, then it streams like rain down a window in a tropical storm, and then Mikey starts getting happy feet, tap-tapping away on the concrete floor, his thighs bouncing. Pretty soon Mikey's rattling like an old heap down a highway and begging for Keller to stop.

"It's not going to get any better, Mikey," Keller says.

Jabs him.

"Oh, fucking shit!"

Wagner's face gets red, his chest heaves, and for a second Keller's afraid of losing his potential source. He lays two fingers on Wagner's neck, takes his pulse, and says, "It's not looking good. A buck ten. You are off to the races."

"Motherfucker, make it stop."

"Give me a name."

"I can't."

"A buck forty, now, Mikey," Keller says. "And you were one Big Mac away from a coronary before you got here, so I don't know . . ."

Keller administers another hit.

Been over a hundred shots now.

Wagner isn't going to last.

But will you do it? Keller asks himself. Can you do this?

He hits him with three more—pop, pop, pop.

Wagner's face goes scarlet, veins pop out, his chest heaves like some bad sci-fi movie.

"Tachycardia on the way," Keller says, holding an ampule in front of Wagner's face. "This one might take you over the top."

"You . . . won't . . . do it."

"Don't test me."

"You . . . won't . . ."

Keller shrugs and goes to plunge the needle into Wagner's vein.

"Carrejos!" Wagner screams. "José Carrejos! They call him El Chavo!"

"You sell him guns?" Keller asks, the needle still pressed against Wagner's arm. "Did you sell him guns, motherfucker?!"

"Yes!"

Keller takes the needle away. "Where do we find Carrejos?"

"I don't know! Please, give me something . . ."

Keller unties Wagner's left hand and then gives him the cell phone he took from him. All the numbers and contacts have already been downloaded. "Call him."

"What . . . do . . . I . . . say?"

"I don't care. Just keep him on the line."

Wagner finds the number and hits it. "Chavo, it's me, Mikey . . . No, I'm good, I'm just high is all . . . really jacked up, 'mano. Hey, do you guys need any more stuff? I just moved that . . . that . . . two pounds and I . . . I . . ."

The FES technician gives Keller a thumbs-up.

They have Carrejos's location.

Keller grabs the phone and clicks it off. He turns to the medic. "Take care of him. Ease him down."

The medic looks at Keller, like, *Why?* But he does it. Half an hour later, Mikey-Mike Wagner is in the front seat of Keller's car, sound asleep, when they cross back over the border. Keller drives him to the bus station in El Paso and then shakes him. "Wake up."

Wagner looks bleary.

Keller hands him a bus ticket. "Chicago. It's Sinaloa cartel turf—the Zetas can't get to you there. If you ever come back here, the Z Company will kill you. If they don't, I will. Now get out."

"Thank you."

"Fuck you. Die."

Driving away, his phone rings. It's one of the FES guys, they already have Carrejos, and he's already talking.

Keller doesn't doubt that. They're holding a Mexican citizen on Mexican soil and there's nothing stopping them from doing what they're going to do—track down the men who killed their comrade's family.

They'll strip Carrejos of everything he knows and then, if he's lucky, put a bullet in the back of his head and dump his body out in the desert.

Keller doesn't care—he just wants the information, even as he knows that the hunt for the Zeta killers takes him further away from his search for Barrera. It's the principle of a river—the deviation of even an inch at the source takes that river on a new course, farther and farther from where it started to go.

Now he drives to meet Marisol.

They're going to a New Year's Eve party.

It turns out to be not a bar or a restaurant but a bookstore café. And she's right, Cafebrería has that feel of a meeting place, a cultural center, a refuge from the insanity that's taken over so much of this city.

Marisol introduces him around. Her friends are nice but he feels out of place, clearly a stranger, a gringo, a North American government official and therefore a curiosity and a little bit of a threat among a crowd of writers, poets, activists, and unironically self-proclaimed intellectuals.

Still, even though he's standing on the periphery, there's a warmth to this circle that he hasn't seen or felt in a long time. The affection is palpable and genuine, the humor of a gentler sort than he encountered in Cuernavaca, and there seems to be no other agenda than friendship and a shared cause, even if he thinks that cause is too inchoate and impractical to ever be realized.

A woman friend of Marisol's, a reporter, invites them over to her house afterward, and as Marisol seems keen to go, Keller agrees.

It's the usual suspects—intellectuals, activists, writers, poets—cheap wine, and cheaper beer, and Keller gets the feeling that joints would be passed around if he weren't there, and he wants to tell them that he just doesn't care, but doesn't know how to broach the subject.

He's standing in the little backyard sipping a beer when a somewhat plump man with long black hair and a day-old beard comes up to him.

"Pablo Mora."

"Art Keller."

"I write for *El Periódico*," Pablo says. He's clearly had more than one beer, and he says, "Some of us have been talking and the consensus is that you're some kind of a spy. If that is the case, what kind of a spy are you?"

"I'm with the government," Keller says, "but I'm not a spy."

"That's disappointing. It would be more fun if you were a spy," Pablo says. "So why are you here?"

"Marisol asked me."

"We love Marisol," Pablo says. "We all love Marisol. I love Marisol. I mean, I *love* her."

"I don't blame you."

"Well, I blame *you*," Pablo says. "How can she love a gringo?"

"Well, I'm only half gringo," Keller says. "Half gringo, half *pocho*."

"A *pochingo*."

"I guess."

"I just made that word up," Pablo says. "I'm a Juarense. Born and bred." Marisol walks over to rescue him. "Pablo, I see you've met Arturo."

"The *pochingo* spy."

"Pochingo?" Marisol asks.

"I'll tell you later," Keller says.

"You're okay, *pochingo*," Pablo says. "I'm going to get another beer. You want another beer?"

"I'm good."

"Okay."

Pablo walks away.

"He's a little over-refreshed," Keller says.

"Kind of a sad story, Pablo."

"I like him," Keller says. "He has a crush on you."

"A small crush," Marisol says. "He'd be in love with Ana if he had any brains. Are you having a good time?"

"I am."

"Liar."

"No, I am."

"Let's go talk with Ana," Marisol says. "I'd love for you to be friends."

They go and sit on the steps with the petite black-haired woman who's in an intense discussion with a bespectacled middle-aged man with a cane. Keller figures that this has to be the famous Óscar Herrera, the eminent journalist whom the Barreras tried to assassinate back in the day.

"Tell me how it's different, Óscar," Ana is saying. "Tell me how this isn't an army of occupation."

"Because it's our own country's army," Óscar answers.

"Still, it's martial law."

"I'm not disputing that," Óscar says. "I'm disputing your notion that it's an army of occupation and I'm also asking, what are the other options? We have a police force that either cannot or will not enforce the law, that is afraid to come out of its precinct houses for fear of being killed, so what is the city government supposed to do? Just surrender to anarchy?"

"This *is* anarchy."

"I'm sorry to interrupt," Marisol says. "I wanted to introduce you to my friend. Óscar Herrera, this is Arturo Keller."

"Mucho gusto."

"The pleasure's mine."

"We were just discussing the sad condition of our city," Óscar says, "but I, for one, am glad to be interrupted. You're a North American, Señor Keller."

"Art, please. And yes."

"But you speak Spanish so well," Óscar says. "Do you read it, too?"

"Yes."

"Who do you read?"

Keller mentions Roberto Bolano, Luis Urrea, and Elmer Mendoza, among others.

"Dr. Cisneros!" Óscar exclaims. "You have done it! You have found a civilized North American! Sit down, Arturo, sit down next to me."

Keller squeezes in next to Óscar, who moves his cane to make room, and they talk about *The Savage Detectives, The Hummingbird's Daughter,* and *Silver Bullets* until Óscar gets up and announces that he needs to leave the late night to the young people.

Marisol walks him out to help him find a cab.

Ana wastes no time. "She's in love with you, you know."

"I hope she is," Keller says.

"I'm not sure you're the man I would have chosen for her," Ana says. "A

North American, and . . . well, we joke about your being a spy, but the joke isn't that far off, is it?"

Keller doesn't answer.

"You be good to her," Ana says.

"I will," Keller says. "What about you and Pablo?"

She looks over at the reporter, who is standing and laughing with Giorgio. "I don't know that there is a 'me and Pablo.'"

"He seems like a nice guy."

"Which might be his problem," Ana says. "He's a nice guy with a soft heart, and he's carrying a torch for his ex-wife, his son, and Marisol."

"Just a crush."

"Oh," she says, "she's so far out of his league it isn't funny. No, the problem with Pablo and me is that we work together and maybe know each other too well."

"It's not a bad basis for a relationship."

Ana's voice turns serious. "If you have any influence with Mari, get her out of this political stuff. It's too dangerous."

"I was going to ask you the same thing."

"She doesn't listen."

"Well, maybe if we both keep trying."

"Deal."

They shake hands. Marisol comes back out. "What are we shaking on?"

"A newfound friendship," Keller says.

"That's good," Marisol says. "I was hoping for that."

She goes back with him to the Candlewood Suites in El Paso, where DEA keeps a room for him, rather than risk a late-night drive back to Valverde. It's one of those extended-stay hotels, hardly luxurious but not so depressing. As they get into the room, she asks, "By the way, what's a *pochingo*?"

"Half *pocho*, half gringo."

"I see. Which half would like to make love to me?"

Both, as it turns out.

New Year Day 2010 is the bloodiest day in Juárez history.

Twenty-six people are murdered in twenty-four hours.

Sixty-nine across Mexico.

Keller kisses Marisol goodbye and then leaves for Nuevo Laredo.

To hunt Zetas.

Carrejos admitted everything.

Yes, I was the one who bought the weapons from Wagner and turned them over to the Zeta team assigned to kill the Córdovas. Yes, Heriberto Ochoa—Z-1, El Verdugo—personally gave the order for the murders, to set an example. Yes, I was behind the wheel, but I didn't go in, I swear on my mother's eyes, didn't participate in the shootings. I just drove. Please stop!—don't do it again.

He even gave up the names of the hit squad.

José Silva.

Manuel Torres.

And the commander, the one in charge—Braulio Rodríguez—"Z-20." They call him El Gigante.

Keller knows the *aporto* Z-20 means that Rodríguez was one of the original Zetas, one of the first group that Ochoa recruited from the special forces. That means he's important, a top guy, so the murder of the Córdova family was a high-priority mission.

Rodríguez was in the extensive FES intelligence file. Sure enough, he'd served with Ochoa in Chiapas, so murdering women wasn't a new thing for him.

Carrejos even gave up the locations of the team.

Silva and Torres were in Nuevo Laredo.

Rodríguez was in Veracruz.

What is he doing in Veracruz? Keller wondered. The port city is a long way from the action, down in territory that had long been a Tapia stronghold, now allegedly being taken over by Crazy Eddie Ruiz.

He relayed the question through the FES guys, who were just wrapping up their interrogation of Carrejos, and he gave them the best answer he knew. It was a promotion, he told them, a reward to Rodríguez for the Córdova mission. Rodríguez would get Veracruz as his own plaza, if he could take it from Ruiz.

Ports are important to the cartels not so much for the product they send out as for the product they bring in—the precursor chemicals needed to fuel their methamphetamine super-factories, the new maquiladoras. Mazatlán, firmly in the hands of the Sinaloa cartel; Lázaro Cárdenas, contested between the Zetas and La Familia Michoacana; and Matamoros, held by the CDG, are all important inlets for the chemicals that come mostly from China. And now Veracruz, which Eddie's using to supply his operations there, but also in Monterrey and Acapulco, as he tries to reassemble the Tapia operation under his own aegis.

The Z Company has other ideas—they want the port for themselves. And Rodríguez—Z-20, El Gigante—is leading the charge.

But first things first, Keller thinks.

José Silva's been spotted in Nuevo Laredo, Eddie Ruiz's old stomping grounds before the Zetas took it for their CDG bosses. He's a whoremaster, running Central American immigrant girls in Boy's Town. The small brothel is on the second floor of a building just off the corner of Front Street and Calle Cleopatra.

Keller looks every inch the drunk middle-aged gringo crossing the border to get laid. Yellow polo shirt, jeans, a white golf cap, the stink of booze. He walks from the taxi stand past the cribs of freelance prostitutes and finds Casa Las Nalgas, which has a shabby bar where he has a beer until the women come out for the "lineup."

There are four of them at this time in the early afternoon. Keller chooses a girl who is maybe seventeen, in an ill-fitting black negligee that barely conceals her thin breasts. She looks drugged as she leads him up the narrow, creaky stairs into a filthy room that looks a little larger than a closet. A mattress sits on old box springs, with a single cover sheet over it.

A button is set in the wall over the bed.

Keller noticed the glance she exchanged with Silva at the bar. He closes the door behind him but doesn't lock it.

The girl says, "Please, the money."

"No."

She looks surprised and scared. "Please."

"I've never paid for it in my life," Keller slurs. He takes a latex glove from his jeans pocket and slips it on. "C'mere."

She backs away from him and presses the button.

Keller pulls the clean, suppressed Beretta that the FES gave him from under his shirt and hears the feet coming up the stairs. The door opens and Silva comes in looking annoyed, saying, "Listen, *pendejo*—"

Keller double-taps him in the chest.

The girl screams.

Standing over Silva, Keller fires another shot into the back of his head, then takes a jack of spades from his pocket—the calling card of the Matazetas—and lays it on the body. He drops the gun, walks down the stairs and out onto Front Street, where an FES work car picks him up.

Manuel Torres holes up.

Doubtless he's heard about Silva, and that Carrejos's brutalized corpse was found in a ditch outside of town with a jack of spades pinned to his shirt, and that the FES is tracking him down. They know he's in Nuevo Laredo, but they don't know where, and he's not using his cell phone or his computer. He's not reaching out to contact his buddies, and they can't find him.

They do find his mother.

Dolores Torres is eighty-seven and not in good health. She lives in the El Carrizo neighborhood in the central part of town, and every day walks down the street on her cane to the little market.

She's on the sidewalk this morning when an ambulance pulls up with its flashers on. Two EMTs get out and, supporting her by the elbows, guide her gently toward the back of the ambulance.

"It's going to be all right," one of the EMTs says. "We have you."

"But I'm fine, I—"

"Just be calm. We're going to take care of you."

They help her into the ambulance and lay her down on the gurney. At least fifty people on the street see this, and see the ambulance take off toward Hospital General. At least three of them phone Manuel Torres to tell him that his beloved mother collapsed on the sidewalk and was taken to the hospital.

Keller waits in a van parked on Calle Maclovio Herrera opposite the entrance to the emergency room. It takes twenty minutes before a Chevrolet Suburban races up. There's a Zeta behind the wheel, a bodyguard in the passenger seat.

Torres in the back.

The car hasn't come to a complete stop before Torres opens the door and hops out.

The two FES snipers have a clear shot. Two suppressed M-4 rifles put tightly patterned bursts into Torres's head and chest.

A jack of spades flutters out of the van before it takes off.

The wind—cold and whirling—blows trash against the tires of Pablo's car as he sits in the parking lot of S-Mart eating breakfast.

He hears the call on the police scanner. *"Motivo 59."*

Another murder.

"One 91."

A woman.

Pablo starts the engine, crumples up the burrito wrapper, throws it on the floor, and heads for the address, a restaurant near the university where he's eaten a few times. Giorgio has beaten him there, but he's not shooting photos now, just standing next to the victim's car, looking down.

Jimena Abarca's body is sprawled by the driver's door, her right arm stretched out in a pool of her blood, her hand still grasping her car keys.

She was shot nine times in the face and chest.

A couple of more photographers roll up to get pics for *la nota roja*. Giorgio steps between them and Jimena's body. "Don't."

"What the hell, Giorgio?"

Giorgio shoves the man back. "I said don't fucking shoot this! *Píntate!* Get the fuck out of here!"

They back off.

Pablo gets back in his car, takes a deep breath, and calls Ana.

They bury Jimena in Valverde.

Hundreds of people come, from Juárez and all over the valley, and Marisol thought it would have been thousands if so many hadn't left and crossed the river. And some are scared to come, afraid to be seen and photographed and become the next person buried.

The army is there, in force, in case a violent demonstration breaks out, and to photograph the people at the funeral.

"They *should* be here," Marisol hisses as they walk the coffin from the bakery to the cemetery. "They killed her."

"You don't know that," Keller says.

"I know it."

Witnesses inside the restaurant said that four men came up to Jimena as she was walking to her car, so they clearly knew her habits and that she had breakfast in that place every morning. A woman who ducked down in her car heard one of the men say to Jimena, "You think you're so fucking cool."

Jimena fought back, clawing at them with her car keys.

"Of course she did," Marisol said when she heard this. "Of course she fought."

One woman with car keys against four men with guns. There was so little left of her face that her casket had to be closed for the wake.

"The army killed her," Marisol says, "because she wouldn't stay silent."

Neither will Marisol.

"Jimena Abarca was my friend," Marisol says at the burial service, "and a friend to everyone in this valley. No one ever came to her for help who didn't get it, for kindness that didn't receive it, for support who didn't find it. She lived with dignity, courage, and purpose . . . and *they* . . ."

To Keller's horror, Marisol points at the soldiers.

". . . killed her for it."

She pauses to stare down the soldiers, including Colonel Alvarado, who goes pale with fury.

"Jimena died as she lived," Marisol continues. "Fighting. May that be said of us all. I hope it's said of me. Goodbye, Jimena. I love you. I will always love you. May God fold you in Her arms."

Now the priest looks angry, too.

Marisol, Keller thinks, is managing to infuriate everyone.

They argue about it that night.

Keller stays with her in Valverde and tries to persuade her to leave.

The town is a shell, he argues. Half the houses are boarded up, only one *tiendita* is open, and that just barely. There's no town government—the mayor and council members have all fled and no one will take the job. The police have all run away, too, and Keller can't blame them. It's not just Valverde—all the little towns on the border are in the same condition.

"It isn't safe here for you," Keller says, and adds, "Especially now that you've made yourself a target."

"My clinic is here, and *they* made me a target," Marisol says.

They glare at each other for a second, then Keller says, "Come live with me."

"I will not run to El Paso," Marisol says. "I will not do that."

"Your goddamn pride, Mari . . . Okay, fine. Come back to Mexico City. You can open a practice—"

"I'm needed here."

"—in Iztapalapa, if that makes you feel better."

"It's not about my *feelings*, Arturo," she says angrily. "It's about the facts. Fact: I am the only physician in the valley. Fact: This is my home. Fact—"

"You could get killed here. Fact."

"I'm not running away."

In fact, she does the opposite.

The next evening, Marisol holds a meeting in her clinic. About thirty people from the valley come, most of them women. It makes sense—so many of the men are dead, in jail, or have crossed the river.

That's Marisol's point.

"What the men can't or won't do," she says, "the women have to. It's always been women's role to create and preserve the home. Now our homes are threatened as never before. The army and the narcos want to chase us from our homes. If we don't stand up to them, no one will."

The meeting lasts for three hours.

At the end, two Valverde women have volunteered for the town council. Three more become mayors and councilwomen in other border towns. A twenty-eight-year-old law student volunteers to become the only police-(woman) in Práxedis; another woman takes over as the only member of the police department in Esperanza.

And Marisol becomes the new mayor of Valverde.

She holds a press conference. La Médica Hermosa has no trouble getting media, and looks straight into the cameras as she says, "This is our announcement—to the politicians, to the army, to the criminal cartels. To you, the thugs who murdered Jimena Abarca, to you, the Zeta cowards who slaughtered the Córdova family as they slept in their beds, I am here to tell you that it didn't do any good. We are here. We will be here. And we will continue to work for the poor people of the valley who tear the souls out of their bodies every day just to feed their children. We are not afraid of you, but you should be very afraid of us. We are women, fighting for our families and our homes. Nothing is more powerful."

The "Woman's Revolution"—spurred by the murder of Jimena Abarca—has taken over the Juárez Valley.

There's only one position missing.

Valverde has no police officer.

Two of the previous cops were killed, the others fled to the United States.

Keller sits with Marisol in her mayor's office in the town building as she ponders this problem.

He's furious with her.

Not only has she not left Valverde, she's put herself squarely in the crosshairs and shone a light on it. He's leaving later in the morning, now he tries to persuade her to at least carry a gun.

"I'll get it for you," he says. "A little Beretta, it will fit in your purse."

"I don't know how to shoot a gun."

"I'll teach you."

"If I'm carrying a firearm," Marisol says, "it will just give them a pretext for shooting me, won't it?"

He's forming a counterargument when there's a knock on the door.

"Come in!" Marisol yells.

The door opens and a young woman stands there. She's tall, probably five-ten. Long black hair, not fat by any means, but not skinny either, with wide hips and big bones.

"Erika, isn't it?" Marisol asks.

The young woman nods. "Erika Valles."

"You work for your uncle, Tomás."

Her uncle is a realtor in the valley.

"There are no houses to sell," Erika says, looking down at the floor.

"What can I do for you?" Marisol asks.

Erika glances up. "I'm here to apply for the job."

"What job?" Marisol asks.

"Police chief."

Keller is appalled.

Marisol smiles. "How old are you, Erika?"

"Nineteen."

"Education?"

"I went to ITCJ for a semester," Erika says, naming the local community college.

"Did you study law enforcement?" Marisol asks.

Erika shakes her head. "Computer programming."

Now Keller shakes *his* head. A nineteen-year-old girl with no training and a semester or two of community college computer science wants to be the town's only police officer. It's cloud cuckoo land.

Marisol asks, "Why do you want to be police chief, Erika?"

"It's a job," she says. "No one else wants it. I think I'd be good at it."

"Why?"

"I'm tough," Erika says. "I've been in a few fights. I play *fútbol* with the boys."

"Is that it?"

Erika looks at the floor again. "I'm smart, too."

"I'll bet you are," Marisol says.

Erika looks up. "So I have the job?"

"Do you have any criminal record?"

"No."

"Drugs?"

"I smoked a little *mota*," Erika says. "When I was young."

When you were *young*? Keller thinks.

"But not anymore," Erika adds.

"Erika," Marisol says, "you know that people have been killed doing this job."

"I know."

"And you want to do it anyway?"

Erika shrugs. "Someone has to do it."

"And you know that there's no one else on the force," Marisol says. "For the time being, anyway, you'd be the chief of yourself."

"Sounds good to me." Erika smiles.

"All right," Marisol says. "I'll swear you in."

Are you out of your goddamned mind? Keller thinks, giving Marisol a look that expresses exactly what he's thinking. She gives him an irritated look back, and then fishes through her desk for the police chief's oath.

After she's sworn in, Erika asks, "Do I get a gun?"

"There's a what . . . an 'AR-15,'" Marisol says, "but do you know how to shoot it?"

"Everyone knows."

Jesus Christ, Keller thinks.

"All right," Marisol says. "When can you start?"

"This afternoon?" Erika asks. "I should go tell my mom."

"She should go tell her mom," Keller says when Erika leaves. "This is insanity, Mari."

"It's all insanity, Art," Marisol answers. "It's not as if she's going to be investigating murders or busting narcos. Parking tickets, routine patrols against break-ins . . . Why can't she do it?"

"Because the narcos don't want any kind of police here," Keller says. "Or any government."

"Well," Marisol says, "we *are* here."

Keller shakes his head.

"But," she adds, "I *will* take that gun."

Weeks later, the messages start to appear in the valley.

White bedsheets, spray-painted in black with the names of those to be executed, are nailed to walls. Banners strung on phone lines read YOU HAVE FORTY-EIGHT HOURS TO LEAVE.

Leaflets threaten to kill police and town officials.

Marisol's name is on the list.

So is Erika's.

So are the names of the councilwomen of Valverde and the police officers in the other towns.

During Semana Santa, Holy Week, leaflets tossed from the backs of trucks tell the entire populations of Porvenir and Esperanza, "You have just a few hours to get out."

On Good Friday, a firebomb is thrown at the Porvenir church, burning its old wooden door.

The exodus begins.

People leave their homes for Juárez, or to family farther south, or they try to cross the border.

Keller urges Marisol to be one of them. He shows up at her office, having driven down from EPIC, and confronts her with the threats.

"How do you know about this?" she asks.

"I know about everything." The hyperbole is not that exaggerated. He gets daily briefings from every important intelligence source, and can't help himself from finding out what's going on in the valley.

"So if you know everything," Marisol says, "tell me—is it the army or the Sinaloa cartel, or is there really a difference?"

Keller does know.

The CDG and the Zetas are expanding west, along Highway 2, through Coahuila and then into Chihuahua.

There are signs that the process has already begun, and Adán Barrera isn't taking any chances on this part of the border. He's already moving Sinaloans into the lands vacated by the people he forced off.

Adán Barrera isn't just depopulating the Juárez Valley.

He's *colonizing* it.

It's a bizarre repeat of the history that brought so many of those families into the valley in the first place, as "military colonists" to fight off the Apaches. Except this time, the Apaches are Zetas. The Zetas and CDG are doing a similar thing in rural northern Tamaulipas, moving suspect people off their land and putting loyalists in their place.

"It's Sinaloa," Keller tells Marisol, "but the army won't do a damn thing to stop them."

"To say the least."

"Mari, you have to go," Keller says. "I admire what you're trying to do, I admire *the hell* out of what you're trying to do, but it's not possible. You and a half dozen women cannot go up against the Sinaloa cartel!"

"Because the people who are supposed to protect me," she said, "are the same people who are going to kill me."

"Yes. Fine. Okay."

"No, it's not okay. If we yield to intimidation—"

"You don't have a choice!"

"We always have a choice!" Marisol says. "I choose to stay."

Keller walks over to the window and looks out at the devastated town, half-deserted. A few folding tables set up under a tent in the park to serve as a grocery store, untended trash blowing across the street. Why does she want to fight and die for this wasteland?

"Mari," he says, "I have to be back in Mexico City on Monday. I'm begging you—please come with me."

Erika picks that moment to come in. She wears jeans and a hooded sweatshirt and has her AR-15 slung over her shoulder.

"Erika," Marisol says, "Arturo thinks we should run away."

"There would be no shame in it," Keller says. "No one would think any less of you."

"I would," Erika says.

Marisol flashes Keller an I-told-you-so smile.

"This is not some Hollywood movie," he says, "where the brave women band together, sing 'Kumbaya,' and there's a happy ending. This is—"

Seeing the look on Marisol's face, he instantly regrets what he said.

She says quietly, "I'm very aware it's not a movie, Art. I have seen my dearest friend killed, the town I grew up in devastated, the people I grew up with pack what little they have and trudge down the road as refugees."

"I'm sorry. That was stupid."

The sunlight, filtered by dust, is beautiful—a dark red-gold—in the sunset as they walk from the office to her house. They go past the Abarca bakery, now closed and shuttered, past the *tiendita*, also closed, its owners now living across the border in Fabens.

Three soldiers, standing behind a barbed-wired sandbag emplacement, watch them walk past.

"They know who you are," Marisol says to Keller, "the big gringo DEA man."

Keller isn't crazy about the fact that he's known, but it's a trade-off he's willing to make if it affords her a little protection when he's there. Erika walks five paces behind them, her rifle in hand now.

She's devoted to Marisol.

Dedicated to her job.

"Thank you, Erika, we're fine now," Marisol says when they get to her house. They kiss each other on the cheeks, and Erika walks back down the street.

Marisol's house is an old restored adobe with a new red tin roof. It's small but comfortable, its thick walls keeping out both the cold and the heat.

The windows now have bars and anti–grenade screens that Keller insisted on putting in.

She slides off her white jacket, revealing the shoulder holster with the Beretta Nano, then pours a glass of wine for each of them and hands one to Keller. He's glad that she's carrying the weapon. He bought it for her and took her out into the desert to teach her how to use it.

Marisol was a surprisingly good shot.

Now she plops into the big old easy chair in her small living room, kicks off her shoes, puts her feet up on a hassock, and says, "Christ. What a day."

"Good Friday," he says.

"I forgot," she says. "No procession. No one to do it."

It's painful, Keller thinks. The traditional Good Friday reenactments of Christ's march to Calvary have been replicated all through the valley by processions of refugees leaving their homes. "Do you want to go to church tonight?"

Marisol shakes her head. "I'm tired. And truthfully? I'm losing my faith."

"I don't believe that."

"That's a funny response if you think about it," she says. "Don't let me stop you from going, but what I really want is another glass of wine, a quiet dinner at home, and an early night."

That's what they do.

Keller finds some chicken in her refrigerator and makes a dinner of *arroz con pollo* and a green salad while Marisol takes a long shower. They eat while watching some American television show and then go to bed.

Marisol sleeps in on Saturday morning, and Keller brings her coffee in bed.

She likes it white and sweet.

"You're an angel," she says, taking the cup.

"That's the first time that's ever been said."

Marisol takes her time getting ready, and then Keller escorts her to her office so she can use the relative quiet of Semana Santa to catch up on some paperwork. He brings his laptop and goes over the classified intelligence briefings.

A top-secret report from DEA and CIA intelligence analysts opines that the Sinaloa cartel has won the war for Juárez and is all but in control there. La Línea has been virtually annihilated and Los Aztecas, while still fighting, has seen its leadership decimated and is in disarray.

Keller has mixed feelings. He hates that Barrera has won, but the victory might bring an end to the hideous violence. That's what it's come to, he thinks ruefully. That's what we can hope for now—a win by one gang of murderers over another.

The memo attached to the report asks for his commentary, and he writes that while the Juárez cartel seems to be finished in the city, its Zeta allies seem to be getting active along the Chihuahua border and the Sinaloa cartel is taking defensive measures.

Then he reads a series of e-mail exchanges between DEA and SEIDO speculating on the whereabouts of Eddie Ruiz. Is he in San Pedro, Monterrey, Acapulco? Another report has him sighted in Veracruz. All agree that he's flying under the radar, hunted by the Zetas and Martín Tapia.

Tapia is back in the country, trying to piece together the remnants of his brothers' organization into something called the "South Pacific cartel." Most of the analysts agree that it's not going particularly well—most of the major Tapia players have sided with Ruiz, who, in any case, seems to have recruited the best killers. And there are reports that Martín, perhaps out of grief for his brother, has adopted Diego's cult of Santa Muerte and is spending more and more time in religious observances, and that his wife isn't happy about it.

Martín's rumored to be in Cuernavaca, Yvette is said to be living somewhere in Sonora.

Keller reads more reports.

CIA warns that the Zeta presence in Central America is getting stronger, especially in Guatemala, in the northern provinces like the Petén and the city of Cobán. The report also indicates that the Zetas are openly advertising for more Kaibiles, but also recruiting MS-13 gang members from the slums of El Salvador.

It makes sense, Keller thinks. The Zetas are fighting on five fronts and need troops.

Keller's own "Zeta front" is bogged down. They know that Rodríguez, Z-20, is somewhere in the Veracruz area, because he surfaced as the leader of a Zeta team that lobbed incendiary grenades into the house of a Veracruz police operations director.

The wooden structure went up in flames. Just to be on the safe side, Rodríguez and his men waited outside to gun down anyone who made it out.

No one did.

The police commander, his wife, and his four young children died in the fire.

———

Keller and Marisol do go to Mass that night, if only because the people of Valverde expect their mayor to be present at Holy Saturday services. The church is only half full anyway, so many people have left town. By tradition, the statue of the Virgin Mary is draped in black for mourning, and the obvious symbolism of the current situation escapes no one.

The whole valley, Keller thinks, is on the cross.

Marisol doesn't take communion and neither does Keller. As they're sitting in the pew, he feels his cell phone vibrate in his pocket and steps outside. It's a computer tech at EPIC.

They've picked up cell phone traffic between Rodríguez's cousin and him in Veracruz and they have an address.

Keller gets on the horn to Orduña. If they move fast, they can get Z-20.

The plan was for Keller to spend the night and then go to Juárez with Marisol for Easter—a dinner with Ana and the crew. Then he was going to fly back to Mexico City and she was going back to Valverde for a meeting with the mayors and city councils from the Valley. When she comes out of the church, Keller tells her that he has to leave. They go back to her house so he can get his things.

"Go to El Paso," he asks.

"I can't. I have things to do," she says. "I'll be fine. I'm going into the city for an Easter party with the crew."

"Te quiero, Mari."

"Te quiero también, Arturo."

Marisol and Ana leave the Easter party in separate cars to go back to Valverde for the meeting tomorrow morning. The plan is for Ana to stay at Marisol's that night and come back after the meeting. She follows Marisol down Carretera 2.

Ana is going to write a story on the meeting as a way of explicating the "Woman's Rebellion" in Chihuahua. In the valley, in Juárez, in little towns all across the state, women are standing up, filling positions in the government and police, demanding accountability, transparency, answers.

Marisol is tired and would have preferred to stay in Juárez, but the meeting is at eight in the morning, and besides, she doesn't like to leave Erika on her own for too long. The young woman has done a good job but she's still nineteen years old.

The party had been fun—good food, good company—although Marisol missed Arturo being there. She's glad that he likes her friends and that they like him; otherwise, it would make the relationship horribly awkward.

It's a crisp Juarense night and she wears a heavy sweater and a scarf. The pistol that Arturo gave her is in her purse, within easy reach on the passenger seat. She wonders about her relationship with Keller. She loves him, she knows that, more than she ever loved her husband, probably more than she's ever loved anyone. He's a wonderful man—intelligent, funny, kind, a good lover—but the challenges to their relationship are formidable.

He needs to understand—well, he does understand, he needs to *accept*, Marisol thinks—that I'm as committed to my work as he is to his. And if I'm under threat, so is he. Arturo's old-school in that regard—being in danger is a man's role, not a woman's.

And Arturo is far more North American than he thinks he is—he has that North American belief that every problem has a solution, whereas a Mexican knows that this isn't necessarily true.

She punches the radio to an El Paso station that plays country-western music, her secret guilty pleasure.

She chuckles. Me and Miranda Lambert.

Despite four bullet wounds, Rodríguez is still breathing with the help of an oxygen mask, his chest heaving as he lies on a gurney in the back of the ambulance now racing across Veracruz toward the hospital.

Keller thinks the man is going to make it. They'd hit Rodríguez's safe house in Veracruz just before dawn and took it by surprise. The raid netted Rodríguez, five armored cars, radio equipment, and Rodríguez's famous gold-plated M-1911 pistol, with his *aportos* encrusted in diamonds.

Now one of the Matazetas, his face disguised under a black balaclava, looks at Keller and asks, "This is one of the *pendejos* who killed Lieutenant Córdova's family?"

Keller nods.

The Matazeta turns to the EMT monitoring the oxygen tank. "Turn around, my friend."

"What?"

"Turn around, my friend," the Matazeta repeats.

The EMT hesitates but then turns around. The Matazeta looks at Keller, who merely looks back, then leans across and takes the oxygen mask off Rodríguez's face. Z-20's chest heaves faster. He starts to panic and gasps, "I want a priest."

"Go to hell," the Matazeta says.

He lays a jack of spades over Rodríguez's heart.

Marisol sees the lights come up in her rearview mirror and wonders why Ana is passing her on this two-lane road at night.

She looks over to see the window roll down and the gun barrel come out.

Then the red muzzle flashes blind her, she feels like something is punching her in the chest, and then her car flies off the road.

An unmarked car picks Keller up outside the hospital where Rodríguez is delivered DOA, and takes him to La Boticaria airfield. His presence in Veracruz is a secret, as is his participation in this, or any, raid. He boards a Learjet 25, provided by Mérida, for the flight back to Mexico City.

Orduña is on the plane. "I hear Rodríguez didn't make it."

"He died of complications on the way to the hospital," Keller says.

Which is true enough, he supposes. It's an unspoken understanding. *Nobody* who participated in the killings of Córdova's family is going to make it into a police station or a hospital. Rodríguez knew that, which is why he pulled his gold-plated pistol and tried to slug it out.

So now they've killed every Zeta who took part.

Mission accomplished.

Yeah, not quite.

Now they have to get the men who ordered it.

Keller takes a seat and pours himself a scotch. As the plane takes off, Orduña hands him *Forbes* magazine and says, "You're going to like this."

Keller gives Orduña a questioning look.

"Page eight," Orduña says.

Keller turns to the page and sees it. Adán Barrera is listed as number sixty-seven on the *Forbes* annual list of the world's most powerful people.

"Forbes," Keller says, tossing the magazine down.

"Don't worry," Orduña says. "We'll get him."

Keller wonders.

He pours two fingers of scotch on the ice and relaxes during the flight. When he lands, his phone rings.

"Keller, this is Pablo Mora."

The man sounds shaken. He might even be crying.

"It's Marisol."

Marisol is not going to make it.

This is what the doctors tell Keller.

She took bullets to the stomach, chest, and leg, in addition to a broken femur, two broken ribs, and a cracked vertebra suffered when the car crashed after the gun attack. They almost lost her three times on the drive to the hospital—twice more on the operating table, where they had to remove a section of her small intestine. Now the issue is sepsis. Dr. Cisneros is running a high fever, is very weak, and is, frankly, *señor,* unlikely ever to emerge from the coma.

Even if she does, there is the possibility of brain damage.

Keller flew directly to Juárez on a military flight. When he got to Juárez General, Pablo Mora was in the waiting room with Erika.

Erika was crying. "I didn't protect her. I didn't protect her."

Mora told Keller what he knew.

They had just left an army checkpoint a mile behind when a car came racing up, pulled around Ana's car, and came up alongside Marisol's. Ana remembers seeing gun flashes out of the passenger window. Marisol's car swerved off the road into a ditch. The attacking car stopped and went into reverse.

Ana hit the brakes and threw herself flat onto the seat.

The attacking car sped off.

Ana had lacerations on her arm where it struck the steering wheel. She managed to get Marisol into her car and start driving back toward Juárez. A Red Cross ambulance met them on the highway, where the EMTs took over.

But Marisol lost so much blood.

A priest is brought in to give her last rites.

Keller goes in after the priest leaves. Marisol's skin is white, tinged with a greenish hue. Her face is sweaty. A tube in her mouth helps her breathe, myriad other tubes going into her arms pump in pain medication and antibiotics. The stomach wound—a gaping, obscene red hole—is left open to prevent further infection.

The mark of holy oil is on her forehead.

Marisol lives through the day and the following night.

Her heart stops again that night but the doctors manage to start it again and wheel her back into surgery to repair the internal bleeding. The doctors are surprised when the sun comes up and she's still alive. She hangs on all that day, that night, and the following day.

A watch is set up in the little foyer outside her room. Keller is there, and

Ana, and Pablo Mora comes in and out. Óscar Herrera spends hours there, and women from all over Juárez and the valley maintain the vigil.

Gunmen have been known to come into Juárez hospitals to finish off the wounded, and they aren't going to let that happen.

Orduña sure as hell isn't.

Two plainclothes FES operatives show up the first night, and then more in shifts, twenty-four/seven.

No one is going to get to Marisol Cisneros.

Nevertheless, Erika refuses to leave.

The third morning, the news comes in that Cristina Antonia, one of the Valverde city councilwomen, was shot dead in her shop in front of her eleven-year-old daughter. Marisol lives through the day and the next, but the other councilwoman, Patricia Ávila, is gunned down outside her home.

Keller has a talk with Erika. "You have to resign. I'll get you a visa on the other side."

"I'm not quitting."

"Erika—"

"What would Marisol think?"

Marisol is in a coma, Keller wants to say. "She would want you to live. She'd tell you to go."

Erika is stubborn. "I'm not running away."

Colonel Alvarado comes to pay his respects. The commander of the army district in the valley brings flowers.

Keller stops him from going into Marisol's room.

"She was a mile from an army checkpoint when she was attacked," Keller says.

"What are you implying?"

"I'm not implying anything," Keller says. "I'm *stating* that your troops let a carload of armed men through their checkpoint and back out again. And your people let two more women get killed in Valverde."

Alvarado turns white with anger. "I know your reputation, Señor Keller."

"Good."

"This isn't over."

"You can count on that," Keller says. "Now get out."

On the third day, Ana persuades Keller to go home and take a shower, change his clothes, and get a little sleep. He notices that two FES follow him the whole way and take positions outside his condo in El Paso.

He's just out of the shower when his phone rings.

"Don't hang up," Minimum Ben Tompkins says.

"What do you want?"

"Someone wants you to know that it wasn't his people who attacked your friend," Ben says.

"Tell that someone I'm going to kill him."

"Think about it," Tompkins says. "He already has everything he wants there. Why would he risk that by killing a bunch of women?"

He makes a point, Keller thinks. Barrera has already won in Juárez and basically taken the valley. But he says, "Marisol Cisneros challenged him on television."

"She challenged the Zetas, too," Tompkins says. "Our friend says to tell you that nothing has changed between the two of you, but that he didn't go after your woman."

Tompkins clicks off.

Barrera doesn't give a damn what I think happened, Keller considers. But he's always been very conscious of his public image. The killing of the women and the attack on a celebrity like La Médica Hermosa would be bad public relations.

On the other hand, the Zetas came into the valley to teach a lesson when they killed the Córdova family. Their idea of public relations is intimidation and terror. Much as he'd like to add the attack on Marisol to Barrera's account, the Zeta explanation does make sense.

He's back in Marisol's hospital room when she opens her eyes.

"Arturo?" she asks weakly. "Am I dead?"

"No," he says. "You're alive."

Thank God, thank God, thank God, you're alive.

Marisol's recuperation is long, painful, and uncertain.

She has another surgery to close up the stomach wound, yet another to fit the colostomy bag.

It's weeks before Keller wheels her out of the hospital, and even then he puts her in a private ambulance for the short drive across the bridge to El Paso.

"I'm not going to El Paso," Marisol says. "I can't."

"The paperwork is already in."

He's obtained a visa for her. There was resistance at first, until Keller told Tim Taylor and the powers-that-be that either Cisneros got the visa or the FES assassination program would be on CNN by morning.

"You're not making any friends with this," Taylor warned.

"I don't want any friends."

Marisol was issued a visa.

"That's all very well," she says now, "but no one asked you to file *any* paperwork. I'm going back to Valverde."

"Marisol . . ."

"I want to go home, Arturo," she says. "Please, I want to be home."

Reluctantly, he tells the driver that they're going to Valverde. The driver is just as reluctant to go.

"See the car behind us?" Keller says. "Marines. FES. Now drive to Valverde."

They get settled in her house.

Keller becomes her nurse, cook, rehab coach, and bodyguard, although shifts of FES stay outside the house. He cleans up after her, makes her the plain food that the doctors say that she can eat, and helps her wean herself off the pain pills.

She's in near-constant pain, and the doctors have said that it will be a matter of "management," not full recovery. But slowly, she gets out of bed, she learns to walk on crutches, then with a cane. The first day that she can walk out into her little garden and back on her own feels like a victory, and she's delighted.

Keller is bitterly amused that the Zetas, blamed now in most of the press for the attack, deny it and launch a public relations campaign of their own. They throw a "Day of the Children" party in a city soccer stadium with bands, clowns, bouncy castles, and hundreds of expensive gifts. A banner hung from the roof reads PRESENTS ARE NOT ENOUGH. PARENTS SHOULD LOVE THEIR CHILDREN—THE "EXECUTIONER" OCHOA AND THE Z COMPANY.

They throw a Mother's Day party in Ciudad Victoria, give away refrigerators and washing machines, and hang banners that read WE LOVE AND RESPECT WOMEN—FORTY AND THE EXECUTIONER.

And their own tame journalists have started to write stories that La Médica Hermosa was in a drunk-driving accident after a party, and that her wounds have been exaggerated by her journalist friends.

Two weeks after that, Marisol announces to Keller that she's ready to go back to work.

"What?" he asks.

"Back to work."

"In the clinic."

"In the clinic and the mayor's office," Marisol says.

"That's insane."

"Be that as it may."

"They almost killed you," Keller says. "You're lucky to be alive."

"Then I shouldn't waste the gift I was given, should I?"

"Is this just ego?" Keller asks. "Or a martyr complex?"

"Look who's talking."

"You're not Joan of Arc," Keller says.

"And you're not my boss," she answers.

He can't dissuade her. That night in bed she asks him, "Arturo? Can you love me like this?"

"What do you mean?"

"I can understand how you might not," she says. "The scars, my stomach, the hideous bag. The limp. I'm not the same woman you fell in love with. You've been wonderful and loyal and faithful, and now I will understand if you want to leave."

He touches her cheek. "You're beautiful."

"Have the decency not to lie to me."

"You want the truth?"

"Please."

"I don't want to live without you."

Two days later she makes him help her into her nicest clothes. She spends extra time with her hair and fixes her makeup impeccably. The effect is stunning. In a little black dress—sexy, powerful—she looks beautiful, even with the cane and the limp.

Then she goes off to give a press conference. For all the cameras, she unzips the dress and raises her arm to display her wounds. She exposes the jagged, still-red scars under her arm and on the side of her breast, the livid wound on her stomach.

"I wanted to show you," she says, "my wounded, mutilated, 'humiliated' body because I am not ashamed of it, because it is the living testimony that I am a whole and strong woman, who, despite my physical and mental wounds, continues standing."

Marisol pulls the dress back up and goes on: "To those who did this to me, to those who murdered my sisters, know that you have lost. I, and other brave women, will not let their sacrifice be in vain. Others have already stepped up to take their place. If you kill me, others will step up to take my place. You will never defeat us."

Then she announces that she is going to the office to go back to work, and that everyone knows where to find her.

Keller watches her limp away, with Erika right beside her, down the dusty street, past the broken buildings, through this village of ghosts.

He thinks it might be the bravest thing he's ever seen in his life.

2

What Is It That You Want from Us?

Shut up! We can't hear the mimes!

—Jacques Prévert
Les Enfants du Paradis

Ciudad Juárez
December 31, 2009

Pablo wearily responds to yet another *"Motivo 59."*
It's almost midnight, and this one is way out in Villas de Salvárcar, a close-knit working-class subdivision squeezed between some factories in the southeast part of the city. A lot of the houses are empty now as workers left the neighborhood with the maquiladoras.

It's cold, and the heater in Pablo's *fronterizo* is for shit, so he shivers as he drives out to Villa del Portal Street, one of the two ways into Salvárcar. He's tired, and was hoping for this Saturday night off. There had been fourteen bodies yesterday, more than he could cover, and he'd driven back and forth across the city to report on as many as he could, even though bodies were no longer news.

It would be news if there *weren't* bodies.

The scanner hadn't indicated whether it was a man or a woman, or how many—just that there had been a murder. Pablo pulls up to 3010 Villa del Portal expecting the same old non-news.

The street is full of people—some screaming, some crying, others holding each other in consolation. There are a lot of other reporters and photographers—even television news trucks.

Something major has happened at 3010 Villa del Portal.

Ambulances pull up behind Pablo, along with a car full of *federales,* and the people start shouting obscenities at them. *It's been forty minutes! Where have you been?! Cowards!* Pendejos!

Pablo gets out and slips on some blood on the sidewalk. He finds Giorgio shooting from outside the house.

"What happened?" Pablo asked.

"Some local teenagers were having a birthday party in the vacant house," Giorgio answers. "Apparently, carloads of gunmen pulled up, went in, and started shooting. Some of the kids ran next door but the *sicarios* chased them down there. The people were calling for help, but no one came."

Pablo remembers that there's a hospital two minutes away.

"The shooters got back in their cars and drove off," Giorgio says. "Then, of course, the *federales* came."

"How many dead?" Pablo asks.

Giorgio shrugs.

It turns out to be fifteen.

Four adults and eleven kids.

Fifteen more wounded.

Over the next two days, Pablo gets more of the story. The kids were just having a party, with the knowledge of their parents and even the permission of the people who owned the vacant house.

The *sicarios* came in. Survivors heard orders to "kill them all." Most died in the living room, their bodies piled in a clump. Others jumped out the window and ran next door, where the gunmen tracked them down.

It was over within fifteen minutes.

The question is, who did it?

And why?

Pablo tracks Ramón down in a Galeana bar.

The Los Azteca lieutenant is slumped in a booth, very drunk, and he stares up through red eyes as Pablo slides into the booth.

"What you want, *'mano?*"

"Villas del Salvárcar."

"Go to hell."

"We're all pretty much living in it, aren't we?" Pablo asks. He sets his glass down on the table. "The fuck happened, Ramón? Who did it?"

Ramón shakes his head. "You want to die, Pablo? Because I don't. I mean, I do, but I got kids, you know?"

"Gente Nueva? La Línea?"

Ramón looks around, leans in, and then says, "It was a mistake, *'mano.* They had the wrong information."

"Who did?"

Ramón taps his own chest. "Us. Los Aztecas."

"Jesus, were you—"

"No, 'mano. I'm going to hell, but not for that." His head slumps, then he recovers, looks up, and says, "Some others. They had orders. They were told it was an AA party."

"Like the rehab?"

"*Nooooo*, like AA, like Aristos Asesinos," Ramón says. "The gang that fights for Barrera. They thought those kids were AA."

"They weren't."

"Know that *now*," Ramón says.

"Who gave the order?"

Ramón shrugs. "Who the fuck knows? No one's in charge anymore. No one knows . . . anything. Someone above you tells you to kill someone, you kill someone. You don't know why, you don't know for who. Then the guy above you is dead, and it's someone else."

"Was it Fuentes?"

"That pussy bitch?" Ramón asks. "He's gone. He ran away. He don't care no more. Fuck, *I* don't care no more. Nobody cares about shit no more."

Ramón starts to cry. Then he says, "You better get out of here, 'Blo. Isn't safe. They're killing us all, man. La Línea, Los Aztecas, they're killing us all."

"Who is?"

"The Gente Nueva," Ramón says. "They're the New People, right?"

Pablo tosses back his drink and slides out of the booth.

"Hey, come to the house sometime," Ramón says. "We'll have a beer, watch some *fútbol*."

"We'll do that."

Pablo walks out of the bar.

The next day, Pablo is in the city room with Ana and Óscar when the president gives a press conference from Switzerland to comment on the Villas de Salvárcar massacre.

"The most probable hypothesis," Calderón said, "is that the attacks were related to the rivalry between drug organizations, and that the youths had some sort of link to the cartels."

"Did he really just say that?" Ana asks.

"He did," Óscar answers. "We run it."

Calderón's statement infuriates Juárez and thousands of other Mexican citizens across the country. Calls for his resignation come from every quarter, not the least of which from the families of those killed.

Óscar Herrera writes a scathing editorial, demanding that the president step down.

The president and members of his cabinet come to visit the families, apologize, offer their condolences, and announce over $260 million in new social programs for the city.

It does little good.

It certainly does little to mollify the Juarenses.

The day after Calderón's visit, a *narcomanta* is hung up over a major Juárez street. It reads THIS IS FOR CITIZENS SO THAT THEY KNOW THAT THE FEDERAL GOVERNMENT PROTECTS ADÁN BARRERA, WHO IS RESPONSIBLE FOR THE MASSACRE OF INNOCENT PEOPLE . . . ADÁN BARRERA IS PROTECTED BY PAN SINCE THEY SET HIM FREE. THE DEAL IS STILL IN PLACE TODAY. WHY DO THEY MASSACRE INNOCENT PEOPLE? WHY DO THEY NOT FIGHT WITH US FACE-TO-FACE? WHAT IS THEIR MENTALITY? WE INVITE THE GOVERNMENT TO FIGHT ALL THE CARTELS.

The next day, hundreds gather at the base of the Free Bridge to protest drug violence.

Villas de Salvárcar comes to symbolize opposition to the government's war on drugs, a symbol of confusion and futility.

It's a watershed moment in the war on drugs.

Another follows in short order.

La Tuna, Sinaloa
February 2010

The CDG and the Zetas have split.

The war is on.

The deck of cartel alliances is going to be shuffled again.

Adán knew that it couldn't last—that eventually the Zeta servants would turn on their CDG masters—but he can't believe it would happen this soon and in such a spectacular fashion.

He goes down to the kitchen to make some breakfast. It's become one of his small pleasures—he likes the solitude of early morning and the simplicity of cooking an egg and making his own coffee.

It's good, quiet time to think before a day of incessant demands.

Adán heats some canola oil and cracks a single egg into the pan. He's picked up a few pounds and his last physical revealed that his cholesterol was a little high, so he's cut his morning eggs in half. Watching the egg crackle, he thinks about Gordo Contreras, the putative head of the CDG.

Gordo made a serious mistake.

Some of his people in Reynosa kidnapped and then killed a high-ranked Zeta, a close friend of Forty's.

Forty was outraged and gave Gordo a week to turn over the killers.

Gordo was in a tough spot. If he turned his own people over, he was done as boss of the CDG and became Forty's bitch; if he didn't, he was at war with the Zetas. Gordo has his own armed force, Los Escorpiones, but they're not a match for the Zetas.

Adán takes a spatula and slides the egg onto his plate. He shakes some Tabasco sauce on it in place of the salt that Eva won't let him have, then sits down to eat.

Gordo didn't turn over the killers.

As a result, Forty kidnapped sixteen CDG *sicarios* and tortured them to death in a basement.

Adán places a private bet with himself to see who will call him first. It would be a smart move for the Zetas to offer to withdraw from Juárez in exchange for his help against the CDG.

But Ochoa and the Zetas are doing stupid things lately.

They've changed.

Their original cadre of veteran special forces has been depleted by arrests and attrition and now they have to recruit men with little or no experience and train them. Some of the people running around calling themselves "Zetas" aren't part of the organization at all, and "Zeta" has become something of a brand name, like "Al Qaeda."

Adán wonders if Ochoa is deteriorating as well. The decision to kill that marine's family after the funeral was so phenomenally stupid as to boggle the mind. The public reacted with predictable outrage, and the marine special forces, the FES, have launched the predictable vendetta and are pounding the Zetas.

With the help of North American intelligence.

Of course Keller would find his way into the elite unit of killers. It's a natural evolution, water seeking its own level. And with the FES relentlessly pursuing the Zetas, Adán is not self-indulgent enough to attract their attention by killing Art Keller.

No, let him do my killing for me.

There will be time enough to deal with him later. Still, it's frustrating. Patience is a virtue, but like most virtues, also a burden.

But if Ochoa thought he could win hearts and minds by slaughtering a hero's grieving family in their beds, he was wrong. Maybe he can intimidate the general public, but he's not going to intimidate Orduña and his men, who are more than willing to get into a fight to the death.

And the Zetas continue to do things that alienate the public—principally kidnapping and extortion. They now make as much money from these activities as they do from drug trafficking, but while the public doesn't pay much attention to trafficking, it deeply resents being held for ransom.

It plays right into my hands, Adán thinks as he puts his dishes in the sink. The Zetas make us look good—or at least the lesser of evils. After the Córdova murders, no one objects to the government making the Zetas its priority.

So now Ochoa and his boys are fighting me in Juárez and Sinaloa, Eddie Ruiz in Monterrey, Veracruz, and Acapulco, La Familia in Michoacán, the marines everywhere, and now the CDG in Tamaulipas.

Nevertheless, the Zetas are expanding, and it's worrisome.

The most worrying expansion isn't in Mexico at all.

It's in Guatemala.

The Zetas have been moving into Guatemala for the last three years, gaining favor with the Lorenzana family by killing their chief rival, Juancho León, and ten others in an ambush at a supposed peace meeting.

In recent months they've fought—successfully—pitched battles against Guatemalan special forces troops to defend airstrips used for bringing in cocaine, and now Adán has word that there are over four hundred Zeta operatives in the country focusing on Guatemala City and the Petén, the province on the border with Mexico, and have advertised for ex-soldiers on pirate radio stations.

It's significant—70 percent of the cocaine that flows through Mexico comes in via Guatemala.

All the cartels have used Guatemala for years.

It goes back to the old "Mexican Trampoline" days of the '80s, because flights from Colombia needed a place to refuel before flying into Guadalajara. With the current war on drugs, Guatemala has become even more important, as a market, but also as a transshipment point. Cocaine flown into the Petén can simply be carried into Mexico and moved up to the border from there. Now the Zetas are forcing peasants from their land so they can use it as a string of bases.

The Guatemalan government has sent a thousand troops, with armored vehicles, helicopters, and surveillance equipment, into the Petén. The Petén has always been neutral territory—safe and quiescent—and now Ochoa, in making a move to control it, has brought government attention, not to mention the DEA.

It can't be allowed—Adán's cocaine imports depend on El Salvador and Guatemala, and he can't yield either to the Zetas.

Adán walks out of the kitchen onto the broad stretch of lawn and walks down toward a grove of *fresno* trees at the bottom of the slope. The morning is cool and quiet, with birdsong just starting as the sun comes up.

Barely aware of the *sicarios* that follow from a discreet distance, Adán walks into the grove. It's peaceful here, it feels so far away from the conflicts and strife that inhabit the rest of his life.

Eva is well, but Eva is also not pregnant.

Which seems to be the central fact of *her* life.

If sex with a beautiful twenty-year-old woman can be deemed a chore, that's what it's become, a chore—Eva running around with a thermometer in her mouth, checking calendars and clocks, summoning him to perform when the moment is ripe, suggesting new positions not for enjoyment but for the efficiency of physics.

Eva is frustrated and fearful—despite his assurances to the contrary—that he'll leave her.

And she's restless.

He understands.

Life on a remote *finca* is not exactly ideal for a vivacious girl her age. Adán understands that she feels like a prisoner here, even with the swimming pool, the home gym, the horses, the satellite dish, and Netflix. She goes on shopping trips to Badiraguato and Culiacán, but he knows that she wants to hit the clubs in Mazatlán and Cabo. He tries to facilitate that, but it's difficult, and she doesn't appreciate the level of organization and planning even a quick trip off the *finca* requires.

She misses her friends, and he brings them in from time to time, but each visitor is a potential security risk, and with two wars going on and the FES rampaging through the narco ranks, he can't afford unnecessary risks.

As a sop, he's arranged for her to go to Mexico City every few weeks for a few days, and she's leaving later this morning, but he knows that it's a temporary respite at best.

The issue is that she's bored, has nothing to do with her time, and refuses to grow up. Some women let the vicissitudes of life make them hard and bitter, but Eva has gone in the other direction—willfully naïve, consciously unaware, almost defiantly childlike. Always cheerful, perpetually, annoyingly "bubbly," still the virgin bride in bed—enthusiastic, energetic, unskillful.

The brutal fact is that Eva has failed in the one job that she was required to do—produce an heir.

"She *has* given you a child," Magda said during one of their assignations in Badiraguato. "Herself."

"Very funny."

"So, seriously, what are you going to do?"

"What are you suggesting?"

"Get a new wife." She let that sit for a second and then continued, "Oh, come on, you don't love her. You can't tell me that you love her."

"I've grown fond."

"I'm fond of my golden retriever," Magda said. "Eva's a child, and she gets younger every day. It's almost creepy. Seriously, I wonder about her mental health, don't you?"

"It's a hard life for a woman."

"Thank you for telling me. I didn't know," Magda said.

How would Nacho react, Adán wonders, if I do divorce his daughter? Would he accept it, or use it as a pretext to break the alliance? No, that's too direct for Nacho—he would pretend to accept it and then use the power base I gave him in Tijuana to move against me. He'd go back to his old allies in Juárez and start stirring up a rebellion, while denying it all the time.

Adán has the fleeting thought that he should kill him now. Easy enough to blame on the Zetas. Then after Nacho is in the ground and a suitable mourning period, send Eva packing, with enough money, of course, to live in the manner to which she's become accustomed.

He walks back up to the house.

Eva isn't up yet, and for some reason it annoys him. He'd like to wake her up on the pretext that she's going to miss her flight, but as they own two Learjets with crews standing by it wouldn't work.

He watches her sleep.

Magda's right, Adán thinks.

She's a child.

Like any civil war, the conflict between the CDG and the Zetas has been extraordinarily vicious.

And it can only be called a war.

Whereas gangs of *sicarios* used to move covertly, now trucks with hundreds of armed men openly roll on the roads of northern Tamaulipas as machine-gun and grenade attacks erupt in Nuevo Laredo, Reynosa, and Matamoros, as well as the small border towns along La Frontera Chica between Matamoros and Laredo.

"The Little Border" is strategically important for three reasons.

One, it lies between the two strongholds of the CDG and the Zetas, Matamoros and Nuevo Laredo respectively.

Two, it lies along the lucrative drug-smuggling border into the U.S.

The third reason has nothing to do with drugs at all, but with that other precious commodity of the twenty-first century.

Energy.

La Frontera Chica contains the Burgo Basin, rich in natural gas. Mexico's national energy company, Pemex, has been exploring and drilling there for years, and there are almost 130 natural gas stations pumping now, with another 1,000 as yet to be exploited. American oil companies are eager to invest and start drilling. The cartels have long wanted to get into the energy business, and La Frontera Chica is the perfect place to do it.

So the little towns like Ciudad Mier, Camargo, and Miguel Alemán become battlefields.

It started in Mier, when fifteen pickup trucks marked with the CDG logo roared into town. *Sicarios* spilled out of the trucks and opened fire with machine guns on the town police station. Then the *sicarios* went in and hauled out six policemen, who were never seen again.

The CDG set up roadblocks, sealed off the town, and started the executions of Zeta loyalists, lining them up against a wall in the town square. The dead were decapitated, their heads set in a corner of the plaza. One young man, accused of being a Zeta lookout, screamed as his arm was sawed off before he was hanged from a tree.

The fighting went on for six days.

The Zetas struck back, and it became a battle of sniper versus sniper in Mier, Camargo, and Miguel Alemán. For all practical purposes, northern Tamaulipas could be Iraq, Gaza, or Lebanon as the rival factions fought in the streets, burned shops and houses, and evicted people from their homes.

Barricades went up.

Towns became ghost towns.

Ochoa doesn't call.

Gordo Contreras does.

Adán says to Magda, "You owe me a hundred dollars."

"I would have sworn it would have been Ochoa."

"He's too arrogant."

"You know the CDG is going to lose," Magda says, "and you don't care. You'll give them just enough help to keep the war going until both sides bleed each other out. Then you'll step in and take Tamaulipas. Matamoros, Reynosa, Laredo—all of it."

Adán shrugs. As usual, she's read both him and the situation exactly.

"Have you thought about your price?" Magda asks. "Gordo will think that you'll settle for just having an ally against Ochoa, but I think we could get more. Free use of their ports. It would be an easier route to the European market."

"You're still on that?"

"You should be, too," Magda says.

It only makes sense, Magda thinks. A kilo of cocaine sells for about $24,000 in the United States, in Europe, more than twice that. Even after cutting in European partners and paying the usual bribes, the profit margin is simply too good to ignore. If Adán doesn't want in on it, she's going to do it anyway, although his protective umbrella would be useful.

"You're talking 'Ndrangheta," Adán says, referring to the Italian Mafia that dominates the drug trade in most of Europe. "The CDG has them wrapped up."

"Because we haven't made the effort," Magda answers. "If I went there, I'm sure I could persuade them to work with us."

Not because of her undoubted sex appeal, but because it's to 'Ndrangheta's advantage to have more than one source of supply. And the European market, especially for cocaine, is rapidly expanding. Most of the heroin still comes in from Afghanistan and Pakistan via Turkey, the marijuana from North Africa via Morocco, but the CDG's cocaine monopoly could be pried open. And if she can buy at $5,500 and sell at $55,000, well, do the math.

Besides, she'd like to see Europe again, through her own eyes instead of as a rapt naïf under Jorge's tutelage. She could mix in some museums and galleries, and maybe a little shopping, with business. The fact is, she could use a vacation—only now does she understand Adán's disciplined, busy days back at Puente Grande—the thousand and one details of running a multimillion-dollar enterprise.

La Reina Amante, indeed.

"But if you don't want in, I'll do it on my own. Just get the CDG out of my way. By the way, have you knocked up your queen yet?"

"Be nice."

"I *am* being nice," Magda says.

"Not yet."

"They say that the doggie position—"

"For God's sake, Magda."

"I don't remember this puritanical attitude in Puente Grande," Magda says. "Let's fuck—I'll give you your hundred dollars in trade."

"In her house?"

"There must be other beds, if you're squeamish," Magda says. "Oh, never mind, if you're going to be such a little *househusband* about it."

He grabs her.

That night, Gordo agrees that Adán will have free use of his ports in Matamoros and Reynosa, and introductions to his drug network in Europe.

Adán agrees to do what he was going to do anyway—continue to fight the Zetas.

Eva lets herself into the condo in Bosques de las Lomas and flops down on the bed.

Her bodyguard Miguel brings in her bag. "Where do you want this?"

"On the bed," Eva says. "Where I want *you*."

Miguel smiles. He sets the bag at the foot of the bed and then lies down on top of Eva.

She unzips the fly of his tight blue jeans. "This is what I want, right here. Hurry. I thought the flight would never end."

Eva makes him hard with her hand, although it doesn't take much. She uses her other hand to unzip her own jeans and then she wriggles out of them. She's already wet and he slides into her easily.

"That's good," she says. "That's so good."

Miguel is twenty-five and strong and lithe and muscled and impatient for his own pleasure, but she likes that. She wants to be taken, and as she feels him near his climax and start to pull out, she grabs his shoulders and holds him inside her and says, "It's all right, you can come in me."

"You sure?"

"The pill."

After, she lies beside him and starts to laugh.

"What?" Miguel asks.

"Do you know what my husband would do to you," she says, "would do to that beautiful cock, if he knew where it had just been?"

"I don't want to think."

"But you're the one who's supposed to tell him these things," Eva said. "You're his spy, aren't you? Are you going to tell him?"

"No."

"Good," Eva says, "because I like this beautiful cock right where it is." She rolls over and takes him in her mouth.

"Can you go again," she asks, sitting up. "Can you?"

"If you keep doing that."

Eva keeps doing that.

She needs a baby.

Ciudad Juárez
September 2010

Pablo shoves the rest of the *torta* into his mouth and wipes the smear of avocado off his lips with the back of his hand.

The *torta*—chicken, pineapple, and avocado in a bun—used to be one of his favorite things about living in Juárez, one of the small local joys that make a city a city. Now he can barely taste it—it's just cheap food to keep the body going.

He needs it, he's tired.

Exhausted, really.

If anyone would ask how Pablo Mora is these days—not that anyone does—he'd say that he's physically, mentally, and emotionally exhausted.

And morally, maybe, if there's such a thing as moral exhaustion.

There is such a thing, he decides.

You start by being idealistic, morally strong if you will, but then the rock of your moral strength is eroded, bit by bit, until you're, well, exhausted, and you do things that you never thought you would. Or you do things that you always feared you would.

Or something like that.

You'd think that there would be a breaking point—a decisive moment—but there is no single moment or event that you can put your finger on. No, it's not that dramatic—it's the dull, monotonous process of erosion.

Maybe it was the day when twenty-five people were killed in a single afternoon. With one of the now tedious *narcomantas* hung by the bodies: ADÁN BARRERA, YOU ARE KILLING OUR SONS. NOW WE ARE GOING TO KILL YOUR FAMILIES.

Maybe it was the next slaughter at a birthday party—fourteen machine-gunned to death. Or the two decapitated bodies of the shooters found the next day.

Or maybe it's just the dull, predictable sameness of it all, that the bizarre has become the norm, like the way Juarenses now unconsciously step over bodies in the street on their way to work.

The unrelenting radio calls, which have now taken on an even more perverse twist as first the cartels took to playing *narcocorridos* over the police band to celebrate the assassination of a rival cop. So now you could tell which side had done the killing by the anthem they played.

Then, in that way that had become the strange normality, the cartels took to playing the songs *before* the killings—just to spread terror through the potential ranks of the victims.

Maybe it was the rituals that now attended the coverage of the killings. The reporters would arrive first, but if the narcos were waiting around for the victim to die, the reporters had to hang back. If the victim was dead, the narcos would either give the okay to cover the story and take photos, or tell them to *píntate*—beat it. Or sometimes the killers would leave a note for reporters on the corpse, telling them what they could write and what they couldn't.

The next on the scene would be the funeral home directors, there to drum up business, dressed in black and looking for all the world like ravens at a roadkill.

Then the police might arrive, depending on the identity of the victim, and then the EMTs, who would only come now once they knew that the police were already there. More than once, Pablo had sat with the EMTs as the killers kept them away at gunpoint until the victim bled out. Then the narcos would wave them in with the words, "Come and get him." Other times, the narcos would get on the EMT radio frequency and simply order the medics not to come to the aid of certain victims.

Maybe it was the sorry fact that he could no longer feel anything when he watched the wife, the mother, the sister, the child, scream and weep. Or that he no longer felt shock or even revulsion at the shattered or dismembered or decapitated bodies. Heads and limbs scattered around his city like so much offal, dogs in the rougher *colonias* slinking away with bloody jowls and guilty looks.

Six bodies . . .

Four bodies . . .

Ten bodies . . .

The army arrested four La Línea members who confessed to a combined tally of 211 murders.

The "New Police," carefully vetted and polygraphed, were mustered in Juárez to great fanfare. One of them—a policewoman—was shot to death on a bus as she rode to her first day of work.

Eleven more people were killed the next day.

Eight the day after.

Everything apparently was going so well in Chihuahua that its state attorney general was promoted to be Mexico's new federal drug czar.

Erosion, Pablo thinks.

Erosion of morality.

Erosion of the soul.

It brings up the question, why?

Not in any grand existential sense—Pablo is beyond thinking he'll get an answer to those questions—but as a practical matter.

After all, the war is supposed to be over.

That's what the politicos have told us—their operations have been so successful that they withdrew the army from the city and handed it over to the "New Police." So if the war is over, why does the killing continue?

Even when you look at the more realistic explanation as to why the war is over—that the Sinaloa cartel won and now controls the Juárez plaza, why does the slaughter continue unabated? Why is there no peace dividend of a day without killing?

And why, again, are the victims mostly the little guys—the poor, the street dealers, the beggars, the driftwood?

Pablo knows the answer.

He just hates what it is.

It has to do not with the cross-border drug trade, but with the internal market. It's not good enough to just blame the U.S. market anymore. The sale of drugs in Juárez is small compared with the volume that goes across the border, but it's still significant.

Most of the killing now is to control the domestic market, especially in heroin and cocaine. It isn't that Barrera wants or needs the money—chump change to him—it's that he can't let the remnants of the Juárez cartel have it. If they're allowed to still dominate the sale of drugs in El Centro, La Cima, and the other *colonias*, the money would be a source of power that might fuel a comeback.

Barrera isn't going to allow that.

When he has his foot on your throat, he isn't going to lift it.

So the killing now is a mopping-up operation.

And the little guy, the nickel-bag street *puchador,* is caught in a vise between Los Aztecas and Sinaloa—if he sells for one, the other kills him. The tiny drug stands—the *picaderos*—are caught in the same vise. Even the addicts are trapped—buy from a Sinaloan and the Juarenses kill you, buy from a Juarense and the Nueva Gente wipe you out. The kids on the corners who are lookouts, the winos and the homeless, the beggars and the buskers, are all there to be killed just in case they're helping the other side.

And the cops? They don't give a fuck, Pablo thinks. Since when has anyone cared about these losers? No, the cops, the pols, the businessmen see it as almost an opportunity to sweep the streets of undesirables and tote it up to the "cartel wars."

The mainstream media love it—they draw neat battle lines with colored zones of which cartel controls which plaza, which *colonia.* It's easier that way, nice and neat and followable—you can even root for one side or the other—but it's bullshit, at least in Juárez.

The truth is that there are no neat lines anymore.

When Barrera, the feds, and the army destroyed La Línea and Los Aztecas, they also destroyed any control over the hundreds of *cartelitos,* the small street gangs in the city, gangs who still are going to fight to sell drugs and practice small-time extortion, extracting the *cuota* from shopkeepers, bus drivers, cabbies, or even just women, children, and the old for the right to walk down the street.

Half the people out there doing the killing now are low-level kids who don't even know which cartel they're killing for. They just get an order from a boss one level up and they follow that order if they want to live. That boss might be Juárez, Azteca, Sinaloa, even Zeta. He might be one thing one day and another thing the next.

The killings might not even be drug-related—the violent chaos covers up murders that might come from an old feud, a jealousy, a lovers' triangle, an unpaid *cuota,* anything.

So they go out and kill, and then they are killed, and then they retaliate, and the killing has a momentum of its own and the grim truth is that there are no generals in command rooms moving colored pins around a map as they direct a grand strategy.

The fact is that *los chacalosos*—the big bosses—lost control.

They couldn't stop it now if they wanted, and Barrera doesn't care. He has his bridges and the violence is wiping the local gangs off the street. So to hell with the city—he'd be just as happy if there was nothing left *except* his damn bridges.

Wouldn't care if the city dies.

Which it is.

So it's chaos here now, and the people who pay the price for it are the people who always do, and who can least afford it—the poor, the powerless, the ones who can't lock themselves up in gated communities, or commute from El Paso.

No one is in charge.

The killing now commands the killing, because no one knows anything else to do. That's the truth that Pablo would like to tell. Like to scream to the country, scream to the U.S., scream to the world.

But he can't.

They won't let him.

Yesterday morning the man who brought Pablo his envelope brought him an order as well.

"The attack on La Médica Hermosa," he said.

"That was months ago." Pablo felt a surge of fear.

"You're going to write that the Zetas were behind it."

"I don't know that," Pablo said. He heard his voice quivering.

"You do know that," the man said. "I just told you that."

He knows why they care. Giorgio's photo essay of Marisol Cisneros's wounds had caused a major outcry across the country, maybe even more than the attack itself. And now he knows who's giving him the money—the Sinaloans, the New People.

Pablo summoned up all his nerve. "Do you have proof?"

"The money in your bank account," the man said, "is all the proof you need."

"I haven't spent it," Pablo says. "I'll give it back."

"What do you think this is?" the man asks. "Marbles? A kid's game? You took the money—there's no 'giving back.' I don't care if you stuck it up your ass. I don't care if you stuck it up your *friend's* ass—the Zetas did it, that's the truth. You want to write the truth, don't you?"

"Yes."

He pushes Pablo up against the wall. "Let me ask you something. Your friends, the people you work with. Do you love them?"

"Yes. Yes, I do."

"If you do," the man said, "then do the right thing here."

The man let him go and walked away.

Pablo stood there, trembling. His legs felt like they were going to give out under him. He walked to the nearest bar and had a whiskey, then another, his mind whirling.

What am I going to do? he asked himself.

What am I going to do?

When Pablo went in to file the story, saying that he had it from unidentified sources on deep background that the Zetas were responsible for the attacks on the Chihuahua women, Óscar called him into the office.

"Unidentified sources?" El Búho asked.

Pablo nodded.

"Who are they? Your Azteca connections?"

"Yeah."

Óscar tapped his cane on the floor. "We need more than that. Go out and get it."

Ramón found *him* that night, drinking beer at Fred's. The Azteca slid up to the bar beside him. "I don't have a lot of time here, so I'll get right to it. You working on a story about those shootings in the valley?"

"Maybe."

"Don't get fucking cute with me," Ramón snapped. "I'm here to tell you, you write anything, you write that those Sinaloan cocksuckers did it."

"I heard differently."

"Yeah? What did you hear? *What did you hear,* 'mano?"

"Zetas."

"Who told you that?"

Pablo shook his head.

"You're taking Sinaloa money," Ramón said, "okay. Nobody gave a shit. Until now. Now we give a very big shit."

"'We'? You're working for the Zetas now?"

"The Zs are taking over," Ramón said. "We're all in the Z Company now. You, too."

Ramón grabbed him by the shoulder. "They *sent* me, 'mano. They sent me to tell you that you write what they want. If I have to come see you again, it won't be to talk. Don't make me do that, 'Blo. Please."

Ramón tossed a few bills on the bar and walked out.

Pablo felt like he could piss himself.

He was trapped—caught between the Sinaloa cartel and the Zetas. He left the bar and found Ana and Giorgio at the Kentucky.

For a man who'd just had a professional triumph, Giorgio was uncharacteristically subdued. Then again, seeing Marisol's wounds was heartbreaking. Such a beautiful woman, such a good person, disfigured and in pain. So it was tasteful of Giorgio not to celebrate, Pablo thought.

Maybe he has some sensitivity after all.

"You're quiet tonight," Ana said to Pablo.

"Just tired."

"That's it?"

"That's it."

They had a few drinks, then Giorgio left to go to El Paso to sleep with his current girlfriend, an American sociologist who was doing her doctoral dissertation on "the phenomenon of violence in Ciudad Juárez."

"Is that what we are?" Ana asked. "A phenomenon?"

"Apparently," Giorgio answered.

"Can you use photographs in a dissertation?"

"I'm sort of deep background," Giorgio answered. "See you tomorrow."

Pablo didn't sleep that night. There seemed to be no way out of the trap he was in. When he went into the office, Óscar asked him if he'd made any progress on the story. Pablo was evasive, and when he went out to his car there was a note on the seat—"Where is our story? Don't fuck with us, *cabrón*."

I'm shrinking with my city, Pablo thinks as he bunches up the *torta* wrapper and tosses it on the floor of the car. The once thriving *mercado* is almost deserted because the tourists don't come anymore; one famous bar or club after another has closed; even the Mariscal, the red-light district just by the Santa Fe Bridge, has been shut down because men won't take the risk of going, even for whores.

Now he forces himself to get out of the car for yet another corpse. Just one more *malandro*, one more piece of garbage swept up in *la limpieza*.

The cleansing.

Usually Giorgio beats him to the scene, but he's probably still in bed with the North American.

Then he spots Giorgio.

It's Pablo who tells Ana.

He goes into the city room, holds her tight, and tells her, and she screams and her knees buckle and she falls into him and he almost tells her. *It's my fault. It's my fault, if I had said something, told him, maybe . . .*

But you didn't, Pablo thinks.

And you still don't.

Because you're a coward.

And because you're so ashamed.

Óscar writes an editorial about Giorgio's murder, a classic El Búho piece full of moral outrage and grief mixed with erudition.

Giorgio's funeral is a horror show.

The whole Juárez journalist community is there, and Cisneros and Keller. The service at the cemetery goes about as usual, then Pablo notices a car parked just outside the gates.

He walks over.

A severed head, its mouth fixed in a macabre grin, is set on its hood.

With Óscar's editorial pinned to its neck.

There's a subdued gathering at Ana's that night. Pablo, Óscar, Marisol, and her North American. A few others. A shrunken group, Pablo thinks, with our shrunken souls.

People drink sadly, sullenly.

A few attempts are made to tell funny stories about Giorgio, but the effort falls flat.

The gathering breaks up early. Marisol, looking tired and in pain, says that she has to be getting back to Valverde, and the others quickly use the opportunity to make their escapes.

When people were gone, Ana, in her cups, says, "Make love to me. Take me to bed."

"Ana."

"Just fuck me, Pablo."

Their lovemaking is angry and afterward she sobs.

The day after Giorgio's funeral, Óscar shows Pablo and Ana an editorial he intends to publish.

"*Señores* of the organizations disputing the plaza of Ciudad Juárez," he reads, "we would like to bring to your attention that we are reporters, not fortune-tellers. Thus, we would like you to explain what is it that you want from us? What do you want us to publish or refrain from publishing? You are, at present, the de facto authorities in this city, due to the fact that the legally established rulers have not been able to do anything to keep our colleagues from falling, despite our repeated demands that they do so. And it is for this reason that, faced with this unquestionable reality, we are forced to pose this question, because what we least want is for another of our colleagues to fall victim.

"This is not a surrender on our part, but an offer of a truce. We need to know, at least, what the rules are, for even in a war, there are rules."

The editorial itself makes headlines internationally. It resonates among the journalistic community in Mexico because so many journalists have been murdered in Chihuahua, Tamaulipas, Nuevo León, and Michoacán.

The Zetas, especially, have established a virtual silence born of terror in the areas that they control, with media in Nuevo Laredo and Reynosa having stopped running stories on the narcotics trade at all, and average people in the street afraid even to speak their names, referring to them instead as "the last letter."

The paper receives hundreds of letters and e-mails.

No answer, however, comes from the cartels.

No rules, no stated expectations.

Pablo knows what the expectations are; he doesn't need a rulebook to know the rules: Write what we tell you, and only what we tell you, or we'll kill you. Take the *sobre*, or we'll kill you. Sell us your soul, or we'll kill you.

It's a bitter lesson—you think you can rent your soul, but it's always a sale, and all sales are final.

That night, the envelope man Pablo finds him on the street.

"Tomorrow, *pendejo*, we see that story or—" He smiles, sticks his two fingers out like a gun, and squeezes the "trigger."

Ana's in bed when Pablo gets back. He doesn't want to wake her so he sleeps on the couch. Or tries to, without a lot of success. He thinks of writing Mateo a goodbye letter, but decides that's too melodramatic.

He decides to write the Sinaloa article.

Then the Zeta one.

Then neither.

In the morning, he decides, I'll go into the office and hand Óscar my resignation.

Then I'll cross the bridge.

In the morning Pablo tries to find a way to tell Ana what he's going to do.

But he can't find the words.

Or, face it, he tells himself, the courage.

Maybe that's the way, though, Pablo thinks. Just tell her that you're afraid, that you don't want to end up like Armando or Giorgio. She'll think less of you, but she won't hate you the way she will if she knows you took money.

Just tell her that you're afraid.

She'll believe that.

Five times he tries to open his mouth, but nothing comes out. He tries again as they drive to the office together. He feels like he's on a conveyor belt headed inexorably for the blades of an abattoir, but can't yell to stop it.

They get to the office and park the car, cross the street to get a coffee.

Pablo can picture the crushed, disappointed look on El Búho's face.

He thought about simply typing up his resignation and e-mailing it, but decided that would be too cowardly. Óscar deserves a face-to-face explanation, and an apology, and somehow Pablo feels that he deserves it, too. Deserves to look into Óscar's hurt eyes and remember his expression. Deserves to hear Óscar's disappointed words and have them replay in his head. Deserves to walk out of the office in shame, clean out his desk, feel the stares on his back, and then (try to) explain things to Ana.

And then what? he thinks as he sips his café con leche and looks across the street at the office building that's been the only professional home he's ever known. You're done in journalism—no decent paper will hire you. The best you can hope for is to freelance for *la nota roja*, circling the city like a vulture, picking at its bones.

A creature that makes its living from corpses.

Can't do it, he thinks.

Can't and won't.

Then again, you might not have the chance—you might *be* one of those corpses, if the narcos get angry that they've wasted their money on you and decide to do something about it. Face it, there's no future for you in journalism and there's no future for you in Juárez.

Or anywhere in Mexico, for that matter.

You're going to have to cross the bridge.

Become a *pocho*.

"You're particularly uncommunicative this morning," Ana says.

"Ummm."

"That's more like it."

He sets his cup down and gets up. "I'm going in."

"I'll go with you."

He crosses the street and shows his ID badge to the security officers at the front door, who know him anyway. Getting into the elevator, he acknowledges that this might be the last time and almost changes his mind, but knows he can't.

He has to say something now, before he goes into Óscar's office.

"Ana—"

"What?"

"I—"

Óscar appears in the doorway and announces that he wants to see the entire reportorial staff in the conference room immediately.

"I am no longer willing to risk the lives of the people for whom I am professionally and personally responsible," he says when they've assembled, "to report upon a situation that even the best of journalists—and that's what you are—cannot affect. We will no longer report on the drug situation."

Ana objects. Red in the face, almost tearful, she asks, "We're just going to give in to them? Knuckle under? Allow them to intimidate us?"

Óscar has tears in his eyes as well. His cane taps on the floor and his voice quivers as he answers, "I don't feel that I have a viable choice, Ana."

"But how is this going to work?" Pablo asks. "Say there's a murder. We just don't report it?"

"You report the fact of an apparent homicide," Óscar says, "but leave it at that. You make no connection to the drug situation."

"That's absurd," Ana says.

"I agree," Óscar answers. "Our civic life, however, has become an absurdity. This is not a suggestion, this is an instruction. I will wield a heavy editorial pen and simply delete anything you write that might jeopardize the safety of anyone on this paper. Do you understand?"

"I understand that it's the death of a great newspaper," Ana says.

"Which I will cheerfully bury," Óscar says, "before I will bury another one of you. I will announce our new policy in tomorrow's edition so that the narcos will be notified."

"What about Giorgio?" Ana presses.

El Búho raises an eyebrow.

"Are we going to investigate it?" Ana asks. "Or just let it go?"

Because the police *have* let it go, Pablo thinks. Of the over five thousand murders in Juárez since the cartel war began, not a single one has resulted in a conviction. They all know the reality—no one has investigated Giorgio's murder, and no one is going to. And now Óscar is telling them that they're not going to, either.

This man, this hero, who once took a narco gun blast and wouldn't let it stop him, now leans on his cane, and looks tired and old, and says with his silence that he, and they, have been silenced.

Not Ana.

They're drinking at Oxido that night, one of the clubs still open in the PRONAF Zone, and she has a couple more than she usually does.

"I might as well have taken the money," she says.

"What do you mean?" Pablo asks.

"When the narcos offered me a bribe," Ana says, "I should have taken it. They're our bosses now, right? So they should pay us."

Pablo drains his beer.

"I'm not letting it go," Ana says. "They killed our friend and our colleague and I'm not letting it go."

"Ana, you heard Óscar. What are you going to do?"

"Push," Ana said. "Push the authorities until they do something about it."

"Like they did something about Jimena's murder?" Pablo asks. "Like they did something about the attack on you and Marisol? How about those two women up in the valley? Or the dozens of murders we see every week? Are those the authorities you're going to?"

"I'll shame them," Ana says.

"Ana, they're shameless."

He's scared. If she pushes on this, she could be next.

"Well, I'm not," Ana mutters. "I'm not shameless."

"Óscar won't print what you write."

"I know," Ana says.

A little while later Pablo pours Ana into a taxi and takes her home. Puts her to bed and then he goes out again.

Pablo is not by nature heroic.

He knows this about himself and he's okay with it. But tonight he goes back out because he has to do something to prevent Ana from running headlong off the edge of the cliff. If I can get an answer, he thinks, about who killed Giorgio and why, maybe I can get the story published in a North American paper under a phony byline. Maybe that would satisfy Ana, or even pressure the police to do something about it.

Nor does Pablo look particularly heroic, and he knows that, too. He wears a black, somewhat soiled T-shirt under a black, somewhat soiled untucked shirt with a light windbreaker and a red Los Indios ball cap, and he's aware that his stomach hangs over his belt.

Now he rings Ramón's doorbell. It takes a few minutes, then some lights come on and the door cracks open behind the security chain.

"Ramón, it's me."

The door opens and Ramón has a pistol pointed at Pablo's face. "*Mierdito,* '*mano,* what the fuck?"

"I have to talk to you."

Ramón lets him in. "Don't wake up the kids, okay?"

They walk into the kitchen. The house is a mini McMansion out in the new suburbs and looks like the generic home of any midlevel manager.

"I haven't seen our fucking story, Pablo," Ramón says.

Pablo tells him about Óscar's decision.

"I guess you're off the hook, then," Ramón says. "That's good—spares us both a lot of pain."

"Why was Giorgio Valencia killed?"

"Fuck, you just got *out* of the hot water—"

"Why?"

"He took the wrong pictures."

"Which wrong pictures?"

"That Cisneros *chocha,*" Ramón says. "You tapping that, Pablo? You know her, right? Jesus shit, I would like to bang that, I mean before she got, you know, fucked up. Don't look a gift horse in the mouth, Pablo, it could have been you."

"Why wasn't it?" Pablo asks.

"You weren't on the Zs' payroll."

Pablo feels his head spinning. "What are you saying?"

"Your boy Giorgio was *sucio,*" Ramón says. "Dirty. Like you. Only he was taking the Zs' money and then he fucked them by doing those pictures of the broad showing off her scars. You want to see *my* scars, 'Blo? I have some beauties."

"You have names? Who did it?"

"Fuck, you want to get me killed with you?" Ramón asks. Then he shuts up because he hears Karla coming down the stairs. His wife comes into the kitchen and looks blearily at Pablo.

"Hi, Pablo."

"Hello, Karla. Nice to see you."

"Nice to see you." She looks curiously at Ramón.

"Go back to bed, baby," Ramón says. "I'll be back up in a few minutes."

"Come by sometime for dinner," Karla says to Pablo.

"I will."

She walks back upstairs.

"Names?" Ramón asks. "*Names?* Grow up. What the fuck difference does it make? They're all the same cat. I'm telling you, Pablo, leave this the fuck alone. Leave it all the fuck alone. Me, I've decided to get out of here. Karla's pregnant again, I got some money set aside on *el otro lado*. A few little things to take care of and then I'm out of here. You should do the same."

"I'm a Juarense."

"Yeah, that's great," Ramón says. "Except there ain't no more Juárez. The Juárez we knew is gone."

When Pablo gets back to Ana's she's still up. "Where did you go?"

"We're not married, Ana."

"I just asked."

"Ana, leave this thing with Giorgio alone, okay?"

"What do you know about it?"

"Just leave it be." It will only break your heart, if it doesn't get you killed first.

"Pablo, what do you know?"

"I know that Sinatra's not coming back."

"What does that mean?"

He doesn't answer.

There are no answers.

Victoria, Tamaulipas
October 2010

Don Pedro Alejo de Castillo hears a commotion outside his hacienda and goes to see what is happening.

His cook, Lupe, looks terrified, and Don Pedro doesn't like people upsetting Lupe. She's been with him for over thirty years, the only woman in his household since his wife, Dorotea, passed away six years ago.

Don Pedro is seventy-seven, still tall and straight-spined. He goes to the door to see men driving around the front of the house in trucks and SUVs, firing AK-47s and AR-15s into the air, honking their horns and shouting obscenities.

Don Pedro doesn't like that either.

Only a *malandro* uses obscenity in front of a woman.

Three of the men get out of an SUV and walk up to his front porch. They're dressed like *vaqueros,* but he sees right away that they've never worked a day in their lives on a ranch.

His has five hundred acres, not large by local standards, but perfectly suited to him. And it sits on the edge of a beautiful lake with ducks and geese and good fishing. He goes out there just before dawn most mornings.

"Are you Alejo de Castillo?" one of the men demands.

Rudely.

"I am Don Pedro Alejo de Castillo, yes."

"This is your ranch?"

"Yes."

"We are the Zetas," the man says, as if it's supposed to frighten him.

It doesn't.

Don Pedro has a vague notion that the Zetas are some sort of drug gang that has been causing trouble in the cities, but he is not frightened. He has little to do with the cities, and less to do with drugs.

"What do you want?" he asks.

"We are confiscating this property," the man says.

"I don't think so, no."

"Old man, we're not asking you. We're telling you. You have until tonight to leave, or we'll kill you."

"Get off my land."

"We'll be back."

"I'll be waiting."

Don Pedro has an aristocratic manner and bearing, but he is not an aristocrat. His father ran a sawmill, and Pedro grew up working very hard. He turned the one sawmill into two, then five, then twelve, and eventually became a rich man. Don Pedro didn't inherit this ranch, he earned it the same way he earned the "Don," from his own hard work.

And he is not going to give it to anyone.

He built the two-story hacienda himself, with the help of local men, and lovingly supervised each detail. The walls are of thick, mud-colored adobe, with deep-set windows. The front door, of heavy wood, is shaded by a deep portal supported by hand-carved *zapatas* from his own sawmills.

Inside, large log roof beams, called *vigas*, stretch across the large, white-washed living room, jointed to the walls with hand-carved corbel brackets. Thin *latillas* are laid crosshatched across the ceiling. The floors are polished terra-cotta tiles, with Indian carpets laid out. A clay fireplace sits in one corner.

The house is beautiful, understated, and dignified.

Don Pedro is impeccably dressed, as always. Dorotea always dressed well, like a lady, and he would never let her down by dressing as anything other than a gentleman. When he goes to put flowers on her grave, on consecrated ground on the little knoll overlooking her beloved lake, he wears a suit and a tie.

Today he wears a tweed shooting jacket, knit tie, khaki trousers, and hunting boots. Don Pedro is a founding member of the Manuel Silva Hunting and Fishing Club and the ranch will go to the club when he dies, on the stipulation that Lupe and Tomás, who has worked for him for thirty-eight years, can live their lives out here.

He has no children to leave his land to. When Dorotea tried to apologize to him once for not being able to give him children, he put his finger to her lips and said, "You are the sunrise of my life."

Now Lupe is crying.

She must have heard everything, and Don Pedro doesn't like this, because he does not like to see a woman cry, and it makes him have even less respect for these "Zetas," because gentlemen do not conduct business in front of women.

"I think," Don Pedro says, "that you should go into town so you can spend the weekend with your grandchildren."

"Don Pedro—"

"Don't cry. Everything will be all right."

"But—"

"I have that beautiful duck that you made me last night," Don Pedro says. "I can warm that up for dinner. Go pack a few things, now."

He finds Tomás in the barn, cleaning the heads on the new John Deere tractor that they are both so proud of.

"Who were those men?" Tomás asks.

"Some *malandros*. Idiots." He tells Tomás to take Lupe into Victoria and to stay there himself, in the hotel where Don Pedro has an account.

"I'm staying with you," Tomás says. His hair has gone silver, and his strong hands are twisted with arthritis. "I can shoot."

"I know you can." He must also have heard everything, Don Pedro thinks. But pigeons and ducks are not men. Not even deer are men. "I need you to take care of the others. I'm sending them, too."

"You will be alone, Don Pedro."

That is the idea, Don Pedro thinks. "An old man needs a little solitude from time to time."

"I won't leave you," Tomás says. "I have served you for thirty-eight years—"

"So now is not the time to disobey me," Don Pedro says. But he knows he has to save this good man's face, preserve his pride. "You will take my shotgun. The Beretta, the good one. I am counting on you to see that everyone gets safely to town. Go on now, wash up. It is not a drive to make at night."

He goes into his study and sits in the old, cracked leather chair and reads a book, his habit in the afternoon. Today it is Quevedo's *The Swindler*. *"I come from Segovia; my father was called Clemente Pablo . . ."*

Don Pedro falls asleep reading.

He wakes up when Tomás comes in and says that they are ready to leave. Don Pedro walks outside to see Lupe in the front seat of the old International Harvester, gripping her small suitcase on her lap, and Paola and Esteban in the back.

They are all crying.

Esteban is a young fool, a nineteen-year-old who is as lazy as all nineteen-year-olds but still worth a hundred of these Zetas. He takes good care of the horses and will be a good man someday.

Paola is a lovely young creature, a dismally hopeless maid who should get married to a lovestruck young man and have beautiful children.

None of these beloved people should be here tonight.

"Have a good weekend and behave yourselves," he says to them. "I will see you first thing on Monday morning, and don't be late."

Paola says, "Don Pedro—"

"Get going now. I will see you soon."

He watches the car rumble down the old road.

When they are gone past the turning, he walks down to the lake. How Dorotea loved this lake. He remembers lying down with her in a bed of wild lilacs and the scent that the flowers crushed under her made.

The priest who married them rode across the Río Bravo on the back of a donkey, and fell off in the river and so was an hour late, and wet and grumpy as an old hen, but it didn't matter.

Don Pedro watches the sun set over the lake.

Watches the ducks swim into the thick green brush at the edge.

Then he walks back to the house.

He unlocks the gun room and carefully selects a .30-40 Krag, a Mannlicher-Schönauer, the Winchester 70, the Winchester 74, and the Savage 99.

Every fine rifle brings a memory with it.

The Savage brings to mind that fine trip to Montana with Julio and Teddy, old friends who have since passed on, and amber whiskeys by the campfire to ward off the chill of night.

The Winchesters recall long slogs in Durango.

The Mannlicher—that was the trip to Kenya and Tanganyika and long slow afternoons under canvas with Dorotea, and her sitting outside the tent reading or painting and the old African cook who made goat better than they do in Mexico.

The Krag . . . The Krag was a birthday gift from Dorotea, and she was so pleased that he was so pleased . . .

Don Pedro takes each rifle and leans it by one of the windows cut into the thick adobe walls. Then he sets a box of ammunition by each rifle.

He heats the leftover duck and sits down with it and a bottle of strong red wine and eats contentedly. He shot the duck himself, as he shoots the pigeon that Lupe makes into such a fine meal with wild rice.

After dinner he goes upstairs and takes a long bath, scrubbing his skin to a pink glow, and then shaves slowly and carefully and trims his pencil mustache because it is important that he look his best for Dorotea.

He puts on a fresh white shirt with French sleeves and the cuff links that Dorotea gave him on their tenth anniversary, and then slips on a tweed shooting jacket, wool trousers, and a silk tie in a rich burgundy color that she particularly favored.

Satisfied with his appearance in the mirror, he goes back downstairs and pours himself two fingers of single-malt scotch and sips it as he reads more of Quevedo and falls asleep again in his chair.

Honking horns, shouts, and laughter wake him up, and he looks at the clock on the mantel. It's a little after four in the morning, just a little earlier than he usually rises. He walks to the window by the Savage and looks out. The idiots are driving around in circles like Indians in a bad North American western film, whooping and shooting into the air and shouting more of their profanity.

They finally stop, and the man who came to his door earlier stands up in the roof hatch of his vehicle and yells, "Alejo de Castillo, you son of a—"

Don Pedro's shot hits him in the forehead.

Don Pedro moves to the next window.

The cars and trucks have stopped and men are jumping out. Don Pedro aims at one who is running, remembers to lead him less than one would a deer, and brings him down with a single shot from the Krag. Moving to the next window, he looks back to see bullets coming through the window that he just vacated.

These idiots apparently believe that everyone is as idiotic as they are.

He lifts the Mannlicher to his shoulder and picks out a Zeta who seems to be second in charge and shoots the man between the eyes, and then moves to the next window.

One of the idiots has the brains to get down, and is slithering like a snake toward the front door. Don Pedro has never shot a snake with a rifle before—he has shot many rattlesnakes with a pistol—but the principle is the same and he dispatches him with a shot from the Winchester 70 as he sees two more Zetas rush the door.

He keeps the Winchester 70, picks up the 74, and stands ten feet away from the door, a rifle in each hand.

There is a small blast, the door swings open, and Don Pedro fires both rifles, hitting both men in the stomach and gutting them.

They writhe on the front porch, screaming in agony, bleeding all over the wood, which is going to have to be sand-stoned now, which will annoy lazy Esteban to no end and require supervision.

Don Pedro goes back to the first window and sees the Zetas run back and take cover behind their vehicles.

He hears them talk, and then he sees the tubes come out and he knows that they're grenade launchers, which is annoying because now he knows that there will be no house for Lupe to move back into. But he has left a will with Armando Sifuentes in town, with specific instructions as to what to do if there were a fire, and he is confident that the lawyer will take care of it.

Don Pedro also knows that he will not be there himself to see the house rebuilt and he feels a little sad, but mostly he feels great joy because he will be with Dorotea soon and he's glad that he shaved.

When the fire starts, he smells not ash but wild lilacs.

When Keller and the FES unit get there, Don Pedro's hacienda is a smoking ruin, four corpses lie in front of the house, and two wounded Zetas in fetal positions twitch on the front porch.

Don Pedro's man, Tomás, had called the marine post in Monterrey and they'd choppered there as soon as they could, and Keller is dismayed to see that they're too late.

Tomás finds Don Pedro's body and kneels by it weeping.

With a little prodding, literally, the wounded Zetas tell the story of what happened. Keller learns that neither of them was involved in the attack on Marisol, but that one of the dead men was.

I owe you one, Don Pedro, Keller thinks.

He must have been a hell of a man. The Zetas were so afraid of him they left behind their dead and wouldn't even go up to the shell of the house to retrieve their wounded.

Keller knows that they'll never come back.

"Where are they now?" one of the marines asks.

The wounded Zeta doesn't want to give it up. "I took an oath."

"You took an oath never to leave a wounded comrade behind, too," Keller says. "What happened to that? You think they'll honor their promise to take care of your families? Those days are over. Tell us where they went and we'll get you to a hospital. I'm not saying you'll make it, but you won't die in agony."

"We have morphine," one of the FES says.

The other wounded Zeta groans and says, "They're in a camp. An hour north of here. Outside San Fernando."

The marine picks up one of Don Pedro's Winchesters and puts two shots into each Zeta's head.

Morphine.

"Don Pedro killed six of them," the marine says to Keller.

"He was a fine man," Tomás says. "You should have known him."

I wish I had, Keller thinks.

Mexico is a country that produces legends larger than life, and Keller knows that songs will be sung about Don Pedro Alejo de Castillo—not trashy *narcocorridas,* but a genuine *corrida.*

A song for a hero.

Keller wakes up sweaty.

With Marisol looking at him.

He knows that she's not stupid. She reads the news, watches television, she has an idea as to what he's been doing and where he goes when he's not with her. They don't talk about it, that's not their arrangement, but he knows that she's aware.

Keller came back a mess—filthy, exhausted, stressed.

And quiet.

What was there to talk about?

She has sorrows of her own, Keller thought. Constant pain, constant worry, constant fear, whether she wants to admit it or not. The last thing she needs is to play nursemaid to some basket case.

So he keeps it to himself.

Now Marisol looks at him and says, "I can turn the air conditioner up."

"It's okay."

He gets out of bed and showers.

You're going to have dreams like that, he tells himself. You just are. He still dreams about the El Sauzal killings, and that was thirteen years ago. Nineteen people lined up and machine-gunned to death.

It was a watershed moment then.

An unimaginable horror.

Now it's an average day's body count that would barely make the news. Even Juárez's Channel 44, "the Agony Station," has cut down on its lurid coverage. You can turn off the television, Keller thinks, but you can't turn off your brain, especially when you're sleeping. So the dreams are going to come and they're probably always going to come and you're just going to have to accept that.

Marisol has breakfast ready when he comes out.

He wishes she wouldn't do that, doesn't want her to exert herself, but she tells him to stop babying her. When he sits down at the table she asks, "Do you think you should see someone?"

"What do you mean?"

"You know what I mean," she says, gently sitting down and propping the cane against the table. "I don't want to be your mother or your therapist, so you need to see someone."

"I'm fine."

"No you're not," she says.

"Don't start."

"Post-traumatic stress—"

"That's starting."

"Sorry."

He digs into the grapefruit, gives up, and takes it to the sink.

A counselor? A therapist? A shrink? What could I say—everything that's on my mind is classified. And what would I say if I could?

Hey, I tortured someone the other day—hooked him up to a battery until he told me all the horrible things they did. Oh yeah, and that time I turned my back so a colleague could execute a prisoner, that kind of bothers me. There's the guy I shot in a whorehouse, another outside a hospital after I kidnapped his elderly mother, and oh, and then there was this mass grave . . .

An American drone located the Zeta camp after Don Pedro's murder.

It's top secret that the U.S. is sending drones over Mexico to help track the narcos. The White House knows it, Keller knows it, Taylor knows, Orduña knows it.

The FES hit the camp, on an old ranch, just before dawn.

The grave was bulldozed out of the red earth, and the bodies, now weeks old by Keller's estimation, were carelessly tossed in.

A Zeta prisoner gave up the story.

The Zetas stopped a bus on Route 1 outside of San Fernando. Most of the passengers were Central American immigrants on their way to the United States. The Zetas came on board and went through the passengers' cell phones to see if they had called any Matamoros numbers. They suspected that the bus was transporting Central American recruits to the Gulf cartel.

Just to make sure, they shot them all.

Ochoa gave the order. Forty carried it out.

It took over two days to recover all the bodies and separate them into discrete skeletal remains.

Even then, they got only an approximate count.

Fifty-eight men, fourteen women.

The marines didn't wait for the count, but stayed on the trail. Over the next three days, they hit five ranches that the prisoner gave up and killed twenty-seven Zetas.

The three captured Zetas died of their wounds.

"Post-traumatic stress disorder"? Keller thinks now.

There's nothing "post" about it. Nothing is over, nothing is in the past.

We live with this shit every day. And "disorder"? It would be a disorder if we *weren't* stressed.

Marisol is an internist, not a psychologist, he grumbles.

So I break out in a sweat.

I'm a little quiet.

I drink a little more than I should.

I look over my shoulder from time to time.

There's nothing crazy about that—that's *sane,* given the circumstances.

It's amazing, Keller thinks, the human capacity—perhaps born of need—to establish a sense of normalcy in the most abnormal conditions. They live in a virtual war zone, under a constant state of threat, and yet they've evolved into doing the little routines that make up a normal life.

They cook dinner, albeit with a pistol on the hip or within easy reach. They sit down and talk about the day's events, even if those events include the body count in Juárez. They watch television and sometimes doze off, with anti-grenade screens on the windows and the doors triple-bolted.

More evenings than not, Erika comes over, and neither Keller nor Marisol has to point out the obvious to each other—that this is as close as Marisol will ever come to having a daughter. Erika never arrives without some kind of offering—cans of soup, some fruit, a flower, a DVD. Lately she's taken to sleeping over in the small spare room, so she's often there when Keller gets up in the morning.

Now Marisol makes a simple steak with rice, Erika contributes a salad, and Keller stopped off for two bottles of decent red on his way back. They eat, drink wine, and then settle in to watch *Modern Family* on a station from El Paso.

Erika is totally into the show and Keller realizes that she's almost five years younger than his own daughter. Five years younger than Cassie and she's laid her life on the line no less than if she'd volunteered for Iraq or Afghanistan.

No—more so, far more so.

Here she's outgunned and outnumbered. She slouches on the sofa in her jeans and sweatshirt, her AR-15 propped against the wall by the door, laughs and looks to Marisol for confirmation that what she's laughing at is really funny.

It's a major case of hero worship, Erika for Marisol.

Marisol knows it.

"Do you think," she asked Keller a few weeks ago, "I should offer her a makeover?"

"A what?"

"A makeover," Marisol said impatiently. "You know, like on the television. Hair, makeup, clothes . . ."

"Why not?" Keller asked, still unsure of exactly what she was talking about.

"I don't know, it might offend her," Marisol answered. "She's a pretty girl, but the clothes and the hair—she's such a *cejona*, a tomboy. A little of the right makeup, if she could lose ten pounds . . . the boys would come running."

Keller had assumed that Erika was gay.

"No," Marisol said. "In fact, she has a crush on this EMT in Juárez. Very cute guy. Nice guy. Sweet."

"I'm sure coming from you, any suggestions would be welcome."

"I don't know, I might bring it up," Marisol said. "I thought one day we could go into El Paso, do girly things. Hair, spa . . . lunch."

"What is it with women and lunch?"

Now he notices that if there hasn't been a makeover, Marisol has had some influence. Erika's long straight hair hasn't been cut, but it has been brushed, and he thinks he detects a trace of eyeliner.

She's a good kid, Erika, and if people treated her taking the police job as a joke at first, they don't any longer. You'd expect looting in a town that's half boarded up, but Erika has kept it to a minimum, and her obsession with enforcing parking regulations has become almost a source of perverse pride in the town.

"Say what you want about Erika," the talk goes, "she does her job."

Even the soldiers have started to treat her with grudging respect, no longer whistling or hooting as she walks by. This came about largely as a result, Marisol reported, of one soldier calling Erika a *marimacha* and her stopping, turning around, and punching him so hard in the face that he went down. His buddies laughed at him, and no one called Erika a lesbian or anything else after that.

When the show is over, she gets up from the sofa. "I have to go."

"Stay and watch another," Marisol says.

"No. Early morning. But can I help clean up?"

"No, that's why I have Keller."

Erika kisses Marisol on both cheeks. "Thank you for dinner."

"Thank you for the salad."

"Are you all right walking home?" Keller asks her.

"Sure." Erika slings her rifle over her shoulder, waves good night, and goes out the door.

"Does the makeover include a different choice of firearm?" Keller asks.

"Some men like that kind of thing."

Later, in bed, Marisol says, "We haven't made love since . . ."

"I haven't wanted to hurt you."

"I thought maybe you were . . . disgusted."

"No. God, no."

"If I lie on my side with my back to you . . ."

She wriggles her butt into him. He holds her by the shoulders or strokes her hair and moves gently inside her, even when she pushes back as if to demand more. When he finishes, she says, "Oh, that's nice."

"What about you?"

"Next time. Can you sleep?"

"I think so." He's not sure he wants to. "How about you?"

"Oh, yes."

Keller does fall asleep.

His dreams are bad and bloody.

Ciudad Juárez
Autumn 2010

The blog first appears just before the Day of the Dead.

It's a national sensation before New Year's Eve.

Pablo first sees *Esta Vida* when he logs in at the office one morning and calls Ana over. "Have you seen this?"

This Life has photographs somehow smuggled out of the San Fernando massacre site. It's grisly, brutal, frank, and asks in red fourteen-point Times New Roman typeface, "Who Are These Zetas and Why Do They Kill Innocent People?"

"Dios mío," Ana says. "That's graphic."

It's nothing a newspaper could or would print, even if they were covering the narco-wars anymore. Skulls, parts of skeletons, bits of clothing sticking up from the red earth. The accompanying article gives details of the mass murder that only the police could have known and is signed "El Niño Salvaje."

"The Wild Child?" Pablo asks.

A new story comes out the next day. Titled "Terror in Tamaulipas," it's an in-depth analysis of the war between the CDG and the Zetas.

"Whoever the Wild Child is," Pablo says, "he knows his stuff."

"It's the new journalism," Óscar opines, looking over their shoulder and wincing at the graphic images. "Some call it the democratization of journalism, others might call it anarchy. The problem is, there's no accountability. Not only are the articles anonymous, but there is no editing process to separate fact from mere rumor. It's self-serving, but I still think there's a role for editors in the media."

The next article, put out the next day, cuts closer to home.

"Who Killed Giorgio Valencia?" is classic investigative reporting. There are photos of Giorgio on the job, snapping pictures, other photos of his body at the murder scene, even an image of the grinning skull left on the car outside his funeral.

"This is offensive," Pablo says.

"His murder was offensive," Ana snaps.

"Jesus . . . Ana . . ."

"Don't look at me, kiddo," she says. "I ain't no Wild Child."

The long article goes on to ask why there has been no investigation into Valencia's death, excoriates both the state and national government for their "supine neglect" on the issue of murdered journalists, and openly accuses the Zetas of Valencia's murder, claiming that they had tried to enforce a news blackout on the attack on Marisol Cisneros.

The next post is harsher than anything seen in even *la nota roja*, showing a hacked-up, limbless body on a Juárez street. "The Cleansing" talks about the murderous chaos in Juárez, how it now seems to affect only the poor, and wonders out loud if the government really cares, or whether it is standing by and letting "social outcasts and undesirables" be hosed off the street like so much garbage.

It directly echoes Pablo's own thoughts on the matter, thoughts that he can no longer write for his own newspaper, thoughts that he has expressed to Ana, who sees the blog and asks him directly, "Are you the Wild Child?"

"I'm anything but a wild child."

It's been a grim autumn for him. He's made one trip to Mexico City to see Mateo—an awkward visit that only highlighted their continuing, gradual estrangement—and have the obligatory quarrel with Victoria, which was only sharpened by her announcement that she's "seeing someone seriously."

"Who?"

"He's an editor here at the paper."

"Has Mateo met him?"

"Well, I'm not going to keep him a secret, Pablo."

"Does he stay with you?"

"Of course not," Victoria said.

"I don't want Mateo waking up and finding him there."

"We're discreet," Victoria says, ending the discussion with that thin-lipped frown that used to challenge him sexually and that now he just hates.

The violence in Juárez has just gone on and on. Attacks on parties seemed to be the popular theme for the autumn of 2010. Six killed at a party, then four, then five more. Pablo dutifully went out to cover them, then wrote bare-bones articles that barely reach paragraph length—the number of dead, the approximate time of the attack, the rough neighborhood. Not the names, not the exact address, and for God's sake not who did it or why, because that might upset the narcos.

He's watched Óscar shrink before his eyes.

Almost literally—El Búho seems to be getting physically smaller, and certainly slower, more dependent on his cane. More and more he stays in his Chaveña home, rarely coming out for parties or even readings.

His newspaper keeps churning out dull, dutiful stories.

Not so *Esta Vida.*

Its next post is called "Our New Vocabulary" and gives a glossary, with accompanying photographs, of the words used to describe murder victims now:

Encajuelados—bodies stuffed in car trunks.
Encobijados—bodies wrapped in blankets.
Entambados—bodies stuffed in metal barrels, often with acid or wet concrete.
Enteipados—bodies wrapped in industrial tape.

"This is the new vocabulary," the article goes on to say, "of our journalism, of our nation. We need specific new words to describe the many varieties of slaughter, for our language, our former concepts of death, fail us. The Black Plague gave us 'Ring Around the Rosie' as a children's game; the war on drugs gives us a new chant for children in our *colonias*—'*encajuelados, encobijados, entambados, enteipados*—all fall down.'"

But *Esta Vida* doesn't restrict itself to Juárez, or even Chihuahua—it reports on La Familia in Michoacán, the Zetas, it takes on the Sinaloa cartel, the police, the *federales,* the army, the marines, city, state, and national governments.

The post "Who Picks the Winner?" causes a national outrage and debate, such as debates exist in the now highly constricted press. Almost blatantly accusing the national government of siding with the Sinaloa cartel to create a *"pax narcotica,"* it runs a statistical analysis—of some 97,516 arrests by federal authorities, only 1,512 have been associated with the Sinaloa cartel, and many of them were people who had fallen into the bad graces of Adán Barrera and Nacho Esparza.

Los Pinos responds with fury and indignation in a nationally televised press conference. The president gets on the screen in defense of his federal police and talks about the sacrifices in blood, and how this "cowardly anonymous verbal sniper" has made a mockery of martyrs.

The result is that thousands of people start logging on to *Esta Vida,* and the *susurro* is that it's the only place where you can get "the real news on the drug war."

The next day, *Esta Vida* runs a story about a woman in Nuevo Laredo whom the Zetas executed for calling the authorities about their extortion business. The accompanying photo shows the woman's head set between her legs, her skirt pulled up. It's as obscene as any pornographic snuff film, and what makes it even more so is the *narcomensaje* left by the body: "We killed this damn old lady because she pointed the police in our direction. This will happen to all careless assholes. Sincerely, the Z Company."

A new development happens the next day, and this time it's Ana who calls Pablo over to her monitor.

"Check this out."

Esta Vida has posted a letter from the Zetas to the Wild Child. "Thank you for doing our public relations work for us. You are helping us spread our message to the world."

But the Z Company isn't so thrilled with the next post, "Eight Zetas Beheaded," which shows the decapitated bodies of eight Zetas in the back of a pickup truck with the message "This is what happens when you support Los Zetas. Here are your *halcones,* you filthy bastards. Sincerely, the CDG."

The blogs start a ferocious debate in the city room.

"You have to ask yourself," Óscar lectures, "whether *Esta Vida* is now reporting on murders or stimulating them. To wit, are the narcos now committing atrocities specifically to have them publicized on this blog? Have we reached the point where murders don't really exist unless and until they appear on social media? Are we now going to have Facebook murders, Twitter murders?"

Not for the first time in his career, Óscar is prophetic. All of that comes to pass in the autumn of 2010, but *Esta Vida* is the star of the Internet, "water cooler talk," to the extent that there is such a thing anymore. Television reporters and social media followers ask the question "Who Is the Wild Child?" and it becomes a national game.

And the Wild Child keeps it up.

Every post graphic, every post provocative.

"Do the Marines Execute Prisoners?" "Families Abandon Ciudad Mier." "Don Alejo de Castillo—An Elderly Hero." "The Women of the Juárez Valley Stand Up to the Cartels." "Whatever Happened to Crazy Eddie?"

But then new *narcomensajes* appear on bridges, monuments, and street corners around the country: WILD CHILD—IF YOU SHOW OUR DEAD AGAIN, YOU WILL BE NEXT—SINCERELY, THE Z COMPANY. WILD CHILD—YOU DON'T KNOW WHAT YOU'RE PLAYING WITH. THE NUEVA GENTE. TAME YOURSELF, WILD CHILD. And, ominously, WILD CHILD, WE'RE TRACKING YOU DOWN AND WE WILL FIND YOU.

Wild Child doesn't back down.

Esta Vida reports that 191 Zetas "disappeared like so many Houdinis" from a Nuevo Laredo prison, and the arrest of 42 guards for "facilitating the escape." It shows a photo of two men whose faces had been skinned off left outside an Acapulco bar. It tells the story of a Christmas party in Monterrey where gunmen came in and took away four university students, who have not been seen since.

There's a New Year's Eve party at Cafebrería, but Pablo can't help but observe what a shrunken group they are. Jimena is gone, Giorgio is gone, Óscar diminished, Marisol in pain, Ana in grief, himself in what . . . malaise? Ennui? Depression?

The gathering is symbolic of the city.

In an article that Óscar did let him write, Pablo reported that as of the end of 2010, there have been 7,000 people killed in Juárez, 10,000 businesses closed, 130,000 jobs lost, and 250,000 people "displaced."

My city, Pablo thinks.

My city of ruins.

And my bleeding country.

Hard to believe that 2010, the *annus horribilis* of the Mexican drug war, has finally come to an end.

The final tally of drug-related deaths in Mexico in 2010 came to 15,273.

That's what we count now, Pablo thinks, instead of counting down to midnight.

We count deaths.

3

Each New Morn

. . . each new morn
New widows howl, new orphans cry, new sorrows
Strike heaven on the face.

—Shakespeare
Macbeth, act 4, scene 3

Acapulco, Guerrero
2011

Eddie's tired.

Tired of moving, tired of running, tired of fighting.

The fact that he's winning almost doesn't matter.

Like, winning *what*? The right to move, run, and fight more?

I'm a multimillionaire, he thinks as he settles into yet another safe house, this one in Acapulco, and I live like a bum.

A homeless man with twenty luxury houses.

Just last week, four decapitated bodies that used to be his guys hung from a Cuernavaca bridge with the message THIS IS WHAT HAPPENS TO THOSE WHO SUPPORT THE TRAITOR CRAZY EDDIE RUIZ.

It was signed by Martín Tapia and "the South Pacific cartel." The cheap motherfucker can't buy a map? Eddie thinks. How close is Cuernavaca to the Pacific Ocean?

Eddie feels aggrieved that Martín thinks he's the informer who betrayed Diego. It's true, but Martín has no reason to believe it's true, so it's not fair. Tapia has this grudge against him, for no good reason at all.

So do the Zetas, but they have a reason.

Same reason they've always had.

They want what I have.

First it was Laredo, now it's Monterrey, Veracruz, and Acapulco. They also want my head on a stick, and they ain't gonna get that either.

He thinks back to, what's it been, shit, five years now when he sat in a car back in Nuevo Laredo with those sleazy cocksuckers. I should have put a bullet in their heads then, except for I wasn't carrying a gun.

Speaking of cocksuckers, he's pretty sure that Ochoa plays for the other team. I mean, I like to keep it tight, but that guy—the hair, the skin products, the military gear. If "the Executioner" showed up dressed like a construction worker, an Indian chief, a biker, or a cop, I wouldn't be surprised.

Well, Heriberto, you can suck my dick.

Figuratively speaking.

Acapulco I can hold, no problem.

Probably Veracruz, too.

Monterrey, that's a problem, given Diego's forward-thinking policy of inviting the Zetas to make themselves at home there. And they did. They have probably hundreds of guns in the city and its burbs now.

And those FES marines are no joke. If anything, they've gotten better since they double-tapped Diego. They even went into Matamoros and took out Gordo Contreras. Biggest battle in Mexico since the Revolution—people in Texas could hear the gunfire. And, thanks a heap, marines, for killing that fat fuck Gordo. Now the Zetas can send more men down here.

And that low motherfucker Keller is worse than any of them.

Talk about not giving a shit.

The jack of spades thing is pretty good, though. Wish I'd thought of something like that—a calling card. Like, have jacks of spades printed up but with my face photoshopped onto it.

Eddie goes into the kitchen and dumps strawberries, blueberries, protein powder, and water into the blender. The blueberries are full of anti-what-do-you-call-'ems and the protein powder is good for the muscle mass he's trying to put on.

The feds have been all over him the past few months, arresting his people, busting his dope, tracking him down. It's serious, because the last thing in the world that the *federales* want is to take Eddie Ruiz alive.

I have too much to say, so if the *federales* take me out, it's on a slab.

Even the DEA has gotten in on the bust-Eddie's-balls act. A week ago, they seized $49 million of his coke as it went across the border, and last month they charged sixty-nine customs agents—half of them Eddie's guys—with corruption.

It's annoying.

In response, he'd made his point to the government again in a letter to the newspapers: "You're always going to have someone selling this stuff, so it might as well be me. I don't kill women, children, or innocent people. Yours truly, Narco Polo."

He's been using Narco Polo in his signed correspondence, trying to wean them off the Crazy Eddie thing.

I'm not crazy, he thinks.

I might be the sanest guy I know.

Eddie makes himself gulp down the smoothie. You don't take the time to savor that crap because there's nothing to savor.

He owns four nightclubs in three cities and shuts them down from time to time so he can party. Stations his guys all around, invites the hottest women in, picks one or two, does some Ecstasy, and parties. Was dating that soap opera star until she got tired of all the security and her "people" started to worry about her "branding." Doesn't matter, she was good while she lasted.

Polishing off the smoothie, he goes into the home gym and starts to pump some iron. He should have one of his guys spot for him, but it would be too easy, wouldn't it, for the guy to do an "oops" on a bench press and drop two bills on his throat.

In this world you can trust yourself and yourself.

He's glad when he hears the doorbell ring downstairs, and after the security screening, Julio comes up.

"You want a water?" Eddie asks him.

"I'd take a water."

They get the waters and then go out on the deck with the view of the ocean. Now *we*, he thinks, should be called the Pacific cartel, not that inland yuppie. He looks across the table at Julio and asks, "Are we ready to go to script?"

"Did you read the treatment?"

"Was that a treatment or an outline?" Eddie asks. Actually, he read up until about page three and then thumbed through the rest of it. The thing was twenty-seven pages long.

"Sort of an outline of a treatment," Julio says. "If you approve the treatment outline, then we'll go to the full treatment."

"*Then* the script?"

"Well, a script outline."

Eddie loves the movies. *The Godfather,* of course, and *Goodfellas,* but also the drug movies. *Scarface, Miami Vice* . . . he'd like to make a contribution to the genre. His own story—the realistic, down-and-dirty tale of a real-life drug lord. The way it really is. No one's ever seen *that* shit before.

They're thinking of calling it *Narco Polo,* and, get this, the main character, the drug lord, actually *plays polo.* Eddie's putting up $100K of his own money and hoping the script will attract investors.

If he ever gets a script from this guy.

Writers.

"Did you like the outline?" Julio asks.

"I did," Eddie says. "I think there are some good things in there, some really good things. But you can't have me getting married twice without getting divorced. It makes me look like a dick."

"I think it makes you interesting."

"Yeah," Eddie says. "Priscilla would think it was a little *too* interesting. You know pregnant women, hormones and shit. And the scene where I escape from the marine raid . . . I think I leave too early. I think I should shoot my way out. You know . . . 'meet my little friend.'"

"That's good, yeah."

"And the ending," Eddie says. "I get killed."

"It's a convention of the genre," Julio says.

Julio wears tight black jeans and black leather shoes even on a sunny day in Acapulco. Eddie thinks this is because he went to film school, which is why Eddie hired him and because he says things like "convention of the genre."

"Pacino didn't get killed," Eddie says.

"He did in *Three.*"

"*Three* doesn't count," Eddie says. "Liotta didn't get killed in *Goodfellas,* De Niro didn't get killed in *Casino* . . ."

"But they couldn't end happily. They had to be punished."

"What are you saying?" Eddie asks. "I have to be punished?"

Julio turns even paler, if that's possible, and mumbles, "For your crimes."

"For what?"

"Your crimes."

"My crimes," Eddie says. "You want to talk about crimes, you talk to fucking Diego, you talk to Ochoa, you talk to Barrera. I'm the good guy in this movie, the anti- . . ."

"Hero."

"Huh?"

"You're the antihero."

"Right." Eddie sulks for a minute and then says, "Casting."

"Are we still thinking about Leo?"

"Leo would be great," Eddie says. "But maybe a little too on the nose, you know what I mean?"

"Sort of. What are you thinking?"

"I'm thinking of going in a different direction," Eddie says, looking out at the ocean. "What if I called my own number?"

"Meaning . . ."

"Cast myself. As me. I mean, what a hook, right? No one has seen that before," Eddie says. *Narco Polo: The Real-Life Story of a Drug Lord,* starring Eddie Ruiz, a Real-Life Drug Lord."

Julio takes a long pull on his water and then asks, "How would that work exactly, Eddie? I mean, you're, you know, wanted. How are you going to be on set? Do promotion?"

"Think outside the box," Eddie says. "I could do TV interviews from remote, secret locations. What a gimmick, huh? The *Today* show . . . *Late Night . . .*"

"Can you act?"

Can I act, Eddie thinks. I have sat at the table pretending to like Heriberto Ochoa. Can I *act*? "How hard can it be? You say the lines, you say them with feeling. I'll take a class. Fucking hire a teacher, I don't know."

They decide to table casting until they have a script. Leo wouldn't commit on just a treatment anyway, so they have a little time. Eddie finishes giving his notes, and Julio goes off to rethink the ending.

After Julio leaves, Eddie wanders upstairs to the room that's been sound-proofed. He's found that it comes in handy to have a soundproof room in all his houses. You can blast music as loud as you want without getting negative attention from the neighbors, and if you need to work on a houseguest, you can do so at leisure without his screams alarming said neighbors or keeping you awake at night.

Now he has such a guest.

Retaliation for the four heads that appeared on an Acapulco sidewalk with the placard THIS IS WHAT WILL HAPPEN TO ALL THOSE STUPID ENOUGH TO SIDE WITH THE HOMOSEXUAL, EDDIE RUIZ.

I do wish they'd stop calling me gay, Eddie thinks.

I'm not.

Ochoa is, not me.

It must be—what does Julio call it?—projection.

The four dead former associates are the last in a streak of killings in Acapulco, and cabdrivers are the ones really taking it in the shorts. Again, it's annoying because using cabdrivers as *halcones* was Eddie's idea and a really good one, too. Who has a better track on who comes in and out of town, at the airport, the train station, the bus station, than cabdrivers? Plus they're the ones on the street all the time—they know the clubs, the bars, the brothels. They keep their eyes open.

The Zetas caught on to this and started hiring cabdrivers of their own and killing Eddie's.

So Eddie had to kill *their* drivers, and back and forth and so on, and anyway, it's not a good time to drive a cab in Acapulco as Eddie and the Zetas try to blind each other, and then you find four of yours with their heads cut off.

You know who really liked to cut off heads, Eddie thinks as he climbs the stairs, was that crazy little fucker Chuy. That skinny goof was something else for taking off heads. He'd clip necks like you'd clip your toenails.

You have to give it to him, though.

That *pocho* could fight.

You want someone to go through the door first, Chuy wouldn't hesitate. You wanted someone to take your back, you could count on him. Shit, we did some damage together.

I wonder what ever happened to him?

Probably still with La Familia if he isn't dead.

Still trimming heads for God.

Anyway, I need to back off Martín Tapia and his Zeta bum-buddies a little bit. It's one thing to fight for territory—that's part of the game—but these "crazy" and "homosexual" messages have to stop.

Osvaldo sits outside the door to the soundproof room. Osvaldo is Eddie's new second in command and chief bodyguard. He was a former marine and trained with the Kaibiles down in Guatemala, so he's another guy who doesn't mind lopping off a head or two if it comes to it. He claims to have killed over three hundred people, but Eddie thinks that's exaggerated.

"Everything good in there?" Eddie asks. "Copacetic?"

"Everything's good."

Yeah, Osvaldo doesn't know what "copacetic" means. Osvaldo can do a lot of things, but crossword puzzles probably ain't among them.

Eddie goes into the room.

Even hog-tied, this is one great-looking piece of ass.

Hell, Eddie speculates, maybe *because* she's hog-tied. Bound hand and foot in that black blouse with the black bra and panties and the stockings, lying on a mattress in a fetal position, her mouth clamped on a gag—now that is *hot*—and he makes a mental note to tell Julio to make sure that's in the script.

Eddie looks down at Yvette Tapia.

"Lady," he says, "what am I going to do with you?"

The Ice Maiden.

He snatched her for protection.

Not his so much as his family's.

Okay, "families'."

The Zetas have a well-earned rep for killing women and children. Priscilla is in Mexico City with her mother and is pretty safe, but Eddie thought that having Señora Tapia as a hostage would be insurance. And she made it so easy, just strolling down a street in Almeda, apparently separated from her old man.

Then he sent a message to Martín. "I have the lovely and charming Mrs. Tapia. If you do not want her parts sent back to you in dry ice delivered once a week, you will leave my family alone. FYI, I am not a homosexual. Yours truly, Narco Polo."

He got a message back—"Please do not hurt her. We have an understanding."

Yeah, me and Martín have one understanding. Turns out me and the Zetas have a different understanding, because he got a message from his pal Forty. "We don't give a fuck what you do to her. She's not our woman. We don't think you have *los ping-pongs* to kill her anyway, faggot."

There's that "faggot" again.

It's bad news for Martín because it means he's become the junior partner and not a very valued one at that, if they're willing to throw away his wife. And it's bad news for her, because if I don't show them that I *do* have the balls . . . they might go after my family. *"Los ping-pongs"* is pretty good though, and he makes a note to tell Julio to work that into the script somewhere.

Eddie leans over and takes the gag out of her mouth.

"I'll do anything," she says. "Martín will send you millions."

"See, I have money."

"Anything," she says. "I'll blow you, I'll do you. I'll let you fuck me in the ass. Would you like that? Would you like to fuck me in the ass?"

Jesus, he thinks, *everybody.*

"You can make a tape," she says. "You can make a sex tape and show it to everybody, put it out on the Net . . ."

"You're embarrassing yourself," Eddie says, "and I hate to see that, because you're a classy lady."

"I'm a MILF," she says. "But I've never had a baby, so it's still nice and tight."

"Stop."

"You keep me," Yvette says. "I can do things those young girls have never even heard of. I can show you things . . . Do you know what a rim job is? I'll do that to you. I'd like to do that to you. And when you get tired of me you can just throw me out. Please."

It's pathetic, Eddie thinks.

He decides to put an end to it.

"Look," he says, "you need to know it wasn't Martín. Your husband loves you. It's Ochoa and those guys. They don't care. And it's put me in a very difficult situation."

His phone rings.

It's his wife, Priscilla, and she's crying. Eddie steps outside to take the call. "What is it? Is it the baby? Are you and Brittany all right?"

She's almost hysterical. *The police were here, looking for you.*

"Which police?" Eddie asks. It makes a difference. He's told her a hundred times.

The federales.

God damn them, Eddie thinks.

"Are you okay?" he asks again. "Did they hurt you?"

"They pushed me around a little," she says, calming down, *"but I'm all right. They said I knew where you were, they'd put me in jail . . . They about wrecked the condo. They said they'd be back."*

"Is your mom there now?" Eddie asks. When Priscilla's mother gets on the phone, Eddie says, "Move to the house in Palacio. I'll send people. They'll get you on a plane to Laredo."

Priscilla gets back on the phone.

"It's okay, baby," Eddie says. "Don't worry. Everything's going to be okay."

But it isn't, he thinks when he clicks off.

It won't be. One of his guys must have gotten picked up by the *federales* and gave up the location.

Things are going to unravel from here.

He grabs Osvaldo and goes back into the room with Yvette Tapia. She tries to squirm across the floor like a snake to get away from them, but they grab her. When they've done what they need to do, they take her out and dump her in a vacant lot.

"I want an ice-cream cone," Eddie says.

"What?" Osvaldo says.

"I want an ice-cream cone," Eddie repeats. "How fucking hard is that to understand? I just want some freakin' ice cream."

They go down to the Tradicional, to the old boardwalk, where John Wayne used to own a hotel, and Eddie gets his ice-cream cone.

Strawberry.

He sits on a bench outside, checking out the tourist chicks, the pussy coming in off the cruise ships, the old men with their faces toward the sun, the young mothers with their kids.

Eddie looks out at the cliffs, the ocean.

A guy trips over the age thirty wire, he realizes that certain things he wanted in his life just aren't going to happen. He's never going to play in the NFL, he's never going to sail around Tahiti, he's not going to star in his own movie.

He's not even going to kill Forty and Ochoa.

Sorry, Chacho.

"We shouldn't be out here like this," Osvaldo says, nervous.

"No shit," Eddie says.

Tapia's people, the Zetas, the *federales*, they've all probably already heard he's here. There are *halcones* everywhere. He gets up and walks away along the boardwalk, takes out his phone, and hits a number.

The thing of it is, he's just tired of it all.

Been there, done that.

"I want to cash in my chips," Eddie says. "Turn myself in."

"Go ahead," Keller says.

"Not in Mexico," Eddie answers. He'd last maybe five minutes in a Mexican lockup. If Diego's people didn't get him, the Zetas would. If they swung and missed, Barrera wouldn't. That's if he got as far as a cell anyway, which is doubtful. "You got to get me out of here."

"Have you ever killed an American citizen?" Keller asks.

"Not since I was seventeen, and that was an accident."

"You know where the U.S. consular agency is?"

"The Hotel Continental."

"Walk there now," Keller says. "Are you heavy?"

"What do you think?"

"Drop it somewhere," Keller says. "Any dope, anything else. Walk straight there, use the name Hernán Valenzuela. Do whatever the consul tells you to do. I'll see you tonight."

"Keller? I need to tell you something first."

"Shit. What?"

The Acapulco police find Yvette Tapia in a vacant lot, bound hand and foot, blindfolded and gagged, dirty, but otherwise fine.

A cardboard sign is draped around her neck with the message THIS IS TO TEACH YOU TO BE MEN AND TO RESPECT FAMILIES. I'M GIVING YOU BACK YOUR WIFE, SAFE AND SOUND. I DO NOT KILL WOMEN OR CHILDREN. EDUARDO RUIZ—NARCO POLO.

Crazy Eddie is gone.

San Fernando, Tamaulipas
2011

Chuy sits on the crowded bus as it rolls up Highway 101, which they call the "Highway of Hell," and looks out the window at the flat, dusty Tamaulipas terrain, so different from the green hills of Michoacán.

He helped bury Nazario on one of those hills.

Chuy and some others spirited the Leader's body away to the hills for a secret burial, and in the weeks since, shrines have appeared all over Michoacán, and it is said that Nazario is a saint whose spirit has already performed miracles.

A new leader took over, but Chuy is finished.

Now he is heading home.

To Laredo.

There has been so much fighting, and Chuy was in on most of it.

He was there when they attacked the convoy of *federales*. His unit killed eight policemen, but the convoy got through. And when the army captured Hugo Salazar, Chuy personally led fifty men in an attack on the police station, with rocket launchers and machine guns. They ambushed police and army convoys, made attacks on eleven cities in eight days.

But they couldn't rescue him.

They did capture twelve *federales* in those attacks, tortured them to death, and dumped their bodies on the highway outside La Huacana.

The army sent in more than five thousand troops then, with helicopters, airplanes, and armored cars, and the war went on. Sometimes La Familia won, sometimes the army won, capturing more La Familia leaders, but always more leaders took their place.

Sometimes they fought the *federales*, sometimes the army, sometimes the Zetas, and after a while Chuy wasn't always sure who they were fighting and it didn't really matter to him—he fought for Nazario and he fought for God. Chuy was vaguely aware that an order had come down to keep fighting the Zetas, which was fine with him—he'd never stopped fighting the Zetas.

He never stopped taking heads.

He lost count.

Six? Eight? Twelve?

He left them by the sides of roads, he hung them from bridges, he did it again and again as if in a dream.

Some things he remembers.

Others he doesn't.

He does remember the ambush on the convoy of *federales,* when he led twelve men onto a highway overpass outside Maravatío and waited for the convoy to finish getting gas at a station down the road. When the convoy came close, they popped up from behind the railing and opened fire, killing five and wounding seven others.

They used the same trick again a month later, this time killing twelve, and then the *federales* caught on and started sending helicopters ahead of their convoys, but Nazario himself praised Chuy for those attacks.

He remembers the day when they marched six thieves around the traffic circle in Zamora and whipped them with barbed wire and made the thieves carry placards that read I AM A CRIMINAL AND LA FAMILIA IS PUNISHING ME. And they hung up a banner—THIS IS FOR ALL THE PEOPLE. DON'T JUDGE US. LA FAMILIA IS CLEANSING YOUR CITY.

Chuy remembers when Nazario announced "La Fusión de los Antizetas," allying them officially with Sinaloa and the Gulf to rid the country of the Zeta menace, and this was one of the best days, because the Zetas had raped and murdered Flor.

He took four Zeta heads in Apatzingán that week.

And Nazario made him one of the Twelve Apostles, his personal bodyguard. He went everywhere with the Leader, keeping him safe as he gave out loans to needy farmers, built clinics and schools, dug wells and irrigation ditches.

The people loved Nazario.

They loved La Familia.

Then it happened.

Nazario was giving a Christmas party for the children of El Alcate, outside Apatzingán. It was a happy day, and Chuy stood guard as Nazario handed out toys, clothes, and candy. Chuy heard the helicopters before he saw them, the bass rumble splitting the sky. He grabbed Nazario by the elbow and ran him toward a house as *federales* and troops came in with trucks and armored cars.

With Nazario inside the house, Chuy and some of the others set fire to cars and tried to block the roads, but the troops came in by helicopters. Bullets ripped through the air, striking, yes, La Familia soldiers, but also parents and children who were outside for the fiesta.

Chuy saw the teenage girl go down, smoke coming from the back of her blouse where the bullet hit. He saw a baby shot in its mother's arms.

He made it back into the house, knocked the glass out of a window, and started to return fire with his *erre*. Another man in the house phoned comrades in Morelia to block roads and attack barracks to keep the army and *policía* from sending reinforcements.

All that afternoon, that night, and all the next day they fought. Chuy led the covering fire as they moved Nazario from house to house and the soldiers came on with grenades, rockets, and tear gas, setting fire to houses and little shacks. The townspeople who could, fled; others huddled in bathtubs or lay flat on floors.

The comrades in Morelia told them that there were two thousand soldiers surrounding the village. Bullhorns called for Nazario to surrender, but he wouldn't, saying that if this was the garden of Gethsemane only God could take the cup from his hand.

By the afternoon of the second day, the La Familia troops were out of ammunition and the six Apostles who were still alive decided that they would try to punch a hole in the soldiers' line and break Nazario out when the sun went down.

They settled into a siege as the battle slowed to a match of sniper against sniper. Marshaling ammunition, two rocket launchers, and some grenades, the six gathered with Nazario in a house at the west edge of the village, nearest a tree line, and waited for dark.

Two of the six were already hit, their wounds bound up with strips torn from their shirts.

As the sun went down, Nazario led them in prayer.

Our Father, Who art in Heaven
Hallowed be Thy Name
Thy Kingdom come
Thy will be done . . .

Two comrades who volunteered to stay laid down cover fire as Chuy burst from the door, shielding Nazario behind him. Another comrade had Nazario's left arm, a third his right.

The rocket from a launcher blasted the soldiers and Chuy ran for that space. Tracer fire cut the night. The man to Nazario's right went down, and Chuy dropped back and took his place, firing his rifle with his left hand and running, and then they were in the trees and then they were through and then Chuy felt Nazario slow down and get heavier and when he turned to look he saw the gaping hole and then he was too small to hold the Leader up, and Nazario staggered and fell to the ground. They picked him up and carried him but he died before they got a hundred yards.

They hid in some trees until some comrades made it in from Morelia, and then they put the Leader in the back of the truck and drove into the hills and buried him in a secret place where no one could desecrate the grave.

But three days later people were saying that they had seen Nazario, that he came to them and told them that everything would be well, that he would never leave them, but Chuy didn't see Nazario and didn't hear him say that everything would be well.

Chuy walked into Morelia.

He found a cheap room in a slum and slept for two days. When he finally got up, he realized that it was over.

Flor was dead.

And now the Leader was gone.

Chuy decided to go home. He took what money he had and bought a bus ticket to Uruapan, and from there to Guadalajara, and from there to Nuevo Laredo. From there, he planned to cross the bridge one more time and be home.

He hasn't seen home in five years.

A war veteran, he's just sixteen years old.

Now he looks out at the mesquite, creosote, and prickly pear, and beyond them the reddish-brown fields of sorghum.

The bus is hot and crowded.

There are maybe seventy people on board, three-quarters of them men, most of them immigrants from El Salvador and Guatemala trying to make it *el norte* for the work. Chuy sits beside a woman and her small child, a little boy. Chuy figures that she's Guatemalan, but she keeps mostly to herself and so does he.

Chuy looks like any other teenager.

Blue jeans, a black T-shirt, a dirty old L.A. Dodgers ball cap.

The bus stops in the town of San Fernando, where Chuy buys an orange soda and a burrito and gets back on board, eats the burrito, drinks the soda, and falls asleep.

The hissing of the bus's brakes wakes him up and he's confused. It's way too soon to be stopping in Valle Hermoso. Chuy looks through the windshield and sees four pickup trucks pulled across the road, blocking it. Men with AR-15s stand beside the trucks and Chuy knows they're either CDG or Zetas.

The men come up to the bus and one of them hollers, "Open up, asshole! Unless you want me to shoot you dead!"

He wears a black uniform, bulletproof vest, and kit belt.

It's Forty.

Chuy slowly pulls the bill of his cap lower over his face.

If Forty recognizes him, he's dead.

Trembling, the driver opens the door and the men get on the bus, point their guns at the passengers, and shout, "You're all fucked!"

Forty orders the driver to pull off on a dirt road, and the bus bounces for about ten miles until they're on a flat, desolate piece of ground in the middle of nowhere. Chuy sees some old army trucks with canvas hoods and a few old buses with broken windows and flat tires.

The Zetas order all the men off the bus.

Chuy gets off, looking at the ground. It's hot out. No shade under the blazing summer sun.

The Zetas push the men into a line and then start to sort them by age and physique. The older and the weaker are cut out, tied foot to foot, and shuffled off into one of the trucks. Chuy watches as Zetas take the better-looking young women off the bus and load them into a different truck, separating them from their children.

The woman who was sitting next to him screams as a Zeta puts his hand over her mouth and drags her away from her little boy. Chuy knows that she'll be raped, and, if lucky, survive to be put out on the streets. Other Zetas take the older or homelier women off the bus and put them into another truck.

Chuy knows their fate, too.

Now Forty stands in front of the rest and asks, "Okay, who wants to live?"

A teenage boy pisses himself. Forty sees the stain spread across the front of the boy's faded jeans, walks up to him, pulls his pistol, and shoots him in the head. "Okay, I'll ask again! Who here wants to live? Raise your hands!"

All the men raise their hands.

Chuy stares off a thousand yards and raises his.

"Good!" Forty yells. "So here's what we're going to do! We're going to test your skills and see who has balls!"

He whistles and the other Zetas bring out baseball bats and clubs with nails driven into them and toss them in front of the men. Then Forty yells, "Pick up a weapon, pair off with the man next to you, and fight. If you win, you become a Zeta, if you don't. Well . . . then you're fucked."

An older man near Chuy starts to cry. He's nicely dressed in a white shirt and khaki pants and talks as if he's from El Salvador. "Please, sir. Don't make me do this. I'll give you all the money I have. I have a house, I'll give you the deed, only please don't make me do this."

"You want to leave?" Forty asks.

"Please, yes."

"So leave." Forty takes the bat from the man's hand. The man starts to walk away. As soon as he steps past, Forty swings his bat into the back of his head. The man staggers and falls to the dirt, raising a small cloud of dust. Forty chops with the bat until the man's head is just a smear on the dirt. Then he turns back to the men and asks, "Anyone else want to leave?"

No one moves.

Forty yells, "Now, fight!"

Chuy's opponent is clearly a campesino—big, hard hands, big knuckles, but not a fighter—and he looks scared. Still, he has six inches and fifty pounds on Chuy and he advances swinging the bat at Chuy's head.

Chuy ducks under, swings his nailed club and shatters the campesino's kneecap. The campesino goes down face first, then tries to push himself back up, but Chuy finishes him with two blows to the back of the neck.

Forty yells, "This skinny one can fight!"

For a horrible moment Chuy thinks that Forty recognizes him, but the Zeta's attention goes to other fights. Most of them last a long time—these men don't have combat skills and their struggles are long, slow, and brutal.

Finally, it's done.

Half the men are left standing, some of them badly wounded with cuts, broken bones, and fractured skulls.

The Zetas march the ones who can walk back to the bus.

They shoot the others.

The bus drives the survivors farther into the countryside, to a camp that Chuy remembers.

The party goes on that night.

As Chuy and the others sit in a line in the dirt, he hears the women's screams coming from inside a corrugated steel building. Fifty-gallon barrels are set outside, and every few minutes a body—dead or still barely alive—is shoved into a barrel and lit on fire.

He hears the screams.

And the laughter.

Chuy will never forget the sound.

Never get the smell out of his nose.

Forty walks over to the eleven survivors and says, "Congratulations. Welcome to the Z Company."

Chuy is a Zeta again.

They don't send him to Nuevo Laredo or to Monterrey.

They send him to the Juárez Valley.

Valverde, Chihuahua

It's the nightmare call.

Keller rolls over in bed to answer the phone and hear Taylor say, *"One of our people has been killed."*

Keller's heart drops in his chest.

It's Ernie Hidalgo all over again.

"Who?" he asks.

"You know him," Taylor tells Keller. "Richard Jiménez. A good man."

Yeah, he was, Keller thinks. "What happened?"

Jiménez and another agent were on the highway from Monterrey to Mexico City. No one knows what the two agents were even doing on that road by themselves, in a car marked with diplomatic license plates. All they know is that their car was run down, forced to pull over, and surrounded by fourteen armed Zetas demanding that they get out of the car.

The agents refused, and yelled that they were American agents.

"Me vale madre," the Zeta leader said.

I don't give a fuck.

The agents phoned the U.S. consulate in Monterrey, and then the American embassy in Mexico City. They were told a federal helicopter would be there in forty minutes.

They didn't get those minutes.

The Zetas emptied their clips through the car windows. By the time the chopper got there, Jiménez had bled to death, the other agent was in traumatic shock, badly wounded but expected to live. He'd been medevaced to a Laredo hospital.

"Get down to Monterrey," Taylor says. "Now."

"What is it?" Marisol asks.

"I have to go."

She's knows better than to ask where. "Is everything all right?"

"No."

Keller gets on the phone again while he's still dressing and gets Orduña on the special line. The FES commander picks up on the first ring. *"I heard. I'm on my way. A plane is waiting for you in Juárez."*

Marisol is out of bed now, balancing on her cane while she puts on her bathrobe. She looks at Keller questioningly.

"One of our guys got killed," he says.

"I'm so sorry," Marisol says.

She's too kind, Keller thinks, to note that Mexicans are killed every single day and that it's considered nothing special.

"Yeah," Keller says, "me too."

Marisol sits at her desk and works her way through piles of paperwork.

The red tape required to manage even a small town is endless, and she wants to finish so that she can get over to the clinic for afternoon hours. She decides to eat lunch at her desk, and calls Erika to see if she wants to join her, but the girl is out in the countryside looking into the theft of someone's chickens.

Chicken theft, Marisol thinks.

She's glad for a bit of normalcy.

Maybe Erika can come for dinner.

"What was the motive?" Keller asks Orduña as they stand at the scene of the attack. The car has been pushed off to the edge of the highway, its body riddled with bullet holes like a Hollywood movie prop. The blood inside is all too real. "Why would the Zetas kill an American?"

Then he sees the answer.

On the floor by the gas pedal, spotted with Jiménez's blood—a jack of spades.

The Zetas know that American intelligence has been working with the FES, and this was payback.

They couldn't get to me, Keller thinks, so they took the first agents they could find. But what were Jiménez and his partner doing on Highway 57, a dangerous road in the middle of the CDG–Zeta war?

Then again, the drug war is getting very real for Americans. A FAST team in Honduras had just been in a firefight with Zeta cocaine traffickers, and several American citizens had recently been killed in the Juárez area. But there hasn't been an American agent killed in Mexico since Ernie, and Keller knows that the response will be massive.

Maybe the Zetas don't care.

Maybe they think they're invincible.

Just a week ago, another mass grave site was discovered near San Fernando, with the story that the Zetas had once again hijacked a bus off Highway 101 and killed most of the passengers.

Stories of grisly torture and forced gladiator-style combat were making the rounds. Hard to know if they're true, but this much is a fact—the Zetas are establishing a reign of terror over whole parts of Mexico, and Americans have no immunity.

Later that day, while Keller, Orduña, and FES are combing the countryside for the attackers, the Zetas make their position absolutely clear. Heriberto Ochoa releases a communiqué in the press that directly challenges the governments of both Mexico and the United States:

"Not the army, not the marines, not the security and antidrug agencies of the United States can resist us. Mexico lives and will continue to live under the regime of the Zetas."

Chuy's *estaca* moved in like morning fog.

They came up Carretera 2 from the east, got out of the vehicle before they hit the army roadblock at Práxedis, and then hiked the countryside, using the riverbank as cover, until they came to the outskirts of Valverde.

Now they wait.

Chuy takes a nap.

Wakes up when an elbow digs into his side and he sees the woman come out of the building, walking with a cane.

The woman police they told him about is nowhere to be seen.

Neither is the North American DEA agent.

Forty told Chuy that he'd get the man out of the way, and he did.

Marisol stands at the kitchen counter and chops onions for the stew she's making. Erika is coming over and she's already late. Where is that girl? Marisol wonders.

She puts some butter and olive oil in the pan, smashes a clove of garlic into it and turns on the heat to brown the chicken before she puts it in the pot. It's one of Arturo's favorite dishes and she wishes he were here to enjoy it. But he's out doing whatever it is that he does, so he'll just have to miss out.

Marisol hears something outside.

A car engine. Must be Erika.

Peeking out the window, she sees headlights pass by. For some reason it spooks her. She dismisses it as silly but nevertheless looks to see that the Beretta is on the chopping block, within reach.

The way we live now, she thinks.

And where is Erika? Where is that girl?

She calls her on her mobile but just gets voice mail.

Keller turns onto Carretera 2.

After a futile hunt, he'd flown back to Juárez. There'll be an emergency meeting at EPIC tomorrow, Taylor's flying in from D.C., and Keller figures he can get an evening in with Marisol before going up. All DEA and ICE personnel in Mexico have already been called back or put under heavy security in the consulates, but Keller decides he's exempt from that.

He's been under a death threat since the day he came here, so what's the difference? He's been in Mexico—just on this last incarnation—longer than the U.S. was in World War II. When you ask people, "What's America's longest war?" they usually answer "Vietnam" or amend that to "Afghanistan," but it's neither.

America's longest war is the war on drugs.

Forty years and counting, Keller thinks. I was here when it was declared and I'm still here. And drugs are more plentiful, more potent, and less expensive than ever.

But it's not about the drugs anymore, anyway, is it?

He calls Marisol to tell her that he'll be there for dinner. The line is busy. He's asked her to get call waiting but she's so stubborn about "being rude."

He dials Erika.

No answer. Voice mail.

Magda likes her new car—a powder-blue Volkswagen Jetta perfect for navigating the traffic of the greater Mexico City metropolitan area and easy to park, as it is now at the Centro Las Américas shopping mall in the suburb of Ecatepec.

As much as she enjoyed Europe, and as successful as her trip was, she's glad to be home. And it's somehow symbolic of the "new Mexico" that her gynecologist's office is in a sparkling new shopping mall with the Nordstrom, the Macy's, the Bed Bath & Beyond.

Everything is commerce now, she thinks, even babies.

She wonders how Adán will react to the news she just got.

Or should she even tell him?

A lot of women have children on their own these days, and certainly she has the economic wherewithal to raise a child by herself. The fact that she's a multimillionaire still surprises her, but certainly she doesn't need a man to provide formula, diapers, and all the other paraphernalia that comes with a baby. She can hire platoons of nannies, if she wants, and she doesn't have to worry about some company granting her maternity leave.

After her diplomatic mission to Europe, she's going to be even richer.

The Italians, the 'Ndrangheta, loved her—more important, they respected her—and she's confident that they'll give her new customers not only in Italy but in France, Spain, and Germany as well.

So which good news shall I give Adán first, she asks herself as she slips behind the wheel: that he's going to make billions of dollars in new money in Europe, or that he's finally going to be a daddy?

And how will he react?

Will he divorce his young queen to marry me?

Do you want him to?

She's become used to her freedom and independence; she's not sure she wants to saddle herself with a husband. At the same time, the son of Adán Barrera—if it does turn out to be a boy—will inherit vast wealth and power. And if it's a girl? Fuck them all—she'll inherit a nice piece of change and influence herself.

Her mother is a *buchona*.

Magda pulls out of the mall parking lot and has only gone a couple of blocks when she sees the flashers behind her.

"Damn it," she says.

Ever since the arrest that put her into Puente Grande, she's had a fear of the police. It's irrational, she has no reason for fear, because Mexico City is Nacho Esparza's plaza, and she's protected.

She pulls over, looks in the rearview mirror, and sees two cops get out of the car. One of them comes up, and she winds down the window. The cop wears a mask over the bottom half of his face, but this doesn't worry her. Most police disguise themselves these days. She gives him her best beautiful-woman smile. "What did I do?"

"Did you know that one of your rear taillights is out?"

"No, I—"

The second cop gets into the backseat and sticks a gun barrel into her neck. "Just be quiet and you'll be fine."

The first cop slides in beside Magda and says, "Drive."

As she pulls out again and drives, she says, "You're making a big mistake. Do you know who I am?"

The cop takes off the mask.

It's Heriberto Ochoa—Z-1.

Now Magda is scared, especially when Ochoa gives her directions and tells her to pull off in a vacant lot next to a construction site. A gun is pressed into the back of her neck, so she does it.

"How was Europe?" Ochoa asks. "Good trip?"

God, she thinks, he knows about that. "It was fine."

"Who did you talk to?"

"You already know."

"Yes, I do," Ochoa says. "You're not going to talk to them anymore."

"That's fine. I won't."

"I know you won't. Take off your blouse."

Her hand shakes as she starts with the top button. It's black silk. New. Expensive.

"Slow," Ochoa says. "Tease me."

She does it.

"Now the bra."

Magda takes it off.

Ochoa leers at her breasts. "Nice. Does Barrera like to suck on them? I asked you a question—does he?"

"Yes."

"The skirt."

Magda unzips it along the side and slides it down her hips. It's hard to do from behind the wheel, but she gets it done and the skirt pools at her feet. She's terrified, but underneath that is fury. Fury that men do this, that they can do this, that they do this *because* they can. She knows it's not about sex but humiliation, and she *is* humiliated and it makes her furious. Then she sees the knife in his hand. "No. Please. I'll do anything you say."

"Anything?" Ochoa asks. "What do you do for Barrera?"

"Everything."

Ochoa says, "I'm not interested in Barrera's leftovers."

The man in the backseat grabs her by the shoulders and holds her as Ochoa forces a plastic bag over her head. Magda can't breathe, she sucks for air, but all she gets is plastic in her mouth. Her legs kick out spasmodically, her back arches, her hands grab at the bag and try to take it off.

She's almost dead when Ochoa pulls the bag off. Magda gasps for air. When she can speak, she croaks. "Please . . . I'm going to have a baby . . ."

"Barrera's?" Ochoa asks.

Magda nods.

He puts the bag back on.

The pain is horrible. Her body spasms violently, she wets herself. And then he pulls it off again.

"The world doesn't need another Barrera," Ochoa says.

He leans away and the man in back pulls the trigger.

Two hours later police responding to an anonymous tip go out to the corner of 16th Street and Maravillas, where they find a female body in the trunk of a powder-blue 2007 Jetta.

Her stomach has been sliced open and a large "Z" carved into her chest and stomach.

Marisol hears something.

She feels alone, and embarrassed that she also feels a little spooked. It's the wind blowing through the trees, she tells herself. It's nothing.

But she jumps when her phone rings.

It's Arturo.

"I'm about twenty minutes out," he says.

"Oh . . . that's good."

"Are you all right?"

"Yes, of course fine," Marisol says. She walks to the window and looks out. "Erika is supposed to come but she hasn't shown up yet."

"She didn't call?"

Marisol hears the worry in his voice. "She's probably with Carlos."

"Stay in the house until I get there," Keller says. *"Do you have the Beretta?"*

"I'm sure it's nothing, it's—"

"Do you have the Beretta? Go into the bathroom. Lock the door."

"Arturo, don't be silly—"

"God damn it, Mari, do what I tell you! I'm going to call you back in two minutes."

Marisol thinks she sees people in the trees now. Must be my imagination, she thinks. Arturo has made me nervous.

"What?" he asks, sensing her anxiety on the silence.

"Nothing. I just think I see some people is all."

"Get into the bathroom now."

She goes into the bathroom and locks the door.

Chuy watches the police car roll slowly past.

It's time.

He hefts his *erre*.

Chuy has never killed a woman before.

There was a time when that would have made a difference, but it doesn't anymore. He doesn't even contemplate the distinction, it doesn't occur to him that he took an oath in La Familia to cherish and protect women.

Now he's seen so many killed, and they die like anyone else.

They want this one hurt first.

Taken, hurt, and cut up.

As a lesson.

Erika pulls up at Town Hall and runs upstairs to grab a sweatshirt. Then she gets back in her car for the short drive to Marisol's. She can recharge her phone there.

Keller phones Erika.

Still no answer.

He calls Taylor. "Get people over to Marisol Cisneros's house in Valverde now."

"Keller—"

"We'll talk about it later. Just do it now."

"I don't have people in—"

"Do it *now*." He gets on with Orduña. "I need men in Valverde right away."

"The closest we have are in Juárez."

"Chopper them out. Now."

He gets back on with Marisol.

"Stay on the line with me," he says. "It's going to be all right. Stay on the line with me. I'll be there in five."

"I hear something outside," Marisol says.

"It's probably nothing," Keller says, his heart racing. "But if they come in, shoot through the bathroom door. Aim stomach high, by the doorknob. Do you understand? Stomach high, by the doorknob."

"Stomach high. Arturo . . . I'm afraid."

"I'm five minutes away."

Chuy sees the woman police get out of the car.

As she reaches back inside to get her rifle, Chuy's men are already on her. She puts up a fight but they rip the gun from her hands, open the back door of her car, and push her in.

She yells, screams, and punches.

Marisol hears Erika.

Screaming, cursing.

She wants to stay inside. Put her hands over ears, close her eyes, and wait for Arturo to come. But she can't. She pulls herself up off the floor on her cane, and walks out. She hears Arturo's voice—*Are you okay? I'm almost there. You're going to be fine*—and she says. "Good, good, I'm fine."

Marisol opens the door to the house to see men shoving Erika into her car. Shaking, she raises the pistol and shoots.

Chuy feels the bullet zing past his head. He looks up to see a woman in the doorway of the house, shooting a little pistol at them. Raising his rifle, he goes to blow her away, but then he remembers that Forty wants her alive. Then he hears an engine, turns to see headlights coming at him, and hears shots coming from the car that's roaring down on them.

So he lowers the gun, climbs into the passenger seat, and says, *"Vamanos!"*

Keller sees Marisol standing in the doorway, the pistol in her hand. She yells, "They have Erika!" and points down the road.

He keeps going.

Out into the countryside.

Off the pavement, onto dirt.

Down along the south side of the river under the cottonwoods. He can hear the car in front of him but it's gaining ground, the sound of the engine fading.

A bullet hits his windshield, spiderwebbing the glass.

Keller keeps going but then the sniper takes out the front right tire. It blows out and he goes into a skid, fishtailing into the ditch. Opening the passenger door, he doesn't make the mistake of using it as cover, because the professional *sicarios* shoot through car doors. So he dives out onto his stomach, rolls away from the car, and crawls back to the edge of the ditch.

He can hear the car getting farther away and knows what's happened. They dropped a shooter off to stop the pursuit.

A bullet comes by his face.

The shooter must have a night scope.

And a high-powered rifle.

All Keller has is his pistol.

And no time if he's going to help Erika.

He moves to make some noise, waits for the next shot and then yells in pain, and slides back into the ditch. It takes thirty seconds but then he hears the shooter coming toward him.

Keller waits.

The shot could come any second, but he waits until he hears the shooter's feet crunch on some dry leaves. Then he lunges for the shooter's ankles. Feels the burn of the muzzle flash on the side of his face, but takes the shooter's feet out from under him and jumps on top of him, trapping the rifle against his chest.

Keller slams the pistol butt into the side of the shooter's face again and again until he feels the body go limp. He pulls the SAT phone off the shooter's hip, hits the button, and says, "I have one of your guys. Bring her back or I'll kill him."

He hears a thin, young voice answer casually, "Kill him."

The line goes dead.

Keller goes back to the car and tries to get it out of the ditch, but it's no good. Then he walks back to the wounded man.

He's groggy, but conscious.

That's good. Keller wants him conscious.

"Where did they take her?!" Keller yells.

"I don't know."

I don't have time for this, Keller thinks. Erika doesn't have time for this. He picks up the man's rifle and slams the stock down onto his left leg. The bone shatters and the man screams.

"I don't know!"

Keller grabs the man's foot and shoves it toward his chest, driving the sharp jagged shin bone up through his flesh.

The man howls.

"Listen to me," Keller says. "I'm going to hurt you bad. You're going to beg me to kill you. But first you're going to tell me where they took her."

"I don't know!"

Keller drives the gunstock onto the broken bone.

"I don't *knoooooooowwwwwwww*!!!"

Keller grabs a piece of the torn flesh in his hands and rips downward, skinning it off the man's leg.

The man babbles.

He's a Zeta . . . He doesn't know where they took the policewoman . . . Somewhere out in the countryside . . . Yes, he does know who the leader of the team was . . . They call him Jesus the Kid . . . they were supposed to take the policewoman and La Médica Hermosa . . .

"Where? Where is she?"

Keller rips more flesh off the leg.

The man vomits.

Cries, whimpers, tries to crawl away, his fingers digging in the dirt, a smear of blood behind him.

They search all night.

Marine and army helicopters shine searchlights down on the river-bed. Military vehicles cruise up and down every road and track. Ordinary citizens—if such courage can be described as ordinary—go out in their own pickup trucks to look for Erika Valles.

They don't find her.

They do find her car, pulled off along the riverbank.

Chuy lies in an arroyo and watches all the commotion.

They dumped the car along the river and then dragged the woman police off to the south, through the old cotton fields and then into the desert.

Now she lies beside him.

He'd cut the sleeve off her shirt and stuffed it into her mouth, so she didn't scream, not too loud anyway.

It's time to go now, while the soldiers are looking along the river.

Using the arroyo as cover, he leads his team away.

They find Erika a little after dawn.

The vultures led them to the site.

Keller squats beside her, then personally collects what's left of Erika Valles and gently places the pieces of her into a body bag.

He puts the jack of spades he found on her chest in his pocket.

The marines take him to Marisol's house.

Now there are soldiers on guard out front, now there are *federales* and Chihuahua state police.

Now.

Colonel Alvarado stands outside the house by a knot of his soldiers. When Keller walks up to him, he says, "I'm so sorry to hear about—"

Keller launches the punch from the ground and hits him square in the mouth. Alvarado falls back into one of his soldiers, then, as his men start toward Keller, pulls his pistol.

Keller pulls his Sig Sauer and points it at his face.

A dozen rifle barrels come up, aimed at Keller.

"Do it," Keller says. "Tell them to do it. Or my hand to fucking God I'll kill you where you stand. I don't care anymore."

Alvarado wipes a smear of blood from his mouth. "Get out. Get out of my country."

"It isn't your country," Keller says. "You don't deserve this country."

He feels someone grab his elbow and turns to swing.

It's Orduña.

"Come on," Orduña says. "These pigs aren't worth it."

He walks Keller into the house.

Marisol is sitting at the kitchen table, an untouched cup of tea on the table by her hand.

She looks up when Keller comes in.

A look that asks him to give her the world back.

He wishes he could. He'd give anything if he could.

But he shakes his head.

The look on her face is horrific. She grows old in an instant. Then she gets up. "I want to see her."

"You don't, Mari."

"I have to go to her!"

Keller grabs her and holds her tight. "You don't. I'm begging you. It's nothing you want to see."

"I want to take care of her."

"I will," Keller says. "I'll take good care of her."

Marisol breaks down sobbing. Keller finally persuades her to take a pill, and when she finally falls asleep, he walks outside.

The soldiers are gone, replaced with FES troopers.

"I need a vehicle," he tells Orduña. "I need a jeep."

"*We* can bring the body in," Orduña says.

"I have to do it."

Orduña orders a man to bring around a jeep, and the marines help Keller load the body bag onto the back and then strap it on.

There's no undertaker in Valverde anymore, one of the bitterest ironies of the whole thing. Keller has to drive to Juárez, where the undertakers have become rich in the city's one thriving industry. He asks Orduña, "Look after her."

"She'll be safe."

Keller gets in and starts west toward Juárez.

The soldiers respectfully let him through the checkpoint, and he delivers the body to a funeral home that Pablo Mora refers him to. The reporter knows all the funeral homes and he and Ana meet Keller at the one he recommends.

"How's Marisol?" Ana asks.

"Not good."

"I'll go," Ana says.

"That would be nice."

The funeral director isn't shocked at the condition of Erika's body. He's seen too much of it. He gives Keller this Humpty-Dumpty line that would be sick if it weren't sincere. "We will put her back together again."

"Okay."

"We'll make her look nice. You'll see."

She looked nice before, Keller thinks.

She looked plenty nice.

A twenty-year-old woman brave enough to volunteer for a job in which everyone else had been killed? And they murdered her for it, and cut her up, just to show everyone who's really in charge.

No, Keller thinks, just to show *you* who's really in charge.

He heads back out to the jeep.

They take him on the street and they're very good.

He hears the footsteps but someone has a pistol jammed into his kidneys before he can pull his weapon, and they move him into the van, push him to the floor, get a hood over his head, and have the van moving again within seconds.

Keller feels the van drive out of the city.

The urban sounds fade and they're in the country.

They drive for hours. Finally, the van pulls over and Keller tries to prepare himself, knowing that you're never prepared for this. He hears the van door slide open, then feels hands picking him up, taking him out, and guiding his steps.

The air feels good.

He hears someone give an order and recognizes the voice as that of Colonel Alvarado.

Alvarado works for Adán Barrera, so Keller wonders how long it will be before they force him to his knees and put a bullet in the back of his head.

The hood comes off, and Keller sees Alvarado.

He expected that.

He didn't expect Tim Taylor.

Adán heard a gurgling sound in the distance and then realized that it was close, that it came from his own throat as he heard about Magda.

It was Nacho who brought him the news.

Nacho, the harbinger, the raven, with the discreet bearing and hushed solicitous voice of a funeral director. And yet there was this salacious undertone, this frisson of pleasure as he described what the Zetas did to her.

"I'll call you back," Adán said.

He staggered up the stairs.

Did they have to do that? Strip her, torture her, slice her up, carve their filthy calling card into her? Did they have to do *that*?

He went to the bathroom, knelt in front of the toilet, and threw up. He vomited again and again until his stomach muscles hurt and the back of his throat was raw and then he laid his face in his forearms on the toilet.

"*I'm* the one who's supposed to have morning sickness," he heard Eva say.

He turned around and looked up to see her smiling at him.

"Something I ate," he said, "didn't agree with me, I guess."

"You can't eat spicy anymore," Eva said. "I keep telling the cook but she doesn't listen. We should let her go."

"Whatever you want."

Eva ran some cold water, took a washcloth, and held it against his forehead. This was her newest persona—maternal, caregiving, beatific. She'd been honing it since she came back from the doctor with the news that she was pregnant. Two months in, she already had that storied glow, although Adán suspected that was cosmetic.

When Eva had cared for him sufficiently, she went back to bed. Adán brushed his teeth and rinsed his mouth and then went back downstairs.

It's over, he decided.

This overabundance of caution, this sensitivity to time and situation. It's time to deal with his enemies, put an end to things, settle them once and for all.

Time to settle with Ochoa.

Time to settle with Keller.

He called Nacho back and gave the necessary orders.

Now he sits and waits for the man to be delivered to him.

"How long have you been working with Barrera?" Keller asks. "The whole goddamn time?"

"No," Taylor says.

They're standing outside a prefab building out in the country. It could be anywhere in the north, but Keller knows from the length of the drive that they're probably still in the Juárez Valley.

"Just *now*," Keller says. "You're just working with him *now*."

"The Zetas killed one of our guys!" Taylor yells. "And I will stop at *nothing* . . . You of all people should understand that. You think I like it? I've spent my life fighting scumbags like Adán Barrera, but now it's either him or the Zetas, and I choose him."

"So you've made a deal," Keller says. "What am I, the kicker?"

"It's not what you think."

"Go to hell."

Alvarado starts in. "You North Americans are clean because you *can* be. That has never been a choice for us, either as individuals or as a nation. You're experienced enough to know that we're not offered a choice of taking the money or not, we are given the choice of taking the money or dying. We've been forced to choose sides, so we choose the best side we can and get on with it. What would you have us do? The country was falling apart, violence getting worse every day. The only way to end the chaos was to pick the most likely winner and help him win. And you North Americans despise us for it at the same time you send the billions of dollars and the weapons that fuel the violence. You blame us for selling the product that you buy. It's absurd."

And convenient, Keller thinks. "You sided with Barrera and then grabbed with both hands—money, land, power."

"Just listen," Taylor says. "For once in your life, Keller, just goddamn listen."

They take him inside.

He's aged.

Adán Barrera always had a boyish face, but that's gone now, along with the shock of black hair that always fell over his forehead. His hair is cut short, there are hints of gray, and lines around the eyes now.

He's aged, Keller thinks, and so have I.

Keller sees bodyguards stand within sight but out of earshot. They're going to shoot me right in front of him, Keller thinks. Or he'll do it himself if he's grown the balls.

Either way, it's a matter of personal satisfaction for him.

Or it might not be shooting, it might be torture.

Slower, more satisfying.

Despite himself, Keller feels a jolt of pure terror.

Adán still wears the black business suit and the white shirt, Keller notices as Adán sits down across from him. It's strange, to say the least, to be so close to this man he's been hunting for over six years now. But here he is, Adán Barrera in the flesh.

"We need to talk, Arturo," Adán says. "We've put this off too long."

"Talk."

"My daughter choked to death," Adán says. "Did you know that?"

"If you're going to kill me, kill me. I don't need to sit here waiting while you justify yourself."

"If I wanted you dead," Adán says, "you'd already be dead. I'm not a sadist like Ochoa. I don't need to see, participate in, or prolong your death. I asked Taylor to come so that you'd be reassured that I mean you no harm today."

"Just so we're clear," Keller says, "I mean *you* harm. Today and every day."

"The Zetas murdered one of your own," Adán says. "You, of all people, should know how that alters the terrain. Your superiors will stop at nothing to avenge him, just as you will stop at nothing to avenge your fallen comrade. Believe me, I respect it."

"You don't respect anything."

"I know what you think of me," Adán says calmly. "I know you think that I'm evil incarnate—I think the same of you—but we both know that there are far worse demons out there."

"The Zetas?"

"You were at San Fernando," Adán says. "You saw what they're capable of. Now they've apparently done it again."

"And you're telling me you care about that."

"They killed one of my loved ones," Adán said, "and they killed one of yours."

"What do you want?" Keller asks. He's sick to death of all this talk.

Adán says, "I had you brought here to propose a truce between us."

Keller can't believe what he's hearing. A *truce* between them? They've been at war with each other for over thirty years.

"We make peace between us," Adán continues, "to fight the Zetas."

"I have enough hate for you *and* the Zetas."

"I agree that you have an unlimited capacity for hatred," Adán says. "In fact, I'm counting on it. You have ample hatred, what you don't have enough of are resources. Neither do I."

"What are you talking about?"

"The Zetas are winning," Adán says simply. "They'll soon have all of Tamaulipas, Nuevo León, and Michoacán. They're moving in Acapulco, Guerrero, Durango, even Sinaloa. Down south they've sent forces into Quintana Roo and Chiapas, to protect the border with Guatemala. If they succeed in taking Guatemala, it's over. Neither I nor you will be able to stop them. They'll control the cocaine trade, not just in the U.S. but in Europe, too. If it gives you a personal rooting interest, they're moving into the Juárez Valley, too. It wasn't me who slaughtered Erika Valles, who tried to kill Dr. Cisneros. They'll try again. Eventually they'll succeed."

Taylor weighs in. "The Mexican government will do anything to stop the Zetas from becoming the dominant force. They would be virtually a shadow government. But the FES combined with American intelligence is by far the strongest force fighting the Zetas. We can annihilate them."

"What do you need me for?" Keller asks. "You already have the government on your side, apparently on both sides of the border."

"Orduña and the FES are loyal to you personally," Adán says. "The operation you've created together is tremendously effective. I don't want to see it disrupted. Also . . ."

"What?"

Adán smiles ruefully. "You're the best they have, aren't you? Taylor can put you on the shelf and send someone else, but whoever that is would be second best, and I can't afford second best. Neither can you, and I'm by far the best offer you have, the best ally. You hate me, but you need me. And vice versa."

"And if I say no?" Keller asks. "I get a bullet in the neck?"

"If you reject my offer," Adán says, "you walk away from this meeting, your organization puts you on the shelf, and it's business as usual between us."

"I'm not going to help you become the king of the drug world again."

"Do you think anyone is serious about the so-called war on drugs?" Adán asks. "A few cops on the street, perhaps—some low- to middle-management crusaders like yourself, maybe—but at the top levels? Government and business?

"Serious people can't afford to be serious about it. Especially not after 2008. After the crash, the only source of liquidity *was* drug money. If they shut us down, it would have taken the economy on the final plunge. They had to bail out General Motors, not us. And now? Think of the billions of dollars into real estate, stocks, start-up companies. Not to mention the millions of dollars generated fighting the 'war'—weapons manufacture, aircraft, surveillance. Prison construction. You think business is going to let that stop?

"I'll take it a step further—let me tell you why the U.S. won't let the Zetas win—because the Zetas want the oil, because they're interfering with new drilling—and the oil companies are never going to let that happen. Exxon-Mobil, BP—they're on my side, because I won't interfere with their business. In turn, they will not interfere with mine. Bottom line? Someone is going to sell the drugs. Now, it's either going to be Ochoa or me, and I'm the better choice. I'll bring peace and stability. Ochoa will bring more suffering. You know that. And you know that you need to do everything you can to bring him down, or you can't live with yourself."

"I'll give it a try, though."

Adán looks at him for several long seconds. "I'm going to have a child. Twins, and I want to raise them without being hunted. I don't want their lives to be like mine. If you'll end your vendetta, so will I."

End the vendetta, Keller thinks.

After all these years.

After Tío, and Ernie.

The children on the bridge, the dead of El Sauzal.

It's impossible.

But then there's Córdova's murdered family, Don Pedro Alejo de Castillo, the bodies in the mass grave at San Fernando.

Keller sees Erika's butchered body.

Marisol's stricken face.

Barrera is right—the Zetas failed to kill Marisol so they'll have to try again. They won't stop until they succeed. And there's something else, something ugly, and he has to face it. Barrera is right about that, too—my capacity for hatred is infinite.

I want revenge.

And I'll sell my soul to get it.

"I want them all dead," Keller says. "Every one of them."

"Good."

"You have to give me your word," Taylor says. "Your vendetta against Adán is over. Finished."

"You have my word," Keller says.

"On our immortal souls, on the lives of our children." Adán offers his hand.

Keller takes it.

Why not? he thinks.

We're all the cartel now.

"It's a new day," Taylor says.

They say that love conquers all.

They're wrong, Keller thinks.

Hate conquers all.

It even conquers hate.

PART FIVE

The Cleansing

People don't usually go off decapitating each other or committing mass murder just because they hate people in another group. These things happen because soul-dead political leaders are in a struggle for power and use ethnic violence as a tool in that struggle.

—David Brooks
"In the Land of Mass Graves"
The New York Times
June 19, 2014

1

Jihad

The U.S. government has in recent years fought what it termed wars against AIDS, drug abuse, poverty, illiteracy and terrorism. Each of these wars has budgets, legislation, offices, officials, letterhead—everything necessary in a bureaucracy to tell you something is real.

—Bruce Jackson
Keynote address
"Media and War" symposium, University of Buffalo
November 17–18, 2003

Nuevo Laredo
April 2012

The bodies of fourteen Zetas, skinned, lie in the backs of garbage trucks. The symbolism, Keller thinks, is deft.

Keller looks at the flayed corpses—Adán Barrera's announcement that he's back in Nuevo Laredo—and thinks that he should be feeling more than he is. Years ago he'd looked at nineteen bodies and his heart had broken, but now he feels nothing. Years ago the machine-gunning of nineteen men, women, and children was the worst atrocity he ever thought he'd see. Now he knows better.

A *narcomensaje* has been left with the bodies: WE HAVE BEGUN TO CLEAR NUEVO LAREDO OF ZETAS BECAUSE WE WANT A FREE CITY AND SO YOU CAN LIVE IN PEACE. WE ARE NARCOTICS TRAFFICKERS AND WE DON'T MESS WITH HONEST WORKING OR BUSINESS PEOPLE. I'M GOING TO TEACH THESE SCUM HOW TO WORK SINALOA STYLE—WITHOUT KIDNAPPING, WITHOUT EXTORTION. AS FOR YOU, OCHOA AND FORTY—YOU DON'T SCARE ME. DON'T FORGET THAT I'M YOUR TRUE FATHER—SINCERELY, ADÁN BARRERA.

Keller finds the paternal language interesting.

Adán is a father again—a year ago, Eva Barrera flew up to Los Angeles and gave birth to twin sons. There was nothing that DEA or the Justice

Department could do about Eva's presence in the United States. An American citizen not wanted for any crimes, she was free to come and go as she pleased. So Eva had her children in the best facility that money could buy, rested for a few days, and then flew back to Mexico, where she "disappeared" into the hills of Sinaloa or Durango, or even into Guatemala or Argentina, depending on which rumor you preferred.

The talk is that the birth of the twins reinvigorated Adán, is perhaps even the cause of his all-out invasion of Tamaulipas. Because he needs a plaza for each son—Nuevo Laredo for one, Juárez for the other, and Tijuana to keep Nacho Esparza happy. In any case, the man who could not produce an heir now has two, named for his late uncle and brother.

Speaking of garbage, Keller thinks.

This isn't Barrera's first venture into "bodies as public relations."

A few months earlier, masked gunmen blocked traffic on a major intersection in the Boca del Río section of Veracruz and dumped thirty-five naked and dismembered corpses, twelve of them women, with the *narcomensaje* NO MORE EXTORTION, NO MORE KILLINGS OF INNOCENT PEOPLE! ZETAS IN VERACRUZ AND THE POLITICIANS HELPING THEM—THIS IS GOING TO HAPPEN TO YOU. PEOPLE OF VERACRUZ, DO NOT ALLOW YOURSELVES TO BE EXTORTED; DO NOT PAY FOR PROTECTION. THIS IS GOING TO HAPPEN TO ALL THE ZETA-FUCKS THAT CONTINUE TO OPERATE IN VERACUZ. THIS PLAZA HAS A NEW PROPRIETOR. SINCERELY, ADÁN BARRERA.

While most of the major papers and television stations shied away from coverage, *Esta Vida* did not, posting graphic photos of the naked bodies dumped into the street like so much, well, garbage. The Zetas were almost as infuriated by the coverage as they were by the event, and threatened horrific retaliation when they found "Wild Child."

The next day, it was discovered that the thirty-five dead probably had no connection whatsoever with the Zetas. A masked vigilante group held a press conference, apologized for the mistake, but declared that it was still at war against the Zetas.

Over the next three weeks, the vigilante group killed seventy-five more Zetas in Veracruz and Acapulco, both cities vacated by the demise of the Tapia organization and then the "disappearance" of Crazy Eddie Ruiz. The *susurro* has it that the Sinaloans are moving into Veracruz as a port of entry for the precursor chemicals they need for their expansion into methamphetamine; rumor further has it that Adán Barrera himself has been spotted in the city.

Bodies from both sides piled up, almost literally, in Durango. Eleven here, eight there, then sixty-eight in a mass grave—eventually the number rose to over three hundred.

Zetas invading Nayarit stumbled into an ambush in which Barrera *sicarios* gunned down twenty-seven of them on the highway. Almost, Keller thinks, as if the Sinaloans had been forewarned, as if they'd been handed American satellite images of the Zeta trucks moving in.

The U.S. intelligence apparatus in Mexico has expanded dramatically since the Jiménez murder. There are now over sixty DEA agents, forty ICE, twenty U.S. marshals, and dozens of FBI, Immigration and Customs, Secret Service, and TSA personnel, as well as seventy people from the State Department Narcotics Affairs Section in-country as a response to the murder of Richard Jiménez.

A lot of their "ISR"—intelligence, surveillance, and reconnaissance—resources are routed via Keller to the FES.

Orduña's unit has been killing Zetas, too—eighteen during a three-day battle in Valle Hermoso, Tamaulipas, with convoys of up to fifty vehicles full of armed Zetas bringing in reinforcements.

An FES patrol hit a Zeta training base on Falcon Lake, bordering Texas, and killed twelve. Another pitched battle was fought in Zacatecas, where more than 250 Zetas fought the FES in a five-hour running gunfight. The FES killed fifteen Zetas and arrested seventeen more. In another action, FES troopers dropped down fast-lines from helicopters and raided another Zeta camp, capturing nineteen more.

And the FES, with the aid of U.S. intelligence, has been pounding the Zeta leadership, arresting gunmen, plaza bosses, and financial officers. Over eighty Zetas alone have been arrested in connection with the first San Fernando bus massacre. Six Zetas, including a character with the *aporto* "Tweety-Bird," have been arrested in connection with the murder of Agent Jiménez, although if Keller had his way, none of the six would have made it into a cell.

A weeklong FES campaign against the Zetas in Veracruz resulted in twenty-one more arrests and the seizure of a payroll list for eighteen Veracruz police officers on the take—depending on rank, they received between $145 and $700 a month.

Two former navy admirals took over the police departments in Veracruz and Boca del Río.

Based on an "anonymous tip"—a euphemism for American intelligence—

the FES captured the Zeta plaza boss for Veracruz, who confirmed that Ochoa had personally ordered Erika Valles's killing.

"Why didn't they kill Cisneros?" Keller asked.

"Z-1 said he wanted to do her last," the plaza boss answered. "Let the big-mouth *chocha* watch her friend die first. But they fucked it up."

"Where is Z-1 now?"

The man didn't know. It turned out under enhanced interrogation techniques that he *really* didn't know. Didn't know where Forty was, either.

Maybe Monterrey.

Once the jewel of the PAN economic revival, the symbol of modern corporate Mexico with shiny skyscrapers, boulevards of exclusive stores, and trendy restaurants patronized by *regios*—the young up-and-coming—Monterrey has become a nightmare.

With police basically paralyzed, crime has gotten out of control.

Downtown stores and restaurants are regularly robbed. There's open fighting in the streets—a man was chased down, shot, and then hanged from a bridge in front of a horrified crowd.

At a trendy restaurant that made the mistake of serving Sinaloan cuisine, about a hundred *regios* were enjoying beers and *aguachile* about midnight when seven Zeta gunmen came in, made everyone lie on the floor, collected wallets and cell phones, then separated the men from the women and systematically took the women into the restrooms and raped them.

The women were afraid to press charges because their assailants kept their identification cards for purposes of retaliation.

It got worse.

A Zeta cell in the city tried to extort a casino known for laundering narco money through its accounts. The casino owners refused to pay. Keller has seen the videotapes of two pickup trucks pulling up to a Pemex station and filling plastic barrels full of gasoline. Other security cameras caught the trucks pulling up to the Casino Royale on a Saturday afternoon at about two o'clock in the afternoon. Seven gunmen get out of the trucks. They walk into the casino lobby and start to shoot. They come out, and the other Zetas roll the barrels into the casino and set them on fire.

The emergency exits were padlocked and chained.

Fifty-three people died of flame, smoke, and toxins.

Five of the attackers arrested later in the week said that they didn't mean to kill anyone, that they were just trying to scare the owners into paying the 130,000 pesos a week.

More critical than Monterrey, the Zetas are taking ground—literally taking ground—in Guatemala, especially in the north, in the Petén district bordering Mexico. Last year, the Zetas slaughtered twenty-seven campesinos in the province, terrifying countless others off their smallholdings, and now Ochoa is consolidating power there. If he controls Guatemala, he takes Barrera's main cocaine route into Mexico.

And the weakened CDG is (barely) hanging on against the Zetas in Matamoros, Reynosa is once again under contention between the Zetas and the CDG, and the border towns are a howling wilderness.

Despite the FES and Sinaloa pressure, the Zetas control—*rule*, really—large swaths of Mexico. They dominate numerous state and municipal police forces, have effectively silenced the mainstream media, and have established a virtual reign of terror.

And now Barrera has taken the war right into the Zeta stronghold of Nuevo Laredo.

Again.

This poor city, Keller thinks as he walks away from the garbage truck display—that's all you can call it, truly, a "display."

First Sinaloa fights the Gulf and the Zetas for it.

Then the Gulf and the Zetas fight each other.

Now Sinaloa fights the Zetas.

Well, Sinaloa and us.

Me.

Me and my new best friend Adán Barrera.

Barrera has shifted his focus to Nuevo Laredo, so Keller has, too, taking up residence in a nondescript "long-stay" hotel across the bridge in Laredo. He moves between Laredo and Mexico City, with only occasional stops in Valverde to see Marisol.

There's "light" as in the opposite of "dark," Keller thinks as he gets back in his car for the trip back across the bridge, and "light" as in the opposite of "heavy," and his relationship with Marisol now has aspects of dark weight.

The weight of guilt, for one—Marisol's guilt for having let Erika take the dangerous job. Keller's guilty for not having been there to protect her, for failing to have rescued her.

Add to that a sense of immutable loss.

"Let's be honest," Marisol said one night during one of her starkly darker moods. "We had this little faux family going here, didn't we? Faux marriage, faux child? Then reality hit, didn't it?"

"Let's get married for real, then," Keller suggested.

She stared at him incredulously. "Do you seriously think that's going to help?"

"It could."

"How?'

He didn't have an answer for that.

The rest of their mutual ennui, he supposes, is simply cumulative. He had read that the Puritans used to execute heretics by placing stones on their chests until their rib cages were crushed or they suffocated. And that's a little what he feels like—and he supposes that Marisol does as well—the sheer cumulative weight of death after death, sorrow after sorrow, crushing them, taking the air out of their lives.

But they don't split up. They're both too stubborn and honorable, he thinks, to go back on the unspoken vow, the silent understanding that they would see this through together, wherever it led.

So they stay together.

Well, sort of.

He spends more and more time in the Mexico City bunker, in Laredo, on raids with FES, or on whatever front of the Mexican drug war is especially hot at the moment. Marisol is kind enough to feign sadness when he leaves, but they're both (guiltily) relieved for the breaks from the weight that they enforce on each other.

The painful truth is that they can't look at each other without seeing Erika.

Despite his urgings, his imprecations, his angry arguments, Marisol has stayed in Valverde, and stayed in office. She forced herself to make a brilliant, defiant speech at Erika's funeral, made herself go through a press conference in which she again openly defied both the government and the cartels while managing to imply that there was small, if any, difference between the two. She once again made herself a target, almost as if she could not tolerate living after so many have died.

"Survivor guilt," Keller said to her one night.

"Just as you did not appreciate my amateur psychoanalysis," Marisol answered, "I don't appreciate yours."

"I don't care if you appreciate it—"

"Thank you."

"—I care only that you don't carry out this death wish."

"I don't have a death wish," Marisol said.

"Prove it. Move to the States with me."

"I'm a Mexican."

"Then come to Mexico City."

"No."

He'd already sold his soul to the devil, so a bonus payment that bought security for Marisol didn't matter. Keller put out word to Adán, who sent word back to the army in the valley that La Médica Hermosa was now a friend, the lady of an important ally, to be protected at all costs.

"Do you think I'm stupid?" Marisol asked a few days later. "Did you think I wouldn't notice soldiers patrolling outside the house? The office? The clinic? They've never been there before. Nor have they ever followed my car except to harass me."

"Are they harassing you now?" asked Keller, concerned that his demand hadn't been met.

"In fact they're elaborately polite," Marisol said. "What did you do?"

"What I should have done sooner," Keller said. Except I didn't have the power then, the goddamn alliance with Adán.

"Such a powerful man," Marisol said. "I don't want them."

"I don't care."

"You don't care what I want?" Marisol asked, arching an eyebrow.

"Not in this case." He hated arguing, but it was better than the long silences, the averted eyes, the sidelong glances, the lying in bed side by side wanting to touch or at least speak but not being able. "I'm trying to protect you."

"You're patronizing me."

That's exactly what I'm doing, Keller thinks now.

Being a *patrón*.

It's what I do now.

Fourteen Zetas skinned alive.

And I provided the intelligence that located them.

He buys "dinner" at 7-Eleven before going back to his room.

The Zetas strike back less than two weeks later, killing twenty-three of Barrera's people. Fourteen of them are decapitated and nine hang from a bridge next to a banner reading FUCKING BARRERA WHORES, THIS IS HOW I'M GOING TO FINISH OFF EVERY FUCKER YOU SEND TO HEAT UP THE PLAZA. THESE GUYS CRIED AND BEGGED FOR MERCY. THE REST GOT AWAY BUT I'LL GET THEM SOONER OR LATER. SEE YOU AROUND, FUCKERS.—THE Z COMPANY.

The Nuevo Laredo police quickly come out and deny that the Sinaloa cartel is in the city, prompting Barrera's people to leave six severed heads in ice chests outside the Nuevo Laredo police station with the message YOU WANT CREDIBILITY THAT I'M IN NL? WHAT WILL IT TAKE, THE HEADS OF THE ZETA LEADERS? KEEP IT UP AND I ASSURE YOU THAT HEADS WILL KEEP ROLLING. I DON'T KILL INNOCENT PEOPLE LIKE YOU DO, FORTY, ALL THE DEAD ARE PURE SCUM—IN OTHER WORDS—PURE ZETAS. SINCERELY, YOUR FATHER, ADÁN.

Once again, the grisly images appear on *Esta Vida*.

Once again, the Zetas vow that they will find Wild Child.

The problem, Keller thinks, is that we can't get to Forty or Ochoa, and until we decapitate that two-headed snake, we won't crush the Zetas. We can take down as many underbosses as we want, but until we get Forty and Ochoa, the Zetas just keep marching on.

Forty is apparently again in charge of defending Nuevo Laredo from Barrera, but he's never spotted in the city. Barrera's people are looking for him, the FES is looking for him, American intelligence is looking for him, but so far, he's invisible. They just find his handiwork, hanging from bridges or dumped on the sides of roads.

And Ochoa is easily the most elusive cartel leader since, well, Adán Barrera. He moves from safe house to safe house, in Valle Hermoso, in Saltillo out in Coahuila. He's said to meet with Forty once a month at ranches in Río Bravo, Sabinas, or Hidalgo. Or they go hunting zebras, gazelles, and other "exotics" at private game ranches in Coahuila or San Luis Potosí. Or they watch their horses race as they sit in armored cars near the track, surrounded by bodyguards.

In all the Zeta territories, they hire *ventanas*—lookouts. *Ambulantes*, store clerks, neighborhood kids, who watch for the police or the marines, and use whistles or cell phones to give warnings. Los Tapados—"the Hidden Ones"—are poor children hired to put up pro-Zeta banners, chant slogans, and protest the presence of the military and the *federales*.

The government can't find Ochoa, and he shoves the fact in their faces. Just three hundred yards from an army base in the 18th Military Zone, he endowed a church, where a plaque reads CENTER OF EVANGELIZATION AND CATECHISM. DONATED BY HERIBERTO OCHOA. He uses a Nextel phone once, and then throws it away. Like Barrera, Z-1 eschews the showy persona of other narcos. He doesn't frequent clubs and restaurants, doesn't show off his wealth.

He just kills.

It's the hunt for Barrera redux, except this time the Mexican government is putting massive resources into the effort. MexSat, the national security system, operates two Boeing 702 HP satellite systems, costing over a billion dollars, from ground control stations in Mexico City and Hermosillo. It scans the country for signs of Forty and Ochoa and finds nothing.

American drones fly over the border area like hawks hunting for mice.

And find nothing.

"What if we're looking on the wrong border?" Keller asks Orduña one day in Mexico City. "What if they're not in Mexico at all? What if they're in Guatemala?"

Ochoa has a grasp of military history. What if he's adopted the classic guerrilla strategy of basing himself in an extraterritorial sanctuary across a border in a neutral country?

Where Barrera is relatively weak, and where the FES can't get to him. Even Orduña won't cross an international border. It makes sense—the Zetas have been increasingly active in Guatemala, and maybe Ochoa has decided to run his war from there.

"We're still talking about eight hundred miles of border," Orduña says. "Rain forest, jungle, hills."

"Wasn't there a mass killing in Guatemala recently?" Keller asks. "Twenty-seven people in a village? Where was that?"

The sort of thing that used to make headlines and is now considered just another day of business as usual. But Orduña goes back through the intelligence files and locates the site.

Dos Erres is a small village in the Petén district, in a heavily forested area not far from the border.

Orduña orders a satellite run.

Two days later, he and Keller look at the photographs.

The village itself looks pretty standard—a dirt road runs through a hamlet of small houses and huts, with a small church and what looks to be a school. But to the east of the village there's a freshly cut rectangle with the outlines of what seem to be neatly ordered rows of tents.

"It's a military camp," Orduña says. "A bivouac."

"Like special forces might build?" Keller asks.

They do another satellite run for closer images and get them. Perusing the new photos, Keller can clearly see men dressed in military-style uniforms around the tent sites, jeeps with mounted machine guns, "bush kitchens," and latrines.

The village itself seems oddly deserted.

No kids in the schoolyard.

Few people around the church.

There are some civilians, most of them seem to be women, but not as many as you would expect from the number of houses.

"The Zetas have taken over," Orduña says, "moved most of the people out and kept only enough to service their basic needs."

Cooking, Keller thinks.

Cleaning.

Sleeping with the men.

"Look at this," Keller says, pointing to images of the church and the school. Both buildings have men in the front and rear.

"Sentries?" Orduña asks. "Guards? Are Forty and Ochoa living in the church and the school?"

The old military saying, Keller thinks—"Rank hath its privileges." The two top-ranking officers don't live under canvas but in the two biggest buildings in the village. It's SOP.

The next satellite run yields gold.

Keller stares at the photo.

Then he flies to El Paso.

Fort Bliss is the living definition of a misnomer, Keller thinks as he drives onto the base on the semidesert flats east of El Paso.

He's seen little of Crazy Eddie since he lifted him out of Acapulco. Literally. One of those black-helicopter jobs that the right-wing crazies are always muttering about. Two minutes after getting Eddie's call, Keller was on a secure SAT line, exchanging coded messages with Washington that even his Mexican colleagues couldn't access. There was no telling how even Orduña would react to the U.S. snatching one of the most wanted men in Mexico.

An hour later, Keller was on a helicopter owned by a CIA shell corporation, which landed him on the roof of the Hotel Continental. He met a very nervous consular agent who took him into a small conference room where Eddie Ruiz sat.

Narco Polo, Keller thought. Eddie had on a sky-blue polo shirt with white chinos and a pair of sandals.

He looked tired but calm.

"We're going to get on a helicopter that will fly us to Ciudad Juárez," Keller said. "From there another helicopter will take us to Fort Bliss army base in Texas. If at any time during that process you try to run, I will put a bullet in the back of your head. Do you understand?"

"This *is* running," Eddie answered.

The flights went smoothly.

During the entire time, Eddie didn't say a word.

The suits were waiting when they got to Fort Bliss. A State Department attorney read him his rights, so to speak. "You are here as an American citizen, under protective custody based on prior, present, and future cooperation in ongoing investigations. Do you understand?"

"Sure."

It was a tag-team match. A federal deputy AG took over. "You have been indicted under the so-called Kingpin statutes for drug trafficking. But we are not arresting you at this moment. If you try to leave, or cease cooperating, you will be arrested and placed in the custody of the federal corrections system and be taken to trial. That being said, you do have the right to an attorney. If you cannot afford an attorney—"

Eddie chuckled. He had attorneys who owed *him* money.

"—one will be afforded to you. Do you wish an attorney?"

"No."

"In all probability," the prosecutor continued, "you will face trial on the trafficking charges. However, your past and future cooperation will be noted in your file for those prosecutors with a view toward charges and to the presiding judge with a view toward sentencing. Do you have any questions?"

"Can I get a Coke?"

"I think that could be worked out."

"One other thing," Eddie said. "I want to see my family."

"Which one?" Keller asked.

"Both of them. Asshole."

It was complicated, bringing first one and then the other of Eddie's family in to see him.

The Mexican narco-world was buzzing about the disappearance of Crazy Eddie Ruiz. Phone and Internet traffic exploded, and both the narcos and law enforcement were busy trying to chase it down.

Some said that he'd been killed in retaliation for kidnapping Martín Tapia's wife; others said that was bullshit because he'd released her. Still others responded that he was killed exactly because he *did* release her, by his own people, because they were afraid that he was weak.

They all agreed on one thing—Eddie was spotted in Acapulco the day of his disappearance, on the boardwalk eating an ice-cream cone.

But they were all out looking for him, or his body. They might also be watching his families.

His second wife, an American citizen, had crossed the border and was said to be with family in the area, but then again, she was nine months' pregnant and would have come into the States to have the baby anyway.

Keller made both contacts personally.

It was tricky.

Ex-wives—or in this case not exactly an *ex*-wife—are renowned snitches, but Eddie faithfully sent Teresa more than enough money to live well, and her parents were, until they got busted, involved in laundering his coke money, so Keller doubted that she'd be a problem.

Teresa was living in Atlanta, and when she came to the door and saw Keller she turned pale.

"Oh my God."

"Your husband is all right, Mrs. Ruiz."

She packed up the kids, nine and twelve years old, and they flew not to El Paso, where the airport might be under watch, but to Las Cruces, New Mexico, and drove down from there. Keller brought them to Eddie's quarters on the fort and then left them to have some privacy, picking them back up and taking them back to Las Cruces in the morning.

It was more complicated with Priscilla.

Their daughter, Brittany, was two and Priscilla was expecting any day. Keller was loath to drive her to El Paso, where there were about as many *halcones* as there were in Juárez. Instead, they dressed Eddie up in an army uniform and drove him to Alamogordo, where Priscilla, Brittany, and Priscilla's mother met them at a motel. Keller had their car followed from El Paso to make sure they didn't have a tail.

He gave Eddie the afternoon with his second family and then drove him back to Bliss, where he was comfortably ensconced in a bachelor officer's apartment on base, with a twenty-four/seven guard of U.S. marshals.

Eddie had other demands—he wanted an iPod, loaded with the Eagles, Steve Earle, Robert Earl Keen, and some Carrie Underwood. He wanted more visits with his families. And he wanted to watch the Super Bowl on a flat-screen HDTV, preferably with some decent chili and some cold beer.

"Shiner Bock," Eddie specified.

He watched the Packers beat the Steelers on a sixty-inch LED with two federal marshals, chili, and beer.

Keller turned down Eddie's invitation to join them.

Now he spreads the Dos Erres photos out on the coffee table in front of the sofa. "Is that them? Forty and Ochoa?"

"Yup."

Keller looks down at the photos that show two men standing outside the school in Dos Erres. Both are wearing black ball caps, but their faces are still visible. One is full-fleshed with a thick black mustache. The other is thin and hawklike. Handsome.

"You're sure," Keller says.

"They burned Chacho García to death in front of me," Eddie says. "You think I'm going to forget those faces? I promised myself I'd kill both those motherfuckers."

Well, we have that in common, Keller thinks.

He leaves Eddie at Fort Bliss and flies to Washington.

Keller slams his fist on the table. "We goddamn know where they are! We have positive IDs and we know exactly where they are!"

He points to the photos spread on the table.

The State Department rep from its Narcotics Affairs Section yells back, "And that's exactly the problem! They're in a foreign country!"

Keller had flown straight from El Paso to Washington to make his case for a strike on the Zeta camp at Dos Erres. It isn't going well—the administration, drone-happy as it is in South Asia, won't authorize a strike of any kind, manned or unmanned, in Guatemala.

"We already have marines there," Keller argues, "on an antitrafficking mission."

Operation Mantillo Hammer has placed three hundred U.S. Marines and FAST teams in Guatemala to combat drug trafficking.

"They are there in a strictly advisory capacity," the NAS guy says, "with authority to only use their weapons in self-defense. We can't just go cross international borders to sanction anyone we want."

"Tell that to bin Laden," Keller says. "Oh, that's right, you can't—he's dead."

Like most other Americans, Keller had sat transfixed by the news of the bin Laden raid, and remembered 9/11, and quietly celebrated alone in his room with a single beer.

The president was one cool cat during all that, Keller remembered thinking. Cracking jokes at the White House Correspondents' Dinner like Al

Pacino at the baptism in *The Godfather* while he knew he was ordering hits.

"That was bin Laden," the NAS rep says now.

"Ochoa is as bad."

"Get a grip."

"You think Ochoa *isn't* a terrorist?" Keller asks. "Define terrorist for me. Is it someone who kills innocent civilians? Commits mass murder? Plants bombs? What criteria are we missing here?"

"He has committed none of those acts in the United States," the rep answers.

"Ochoa sells millions of dollars' worth of drugs in the United States," Keller says. "He traffics human beings into the United States. He has caches of arms and cells of armed men in the United States. He ordered the killing of a United States federal agent. How is he not a terrorist threat to the United States?"

"The Zetas have not been officially designated a terrorist organization," the rep says. "And even if they were, it's more complicated than you think. Even with the jihadists, authorizing a strike requires convening a 'kill panel' to evaluate the necessity, the legal ramifications, the ethical justification . . ."

"Convene it," Keller says. "I'll testify."

I'll give you ethical justification.

The horrors go on and on.

Just last week, the Zetas tried to tap into a pipeline to steal Pemex oil and caused an explosion that killed thirty-six innocent people. If it had happened inside the United States it would be all over the news for days, with Congress screaming for action. Because it's Mexico, it doesn't matter.

"It's a nonstarter," the rep says.

"We have spent months," Keller says, "and millions of dollars finding these people, and now that we have, we're not going to do a goddamn thing about it?!"

Yes.

Ochoa has found himself a sanctuary where the U.S. won't touch him.

Because he's a Mexican narco, not an Islamic jihadist.

That's when Keller gets the idea.

But he needs a break to implement it.

He gets it from a horse ranch in Oklahoma.

Forty's little brother raises horses at a ranch outside of Ada.

Rolando Morales has been very successful, and recently rocked the quarterhorse world by buying a colt at auction for close to a million dollars. It strikes a few people as odd, because prior to buying the multimillion-dollar ranch, stables, and the thoroughbred horses to put in them, Rolando was a bricklayer. The FBI shows his highest annual income was $90,000.

There are whispers in the quarter-horse world about where Rolando's money comes from, but to the FBI they're more than whispers. They know it comes from big brother down in Nuevo Laredo—the ranch near Ada is a money laundry on hooves.

The technique is simple.

The Zetas send cash north to Rolando, who buys a horse for well over market value and then sells the horse back to the Zetas for true market value.

Money laundered.

And you still have your horse.

And participation in an expensive hobby, the sport of kings. It's almost pathetic, Keller thinks, how badly the narcos want social status—polo, horse racing. What's next, America's Cup yachts?

The crowd here is different from the polo set in Mexico City. Here there are a lot of cowboy hats, and thousand-dollar custom boots, and denim, and turquoise jewelry. This is western American aristocracy, people with the money and leisure to play with expensive quarter horses.

The particular horse in question today is a colt named, with an almost unbelievable sense of impunity, Cartel One, and the race is the All American Futurity, the Kentucky Derby of quarter-horse racing.

Keller watches the jockey take him into the gate.

"You have money down?" Miller asks him. Miller is the FBI agent assigned to Operation Fury, the bureau's surveillance of the Morales quarter-horse scam. Miller had contacted Keller because there was a red flag, an interdepartmental alert that anything to do with "Forty" Morales was to be forwarded to Art Keller.

"I'm not a gambler," Keller says.

"Put a few bucks on Cartel One."

"He's an eight-to-one shot."

"He's a lock," Miller says.

The horses come out of the gate. Cartel One starts slowly and gets trapped along the inside rail. But then a gap miraculously opens, the jockey works the colt to the outside, and Cartel One is third as they go into the home stretch. The two lead horses fade, and Cartel One comes in by a nose.

Keller looks down into the paddock, where Rolando and his wife and friends are jumping up and down, yelling, screaming, and embracing. Quite a celebration for a race that was fixed, Keller thinks. Miller has established that tens of thousands were passed out to other jockeys and trainers.

The prize money for the All American Futurity is a flat million.

Not a bad day's pay.

Still, chicken feed for the Zetas, who would have paid over a million to "win" the million. What they want is the bragging rights, the status. Rolando looks like his older brother, the same stocky build, the same curly black hair, even the thick mustache. Except he wears a white cowboy hat instead of a black ball cap.

"We thought we'd pick him up at the airport," Miller says.

"You have enough to charge?"

"Money laundering, conspiracy to traffic narcotics, tax evasion," Miller says. "Oh yeah."

"Do me a favor?" Keller asks. "Hold off a little?"

"Can't hold off for long," Miller answers. "Rolando is planning a trip to Italy."

"What?" Keller asks, feeling a jolt of excitement.

"He's going to Europe," Miller says. "Starting in Italy but going on some kind of Grand Tour, I guess—Switzerland, Germany, France, Spain. We've had a tap on his e-mail."

"Family vacation?" Keller asks, trying to keep the excitement out of his voice.

"Nope, just him."

Yeah, just him. No married man takes a "vacation" to Europe without his wife. It just doesn't happen. Rolando is going for work, and Keller hopes he knows what the work is.

He's praying that Rolando is going to Italy as the Zetas' ambassador to 'Ndrangheta.

The wealthiest criminal organization in the world.

'Ndrangheta is based in Calabria, in southern Italy at the toe of the boot, and it makes the older, more famous Sicilian Mafia look like a poor country cousin. Eighty percent of the cocaine that flows into Europe comes through 'Ndrangheta at its port of Gioia Tauro. The organization's income from drug trafficking is estimated at $50 billion annually, a whopping 3.5 percent of Italy's gross domestic product.

They're untouchable.

The Gulf cartel used to have an exclusive relationship with 'Ndrangheta—now Barrera is competing with the Zetas for the European market. The apparent motive behind the sadistic murder of Magda Beltrán was that she had been making successful inroads with 'Ndrangheta.

Is Rolando Morales going on a diplomatic mission to secure an alliance with 'Ndrangheta for the Zetas? Keller wonders.

Wars are fought with money, and the European market would give either cartel an insurmountable financial advantage with which to buy weapons, equipment, protection, and, most of all, gunmen.

If the Zetas can become 'Ndrangheta's suppliers, while at the same time cutting Barrera's Guatemalan route, they'll have the money and resources to beat him in Mexico.

So Rolando's diplomatic mission—if that's what it is—represents an enormous opportunity for the Zetas.

It's an enormous opportunity for Keller, too.

"Let him go," he says to Miller.

"Back to Oklahoma?"

"To Europe," Keller says.

They pick him up in Milan's San Siro stadium, where the red-and-black-clad AC Milan players are going up against the black-and-white-striped Juventus rivals.

Keller watches the video feed from a situation room at Quantico, supervised by the FBI, which is understandably reluctant to jeopardize an operation that has taken them years, cost them millions of dollars, and would result in convictions and headlines. DEA is equally reluctant to allow a Zeta ambassador freedom to leave the country and possibly escape arrest.

That's just the domestic side.

Keller's plan demands a complex multinational effort involving not only Italy's Direzione Antidroga, but INTERPOL, as well as Switzerland's Einsatzgruppe, Germany's BND, the French Sûreté, Belgium's Algemene Directie Bestuurlijke Politie, and Spain's CNP—the Cuerpo Nacional de Policía.

The protocols are complicated, language barriers difficult, and negotiations intricate, requiring Keller to adopt a diplomatic persona that he hasn't used for years. If it weren't for the common umbrella of INTERPOL, the operation wouldn't happen, but in the end everyone agrees to track Rolando's movements and not make arrests, with each country free to do what it likes regarding its own territory after the operation is concluded.

The logistics are at least as complicated, with detachments of elite police swapping surveillance while keeping each other in touch, exchanging video, audio, and photos, keeping a loose net around Morales while not getting in close enough to spook him.

They're going to use him as a dye test, let him run all the way through the bloodstream of the European drug-trafficking body.

The first place he goes is Milan, where Direzione Antidroga picks him up, and now their agents have him under surveillance, sending live video feed back to Quantico as Rolando talks into the ear of a translator who in turn talks to Ernesto Giorgi, the *quintino,* the underboss, of the 'Ndrangheta's Milan *'ndrine*—the equivalent of a Mexican plaza.

The noise in the stadium—the chanting, singing, banging of drums—is terrific. So there's not a chance of grabbing audio in the noisy stadium—doubtless why Rolando and Giorgi chose to meet there. Keller can't read lips, but the DEA techie at his side can—Giorgi had been friends with Osiel Contreras, and Rolando is explaining why the Zetas went against their old bosses, and why 'Ndrangheta should side with them.

Keller knows that Giorgi will forgive the treachery—business is business. What he won't tolerate is losing, and the 'Ndrangheta mob boss would have been briefed on the recent Zeta defeats in Veracruz.

The crowd erupts in a cheer.

Giorgi jumps up and pumps his fist in the air as a Milan player runs around the stadium celebrating the goal he just scored. When Giorgi sits back down, he leans over to Rolando and says something.

Keller looks to the translator.

"'We were thinking of doing business with the woman,'" the translator says. "'Magda Beltrán.'"

Keller doesn't need the translator to catch Rolando's response in Spanish. The words are clear on his lips. *"Está muerta."*

She's dead.

Rolando and Giorgi dine in a private room at Cracco.

Two Michelin stars.

Rolando spent the afternoon in Milan shopping, and now he wears a gray Armani suit with brown Bruno Magli shoes, a red silk shirt, and no tie. Giorgi is more conservative in a brown Luciano Natazzi cashmere jacket.

A camera hidden in an overhead pin light provides an image, and this time, the audio is crystal clear as Rolando repeatedly asserts that the Zetas have control of the Petén and will dominate the cocaine trade. Giorgi isn't convinced, and he brings up another issue.

GIORGI: *Barrera has the government.*

MORALES: *That's overstated.*

GIORGI: *He has the military and the federal police. Don't blow smoke up my ass.*

MORALES: *But there's an election coming up. PAN will lose. The winner is not going to prosecute the so-called war on drugs for the benefit of Adán Barrera. It will be up for bids.*

GIORGI: *You have the money?*

MORALES: *If we have your business, we'll have the money.*

Rolando is right, Keller thinks.

The PRI candidate, Peña Nieto, is making the end of the drug war a platform of his campaign. The other front-runner, PRD's López Obrador, would go even further, refuse the Mérida funds, and boot the DEA and CIA out of Mexico altogether. It's the wild card in all of this. No wonder Adán is in a hurry to grab all he can before the July elections, and before Peña Nieto would take office in December.

The irony is that we are, too.

We have to take the Zetas out before we get shut down.

"Who are they?" Keller asks as two men come in and sit down at the table.

No one in the room—not the FBI guys or the DEA people—knows. Keller gets on the phone to Alfredo Zumatto, his counterpart in DAD, who is also watching the video feed from Rome. He runs still frames through his database. Thirty minutes later an ID comes back—the two men are the *vangelista* and *quintino*—the second and third in command for Berlin.

"'Ndrangheta has 230 *'ndrines* in Germany," Zumatto says on the phone. "Your boy is making some impressive connections."

He's also trying to assure Giorgi that the Zetas won't do business in Germany except through 'Ndrangheta, Keller thinks.

He watches as the men socialize. The rest of the talk is mostly about *fútbol*, horses, and women.

From Milan, Rolando takes the train to Zurich, meeting with bankers and potential dealers; from there he trains to Munich, meeting the local 'Ndrangheta members and some German nationals.

From Munich, Rolando goes to Berlin, where he hooks back up with the two men from the restaurant, who pick him up at his hotel near the Brandenburg Gate. The German counterpart in BND tails them to the Kreuzberg neighborhood, down the Oranienstrasse, where they go into a nightclub and meet three men that the BND guy identifies as Turkish immigrants.

From Berlin, Rolando trains to the ancient Baltic port city of Rostock, where 'Ndrangheta has a strong presence. He goes to a yacht moored at the marina, stays for two hours, and then goes to his hotel on Kröpeliner Strasse. BND personnel track the yacht owners to a drug ring known for trafficking throughout the former East Germany.

Rolando backtracks by train to Hamburg. He connects with the local 'Ndrangheta and a Hamburg local and together they go down to the Reeperbahn, an upscale version of Nuevo Laredo's Boy's Town, only with more neon in lurid pinks, reds, greens, and purples. Rolando and his escorts walk past clubs with names like the Dollhouse, Safari, and the Beach Club and finally go into Club Relax, a brothel featuring women clad in masks and lingerie.

Rolando isn't just a dye test, Keller thinks, when he comes back out a few hours later. He's a germ, bacteria spreading through the *corpus narcoticus*. He infects everything he touches, and the infection spreads like a plague. Spider diagrams go up on police walls all over Europe, connecting Rolando's connections to their connections and *their* connections. The brothel metaphor works—Rolando Morales is venereal. That's part of Keller's plan, and he's pleased that it's working, but it's only part.

Rolando flies from Hamburg to Paris but doesn't leave the airport, connecting instead with a local flight to Lyon, where the Sûreté pick up the surveillance. Everywhere he goes it's the same drill—meeting with the organization, with dealers and financiers, and spreading the gospel of Heriberto Ochoa—the Zetas will win in Guatemala, they will win in Mexico, Barrera is finished once the elections happen, so hook your fate to the Zetas' rising star. The meetings take place in parks, soccer stadiums, restaurants, strip clubs, and brothels.

Rolando picks up the checks.

He trains from Lyon to Montpellier, and from Montpellier across the Spanish border to Gerona and then to Barcelona.

It's good that Rolando has gone to Spain, Keller thinks.

What cocaine doesn't come into Europe through Gioia Tauro comes in through Spain, mostly through the small fishing towns on the Galician coast, but also increasingly through Madrid airport.

Spain is also an important market in itself, with the highest rate of cocaine use in Europe. Most of the coke comes directly from Colombia, the deal being that the Galician mob, Os Caneos, keeps half the shipment and sells it domestically in exchange for allowing the other half to flow through their territory into the rest of Europe.

Through his Spanish CNP liaison, Rafael Imaz, Keller learns that Rolando is going to host a party at Top Damas, the city's most exclusive brothel.

"That's a piece of luck," Imaz tells Keller over the phone.

"You have contacts at the brothel?"

"We own it," Imaz says.

It's wired for video and sound, and Keller and Imaz get a good look at the guests as they roll up to the brothel. Imaz quickly identifies them as two Barcelona port officials.

Keller has to sit and listen to sounds that he'd rather not hear as Rolando and his guests partake of the specialties of the house, but when they finish, they settle into a back room for a relaxed business discussion.

> MORALES: *We bring it in shipping containers—small amounts at first— eight to ten kilos.*
> PORT OFFICIAL: *How much for our consideration?*
> MORALES: *Five thousand.*
> PORT OFFICIAL: *Euros or dollars?*
> MORALES: *Euros.*
> PORT OFFICIAL: *Have you talked to Os Caneos?*
> MORALES: *Why bring them into it? They're a long way away.*
> PORT OFFICIAL (laughs): *You don't want to split the coke with them.*
> MORALES: *Let's just say we're looking at other distributors.*
> SECOND PORT OFFICIAL: *Have you cleared this with our Italian friends? I don't want to get sideways with them.*
> MORALES: *They don't care what we do here.*

Keller listens to the discussions go on until they finally arrive at a figure—8,000 euros per shipment of coke that passes through the port.

A CNP tail picks up Rolando as he walks out of the brothel, tracks him downtown into the El Raval district, and radios Keller and Imaz as the Zeta walks down a narrow, twisting street in this ancient part of the city.

Barcelona has the largest Islamic population in Spain, mostly Pakistanis, but also Moroccans and Tunisians. Keller knows that the U.S. consulate here has a secret antiterrorist section, concerned that Barcelona will become the next Hamburg, a European base for jihadists.

The bin Laden mission was less than a year ago, and everyone is waiting for the retaliatory strike.

"He's in the Pakistani quarter," Imaz says.

It's working, Keller thinks. Please let him go where I hope he's going, please let him walk into the trap. It's been weeks in the making, weeks of private talks with Imaz, secret negotiations with CNI, exchanges of information and assets.

Now it will either work or not.

The tail follows Rolando to the tenement building, where he knocks on the door, waits a few seconds, and then is let in. CNI, the Central Nacional de Inteligencia, Spain's CIA, has had the place under surveillance as a known location for the Tehrik-i-Taliban, a loose affiliate of Al Qaeda.

Keller sits and listens to the audio feed. So do the FBI guys, whose ears have really pricked up now. They know what this could mean—that they're about to lose the Rolando Morales case and all their work—to other agencies, and they either give Keller dirty looks or avoid eye contact altogether as they all listen.

> MORALES: *What's your name?*
> ALI: *Call me Ali Mansur. It's my jihad name.*
> MORALES: *Okay. You speak good English.*
> ALI: *I went to college in Ohio. Do you want to swap biographies or do business?*
> MORALES: You *reached out to* us.
> ALI: *You can sell us cocaine?*

As much cocaine as they can buy, Rolando assures him. High quality, brought in through the port of Barcelona. Cash on the barrelhead.

That's good, Keller thinks. That's great. But he needs the other boot to drop. Come on, Ali, do it.

> ALI: *Can you get me guns?*

Keller holds his breath. Then he hears—

> MORALES: *AR-15s, rocket launchers, grenades, you name it.*

One of the FBI guys curses.

ALI: *Where do you get them?*
MORALES: *What do you care?*
ALI: *I care that they're good.*
MORALES: *They're good.*

Rolando is in the house for an hour. The tail gets photos of him when he comes out and hails a cab back to his hotel, the five-star Murmuri.

"You owe me," Imaz tells Keller over a private line.

Keller hangs up and starts setting the hook. He gets on the horn to the station chief of the secret antiterrorist unit embedded in the Barcelona consulate.

"What do you know about a group called Tehrik-i-Taliban?" Keller asks.

"A lot." CIA has had Tehrik-i-Taliban in Barcelona "up" for the past eighteen months. *"Why? Is there a drug connection?"*

"There might be." Keller tells him about Rolando's visit to the house in El Raval.

"These Zetas, what are they, some kind of cartel?"

"Jesus, where have you been?" Keller asks.

"Here."

"Well, they're about to be there," Keller says.

"Great. Anything you can share with us, I'd appreciate."

I've already shared with you what I want to share with you, Keller thinks—the lie that "Ali" is in good standing with TTP and not an agent provocateur, one of Imaz's assets, buried deep inside the Spanish CNI.

You don't need to know that, State doesn't need to know that, CIA, FBI, and Homeland Security don't need to know that. All any of you need to know is that the Zetas are willing to sell weapons to Islamic terrorists.

You say "narco" anymore in D.C. outside the hallways of DEA, you get a yawn. You say "narcoterrorism," you get a budget. A free hand and a blind eye. The Sinaloa cartel has been immaculate about not dealing with anything that looks like terrorists. If the Zetas are going to go into business with an AQ affiliate, they'll bring the whole antiterrorist structure down on their heads.

So Keller knows that his call to Barcelona is a poison pill, a shot of mercury into the Zeta blood system. Memos flying around CIA will make their way to DEA, then there'll be a coordinating committee.

And then there'll be action.

In one month, the Zetas are going to deliver twenty kilos of cocaine and a smorgasbord of weapons to what they think is an Islamic terrorist cell. The shipment will be busted, the Zetas' contacts in Europe rolled up like a cheap rug, and 'Ndrangheta will run away from the Zetas as fast as they can.

Barrera will get the European cocaine trade.

Sinaloa
May 2012

Adán lays flowers and a bottle of very good red wine on Magda's grave. It's sentimental, he knows, the same wine he gave her on their first "date" back in Puente Grande prison, a lifetime ago. He says a prayer for her soul, just in case there is a God and in case her soul needs prayer.

There have been two great loves in his life.

Magda.

His daughter, Gloria.

Also in the grave.

Adán gets up and brushes off his trousers. It's time to put the past away, and with it the bitterness, and think only of the future. You have children now, two healthy sons, and you have to make a world for them.

He walks back to the car where Nacho waits.

"Don't mention this to Eva," Adán says as he gets in.

"Of all things," Nacho says, "I understand mistresses."

"I don't have one now, if you're wondering."

"I wasn't," Nacho answers. "But it's none of my business, as long as you treat my daughter well. And my grandsons."

Nacho has become the doting grandfather. He comes to visit Raúl and Miguel Ángel all the time, bringing presents that infants cannot possibly appreciate or understand. Their birthday is coming up soon and Adán is dreading it, with Eva and her family planning a celebration that is almost royal in its scope and complexity.

And you're going along with it, Adán thinks.

Admit it, you're the doting father.

He didn't think that having children at his age would really change his life—they were more for the sake of a business succession—but in his secret soul he has to admit that he loves those boys with a passion that he almost can't believe.

All the clichés are true.

He lives for his children.

He would die for them.

Sometimes at night he sneaks out of bed, goes into the nursery, and watches them sleep. Part of this, he knows, is the anxiety of a parent who once lost a sick child. But most of it is pure pleasure, an actual physical joy of just looking at his children.

"The elections," Nacho is saying. "PAN is going to lose."

"The war on drugs is very unpopular," Adán says drily. "Have you made inroads?"

"Into the new people?" Nacho asks. "Some. I can't guarantee it will be enough."

"It's us or Ochoa," Adán says. "The new government will choose us."

"It's us or Ochoa as long as there *is* an Ochoa," Nacho says. "Once the Zetas are no longer a threat . . . the government might decide to go after us."

"What are you saying?"

"That our best course of action might not be to destroy the Zetas but to damage them," Nacho says. "Keep a remnant of them active as a counterweight to assure that we remain the lesser of evils."

Adán looks out the window as the car slowly rolls through the cemetery. So many friends buried here. So many enemies, too. Some of them you put here.

"They killed Magda," Adán says. "You can't be seriously suggesting that we make peace with them."

The Zetas are animals. Ochoa, Forty, and their minions are savage, sadistic murderers. Look what they did to the people on those buses, what they do to women and children. The extortion, the kidnapping, the firebombing of the casino . . . no wonder the country is turning against the narcos. The Zetas have made us into monsters, and they have to be destroyed.

"I'm not getting any younger," Nacho is saying. "I would like to sit back and play with my grandchildren."

"You want a rocking chair, too?"

"No, but maybe a fishing pole," Nacho says. "We have billions. More money than our children's children's children could spend in a lifetime. I'm thinking of getting out, handing the business over to Junior. I don't know, maybe taking the whole family out of the trade."

"And how would that work?" Adán asks. "We make an announcement, have a party with toasts and gold watches, and the Ochoas of the world just let us live in peace?"

"No, I suppose not," Nacho answers. "But if we made peace with them first, divide up the plazas—"

"We're winning."

"We're not winning in Guatemala," Nacho says, "and we're running out of time. The new president will throw our friends out and the North Americans with them."

Adán says, "We had good relations with the PRI once, we'll have them again."

"Different times, Adanito."

The diminutive form of his name annoys Adán. Nacho is playing the foxy grandpa and Adán doesn't like it. All the less because Nacho is right—those were different times. We ran our businesses, and if things got out of hand, we kept civilians out of it. Now the country is fed up with the violence associated with the drug trade. The chaos that—face it—*you* unloosed in Juárez alone has been catastrophic and you can't reel it in anymore if you wanted to.

And the war with the Zetas—just yesterday sixteen of his men were found dumped along the highway outside Badiraguato with their heads cut off. We're winning the war, but at a horrific cost.

And Nacho is right about Guatemala, too.

We are losing there, and if we lose Guatemala . . .

We can't lose Guatemala.

The irony is bitter.

It all depends on Art Keller now.

"Let me ask you something," Tim Taylor says. "Are you out of your fucking mind?"

Keller looks across the desk at him in the meeting room in EPIC. "No, I don't think I'm out of my fucking mind, Tim."

"I ask," Taylor says, "because I think you just requested that we allow a shipment of armaments to leave the United States en route to Spain."

"Strictly speaking," Keller answers, "I'm requesting that we allow a shipment of armaments to go to Mexico, *then* go to Spain—with a load of cocaine."

"You never heard of Fast and Furious?" Taylor asks.

"I have."

Everyone's heard of DEA's notorious "gun-walking" operation that went south, literally and figuratively. In an effort to trace arms sales, the agency allowed weapons to go into Mexico, and then lost track of them. The weapons were used by the Sinaloa cartel and the Zetas in the commission of a number of killings, including the murder of Agent Jiménez. In fact, there's been speculation that Jiménez and his partner were on that highway heading to collect a shipment of Fast and Furious weapons and bring them back.

"Because I can turn on the TV if you want," Taylor says. "I think the congressional hearings are on C-Span."

"That's all right."

Taylor says, "But you want to repeat the fiasco, only in Europe. So if you lose track of these weapons, we'll have an international incident."

"Rolando won't be delivering the weapons to narcos," Keller says. "He'll be delivering them to our own agents."

"Because you, on your own boot, set up a phony terrorist cell—"

"With the cooperation of Spanish intelligence—"

"—to entrap an American citizen—"

"Which is what a sting operation is," Keller says. "What, Tim? You have ethical problems with setting up the Zetas? We're just lucky we did set them up and they're selling the weapons to us instead of some *real* AQ affiliate."

"Still and all, you should have asked permission."

"Would I have received it?" Keller asks.

"No."

"I'm asking now."

"Now that you're eight months pregnant."

"The clock is ticking," Keller says. "If the PRD wins the election, they're going to throw our asses clean out. If PRI comes through, they're going to tolerate us, but they're not going to let us or FES go after Ochoa. If we're going to get the Zetas, we have to do it soon. You know and I know that if they get caught selling weapons to jihadists, we go to Pennsylvania Avenue and come back with a sanction on Ochoa and there won't be a thing that State or Justice can say about it."

"You're piece of work, Art."

"You want Ochoa or you don't?"

"You know I do."

"So?"

Taylor gets up from his chair. "I don't want to know a fucking thing about it until it succeeds."

"You got it."

"If it blows up," Taylor says from the doorway, "do me a favor. Stay in Mexico. Better yet, go to Belize. Somewhere you can't be subpoenaed. I'm going to retire soon, and I want to retire to a cabin near a lake, not a federal prison."

There are seven thousand arms dealers within a few hours' drive of the Mexican border.

That's three a mile.

Most of those guns aren't going to shoot deer in Minnesota.

Now Keller sits across the street from one of them, in Scottsdale, Arizona, and watches the straw purchaser go in.

The Mexican government claims that 90 percent of the weapons used by the cartels come from the United States, but Keller knows that isn't true. Most of the weapons the cartels use are looted from the armories of Central American military, but the gun stores that line the border are there for a reason, just like the narcos on the other side are *there* for a reason.

As soon as Keller got the go from Taylor, he put a tap on Rolando Morales's cell phones and e-mail, which led him to five gun stores in Scottsdale, Phoenix, Laredo, El Paso, and Columbus, New Mexico.

Now he watches the straw purchaser go in and buy three Romanian-made AR-15 assault rifles—any more would get the attention of ATF. The purchaser fills out a Form 4473 with himself listed as the real buyer. The store owner knows exactly what's going on and who the guns are ultimately for.

It's so pat that this particular guy is only in the store for about thirty minutes before he comes out and puts the newly acquired weapons in the trunk of his Dodge Charger. A tail follows him to his house in the suburbs. He goes inside, has dinner, watches some television, then later that night drives to a house out in the desert where he delivers the guns to a Zeta cut-out.

This transaction is being repeated all along the border until Morales collects the fifty assault rifles he's putting in the package for delivery to the "jihadists."

To cross the border, a similar process is used for guns going south as for drugs coming north. The weapons are loaded into compartments in cars and trucks and driven across the border. Keller's people follow the shipments to Veracruz, where the guns and cocaine are put in containers and loaded onto a freighter bound for Barcelona.

Rolando buys a first-class air ticket.

Keller looks at the video feed—coming from inside the warehouse on the industrial dock at Barcelona's Free Harbor—and profoundly wishes that he could be there instead of in the situation room at Quantico.

But Rafael Imaz is in the warehouse with twenty heavily armed CNP troopers. More troops wait several blocks away in unmarked vehicles. Looking into the surveillance monitor, Keller watches the man they know as "Ali" and three of his jihadist comrades wait for Rolando.

It's tense.

Keller believes that they've tracked the drug and weapon shipment and that Rolando will make his rendezvous with Ali. But if they're wrong, if there's been a leak, if the Zetas' own impressive intelligence network has sniffed out the trap, then Rolando doesn't show up, and the drugs—and more important, the weapons—are headed somewhere else.

Fast and Furious—the European version.

Rolando has been in Barcelona for two days, enjoying the sun, the food, the pretty women on La Rambla. He treated the two port officials to another night at Top Damas, another reason that Keller believes the arrangement with Ali is still on. But it could all be misdirection—Ochoa is well versed in military intelligence, and Keller wouldn't put it past him.

The freighter arrived early yesterday morning and started offloading right away, but so far, Rolando hasn't gone close to the port. And Ali had made it very clear that he would only deal with Morales personally—no cut-outs, no wire transfers. Now Rolando is thirty minutes late. It's worrisome. The delivery could be going somewhere else while we're chasing Rolando around Barcelona.

Ali is wearing an earpiece.

"Anything?" Keller hears Imaz ask.

"Not yet."

Then a call comes through from the tail that Imaz has on Rolando. He and two other men left the hotel in a car headed in the direction of the harbor.

They wait.

An hour later, a loader pulls into the warehouse with two shipping containers. Rolando and his two guys come in right after it.

Rolando is in a jovial mood. "Allahu akbar!"

Ali plays his role. *"You're late."*

"We just wanted to make sure there were no other guests at the party," Rolando says.

"Next time," Ali says, *"if there* is *a next time, be* on time."

"Next time, don't make me come personally."

"You don't like Barcelona?" Ali asks. *"My people seemed to think that you're having a nice time for yourself."*

"We have whores in Oklahoma," Rolando says.

"Let me see the merchandise."

Rolando's guys open one of the containers. He takes a package of cocaine and holds it up.

Keller watches through the monitor. The whole thing is on tape, with audio.

"You want to sample?" Rolando asks.

"You're too smart to cheat me on the dope," Ali says. *"I want to see the weapons."*

They open the other container.

Ali steps over and looks in.

"Be my guest," Rolando says.

Ali picks up one of the rifles and hefts it in his hand. *"Ammunition?"*

"Gun isn't worth much without ammo," Rolando says. *"It's all there."*

Sticking with the script, Ali asks, *"Can you get me grenade launchers?"*

"Grenade launchers," Rolando says. *"Wow."*

"Can you?"

"For a price," Rolando says. *"We can get them out of Guatemala, El Salvador. And speaking of a price . . ."*

Ali gives a curt nod and his guys bring up four attaché cases. They open them and Ali shows Rolando the U.S. dollars wrapped in neat packages inside. *"Do you want to count it?"*

"No, I trust you."

Ali's guys shut the cases and then hand them to Rolando's men.

"Go!" Imaz says into his mike.

His CNP troopers burst out of the back room into the warehouse. At the same time, the men outside rush to shut off the exit. They're very fast and very good, and Morales has no choice except to throw his hands in the air.

Keller watches Imaz walk up to him. *"Sorpresa, hijo de puta."*

Surprise, motherfucker.

"Can you get me grenade launchers?"

"Grenade launchers. Wow."

"Can you?"

"For a price. We can get them out of Guatemala, El Salvador . . ."

The State Department NAS rep turns off the tape player and looks across the table at Keller.

Keller looks back at the NAS rep as if to say, *Well?*

"I get it," the rep says. "But you stopped the purchase and busted the network. Case closed. Well done."

"You don't think they'll try again?" Keller asks. "I've just given you proof positive that the Zetas supplied weapons to Islamic terrorists and therefore—"

"No, I get it."

All the usual players are there—Keller, Taylor, the head of DEA, CIA, Homeland Security, Justice, State, and the White House.

In short, Keller thinks, a clusterfuck.

With a lot more cluster than fuck.

"I still don't see," the White House guy says, "why we can't hand this over to the Guatemalans and provide an assist from the marines already there."

"Same reason," Taylor says, "that you guys couldn't inform the Pakistanis about the bin Laden mission. You don't know who in their government the Zetas have compromised."

"The Guatemalans aren't up to it yet," the Guatemalan CIA station chief adds. "Every time they go up against the Zetas they get their asses kicked. They won't go near them."

The CIA rep suggests a drone strike.

"In Central America?" the Homeland Security rep asks.

"We have the assets there," the CIA rep says. "We have the drones. It's only a matter of sticking on a missile."

"Collateral casualties would touch off an incident," the State rep says.

"One thing that cannot happen," the Homeland Security rep said, "is that the Zetas go back in business selling drugs and weapons to the jihadists. That's not on the table."

"So we have to go in with boots on the ground," Keller said.

"Boots on the ground," the White House guy says, "are exactly what we *don't* want. For Chrissakes, we've been trying to get boots *off* the ground in Iraq and Afghanistan."

"You did it for the bin Laden mission," Taylor says.

"The American public would accept casualties to get bin Laden," the White House rep says, "not a couple of drug dealers they've never heard of. We get guys shot up on some covert mission in Central America, the Republicans will be screaming for impeachment."

"We have men there now," Keller repeats.

"As advisers," the NAS rep repeats.

Keller sits back and throws his hands in the air.

"At the end of the day," the White House guy says, "the only person here whose opinion matters is mine. Strictly speaking, DEA has no fucking business even sitting in on a discussion like this. The answer is no—if the two subjects show up in Mexico and your Mexican FES boys can pop them, hey, great. *Salud!* But there is no way we are going to okay some Rambo-style mission in the jungles of Guatemala. Subject closed. This meeting never happened."

He gets up and walks out.

Keller broods in his hotel room that night.

Ochoa and Forty will sit safely in Guatemala, and no one will touch them. From their safe haven, they'll kill more people, launch more terror and suffering. And we'll sit safely on this side of the border, fat and happy, and buy their dope and fund more killing.

His phone rings.

Tim Taylor calling to commiserate, an unusual harmony between them, Keller thinks as Taylor bitches about gutless politicians and castrated bureaucrats. Taylor fought the losing battle hard, and has to be feeling it, too.

"You want to have a beer?" Taylor asks.

"Yeah, okay."

"I'll come to your room," Taylor says. "Oh, and I'm bringing a couple of people."

Five minutes later Taylor shows up with the CIA rep from the meeting and a guy that Keller's never met. The guy looks to be in his early sixties, wears an expensive gray suit with no tie and cowboy boots, and doesn't introduce himself.

They all sit down and Keller gets four beers out of the refrigerator.

The CIA rep starts. "My colleague is from the energy sector. We agree that we want this Guatemalan mission to happen."

His colleague says, "The Zetas are interfering with oil and gas exploration in Tamaulipas, putting potentially billions of dollars at stake. And, of course, there are the humanitarian aspects."

"Of course," Keller says.

He doesn't give a shit *why*, only *that*.

"We can't use our own people," the CIA guy says, "so we'll have to hire this out to a private security firm. Most of those guys are retired U.S. special forces—SEALs, DEVGRU, Delta Force. It's what they did in Afghanistan and Iraq, isn't it? Drop in, get the bad guy, get out."

"What about funding?" Taylor asks. "There's no way to run this through DEA."

"I can arrange the money," the colleague says. "In exchange for certain assurances."

"What are they?" Keller asks.

"Well," the colleague says, "we don't want to clear one group of narcos from the oil and gas fields just to let another in."

"So you want assurances from Adán Barrera," Keller says, "that he'll keep his hands off the oil and gas fields."

"That's about right. Can you give us those assurances? Can you speak for Barrera?"

It's a strange goddamn world, Keller thinks. "Actually, I can."

"You and him are tight, huh?"

"We're the same guy," Keller says.

"Then money is no problem."

So it's decided. The oil people will hire a firm out of Virginia. A private force of elite counterinsurgency troops will drop into the Petén and take out Heriberto Ochoa and Forty.

"How are we going to be sure they're there?" the CIA guy asks. "We'll have to have a date certain when they're locked in place."

"I'll take care of it," Keller says. "Of course, I'm going on the mission."

"No way," Taylor says.

"What if you get killed?" the CIA guy asks. "How do we explain that?"

"I won't care, will I?" Keller asks.

"You're too personally involved," Taylor says.

You're goddamn right I am, Keller thinks. Ochoa gave the order to attack Marisol. He gave the order to kill Erika.

You're goddamn right it's personal.

"I go or there's no deal," he says.

"It's your funeral," Taylor says. "But first you hand in your resignation. Then we'll see that the firm hires you. In no way do I want you traceable to the agency if this goes sick and wrong."

"I've been trying to resign for seven years, Tim."

"This time it's permanent."

This time it will be, Keller thinks.

"One other question," Taylor says. "What about the White House?"

The oilman scuffs the toe of his boot across the floor and smiles. "Jesus shit, who do you think sent us over here?"

Keller pulled his papers, and a rumor was sent around that Art Keller had been forced out for an overly close relationship to the former Tapia organization, but that DEA had quietly arranged a soft landing for him at a security firm in Virginia to avoid another scandal.

After Fast and Furious, no one wanted another scandal.

To Marisol, Keller tells the truth.

As much as he can, anyway.

"A private security firm?" Marisol asks, raising an eyebrow. She's no fool, she can read between the lines.

"Just for one mission," he says.

"Famous last words."

"Did I hear glass breaking when you threw that stone?" Keller asks. "*I'm pulling the pin after this.*"

They've seen so little of each other over the past few months. He's been out with FES tracking down Zetas or in Washington. Even his time at EPIC has been jammed, and more and more often he's stayed in his condo in El Paso rather than make the drive out to Valverde.

Marisol has been busy as well, still running what's left of the town government, trying to maintain some order without a single cop, applying to the state and federal government for renewal funds, running her clinic. The violence in the valley has subsided somewhat, and she knows that the army is protecting her at Keller's behest, and he's assured her that this won't change.

Slipping his punch about retiring, she says, "So your 'retirement' is a bit of a farce. You're still a power in the antidrug world. What's this mission?"

He's chopping vegetables for dinner, keeps chopping, and doesn't answer.

"You're going to kill more people, aren't you?" Marisol presses. He doesn't answer, but she won't let it go. "Haven't you had enough of that? Haven't we all had enough of that?"

"It's Ochoa," he says, without looking at her. "Happy now?"

"Do you think that will make me happy?" she asks.

"He killed Erika!"

"I know that!" Marisol leans back and stares at him. "But you don't know me at all."

"Good—let's just spout clichés."

"Fine—go fuck yourself."

Marisol grabs her cane and limps out of the kitchen. Keller hears the bedroom door slam. He takes a deep breath, sets the knife down, and goes after her. When he walks into the bedroom, she's changing out of her office clothes and he can see the scars on her body, the colostomy bag, and he recalls her bitter jibe about how symbolic it is that she carries a bag of her own shit around with her.

"Yes," Marisol says as she pulls the blouse over her head and sees him looking, "Ochoa did this to me. Ochoa had Erika killed. But who killed Jimena? Who slaughtered people in the valley? That was your new best friend Adán Barrera. You all work together now, don't you? Your government, my government, they've always worked with him."

"What are you saying?" Keller asks. "I'm part of the cartel?"

"Forgive me, but aren't you?"

"I made the devil's deal to take down the Zetas," he says, the bitterness clear in his voice.

"For me?" Marisol asks. Sarcastically. "You sold your soul to avenge me? I didn't ask you to do that. I don't want you to do that now. If you do this for revenge, own it yourself. Don't put it on me."

"What *do* you want?"

"I want it to end!" she yells. "I want all of this to be over!"

"So do I."

"Then end it," she says. "Stop it. Say you do kill Ochoa. Someone even worse will just take his place. You know that. I don't even know how many people you've killed since we met, Arturo. Maybe they all deserved it, I won't even argue that they didn't, but I do know that you don't deserve it . . . *I* don't deserve it."

"It's this one last time."

"Just go," she says. "Please, just go and do whatever it is that you think you have to do. Only . . ."

"What?"

She looks into his eyes for what feels like a long time.

"If you do this," Marisol says, "I don't know if I want you back."

"Okay."

"Art—"

"No," he says, "you've made yourself clear. Goodbye, Marisol. I only wish you every happiness."

Keller leaves, the engagement ring purchased in El Paso still in his pocket as he goes off on his jihad.

2

La Plaza del Periodista

There is no water to put out the fire.
Mi canto la esperanza.

—Carlos Santana
"Maria Maria"

Ciudad Juárez
June–July 2012

Guiltily, Pablo logs on to *Esta Vida*.

Today's post features a vid-clip of five men, shirtless, kneeling on a warehouse floor. The letter "Z" has been painted on their bare chests, and hooded men with CDG logos on their military-style shirts stand behind them.

The soundtrack has one of the CDG captors, offscreen, asking the prisoners questions. One by one, the captives confess that they are Zetas and have committed crimes.

Then comes the sound of a chainsaw starting up.

The camera stays on the scene, but Pablo turns his head. He looks back a few moments later to see the severed heads on the floor as the offscreen voice announces that this will happen to "all Zeta scum" in Tamaulipas.

It's terrifying for more than the obvious reasons.

The blog is virtually taunting the Zetas by showing the execution of their people. To make matters worse, this day's post also has a story about the kidnapping of a *Milenio* reporter in Veracruz, taken from his office parking lot by three men in a van. His body was found in a downtown park with the message THIS IS WHAT HAPPENS TO TRAITORS AND THOSE WHO ACT SMART. SINCERELY, THE ZETAS.

He was the fourth journalist killed in Veracruz over the past two months. Three crime-beat photographers were dumped in plastic bags in a canal. A woman reporter was beaten and strangled.

Reading the story, Pablo feels his bowels turn to water. He'd like to ascribe it to the too-many beers along with the fiery *aguachile* he consumed last night, but he knows that it's really fear.

No, not fear.

Terror.

He logs off quickly when he hears Ana walk up behind him.

"You know the paper monitors your downloads," she says. "You could get fired for 'Backdoor Mamacitas.'"

"Research," Pablo says.

"That's what they all say."

Pablo has spent more time in the office lately because there's been less crime on the streets. The violence in Juárez is by no means over, but the crest seems to have receded.

Some attribute it to the new police chief, a retired army officer named Leyzaola who came in a year ago now after "cleaning up" Tijuana. His first day on the job he was greeted by a bound, duct-taped body left on his doorstep with a note of greeting from the narcos, followed by the usual threat that one of his men would be killed every day until he resigned.

But Leyzaola didn't flinch when the first five officers were gunned down. He ordered his men to leave their homes and he got them hotel rooms. Then he held a press conference and said, "In the end, the criminal needs to be overpowered. There's all this legend, this mystique, around the narcos, that they are invincible, omnipotent. We need to dispel that and treat them like what they are—criminals."

Of course they tried to kill him, ambushing his motorcade, opening fire and killing one officer, but not even winging Leyzaola. He responded with another press conference, announcing that he was going to clean up Juárez one neighborhood at a time, starting with El Centro.

He did. He put "boots on the pavement" and those cops survived. Some say it was because the narcos were afraid of Leyzaola—stories about his torture of narcos and corrupt police in Tijuana hit the street faster than his cops—others say that the violence was receding because Adán Barrera had already won the war. Some went a little further, claiming that Leyzaola had made a separate peace with Barrera to tame Tijuana and was simply doing the same now in Juárez, although he once publicly claimed that he had turned down an $80,000-a-week bribe from El Señor.

Pablo was more cynical. If there was less killing, he opined, it was probably because there was no one left to kill.

Other theories had it that the narco-war had merely changed fronts, and was now being fought more in Tamaulipas, Nuevo León, and Veracruz.

To most, it didn't matter.

The killing, if not stopped, was slowing down. Slowly, very slowly, businesses that were shuttered up were starting to return to El Centro and other neighborhoods. Juárez, "the most murderous city in the world," was showing signs of life.

There were other signs of hope.

An army general in Ojinaga was actually arrested and charged with the murder and torture of civilians, a major victory for the "Woman's Rebellion" in the Juárez Valley, although Pablo wishes that Jimena Abarca, Erika Valles, and the others had lived to see it.

But still, a sign of hope, and people were starting to quietly talk about a "Juárez spring."

Even Pablo—cynical, chronically depressed Pablo—secretly harbored a delicate seed of hope that the worst was over and his city was going to come back. Not the same, of course, it could never be the same, but come back as something different and at least survive.

"What *are* you working on?" Ana asks.

"Pirated DVD sellers," Pablo answers. "In El Centro. Human-interest, color kind of piece. You?"

"The elections," she says, as if the answer is obvious.

It is.

The elections are on everyone's mind.

Victoria is thrilled about the PAN candidate.

"A conservative *and* a woman," she chirped during Pablo's last visit to Mexico City, a sop from Óscar to write a story about a literary festival. "As I've always tried to tell you, PAN is the progressive party, not PRI or PRD."

"You like her mostly because of the title of her book," Pablo answered. The PAN candidate, Josefina Vázquez Mota, had written a self-help bestseller entitled *God, Make Me a Widow*.

"At least she writes." Veronica chuckled. "Your guy can't even *read*. My God, Pablo, he's Rick Perry!"

The PRI candidate, Enrique Peña Nieto, had stumbled when a reporter asked him which three books had influenced him most. He couldn't come up with three, and finally muttered something about the Bible. And he has Perry's carefully coiffed hair, not a strand out of place, and he couldn't tell another reporter the price of a pack of tortillas.

"He's a serial adulterer," Victoria went on cheerfully, "has fathered not one but two children out of wedlock, and then he has an affair with that actress."

"He married her," Pablo responded weakly. And a little jealously—Peña Nieto scored a gorgeous soap opera star, the aptly named Angélica Rivera. "Anyway, he's not my guy."

"No, of course not," Victoria said. "You're going for the lefty. López Obrador is only running because he thinks he was robbed the last time."

"He *was* robbed the last time."

"So he's Al Gore?"

"And your choice is, who, Sarah Palin?" If we're going to play the American comparison game.

"She's much smarter than Palin."

"Well, don't set the bar *too* high."

He kind of enjoyed bickering with Victoria over politics, and it was indicative of a thaw in their relationship. Pablo had come to accept her getting remarried, even accept that Mateo had a "stepfather," who seems, actually, to have had a good influence on Victoria. She's become much more liberal about Mateo's visits and is even open to Mateo coming to see him, maybe on a holiday to Cabo or Puerto Vallarta or even El Paso.

The last option is more in Pablo's budget, and he's already started planning the trip. He'd pick Mateo up in El Paso and take him to Western Playland Park for the waterslide and the roller coaster, and then drive out to Big Bend and go camping.

He can't decide whether to ask Ana to come with them.

Victoria, with her unerring radar, had brought that up, too. "So you and Ana are a thing now?"

"I don't know what a 'thing' is," Pablo answered disingenuously.

"Sleeping together," Victoria prompted. "Having sex. It's all right, Pablo, we're divorced. You have every right. I get it. I like Ana, actually."

"So do I."

"Well, I should hope so. If you're doing her."

"For God's sake, Victoria."

"And you've lost a little weight, too," Victoria said. "Men only become conscious of their waistlines when they're doing someone, although you didn't bother with me."

"I was thin when we met."

"Yes, you were."

Victoria was always nagging him to eat better, drink less, and go to the gym, but then again, Pablo has long felt that she (barely) sublimates her innate fascism with exercise and diet regimens and has recently taken to attending weekly "boot camp" sessions where she probably achieves orgasms as some steroid-enraged instructor screams at her.

Ana doesn't nag him about anything, another of their many unspoken understandings. Pablo recognizes that they have a common survivor's mentality, something that can only be shared by people who have lived together in a war zone. The resultant attitude is one of "whatever gets you through the day."

For Pablo that's usually beer and junk food. For Ana, it's wine and cigarettes and the occasional blunt. And work. She's always been diligent, but for the past year Ana has brought an almost demonic energy to her reporting. When she's not at the desk in the office, she's on her laptop, and it's harder and harder for Pablo to get her out to a bar for a drink.

They see each other in the city room and late at night at her place (okay, *their* place), when he rolls in from the bars and Ana is just back from covering whatever it is she's covering. She has a glass of wine and a cig, maybe a puff or two on a joint, and then they go to bed and have what can only be described as "desperate sex."

Victoria was a machine in bed. Not at all the ice maiden that one might expect, but an orgasm-producing mechanism of staggering efficiency, both for him and herself. Ana is nothing like that—Ana in bed is chaos. She approaches climax like a galloping, out-of-control horse that suddenly sees the cliff ahead but can't stop running.

Victoria's orgasm was usually announced with a triumphant shout (another item on her checklist successfully ticked off), Ana's with an "oh-no" whimper followed by tears and a desperate clutching at him as if he were all that kept her from falling into the abyss.

That's all that Ana seems to want from the relationship. She doesn't want to "improve" him, doesn't ask "where this is all going." She seems satisfied with the companionship at night, the friendship, the love, if that's what you can call it.

For Pablo, sex is more of a delay of sleep.

He used to love to sleep, relish sleep, bury himself in the blankets and roll in sleep.

Now he hates and fears it.

Because with sleep comes dreams.

Not a good thing for a man who has covered thousands of murders. That's not a figure of speech or hyperbole, he realized one night while doing the math. He has literally attended thousands of killings. Well, not the actual killings—although a few he missed only by moments—but the aftermaths. The dead, the dying, the grieving. The dismembered, the decapitated, the flayed.

He doesn't need a website to see these images.

Doesn't need *Esta Vida* because this *is* his life and he has his own vid-clips running on the insides of his eyelids, which is why he hates to close his eyes and yield to sleep.

So Pablo looks perpetually tired, but then again, Pablo has always looked perpetually tired. And he is trying to get into better shape, eat a little better, drink a little less, and while he will never get his ass into a gym, he is going out to the park one or two times a week to kick the *fútbol* around a little bit.

Now Óscar comes out of his office, his cane clicking on the floor. "What are you working on?"

"I thought I'd go to Mexico City to do a piece on Peña's hairdresser," Pablo answers. "The hours, the stress . . ."

"That is a joke."

"Yes."

"Mildly amusing."

"No, I thought I'd do a classic on-the-street survey," Pablo says. "Slice-of-life interviews from various barrios. What people are thinking, who they support and why. Give the Juarense point of view."

The election promises to be close, at least vis-à-vis Lopez Obrador and Peña Nieto. The polls have Peña Nieto with a five-point lead as of two weeks ago, although the other parties have complained bitterly and loudly about perceived media bias toward the PRI. PAN is far behind, in the 20 percent range.

"Go to El Paso, too," Óscar tells Pablo. "See what they're thinking *el otro lado.*"

"Do they even know we're having an election?" Pablo asks.

"Find out," Óscar says. "It's a story either way."

"Got it." Pablo sighs. He hates crossing the border. The traffic, the lines, the waiting at the checkpoints . . .

"Be careful to write your story in a neutral way, please," Óscar says. "No slant that one party or the other has a bias toward a cartel."

"All the parties have a bias toward Sinaloa," Ana says. "I mean, the Zetas practically declared themselves their own government."

"We don't need to print that," Óscar says.

"*Esta Vida* will," Ana says.

"Let them," Óscar snaps. "It's irresponsible 'journalism' as its worst. Unedited rumors and innuendo pandering to the basest instincts."

Pablo understands his bitterness. El Búho has spent his life in mainstream newspapers producing quality journalism, believing that a free press is the lifeline of a democracy. Now he has to sit and watch as the public turns to websites and blogs to get real information on the narcos.

It has to be galling.

"I would like to give 'Wild Child' a good spanking," Óscar adds before he limps back to his office.

"Well, *there's* an image," Ana says.

"If we knew who El Niño Salvaje is," Pablo answers.

"Did you see this morning's post?"

"Horrible," Pablo says.

Horrible.

Pablo hits the streets in his *fronterizo*, which has maybe one more year in it. The air-conditioning is shot, more of a wheezing protest against the heat than any true cooling, so he keeps the windows rolled down and just sweats as he makes his way from El Centro to Anapra, Chaveña, and Anáhuac.

He could already predict the favored candidate by the relative wealth of the neighborhood. The rich sections of Campestre and Campo Eliseos will vote their wallets for PAN. The working-class—or unemployed-class—*colonias* will vote PRD, while some of the older, more genteel neighborhoods like Colonia Nogales and Galeana will likely go PRI.

Some of the neighborhoods don't exist anymore, he thinks sadly as he drives around. Riviera del Bravo, for instance, once a thriving new section of apartments and strip malls, is a virtual ghost town of abandoned houses and graffiti-sprayed walls, the inhabitants having fled from the incessant violence. The old Mariscal red-light district has been bulldozed, scraped clean, if you will. His route takes him past Benito Juárez Stadium, where his beloved Indios used to play until the city's financial demise caused the owners to shut them down.

Another casualty, Pablo thinks, of the war on drugs.

He goes back downtown, buys a *torta* from a truck, and eats his lunch in Chamizal Park as he watches kids play *fútbol* in the bone-dry canal or taunt the Border Patrol agents on the other side of the fence.

There's no putting it off, Pablo thinks. He gets back in his car and drives across the bridge. The line in the express lane isn't too bad, and he's in the U.S. before he wants to be.

Just another Juarense on the way to El Paso, he thinks.

The mayor lives in El Paso now, for safety. So do the chief of police and the editors of two of the city's newspapers.

Not Óscar, Pablo thinks with some pride.

You couldn't pry El Búho out of his Chaveña house with a crowbar, and the editor views El Paso as a redneck backwater with no cultural life. Óscar is *anclado,* "anchored," a Juárez fixture, but a lot of people who can afford to move have and now drive across the bridge in the morning and back before dark in modest cars that hopefully won't draw the attention of potential kidnappers. They've started social clubs, restaurants, country clubs, private schools, and fueled an El Paso real estate boom.

Pablo can't help but think of them as traitors.

He knows it's a stupid attitude—El Paso and Juárez are and always have been joined at the hip, and most people in both cities have family on the other side. A lot of Juárez women go *el otro lado* to have their babies, so the child will have dual citizenship and better choices. If you sneeze in Juárez, someone in El Paso will say, "Gesundheit," and for a lot of people the border doesn't exist as a reality but more a mere annoyance, a technicality.

For Pablo, the border *exists.*

As a reality and a state of mind.

For one thing, the reality is that the border is the raison d'être of the cartels. No border, no profit, no "plaza." No violence.

For another, the border is the reason for the maquiladoras. The largest consumer market in the world is a mile north, over that border, so what better place to make those consumer goods?

Well, China now, but the mushrooming of the maquiladoras changed the landscape of Juárez forever, creating the vast *colonias* where the people who can find jobs now struggle to survive on a third of what they used to make. Their poverty makes them targets for narco recruitment, their despair makes them customers for the narcos' product.

And their lives are cheap.

That's the reality.

And the reality is that there's a different state of mind on the other side of the border. You live in El Paso, you're a *pocho,* an Americanized Mexican, and no one can tell Pablo that it doesn't change you. You shop in malls instead of *mercados,* you watch football instead of *fútbol,* you become another consumer in a giant machine that consumes consumers.

Dios mío, Pablo thinks, Óscar would throw that sentence in the garbage, but it's true nevertheless. There's a different state of mind in the States—no, it's more than that—there's a different state of soul.

As he expected, outside El Paso's barrios no one gives a shit who's going to be the new president, and when he asks the question in the affluent West El Paso neighborhoods with names like "The Willows" and "Coronado Hills," the answer is usually, "Romney."

I don't think so, Pablo said to himself, primarily because the "Latino" vote will be almost as crucial in the United States as it will be in Mexico. Being in the U.S. always makes Pablo feel vaguely uncomfortable, like an unwanted guest at a party whom everyone wishes would leave. He knows how North Americans feel about Mexicans, and it's the same way that many Mexicans feel about Juarenses.

We're the "Mexicans" of Mexico.

Well, fuck 'em all.

He drives into Barrio El Segundo, the original breeding grounds of the Aztecas, and finds a congenially dark bar where he can sit and have a beer without feeling that he doesn't belong. The anxiety that he's felt since reading *Esta Vida* this morning won't leave him, and the three cold beers don't chase it away.

It only gets worse as he leaves and crosses the bridge back into Juárez.

Call it paranoia, or the insecurity from being *el otro lado,* but Pablo can't escape the feeling that someone is following him. It's ridiculous, he thinks as he looks into the rearview mirror, but he can't help but think of the other reporters ambushed in their cars, in their driveways, outside their offices. Murdered on the spot or driven off somewhere to be tortured and killed, and now the sweat is not just from the heat, it comes from fear as well and smells different—a detail he thinks that he should put in a story somewhere.

Pablo drives out to Las Misiones, the new shopping mall across from the U.S. consulate, and walks the polished marble floors and new "fitness center" and then stands outside the new twelve-screen IMAX theater to ask people their opinion of the upcoming election. Not surprisingly, the mallgoers are overwhelmingly PAN or PRI.

This is the "new Juárez," Pablo thinks—suburban, affluent, and soulless just like its counterpart across the river. But this is what we aspire to be, Pablo thinks. We took all that "new money" and built a faux U.S. He's leaving the mall when Ramón walks up to him.

"Hola, 'mano."

"Ramón. Hi. What are you doing here?"

"Looking for you. You sick, *'mano?* You're sweating like a pig."

"No, I'm good."

"We have a job for you."

"You know I can't write—"

"No one's asking you to write shit," Ramón says. "Some people at the end of the alphabet are very angry at this morning's blog post. You're going to tell us who El Niño Salvaje is."

"I don't know."

"Find out." Ramón pulls out his cell phone and shows Pablo a picture of Mateo standing outside his school in Mexico City. "Cute *hijo* you got."

"You fucking son of a bitch."

"Careful, *'mano.* Watch your mouth." Ramón puts the phone back in his pocket. "Their computer what-do-you-call-them, geeks, say the blog comes out of Juárez. That puts a lot of pressure on me, *'mano.* So I have to put a lot of pressure on you. It's not you, is it? Tell me it's not you, Pablo."

"It's not," Pablo says.

"That's good," Ramón says. "I'm relieved. But it has to be someone you know. Some fucking reporter."

"I told you I don't know."

"I didn't *say* you know," Ramón snaps. "I said it's *someone* you know. There's a difference—pay attention. You find out, Pablo, and you tell me. If you don't, we're not going to hurt *you* first, you understand? You'll get the pictures on your phone. Hey, maybe El Niño will put them up on the blog."

Pablo is literally speechless with fear.

"Tell me you understand," Ramón says.

Pablo croaks, "I understand."

"Good," Ramón says. He lays his hand on Pablo's shoulder. "'*Mano,* I don't want to hurt your kid. It's the last thing I want to do. So don't make me, okay? A week, ten days, I want to hear something from you. A name."

He walks away.

The terror runs through Pablo like an icy stream.

He has to stop shaking.

Pablo has two whiskeys at San Martín, and then steps outside to call Victoria. "Listen, I've been thinking. About that vacation. Could you fly with Mateo to El Paso and I'll meet you there?"

"I suppose, but why?"

"I was thinking you and Ernesto should come," Pablo says. "We could have dinner. I should get to know him, don't you think? If he's going to be Mateo's stepfather."

If the narcos can't lay their hands on Mateo, Pablo thinks, they'll go after Victoria. He has to get her out of the country and then find a way of explaining to her that she can't go back.

Not for a while.

Not like you.

You can't *ever* come back.

"Pablo, are you all right?"

"I'm fine," Pablo says. "You're always after me to be more mature, I'm trying to be more mature."

"All right."

"I'm thinking next week."

"Next week?" Victoria says. *"Are you joking? The election?"*

"We're talking one day, Victoria."

"The soonest I could do this," Victoria says, *"is two days after. And you just can't uproot Mateo all of a sudden. He has play dates, tutoring . . ."*

"Let's don't argue, okay?" Pablo asks. "Please, Victoria, I need you to make this happen."

"All right." She sighs.

"Yes?"

"Yes."

Pablo clicks off and goes home. Ana is already there, sitting on the back step drinking wine and smoking a cigarette. He sits down next to her. "Listen, I'm taking Mateo on a little trip."

"That's wonderful," Ana says. "Where are you going?"

"Across the river," Pablo says, trying to sound as casual as possible. "Do some theme parks in El Paso, but then we're going camping in Big Bend."

"Sounds nice."

"You want to come with us?"

"When is it?"

"Next week."

Ana laughs. "There's this little thing, the election . . ."

"After the election."

"I'll be writing follow-ups, analysis . . ."

"There's also this thing called the Internet," Pablo says. "You could write your stories from the road. Might be kind of fun."

Ana looks at him curiously, her antennae up and quivering. "What's going on?"

"Nothing. I'd just like to have you with us."

"I don't know . . ."

"What?"

"Is Mateo ready for that?"

"He's known you all his life," Pablo says.

"As his 'Tía Ana,'" she answers. "Not as his father's girlfriend. That's a lot to get used to."

"Mateo's getting used to a lot of new things," Pablo says. "Ernesto, for starters."

Ana asks, "Are you just trying to get even with Victoria?"

"That would be pretty childish."

"Yeah, that eliminates *that* possibility." She sips her wine and sets the glass down. "Pablo, if this is your way of trying to 'take things to the next level' . . ."

"I'm talking about a few nights camping," Pablo says. "Flies, mosquitoes, lousy food cooked badly over an ineptly built fire, smoke in your eyes, sand in your crotch—"

"You make it sound so attractive, how can I refuse?"

"Then you'll come?"

"I'll think about it," Ana says.

Come with me, Pablo thinks.

Please, Ana. Cross the river with me.

Pablo puts on the best clothes he owns—a collared blue shirt, relatively clean jeans, and a "travel" sports coat that was not supposed to wrinkle but has, and goes to the U.S. consulate the next morning. He feels like a traitor, plotting his escape to the United States, as so many others have done, as so many others have had to do.

The consular official he finally sees is not particularly helpful. "You have to be physically present in the United States to apply for an asylum visa. You have a seventy-two-hour guest visa anyway. Once there, you can apply for asylum. If it's not granted, you can apply for defensive asylum, show cause why you shouldn't be sent back. If you have a well-founded fear that you're going to be persecuted—"

"I do."

"On the grounds of ethnicity, religion, or political opinion—"

"I'm a journalist"—Pablo sighs, repeating himself—"and I feel that I'm under threat. Certainly you're aware that other journalists have been—"

"Are you under a specific threat?" the official asks. "Or just a general sort of threat?"

"A 'general threat'?"

"Have you been specifically threatened," the official says impatiently. "Has a specific person made an explicit threat on your life? Or do you just feel generally threatened as a journalist?"

"Is there a difference?"

"There's a very big difference," the official says. "Just a general feeling that you might be killed is not enough for us to issue asylum. On the other hand, if you're under an explicit threat—"

"I am."

"What is it?"

"Do you need to know?" Pablo asks.

"If we're going to consider giving you asylum, yes." The official pushes some papers across the desk. "Here's the form they'd give you in the U.S. Write down the nature of the threat, the date of the threat, the individual issuing the threat, why you consider the threat to be serious . . ."

"Is there any way that you can expedite this?"

"Yes, by your filling out the paperwork."

"I need it for another person as well," Pablo says.

"Immediate family?"

"No."

"Then that person will have to go in on his or her own."

"His or her own," Pablo repeats.

"Yes."

"We really don't have a lot of time here."

"Then . . ."

"You understand that they're going to *kill* us."

"I'm doing the best I can for you, Mr. Mora."

"Thank you."

Pablo walks out of the consulate and sits in the *fronterizo*. The "nature of the threat." *What am I supposed to write? They are going to kill me because . . .*

His phone rings.

"You thinking about running, you fat fuck?" Ramón says.

"What do you mean?"

"You went to the consulate?" Ramón asks. "You don't think we watch who goes in and out of there? We have *halcones* everywhere. Hey, you want to see a live video feed of your kid? I got one."

"No. Shit. I'm doing a story."

"What kind of a story?"

"You know," Pablo says, forcing himself to sound calm. "Every few months we track the immigration numbers. See how many people are leaving Juárez. So I check in with the U.S. consulate. That's all."

There's a long silence, then Ramón says, "You made any progress? On that other thing?"

"A little. Not much. I mean—"

"That's the story you should be working on."

Pablo sits at his desk and pounds out his story about voting trends.

He feels like he's walking underwater—every keystroke is like swinging a hammer, and he makes typo after typo.

"What's with you today?" Ana asks.

"Nothing. What do you mean?"

"You seem out of it."

"Hungover," Pablo says.

Ana doesn't buy it. Pablo didn't have that much to drink last night, and he's probably better at writing with a hangover than without one. And he's doing very un-Pablo-like things, like asking for more out of their relationship. Pablo is not a "more" person—he's usually looking for "less."

"Are you okay?" she asks.

"I'm fine," Pablo says. "Have you thought about the camping trip?"

"I'm still thinking."

"Could you think a little faster?" Pablo asks. "I have arrangements to make."

"Like how many s'mores?"

"Camping permits," Pablo says. "How many people."

"Oh. I'll let you know this afternoon."

She goes back to her desk and goes online and quickly finds out that Big Bend National Park doesn't require individual camping permits.

Why would Pablo lie about something like that? Unless he's just wrong about it. Unlikely—Pablo is personally sloppy but professionally immaculate. He checks his facts. One thing you can never say about Pablo is that he gets his stories wrong.

Ana logs on to *Esta Vida*.

The featured article is "Who Picked the Winner in Juárez?" and asks the question whether the PAN government, through the army and federal police, cooperated with the Sinaloa cartel to help Barrera control Juárez and the valley. "Is the government biased," Wild Child asks, "or just singularly inept at arresting people from Sinaloa?"

It's exactly what they're all thinking and exactly the kind of story that Óscar won't let them write anymore.

The next story is even more provocative, addressing the threats that Wild Child received about running photos of dead Zetas. "Don't Dish It Out If You Can't Take It" reprints the photos, along with photos and vid-clips that the Zetas have put out on websites.

She glances over at Pablo, who is ham-handedly beating out his article.

What does he know about this?

Chuy looks at the Bridge of Dreams.

All he would have to do is walk across. He'd be in El Paso, true, not Laredo, but it would be only a bus ride home.

Home.

The word has almost no meaning.

Chuy hasn't been home in six years. Hasn't talked to his family, doesn't even know if they still live in the same house. Or even if they're alive. If they know *he's* alive, if they even care.

After killing the woman police, his *estaca* got orders to fade into the city. They live in a safe house in the center of town so they can keep an eye on the newspaper office. Chuy doesn't know why, he doesn't care. Forty has a mission for them, but Chuy has a mission of his own.

Which is all that keeps him from walking across the Bridge of Dreams.

Eddie Ruiz is already back in Texas.

But he's thinking about Mexico.

Sitting in his apartment on Fort Bliss, his babysitters playing cards at the kitchen table, he sips on a cold Dos Equis as he watches Univisión coverage of the elections.

Eddie figures he has a dog in that fight.

Face it, man, he tells himself, your chips are stacked with PAN. All the valuable information you have is on PAN politicians and their police. If PAN loses, like the analysts on TV are predicting, your value goes way down. The people you're going to rat out are going to be gone anyway.

Prosecutors get hard-ons for corrupt politicians who are in office. Once they're out their appeal fades like an old girlfriend you're tired of tapping. No one writes headlines about politicians who are finished, and prosecutors love headlines like goats love garbage.

Eddie figures he's looking at a wilting dick.

The negotiations with the prosecutors have dragged on for months. Eddie's is a good poker player who knew he was holding face cards and played them well. He was in no hurry because he knew he was looking at fifteen-to-thirty and would get credit for time served.

Eddie just sat tight.

Because, what the fuck, right? Let the suits argue as long as they want.

Sit here or sit somewhere else.

The AG came back with an offer of fifteen years, seizure of Eddie's personal assets (Eddie don't give a shit because everything is in his wives' names anyway), and a $10 million fine (serious money but not *serious* money). Eddie's lawyer countered with twelve years, seizure, and $7 million.

Eddie's going to take it. He'll be at least four years testifying, with time credited. That left six, but it was really four, federal time. By the time he got to prison, he'd be old news in the narco-world. Then into the program, a whole new life ahead of him, selling aluminum siding in Scottsdale or something.

But that deal still has to be approved by a judge at the time of sentencing, and the judge might get buyer's remorse if he sees that what he's purchasing is a collection of out-of-office politicians and retired (or dead) cops.

I'm a used car, Eddie thinks.

As election day drags it's like that old song, "Fast Women and Slow Horses." The Ken doll candidate from PRI is in the lead, closely followed by the old whiner from PRD, and PAN . . . that filly is bringing up the rear.

You might as well just rip up your ticket, Eddie thinks, you ain't goin' to the window to collect.

Then Art freakin' Keller walks through the door.

And makes Eddie an offer he can't refuse.

Adán walks away from the television.

It's over.

At least as far as PAN is concerned.

Neither Peña Nieto nor López Obrador is going to win. There will be the routine accusations of voter fraud, the usual protest marches, and then the electoral officials will do the intelligent thing and install Peña Nieto as the winner.

The election is not a disappointment, as he had expected that PAN would lose. Peña Nieto won't throw the North Americans out, but he will neutralize them. Which would have been a dream just a few months ago, but now is a problem in that they're allies in his war against the Zetas.

All the new government wants is peace, an end to the violence, Adán thinks. It will accept whatever arrangement we make in order to achieve peace and order. It will accept a Sinaloa-Zeta division of the plazas, it will accept a Sinaloa victory, it will accept a Zeta victory.

It only wants a *pax narcotica*.

Five months, Adán thinks.

We have five months until the new president takes office.

One hundred and fifty days to destroy Ochoa. Can it be done? Or is Nacho right, should we try to make peace?

It's a hard calculation. So tempting to push for victory. Even now the Zetas are in the process of losing their deal with 'Ndrangheta, in fact, losing all of Europe. The prince of darkness himself, Arturo Keller, personally saw to it, and the Zetas waltzed into his trap that will also set the North American antiterrorist apparatus against them.

Then again, a hundred things could go wrong.

Ochoa still has the upper hand in Guatemala.

He has thousands of fighters. He is without morals, restraint, or scruples—the truly ruthless man.

And that is the hell of all this, Adán thinks.

The unvarnished truth is that Mexico would be better off with you, rather than under the Zetas. You would run a business that didn't touch the ordinary person's ordinary life; Ochoa would preside over a reign of terror.

The current government understands this, the future one thinks like a goat bleating "just make it stop."

"Where are you going?" Eva asks him.

For some reason, she is glued to the elections, her attempt, Adán thinks, to display that she's a serious person with a real interest in current affairs. It's part of her new maturity campaign. Eva has adopted the "concerned young parent" role. Now she reads—articles about early education, organic nutrition and climate change, global warming and rising sea levels.

"What kind of a world," she has asked Adán several times, "will our children grow up in?"

The same world we did, Adán thinks, only hotter.

And with more beachfront property.

And yet it is time for a change.

For the country.

For yourself.

For your family.

Nacho is right—we have billions of dollars but live like refugees. We have to hide, look behind our backs, always have to wonder if this day is our last.

It's not the life you want for these boys in their cribs.

You could be El Patrón again, if you win. But you could also do what no *patrón* has ever done.

Walk away.

With a life and family intact.

No one has ever done that.

Every "drug lord" before you has ended up either dead or in prison.

You could reinvest your billions in legitimate concerns and your sons could grow up and live as titans of business.

You could live to see your grandchildren.

It could be done.

He goes upstairs to the nursery, where an *abuela* sits asleep in a chair beside the boys' cribs. Eva has decorated the nursery in soothing "womb tones" with letters from the alphabet painted on the walls and ceilings in the belief that it's never too early for them to start learning.

The boys have nannies, but Eva is what they now call a "helicopter parent," hovering over them constantly, supervising every detail of clothing, diet, and environment.

Ah well, he thinks, be patient. She tried for so long and so hard to have a baby, it's natural that's she's going to be overprotective for a while. She'll get over it and start a new phase. With any luck it will be "I'm sexy even though I'm a mother."

The *abuela* wakes with a start when Adán comes into the room and he shakes his head quickly to let her know that he doesn't mind her dozing. He looks down at the two babies, who are breathing softly and evenly, their foreheads dewy with a sheen of sweat.

They're beautiful.

He remembers Gloria when she was a baby. She was *not* beautiful, with her heavy misshapen head, except to him.

To him, she was lovely.

Adán looks down at his boys and then suddenly he doesn't see them but two other children and he gets hot and dizzy as he sees those two children on a bridge in Colombia, a boy and a girl, not babies but little, and he'd already had their mother killed and the little girl screamed *Mi mamá, mi mamá* and he gave the order and his man threw them over the side and he made himself watch as they plunged onto the rocks below and now he sees their faces in the faces of his sons and he recoils, staggers away from the crib, his children are dead children, all his children are dead.

He leans against the wall trying to catch his breath.

Then he forces himself to look into the crib again.

His boys are sleeping.

Adán kisses them on their cheeks and goes back downstairs and makes the call that will set up the peace meeting with Ochoa.

The election is called by 8 p.m.

The following morning, the numbers are in:

Peña Nieto receives 38.15 percent of the vote.

López Obrador gets 31.64.

Vázquez Mota comes in with 25.40.

PAN is finished, Los Pinos will go back to the PRI, which also gets a heavy plurality in the Chamber of Deputies.

Victoria is bitterly disappointed.

"Did you call to gloat?" she asks Pablo.

"No," Pablo says, "just to firm up our plans."

"She should have won," Victoria says. *"The country would be so much better off than with this . . . this . . ."*

"I need your flight information."

"It's the media," Victoria says. *"Media bias."*

"You *are* the media."

"I mean the rest of the media."

"Of course."

"You, for instance," Victoria says. *"And Ana. And El Niño Salvaje. How* dare *that . . . blogger . . . write a story the day before the election, accusing PAN of supporting the Sinaloa cartel?"*

Perhaps because it's true, Pablo thinks. "I don't know, Victoria. Give me a clue—morning, afternoon, or evening?"

"Morning, afternoon, or evening what*?"*

"When you and Mateo are coming," Pablo says. "Is Ernesto coming with you?"

"I don't know, I don't know yet," Victoria says. *"Pablo, I have stories to write, unfortunately. Stories on how this election will damage the economy. Now all we need is for the Democrats to get elected and we'll all be selling apples."*

"Flight times?"

"I don't know." She sounds confused, impatient. *"I'll have Emilia call you."*

"Who's Emilia?"

"My new assistant."

"But you *are* coming," Pablo says.

"Yes."

"Tomorrow."

"Yes!"

"Okay, have Emilia call me."

"I will." She clicks off.

"Is Victoria beside herself with disappointment?" Ana asks, rolling her chair up to his. "I am sorry we won't have a woman president, only not *that* woman. Our answer to Maggie Thatcher."

"Ana?"

"Yes?"

"I don't care."

Óscar comes into the room. "Ana, write the story, straight news, facts and figures. Then get a jump on the inevitable fraud angles. Pablo—"

"Man-in-the-street."

"How did you know?"

"I just knew."

Pablo grabs his laptop, goes out into the parking lot, and gets into the *fronterizo*. He has no intention of going out and doing man-in-the-street interviews, because he already knows what man in which street is going to say.

And it doesn't matter.

He's leaving the paper, leaving journalism, leaving Mexico.

Leaving Juárez.

Pablo drives back to Ana's apartment and throws what little he has into a backpack.

Manuel Godoy is a self-described geek.

A graduate student at Juárez Autonomous University, he's the best computer hacker in the city, maybe in all of Chihuahua.

Now he has a gun to his head.

Literally.

Three men picked him up as he left campus, shoved him into a car, hooded him, and drove him to this nondescript building. They sat him down in a chair in front of a computer, removed the hood, and stuck the pistol into the back of his head.

"You want to live?" the man they called "Forty" asked him.

"Yes."

"Good answer," Forty said. "You know *Esta Vida?*"

Manuel didn't know how to answer. This wasn't some oral exam at the university, defending his thesis. The wrong answer could get that trigger pulled. He dissembles. "I've heard of it."

"All you have to do," Forty said, "is tell us who's behind it. We know it comes from Juárez. You tell us who, we'll pay you very well. You don't, we kill you. It's that simple. Go."

"I can't do it on this computer."

"Why not?"

"It's a piece of shit."

Forty laughed. "What do you need?"

Manuel gave him a list of hardware and software and Forty sent his guys out to get it. When they got back, Manuel assembled the hardware, downloaded the programs he needed, and went to work.

Now he sits at the computer and hacks for his life.

"What do you mean?" Pablo asks Victoria over the phone.

"What do you mean, what do I mean?" she answers, sounding aggrieved. *"I have* work, *Pablo—stories to file—and can't come until tomorrow, at the earliest. You and Mateo can meet us in El Paso."*

Pablo thinks he might throw up. "Mateo can't come to Juárez."

"Why not?"

"It's not safe."

"You pick him up at the airport and go straight over to the U.S.," Victoria says. *"Ernesto and I will meet you there. I don't see the problem."*

"The problem is that Mateo can't come to Juárez."

"He's dying to see you," Victoria says. *"When I told him it would be another day or two he threw a fit, and he can throw a fit these days, believe me."*

"For God's sake, Victoria, just tell him no."

"Too late," Victoria says. *"Emilia is putting him on a flight now."*

"Stop her."

"Aeroméxico 765. He gets in at 8:10. Be there."

She clicks off.

It will be all right, it will be all right, Pablo tells himself. Ana goes with you to pick up Mateo and you drive straight across the border. But the airport is on the southern edge of the city, a long drive down the 45 and back.

He looks over.

Ana's not at her desk.

Pablo leaves the office and crosses the street to the coffee shop. Ana is at the counter, smoking a cigarette and banging away on her laptop. She closes it when she sees him come in.

"Okay," Pablo says, "are you coming with us?"

"If you really think it's a good idea."

"Yes," Pablo says. "Go home right now and pack your things. Then we're going out to González to pick up Mateo. There's been a change of plans."

He tells her about Victoria.

Ana says, "Listen, I'm just okay with Mateo. I don't know about seeing Victoria and her new man. I mean, the whole 'exes meet' scene—"

"You've known Victoria for years."

"Exactly," Ana says. "Look, you go do your thing with the Ice Maiden and I'll meet you and Mateo when you're done."

"No."

"No?"

"Ana, come with me now," Pablo says. "We'll get Mateo and go to El Paso tonight?"

"*Tonight?* What's the hurry?"

"Ana."

"Pablo."

They stare at each other.

"We're leaving tonight," Pablo says. "Please. Just do this for me."

"I'll tell you what," Ana says. "I'm a woman, in case you don't recall. I need a little more time to pack. You go get Mateo, then swing by my place, I'll be ready and we'll go."

"Okay, but be ready."

"*Okay*, Pablo."

"I have to go talk to Óscar," Pablo says. "I'll meet you at your place and we'll go, okay?"

"As previously stated, okay."

Pablo walks out of the coffee shop.

Chuy watches him cross the street.

Pablo knocks on Óscar's door.

"Come in!" Óscar is sitting in his office, his bad leg propped up on a stool, his cane leaning against the desk.

"Óscar, I need a few personal days."

"All right, Pablo. When?"

"Now. Tonight."

"Tonight?" Óscar asks.

"It's a family matter."

"I'm sorry," Óscar says. "Is Mateo all right?"

"He's fine. He's coming to Juárez. I'm going to take him away on a small holiday."

"Usually, a little more notice would be appreciated," Óscar says.

"I'm sorry. I am."

"Well, don't be too sorry," Óscar says. "An excess of contrition is bad for the digestion. A small joke, Pablo—you look like your best friend just died."

Pablo stands there.

"Is there something else?" Óscar asks.

"I just wanted," Pablo stammers, "to thank you."

"It's a small thing."

"No, I mean for everything," Pablo says. "For everything you taught me, and . . . for being who you are."

El Búho blinks at him. "Well, thank you, Pablo. That's very gracious."

Pablo nods, turns, and leaves.

Manuel sits back from the keyboard.

"I've got it," he says.

The address from which 80 percent of the *Esta Vida* articles have been posted. The rest were posted from the offices of *El Periódico* or a coffee shop just across the street.

Forty calls Ramón and gives him the address.

Pablo drives down the 45 to Abraham González International Airport.

The trip takes only twenty minutes but feels like forever, and he also has the sense that he's being followed. Paranoia again, he tells himself. Shake it. They gave you a couple of weeks. Please God, he thinks as he parks in the short-term lot and walks into the terminal, for once let Aeroméxico be on time.

"Papi!"

Mateo has grown.

He looks skinny now. Not underfed, by any means, but his body is in the process of becoming lanky like his mother's. Pablo picks him up and swings him around. *"M'ijo! Sonrisa de mi alma!"*

The smile of my soul.

"Are we going on a holiday?" Mateo asks.

"Yes, we are."

"Can I go down the waterslide?!"

"As many times as you want," Pablo says.

"I'm not too small?"

"If I'm not too fat."

"You're not fat, *Papi*."

"You are a very kind boy, *m'ijo*." He takes Mateo's bag, slings it over his shoulder, then takes his son's hand and starts to walk out of the terminal. "How was your flight?"

"I had a Coke. Don't tell."

"Don't worry."

They walk outside.

The night is warm and close. Pablo throws Mateo's bag into the backseat, then opens the passenger door and straps him into his seat.

"*Papi*, your car is a mess!" Mateo laughs.

"You can help me clean it when we get to El Paso."

"When are we going?"

"When?! Now!"

"Now!?" He's delighted. Little boys so rarely hear the word "now." Usually, it's "later" or "we'll see."

"*Right* now," Pablo says, sliding behind the wheel. "We're going to go pick up Tía Ana first. She's coming with us. I hope that's okay."

Mateo looks very serious. "Is Tía Ana your girlfriend?"

"Well, she's a girl," Pablo says, "and she's my friend. Are you hungry? Did they give you anything to eat on the flight?"

"*Is* she?" Mateo asks.

He's a reporter's son, Pablo thinks as he starts the car and pulls out of the lot.

The car, a silver Navigator, pulls up in front of Pablo and stops.

Pablo hits the brakes.

He starts to back up but another SUV pulls up behind him. Then he sees Ramón get out of the car in front and walk back toward him. A short, skinny kid who can't be more than a teenager is behind him. Ramón taps on the window and motions for Pablo to roll it down. When he does, Ramón says, "This is a fine automobile you have, *'mano*."

"It's just a *fronterizo*," Pablo says, his voice shaking.

"When you headed out to the airport I thought maybe you were going on a trip," Ramón says, "but you were just picking up little Mateo. *Hola*, I'm your Tío Ramón."

"Hello."

"He's a cute one," Ramón says to Pablo.

Pablo can't breathe. His throat tightens as if he's being choked from the inside. "Please, Ramón—"

"You're out of time. We want an answer. Tonight. Otherwise we're going to come visit you." Ramón leans in and smiles at Mateo. "Maybe I'll see you later, okay, *mi sobrino*?"

"Okay."

Ramón smiles, makes a *phone me* signal to Pablo, and then walks away. His car takes off and Pablo, his hands shaking, pulls back onto the road.

"Who was that man, *Papi*?" Mateo asks.

"An old friend."

"What did he want?"

"Just to say hello, I guess."

Pablo's in agony as he drives to Ana's. He doesn't have a choice now.

He has to tell them what he knows.

Ana stuffs a flannel shirt into her backpack.

Even in July, it can get cold in the desert at night.

She's still not so sure about this, not at all sure she should be making this trip. The thought of an awkward dinner with Victoria and her fiancé is appalling, and Mateo is too smart and sensitive a kid not to pick up on that, and react to it, so the whole thing could turn into a hot mess.

But it seems important to Pablo that she goes, so—

She hears a car door shut, and then another.

That must be them, she thinks.

Pablo lets himself into the house.

Ana is just finishing packing. She takes Mateo into her arms and gives him a long hug. Then she leans back, looks at him, and says, "You've grown so much!"

"I know."

"I'm almost ready," Ana says to Pablo.

"That's okay," Pablo says. "I need to make a phone call."

He walks out into the backyard, where he's spent so many great evenings. The parties, the music, the conversations and arguments . . . Ana shouldn't have done it, he tells himself. She put us all in danger, writing that god-damned blog. She knew what she was doing, knew the chance she was taking, knew that it would come to this eventually . . .

He takes his phone from his jeans pocket and hits the number.

It's his last chance.

Keller doesn't answer—the call goes straight to voice mail.

Where the hell are you? Pablo thinks. You're the last chance I have, the last chance Ana has, you . . . North American . . . could get us out of this. Whisk us across the border and hide us the way you hide narcos who change sides.

Narcos can get asylum visas. The journalists who write about them can't.

And now it's too late anyway.

All you can think about is Mateo, he tells himself.

Do what you have to do for your son.

But, oh, Ana.

Chuy gets his orders from Forty.

When we get the Wild Child . . .

Make it long, make it last.

Make it hurt.

Send a message.

Pablo walks back into the house.

"Where's Mateo?" he asks, panicked.

"In the bathroom," Ana says.

"Listen, something's come up," Pablo says. "Could you do me a huge favor? Take Mateo to El Paso and I'll meet you there tomorrow?"

"Why don't you just do what you need to do and we'll all go then?" Ana asks.

"Ana . . ."

"What?"

"Just go. Please."

"What is it you need to do?" Ana asks. "Can I help?"

"Yes. Take my son across tonight."

"Pablo—"

"Ana, it's okay."

"Come with us."

He shakes his head. It's no good anyway. The North Americans will only toss them back into Mexico, sooner or later, and even if they don't the narcos will track her down and kill her there.

There's only one way to save her.

And protect Mateo.

Pablo says, "I need you to get Mateo across. I'll come over tomorrow, I promise."

Mateo comes out of the bathroom. Pablo kneels in front of him, takes his face in his hands, and says, *"M'ijo*, I have a nice surprise for you. I have a little more work to do, so Tía Ana is going to take you and I'll see you tomorrow, okay?"

Mateo looks uncertain.

"You love Tía Ana, don't you?" Pablo asks.

"Yes."

"So you'll have a great time," Pablo says. "Tía Ana will let you get a Coke out of the machine at the motel."

"We'll have fun," Ana says.

"Okay."

Pablo holds him tight. Feels his soft warm little chest against his own. *"Papi* loves you very much. You know that, don't you?"

"I love you, too."

Pablo kisses him on both cheeks. "Okay, you'd better go. I'll see you both tomorrow and we'll go to the waterslide. Did I ever tell you that I'm the world's champion waterslider?"

"Why are you crying, *Papi*?"

"Just because I love you so much."

Ana takes Mateo's hand and walks him outside. Pablo stands in the door and watches them drive away.

He waves.

Then he goes back inside and finds a bottle of Johnnie Walker Black in the kitchen cupboard. He pours himself a glass, goes into the bedroom, and once he's drunk enough to stop his hands from shaking, he sits down at Ana's desktop computer and starts to type.

"Look at this," Forty says to Ramón.

It's *Esta Vida*—the latest post.

An article signed by the author.

"Son of a bitch," Ramón says.

It takes him less than an hour to track Pablo down at Ana's house. He and the kid Chuy go out, and when they get there Pablo's sitting on the back step drinking a beer, a dead bottle of scotch beside him.

Pablo looks up at him.

"Time to go," Ramón says.

"For old time's sake," Pablo says, "I don't suppose you could just do it here? You know . . ."

He mimes pointing a pistol and pulling the trigger.

"It doesn't work that way," Ramón says. "I don't know why you had to go and do this."

"I don't know why, either." Pablo grabs the railing and slowly pulls himself to his feet. His legs start to go out from under him and Ramón grabs his elbow. "You're pretty drunk, *'mano*."

"Probably better, huh?"

"Probably."

"I'm really scared, Ramón."

"Yeah, well . . ."

They take him out to the car and drive to one of the old maquiladoras that's been shut down.

The street sweepers find him just before dawn.

Paper wrappers, old newspapers, and other trash blow across Pablo Mora on the Plaza del Periodista.

His killers took great trouble to arrange the pieces of his body around the statue of the newsboy—Pablo's amputated arms and legs frame his trunk, which is disemboweled and emasculated. His head is carefully set at the base of the pedestal, his mouth stuffed with the severed fingers with which he used to type, his tongue has been pulled through a gash in his throat, his empty eye sockets are bloody and raw.

A placard is set at his neck.

NOW WRITE YOUR STORIES, WILD CHILD—THE Z COMPANY.

But later that morning, it seems as if everyone in Mexico is reading Wild Child's last words:

FOR THE VOICELESS
by El Niño Salvaje

I speak for the ones who cannot speak, for the voiceless. I raise my voice and wave my arms and shout for the ones you do not see, perhaps cannot see, for the invisible. For the poor, the powerless, the disenfranchised;

for the victims of this so-called "war on drugs," for the eighty thousand murdered by the narcos, by the police, by the military, by the government, by the purchasers of drugs and the sellers of guns, by the investors in gleaming towers who have parlayed their "new money" into hotels, resorts, shopping malls, and suburban developments.

I speak for the tortured, burned, and flayed by the narcos, beaten and raped by the soldiers, electrocuted and half-drowned by the police.

I speak for the orphans, twenty thousand of them, for the children who have lost both or one parent, whose lives will never be the same.

I speak for the dead children, shot in crossfires, murdered alongside their parents, ripped from their mothers' wombs.

I speak for the people enslaved, forced to labor on the narcos' ranches, forced to fight. I speak for the mass of others ground down by an economic system that cares more for profit than for people.

I speak for the people who tried to tell the truth, who tried to tell the story, who tried to show you what you have been doing and what you have done. But you silenced them and blinded them so that they could not tell you, could not show you.

I speak for them, but I speak to you—the rich, the powerful, the politicians, the *comandantes,* the generals. I speak to Los Pinos and the Chamber of Deputies, I speak to the White House and Congress, I speak to AFI and the DEA, I speak to the bankers, and the ranchers and the oil barons and the capitalists and the narco drug lords and I say—

You are the same.

You are all the cartel.

And you are guilty.

You are guilty of murder, you are guilty of torture, you are guilty of rape, of kidnapping, of slavery, of oppression, but mostly I say that you are guilty of indifference. You do not see the people that you grind under your heel. You do not see their pain, you do not hear their cries, they are voiceless and invisible to you and they are the victims of this war that you perpetuate to keep yourselves above them.

This is not a war on drugs.

This is a war on the poor.

This is a war on the poor and the powerless, the voiceless and the invisible, that you would just as soon be swept from your streets like the trash that blows around your ankles and soils your shoes.

Congratulations.

You've done it.

You've performed a cleansing.

A *limpieza*.

The country is safe now for your shopping malls and suburban tracts, the invisible are safely out of sight, the voiceless silent as they should be.

I speak these last words, and now you will kill me for it.

I only ask that you bury me in the *fosa común*—the common grave— with the faceless and the nameless, without a headstone.

I would rather be with them than you.

And I am voiceless now, and invisible.

I am Pablo Mora.

3

The Cleansing

Wash me throughly from my wickedness and cleanse me from my sin.

—Psalm 51

San Diego, California
October 2012

A thousand years ago, Keller learns, the Petén was one of the most densely populated areas on earth.

As a center of the Mayan civilization, the heavily forested lowlands—rain forest, jungle—held dozens of cities with stone temples and courtyards, and vast terraced fields irrigated with canals, and *chinampas,* floating farms on lakes.

Then it went into decline.

No one is sure why, whether it was drought, or disease, or invasion, but by the time Cortés arrived in the 1520s the rain forest had taken back most of the towns and the farms, and what people survived the spread of the foreign smallpox lived off slash-and-burn agriculture in isolated villages.

Still, it took the Spanish almost two hundred years to finally and fully subdue the Mayan descendants in the Petén and set up a system of colonization that made the white Spanish and their mestizo offspring the landowning masters, and the native Mayan "Indians" the landless peasants.

The system held for almost four hundred years, even as the new American imperialists of the United Fruit Company came into power in Guatemala. It wasn't until 1944 that the "October Revolutionaries" launched liberal reforms and in 1952 put through Decree 900 that mandated the redistribution of the land.

The masters reacted.

The 2 percent of the population that owned 98 percent of the land weren't about to see their position altered and with CIA backing staged a coup that overthrew the civilian government.

The left—a loose coalition of students, workers, and a few peasants from the countryside—formed "MR-13," a guerrilla movement that started to fight the Guatemalan army and police. After five years of sporadic fighting, the United States sent in its army special forces—the Green Berets—to help combat the "communist guerrillas."

What followed was called the "White Terror" as the "Special Commando Unit" and the paramilitary Mano Blanca—actually police and soldiers— committed thousands of "disappearances" against leftists in Guatemala City and out in the countryside. Guatemala's president, Carlos Arana Osorio, in declaring a "state of siege" announced, "If it is necessary to turn the country into a graveyard in order to pacify it, I will not hesitate."

Seven thousand people "disappeared" over the next three years.

The left responded, forming the CUC (Committee for Peasant Unity) in the south and east and the EGP (Guerrilla Army of the Poor) in the Mayan north, and the Guatemalan Civil War went on.

If ever there has been a greater misnomer than "Mexican drug problem," "Guatemalan Civil War" has to be it. Certainly it was a one-sided civil war, mostly the disappearances and slaughter of a few poorly armed leftist guerrillas by a professional army and police forces well supplied with American weapons and training.

In 1978 the special forces, the Kaibiles, opened fire on an unarmed group of protestors in Panzos and killed 150. By 1980, 5,000 had been killed.

Keller made it a point to study the history of a particular Guatemalan village in the Petén—Dos Erres.

It's one of tragedy.

In October 1982, EGP guerrillas ambushed an army convoy near Dos Erres, killed twenty-one soldiers, and took nineteen rifles.

On December 4, a unit of fifty-eight Kaibiles disguised as guerrillas flew into the area. Two days later, they walked into the village at 2:30 in the morning. They roused the people from their houses and separated the men from the women, putting all the men into the village schoolhouse, and the women and children into the church. Then they searched the village for the missing weapons. They didn't find any because the EGP who ambushed the soldiers hadn't come from Dos Erres.

It didn't matter.

The Kaibiles announced that after they'd had breakfast, they were going to "vaccinate" the inhabitants of Dos Erres.

The Kaibiles went berserk.

They grabbed children by the ankles and swung their heads into tree trunks and walls. Not wanting to waste ammunition, they smashed the adult men's heads with hammers. They ripped babies from pregnant women's stomachs, and then, over the course of the next two days, raped the rest of the women before killing them and dumping their bodies on top of their families in the village well.

On the last morning of the slaughter, fifteen more Mayan peasants wandered into Dos Erres. Because the wells were too full, the Kaibiles drove them half a mile away before slaughtering all but two teenage girls whom they raped as they left the area, then strangled them.

The Guatemalan "Civil War" went on for fourteen more years after the massacre of Dos Erres. Over two hundred thousand people were killed, including forty to fifty thousand who "disappeared." A million and a half people were displaced from their homes, another million emigrated, mostly to the United States.

But the suffering of the Petén goes on, this time by narco cartels wanting the area for its proximity to the border. The Zetas and the Sinaloa cartel were ready to go to war for the Petén until Barrera brought Ochoa to the peace table.

Now Keller studies the latest satellite photographs.

The clearing outside Dos Erres is fresh, a small rectangle hacked out of the rain forest. He counts the number of tents and the two small buildings, but doesn't have to do a calculation as to how many Gente Nueva are there. He already knows—Barrera has told him he was bringing a hundred men.

His intel team has done a calculation as to the numbers of Zetas, based on the small houses, huts, and tents in Dos Erres, the number of vehicles, and whatever satellite imagery they could grab of the village itself. Their best estimate was two hundred Zetas, among them maybe two dozen former Kaibiles.

We're bringing twenty men, Keller thinks.

All elite operatives.

Keller has gotten to know and like the team members during the long weeks of training. It's hard to get to know these men—they're quiet, reticent, don't swap biographies. The general, unspoken rule is that the less they know about each other the better, but Keller has gleaned that John Downey, "D-1," the team leader, was an army full colonel, a Ranger with combat experience in Somalia, Iraq, and Afghanistan. Late forties, built like a fire hydrant, short red hair, pug nose, and an easy air of command.

It's the only name he's allowed to know. The rest are just first names—Keller has no idea if any or all are real—or nicknames. What they have in common is that they're all professional, efficient, athletic, and educated. Through conversation over meals and beers he's learned that most have advanced degrees in history, sociology, or the hard sciences and most are at least bilingual, but can curse fluently in English, Spanish (Downey recruited only Spanish speakers), Arabic, Kurdish, Pashto, and Dari.

Keller feels that he knows Dos Erres as well as you can know a place you've never been. He's studied satellite photos, maps, and video. When the team moved from Virginia to a private training camp at Sunshine Summit, in remote hills about seventy miles north of San Diego, they built a mockup of the village with PVC pipe and cords.

They've practiced the operation a few hundred times.

Their best intelligence says that Ochoa has turned the empty church into his personal quarters, whereas Forty resides in the abandoned school just next to the church, on the west end of the village.

Each seems to have four personal bodyguards living in quarters with him, while the rest of the Zetas are quartered to the east of the village in the bivouac that had first been detected from the satellite reconnaissance.

A new clearing has been made to the west of the village. Another neat military rectangle, it has tents and what appear to be two C-containers that have been turned into living quarters, with small wooden porches covered with corrugated tin shade roofs.

Keller and the team have surmised that this new camp is for the Sinaloan guests, with the C-containers for Adán and Nacho.

The operational plan is simply but tightly timed.

Two MH-60 Black Hawk helicopters, each carrying ten men and a pilot, will fly the team across the Mexican border into Guatemala. The first chopper will hover over Dos Erres itself while its team fast-lines into the village and then separates into two "kill teams" of four men each. Kill Team "F" will attack the school and eliminate Forty. Kill Team "G" will hit the church and take out Ochoa. Downey will stay back with a medic who will double on communications.

The second chopper will land at the eastern edge of the village, along the narrow belt of jungle between the village and the Zeta camp. Its men will deploy and screen the kill teams from any counterattack coming from the camp.

There shouldn't be one—the raid should be quick. Just in, just out, and then the first chopper will land, the kill teams will board, and then a fast "exfil" back across the border into Campeche, where the FES will pick them up and fly them to a military base outside Juárez.

From there they'll "smurf" into small units, cross back into the States, and disappear.

The element of surprise will be critical.

Keller will be on Kill Team G with Eddie Ruiz. The special-ops guys didn't really want Keller there; in fact, they wanted him to stay in the chopper. He's too old, too slow, not a highly trained combat fighter, and there's no time for him to catch up on the learning curve.

Keller told them to go fuck themselves.

"This is my op," he told them. "I go, and I go in the front, or nobody goes."

They grudgingly accepted it, more so as they learned more about "Killer Keller," his background, and his personal losses. Rumors went around the camp about his relationship with the beautiful Médica Hermosa—who was promptly Googled and ogled—and how the Zetas shot her to pieces. The guys also learned about Erika Valles and Pablo Mora, and they decided that if Keller wanted to get some revenge, they were going to walk him in and take his back.

They've given him the radio call name "K-1."

He surprised them in training.

Slow, yes, but precise.

And motivated.

And his briefings on the Zetas were comprehensive—their habits, their tactics, their training, their armaments—even the psychology of the two targets. He brought a treasure trove of photographs and video clips.

Eddie Ruiz brought something different.

Eddie was chilling out in his pad at Bliss when Keller came in and dismissed the babysitters.

"Pack," Keller said.

"Where am I going?" Eddie asked.

"You're coming with me," Keller said. "To kill Forty and Ochoa."

Eddie whistled. "Holy shit. That couldn't have been easy."

It wasn't. Everyone and his dog had fought the idea of taking Crazy Eddie on the mission to Guatemala, but Keller argued that Ruiz was the only person who could personally identify both targets, that he was certainly a proven fighter, and that, at the end of the day, Ruiz was a free citizen who could walk out of Bliss anytime he wanted.

"We'd charge him five seconds later and arrest him," Taylor answered.

"I promised him," Keller said.

"You had no authority to do that."

Keller shrugged.

"What if he runs?" Taylor asked.

"He won't."

Keller knew that he'd prevail on the issue. Eddie was damaged goods now that PAN had lost the election.

"You take him," Taylor said, "you bring him back."

"Sure."

Eddie's briefings—if you can call them that—have been invaluable. Ruiz had sat down with Zetas, ate with them, talked with them, partied with them. He knows how they talk, how they think, how they react. Along with Keller, he's the only one who's fought them, who's killed them.

The ex–special ops on the team were resistant to him, too—at first—looking on him as an undisciplined, drug-dealing, homicidal dirtbag. But once Eddie freely admitted that's exactly what he was, they relented a little. And there was no question about one thing—Crazy Eddie could shoot the balls off a mosquito if mosquitoes had balls.

He told them so, and backed it up on the range.

So did Keller.

But the physical training, Keller has to admit as he studies the latest intel images, about killed him. The guys are right—he is too old and too slow. His legs and reflexes just won't do what his mind tells them to do, and it's infuriating. He's in the best shape of his life, and exhausted. If there were two missions instead of one, he wouldn't make it. This is his last operation.

The other thing that's killing him is the waiting.

He waited for weeks, sweating out whether Barrera could even get the meeting with Ochoa. Then weeks more to learn where the location was going to be. Once they knew that, the tactical planning and training went into overdrive, but then it was more waiting to find out the exact date. When the date was established, there were five more days of excruciating tension to see whether it would actually come off.

Now it has, Keller thinks as he studies the photos.

Barrera is in Dos Erres.

The meetings are scheduled to begin in the late afternoon tomorrow.

They'll go all day and into the night—at which point there will be a fiesta and partying, if everything goes well. There will be no more meetings the next day because by the time the sun comes up, the Zeta leaders will be dead.

Adán Barrera will be the undisputed patron.

And the *pax narcotica* can begin.

Because that's the deal.

There will be one cartel trafficking drugs into the United States and we can all go back to playing the perpetual game of coyote and sheepdog along the border. Business as usual, and the gigantic trafficking and antitrafficking machines can grind on. Without me, Keller thinks.

In two days, I'm out of it.

Maybe less than that, he admits, if you die in Dos Erres, which is a very real possibility. Face it, they're all right—you have no business coming on this mission, you're the weakest link, probably the least skilled combatant on the ground. There's a very good chance you won't come back.

But what if I do? he asks himself.

What then? What next? What do you do with what's left of your life? You can't go back to Marisol, she doesn't want you, so the happy retirement you pictured with her is out of the picture. You can't go back to tending the bees—the monastery won't have you, and besides, you're not that guy anymore. That guy believed in the possibility of serenity and faith. The past seven years have beaten that out of you.

There is no such thing.

Not in this world, anyway.

So what are you going to do?

Take your pension, find a condo in Tucson, become that pathetic middle-aged guy you find at sports bars at two in the afternoon? Take up golf? Brew your own beer? Read the great books? Hang around until you get the bad biopsy and in the meantime try to convince yourself that you haven't done what you've done, seen what you've seen, that your nightmares are the stuff of fantasy and not just a slightly more surreal depiction of your surreal life?

Maybe there are worse things than dying in Dos Erres.

They break up the camp in Sunshine Summit and go to the staging area in San Diego. Then it will be separate flights to Mexico City, on to Campeche, then into the chopper and across the border for "Operation XTZ."

"Cross Out the Zetas."

In his hotel room out by the airport, Keller sits on his bed with his phone in hand and thinks about calling Marisol. But what would he say? I miss you? Goodbye? Nothing he's going to say will change anything, but he isn't going to say that he's changed his mind about going.

He doesn't call.

Restless, he goes for a walk through the old neighborhood known as Little Italy. He used to come down here from his office in the old days, to get a sausage at Pete's—now gone—or a good espresso at a place that he sees is now a Starbucks.

He turns up Columbia Street to Our Lady of the Rosary, built back in the '20s to serve the Italian tuna fishermen who dominated the neighborhood. Keller used to come here often, for early morning Mass, to make confession, take communion, or just look at the frescoes in the back of the sanctuary.

The tuna fleet is long gone, the Italian fishermen with it.

The neighborhood is "hip" now—coffeehouses and nightclubs, new condo buildings. The Italian restaurants are expensive and cater mostly to tourists.

Keller stands outside the church and thinks about going in. It's too late for Mass, but there might be a priest inside to hear confession.

But how much time could he have? Keller asks himself ruefully.

Bless me, Father, for I have sinned and sinned and sinned and sinned . . .

And I'm about to go commit (another) murder.

At least one.

Keller keeps walking.

He has no need of God, he decides, and God has no need of him.

The Petén District, Guatemala
October 31, 2012

Chuy kicks a soccer ball against the remnant of a stone wall he doesn't know is Mayan in origin.

The jungle is full of such ruins and he doesn't care. Chuy wanders across the old stone terraces that were once altars without knowing what he's walking on, or his own connection to them, that they were places where victims were decapitated in sacrifices to the Mayan death gods. He does like the caves that permeate the forest, cracks in the limestone floor of the jungle into which he can crawl and hide, take a nap, or just lie and think.

Forty brought Chuy and his *estaca* down to Guatemala and it was his first time on an airplane. He hated the crowded heat of Guatemala City but felt better when they drove north across the broad grasslands and then into the jungle. It still feels too close and too green, but he's starting to get used to it, even though he's a little scared at night because the men who'd been there longer told him that there are jaguars and pumas, and crocodiles in the swamps outside the village.

The village itself is pretty empty, except for some women and girls the men keep to do the cooking and the cleaning, and some men to do the grunt work. Otherwise, they had killed the villagers or chased them out, so it's pretty much just Zetas living there in an armed camp.

The men had offered Chuy a girl for his bed, but he didn't want her because he remembered Flor talking about her childhood in the Petén and how the Kaibiles forced her family off their land. So he doesn't want a girl because it would remind him too much of her and also because he wakes up in the night crying and sometimes he pisses the cot, so he likes to sleep alone.

Some nights he doesn't even sleep in the tent, but crawls into one of the caves and pulls a sweatshirt around him and sleeps there, even though he's afraid of the jaguars and the pumas, but he has a rifle and a pistol and a knife so he's not too afraid, and anyway, he only sleeps in fits and starts because in his sleep he sees faces—the faces of the boys who took him in the reformatory, the face of the first man he killed, the face of Forty, the face of Ochoa when he made him take the man's head. He sees the faces of the people he's killed, they're like masks that float around the inside of his head when he closes his eyes.

Chuy sees the face of the woman police when he started to saw on her throat, and now he sees the face of the man they took away a few weeks ago, the drunk man who was so afraid and who cried and wept and begged and screamed until they shoved his shirt in his mouth to shut him up and he sees Forty's face laughing, always laughing, telling him to do it, keep doing it, keep hurting him, you little bitch, you're a little bitch, aren't you.

And Chuy remembers his mission.

He kicks the ball into the wall hard and it bounces back to him and he juggles it on his foot twice before kicking it again. Maybe he should have been a *fútbol* player, maybe he should have done that instead of what he did, and it seems like a long time ago that he picked up that pistol and fired it into the air and they put him in jail.

Forty brought him down here to fight the Sinaloans, but now it turns out that they may not fight because Chuy has heard that Barrera himself is coming to sit down with Ochoa and make a deal and he wonders if that means he'll stay in Guatemala or they'll send him back to Mexico or even let him go home.

Maybe I'll just stay here, Chuy thinks, and live in a cave. Hunt my food and live like they do on *Survivor.* Or go to Alaska like on one of those shows. Or maybe just walk into a shopping mall or a movie theater, open up with the *erre* and kill everybody.

See my face on television.

He kicks the ball against the wall again. It feels good, comforting, the simple repetitive action, and it keeps him absorbed until he hears the shout to "fall in." He trots back to the center of the village where the men are forming up.

The word goes around quickly.

Adán Barrera is in Dos Erres.

Adán brings an army with him made up of a hundred of the best Gente Nueva, the ones who have been fighting the war in Juárez, Durango, and Sinaloa, and they're well armed with assault rifles, grenade launchers, and enough ammunition to handle the situation if things go badly.

Nacho is there, of course.

He'd reached out across complicated layers of connections in the narco-world to get the message to Ochoa that they wanted to discuss peace. It seemed like a ludicrous proposition at the time, given the mutual carnage they were inflicting on each other across Mexico, but Nacho persisted with his trademark patience.

It helped that Ochoa was motivated—his recent European debacle was a major setback. The fighting on all fronts was at a stalemate, and no one could be sure what the new government was going to do.

The Zetas' strongest card was their hold on the Petén, and Ochoa insisted that the meeting be there, not in Mexico, where Barrera's tame *federales,* army, and FES could swoop in.

Nacho responded that the Petén was unacceptable, that they would have to find neutral territory in Colombia or even Europe, if it came to that, but Ochoa was adamant and Nacho finally gave in with the assurance that the Sinaloans were welcome to bring as much armed force as they wanted.

The sight of Dos Erres isn't particularly reassuring, Adán thinks as they roll toward it in a convoy of jeeps and trucks. The place is the visual definition of a backwater—jungles and swamps and a virtually abandoned village.

The heat is oppressive, the humidity more so, the jungle tight and close, and the tension is bowstring taut. Fifty of his fighters are in front of him, fifty more behind as they drive along a dirt road guarded by Zetas dressed in paramilitary garb.

Every man in this parade is a blood enemy to the other side, with grudges, vendettas, and deep hatreds. A casual glance, an untoward word, a rumor. Anything could set if off before—

He doesn't even let himself think it.

Nothing can be allowed to go wrong.

The convoy stops.

Adán knows it's just a strict protocol being followed. He can't meet Ochoa until Nacho meets with Forty. Their conversation takes only a few minutes and then the convoy is directed to a clearing about a quarter mile west of the village proper. The Zetas have chopped away the forest to create a campsite for their guests—tents have been set up and two cargo containers have been converted into living quarters for Adán and Nacho.

Adán's men go into the camp first in case it's an ambush, and check the grounds for booby traps and the dwellings for microphones. When they declare it clean, Adán's jeep comes in and he takes possession of his "quarters"—the C-container with a bed and real mattress, a latrine, a sink, and, thank God, air-conditioning run off a generator.

He has a woman, clearly a local Mayan captive, for a servant. She looks terrified, and he smiles and does his best to reassure her as one of his men brings in his bags. His traditional black suit is clearly out of place here, and he changes into a clean white guayabera, jeans, and tennis shoes.

Reflecting that he hasn't worn one of these shirts since his wedding, he thinks about Eva and the kids. At his insistence, they've all gone to the U.S. on a holiday while he's away and should now be on the beach in La Jolla. The strange irony that they are under the protection of Art Keller is almost painful.

As is the knowledge that his own life might be in Keller's hands.

The raid to kill the top Zetas is on for tomorrow morning—the peace meeting he arranged "locked the target in place," to use Keller's term. Now it's just a matter of keeping Ochoa and Forty in place, lulling them into complacency with sweet talk of peace on favorable terms.

If everything goes well, Ochoa will be dead before the sun comes up.

Magda was pregnant, the autopsy had said.

With my child, Adán thinks.

He flops down on the bed to get a little rest before the meeting starts.

Outside, he hears a soft, odd thumping noise.

Rhythmic.

He doesn't know what it is, and then realizes that someone is kicking a *fútbol* against a stone wall.

There are no jokes this time when Adán meets Ochoa.

No banter, no efforts to cut the tension. There's only mutual hatred but also mutual need, and they sit down at the table quietly.

Armed men stand in an oval around them, out of earshot but within sight, their fingers on the triggers, their eyes on their opposite numbers. This could turn into a bloodbath in a second, Adán thinks.

Ochoa and Forty sit on one side of the table, Adán and Nacho on the other.

Z-1 has aged since the last time, Adán thinks.

The burden of command, I suppose. He's just as handsome, but in a different way, and for the first time Adán can see the latent psychosis in his eyes. It's disgusting sitting so close to him, talking peace with this sadistic killer, this mass murderer. The man is Satan, and his familiar Forty is, if anything, worse.

"Let's get right down to work," Nacho says.

Basically they agree on an east-west division of the plazas, which reflects the reality on the ground. Adán concedes that the Zetas will retain Nuevo León, Monterrey, and Veracruz, as well as Matamoros, Reynosa, and La Frontera Chica in Tamaulipas. In turn, Ochoa agrees that Tijuana, Baja, Sonora, and even Juárez, with the valley, will go to the Sinaloans.

The sticking point is Nuevo Laredo.

Adán puts up a fight, because to do otherwise would arouse suspicion. At first he demands the city outright, then offers to allow the Zetas to use it for a *piso*. Then he offers to discount the *piso* to three points.

It's amusing, a small pleasure, to watch Ochoa get angry, and time and again Adán pushes him to the edge of calling off the negotiations, and then reels him back.

Finally, Nacho makes the proposal that they'd agreed upon beforehand. They'd revert back to the old days when the Floreses and the Sotos divided the plaza east and west. The Sinaloans would keep the western part of Nuevo Laredo, and the Zetas the east. That settled, Ochoa moves the topic to Europe and the relationship with 'Ndrangheta.

"I don't know that I can help you there," Adán says drily, making a point to smile at Forty. "'Ndrangheta shied away from you when you tried to do business with Islamic terrorists."

"We need a piece of the European market," Ochoa says.

It's a risky topic because they all know it could bring up the subject of Magda Beltrán's murder.

Adán lets it go. "Be that as it may . . ."

"You need our Gulf ports to do business in Europe," Forty says.

"Not really," Adán answers.

But he really does. It would be much more efficient to ship directly from Veracruz or Matamoros. He drags it out, but eventually pretends to reluctantly agree to Nacho's suggestion that he "factor" Zeta cocaine to the Europeans in exchange for free use of the Gulf ports.

They break for lunch, an awkward hiatus over some mango and an execrable chicken dish.

There's no small talk. They eat at separate tables, and Adán confers quietly with Nacho, then walks off to call Eva in La Jolla. The boys are fine, playing on the beach, she's slathered them in sunblock, no they're not too close to the water, yes, the North Americans are keeping close watch over them.

After lunch they tackle the subject of Guatemala.

It's a deal-killer, Adán insists. Ochoa must share Guatemala. Sinaloan planes must have free access to landing strips and be allowed to transport their product across the border unmolested. They will, of course, pay their share of police and political protection.

Ochoa balks. Guatemala is his "by right of conquest"—which Adán finds amusing—and if the Sinaloans want to use the territory, they must pay for the privilege, and by the kilo. Adán gets up from the table. "Thank you for lunch. We won't be requiring dinner."

"Sit down."

"Don't tell me what to do."

Nacho says, "Gentlemen—"

"If I pay you for every kilo of coke that I bring through Guatemala," Adán says to Ochoa, "I might as well just go to work for you."

"That would be acceptable." Ochoa smiles.

Adán is growing tired of the game. But the game must be played, and on the chance that the raid doesn't come off or fails, he needs an arrangement with the Zetas, so he says, "We've bled each other dry, it makes no sense to come to the peace table and try to bleed each other to death financially. I'm offering you a market in Europe in exchange for a supply route in Central America."

Ochoa confers with Forty and then agrees.

What follows is a long, tedious discussion about security arrangements between now and the end of the present administration. Adán verifies that the AFI and the army will make no overt moves against the Zetas if they will not fire on agents or soldiers.

"What about the FES?" Ochoa asks.

"I have no influence there," Adán says.

"Then why do they only come after us and not you?"

"Perhaps because you killed their families," Adán suggests. Perhaps because you're animals without the slightest restraint. Perhaps because you're sociopaths and sadists. Perhaps because you crippled Keller's woman and butchered a young woman he thought of as a daughter. Perhaps because you killed my unborn child. "I can't help you there."

Ochoa seems to accept it, and then asks, "What do you intend to do about the new administration?"

"Same thing we've done with every administration," Adán says. "Try to influence it with money and reason. If we pool our resources and present a common front we might gain some ground there. The best thing we can do is to stop fighting. I truly believe that if we give this government peace, it will reciprocate."

"And the North Americans?"

"Are the North Americans," Adán answers. "They'll do everything they can to force the government to come after us. The government will make a show of it but be ineffectual. That is, unless you continue to commit atrocity after atrocity, and continue to do frankly idiotic things such as challenging them with press releases boasting that you rule the country, in which case you force the government's hand."

"We do rule the country," Forty says.

"Which is totally irrelevant to the point I'm making," Adán says. He tries again. "We can have a business. We can have the most profitable business in the history of the world—outside of oil, which I believe you're moving into—if we manage it in an orderly way. Or we can have chaos that will eventually ruin us."

The talks continue, focusing on details of how to disengage on the various fronts, how to announce the cease-fire, how to enforce it and make sure that no small organizations go off on their own and break the truce.

Much of this is delegated to Forty and Nacho.

By the time the sun starts to go down, they have achieved the *pax narcotica*.

Adán and Ochoa shake hands.

"We've arranged some entertainment for this evening," Ochoa says. "A small party to celebrate the peace and the Day of the Dead. Some refreshments, some women from Guatemala City."

"No offense, but I'm a married man."

"But not a dead one," Ochoa says.

"But a faithful one," Adán answers.

He goes back to the camp, takes a hot shower from a Lister Bag hung from the ceiling, and then lies down to sleep under the mosquito netting that the servant opened over his bed.

He knew there'd be a fiesta, but it worries him. More than one narco has been murdered while celebrating a peace with his enemies, so he only let half the men attend the party, withdrew the other half to the camp, and reminded Nacho that the men should stay relatively sober and completely alert.

Adán looks at his watch, the gaudy expensive affair that Eva gave him and which he wore only to impress Ochoa, a vulgar hick who would *be* impressed by that sort of thing.

In twelve hours, he thinks, if everything goes according to plan, my enemies will be dead.

Forty.

Ochoa.

And, with any luck, Art Keller.

If there is a God, Keller will die a hero's death, gunned down in a firefight against the Zetas in the jungles of Guatemala. There will be a private—secret, in fact—ceremony in the back halls of the DEA building, maybe even the White House, and then he will be forgotten and unmourned.

But every year, on the Day of the Dead, I will arrange for poppies to be placed on his grave.

A private joke, just between the two of us.

Ochoa watches the party.

It's quite a scene, lit by a bonfire in the middle of the Zeta camp, men and women in black-and-white skull masks dancing to the blaring music, women going down on the men right out in the open, or sneaking off to the edge of the light to fuck. His only disappointment is that Barrera chose not to attend.

That will complicate things.

Barrera is a slimy piece of shit, not nearly as clever as he thinks he is. Ochoa knew that "El Patrón's" peace offering was disingenuous when Barrera didn't as much as mention his dead mistress, even when practically invited to. If he'd demanded something—some sort or recompense, even an apology—Ochoa might have believed him. Now Barrera will do what he always does: pretend to make peace and then buy off the government to make war.

Except this time, he won't have the chance. Ochoa watches the party—beer, whiskey, and champagne flow generously, and most of the partiers are snorting cocaine.

Well, the Sinaloan guests are snorting cocaine laced with heroin, and the women aren't whores, they're Panteras.

Nacho Esparza is having a hard time getting it up, and he doesn't understand it. Coke usually makes him harder than a diamond, he took a Viagra, and the girl is beautiful—lustrous black hair, big tits, and, under the half mask, full lips that are made for giving blow jobs, which she's doing now, on her knees the way he likes it.

She tilts her head back and just flicks at the head of his dick with her tongue, like a snake, and that does the trick. He feels himself getting hard, the pornographic scene of the orgy around him helps, and then she swallows him deep and he's relieved when he feels the blood pump down into him, he gets hard and thick in her mouth, and he closes his eyes in pleasure.

The pain is horrific, unimaginable.

Nacho looks down to see his blood seeping around the knife blade embedded in his stomach, and then the girl with the lustrous hair and full lips smiles and pulls out the blade, and his blood squirts out into the dirt.

Staggering backward, Nacho looks around at a nightmare. In the red of the firelight, beautifully dressed, elegantly masked women slaughter their lovers with knives and guns, with garrotes or just their bare hands. Zetas pull pistols from their belts and gun down Sinaloans at close range. Other demons come out of the shadows and drag dead and wounded men into the bonfire. Nacho hears their screaming as he feels a deep dull ache in his belly and then he realizes through his disbelief that he's going to die and then the beautiful woman with the lustrous hair behind the white skull takes him by the hand and walks him toward the fire.

Chuy watches the Sinaloan camp from the brush at its edge.

The Sinaloans have sentries out, two each in front of the quarters where their bosses are. There are probably more, peeking out from tents or, like him, lying in the brush outside the camp, but he can't see them.

He doesn't drink, do drugs, or fornicate with women, so other than the music—*norteño* mariachi that he doesn't like anyway—the pagan Day of the Dead fiesta held nothing for him. And Forty had told him and the rest of his cell to refrain—there would be work for them later and he wanted their heads on straight.

Chuy was just as glad—the scene at the party was satanic, disgusting. Now he hears screams coming from the camp, sights in on the sentry outside Barrera's cabin, and waits for the signal, one blink from a laser.

It comes just seconds later and he squeezes the trigger.

The sentry's head snaps back, his rifle clatters on the cabin's porch.

Chuy swings his *erre* onto the second sentry, who is looking to see where the shot came from. A dumb mistake—he should have hit the ground and then looked. Chuy's shot takes him in the chest.

Five yards away from Chuy, the muzzle flash of a grenade launcher goes off and the armor-piercing missile spins its way toward Barrera's quarters.

Now gunfire is coming back toward him and the fight is on.

Then, in the distance, Chuy hears helicopter rotors. Shit, do the Sinaloans have a chopper? Where did they hide it? He shifts position and looks up into the night sky. A helicopter gunship like the army and the *federales* had in Michoacán could wipe them out in seconds.

He sees the chopper.

The man with the grenade launcher panics, drops the weapon, and runs. Chuy picks up the launcher, hefts it onto his shoulder, and points it toward the sky until the chopper comes into the range finder.

A red streak comes up out of the predawn darkness.

A loud bang, a flash of yellow light, and the helicopter jolts sideways like a toy that's been hit by a bat.

The blast tosses Keller to the deck.

Shrapnel sprays, exposed wires spark, the ship is on fire. Red flame and thick black smoke fill the cabin.

The stench of scorched metal and burned flesh.

Keller struggles back up and sees that Ruiz's face is a bloody smear. Then Ruiz wipes the blood off and Keller sees that it came from one of the other men, whose carotid artery spurts in rhythm with his racing heartbeat. Another keels over, shrapnel obscenely jutting from his crotch, just below his protective vest, and the team medic is already crawling across the deck to help.

Now the voices come from grown men—howls of pain, fear, and rage as tracers fly up and rounds smack the chopper's fuselage like a sudden rainstorm. But it's too late to abort the mission, Keller thinks, even if we wanted to, because we're going down.

The chopper spins crazily as it falls toward the earth.

Adán topples out of his quarters.

His hair is singed, his face scorched, and he's deaf—all he can hear is a horrible ringing. He realizes that he's on his stomach in the dirt, and thinks that he should be doing something, but he can't figure out what it is.

Looking up, he sees one of his men run toward him, yelling something, but Adán can't hear his words, only sees his mouth open and close in what seems to be slow motion, and then Adán slowly comes to the realization that he's concussed.

The man runs right past him. It's almost funny because he has no pants on, only a shirt, and his ass is skinny and flabby at the same time, and then Adán realizes that *he's* naked as well and he yells out—or thinks he does, because he can't hear his own voice. Yells out to stop and wait for him, come back and help him get up, but the man just keeps running, his ass bouncing, then bullets cut him down from behind and he claws at the air before toppling forward into the dirt.

Adán thinks he should be doing something but can't think of what it is and then remembers that he's the leader, El Patrón, he should be taking command, giving orders, organizing his men who are running around shooting in all directions, but then he realizes that would mean standing up and he's too afraid to do that. A bullet smacks into a man near him and he wants to get up and take command but his legs won't let him do it, they're like water under him.

Adán belly-crawls toward the bush.

The landing is "hard."

The pilot manages to bring the spinning helicopter down at the western edge of the village, but it hits hard, rattling Keller's spine and snapping his head back against the bulkhead, and he almost blacks out.

The interior of the chopper is on fire. A couple of men work to suppress the flames as others get the wounded men out. Keller realizes that half his kill team is already out of action and then he hears Downey yell, "Out! Out! Deploy!" so he jumps out of the chopper bay.

Muzzle flashes crackle and bullets zip around his ears, so he flattens himself to the ground, flips his night-vision goggles over his eyes, and then risks looking up to get his bearings.

The school and the church are ahead to his right; in front of him and to the left, Zetas are taking position in huts, houses, and in the bush. Heavy firing is coming from about a quarter of a mile ahead, and Keller realizes that Zetas were attacking Barrera in his camp when the chopper came in. The Zeta camp is directly behind him, on the other side of the narrow belt of jungle, so they have enemy on all sides.

The second chopper has landed safely and its men are deploying, creating a firing line between them and the Zeta camp behind them. But there's no screen between them and the Sinaloan camp in front, and Zetas are starting to come back from there.

Our only advantage is chaos, Keller thinks. The Zetas seem to be confused as to who the crashed helicopter belongs to, and they're running in all directions, pouring fire at the chopper but also fighting in the Sinaloan camp and back in their own.

He notices that some of the fighters are women, dressed up as if to go to a party, some in masks, but carrying AR-15s and pistols, even lobbing grenades. They must be Panteras—he thought it was an urban legend, the "Zeta Amazons," but now he sees that it's true as figures move in and out of the darkness toward cover and good firing positions.

The old dictum is that "no plan survives first contact with the enemy," and the special-ops team is already regrouping and improvising a new plan. He hears the sharp, disciplined fire as they use their night-vision advantage to pick out targets and create space to form a defensive perimeter. Short bits of talk come across the earpieces as Downey distributes his people and firepower.

They had expected to go into a sleeping village in an environment of surprise, not a hot combat zone. The plan was to perform the sanction and get out, not take on the entire Zeta force, and now the helicopter is destroyed and they're going to have to fight their way out across the border.

"K-1," Keller hears on the bone-phone. "This is D-1."

"Acknowledge."

"Aborting mission."

"That's a no."

"Not a lot of time here, K-1," Downey says. "Kill Team G is fifty percent down, Kill Team F is engaged and I can't spare them. And we're going to have to get our wounded back to Chopper 2 and medevac."

Keller gets what Downey is saying—

He and Ruiz are the only members of Kill Team G left, and Team F has all it can do just to keep from getting overrun themselves.

The mission is fucked.

And where is Barrera? Dead already, or did he survive the Zetas' attack?

First things first, Keller thinks as he hears Downey say, *"We're going to hold this perimeter until we can evac two eagles down."*

"Acknowledge."

It's the right move, Keller thinks. They have to get two wounded men back to the second chopper and then hold until it can deliver the wounded and then come back for them, because twenty men are too heavy a load for a single Black Hawk, already weighed down with special noise-suppressing gear.

Looking over his shoulder, he sees F start to move back into the jungle toward the Zeta camp. Bullets zing over his head and he trains his M-4 on a house to his left and returns fire. It feels good to be doing something, it lets loose his adrenaline, and he realizes that he didn't come here to *not* kill Forty and Ochoa.

"Moving," Keller says into the bone-phone.

"Negative that," Downey answers.

Keller gets up into a crouch and sees Eddie Ruiz to his left.

Eddie nods.

It's on.

Keller dashes toward the school.

Forty's bodyguards lay down a sheet of fire.

Eddie hits the ground and looks up to see a woman with a pink Uzi trying to spot him, but he shoots and blows Commander Candy away first. She clutches at her stomach as if she can't believe that this has happened, drops the pretty pink gun, and sits down and howls for her mother.

Then Eddie sees Forty make a dash for the jungle. Eddie leads and pulls the trigger. Forty stumbles and then goes down, gets up again, and Eddie's about to finish him when another spray of gunfire from the Zetas forces him to squeeze the earth.

Then there's a whoosh and an explosion and Eddie sees the bodyguards blown off the school's porch like toy soldiers in a kid's game. He looks to find Forty but can't see him.

He does see Keller get up and head for the church.

Ochoa.

Z-1.

El Verdugo.

Works for me, Eddie thinks.

He gets up and follows.

Chuy's done.

He drops the rocket launcher and walks back into the brush. Carefully picking his way along the narrow trail he's walked so many times, he crosses the stone terrace of the Mayan temple, picks up his *fútbol,* and crawls into his cave.

There is nothing to fight for here.

Not Flor.

Not Nazario.

Not Hugo, or God.

One side will win, one will lose, and it doesn't matter which. He has his own mission now and he can't carry it out during this fight.

He curls up into a fetal position and hugs the ball tightly to his chest.

Adán trips over a root and falls face first.

He hurts.

His right leg is burned and blistered, he's scratched and cut from the thorns and razorlike leaves, the soles of his feet are cut and bleeding. He's exhausted, and part of him just wants to stay down and sleep, but if he sleeps they might catch up with him, and he wants to live to see his sons again, to hold them. That's all he wants in the world, all he wants from life.

Nacho was right.

What are they doing this for?

If Ochoa survives and wants to be *patrón,* let him.

All I want is to live.

Adán fights to his feet and keeps going. The jungle is dark in the predawn and he can't see where he's going, he can only move away from the sound of shooting and hope that the North Americans find him before the Zetas do.

His only hope now is that Keller is winning and will come find him and get him out. That was their deal, and for all his faults, and they are many, Keller is a man of honor, a man of his word. But Adán saw the helicopter crash and wonders if Keller was in it, if he's dead, if even now the Kaibiles are cutting up his body.

As they'll do to you, Adán thinks, if they catch you. He's lost and has nowhere to go, but he keeps stumbling through the jungle, away from the sounds of shooting, trying to find a refuge.

Chuy wakes up.

Something is coming, burrowing into his cave. He turns on his flashlight and sees—

Forty.

He's bleeding, holding a wound in his stomach. An exit wound, Chuy sees. Forty was shot in the back and the bullet came out his stomach and now there's a big gaping hole that Forty can't cover even with his big hand.

Forty recognizes him. Croaks, "It's you. Thank God. Help me."

Chuy looks at his face.

Doesn't see the face grimacing in agony, but sees the face laughing at him, laughing at him while he hurts him, laughing while people scream.

"Help me," Forty begs.

Chuy takes his knife, plunges it into Forty's wound, and then rips the blade up through his stomach, up into his chest, just the way they taught him.

Forty bellows.

"Bitch," Chuy says.

Forty huffs in agony.

Chuy takes out the knife, makes a horizontal incision across the top of Forty's head, near the scalp line. Then he grabs the flap of skin and peels down as Forty screams.

The face won't haunt Chuy anymore.

Then Chuy grabs his *fútbol* again.

His mission is done.

Almost.

He takes a little sewing kit out of his pocket.

Keller rushes the church.

Runs for the count of three, dives to the ground. Looks, fires ahead of him, gets up and runs for the count of two. Mixes up the rhythm so the four Kaibile guards firing from the church doorway and windows don't anticipate his move.

He hears the chopper come over him and realizes that the wounded are up and off. Thirty minutes, at least, before it comes back to get them. Downey would have sent the medic with it, and seven others. Ten of us left. Downey's reconfigured his men—four screening the line from the Zeta camp, four covering the village and the Zetas coming back from the attack on the Sinaloan camp. Ruiz and I moving on Ochoa.

Ruiz dives to the ground five yards to his right.

Ochoa is in the church. Keller knows it, feels it, because otherwise the Kaibiles wouldn't put up a fight there. But they have him and Ruiz pinned down and will kill them the second they get up.

"*K-1, this is D-1.*"

"Acknowledge."

"*Wait for my 'go.'*"

"Acknowledge."

Keller listens to the traffic between the team members. "*Target acquired. Target acquired. Target acquired. Target acquired.*"

"*Joy.*"

Four shots, four hits.

"*Go!*"

Keller gets up and runs for the church. Shots come at him from the left, but he keeps running, and then bursts of fire from the team cover him and he makes it to the church doorway and steps over the two Kaibile bodies, neatly shot in the head. He flattens himself against the wall and sees Ruiz come up right behind him.

Keller pivots, swings his M-4 in front of him, and goes in.

The church is small, more of a chapel. Two more dead Kaibile lie by the windows. Some of the rough wooden pews have been torn out, a small bedroom built in their place, a bed, a nightstand—very basic. Oil lanterns hang from the walls and cast the church in a pale golden light.

A woman crouches by the side of the bed, clutching a baby.

She looks up at Keller in fear.

"No one is going to hurt you," Keller says.

But she doesn't believe him, clutches the baby tighter against her, and waits for him to do whatever he's going to do.

Keller moves past her, down the center aisle.

He doesn't see Ochoa.

Then he does—a slim shadow behind a cheap plaster statue of Mary, the baby Jesus in her arms.

Eddie sees it, too.

No respecter of saints—or for that matter, virgins—he blasts away at the statue, and chips of the Madonna and child spray the wall.

Ochoa rolls away and fires.

Keller feels a round hit the protective plates in his vest, like the blow of a baseball bat. He drops to his knees behind the wooden pew and swings his M-4 to find Ochoa, now slithering across the base of the altar, and fires.

The bullets rip into Ochoa's feet, then up his legs, across his knees.

Eddie's burst takes him in the stomach.

Ochoa lies by the front of the altar, his .45 in one hand, his other clutching his stomach, trying to keep his guts in. His eyes are half open, his legs twitch, his once handsome face is distorted in agony.

Keller knows that a bullet has snapped his spine.

Then Keller sees Eddie look around, and then spots what he's looking *at*—a tin of paraffin, used to light the lanterns. He should stop Eddie, but then he thinks about Erika's and Marisol's mutilated bodies and decides to let Eddie Ruiz do what he's going to do.

Keller turns his back and holds his hand out to the woman. She takes it, and he helps her up, then puts his arm around her and leads her and the baby out of the sanctuary and into the doorway. The shooting outside has slackened—when the Zetas saw that Ochoa was captured, they started to withdraw back to their camp.

Eddie takes the tin and pours the paraffin over Ochoa.

Eyes wide, Ochoa stares up at him.

Helpless.

"You think you hurt?" Eddie asks. "You don't hurt yet."

He tosses the match on him.

Keller steps out of the church.

But he hears Ochoa's shrill screams, like a strong, fast wind scouring stone.

The sun comes up, red as blood, fire, and raw truth.

Adán sees it as good and bad.

Good in that he can see, bad in that he can be seen. Sheltering in the jungle like a small animal, he wonders if prey is grateful for the end of night. He's tired and sore, the burns on his skin raw and painful, his head throbbing, his arms cut and scratched from the thorny branches, his bare feet a raw mess.

He's walked in circles and figure eights, avoiding the Zetas, trying to discern what's happened in the village, if his men have won or lost, if Keller has succeeded or failed. The shooting has faded into sporadic desultory bursts, but trucks have roared by on the narrow dirt road, men have trotted through on trails, and Adán has been afraid to lift his head and call out.

The bitter irony is that he's waiting to see Keller.

His persecutor has become his savior.

He staggers ahead.

Lost.

Eddie comes out of the church. "I was lighting a candle."

"We're pulling out," Keller says.

"I'm going to find Forty."

"We don't have the time," Keller says.

"Maybe *you* don't."

He pushes past Keller and starts to walk away.

"I told you if you ran I'd put two in your back!" Keller shouts.

"Do it!" Eddie keeps walking.

Keller doesn't.

Because Crazy Eddie's right.

You finish what you start.

Keller follows him into the jungle.

Eddie sees a pair of legs sticking out of a crack in the earth. He walks up to them, looks down and sees Forty's body.

Or what's left of it—the trunk.

The head is missing.

Which is kind of random.

Anyway, Eddie thinks, my list is complete.

Segura, Forty, Ochoa.

RIP, Chacho.

Then he hears something and jerks the rifle to his shoulder. It's in front of him, through some jungle, maybe forty or fifty feet, a dull rhythmic sound. Keeping the rifle pointed, Eddie walks through the brush until he comes to some kind of stone court, and then he sees what's making the sound.

A skinny kid is kicking a soccer ball against an old stone wall.

"Hey!"

The kid turns around.

Eddie recognizes him and grins.

Chuy stares at him for a second, then turns his back and kicks the ball again, and then Eddie gets a closer look, hunches over, and throws up.

Forty's face has been carefully stitched to the soccer ball. His mouth stretched open, grinning. Eddie thinks he's seen some weird shit before, but this takes the freakin' cake.

Chuy gets the bounce, dribbles it off the top of his foot, turns and kicks the ball to Eddie, who lets it roll off the stone into the bush.

"You remember me?" Eddie asks.

The kid just looks at him and stares.

Like we didn't kill a few dozen people together, Eddie thinks. Like that didn't happen, or it was nothing. Eddie asks, "What do you say we go home, *pocho*? Back to the 867?"

Chuy thinks about this for a second and nods.

He walks past Eddie and picks up his ball.

"No, why don't we leave that here?" Eddie says.

Chuy shrugs and drops it, just as Keller comes into the clearing.

Keller looks down at the football with Forty's skinned face stitched across it. Then he looks up at Ruiz and the teenage boy beside him.

"Who's this?" Keller asked.

"Chuy," Eddie answers. "Jesus the Kid."

It's the one who killed and butchered Erika. He's a kid, a child—scrawny under his "uniform." Thin face, stooped shoulders, a wisp of a mustache forming on his lip, about as lethal-looking as a mongrel pound puppy. Yet he killed Erika and cut her up like a chicken. Stuck the ironic calling card into her, and walked away.

Keller aims the M-4 at the kid's head. Chuy doesn't flinch, but just stands there staring at him, uncaring.

Catatonic.

Insane.

"You don't want to do that," Keller hears Ruiz say. "I mean, it's not what we do, is it? Women and kids."

This is no kid, Keller thinks. This is no child.

This is a monster.

The boy looks at him with flat, dull eyes, and Keller knows what those eyes have seen.

He lowers his gun.

"Get him out of here," Keller says.

"What about you?"

"I have to find Barrera," Keller says. "I have to take *him* home."

"The hell you do."

"Without him," Keller says, "all this has been pointless, hasn't it? Without him, it will just be more chaos, more killing. If he's alive and out there, I have to find him."

"Suit yourself."

Eddie shrugs and leads the boy away.

Keller walks into the Sinaloan camp.

Deserted save for the dead.

The survivors must have run, Keller thinks. Gotten in their vehicles and tried to make it out.

Is Adán with them? Keller wonders.

Barrera triumphant?

The Once and Future King?

Or is Barrera dead, the victim of his own treachery? He underestimated Ochoa, didn't think he was as cunning as himself. But that's Adán; he always thought he was smarter than everybody else.

And maybe he's right.

Keller sees the C-container that was one of the guest quarters, kicks the door open, and goes in. The place is a blackened tomb, and he looks around for Adán's charred body but doesn't find it.

Over the bone-phones he hears Downey. *"K-1, this is D-1. We're bugging out. What is your location?"*

Keller doesn't answer. Stepping out of the C-container, he can hear the chopper's rotors coming in.

Good.

"K-1, repeat—what is your location?"

The sun is coming up, and it feels warm on his face.

"K-1, we will not wait for you. Repeat, we will not wait for you."

"Acknowledge. Go."

A silence.

"K-1, what the—"

"I'm not coming."

Keller walks into the jungle.

Adán comes to a clearing.

A flat stone terrace with ruins around it. The remnants of carved pillars, a slab that must have been a sacrificial altar. It's overgrown now with vines, and has been looted of its statues and stone heads, but it provides a place to rest and he lies down.

More like falls down. Beyond exhaustion now, beyond hope, he collapses onto the stone, still cool on his skin in the early morning, and lays his head on his outstretched arms and closes his eyes.

He hears a scuffling sound and opens his eyes to see a small lizard racing across the stone and then the lizard stops and they stare at each other for a few seconds before the lizard skitters away.

Adán's thirsty, more thirsty than he ever thought possible, and thinks that he might die of thirst in this rain forest. He doesn't know where to go, how to get there, or what he'll find when he does. He doesn't have the strength to go anyway, and for the first time, perhaps in his life, he doesn't know what to do, and he starts to cry.

The heat rises with the sun.

There is a cool of the morning in the rain forest, but it's as brief as a summer love, and Keller feels enervated as he pushes through the heavy brush, feels an exhaustion like he's never felt before, pushing through to the end of . . .

What?

This holy quest, this unholy vendetta?

You made your peace with the devil, Keller thinks. Now you live with it. If it's *worth* living with it, worth living with the knowledge of the *cost*.

What it's cost you.

What it's cost others.

Luis Aguilar, Erika Valles, Pablo Mora, Jimena Barca.

Marisol.

Thousands upon thousands of others—Mora's faceless and nameless, the guilty and the innocent and the somewhere-in-between, where most of us live and die in our variegated grays.

Eighty thousand lives and all we've done is crown a new king.

And the new king is the old king.

World without end, amen.

Keller doesn't really know where he's going. Only knows that if Adán ran he would have run away, away from the fighting, he would have looked for a place to hide, and this is certainly a place to hide. You could disappear in here, under this canopy of green, hidden from the air, in this very old place that was once the home of ancient people and ancient gods that themselves disappeared, and then the jungle came back.

The jungle always does. As much as you chop away at it, the jungle always comes back. He can *feel* Adán in here—his severed limb, the phantom part of himself, always there, always lurking, the jungle waiting to reclaim itself.

Keller is aware of the sun because of the heat, but he can't see the sky.

The jungle is too close and too dark.

Adán hears the footfalls in the bush.

Feels the prey's pang of fear.

A puma? A jaguar? A human enemy come to kill him?

He opens his eyes and sees Keller.

Keller looks at Adán stretched out on the stone.

His face is black with soot, his naked body scratched and bloody and burned, his hair singed, his skin filthy with dirt, caked sweat, and raw, open blisters.

Small and pathetic, he blinks at Keller. Then he says weakly, "You came for me."

Keller nods.

Adán starts to cry. Bubbles of snot come out of his nose. Struggling to sit up, he asks, "Do you have water?"

Keller unclips the small canteen from his belt and hands it to Adán, who screws off the cap and takes long, greedy gulps. The water seems to revive him, and he asks, "Ochoa?"

"Dead," Keller says. "So is Forty."

Adán's cracked lips form a slight smile. "Killer Keller."

"I have to get you home." Keller offers his arm. Adán grabs on to it, and Keller pulls him to his feet.

"Thank you," Adán says, finding his legs under him. "I want you to know I'm getting out of the trade. I'm giving it up. I just want to live my life with my family."

"Amplius lava me ab iniquitate mea; et a peccato meo munda me."

"What?"

"Latin," Keller says. "A psalm: 'Wash me throughly from my wickedness and cleanse me from my sin.'"

He points the gun at Adán.

Adán blinks in disbelief. "You gave your word. You swore on your soul."

Keller shoots him twice in the face.

Then he drops the gun and walks back into the jungle's darkness.

CIUDAD JUÁREZ

And I believe in God.
And God is God.

—Steve Earle
"God Is God"

Ciudad Juárez, Mexico
2014

Keller finishes stirring the eggs in the pan, then slides them onto a plate and sets it down at the kitchen table in front of Chuy.

Chuy eats with abandon, like an animal.

Keller waits until he finishes and then says, "Go get dressed now and we'll go. And brush your teeth."

The kid gets up and goes into his room.

He rarely speaks, lives in his own world, impenetrable as a severe autistic. He still wets the bed and cries at night, wakes up screaming and Keller goes to him and does his best to soothe him, and even after almost two years of weekly therapy and daily medication, it doesn't get much better. Keller is wryly amused that sometimes Chuy's nightmares wake him from his own.

After the Petén raid, Keller had walked out of the jungle back into Mexico. Made his way to El Paso and told Tim Taylor that he was done for good this time.

Taylor had no problem with that.

"What happened to Barrera?" he asked angrily.

Keller shrugged. "I guess he didn't make it."

Then Keller walked out and never looked back. He went down to Juárez the same day and made Ana an offer on her little house. She was living out in Valverde with Marisol anyway, had quit her job at the paper to work at the clinic. She described it as penance, but never said for what, and Keller didn't ask.

Eddie Ruiz turned up two days later, with Chuy in tow like a stray puppy. "I don't know what to do with him."

"Turn him in," Keller said.

"They'll kill him," Eddie said.

Chuy walked past them and curled up on the couch. He's pretty much been there ever since. The police didn't care, if they even knew. Chuy had yet to turn eighteen, and as a juvenile could only serve three years in Mexico anyway. No one wanted to go through the trouble to prosecute.

No one wanted to be reminded.

"What are you going to do?" Keller asked Eddie.

"Cross the river and turn myself back in," Eddie said. "Four years and I'm out."

"Sounds like a plan."

"How about you?"

"I don't have a plan," Keller says. "Just live, I guess."

He has a little money put away and a pension. It's not a lot, but it's enough, and he doesn't need much. He thought about going back to the States, but somehow he wanted to stay in Mexico, in Juárez, to assist in the recovery of the ruined city, if only by buying his groceries there.

By being there.

Chuy's story came out little by little, and it was horrific. Marisol said that he would probably never fully recover from the sort of traumas that he'd experienced, that the best they could hope for would be a kind of base functionality, a twilight existence. She found the best therapists, but the best anyone can do is to see that he's not a danger to himself or anyone else. He's pushing twenty now, but with the affect of an eleven-year-old, because as Marisol explained, the traumas stopped his growth when they started.

"I'll look out for him," Keller said.

Because he needs to. Call it penance, call it atonement or whatever the hell you want, he only knows that he needs to do it, that he can only find redemption by helping this boy find his, by showing love to what he hates, that at the end of the day or the end of the world, there are no separate souls. We will go to heaven or we will go to hell, but we will go together.

"That's going to be a full-time job," Marisol said.

Her own health is fragile, her limp more pronounced, and she relies more on her cane. The clinic is busy—many of her patients now are transplanted Sinaloans, but still poor and still without medical care if it weren't for her.

She and Keller see each other occasionally, at rare social functions, sometimes at a bookstore or a café, and they talk pleasantly, like old friends. Sometimes they're tempted to go back, to try to find what they lost, but they know that some things once destroyed can't be rebuilt.

Loss is loss.

Chuy comes out of his room and they go outside, walk down to the corner, and catch a *rutera* downtown.

The city is coming back.

Not fully yet, not even close.

But stores have opened their doors, houses have people living in them again, there are no corpses on the sidewalks. This is Keller's city now, and will be, two ruins inhabiting each other.

The war on drugs drags on in its desultory fashion. In Mexico, in the States, in Europe, Afghanistan. The drugs still flow out of Mexico into the American Southwest, a more abundant commodity now than water. A few of the machine's most monstrous cogs are missing, but its wheels still turn. Banking, real estate, energy, politics, armaments, walls, fences, cops, courts, and prisons—the cartel carries on.

Keller rarely thinks about any of it. He had read—in the newspapers like any ordinary citizen—that Martín and Yvette Tapia had been captured, and he wonders how Yvette will fare in Puente Grande. Probably not well. And Eddie Ruiz is scheduled for release soon, to a new identity and an ordinary life that he will find impossibly mundane.

Eva Barrera is living in the States now, in California with her two little boys, and they have plenty of money to live well, and he wonders if Adán ever knew that they weren't his, that she has officially changed their paternity to spare them the shame of their legacy.

Someone else will take the throne, Keller thinks.

He doesn't care who it is.

People don't run the cartel; the cartel runs people.

The bus's brakes hiss, and Keller and Chuy get off in El Centro and walk together toward the medical building where Chuy has his regular appointment that can do little more than maintain him where he is.

We are all cripples, Keller thinks, limping together through this crippled world.

It's what we owe to each other.

Chuy goes inside.

Keller sits outside on a bench and waits. The words of the psalm come back to him—

"Be still and know that I am God."

There is nothing to do but be still.

Acknowledgments

This is a work of fiction. However, any observer of the "drug war" in Mexico will realize that the incidents in this book are inspired by actual events. That being the case, I consulted a number of journalistic works that I would like to acknowledge here: Ioan Grillo—*El Narco*; George W. Grayson and Samuel Logan—*The Executioner's Men*; Anabel Hernàndez—*Narcoland*; Charles Bowden—*El Sicario: Confessions of a Cartel Hitman* and *Murder City*; George W. Grayson—*Mexico: Narco-Violence and a Failed State?*; Blog del Narco—*Dying for the Truth*; Howard Campbell—*Drug War Zone*; Ed Vulliamy, *Amexica*—*War Along the Borderline*; Malcolm Beith—*The Last Narco*; Jerry Langton—*Gangland: The Rise of the Mexican Drug Cartels from El Paso to Vancouver*; Robert Andrew Powell—*This Love Is Not for Cowards*; Ricardo C. Ainslie—*The Fight to Save Juárez: Life in the Heart of Mexico's Drug War*; John Gibler—*To Die in Mexico: Dispatches from Inside the Drug War*; Melissa Del Bosque—"The Most Dangerous Place in Mexico," *The Texas Observer*. I also consulted articles from *The Los Angeles Times*, *The New York Times*, *The Washington Post*, *The San Diego Union-Tribune*, *The Guardian*, and a number of Mexican newspapers, including, but not limited to, *Milenio Diario*, *La Prensa*, *El Norte*, *La Mañana*, *Primera Hora*, and *El Universal*.

The recent era of the drug wars is unique in that it was "covered" in real time, often through Internet postings from the participants themselves, and also from blogs. Among the latter, I principally consulted *Borderland Beat*, *Insight Crime*, and, of course, *Blog del Narco*.

A special thanks to my good friend and coconspirator Shane Salerno and The Story Factory for pushing and pulling me into writing this book, making it possible, and for being that guy who handles business differently, thinks globally, and truly cares about writers. Thanks to Sonny Mehta for his sage and patient editing, and to the whole crew at Knopf—Edward Kastenmeier, Diana Miller, Leslie Levine, Paul Bogaards, Gabrielle Brooks, Maria Massey, Oliver Munday, and all the rest.

And, finally, to my wife and son for their love, patience, and support.

A Note on the Type

The text of this book was set in Ehrhardt, a typeface based on the specimens of "Dutch" types found at the Ehrhardt foundry in Leipzig.

Composed by North Market Street Graphics,
Lancaster, Pennsylvania

Designed by M. Kristen Bearse